PENGUIN CLASSICS

NEW SCIENCE

GIAMBATTISTA VICO was born in Naples in 1668 of humble origins. Though he was Professor of Rhetoric at the city's university, his masterpiece was a philosophical work entitled *Principii di una scienza nuova d'intorno alla natura delle nazioni* (*The Principles of a New Science of the Common Nature of Nations*, 1725). This wide-ranging and later highly influential text was Vico's response to the devaluation of social and historical knowledge implicit in Cartesian thought. The work centred on the notion that the legitimate area for Man's scientific enquiry was that which he had created – the social rather than the physical universe, the latter being for God alone to understand.

Despite their influence on later thinkers, Vico's theories (being concerned with an area of study unfashionable at the time) were not well received during his life, and his career cannot be described as successful. He held an obscure academic position and had to take private teaching work and writing commissions to supplement his poor income. He received little public recognition for his work and rarely travelled, despite his interest in other cultures and societies. Still, he continued to work on and revise his great work, and a second edition of *New Science* appeared in 1730, followed not long after his death in 1744 by a third and final version.

Giambattista Vico died in Naples, the city he had lived and worked in all his life, but which had never given him the recognition he desired and deserved.

DAVID MARSH is Professor of Italian at Rutgers University in New Brunswick, New Jersey. He is the author of *The Quattrocento Dialogue: Classical Tradition and Humanist Innovation* and *Lucian and the Latins: Humor and Humanism in the Early Renaissance*, and has translated Leon Battista Alberti's *Dinner Pieces*.

ANTHONY GRAFTON teaches European intellectual hi— ceton University. He is the aut! ory of *Classical Scholarship, Defe* rious *History*.

GIAMBATTISTA VICO

NEW SCIENCE

PRINCIPLES OF THE NEW SCIENCE
CONCERNING THE COMMON NATURE OF NATIONS

THIRD EDITION
THOROUGHLY CORRECTED, REVISED, AND
EXPANDED BY THE AUTHOR

Translated by DAVID MARSH
with an introduction by
ANTHONY GRAFTON

PENGUIN BOOKS

PENGUIN BOOKS

UK | USA | Canada | Ireland | Australia
India | New Zealand | South Africa

Penguin Books is part of the Penguin Random House group of companies
whose addresses can be found at global.penguinrandomhouse.com

Penguin
Random House
UK

Third edition first published in 1744
Published in Penguin Classics 1999
Reprinted with corrections 2001, 2013
028

Set in 10/12 pt Monotype Bembo
Typeset by Rowland Phototypesetting Ltd, Bury St Edmunds, Suffolk
Printed in England by Clays Ltd, Elcograf S.p.A.

ISBN: 978-0-140-43569-6

www.greenpenguin.co.uk

CONTENTS

v

CONTENTS

CONTENTS

ix

BOOK 5: THE RESURGENCE OF NATIONS AND THE RECURRENCE OF HUMAN INSTITUTIONS

CONCLUSION OF THE WORK

INTRODUCTION

Anthony Grafton

Giambattista Vico bestrides the modern social sciences and humanities like a colossus. Historians, anthropologists and philosophers around the world agree in seeing his *New Science* as a work of dazzling prescience. Vico argued systematically that the understanding of a past society – even of an earlier period in the history of one's own society – was a demanding, if rewarding, intellectual task. The modern reader opening a work by Homer or Livy had to realize that it did not describe individuals like himself, men and women whose experiences, feelings, and ideas would be immediately recognizable. Only by mastering the general laws of social and cultural evolution that Vico himself had formulated could one avoid committing basic errors. Vico's contemporaries envisioned the ancient Greeks and Romans as robed sages moving decorously down perfect colonnades. In fact, they had been brutal, primitive warriors. Any modern who sincerely desired to enter into their minds and understand their actions must first undergo a long process of training and self-discipline, learning that language itself had evolved over the centuries, that feelings had been far more intense and ideas far more crude in primitive societies and cultures than they were in modern ones, that ancient poetry contained not moral lessons but historical clues to the life of the heroes who had created it. Vico's *New Science*, the massive decoding of ancient history, mythology, and law in which he argued these points, is commonly recognized as one of the founding works of the modern human sciences, a work in some ways as deep and original as the contemporary work that transformed the natural sciences, the *Principia* of Isaac Newton.

In life, however, Vico was no hero. Newton received many honours for his scientific work, becoming one of the greatest celebrities of his age. Vico, by contrast, lived the life of an obscure – a very obscure – academic. His modest professorship of rhetoric paid only one-sixth as much as the professorship of law that he failed to win. He treasured every reference to his books in the foreign journals that could bring his name and ideas to a European public. But these were few, and some were negative. At home in Naples he walked the crowded streets in misery, avoiding the gaze of the acquaintances who failed to acknowledge the copies of his works that he sent them. He never managed to travel abroad – not even to Rome, to the unravelling of whose history he devoted much of his life. Even his funeral degenerated into a public quarrel, as the professors of the University of Naples and the members of the Confraternity of Santa Sofia, to which Vico had belonged, argued over which group should provide his pallbearers. In the end, his body had to be carried back into the house, where it awaited burial overnight.

Vico's great book fared just as badly, at first, as its author. A massive defence of the humanities, it appeared in an age when the philosophy of Descartes had triumphed in much of continental Europe and natural philosophy seemed the cutting edge of human thought. Vastly erudite – though also vastly inaccurate – it challenged the canons of taste in a period when the *philosophes* were beginning to denounce the study of historical details, which Voltaire memorably described as 'a vermin that kills great works'. Throughout the period in which the three editions of the *New Science* appeared, prices for erudite Latin books were falling. The whole style of the book seemed archaic and remote. With its allegorical title-page, pullulating erudition, and strange language (even some central and north Italians prefer to read Vico in English), the *New Science* was generally declared dead on arrival: out of scale, out of date, and doomed to be thoroughly out of mind.

Yet Vico and his book have had an afterlife as exciting as their original life was depressing. Italian readers continued to admire him. In the second half of the eighteenth century, the creators of the new sensibility that became known as Romanticism began to appreciate the depth and value of his work. Vico's evolutionary approach to ancient culture was independently revived by the heroes of German historicism after 1770. Some of Vico's more specific theses – like his arguments that Homer was a man of the people, not a polished poet, and that the myths about Romulus and Remus, Tarquin and Lucrece concealed a true and instructive social history of Rome's growth – found academic exponents at the same time. Long before the classical scholars and historians of late eighteenth-century England and Germany embarked on their discovery of the pastness of the past, Vico was already there – as more than one prophet of modern historicism discovered belatedly, to his chagrin. The *New Science* gradually began to be cited, summarized, and translated.

Early in the nineteenth century, the French historian Jules Michelet fell in love with Vico's evocation of the terrible creative power of ordinary people – a central motif of Michelet's own work on the history of France. He produced an abridged French text of Vico's prescient (because pre-Revolutionary) demonstration that man makes his own history. Social scientists from Auguste Comte to Karl Marx approved and embroidered on Vico's theory that each society passed through a recognizable series of stages of development. Later in the nineteenth century, pioneers of modern hermeneutics like Karl Lamprecht and Aby Warburg saw him as one of the creators of their method, with its emphasis on historical empathy, on the need to feel one's way into the strange textures of past cultures. Still later, Vico provided Benedetto Croce with the core of his attack on the positivism that the comparatist parts of the *New Science* had helped to nourish, and inspired James Joyce to devise the complex structure of *Finnegans Wake*. Since Croce's time the study of Vico has engaged the attention of some of the most influential intellectuals in western Europe and America, like Erich Auerbach, Isaiah Berlin, Arnaldo Momigliano, and Hayden White. They have given Vico a firm place in the intellectual pantheon of modernity.

The creator of the *New Science* had to struggle to find the social and mental freedom to do creative work. Born in 1668, Vico was one of the eight children of a poor man – Antonio de Vico, who owned the smallest of the many bookshops that crowded the street of San Biagio in central Naples. In the sharply hierarchical society of Naples, ruled by a Spanish viceroy and dominated by the landed aristocracy, Vico struggled from birth against the terrible handicaps of poverty and modest birth. These were made worse by his traumatic head-first fall from a ladder at the age of seven, which left him with a fractured skull and interrupted his studies. Though he made excellent progress while confined to his home, he found little appreciation at school, and an early effort to master scholastic philosophy with the Jesuits ended in failure. Vico's encounters with injustice and misunderstanding, in other words, began early.

None the less, he studied Roman law more successfully on his own, defended his father in a lawsuit, and attracted the attention of a rich and distinguished jurist named Rocca. Vico became the tutor to Rocca's children, with whom he spent several years, dividing his time between his teaching and study at the University of Naples. He also began to read the classics of Italian poetry and to write his own, and to study the fashionable new natural philosophy of Gassendi and others. Their efforts to replace the traditional Aristotelian natural philosophy of the schools with atomism attracted much interest in Naples, both from younger intellectuals and, in a different way, the Inquisition.

At thirty, Vico entered a competition to become professor of rhetoric – a poorly paid, elementary subject – at the University of Naples. Despite the vagaries of his education, his mastery of the Latin classics and his erudition evidently stood out. He won the post, married, and raised a family, supplementing his meagre income by writing commissioned poems and eulogies, giving private lessons, and evaluating libraries that came up for auction. For all the problems that afflicted Vico, he found much to enjoy and profit from in his immediate environment. Naples had a diverse and lively local culture, as Harold Stone has recently shown in detail. A social and cultural pressure-cooker, the lid of which was periodically blown off by revolutions, the city harboured convents, museums and libraries where innovative intellectuals had gathered for decades. Its natural philosophers and opera librettists were equally innovative. They read the most radical books of the seventeenth century, like the *Tractatus* of Spinoza; treasured manuscript copies gave them access to works too hot to be printed. Ideas were exchanged in Naples as much by public performance as by formal publication: effective formal speeches could make a career.

Vico's skills as poet and orator established his name. He made alert and well-informed friends – like the brilliant Paolo Mattia Doria, who shared his commitment to humanistic studies and with whom he discussed a wide range of philosophical questions. An elegant set-piece Latin oration won him membership in the liveliest intellectual organization in the city, the Accademia Medinaceli, which the Spanish viceroy had founded in 1698. To his fellow intellectuals who avidly studied the Epicureanism of Pierre Gassendi and the metaphysics of René Descartes, Vico owed much stimulation and perhaps some questioning of his original religious convictions.[1]

Gradually Vico gained recognition as a leading figure in this competitive and articulate intellectual field. At the same time he developed a sense of his own distinct intellectual position. In opposition to Descartes and his followers, he began to insist on the vital independent value of humanistic and historical studies. By 1710, he was developing what he called both a 'philosophical philology' and a 'new science' – a radically new approach to the understanding and study of human history. The Latin works on jurisprudence in which he described this project won a favourable review from the Protestant scholar and journalist Jean Le Clerc. In the early 1720s Vico was invited to contribute to a collection of autobiographies of distinguished Italian scholars. In the 1730s he became the official historiographer of Naples. At times he could feel that he was well on his way to attaining celebrity, not only in Naples but in the Republic of Letters, the imaginary society of scholars across Europe who were bound together by networks of correspondence and depended for information about the works of the learned on review journals like those edited by Le Clerc.

Sadly, none of these individual successes radically improved Vico's lot. He failed either to climb the academic ladder at home or to win widespread admiration for his most ambitious efforts as a writer. In 1717 he tried and failed to win one of the much more lucrative chairs of law in the university. The first edition of the *New Science* – the publication of which Vico had to finance by selling a ring – fell almost dead from the press. Vico did not receive so much as a letter from Le Clerc or Newton, to whom he sent copies. The only reference to the book that appeared abroad was a deliberately inaccurate and malicious notice in the influential *Acta eruditorum*, published in Leipzig, which Vico tried to rebut. His sense of isolation and disaffection grew. Vico saw his career as a catastrophe, the normal lot of a prophet in his own country. Other Neapolitan intellectuals, he decided, regarded him as a madman. By the end of his life, as he wrote in one bitter letter, he expected nothing from his native city but the complete isolation which enabled him to work so hard.[2]

Despite his increasing despair, Vico continued to work with admirable determination, revising his great book in 1729–30 and again in 1744. The final edition of the *New Science*, which appeared in the year of Vico's death, became his unruly summa. It defies recapitulation. The sprawling mass and spiralling cross-references of Vico's book effectively subvert its geometric form of presentation – a modern device that Vico borrowed from Descartes, as part of his claim to create a new science of humanity. But its general purport is clear enough.[3] Vico set out to show that his predecessors and contemporaries had misunderstood both the capacities of the human mind and the development of the human race. All too many intellectuals had dedicated themselves to the study of nature – the most fashionable of topics in the age of the New Philosophy of Descartes and Bacon, Copernicus and Gassendi. In doing so, however, they had failed to see that they were attempting something for which the human mind lacked the proper equipment. Understanding, Vico argued, in passages which have spawned much commentary, comes from making: one can truly understand only what one has created. Only God, accordingly, could truly understand the cosmos. Human beings, by contrast, could and should address themselves to the study of the human world – the laws and institutions, customs and practices created by earlier humans. The proper study of mankind was – must be – man.

Even those philosophers who studied society, moreover, had gone radically wrong as they tried to draw from a wide range of texts and experiences, themselves pulled out of context, a theoretical history of the origins of society and the state. Some, like the legal theorist Hugo Grotius, looked for clear, abstractly formulated laws that all men, pagan or Christian, early or late, acknowledged as valid. Others, like Thomas Hobbes, used the absence of an original code of laws as an explanation for the viciousness and fear that drove men to frame the state in the simple, brute hope of finding safety.

The philosophers, for all their disagreements, had converged in reading the wrong lessons into human history. They had created imaginary stories about society, culture and the state instead of teasing out the lineaments of the true history from the clues that remained in myths and texts. Their failure was easy to explain, if hard to redress. From Bacon and Descartes onwards, modern thinkers had despised the mere scholars who read ancient texts instead of dealing with the modern world. Bold speculation and experimentation in the world seemed far more productive than old-fashioned interpretation of books. Bacon condemned the humanists who had confined themselves to imitating Cicero instead of attacking the objects around them. Descartes dismissed the study of old texts as nothing more than a form of virtual travel. History, he explained, could teach only that customs varied from time to time, as they did from place to place. The serious thinker must look elsewhere for certain knowledge about God and the universe.

But the philosophers' wilful ignorance ruined their systematic theories. They could not assess the quality and solidity of the slabs of evidence which they hauled into different positions in the theoretical structures they erected. Samuel Pufendorf, for example, studied societies ancient and modern, civilized and barbarous. But he concluded only that history could not yield the rules that should frame a society, since no single set of laws and institutions appeared everywhere. History seemed mere chaos to this learned natural lawyer. As always, those who did not know how to study history were condemned to distort it.

The philologists, for their part, knew a great many things about the human past. Since the fourteenth century, after all, the Renaissance humanists had worked frenetically to collect and emend the ancient texts and to reconstruct ancient customs and institutions. Professional specialists in texts and commentary, they had direct access to the rich textual data that the philosophers refused to exploit. Antiquaries amassed heaps of information about the rituals and customs, institutions and lifestyles of the ancient world. But the philologists were as blind as the philosophers. They took their texts – and the stories these told – far too literally. They believed that the ancients had been men and women like themselves, with thoughts and feelings like their own. They broke their hearts and bankrupted their publishers bringing out folio after folio in which they tried to weld the divergent claims of Jews and Greeks, Egyptians and Babylonians about the early origins of their states into a single, coherent chronological framework – as if the ancients who had dated the origins of Egypt and Babylon had been rational moderns like themselves, working from precise quantitative evidence.

In fact, the ancients' stories about the early histories and primeval wisdom of Egypt and Mesopotamia derived not from their learning but from their ignorance. The original isolation of each nation led it to overestimate its originality and antiquity – a shared delusion which Vico called 'the conceit of the nations'. Modern scholars, for their part, had failed to see that they must not expect an ancient historian to use the methods and meet the standards of a modern archivist, a systematic error which Vico named 'the conceit of the learned'. The *folie à deux* of ancient writers and modern scholars had twisted the historical record into something as distorted as the image in a fun-house mirror. To that extent, the philosophers had been perfectly right to refuse to learn from books. At best the specialists in books knew only disconnected and insignificant facts – the same sort of facts that Cicero's serving-maid had known by virtue of living in the ancient world. Scholarship of this tedious, compilatory kind could not shed light on the origins of humanity or the state.

Vico's *New Science* set out to reform both philosophy and philology by connecting the two enterprises – by making philology into philosophy. Philosophy would trace the basic path that the march of human history must have followed, in all cases except that of the Jews. Thanks to direct divine revelation, they had had an organized civilization from the start. But other societies and civilizations – whose history Vico separated radically from the sacred history of the Jews – had not taken shape until after the Flood. And the founders of these gentile nations could not have been the sage legislators long celebrated in classical and modern texts, like the Egyptian Hermes Trismegistus and the Spartan Lycurgus. Rather, they must have been *bestioni* – brutish primitives, without masters and without mates, of gigantic size and untrammelled appetites. These antediluvian Frankenstein's monsters of Vico's romantic imagining had wandered the drying marshes left by Noah's Flood. They took what property and women they wished – a vision of the state of nature that owed something both to the ancient Epicurean Lucretius and to the modern atheist Hobbes.

Gradually and inevitably, Vico argued, the *bestioni* turned into heroes, and the heroes into men. Exhalations from the drying earth caused terrifying thunder in the sky. Being primitives, the *bestioni* imagined that the threatening natural phenomenon was an anthropomorphic god, literally threatening them. Hence religion came into being, and with religion shame. The fact that sexual intercourse had been carried out whenever and wherever one of the giants wished, without solemnity and in the open, now seemed horrifying. Sexual relations began to take place only after a religious ceremony sanctified the union of the couple in question, and in private. Over time, stable families were formed. Then a complex, hierarchical society took shape, as those *bestioni* who could not defend themselves became the slaves of those who could, exchanging freedom for safety. Divisions rent the one unified family when the slaves realized that they were as human as their heroic masters. Struggles for power and autonomy led to reforms and the creation of laws. Gradually each society developed laws, codes, and institutions. The state replaced the family. This dynamic history, in which strife played a basically creative role, was exemplified for Vico, as for Machiavelli, by the case of Rome.

In the end, Vico admitted, even Rome's triumphant story closed in disaster and sorrow. Prosperity and sophistication corrupted the original order, and Rome relapsed into a new barbarism as terrible – and happily as temporary – as the old. This course each nation except the chosen one must run – though not, of course, simultaneously. The barbarous peoples of the New World and China, for example, were clearly the contemporaries in development not of the Europeans of their day but of the primitives of ancient Germany or Scythia. Philosophy, rather than philology, provided this conjectural history of man – a history for lack of which the philologists inevitably went wrong. It also sounded the warning that the Europeans of Vico's time could also fall back into barbarism.

Philosophy, however, could lay out only the largest features on Vico's map of the human past. Philology filled in the contours and details, and in doing so it not only bore out Vico's theories about the origins of societies but shed a blinding new light on the most familiar texts. The oldest substantial document of Roman law consisted of the fragments of the Twelve Tables – the tables of statutes, traditionally thought to have been written down by the members of a commission appointed in 451 BC, and traditionally ascribed to the influence of Athenian example on the less civilized Romans. Vico admitted the vital importance of the Twelve Tables. But he rejected the story of their origins, insisting that these laws were not an import from a superior civilization but a 'code' autonomously created by the Romans over a century and more. Many earlier scholars had followed ancient precedent, drawing easy, rapid connections between one people and another and positing cultural borrowings even where the evidence was very slight. They imagined the entire ancient Mediterranean world as a small, well-lighted space, where Jewish patriarchs, Athenian statesmen and Roman generals cosily exchanged ideas.[4] Vico, by contrast, insisted on the autonomous development of societies. Moreover, he not only argued for the native origins of the Tables, but reinterpreted the document as a whole, trying to show that it began as the enactment of an agrarian law, itself passed in the course of the savage struggle for equality that raged between patrician heroes and plebeian *bestioni* in the early period of Roman history. A century before Barthold Georg Niebuhr recast the early history of Rome as one of radical social struggle gradually transformed into the mythical account of Roman origins, Vico rethought the whole Roman historical tradition, insisting that a true account of the early history of the city would bear little resemblance to the stories that had been retold for centuries in classrooms or to the interpretations offered by earlier jurists.[5]

Even in fields where Vico lacked the technical expertise he brought to the law, he proved capable of making extraordinary discoveries. In preparing the last edition of the *New Science*, for example, he devoted himself to a systematic study of Homer. The *Iliad* and *Odyssey*, Vico pointed out, had many curious characteristics, to some of which literary critics had objected since the Renaissance. Homer's heroes lived an

INTRODUCTION

absurdly simple life. Achilles cooked his own meals, the princess Nausi-
caa did her own laundry, and piles of manure reeked outside the palaces
of kings. The heroes were often unheroic: Achilles railed like a fishwife
at Agamemnon and wept like a child at the death of Patroclus. The
gods were even worse: bad-tempered, jealous, sometimes vulnerable
to mortal attack. Homer, moreover, often contradicted himself. How,
for example, could Odysseus' men have stolen the cattle of the sun,
whom Homer described as 'all-seeing'? Long and inept comparisons
between humans and animals filled page after tedious page, while absurd
epithets ruined what could have been powerful emotional effects.

Vico's new science explained away these indelicacies. Homer's heroes
lived simply because they had only recently climbed out of the mire.
They showed their emotions because they were primitives, more like
modern children than like modern adults. They created anthropomorphic gods because primitives and children always imagine deities
in their own form. Homer's apparent self-contradictions arose because
his poems were oral, not written. Over the centuries, the reciters had
made many changes and additions to the original work.

Even Homer's repetitive, inappropriate similes made sense of a
particular kind. In the history of culture, analogy precedes logic as poetry
precedes prose. Comparison between the known and the unknown was
the chief mental tool at a primitive's disposal. Homer's poetry revealed
in its warp and woof the perplexities of a mind still frightened by natural
forces, still unbroken to the dry analytical logic of civilization. Both
the curious style and the indecorous content of his poetry stemmed
from his historical position. Both provided vital evidence about the
way the primitive mind worked and the imaginative power that the
primitive could attain. In short, Vico saw even Homer's errors as
historical clues that revealed the differences of feeling and expression
that had grown up between Homer's time and his own. This insight
has received its full development only in the twentieth century, thanks
to the very different work of such Homeric scholars as Milman Parry
and Moses Finley.

Vico's own imaginative brilliance seems as impressive as that of the
ancient bards he liked to evoke, singing their tales around the fire. He
knew Homer only at second hand, through Latin translations. He knew

the Greek world more distantly still, through scholarly compilations, themselves based on the epics, of the customs and manners of the Homeric heroes. Yet he saw what dozens of more learned scholars had not: that Homer described, and lived in, a world very distant from the present. Vico, in other words, had the sort of prescient structural insight into difficult problems which is more often found in scientists than in humanists. A Feynman of the social universe, he could predict almost without effort, and certainly without research, results that later scholars would take lifetimes of work and masses of new data to confirm. Raising his six children in genteel poverty amid the pastel palaces, stuccoed churches and noisy streets of Europe's most rebellious city, imagining the life of the ancient giants as he trudged to his home in the Vicolo dei Giganti, Vico saw that men could live by radically different codes of value and speak in radically different codes of meaning. His programme for understanding the human past, with its insistence on using the evidence of custom and emotion to recreate the peculiar texture of each past society, adumbrates the achievements of modern anthropology and cultural history. His theory of interpretation often resembles the historical hermeneutics of the late eighteenth and nineteenth centuries. Throughout the twentieth century, the most up-to-date students of culture have repeatedly found inspiration and stimulation in the *New Science*.

The modern reader who seeks not only to follow Vico's arguments, but also to understand the intellectual context in which he framed them, should be aware that he was not the lonely explorer of strange continents of thought that some modern accounts portray. He learned from others who had gone in some of the same directions before him. In fact, he took facts and factoids, theses and interpretations from ancient and modern sources with the undiscriminating zeal of an intellectual magpie. True, it is not easy to identify all the sources on which he drew for inspiration or information. The Inquisition did its best to stamp out atomism and biblical criticism in late seventeenth-century Naples, making it risky even to refer to Spinoza or Hobbes – both of them authors who attacked issues of central importance to Vico. Vico, moreover, was a master of misquotation, whose deft misreadings of ancient and modern classics bewilder and bemuse the modern critic. He knew no English or German. When he listened in on the great debates of his time from his post in lively but distant Naples, he resembled a country telephone operator trying to eavesdrop on lovers whispering on a crackling party line. And even when he claimed to identify his intellectual icons and enemies, he cited authors whose work shows, on the surface, few precise connections with his. It seems genuinely impossible to know exactly what Vico knew, and when he knew it, about such iconoclastic, and even scandalous, figures as Hobbes, Bayle, Simon – the 'moderns' whom he both learned from and attacked. Nor is it easy to see the *New Science*, as Vico described it, as a work deriving from the teachings of Plato and Tacitus, Bacon and Grotius – though, as we will see, he learned something from each of these thinkers. Though Fausto Nicolini, author of a comprehensive commentary on the *New Science*, and later scholars like Paolo Rossi have done a spectacular job of clearing the scholarly ground, much remains to be rediscovered about what Vico read and how he used it.[6]

In general, however, it is clear that Vico responded not only to the discoveries he made on his own, but also to some of the most widespread and dramatic discussions of his own period. When Vico insisted on the value of humanistic and historical study, when he dwelt on the vital importance of classical studies, he took a side in a debate between Ancients and Moderns which had begun well before he was born. Previous participants had staked out positions which strongly resembled his. From the sixteenth century onwards, European intellectuals debated in a lively, even ferocious, way about the value of ancient texts, and the knowledge they enclosed. Advocates of modernity emphasized the gaps in the Ancients' knowledge of the world. They wrote panegyrics to the modern inventions which had enabled Europeans to discover the New World, circumnavigate the globe, and establish empires of unprecedented size: the compass and gunpowder. Printing, which preserved and disseminated the new knowledge brought back by explorers and conquistadors, also came in for praise. Francis Bacon – who placed a ship sailing past the Pillars of Hercules on the title-page of his programmatic work, *The Great Instauration* – found a new way of saying something which many others had felt when he described antiquity as 'the youth of the world' and insisted on the need to surpass the ancients. In the later seventeenth century, advocates of the ancients fought back, admitting the superiority of modern inventions but insisting that the ancients retained pre-eminence in literature and philosophy. The Quarrel of the Ancients and Moderns in France and the Battle of the Books in England represented parallel episodes in a literary war that engulfed academies, universities, and coffee-houses.

By the later seventeenth century, as Joseph Levine has shown, historical thought began to play a vital role in this discussion. Advocates of the Modern position argued that the works cited as inimitable classics by the Ancients were in fact the products of a society so alien from modern life, so primitive, that they could not possibly serve as moral or literary models. Charles Perrault, the French critic whose polemical *Parallel of the Ancients and Moderns* did much to frame the central issues of the debate, insisted as heatedly as Vico that Homer described a primitive, not a noble world. Richard Bentley, the most proficient Hellenist and editor of classical texts in early eighteenth-century Europe, dismissed the idea that Homer had meant to instruct and entertain readers for ages to come: 'Take my word for it, poor *Homer* in those circumstances and early times had never such aspiring thoughts. He wrote a sequel of Songs and Rhapsodies, to be sung by himself for small earnings and good cheer, at Festivals and other days of Merriment; the *Ilias* he made for the Men, and the *Odysseis* for the other sex.'[7] Vico's reading of Homer was far more sustained, and the consequences he drew from it more radical, than these men's remarks. But his approach to the subject bore a clear resemblance to those already sketched out in the last generation or two before his time.[8]

Even Vico's reading of the Homeric text rested on a more distant scholarly precedent. Julius Caesar Scaliger, the sixteenth-century scholar who wrote the first independent treatise on poetics of modern times, saw Homer's literary crimes as clearly as Vico. In his *Poetics*, he did to the *Iliad* and *Odyssey* what Mark Twain would do to *The Last of the Mohicans*. He identified every misplaced epithet and inappropriate action he could in order to prove, to his own satisfaction at least, the superiority of Virgil to Homer. Vico's lists of Homer's primitive forms of expression derived not only from his reading of the text, but also from Scaliger's commentary on it – which had also inspired Bentley.[9]

Some scholars in seventeenth-century Italy held the beliefs that Vico denied. Athanasius Kircher, the German Jesuit whose museum in the Collegio Romano at Rome became one of the most popular gathering places for native and foreign intellectuals in the 1660s and 1670s, firmly believed that the Egyptians had had a primeval revelation, direct rather than scriptural, of all the basic truths about the universe. Only elaborate allegorical decoding of their hieroglyphs and the myths these recorded, he argued, could unveil these lost truths to the forgetful moderns. Vico insisted that the most ancient pagans had been primitive giants, rejected allegorical explications of their myths, and treated hieroglyphs as a primitive form of writing rather than a subtle philosophical code devised by learned priests who did not want their learning sullied by the eyes of ordinary mortals. In this way, he attacked Kirher's impressive, if little read, books – as well as the magnificent Roman monuments, with obelisks at their core, that the Jesuit had helped to design. In Naples as well, scholars like Antonio Costantino, whose *Divine and Worldly Adamo-Noetic Philosophy*, written around 1730, circulated in manuscript, juggled the data of chronology and biblical exegesis in order to show that all nations, gentile as well as Jewish, had inherited a primeval revelation of the basic truths of religion and philosophy.[10]

But Vico had allies as well as enemies when he took the field. Jean Le Clerc, for example – the very journalist whose review he prized so highly – also insisted on the need to read texts historically, and rejected the allegorical tradition as anachronistic and unsubstantiated. He even wrote an elaborate theoretical manual on textual interpretation and emendation, the *Ars critica*, to which he appended detailed treatments of specimen texts and problems. Vico did not cite the works in which Le Clerc advanced theses like his own, but the many resemblances between Le Clerc's work and his own make it highly likely, as Gianfranco Cantelli has argued, that he knew them. Vico's *New Science* was a synthesis of novel work done by others as well as a statement of his individual discoveries.[11]

Vico learned from his enemies as well as his friends. No Modern, he still used the characteristic tools of the Moderns against their creators. Though he rejected Cartesianism, he certainly took from Descartes the idea of presenting his way of understanding the past as a radically new philosophy – a new, independent and structurally coherent method for attacking problems that intellectuals had dealt with piecemeal and ineffectually in the past. His effort to state his findings axiomatically, to make the normally vague disciplines of historical interpretation take on the visible clarity of geometry, reflected his effort to fight the Cartesians on their own ground.

Though Vico disagreed on many points with Bacon, in some ways he owed the man he called 'the pioneer of a completely new universe' even more than Descartes. Bacon, like Vico, held that the ancients were not classic models for the moderns, but their primitive ancestors – an idea that lies at the core of the *New Science*. More important, Bacon argued that the reform of culture in his own time must be prepared for by a systematic effort to collect and explain the cultural achievements of the past. Each century, he argued, had had a different 'spirit', which had promoted certain studies while discouraging others. The modern manager of knowledge needed to understand these in order to create the proper 'spirit' in his own day. And the only way he could attain this knowledge was, quite simply, by surveying as many products of the human mind in each period as possible, in order to see which conditions had brought them into being. A comprehensive history of culture – which Bacon, like others before him, called a 'historia litteraria' or 'literary history' – would have to be compiled before natural and moral philosophy could be completely reformed. Throughout the seventeenth century, intellectuals struggled to produce such a history. Specialized contributions to it – dozens of voluminous monographs on the history of philosophy, for example – poured from the presses.[12]

As early as 1708–9 Vico devoted a Latin oration, *On the Study Methods of Our Time*, to attacking Descartes and Bacon for their failure to appreciate the vital importance of the humanities. In the course of this work, he used Bacon's own method for historical analysis to explain why intellectual tastes changed, so that a given book might find many readers in one period only to drop from sight a decade later. 'Every epoch', he wrote, 'is dominated by a "spirit", a genius, of its own. Novelty, like beauty, recommends certain faults which, after fashion changes, become glaringly apparent. Writers, wishing to reap a profit from their studies, follow the trend of their time.'[13] This argument already summed up, in a nutshell, the larger programme of the *New Science* – the great work in which Vico used his understanding of the differences between historical periods to explain the different forms of feeling and expression that had flourished in them. Despite his dislike of the new natural philosophy, Vico learned a vast amount from its prophets.

The *New Science* presents itself not only as a study of providence, grounded in theological debate, but also – indeed, above all – as a study of myth and law, grounded in scholarly traditions. It offers explanations of a great many textual, mythological, and historical details. And its interpretations of particular details in human history often incorporate intellectual traditions which now seem highly recondite, but were in Vico's time simply in the scholarly air. Vico, for example, made clear that the Roman scholar Varro, who had divided past time into three periods, 'chaotic', 'mythical', and 'historical', inspired his own effort to divide the past into coherent periods. In using and giving credit to Varro, Vico quoted a text and took positions in a discipline familiar to every scholar of his time. True, Varro's own historical works did not survive. But the later Roman scholar Censorinus, writing in AD 238, quoted the passage in question. In the sixteenth century, when Joseph Scaliger and others began to try to establish the framework of dates for ancient history, they seized upon, quoted and interpreted this same passage in the massive, highly technical works they dedicated to what became, for a century and more, a fashionable subject. In making Varro's tripartite periodization a cornerstone of his own work, Vico was not rejecting, but adapting, the chronological scholarship of his own day.[14]

Similarly, in treating the development of law as one of the keys to human history, Vico built on precedents solidly established in the sixteenth century. Philologically trained lawyers like Andrea Alciato, Jacques Cujas, François Baudouin, and Jean Bodin had broken, long before Vico, with the largely unhistorical treatment of Roman law normally offered in the medieval universities. They had insisted that Roman law changed radically over time. They had done their best to dissect the *Corpus iuris* of Justinian and other surviving documents, reconstructing lost or partially preserved sources like the Twelve Tables, on which an enormous literature had grown up before Vico. And they had insisted, polemically, on the need to use legal systems as central evidence about past societies and states. Their works included elaborate treatises, like Baudouin's *Prolegomena* and Bodin's *Method*, on how to study law historically. No earlier jurist anticipated Vico's bold effort to turn the Twelve Tables into evidence for the existence, in early Rome, of social struggles as radical as those that had flared up in Naples a generation before Vico's birth. But the tradition of humanistic jurisprudence was much on his mind for decades. Vico owed at least a part of his historical sensibility to the jurists who, as he wrote in 1708–9, 'gave back to Rome her own laws, instead of adjusting these laws to the needs of our epoch'.[15]

The French jurists of the sixteenth century, like Vico himself, are often seen as pre-eminently modern figures. Accordingly, a number of scholars have been willing to accept that he learned from them. But Vico also drew on much older scholarly traditions. Some of these were classical – like the rhetorical tradition, with its emphasis on the kinds of knowledge that were directly relevant to life in society and its elaborate treatments of hermeneutics, on which he drew heavily.[16] Others he found at less respectable addresses. The case of Vico's giants, for example, tells a story very different from that of his legal scholarship. A number of scholars have suggested that Vico drew his vision of the first men from the *De rerum natura* of Lucretius. The Roman poet described the gigantic sizes early beings attained and evoked the fear that thunder inspired in early men. His account of the primitive world provided the basis for a modern anthropology, just as his discussion of atoms provided part of the basis of a modern physics. In fact, however, Vico's giants were composite figures, historical golems patched together from diverse sources. In his first treatment of the giants, which formed part of his works of the 1710s on law, Vico cited not only Lucretius' poem but also chapter 6 of Genesis. This tells the story of the sons of God, who saw that the daughters of men were beautiful and went in to them, siring mighty men of valour. The text remarks that 'there were giants in the earth in those days'. This verse provided the foundation for Vico's belief that early humans reached enormous size. His later tale of the barbarian giants who lived after the Flood repeated, in updated terms, the history of the antediluvian giants of the Bible.

In fusing history with gigantology – as Walter Stephens has shown in a massive, fascinating book entitled *Giants in Those Days* – Vico followed exegetical traditions of long standing.[17] One of the most influential world historians of the Renaissance, the saintly Dominican forger Giovanni Nanni da Viterbo, portrayed all men before the Flood as giants. Many other writers took him up – not least Rabelais, whose giants, Gargantua and Pantagruel, also have a biblical ancestry and inspiration as well as classical and modern characteristics. Vico's *bestioni*, then, were not by any means the first gigantic brutes to populate world histories. And though Vico gave the story his own twist, he drew on another source – a genuinely classical text – in doing so. Urine and faeces, Vico noted, have a great fertilizing power, as anyone can see by planting a field where an army has made camp. The Jews were cleanly, as their divine law made them. But pagan babies, abandoned by their mothers, played with their own excretions – as Tacitus showed, in a passing remark in his account of the ancient Germans. Pagan babies, accordingly, never stopped growing. These points seem trivial to the modern reader, and are often overlooked by modern interpreters seeking points of contact with the *New Science*. Vico, however, endlessly repeated and developed them – clear evidence that he took them very seriously indeed. Biblical and apocryphal, classical and Renaissance, historical and scientific theories coalesced in the foundations of Vico's work.

The *New Science*, in other words, is nowhere simple, never of a piece. Vico's heroic effort to modernize philology by making it philosophical was a project he shared with many seventeenth-century intellectuals of the most diverse theological views, as Carlo Borghero has shown in his detailed account of historians' and philologists' efforts to counter the Cartesian attack on book-based, historical forms of knowledge.[18] Vico's history of the human race, in short, is less a fresco painted spontaneously than a Watts Tower of found objects, combined in dazzling new ways but often old and battered in themselves. A baroque encyclopedist, he seized upon an incredibly wide range of materials, not only acting upon them but being acted upon by them. As one might expect, his system resembled the muddy vortices of Descartes' physics rather than the lucid structures of his mathematics. Vico's new science grew like a glacier, awkwardly and incoherently, absorbing new elements while shedding older ones.

The peculiar origins, composite character, and complex, twisting argumentation of Vico's book made it hard to interpret even in his own time. For all its use of and references to well-known books and theories, it did not belong to any of the standard genres of Vico's period. Philosophical works, in Vico's day, regularly dealt with the origins of human society and law. But they rarely referred in detail to a vast range of literary and legal sources. Scholarly works, by contrast, often rested on massive erudite foundations. But the leading scholars of the late seventeenth century – men like the great Benedictine scholars Jean Mabillon and Bernard de Montfaucon – pioneered in the precise historical study of objects, from documents on parchment and paper to sculptures in stone. Connoisseurs of detail, they analysed the materials they studied word by word or surface by surface, often providing illustrations to enable their readers to participate in the work of philology. Vico's imaginative decoding of literary texts differed radically in style – if not always in spirit – from their austere, step-by-step decipherment of clearly delimited bodies of evidence. That helps considerably to explain why this ambitious scholar's most ambitious book found so few sympathetic readers among those contemporaries who had read the same texts and confronted the same problems as Vico himself.[19]

The *New Science* fits modern ideas about method and genre even more loosely than it did those of Vico's contemporaries. Moreover, it has spawned a vast range of interpretations, some of them richly informed about Vico's own world, others motivated by more contemporary concerns. In these circumstances, debate is only natural. Scholars disagree sharply over many important points connected with the interpretation of the *New Science* – for example, the religious views that it expresses. Some have seen Vico's history of the human race as radically secular. Man, Vico argued, could understand only what man had made: not the physical, but the social universe. By turning from the cosmos to the human past, the modern scholar would come to see that the ancient stories about the gods had not been a twisted version of Christian sacred history, as many scholars thought, but the creation of primitive men desperately trying to master the universe they inhabited. On this account, Vico's history of humanity strikes a modern, secular note, insisting on its own independence from the sacred histories and emphasizing the creative independence of the human race.

Others see Vico's universe as absolutely determinist. By separating gentile from Jewish history, they argue, he made clear that the human race, unsupported by revelation, could evolve only in one direction – one programmed into it in advance, by the Creator, who destined all races to create religions, institutions, and laws as they wandered the earth after the Flood. Vico's new science of the past did not draw most of its details from the Old Testament account of early human history. None the less it asserted – more powerfully, perhaps, than the traditional histories which did draw on the Bible – the absolute power of Providence. Like the little figures in the eerie drawings of *Prisons* by Vico's contemporary Piranesi, all humans appear, on this account, as prisoners dwarfed and manipulated by a gigantic historical machinery that they could neither comprehend nor control.[20] Disputes on this and many other points will certainly continue: no amount of critical and editorial commentary will produce consensus on all controversial points.

David Marsh's lucid and readable translation brings this massive, difficult text to the English reader more directly than ever before. Precise but not literal, cast in graceful English, it enables the reader to follow Vico's arguments without having to master a special terminology. It should help to stimulate the direct study of Vico's ponderous and puzzling tome, a work both infinitely remote and startlingly contemporary, more cited and less understood, perhaps, than any of the other challenging books produced in the age of the New Philosophy that called all in doubt.

NOTES

1. For the larger context of Vico's thought see H. Stone, *Vico's Cultural History: The Production and Transmission of Ideas in Naples, 1685–1750* (Leiden, New York, and Cologne, 1997).
2. On Vico's life see especially his *Autobiography*, tr. M. H. Fisch and T. G. Bergin (Ithaca, NY, 1944; repr. 1963), and the perceptive commentary on it by D. P. Verene, *The New Art of Autobiography: An Essay on The Life of Giambattista Vico Written by Himself* (Oxford, 1991).

3. For more extended introductions to Vico's thought, see P. Rossi, 'La vita e le opere di Giambattista Vico', *Le sterminate antichità: studi vichiani* (Pisa, 1969), 15–80; P. Burke, *Vico* (Oxford and New York, 1985).

4. See D. C. Allen, *The Legend of Noah: Renaissance Rationalism in Art, Science, and Letters*, Illinois Studies in Language and Literature, 33, 3–4 (1949; repr. Urbana, 1963); A. L. Owen, *The Famous Druids: A Survey of Three Centuries of English Literature on the Druids* (Oxford, 1962).

5. See A. D. Momigliano, 'Roman "Bestioni" and Roman "Eroi" in Vico's *Scienza nuova*', *History and Theory* 5 (1966), 3–23, repr. in Momigliano, *Terzo contributo alla storia degli studi classici e del mondo antico* (Rome, 1966), I, 153–77.

6. See F. Nicolini's *Commento storico alla seconda Scienza Nuova*, 2 vols. (Rome, 1949–50), and his edition of *La Scienza Nuova giusta l'edizione del 1744*, 3 vols. (Naples, 1911–16); Rossi, *Le sterminate antichità*.

7. Richard Bentley, *Remarks Upon a Late Discourse of Free-Thinking, in a Letter to F. H. D. D. by Phileleutherus Lipsiensis*, 8th ed. (Cambridge, 1745), 25–6.

8. See K. Simonsuuri, *Homer's Original Genius* (Cambridge, 1979), and J. Levine, *The Battle of the Books: History and Literature in the Augustan Age* (Ithaca, NY, 1991).

9. See A. Grafton, 'Renaissance Readers of Homer's Ancient Readers', in *Homer's Ancient Readers*, ed. R. Lamberton and J. J. Keaney (Princeton, 1992), 149–72.

10. See the splendid survey by D. C. Allen, *Mysteriously Meant: The Rediscovery of Pagan Symbolism and Allegorical Interpretation in the Renaissance* (Baltimore and London, 1970).

11. G. Cantelli, *Vico e Bayle: Premesse per un confronto* (Naples, 1971).

12. For Bacon's views and their context see E. Hassinger, *Empirisch-rationaler Historismus: Seine Ausbildung in der Literatur Westeuropas von Guicciardini bis Saint-Evremond* (Berne and Munich, 1978), and W. Schmidt-Biggemann, *Topica universalis: Eine Modellgeschichte humanistischer und barocker Wissenschaft* (Hamburg, 1983).

13. G. B. Vico, *Le orazioni inaugurali, il De italorum sapientia e le polemiche*, ed. G. Gentile and F. Nicolini (Bari, 1914), 116; *On the Study Methods of Our Time*, tr. E. Gianturco (Ithaca and London, 1990), ch. 13, 73.

14. See in general P. Rossi, *I segni del tempo: Storia delle terra e storia delle nazioni da Hooke a Vico* (Milan, 1979), translated as *The Dark Abyss of Time: The History of the Earth and the History of Nations from Hooke to Vico*, tr. L. G. Cochrane (Chicago and London, 1984); A. Grafton, *Joseph Scaliger: A Study in the History of Classical Scholarship*, 2 vols. (Oxford, 1983–93), II: *Historical Chronology*.

15. Vico, *Le orazioni inaugurali*, ed. Gentile and Nicolini, 110; *On the Study Methods of our Time*, tr. Gianturco, 65. On the French jurists see e.g. J. H. Franklin, *Jean Bodin and the Sixteenth-Century Revolution in the Methodology of Law and History* (New York and London, 1963); G. Huppert, *The Idea of Perfect History: Historical Erudition and Historical Philosophy in Renaissance France* (Urbana, Chicago, and London, 1970); and D. R. Kelley, *Foundations of Modern Historical Scholarship: Language, Law, and*

History in the French Renaissance (New York and London, 1970). On Vico's debt to this tradition see e.g. I. Berlin, *Vico and Herder: Two Studies in the History of Ideas* (London, 1976; repr. London, 1992), 125–42.

16. See the lucid and informative work by M. A. Mooney, *Vico in the Tradition of Rhetoric* (Princeton, 1985).

17. W. Stephens, Jr., *Giants in Those Days: Folklore, Ancient History and Nationalism* (Lincoln and London, 1989).

18, C. Borghero, *La certezza e la storia* (Milan, 1983).

19. On this point, see Stone, *Vico's Cultural History*.

20. See M. Lilla, *G. B. Vico: The Making of an Anti-Modern* (Cambridge, Mass., 1993). Portions of this introduction appeared in the *New Republic* magazine and are reprinted here with permission.

TRANSLATOR'S PREFACE

The present translation is based on the edition of Vico's works edited by Andrea Battistini (2 vols., Milan, 1990). I have greatly benefited from the classic English translation of the work by Thomas G. Bergin and Max Harold Fisch (3rd edition, Ithaca, NY, 1976), whose introduction and interpretation remain invaluable for any student of Vico. I have also used the French translation by Ariel Doubine (Paris, 1953) and the German translation by Vittorio Hösle and Christian Jermann (2 vols., Hamburg, 1990).

The translation was revised during a sabbatical leave at the Institute for Advanced Study in Princeton, New Jersey. I wish to thank the Institute's faculty, staff, and its director, Phillip A. Griffiths, for making my stay so pleasant and productive. Others who advised me at the Institute were Glen Bowersock, Patrizia Castelli, Fernando Cervantes, Marshall Clagett, Giles Constable, Donald Kelley, Frank Ryan, Homer Thompson, and Peter Zarrow. I also wish to thank my Rutgers colleague James Masschaele for advice on medieval institutions. Anthony Grafton generously read the entire translation and offered many valuable suggestions and corrections.

In the interest of readability, I have translated foreign words and titles throughout; passages from Greek and Roman authors generally follow the version in the Loeb Classical Library. On occasion I have corrected minor lapses and supplied phrases required by the context, taking care that these surface adjustments in no way distort the substance of Vico's argument. Following the example of Bergin and Fisch, I have omitted or abridged most of Vico's obtrusive cross-references.

By present-day standards of scholarship, Vico is often inaccurate and inconsistent. But his larger view of history and society demands our attention, and I have striven to make his work readable for the modern reader.

D.M.

Princeton,
20 January 1997

This printing corrects several misprints and oversights in the first edition, but none of the departures from the Bergin–Fisch Vulgate, which some regard as heretical errors. Bergin and Fisch provide a trot; I provide a translation. Scholars will consult Vico's original text.

D.M.

Princeton,
September 2001

This third version offers the reader new notes on the translation in paragraphs 25(5) and 1106.

D.M.

Metuchen,
April 2013

Dcm. Ant. Vacaro I.

Sescne. Sculp.

Frontispiece from the 1744 edition

IDEA OF THE WORK

Explanation of the Frontispiece Illustration which Introduces the Work

[1] Just as Cebes the Theban once made a *Tablet* of things moral, so I present here a *Tableau of civil institutions.*★ Before reading my work, you may use this tableau to form an idea of my New Science. And after reading it, you will find that this tableau aids your imagination in retaining my work in your memory.

[2] The woman with winged temples who stands on the celestial globe, meaning the world of nature, is Metaphysics: for her name in fact means 'above nature'. The radiant triangle with the seeing eye is God, shown in his manifestation as providence. In her state of ecstasy, Metaphysics contemplates God above the order of natural institutions, through which philosophers have previously contemplated him. In other words, Metaphysics in this work ascends higher and contemplates in God the world of human minds, which we call the metaphysical world. Metaphysics thus seeks to demonstrate God's providence in the world of the human spirit, which we call the civil world or the world of nations.

In the lower part of the picture are represented various hieroglyphs symbolizing the institutions which are the basic elements of the civil world. The globe, which represents the physical or natural world, rests on only one point of the altar. This means that previously the

---

★ From the outset, Vico constantly plays upon the ambivalence of Latinate vocabulary: *tavola* means a table, tablet, or tableau; and *cosa*, 'thing' (like Latin *res*), often means an institution. The so-called *Tablet* of Cebes is a first-century Greek dialogue in which an allegorical painting about human morality is described and analysed.

philosophers have contemplated and demonstrated divine providence only through the natural order, in which God is conceived as an eternal Mind who is the free and absolute sovereign of nature. To this God, humankind offers its worship, sacrifices, and other divine honours, because his eternal counsel naturally grants and preserves our existence. But no philosopher has yet contemplated God's providence under humankind's most characteristic property, which is its essentially social nature.

Since original sin caused people to fall from a state of perfect justice, human intentions and actions generally follow different and even contrary paths. If people were left to pursue their private interests, they would live in solitude like wild beasts. But by His providential care, God ordered and arranged human institutions so that this same self-interest led people, even through these different and contrary ways, to live with justice like *human beings* and to remain in society. In my New Science, I shall show that this social nature is the true civil nature of humankind, and that law exists in nature. This role of divine providence is the first of the principal topics studied in my New Science. Viewed in this aspect, my work becomes a *rational civil theology of divine providence*.

[3] In the Zodiac belt circling the celestial globe, only the signs of Leo and Virgo, and no others, appear full-face or in what is called front view.

The figure of Leo means that the principles of my New Science begin by contemplating Hercules, who is the archetype of the founder celebrated by every pagan nation of antiquity.★ And it contemplates him as he performs his greatest labour, the slaying of the Nemean lion. (Spewing forth flames, this beast set fire to the Nemean forest. When Hercules killed it, he donned its skin as a trophy and ascended to the stars. As we shall see, this lion represents the great ancient forest of the earth, which was burned off and placed under cultivation by Hercules, who is also the archetype of the political heroes, who in fact came before the better-known warrior heroes.) Leo further marks the starting point of human chronology. For the Greeks, who are the source for all our knowledge of pagan antiquities, reckoned their Olympiads from

---

★ Vico's *carattere*, character or sign, is best rendered as 'archetype'.

the first Olympic games, which Hercules founded when he instituted the Nemean games to celebrate his victory in slaying the lion. In this way, the chronology of the Greeks begins with the introduction of agriculture among them.

As for Virgo, the astronomers adopted the poets' description of the goddess as crowned with ears of grain. This means that Greek history began in the Golden Age, which the poets clearly celebrate as the world's first age. Indeed, for many centuries years were reckoned according to the harvests of grain, which was the world's first 'gold'. The Greeks' Golden Age corresponds exactly to the Latins' Age of Saturn, a god whose name comes from *satus*, sowing. During this Golden Age, the gods mingled with heroes on earth, as the ancient poets faithfully record. As we shall see, the earliest pagans, being simple and uncouth folk, were deceived by the fearful superstitions created by their vigorous imaginations, and so truly believed that they saw gods on earth. And we shall also see that the Near Eastern peoples, Egyptians, Greeks, and Latins – while unaware of each other's existence – all shared uniform ideas which led them to elevate their gods to planets and their heroes to fixed stars. Thus from Saturn, whom the Greeks call Kronos or Chronos (meaning 'time'), we derive further basic principles of chronology, the science of time-reckoning.

[4] You must not think it improper that the altar stands beneath the celestial globe and supports it. As we shall see, the world's first altars were raised by the pagans in the primitive, earthbound heaven sung by the ancient poets, whose myths faithfully record the tradition that Heaven once ruled on earth and bestowed great benefits on the human race. As the children of the new-born human race, the first people believed that the sky was no higher than their mountain heights, just as children today think it no higher than the rooftops. Later, as the Greek mind developed, altars were erected on the summits of the highest mountains, such as Olympus, which is where Homer says that the gods dwell in his day. Eventually, Heaven was raised above the celestial spheres as described by today's astronomers, and Olympus was raised above the firmament of stars. At the same time, the altar was carried up into heaven, where it forms the constellation Ara. The fire on the altar passed into the neighbouring house of Leo, which you see

in the picture. (This sign symbolizes the Nemean forest which Hercules burned off to place the land under cultivation.) And as a trophy of Hercules' deed, the lion's skin was raised up to the stars.

[5] The ray of divine providence, which illuminates the convex jewel adorning the breast of Metaphysics, signifies that metaphysics must have a clean and pure heart. (Metaphysics must neither be tainted by pride of spirit, nor soiled by the baseness of physical pleasures. Pride led Zeno to teach fate as his first principle, and pleasure led Epicurus to teach chance; and both denied divine providence.) The jewel also signifies that the knowledge of God must not end in the metaphysics of previous philosophers, who merely sought the private illumination of intellectual virtues as a guide to their personal morality. Such metaphysics would have been represented by a flat jewel. Instead, the jewel in my picture is convex, so that the rays of providence are reflected and refracted outwards. In this way, metaphysics recognizes God's providence in *public* moral institutions, meaning those civil customs by which nations arise and are perpetuated in the world.

[6] The ray of providence is reflected from the breast of Metaphysics to the statue of Homer, who is the earliest pagan author to come down to us. For metaphysics has its origins in the history of human ideas, beginning with humankind's very first civilized thoughts. With the aid of metaphysics, I have finally been able to descend into the confused minds of the first founders of the pagan nations, which were filled with vivid sensations and unbounded fantasies. Such people had only a dull and dim-witted capacity for applying their human reason. And so we find that the origins of poetry not only differ from, but even contradict all our previous conceptions. For they spring from the origins of poetic wisdom, which were previously obscure for the same reasons. This poetic wisdom was the knowledge of the theological poets, and was undoubtedly the world's first wisdom among the pagans. The statue of Homer standing on a broken pedestal signifies my discovery of the true Homer. (This discovery, which I sensed but did not fully comprehend in the first edition of my *New Science*, is here fully worked out and explained.) Our previous ignorance of the true Homer kept hidden from us the true origins and institutions of the nations in three ages: (1) the mythical age; (2) the dark age, which all have despaired of

knowing; and (3) the historical age. These are the three ages of history described by Marcus Terentius Varro, the greatest scholar of Roman antiquities, in his great work, now lost, titled *Divine and Human Institutions*.

[7] In addition, I note that my work employs a new form of criticism, which was previously lacking, in seeking to establish the truth about the founders of the pagan nations. For these founders in fact lived more than a thousand years before those writers with whom previous criticism has dealt. In my Science, philosophy undertakes to examine philology. (By philology, I mean the science of everything that depends on human volition: for example, all histories of the languages, customs, and deeds of various peoples in both war and peace.) Previously, philosophy has had almost a horror of discussing questions of philology, since they involve lamentably obscure causes and infinitely diverse effects. But here philosophy reduces philology to the form of a science, discovering in it the outlines of an *ideal eternal history*, along which the histories of all nations pass in time. Viewed under this principal aspect, my New Science becomes a philosophy of human 'authority', a term I shall explain later. And by discovering new principles of poetry, which in turn reveal new principles of mythology, I show that the Greek myths were true and rigorous histories of the customs of the most ancient peoples of Greece.

First came the myths of the gods, which were histories from the crudest age of pagan civilization, when people believed that all institutions necessary or useful to humankind were deities. The authors of this poetry were the first peoples, who were all theological poets; and tradition relates unequivocally that they founded the pagan nations through their myths of the gods. We shall have occasion to apply the principles of my new criticism to the origin of the pagan gods. For we shall ponder the specific times and particular occasions when the first pagans conceived of institutions necessary or useful to humankind, and which gods they variously imagined then, inspired by the fearful religions which they themselves had invented and embraced. This natural theogony, or genealogy of the gods, arose naturally in the minds of the earliest people, and thus provides a rational chronology for the poetic history of the gods.

Second came the heroic myths, which were the true histories of the heroes and heroic customs which have flourished in every nation during the age of its barbarism. Homer's two epics prove to be two treasuries, in which we may discover the natural law of the Greeks when they were still a barbarous people. My New Science shows that among the Greeks this period lasted until the age of Herodotus. Now, although Herodotus is called the father of Greek history, his books are for the most part filled with myths, and his style contains many Homeric elements. Indeed, this trait persists in later Greek historians, who employ a style that is midway between the poetic and the prosaic. By contrast, Thucydides, who is the first serious and rigorous historian of Greece, admits in the introduction to his history that until his father's day – which was the generation of Herodotus, who was old when Thucydides was a boy – the Greeks knew absolutely nothing about their own antiquities, much less those of other peoples! (And, with the exception of the Romans, today we can only know about these ancient peoples from the Greeks.) These antiquities are the dense darkness shown in the background of the frontispiece. But as Metaphysics reflects the ray of divine providence on the figure of Homer, from this darkness there emerge into the light all the symbols that represent the basic principles of this world of nations – principles which were previously known only by their effects.

[8] Among these symbols, the altar appears most prominently. For the civil world of all peoples begins with religion.

[9] On top of the altar and to the left, there first appears a *lituus*, which is the divining wand that Roman augurs used in taking auguries and observing omens. It symbolizes divination, which among all pagan peoples was the origin of their first divine institutions. For all ancient peoples recognized God's providence. The Jews recognized God's true providence, and believed that God is an infinite Mind who beholds all ages in a single moment of eternity. Their God revealed future events to His people by Himself, through His angels (who are also minds), or through the prophets, to whose minds He spoke. By contrast, the pagans embraced an imaginary providence, for they fancied the gods as physical bodies which foretold the future by signs apparent to the senses. But whether true or imaginary, this attribute of providence led

the entire human race to call God's nature 'divinity'. They all derived this name from one and the same notion, which in Latin was called *divinari*, to foretell the future. But we must bear in mind the basic distinction I just made between Jews and pagans. From it derive all the other essential differences, explained in my New Science, which distinguish the natural law of the Jews from the natural law of the pagan nations.

Now, Roman jurists defined this second kind of natural law as something which divine providence had ordained together with the human customs of civilization. Hence, the divining wand also denotes the origin of the universal history of the pagans, which began with the universal flood, as physical and historical evidence proves. Mythology relates that two centuries after the flood Heaven (Uranus in Greek) reigned on earth and bestowed numerous great benefits on mankind. At that time, the Near Eastern peoples, Egyptians, Greeks, Romans, and other pagan nations shared uniform ideas which caused them to develop parallel religions, all based on their various Jupiters. For at that time, 200 years after the flood, the heavens were filled with thunder and lightning, and each nation began to read in this thunder and lightning the omens of its own Jupiter. (This existence of multiple Jupiters – which accounts for the Egyptians calling their Jupiter Ammon the most ancient of them all – was previously a source of amazement to philologists and historians.)* As we shall see, the same physical and historical evidence proves that the religion of the Jews is more ancient than the religions on which the pagan nations were founded, and thus confirms the truth of the Christian religion.

[10] On the altar next to the divining wand, we see a fire and a pitcher of water, the elements required in divination sacrifices. Among the pagans these sacrifices originated in that custom which the Romans called procuring the auspices, *procurare auspicia*. This meant offering a sacrifice in order to interpret the omens properly, so that the divine admonitions, or Jupiter's commands, could be properly carried out.

---

* By *filologi*, 'philologists', Vico often means the scholars we now call 'historians'. For Vico, philology is the study of historical cultures, as philosophy is the study of eternal ideas: see 139 below.

Such rites were the pagans' divine institutions, from which their human institutions later arose.

[11] The first of these human institutions was marriage, which is here represented by a torch, lit at the altar fire and supported by the pitcher of water. As all political thinkers agree, marriage is the seed-bed of the family, just as the family is the seed-bed of the commonwealth. To signify this, the marriage torch, while symbolizing a human rite, is placed on the altar between the water and the fire, which are symbols of divine rites. In precisely this way, the ancient Romans celebrated nuptials with water and fire, *aqua et igni*. For they saw that it was by divine counsel that these two common elements had led people to live in society. (Even before the discovery of fire, society was made possible by perennial sources of water, which is more essential to life than fire.)

[12] The second human institution is burial. In Latin, it was the verb *humare*, to bury, which gave the primary and proper meaning to the noun *humanitas*, human civilization. Burial is represented by a funerary urn placed to one side in the forest. This means that burials date from the age when mankind fed on fruit in the summer, and acorns in the winter. Inscribed on the urn are the initials *D.M.*, which stand for the Latin *Dis Manibus*, to the Dii Manes, meaning the good souls of the buried dead. This phrase refers to the belief that people's souls do not die with their bodies, but are immortal – a notion which was first approved by the common consensus of all mankind, and later demonstrated by Plato.

[13] The urn also alludes to the origin of the pagans' division of their fields, which we may view as the origin of the later distinctions between cities, peoples, and ultimately nations.

Long ago, Noah's three sons renounced their father's religion, which by its rite of marriage was the only thing that preserved the society of families in that state of nature. There followed a period of brutish wandering or migration, in which first Ham's tribes, then Japheth's, and finally Shem's, were all scattered throughout the earth's great forest. Pursuing shy and intractable women, fleeing the wild animals which were so abundant in the great primeval forest, and searching for pasture and water, they were after many years so widely scattered that their condition was reduced to that of brutes. Then, on certain occasions ordained by divine providence, described in my New Science, they were shaken and roused by a terrible fear of Uranus and Jupiter, the gods they had invented and embraced. Some of them now finally stopped wandering and took shelter in *certain* places. Here they settled down with *certain* women. And in their fear of the deities they perceived, they celebrated marriages, engaging secretly in religious and chaste carnal unions. In this way, they founded families by bearing *certain* children.

Through protracted settlement and the burial of their ancestors, they came to found and divide the first dominions of the earth. The lords of these domains were called giants, a Greek word which means 'sons of the earth', or descendants of the buried dead. These lords were considered patricians or nobles: for in this first stage of human civilization, nobility was justly ascribed to those who had been *humanely* engendered in fear of divinity. Indeed, it was this 'human generation' which gave rise to the expression *humanum genus*, or human race. Then, as various houses branched out into numerous families, this same notion of engendering caused them to be called the first *gentes*, clans or peoples. (We shall see that sciences must begin at the point when their subject matter begins. Hence, since the subject of the natural law of nations, *ius naturale gentium*, begins at this remote point of antiquity, so too must our doctrine of natural law, which constitutes a third basic principle of my New Science.) Now, there are physical and ethical reasons, not to mention historical authorities, which show that these early giants were endowed with enormous strength and stature. By contrast, believers in the true God – who created the world and Adam, founder of the human race – were unaffected by these reasons. This is why, from the world's creation, the Jews possessed the proper human proportions.

The funeral urn thus gives us the third of the three principles which my New Science adopts in discussing the origins of countless institutions. These principles are (1) divine providence; (2) solemn matrimony; and (3) the universal belief in the immortality of the soul, which originated with burial rites.

[14] A plough emerges from the forest where the urn is placed. It signifies that the fathers of the early pagan peoples were history's first strongmen, or men of fortitude. They are the Herculean founders of

the first pagan nations mentioned earlier: because they subdued the world's first lands and placed them under cultivation. (Varro lists some forty Herculean heroes, and the Egyptians vaunted theirs as the most ancient of all.)

These first fathers of the pagan nations possessed all four of the classical virtues: justice, prudence, temperance, and fortitude. They were *just* in their supposed piety of observing the auspices, which they believed to be Jupiter's divine commands. (From his Latin name *Ious*, Jove, derived the ancient word *ious*, law, which was later contracted to *ius*, justice. And in every nation, justice is taught together with piety.) They were *prudent* in making sacrifices in order to 'procure' omens, that is, to interpret them properly, and thus to take proper care to act according to Jupiter's commands. They were *temperate* by virtue of their marriages. And, as noted here, they also possessed *fortitude*.

From all this we may derive new principles of moral philosophy which reconcile the esoteric wisdom of the philosophers with the common wisdom of the lawmakers. These principles ground all the virtues in piety and religion, which alone make virtuous actions possible, and which move people to embrace as good whatever God wills. From this we also derive new principles for the doctrine of household management. In this light, children who are still in their fathers' power should be regarded as members of the family state, and all their studies should strive to form them in familial piety and to confirm them in religion. And until they are able to comprehend the state and its laws, they must revere and fear their fathers as the living images of God. Then, when they are older, they will be naturally inclined both to observe the religion of their fathers, and to defend the fatherland which preserves their families; and thus to obey the laws which were ordained to preserve both religion and fatherland. For divine providence established human institutions according to this eternal counsel: first, the founding of families through religions, and then the creation of commonwealths through laws.

[15] The plough rests its handle against the altar with a certain prominence, which indicates that ploughed lands were the first altars of pagan antiquity. And the prominence of the plough symbolizes the natural superiority which the heroes claimed over their associates, who

are in turn represented by the rudder bending at the altar's base. We shall see that it was on this natural superiority that the heroes based the law and science of divine rites (the auspices), and hence their control of them.

[16] The plough shows only the tip of its share, but hides its curved blade, or mouldboard. (Before the use of iron was known, the mouldboard must have been a curved piece of wood hard enough to break and turn the soil.) The Latin word for mouldboard is *urbs*, from which derives early Latin *urbum*, curved. The mouldboard is hidden to signify that the first cities, *urbes*, which were all founded in cultivated fields, arose only after families had spent many years withdrawn and hidden deep amid the sacred terrors of their hallowed groves. Such groves are found in all the pagan nations of antiquity; and by an idea common to them all, a grove was called *lucus* in Latin, meaning the 'land burned off within a wooded enclosure'. In the Bible, we read that, wherever God's people extended their conquests over other peoples, Moses commanded them to 'burn their groves with fire'. In this way, he obeyed the counsel of divine providence, which prohibited newly civilized peoples from mingling with nomads, who still persisted in abominable promiscuity by sharing their possessions and their women.

[17] To the left of the altar we see a rudder, which signifies that the migration of peoples originated with seafaring. By seeming to bend before the altar, the rudder represents the suppliant ancestors of those who later led these migrations.

Now, these ancestors were at first impious people, since they recognized no divinity. They were abominable, since without marriages they could not distinguish kinships: sons often slept with mothers, and fathers with daughters. And they were solitary, since their infamous sharing of all things made them like wild beasts ignorant of society. This made them weak, and hence miserable and unhappy: for they lacked all the goods which are necessary for making life secure. At length, they sought to flee the hardships they suffered as a result of quarrels provoked by their brutish sharing. Seeking safety and survival, they took refuge in the lands cultivated by the people who were pious, chaste, strong, and even powerful, because they had already united in families.

From such lands, cities everywhere in pagan antiquity were called *arae*, altars, since they were the first altars of the pagan nations. The first fire lit on these altars was the fire used to clear the forests and place them under cultivation. And their first water was the water drawn from perennial springs, which allowed the founders of civilization to end their brutish wandering in search of water, and lose their nomadic habits by permanently settling on well-defined lands. Since these altars were also the first refuges in the world, the first cities were called *arae*, altars. In fact, Livy defines such refuges as 'the ancient counsel of city founders', *vetus urbes condentium consilium*; and we read that Romulus founded Rome within a refuge opened in a clearing.

To this small discovery, I add a greater one, concerning the Greeks, who are the source of all our information about pagan antiquity. Among the earliest Greeks, all the lands of the known world were born *within Greece itself*. Thus, the first Thrace and Scythia (meaning the north), the first Asia and India (the east), the first Mauretania or Libya (the south), the first Europe or Hesperia (the west), and even the first Ocean – all were originally places in Greece. Later, the Greeks travelled out into the world and, finding similar places, applied these names to the four parts of the globe and to the ocean encircling it. From such discoveries, I believe we may derive new principles of geography which, together with the principles of chronology mentioned earlier, allow us to read what I have called ideal eternal history. For geography and chronology are the two eyes of history.

[18] Thus, when the lives of these impious, wandering, and weak people were threatened by their stronger companions, they sought refuge at these altars. There the pious men of strength slew the violent nomads, but received the weak fugitives into their protection. Since these refugees had nothing to offer but their lives, they were adopted as household servants, *famuli*, and offered the means of sustaining themselves. The family, *familia*, took its name principally from these household servants, *famuli*, who were the prototypes of the later slaves captured in war.

From this event springs the origin of several institutions, like branches growing from a single trunk:

(1) refuges;

(2) families, which form the basis of cities;

(3) cities, where people dwell safe from violence and injustice;

(4) jurisdictions, which are exercised within their own territories;

(5) expansions of empires, which are attained through justice, fortitude, and magnanimity, the most glorious virtues of rulers and states;

(6) coats-of-arms, whose first fields-of-arms were the first seed-fields;

(7) fame, from which family servants take their name; and glory, which always consists in aiding humankind;

(8) true nobility, which naturally stems from practising the moral virtues;

(9) true heroism, which lies in conquering the proud and aiding the oppressed, a virtue in which the Roman people surpassed all others and so became masters of the world; and, finally,

(10) war and peace, which first began with wars of self-defence, in which true fortitude consists.

In all these origins, we discern the eternal plan of commonwealths, to which all states must conform if they are to endure, even those acquired by violence and fraud. (Conversely, even commonwealths created by virtuous origins may later collapse through force and fraud.) This plan of commonwealths is based on the two eternal principles basic to our world of nations, namely, the mind and the body of the persons who make up the nations. Each person is composed of these two parts; and the mind, being noble, ought to command, while the body, being vile, ought to serve. But human nature is corrupt, and without the aid of philosophy, which assists only a very few, the vast majority of people cannot individually make their minds command their bodies, rather than serve them. Hence, divine providence organized human society according to the eternal order that, in commonwealths, men who use their minds command, while those who use their bodies obey.

[19] The rudder bows at the foot of the altar. As godless people, the family servants were excluded from the nobles' divine institutions, and thus from their human institutions. Above all, they were excluded from the right of contracting solemn nuptials, which the Romans called *connubium*. For the greatest solemnity of the marriage ceremony was the auspices, a rite by which the patricians distinguished their own divine origins from the bestial origins of their servants, who were

13

conceived in abominable intercourse. Among the Egyptians, Greeks, and Romans, we find that this distinction of a nobler nature lay in the presumption of natural or innate heroism, which is described in such detail by ancient Roman historians.

[20] Finally, the rudder is at some distance from the plough, which stands before the altar pointing its tip in a hostile and threatening manner. For since the family servants were barred from owning land, and all the estates were in the hands of the nobles, they grew tired of constantly serving their lords. After many years, they finally rose up in rebellion, asserting their own claim to the lands, and thus revolting against the heroes in agrarian contentions. (These prove to be much older than, and quite different from, the contentions described in later Roman history.) Many of the leaders of these rebellious bands of servants were put down by the heroes – just as the peasants of Egypt were often subdued by the priests, as Peter Cunaeus notes in his *Commonwealth of the Jews*. Fleeing from oppression and seeking safety and survival, the leaders of these uprisings and their followers committed their fortunes to the sea, and sailed in search of vacant lands on the shores of the western Mediterranean, whose coasts were then still uninhabited.

Thus originated the migrations of peoples whom religion had already humanized. From the Near East and Egypt, such migrations first occurred among the Near Eastern peoples, particularly the Phoenicians; later, for the same reasons, we find them among the Greeks. Now, such migrations were not caused by waves of invading populations, who cannot travel by sea. Nor were they caused by the zeal of nations competing to protect their distant possessions by establishing colonies: for we have no record of the Near Eastern peoples, Egyptians, or Greeks extending their empires to the west. Nor were they caused by trade interests, since the western Mediterranean coast was not yet inhabited. Rather, it was *heroic law* which forced these bands of men to leave their native lands, which people will naturally abandon only when driven by dire necessity. Through such colonies, which I therefore call 'heroic overseas colonies', the human race spread by sea throughout the rest of the world, just as it had spread by land in its brutish wanderings.

[21] In front of the plough, we see a tablet inscribed with two Latin alphabets: above, the ancient one which Tacitus tells us resembled that

of the ancient Greeks; and below, the later alphabet which we still use. The alphabet represents the origin of what we call the vernacular languages and letters. We find that these arose many years after the founding of the nations, and letters much later than languages. To represent this, the tablet rests on a fragment of a Corinthian column, which is the most recent architectural order.

[22] The tablet lies quite close to the plough and rather far from the rudder. This represents the origin of native languages, each of which was formed in its own land, where the founders of nations finally chanced to settle, ending the brutish wandering that had scattered and dispersed them through the earth's great forest. Many years later, these native languages mixed with the Near Eastern, Egyptian, and Greek languages along the shores of the Mediterranean and the ocean, as a result of the migrations of peoples I have just described. We find here new principles of etymology, amply illustrated throughout my Science, which allow us to distinguish the origins of native words from those of clearly foreign origin. The distinction is an important one. For the etymologies of native words contain the history of the things they signify following a natural order of ideas. (Thus, at first there were forests, then cultivated fields and huts, next small houses and villages, thence cities, and at last academies and philosophers. This is the order of all progress from its first origins.) By contrast, foreign etymologies merely record the history of words borrowed by one language from another.

[23] The tablet shows only the beginning of the alphabets, and lies facing the statue of Homer. For Greek tradition tells us that the Greek letters were not all invented at one time. And we must conclude that at least in Homer's day they had not all been invented, for it has been shown that he left none of his epics in writing. As for the origins of native languages, I shall treat them in greater detail later on.

[24] Finally, the foreground is the brightest-lit plane of all, for it displays the symbols of the best-known human institutions, which the ingenious artist shows us with fanciful propriety: the Roman fasces, a sword and a purse supported by the fasces, a balance, and Mercury's caduceus, or herald's staff.

[25] The first of these symbols is the fasces because the first civil

authorities grew from the union of the fathers' paternal powers. Among the pagans, these fathers were *wise men* versed in the science of the auspices; *priests* who made sacrifices to procure or interpret them properly; and kings, or at least *monarchs*, who commanded what they believed was the gods' will revealed in the auspices, and were thus subject only to God. Hence, the fasces consist of a bundle of *litui* or divining wands, which prove to be the first sceptres in the world.

In the agrarian unrest described above, these fathers resisted the bands of their rebellious servants. So they were naturally led to unite, forming the closed orders of the first ruling senates, meaning senates of household kings. The leaders of these senates were the heads of the various orders, who prove to be the first kings of what we call heroic cities. And ancient history tells us, but very obscurely, that in the earliest world of peoples kings were created 'by nature', in a manner which my Science seeks to study and discover. The reigning senates now sought to placate the bands of rebellious servants and reduce them to obedience, and therefore granted them an agrarian law, which proves to be the first civil law in the world. The servants, subdued by this law, naturally became the first urban plebeians. Under this law, the nobles granted the plebeians the *natural ownership* of the fields, but retained the *civil ownership* for themselves as the sole citizens of the heroic cities. From this, there later developed the *eminent ownership*, or eminent domain, of the heroic orders, which were the first civil or sovereign powers of the peoples. All three kinds of ownership were formed and distinguished from each other at the birth of these commonwealths. Among all nations, we find that these commonwealths, by a single idea expressed in various languages, were called Herculean commonwealths, or commonwealths of Curetes, meaning public assemblies of armed men. This sheds light on the origins of the famous *ius Quiritium*, the right of citizens, which the interpreters of Roman law considered peculiar to the citizens of Rome, because it was so in later times. But we find that in the earliest age of Rome this right was the natural law of all the heroic tribes and nations.

From this natural law sprang the origins of many institutions, as many rivers flow from one great source:

(1) *The origin of cities*, which developed from extended families which

included both children and servants. We find that cities were naturally founded on two communities, the nobles who commanded and the plebeians who obeyed: for these two parts make up the entire polity or law of civil governments. I shall show that the first cities could not have arisen at all merely on the basis of simple nuclear families.

(2) *The origins of public authorities*, which were born of the union of the private authorities, or paternal sovereignties, which existed in the family state.

(3) *The origins of war and peace*, by which all commonwealths were born by force of arms and later ordered by laws. From their original nature, these two human institutions preserve the eternal property that wars are waged so that peoples may live secure in peace.

(4) *The origins of fiefs*, which were of two kinds. Under the first kind, the rural fiefs, the plebeians subjected themselves to the nobles. Under the second, the noble or military fiefs, the nobles subjected themselves to the greater sovereignty of the heroic classes, while retaining sovereignty over their families. We shall see that the kingdoms of barbarous times have always arisen from such fiefs. This sheds light on the history of the modern kingdoms of Europe, which arose in the latest era of barbarism, a period even more obscure than the earliest barbarism described by Varro. Now, when the nobles gave fields to the plebeians, they exacted a tax which the Greeks called the 'tithe of Hercules', and which the Romans called both the tribute and the census, which was established by Servius Tullius. In time of war, this tribute also obliged the plebeians to provide military service at their own expense to the patricians, as ancient Roman history makes clear.

(5) This reveals *the origin of the census*, which later became the basis of popular commonwealths, or democracies.* Of all my researches into Roman institutions, the most arduous was to discover the manner in which the popular census replaced the census of Servius Tullius, which proves to have been an essential element in ancient aristocracies.

---

* Here and elsewhere, Vico adopts the Aristotelian division of government into monarchy, aristocracy, and democracy. But he seldom uses the last term, and instead refers to *repubbliche popolari (libere)*, 'popular (or free) republics'. In accordance with Vico's observations in paragraph 620, I have used 'democracy' and 'democratic', but these terms should not suggest our liberal concept of such governments.

Confusion about the census has misled all previous scholars into mistakenly asserting that Servius Tullius instituted the census as the basis of popular liberty.

[26] There also sprang from the same source:

(6) *The origin of commerce.* Commercial transactions began in the manner I have described, with the real estate exchanged when cities were founded. Commerce took its name from the world's first *pay*, *merces*, which consisted of the fields given by the heroes to their servants under the legal obligation of service, as described above.

(7) *The origin of public treasuries.* Crude precedents existed from the birth of commonwealths. But what are properly called public treasuries – *aeraria* from Latin *aes, aeris*, bronze, meaning money – were organized later, when it proved necessary to supply public funds to the plebeians in time of war.

(8) *The origins of colonies.* We find that these were bands of people, first peasants who served the heroes in order to sustain themselves, and later vassals who worked the fields for themselves under the real and personal obligations described above. I shall call these 'heroic inland colonies' to distinguish them from the heroic overseas colonies described above.

(9) Lastly, *the origins of commonwealths.* These arose in a severely aristocratic form, in which the plebeians were denied any share in civil rights. Accordingly, we find that the Roman commonwealth was originally an aristocratic kingdom. It fell during the tyrannical reign of Tarquinius Superbus, who governed the patricians so badly that he destroyed nearly all of the senate. So, when Lucretia was raped, Junius Brutus seized the occasion to incite the plebeians against the Tarquins. Having liberated Rome from their tyranny, he re-established the senate and reorganized the state according to its original principles. Yet by replacing a lifelong king with two consuls elected annually, Brutus did not introduce popular liberty, but in fact re-established aristocratic liberty. This type of liberty proves to have flourished until the Publilian Law framed by Publilius Philo, who was called 'the people's dictator' because he declared the Roman republic popular in constitution. And it finally expired when the Poetelian Law effectively liberated the plebeians from the rural feudal right of patricians to imprison them for debt.

Now, although these two laws, the Publilian and the Poetelian, constitute two milestones in Roman history, no political thinkers, jurists, or scholars of Roman law have bothered to study them. For they believed the myth that the Law of the Twelve Tables came from the free city of Athens to establish popular liberty at Rome. (I exposed this myth in my *Principles of Universal Law*, published many years ago.) But these two laws clearly prove that popular liberty was established internally by the Romans' own natural customs. These principles of the Roman state accordingly establish new principles for Roman jurisprudence: for the laws of a commonwealth must be interpreted in accordance with its constitution.

[27] The sword rests on the fasces because heroic law, while a law of force, was tempered by religion. For only religion can hold force and arms in check when judiciary laws do not yet exist, or when those existing are no longer observed. This heroic law is precisely that of the hero Achilles, whom Homer sang to the peoples of Greece as a paragon of heroic virtue, and who determined every question of right by armed combat. In this, we discover the origin of duels. For just as duels were clearly prevalent during the medieval return of barbarism,* so we find them practised in the barbarous age of antiquity, when powerful men had not yet learned to use judiciary laws to avenge each other's offences and wrongs. Duels were fought with appeals to the certainty of divine judgments: the duelling parties called on God as their witness, and turned to him as judge of the offence. No matter what the outcome of the combat, they accepted its decision with such great reverence that even the wronged party, if defeated, was deemed guilty. This was a profound counsel of divine providence: for in a fierce and barbarous age, it led men who were ignorant of law to gauge it by God's favour or disfavour, thus preventing their private feuds from sowing the seeds of wars that could eventually destroy the human race. This natural sense in the barbarian mind could spring only from the innate concept which people have of divine providence, to which they must submit when

---

* Here and elsewhere, Vico simply writes 'the return of barbarism' in accordance with his cyclical notion of history. For the sake of clarity, I have consistently added the adjective 'medieval' to such expressions, even though he never refers to the Middle Ages.

they see the good oppressed and the wicked prospering. For all these reasons, duels were considered a sort of divine purgation. And just as duels are prohibited by today's civilization, in which law regulates criminal and civil judgments, they were deemed necessary in that age of barbarism. In this manner, duels or private wars reveal the origins of our public wars, which are waged by civil authorities who are subject to God alone, so that God may settle them by granting victory, and the human race may repose in the certainty of their civil states. This is the so-called principle of the 'external justice' of wars.

[28] Also resting on top of the fasces is a purse, which signifies that commerce using money began late, only after civil powers had been constituted. This is why coined money is not mentioned in either of Homer's epics. The symbol of the purse also represents the origin of coined money, which ultimately derived from family coats-of-arms. Now, like the first fields-of-arms, the first coats-of-arms represented rights and privileges of nobility which pertained to one particular family, rather than another. Later, they gave rise to public emblems, or ensigns of the people; then they were raised as military ensigns, which are still employed as wordless signals in military discipline; and eventually they were used by all peoples as designs for striking coins. From this we derive new principles for the science of medallions, or numismatics, as well as new principles for the science of what is called blazonry, or heraldry. (The first edition of my *New Science* contains three sections which I still find satisfactory; this is one of them.)

[29] After the purse, we see a balance, which indicates that after the heroic governments, which were aristocratic, came what I call human governments, which were initially democratic. These arose when peoples finally understood that our rational nature, which is our true human nature, is equal in all. Then, on the basis of this natural equality, these peoples gradually drew the heroes into the civil equality of democracies. (The events which occasioned these changes are studied in my ideal eternal history, and are found to correspond precisely to moments in Roman history.) Now, civil equality is represented by the balance, because the Greeks used to say that in a democracy everything is settled by lot or by the balance. But eventually the factions of the powerful made it impossible for free peoples to retain their civil equality

by means of laws, and they began to destroy each other in civil wars. As they struggled to survive, it naturally happened that they obeyed a 'natural royal law', or rather a custom natural to human nations, and sought the protection of a monarchy, which is the second human form of government. (This natural royal law is common to all peoples in all ages, when their democracies become corrupt. By contrast, the 'civil royal law', which the Roman people supposedly enacted to legitimize the Roman monarchy in Augustus' person, is exposed as a myth in my *Principles of Universal Law* – as is the myth that the Law of the Twelve Tables came from Athens. If my treatise has any merit, it lies in exposing these two myths.)

In the present civilized age, these two forms of human government, democracy and monarchy, alternate one with the other; but neither of them naturally passes into an aristocracy, in which the nobility alone commands and all others obey. Indeed, there are today only a handful of aristocracies governed by nobles: Nuremberg in Germany; Dubrovnik in Dalmatia; and Venice, Genoa, and Lucca in Italy. Divine providence created these three types of states, which succeed each other in this natural order, together with the natural customs of such nations. But the nature of nations does not tolerate mixed constitutions devised by human minds. Even though he only noted the outward effects of the political causes analysed in my Science, Tacitus characterized such mixed states as 'more laudable than feasible, and shortlived when they happen to arise'. This discovery gives us new principles for political science, which not only differ from, but even contradict, our previous conceptions.

[30] The last of the symbols is the caduceus, or herald's staff. It reminds us that, as long as the heroic age was ruled by the natural right of force, the earliest peoples regarded each other as perpetual enemies. Indeed, they continually practised brigandage and piracy: for since their wars never ceased, they saw no need to declare them. (In the barbarous age of antiquity, heroes considered the title of thief a badge of honour, just as in the medieval return of barbarism, powerful men vaunted the title of corsair.) But with the rise of human governments – whether democracies or monarchies – the law of the civilized nations introduced heralds to declare war, and hostilities began to be concluded by peace treaties. Here too we perceive the lofty counsel of divine providence

in the age of barbarism. For when they were new and had to grow, the nations remained within their own borders; and despite their fierce and untamed natures, they did not march forth and destroy each other in foreign wars. Then, as time passed, these nations matured, growing at once more civilized and more tolerant of each other's customs. As a result, victorious nations found it easy to spare the lives of the vanquished under the just laws of victory.

[31] Thus, by studying the common nature of nations in the light of divine providence, my *New Science*, or new metaphysics, discovers the origins of divine and human institutions in the pagan nations. And on the basis of these origins, my Science establishes a system of the natural law of the nations, which progresses with great regularity and consistency in all three ages through which the Egyptians said they had passed in the entire course of world history. These three ages are the following:

(1) The age of the gods, when the pagan peoples believed that they were living under divine government, and that all their actions were commanded by auspices and oracles, which are the most ancient institutions in secular history.

(2) The age of the heroes, when heroes ruled everywhere in aristocratic states by virtue of their presumed natural superiority to the plebeians.

(3) And finally, the age of men, when all recognized their equality in human nature, so that they first established democracies and later monarchies, which are the two forms of human government.

[32] Corresponding to these three types of nature and government, three kinds of language were spoken, which constitute the lexicon of my New Science:

(1) The first dates from the age of families when pagan peoples had just embraced civilization. We find that it was a mute or wordless language which used gestures or physical objects bearing a natural relationship to the ideas they wanted to signify.

(2) The second language used heroic emblems – such as similes, comparisons, images, metaphors, and descriptions of nature – as the principal lexicon of its heroic language, which was spoken in the age when heroes ruled.

(3) The third language was the human or civilized language which

used vocabulary agreed on by popular convention, and of which the people are the absolute lords. This language is proper to democracies and monarchies, for in those states it is the people who determine the meaning of the laws, which are binding for nobles and plebeians alike. Hence, once the laws of any nation are written in the common speech, knowledge of them is no longer in the hands of the nobility. Previously, the nobles of every nation, who were also priests, kept their laws in a secret language like a sacred object. This is the natural reason for the secrecy in which the Roman patricians kept their laws before popular liberty was established.

These are precisely the three languages which the Egyptians said had been spoken earlier in their world, corresponding exactly in both number and order to the three ages through which their world had passed:

(1) The first was the *hieroglyphic* language, a sacred and secret language using mute gestures, as befits religions, in which observance is more important than speech.

(2) The second was the *symbolic* language using resemblances, like the heroic language I have just described.

(3) Finally, the third was the *epistolary* or vernacular language, which was used for the common business of everyday life. These three kinds of language were found among the Chaldaeans, Scythians, Egyptians, Germanic peoples, and all the other nations of pagan antiquity. (Hieroglyphic writing persisted later among the Egyptians simply because they were closed to foreign nations longer, which also explains why the Chinese still use ideograms. But the use of hieroglyphics by other nations proves that the Egyptians' presumption of their own remote antiquity is groundless.)

[33] My Science sheds light on the origins of both languages and letters, which were previously the despair of historians and philologists, whose bizarre and grotesque opinions I shall review. The unfortunate reason for their error is obvious: they simply assumed that nations developed languages first, and then letters. Yet languages and letters were born as twins and developed at the same pace through all three kinds. We find precise evidence for such origins in the stages of the Latin language which I discovered in the first edition of my *New Science*.

(Earlier, I remarked that this work contains three sections which I do not regret writing; this is the second of them.) This evidence has offered me many discoveries about the history, government, and law of the ancient Romans, as the reader will find in countless passages of the present work. Following my example, scholars of Oriental languages, of Greek, and especially of German among the modern languages, which is a mother tongue, will be able to make discoveries about antiquities that surpass their expectations and mine.

[34] In seeking the basic principle of the common origins of languages and letters, we find that the first peoples of pagan antiquity were, by a demonstrable necessity of their nature, *poets* who spoke by means of *poetic symbols*. This discovery provides the master key of my New Science, but making it has cost me nearly an entire scholarly career spent in tireless researches. For to our more civilized natures, the poetic nature of the first people is utterly impossible to imagine, and can be understood only with the greatest effort. Their symbols were certain *imaginative general categories*, or archetypes. These were largely images of animate beings, such as gods and heroes, which they formed in their imagination, and to which they assigned all the specifics and particulars comprised by each generic category. (In precisely this way, the myths of civilized ages, such as the plots of the New Comedy, are rational archetypes derived from moral philosophy; and from these myths, our comic poets create in their characters these imaginative archetypes, which are simply the most complete ideas of human types in each genre.) We find, then, that the divine and heroic symbols were true myths, or true mythical speech. And we discover that, in describing the early age of the Greek peoples, the meaning of their allegories is based on identity rather than analogy, and is thus historical rather than philosophical.

These archetypes – which is what myths are in essence – were created by people endowed with vigorous imaginations but feeble powers of reasoning. So they prove to be true poetic statements, which are feelings clothed in powerful passions, and thus filled with sublimity and arousing wonder. We further find that poetic expression springs from two sources: the poverty of language, and the need to explain and be understood. This engendered the vividness of heroic speech, which was the direct successor of the mute language of the divine age, which had conveyed ideas through gestures and objects naturally related to them. Eventually, following the inevitable natural course of human institutions, the Assyrians, Syrians, Phoenicians, Egyptians, Greeks, and Romans developed languages, which began with heroic verse, then passed to iambics, and finally ended in prose. This progression is confirmed by the history of ancient poetry. And it explains why we find so many natural versifiers are born in German-speaking lands, particularly in the peasant region of Silesia; and why the first authors in Spanish, French, and Italian wrote in verse.

[35] From these three languages, we may derive a conceptual diction-ary, which properly defines words in all the different articulate languages. In this work, I shall refer, when necessary, to this dictionary, of which the reader will find a detailed sample in the first edition of my Science. In that passage, I studied the timeless attributes of the fathers who lived in the age when languages were formed, both in the state of families and in the first heroic cities. Then, in fifteen different languages, both living and dead, I derived proper definitions of the words for father, which varied according to their different attributes. (Of the three sections in that edition which satisfy me, this is the third.) This lexicon proves necessary if we are to learn the language of the ideal eternal history through which the histories of all nations in time pass. And it is necessary if we are to be scientific in citing authorities that confirm our observations about the natural law of nations, and about particular kinds of jurisprudence.

[36] There were, then, *three* languages, proper to *three* ages in which *three* kinds of government ruled, conforming to *three* kinds of civil natures, which change as nations follow their course. And we find that these languages were accompanied by an appropriate kind of jurisprudence, which in each age followed the same order.

[37] (1) The first kind of jurisprudence was a *mystical theology*, which was practised in the age when the pagan peoples were commanded by gods. Its wise men were the theological poets, commonly called the founders of pagan civilization, who interpreted the mysteries of oracles, which in all nations gave their responses in verse. Hence, we find that ancient myths contain the hidden mysteries of their vernacular wisdom.

This leads us to ponder the following questions. Why were later philosophers so eager to attain the wisdom of the ancients? What causes moved these philosophers to aspire to lofty philosophical speculations? And what encouraged them to impose their own esoteric wisdom on the ancient myths?

[38] (2) The second kind was *heroic jurisprudence*, which was exclusively concerned with scrupulous attention to words – the sort of prudence Ulysses reveals. This kind of jurisprudence was directed towards what Roman jurists called civil equity, and what we call 'reason of state'. With their limited ideas, the heroes deemed that they naturally had a right to precisely *what*, *how much*, and *what sort* had been defined in words. Even today, we can observe this in peasants and other uncouth folk: for in their contentions involving words and sense, they obstinately insist that their right lies in the words. Here too we see the counsel of divine providence. For while the pagan peoples were still incapable of grasping universal concepts, which good laws must contain, their particular care for the words moved them to a universal observance of the laws. And if in some cases this equity made their laws harsh and even cruel, they naturally tolerated it because they deemed this to be the nature of their justice. The heroes were also encouraged to observe the laws by that supreme private interest which, as the only citizens, they identified with that of their homelands. Hence, to protect the safety of their homelands, they did not hesitate to sacrifice themselves and their families to the will of the laws. The laws in turn, by protecting the common safety of their homelands, protected their private monarchical reigns over their families. This powerful private interest, moreover, joined to the supreme arrogance of a barbarous age, shaped their heroic nature, which inspired so many heroic deeds to protect their homelands.

Yet next to these heroic deeds, we must place the intolerable pride, the insatiable greed, and the merciless cruelty with which ancient Roman patricians treated the unfortunate plebeians. Roman history explicitly records such events during the period which Livy himself calls the age of Roman virtue, and the greatest flowering of popular liberty ever dreamed of in Rome. We find that such public virtue was merely the good use to which providence turned grievous, filthy, and savage private vices. For it preserved cities during an age when the minds of men, being concerned with particulars, were naturally incapable of grasping the notion of a common good. From this, we derive new principles to prove the point which St Augustine makes in his chapter on the virtue of the Romans. And we shall dispel the opinion which scholars previously held concerning the heroism of the earliest peoples. We find that this sort of civil equity was observed naturally by heroic nations in both war and peace, and I shall adduce striking examples of it from both the ancient and medieval periods of barbarism. And we find that the Romans practised this civil equity in their private affairs as long as their republic remained aristocratic, that is, until the age of the Publilian and Poetelian Laws, before which civil equity was entirely based on the Law of the Twelve Tables.

[39] (3) The third and last form of jurisprudence was *natural equity*, which rules naturally in free commonwealths. In these, each person seeks his own particular good, which is in fact the same for all, so that the people are inadvertently led to enact universal laws. Hence, they naturally desire laws which are generously flexible when applied to specific circumstances that call for the distribution of equal benefits. This good was called *aequum bonum* in Latin, and was the subject of later Roman jurisprudence, which by Cicero's day was beginning to be recast by the edicts of the Roman praetors. This jurisprudence is still compatible with the nature of monarchies, perhaps even more than with democracies. For in these, monarchs have accustomed their subjects to attend to their own private interests, while they themselves have taken charge of all public affairs. And monarchs want all their subject nations made equal by laws, so that they will all take an equal interest in the state. This is why the emperor Hadrian reformed all of Rome's natural heroic law according to the natural human law of the provinces. And he decreed that jurisprudence be based on the *Perpetual Edict*, which Salvius Julianus compiled almost exclusively from provincial edicts.

[40] We may now review all the basic elements of our world of nations, using the symbols that represent them. The lituus or divining wand represents divination; the water and fire on the altar represent sacrifices and the first nuclear families. The funerary urn in the forest represents burial rites. The plough supported by the altar represents the

cultivation and division of the fields, the refuges, the later extended families including servants, and the first agrarian disputes. The rudder at the foot of the altar represents the earliest heroic colonies – first the inland colonies, then, as these waned, the overseas colonies – and with them, the earliest migrations of peoples. All these institutions arose in the age of the Egyptian gods, which through ignorance or oversight Varro called the dark age.

The fasces represent the first heroic commonwealths; the distinction of three kinds of ownership: natural, civil, and eminent domain; the first civil powers; and the first unequal alliances formed by the first agrarian law. (By this law, cities were established on the rural fiefs of the plebeians, who became feudal subjects of the noble fiefs of the heroes. And the sovereign heroes in turn became subjects of the greater sovereignty of the heroic ruling orders.) The sword supported by the fasces represents the public wars waged by the cities, which originated in brigandage and piracy. (Duels, or private wars, must have arisen much earlier within the state of families.) The purse represents the emblems of nobility, or family coats-of-arms, which were later transferred to medals. These first ensigns of the people later became military ensigns, and finally were used on coins, which imply trade in movable goods using money. (Trade in real estate, using natural payments in produce and labour, had begun earlier during the divine age, as a result of the first agrarian law, from which commonwealths were born.) The balance represents the laws of equality, which are properly speaking the only laws. And finally, the caduceus, or herald's staff, represents the formal declaration of wars, and their conclusion by peace treaties.

All these symbols are distant from the altar, because they represent the civil institutions established in the period when false religions were gradually disappearing. This period began with the heroic agrarian disputes, which gave their name to the Egyptian age of heroes, which Varro calls the mythical age. The tablet with the alphabets is placed between the divine and human symbols because false religions began to vanish as letters were introduced and gave rise to philosophies. By contrast, the true religion, which is our Christian religion, is confirmed in human terms by the sublimest philosophies: by Plato, and by Aristotle, insofar as he agrees with Plato.

[41] The entire idea of this work may be summarized as follows. The darkness in the background of the picture represents the uncertain, formless, and obscure material of this Science, which is outlined in my *Chronological Table* and in the accompanying *Notes*. The ray by which divine providence illuminates the breast of Metaphysics stands for the axioms, definitions, and postulates which my Science adopts as *Elements* in establishing both its underlying *Principles* and its consistently applied *Method*. All these topics are contained in Book 1. Next, the ray reflected from the breast of Metaphysics to the statue of Homer is the proper light we shed on *Poetic Wisdom* in Book 2, and on the true Homer in Book 3. The *Discovery of the True Homer* in turn elucidates all the institutions of our world of nations, tracing their origins in the order in which the symbols emerge in the light of the true Homer. This is the *Course of Nations*, which is discussed in Book 4. When they finally reach the base of Homer's statue, they *recur*, beginning in the same order. This is discussed in my final Book 5.

[42] In conclusion, let me summarize the idea of this work as briefly as possible. The entire picture represents three worlds in the order in which the human minds of pagan antiquity ascended from earth to heaven. (1) The symbols seen on the ground denote the world of nations, the very first things to which people applied themselves. (2) The globe in the middle represents the world of nature, which was subsequently observed by natural scientists. (3) And the symbols above these signify the world of minds and of God, which were eventually contemplated by the metaphysicians.

BOOK I
ESTABLISHING
PRINCIPLES

Chronological Table* Based on the Egyptians' Three Epochs of World History: The Ages of Gods, Heroes, and Men (1)

Jews (2)	Chaldaeans (3)	Scythians (4)	Phoenicians (5)	Egyptians (6)
Universal Flood				
	Zoroaster: Kingdom of the Chaldaeans (7) Nimrod: The confusion of languages (9)			
Calling of Abraham				Dynasties in Egypt Hermes Trismegistus the elder: Egyptian age of the gods (12)
God gives the written law to Moses				
				Hermes Trismegistus the younger: Egyptian age of heroes (18)

* According to tradition, the creation took place in 4004 BC, and Rome was founded in 753 BC. In my translation, I have often added equivalent dates in parentheses.

Greeks	Romans	Year of the World	Year of Rome
		1656	
		1756	
Iapetus, ancestor of the Giants (8)			
The giant Prometheus steals fire			
from the sun (10)		1856	
Deucalion (11)			
The Golden Age: Greek age of the			
gods (13)			
Three dialects are spread through			
Greece by the three sons of Hellen,			
son of Deucalion, grandson of			
Prometheus, and great-grandson of			
Iapetus (14)		2082	
Cecrops the Egyptian leads twelve			
colonies into Attica, which Theseus			
later unites to found Athens (15)			
Cadmus the Phoenician founds			
Thebes in Boeotia, and introduces			
vernacular letters into Greece (16)		2448	
	Saturn: Latin age of the gods (17)	2491	
Danaus the Egyptian drives the			
Inachids out of Argos (19)			
Pelops the Phrygian rules in the			
Peloponnese		2553	
Scattered throughout Greece, the			
Heraclids introduce the age of			
heroes			
In Crete, Saturnia (Italy), and Asia,			
the Curetes introduce priestly			
kingdoms (20)		2682	

Jews (2)	Chaldaeans (3)	Scythians (4)	Phoenicians (5)	Egyptians (6)
	Ninus rules with the Assyrians			
			Dido leaves Tyre to found Carthage (21) Tyre is famed for navigation and colonies	
			Sanchuniathon writes history in vernacular letters (24)	
Kingdom of Saul				
				Sesotris rules in Thebes (26)
				Psammeticus opens Egypt to Ionian and Carian Greeks (31)

Greeks	Romans	Year of the World	Year of Rome
		2737	
Minos, king of Crete, the first pagan lawmaker and first corsair in the Aegean			
		2752	
Orpheus and the age of theological poets (22)			
Hercules, culmination of the Greek heroic age (23)	Arcadians		
Jason initiates naval wars in Pontus			
Theseus founds Athens and organizes the Areopagus			
	Hercules visits Evander in Latium: age of heroes in Italy	2800	
Trojan War (25)		2820	
Wanderings of the heroes, particularly Ulysses and Aeneas			
	Kingdom of Alba	2830	
		2909	
Greek colonies in Asia, Sicily, and Italy (27)		2949	
Lycugus gives laws to the Spartans		3120	
The Olympic games, first established by Hercules and later suspended, are reinstated by Isiphilus (28)			
		3223	
	Founding of Rome (29)		1
Homer, who lived before vernacular letters were invented and who never saw Egypt (30)	Numa Pompilius king	3290	35
Aesop, popular moral philosopher (32)		3334	

Cyrus and the
Persians rule in
Assyria

Idanthyrsus king
of Scythia (38)

Greeks	Romans	Year of the World	Year of Rome
Seven Sages of Greece: Solon establishes popular freedom in Athens, and Thales of Miletus introduces philosophy by his study of natural science (33)		3406	
Pythagoras, whose very name (Livy tells us) was unknown in Rome during his lifetime (34)	Servius Tullius king (35)	3468	225
Pisistratus' sons, tyrants of Athens, are driven out		3491	
	Tarquins, tyrants of Rome, are driven out	3499	245
Hesiod (36); Herodotus and Hippocrates (37)		3500	
Peloponnesian War. Thucydides writes that he decided to recount it because in his father's day the Greeks knew nothing about their own antiquities (39)		3530	
Socrates introduces rational moral philosophy. Plato excels in metaphysics. Athens radiant with all the arts of advanced civilization (40)	Law of the Twelve Tables	3553	303
Bearing Greek arms into the heart of Persia, Xenophon is the first to learn about Persian institutions with any certainty (41)		3583	333
	Publilian Law (42)	3658	416
Alexander the Great of Macedonia overthrows the Persian monarchy. Aristotle visits the Near East and observes that previous Greek accounts were myths.		3660	
	Poetelian Law (43)	3661	419
	War with Tarentum, in which the Greeks and Romans begin to know each other (44)	3708	489
	Second Punic War, the first certain part of the history of Rome of Livy, who yet declares his ignorance of three important facts (45)	3849	552

SECTION I
NOTES ON THE CHRONOLOGICAL TABLE IN WHICH THE HISTORICAL MATERIALS ARE ORGANIZED

I *Chronological Table Based on the Egyptians' Three Epochs of World History: The Ages of Gods, Heroes, and Men*

[43] My Chronological Table gives an overview of the nations of the ancient world from the universal flood through the Second Punic War, passing from the Jews to the Chaldaeans, Scythians, Phoenicians, Egyptians, Greeks, and Romans. On it, there appear the most renowned people and events, as they are commonly assigned by scholars to specific times and places. But in fact these people and events did not exist at the times and places commonly assigned to them, or never existed at all. By contrast, from the deep and impenetrable darkness in which they lay buried, there emerge other notable people and consequential events that produced or witnessed decisive moments in human history. My Notes will show this, and will thus make clear how the civilization of the nations arose from uncertain, unseemly, imperfect, and insubstantial beginnings.

[44] In addition, the reader will find my Table quite at odds with John Marsham's *Canon of Egyptian, Jewish, and Greek Chronology*. Marsham tried to show that the government and religion of the Egyptians antedate those of all the other nations of the world; and that their sacred rites and civil statutes passed to other peoples, and were eventually adopted with some modifications by the Jews. Marsham's opinions were soon embraced by John Spencer, who in his treatise *On Urim and Tummim* asserts that, through the sacred Cabala, the Israelites borrowed all their theology from the Egyptians. At length, Marsham's work was

applauded in the *Pagan Philosophies of Antiquity* of Otto Van Heurn, who writes in his discussion of the Chaldaeans that the Egyptians instructed Moses about divine rites before he introduced them to the Jews in his laws.* Against these positions, Herman Wits mounted a counter-attack in his *Comparison of Egyptian and Jewish Rites*. He asserts that the first pagan author to give us accurate information about the Egyptians is Dio Cassius, who flourished under the philosopher-emperor Marcus Aurelius. In fact, this view is refuted by a passage in Tacitus' *Annals*, describing Germanicus' journey in the Near East. When he travelled to Egypt to see the famous antiquities of Thebes, Germanicus asked a priest to explain the hieroglyphics on some obelisks. Talking nonsense, the priest explained that they commemorated the boundless might of king Ramses, which once extended to Africa, the Near East, and even Asia Minor – an area nearly equal to the vast Roman empire of the time! But perhaps Wits omitted to mention this passage because it contradicted his thesis.

[45] Egypt's boundless antiquity yielded little esoteric wisdom to the Egyptians who lived inland from Alexandria. In his *Miscellanies*, Clement of Alexandria tells us that in his day about forty-two of the Egyptians' 'priestly' books were in circulation. But they contained gross errors in philosophy and astronomy: Strabo often ridicules Chaeremon, the teacher of St Dionysius the Areopagite [Dionysius Glauci], for repeating them.† In turn, the Egyptians' medical notions are impugned in Galen's treatise *On Hermetic Medicine* as rank nonsense and mere quackery. The Egyptians' morals were dissolute: for they not only tolerated and permitted prostitutes, but also made them respectable. Their theology was full of superstitions, illusions, and witchcraft. And the magnificence of their obelisks and pyramids is the product of barbarism, which has an affinity for the colossal. Even today we criticize Egyptian sculpture and casting as hopelessly crude. By contrast, subtlety is the fruit of philosophy. This is why Greece, the nation of philosophers, was alone resplendent with all the fine arts devised by human genius: painting,

* Vico is mistaken: Van Heurn's work was published in 1600; Marsham's in 1672.
† For the philosopher Dionysius Glauci (1st century), Vico mistakenly writes 'Dionysius the Areopagite'.

sculpture, casting, and carving in relief. These are the subtlest arts, because they must conceive abstractly the surface contours of the objects they depict.

[46] By contrast, in Alexandria, the city which Alexander the Great founded on the sea, the ancient wisdom of the Egyptians was praised to the heavens. By uniting African acumen with Greek subtlety, Alexandria produced illustrious philosophers of divinity, and gained great renown as a seat of divine learning. Indeed, the Museum at Alexandria became as celebrated as all the schools of Athens put together: the Academy, the Lyceum, the Stoa, and the Cynosarges. Alexandria was called the 'Mother of the Sciences'. And for its excellence, the Greeks simply called it *Polis*, the city, just as Athens was called *Astu* and Rome *Urbs*. Alexandria was the birthplace of Manetho, the Egyptian high priest who transformed all of Egyptian history into an exalted theology of nature. (Earlier, Greek philosophers had treated their own myths in precisely the same way. Yet these myths were their most ancient histories, which shows us that Greek myths and Egyptian hieroglyphics underwent the same process.)

[47] Such great vanity for profound wisdom suited the Alexandrians, whose conceited nature caused them to be mocked as 'glory-hungry beasts'. Alexandria was an important trade centre both for the Mediterranean and, through the Red Sea, for the Indian Ocean and the East Indies. So when the Alexandrians heard merchants of various nations describe false deities scattered throughout the world, they believed that all of them had originated in Egypt. (In a golden passage listing the city's reprehensible customs, Tacitus calls it 'eager for strange religions'.) Since every pagan nation had a Jupiter, they presumed that their Jupiter Ammon was the most ancient of all. And they likewise presumed that the Herculean heroes in other nations, of which Varro counted forty, all derived their name from the Egyptian Hercules. Both of these claims, which are reported by Tacitus, derive from two sources. First, the Egyptians were blindly persuaded of their own immeasurable antiquity, and therefore vaunted their superiority over all the other nations, even claiming that they had formerly ruled a great part of the ancient world. Second, they were unaware that pagan peoples had separately developed uniform ideas about gods and heroes, even though

they had no contact with each other, as my New Science will clearly show.

Even the Augustan historian Diodorus Siculus, who lavishes overly flattering judgments on the Egyptians, does not credit them with more than 2,000 years of ancient history. And Diodorus' conclusions are discredited by Jacques Cappel, who in his *Sacred History of Egypt* puts them on a level with those which Xenophon bestowed on Cyrus the Great and with those, I might add, which Plato often invented about the Persians. In sum, all these observations about the vanity of the ancient Egyptians' profound wisdom are confirmed by the case of the forgery *Pimander*, which was long palmed off as Hermetic doctrine. For Isaac Casaubon exposed the work as containing no doctrine older than the Platonists, whose language it borrows. And Claude Saumaise dismissed the entire work as a jumbled and disjointed compilation.

[48] The Egyptians' mistaken belief in their own great antiquity sprang from the indeterminacy of the human mind, a property which often causes people to exaggerate immeasurably the magnitude of the unknown. In this, the Egyptians resembled the Chinese, who developed into a great nation isolated from all others, like the Egyptians until the reign of Psammeticus. The same isolation affected the Scythians up to the reign of Idanthyrsus. Indeed, one popular tradition made the Scythians surpass even the Egyptians in antiquity. This tradition must perforce date from the starting-point of secular universal history, which in Justin's account began with two mighty kings who antedate even the Assyrian monarchy. These were Tanaus the Scythian and Sesotris the Egyptian, whose supposed existence previously made the world seem much older than it really is. It is said that Tanaus first led a vast army through the Near East to conquer Egypt, even though its terrain makes it naturally resistant to invasion, and that Sesotris then led equal forces to conquer Scythia. (In fact, Scythia was unknown to the Persians even after they conquered the neighbouring Medes, and remained so until the age of Darius the Great, who declared war on the Scythian king Idanthyrsus. And in an age when Persia was quite civilized, Idanthyrsus was so barbarous that in his reply to Darius he used five physical objects instead of words, because he could not even write in symbols!) Yet we are to suppose that these two mighty kings crossed Asia with their vast armies,

but failed to conquer a single province for either Scythia or Egypt. Indeed, they left the region in such freedom that it later gave birth to the first of the four most famous monarchies in the world – Assyria!

[49] For similar reasons, perhaps, the Chaldaeans did not fail to enter the contest for greatest antiquity. They too were an inland nation and in fact older than the other two. The Chaldaeans vainly boasted that they had preserved astronomical records dating back some 28,000 years. This may explain why the Jewish historian Flavius Josephus mistakenly believed that such records actually survived from before the flood. He writes that these were inscribed on two columns erected before the two floods: one of brick, and another of marble, which he claims to have seen in Syria. Such great importance did the ancient nations attribute to preserving their astronomical records – a sense which evidently died out in later nations! We must assign Josephus' column a place in the Museum of Credulity.

[50] We find that the Chinese also write using hieroglyphics, as did the ancient Egyptians, to say nothing of the Scythians, who in fact were ignorant of writing! For many thousands of years, these three peoples had no contact with any other nations that could have taught them the true antiquity of the world. Now, imagine someone sleeping who awakes to find himself locked in a tiny dark chamber. Terrified by the darkness, he will believe that the room is much larger than what he can touch with his hands. In the obscurity of their chronology, this is just what has happened to the Chinese, the Egyptians, and the Chaldaeans as well. To be sure, the Jesuit father Michele Ruggieri asserts that he has seen Chinese books that were printed before the coming of Jesus Christ. And the *History of China*, by Father Martini, another Jesuit, places Confucius in remotest antiquity. (According to Martin Schoock, this view has converted many to atheism. In his book *Noah's Universal Flood*, he notes that it may even have moved Isaac de la Peyrère, author of *Adam's Predecessors*, to renounce the Catholic faith and to write that the flood was limited to the lands of the Jews alone.) But Nicolas Trigault is better informed than either Ruggieri or Martini. In his *Christian Mission to China*, he writes that the Chinese invented printing not more than two centuries before the Europeans, and that Confucius lived not more than 500 years before Christ. Indeed, like the Egyptians' priestly

books, the philosophy of Confucius is crude and inept, and almost entirely concerned with popular morality, meaning the morality imposed on the people by their laws.

[51] We have reviewed the vain opinions held by the pagan nations, and especially the Egyptians, concerning their own antiquity as a necessary preamble to all our knowledge of the pagan world. We proceed in two ways: (1) by seeking to determine methodically this important starting-point, the precise time and place in which pagan civilization began in the world; and (2) by seeking to offer human reasons to support our Christian faith. (This faith begins from the truth that the first people in the world were the Jews, descended from Adam, who was created by the true God at the world's creation.) Accordingly, the first science we must study is mythology, meaning the interpretation of myths: for all pagan histories have mythical origins, and the myths of the pagan nations were their first histories. By applying this method, we shall discover the beginnings of the sciences as well as of the nations: for the sciences could only arise within nations that were already formed. Throughout my New Science, I show that the sciences sprang from institutions necessary or useful to humankind, which were later perfected as ingenious individuals refined them. This must be the starting-point of universal history, whose origins and principles were previously lacking, as all scholars agree.

[52] In this study, we shall greatly profit from the antiquity of the Egyptians. For they have preserved two fragments of their history which are no less amazing than the pyramids and which contain two great historical truths. The first is recorded by Herodotus, who says that the Egyptians divided all of the world's history into three ages: (1) the age of the *gods*, (2) the age of *heroes*, and (3) the age of *men*. The second fragment is reported by Johannes Scheffer in his *Pythagorean Philosophy*. He says that in these three ages the Egyptians spoke three languages, corresponding to them in number and order: (1) a *hieroglyphic* language, using sacred characters; (2) a *symbolic* language, using heroic characters; and (3) an *epistolary* language, using characters agreed on by the people.

Now, when Varro did not follow this historical division, he must have acted by choice, rather than from ignorance. For by virtue of his boundless erudition, Varro was deservedly eulogized as 'the most learned of the Romans', and this was in the age of Cicero, when the Romans were most enlightened. It may be that Varro saw in the Romans what my principles will show to be true of all ancient nations, namely that all their divine and human institutions were indigenous, or native to Latium. Hence, in his masterpiece *Divine and Human Institutions*, of which the injustice of time has deprived us, Varro was at pains to assign Latin origins to Roman institutions. (This shows how much he believed in the myth that the Law of the Twelve Tables came to Rome from Athens!) At any rate, Varro divides all the ages of the world into three ages: (1) the *dark* age, or age of the gods; (2) the *mythical* age, or age of heroes; and (3) the *historical* age, which the Egyptians called the age of men.

[53] We may further profit from the antiquity of the Egyptians by reflecting on two of their conceited traditions. These exemplify what is called the *conceit of nations* by Diodorus Siculus, who observes that every nation, barbarous or civilized, regards itself as the most ancient, and believes that it preserves traditions dating from the beginning of the world. (We shall see that this was the privilege of the Jews alone.) I mentioned earlier two of the Egyptians' conceited traditions: first, that their Jupiter Ammon was more ancient than the others, and second, that all the Herculean heroes of other nations took their name from the Egyptian Hercules. In other words, all nations passed first through an age of the gods, whose king was everywhere believed to be Jupiter, and then through an age of heroes claiming to be sons of the gods, of whom Hercules was reputed the greatest.

2 The Jews

[54] The first column on my Table is dedicated to the Jews. We know by the solemn authority of Flavius Josephus and Lactantius Firmianus, whom I shall cite later, that the Jews lived unknown to all the pagan nations. Yet they had an accurate chronology of the world, which is today accepted as true by even the most rigorous critics, according to the estimate given by Philo the Jew. Indeed, if Philo differs from Eusebius, the discrepancy amounts to a mere 1,500 years, which is a minor amount, compared to the distortions made by the ancient

Chaldaeans, Scythians, Egyptians, and by the Chinese today. This is an irrefutable argument that the Jews were the first people in the world, and that in their sacred history they have truthfully preserved traditions dating from the beginning of the world.

3 The Chaldaeans

[55] The second column represents the Chaldaeans. Geographically, the kingdom of Assyria was the farthest inland of the inhabited world; and my Science shows that the formation of inland nations preceded that of coastal nations. It is certain that the Chaldaeans were the first sages of pagan antiquity, and their Zoroaster is commonly regarded by historians as the first sage in history. There is no doubt that the starting-point of universal history is the monarchy of Assyria, which must originally have been formed of the Chaldaean people. As these grew to a great multitude, they must have developed into the nation of Assyrians ruled by Ninus, who founded his monarchy with native peoples rather than foreigners. Ninus abolished the name of the Chaldaeans and replaced it with that of the Assyrians, because the plebeians of that nation had supported his ascent to the throne. (My work shows that almost every nation underwent this political process, as the Romans clearly demonstrate.)

History further tells us that Zoroaster was killed by Ninus. In heroic language, this means that the Chaldaeans' aristocratic kingdom, symbolized by the heroic Zoroaster, was overthrown by the popular freedom of the native plebeians. For we shall see that in the heroic age the plebeians were a nation distinct from the nobility, and that Ninus set himself up as monarch with their support. If this were not the case, there would arise a sort of chronological monster in Assyrian history. For within the lifetime of one man, Zoroaster, Chaldaea would have grown from a region of lawless nomads to a dominion of such magnitude that Ninus easily transformed it into a great monarchy. Without my historical principles, the figure of Ninus at the starting-point of universal history previously made it appear that the Assyrian kingdom was born overnight, like frogs after a summer storm.

4 *The Scythians*

[56] The third column represents the Scythians, who surpassed the Egyptians in antiquity, according to the popular tradition I have just cited.

5 *The Phoenicians*

[57] The fourth column represents the Phoenicians, who antedate the Egyptians. Popular tradition says that the Phoenicians, who had learned from the Chaldaeans, taught the Egyptians how to use a quadrant to measure polar latitude. Later we shall show that they also brought vernacular letters to other nations.

6 *The Egyptians*

[58] For various reasons given above, the Egyptians merit the fifth place in my Table, even though in his *Canon* Marsham declares them the most ancient nation of all.

7 *Zoroaster: Kingdom of the Chaldaeans*
Year of the World 1756 (2249 BC)

[59] My Science will show that Zoroaster was the poetic archetype of the founders of peoples in the Near East. We find as many Zoroasters scattered throughout that vast part of the world as there are Herculean heroes in the opposite part to the West. As for the Herculean heroes with European traits whom Varro noted in Asia Minor, at Tyre and in Phoenicia, they were perhaps considered Zoroasters in the Near East. But through the conceit of scholars, who assert that what they know is as ancient as the world, all these many founders were conflated into one man crammed with profound esoteric wisdom. And they thrust on this man the philosophical Oracles of Zoroaster, which palm off recent doctrines of Pythagoras and Plato as ancient ones. Not content with this, the conceit of scholars then puffed itself up even further by inventing a succession of national schools. Supposedly, Zoroaster taught

Berosus of Chaldaea; Berosus taught Hermes Trismegistus of Egypt; Hermes Trismegistus taught Atlas of Ethiopia; Atlas taught Orpheus of Thrace; and finally, Orpheus founded his school in Greece. Yet we shall soon see exactly how easy such long journeys were between the early nations. For since they had only recently emerged from savagery, they all lived in isolation, unknown even to their neighbours, and only came to know each other in the event of war or by reason of trade.

[60] Confused by the various popular traditions they have themselves collected, historians do not know whether the Chaldaeans were individuals, families, or an entire people or nation. But we may resolve these ambiguities by the following principles. First there were individuals, then whole families, later an entire people, and finally a great nation, on which the Assyrian monarchy was founded. The first wisdom of the Chaldaeans lay in the vernacular science of divination, by which they divined the future from the nightly paths of falling stars. Later, it extended to judicial astrology, which is why in Roman law a judicial astrologer was called a Chaldaean.

8 Iapetus, ancestor of the Giants
Year of the World 1856 (2239 BC)

[61] Giants naturally existed among all the earliest pagan nations. This is clear from the references to natural history found in Greek myths, as well as from physical and moral proofs we find in civil history.

9 Nimrod: The confusion of languages
Year of the World 1856 (2239 BC)

[62] The confusion of languages happened miraculously, creating many different tongues all at once. According to the Church Fathers, this confusion of languages gradually destroyed the purity of the sacred language which was spoken before the flood. We must take this to mean the languages spoken by the Near Eastern peoples among whom Shem propagated the human race. By contrast, the nations in the rest of the world fared differently. The races descended from Ham and Japheth were destined to be scattered throughout the earth's great forest,

where they wandered like beasts for 200 years. Solitary and aimless, they bore children whom they raised like beasts, lacking human customs and speech, and living in a brutish state. Precisely this much time had to elapse before the earth, drenched by the universal flood, could dry out. The earth then sent forth what Aristotle calls dry exhalations into the atmosphere, which generated lightning bolts that stunned and terrified humankind. In their fright, people abandoned themselves to false religions worshipping various Jupiters. (These were so numerous that Varro counted as many as forty of them, among which the Egyptians claimed their Jupiter Ammon as the most ancient of all.) In these religions, they developed a sort of divination which divined the future from thunder and lightning, and from the flight of eagles, which they considered birds sacred to Jupiter. The Near Eastern peoples, by contrast, developed a subtler system of divination, which observed the motions of the planets and the aspects of the stars, *astra*. This is why Zoroaster is celebrated as the first sage of pagan antiquity, and Samuel Bochart takes his name to mean 'star-gazer'. Thus, just as the Near Eastern peoples gave rise to the first vernacular wisdom, which was astrology, so the first monarchy arose among them, which was Assyria.

[63] This account confutes all the recent etymologists who would derive all the world's languages from Semitic sources. In fact, all the nations descended from Ham and Japheth first formed their languages inland. Only later did they descend to the coast, where they began to trade with the Phoenicians, who were famed along the shores of the Mediterranean and the ocean for their navigation and colonies. In the first edition of my *New Science*, I showed that this is true of the inland origins of the Latin language, and thus that it is true by extension of all other languages as well.

10 *The giant Prometheus steals fire from the sun*
Year of the World 1856 (2239 BC)

[64] This myth implies that Heaven reigned on earth, in an age when Heaven was believed to be only as high as the mountain tops. Popular tradition also relates that Heaven conferred many great benefits on humankind.

11 *Deucalion*

[65] In the same age, Themis, the goddess of divine justice, had a temple on Mt Parnassus, and judged men's affairs on earth.

12 *Hermes Trismegistus the elder: Egyptian age of the gods*

[66] According to Cicero's *On the Nature of the Gods*, this is the Hermes whom the Egyptians called 'Thoth' – from which the Greeks supposedly derived *theos*, god – and who gave the Egyptians their letters and laws. According to Marsham, the Egyptians then taught them to the other nations of the world. But in fact the Greeks wrote their laws not in hieroglyphics, but in vernacular letters. And it was previously thought that Cadmus introduced such letters into Greece from Phoenicia. But if that were the case, then the Greeks made no use of them for more than 700 years. Witness Homer, who lived during this period, but never uses the word *nomos*, law, in either of his epics – a fact noted by Everard Feith in his *Homeric Antiquities*. Instead, Homer entrusted his epics to the memory of the rhapsodes, because in his day Greek vernacular letters had not yet been invented – as the Jewish historian Flavius Josephus stoutly maintains against the Greek grammarian Apion. Besides, when Greek letters emerged after Homer, how different they were from their Phoenician models!

[67] Still, all these difficulties appear minor, when we ask the following questions. How could any nations be founded without any laws? How were dynasties founded within Egypt before the arrival of Hermes Trismegistus?

As if letters were essential to laws! As if Spartan laws weren't legal, when a law of Lycurgus himself prohibited the knowledge of letters! As if our civil nature prevented laws from being framed and proclaimed orally! As if we did not in fact find in Homer two kinds of assembly, the *boulé* or secret council, in which heroes deliberated orally about their laws, and the *agorá* or public assembly, whose decisions were also proclaimed orally!

And, finally, as if divine providence had failed to provide for our human needs! For providence ensured that, even without letters, all barbarous nations were founded on the basis of their customs, and were governed by written laws only later when they had become civilized. During the medieval return of barbarism, the first laws of the new-born European nations sprang from their customs, and the most ancient of these were their feudal customs. (We shall return to this point later, when I show that fiefs were the first sources of all the laws that developed in nations both ancient and modern; and hence that the natural law of nations was established not by laws, but by civilized customs.)

[68] Let us now consider a critical issue in the history of Christianity, namely, the view that Moses was not indebted to the Egyptians for his sublime Jewish theology. At first glance, chronology would seem to pose a great obstacle, since it places Moses after Hermes Trismegistus. Yet this difficulty has been met by my earlier arguments, and it may be completely eliminated if we cite the principles implied by a truly golden passage in Iamblichus' *Mysteries of the Egyptians*. For Iamblichus writes that the Egyptians attributed to Hermes Trismegistus every invention that proved necessary or beneficial to their civil life. Thus, Hermes could not have been an individual rich in esoteric wisdom who was later consecrated as a god. Instead, he must have been a *poetic archetype* of the earliest Egyptian sages who, being wise in vernacular wisdom, founded first the families and then the peoples who eventually made up that great nation. Furthermore, if we are to preserve the Egyptian division of history into the three ages of gods, heroes, and men, and if Hermes Trismegistus was their god, then it follows from this same passage in Iamblichus that the life of Hermes corresponds to the entire Egyptian age of the gods.

13 *The Golden Age: Greek age of the gods*

[69] As a particular aspect of the divine age, mythology relates that the gods mingled with men on earth. In order to insure the certainty of my principles of chronology, my New Science envisions a *natural theogony*. This means a genealogy of the gods as it naturally formed in the imagination of the Greeks on certain occasions, when they perceived that institutions necessary or useful to humankind had relieved or assisted them in the early childhood of the world. (The world of these first people

was subject to fearful religions, for whatever they saw or imagined, and even did themselves, they regarded as something divine.) Since there were twelve famous gods of the so-called major tribes, meaning the gods that men consecrated during the age of families, we may accordingly divide this age into twelve shorter periods. Hence, a rational chronology of poetic history reckons the age of the gods as lasting 900 years. This gives us the beginnings of universal secular history.

14 *Three dialects are spread through Greece by the three sons of Hellen, son of Deucalion, grandson of Prometheus, and great-grandson of Iapetus*
Year of the World 2082 (1923 BC)

[70] Taking their name from Hellen, the native Greeks were called Hellenes. By contrast, the Greeks in Italy were called *Graii*, and their land *Graikía*, so that in Latin they were called *Graeci*. This shows how well the Greeks in Italy knew the name of their homeland across the sea, which they left to colonize Italy! Indeed, the name *Graikía* is found in no Greek author, as Jacques Le Paulmier observes in his *Description of Ancient Greece*.

15 *Cecrops the Egyptian leads twelve colonies into Attica, which Theseus later unites to found Athens*

[71] Strabo objects that the landscape of Attica was too harsh to encourage foreigners to settle there, for he wishes to prove that the Attic dialect is one of the earliest native dialects in Greece.

16 *Cadmus the Phoenician founds Thebes in Boeotia, and introduces vernacular letters into Greece*
Year of the World 2448 (1557 BC)

[72] If Cadmus had introduced the Phoenician alphabet there, Boeotia's literary foundations would have made it the most ingenious region of Greece. But it produced men of such stupidity that the adjective Boeotian became proverbial for a dullard.

17 Saturn: Latin age of the gods
Year of the World 2491 (1514 BC)

[73] This age of the gods marks the beginning of the nations of Latium, and its features correspond to those of the Greeks' Golden Age. My study of myths reveals that the Greeks' first gold was grain, which is why for many centuries the earliest nations reckoned their years by their harvests of grain. The Romans named Saturn after *satus*, sowing; and the Greeks called him *Chronos*, which means time, and is the root of the word chronology.

18 Hermes Trismegistus the younger: Egyptian age of heroes
Year of the World 2553 (1452 BC)

[74] Hermes the younger must be the poetic archetype of the Egyptian age of heroes. In Greece, this heroic age comes after an age of gods which lasted 900 years. But in Egypt the age of the gods corresponds to only three generations: a father, son, and grandson. We have noted a similar anachronism in Assyrian history, in the figure of Zoroaster.

19 Danaus the Egyptian expels the Inachids from Argos
Year of the World 2553 (1452 BC)

[75] These royal successions offer us important standards* for chronology. For example, Danaus seizes the kingdom of Argos, which had previously been been ruled by nine kings of the house of Inachus. If we apply a chronological rule of thumb, this must have been a period of 300 years, just as the fourteen Latin kings of Alba ruled for nearly 500 years.

[76] But Thucydides says that in the heroic age kings dethroned each other almost daily. Thus, Amulius expels Numitor from the kingdom of Alba, but Romulus expels Amulius and reinstates Numitor. This happened because of the ferocity of the age, because heroic cities had

---

* I translate Vico's *canoni di chronologia* by 'standards of chronology'. In Greek, *canon* means both standard measure and chronological table.

no walls, and because the use of fortresses was still unknown. Later, we shall encounter similar conditions during the medieval return of barbarism.

20 Scattered throughout Greece, the Heraclids introduce the age of heroes. In Crete, Saturnia or Italy, and Asia, the Curetes introduce priestly kingdoms
Year of the World 2682 (1323 BC)

[77] Denis Petau observes that these two great fragments of antiquity occur in Greek history before the Greeks' heroic age. In fact, the Heraclids, or sons of Hercules, were scattered throughout Greece more than a century before the appearance of their father Hercules, who would have had to be born many centuries earlier to beget so many descendants.

21 Dido leaves Tyre to found Carthage

[78] We place Dido at the end of the Phoenicians' heroic age. She must have been exiled from Tyre after losing a heroic contest: indeed, she admitted that her brother-in-law's hatred had forced her to depart. In heroic language, the Tyrian masses were called a woman because they were made up of weak and defeated men.

22 Orpheus and the age of theological poets

[79] Orpheus, who supposedly reduces the wild beasts of Greece to human civilization, turns out to be the vast den of a thousand monsters. For he comes from Thrace, which was the homeland of fierce Mars-like warriors, rather than civilized philosophers. Indeed, the Thracians remained so barbarous even in later ages that the philosopher Androtion removed Orpheus from the number of sages solely because he had been born in Thrace. As that nation emerged, Orpheus supposedly grew so learned in Greek that in it he composed verses of wonderful poetry, which civilized the barbarians by appealing to their ears. Yet later, when they had already formed nations, these same Thracians were not

restrained from destroying cities whose wonders appealed to the eyes! And Orpheus finds the Greeks still living like wild beasts, even though a thousand years earlier Deucalion had taught them piety by his reverence and fear of divine justice.

Now, a thousand years before Orpheus, Deucalion had built a temple to divine justice on Mt Parnassus, which later became the dwelling of Apollo and the Muses, who are the gods of civilization and its arts. With reverent fear, Deucalion and his wife Pyrrha stood before this temple with their heads veiled, as a sign of modesty in intercourse, which signifies marriage. They picked up the stones at their feet, which symbolized their previously brutish life. They changed the stones into people by casting these stones over their shoulders, that is, by means of household instruction within the family state.

Then, some 700 years before Orpheus, Hellen unified the Greeks with a single language, which spread throughout Greece as the three different dialects spoken by his sons. We have seen that 300 years earlier the house of Inachus had founded its kingdoms, which continued by royal successions throughout this period. At last, Orpheus arrived to teach human civilization to the Greeks. From the savage state in which he found it, he raised Greece to such splendour as a nation that he himself was Jason's shipmate in the quest for the Golden Fleece. But this allusion to a nautical expedition must remind us that navies and navigation are the last of a people's achievements. Also on board were Castor and Pollux, the brothers of Helen of Troy, who caused the celebrated Trojan War.

Thus, in the life of this one man, so many civil institutions were established for which a thousand years would hardly suffice. As a monster of Greek chronology, Orpheus resembles two others noted earlier: Zoroaster in Assyrian history, and Hermes Trismegistus (both the elder and the younger) in Egyptian history. This would explain why Cicero in his *On the Nature of the Gods* suspects that such a person as Orpheus never existed.

[80] These great difficulties of chronology are compounded by others, no less serious, of a moral and political nature. For Orpheus founds Greek civilization using the following mythical examples: Jupiter the adulterer, Juno the mortal enemy of Hercules' virtues, Diana the virgin

who seduces the sleeping Endymion, Apollo who gives oracles but hunts the chaste maiden Daphne to her death, and Mars who commits adultery with Venus in the sea – as if the crime on land were not enough. Nor is the gods' unbridled lust satisfied by illicit intercourse with women. Jupiter burns with perverted love for Ganymede. His lust does not stop here, but at last turns to bestiality, when Jupiter transforms himself into a swan and couples with Leda. Such lust practised on men and beasts was in absolute form the execrable abomination of the lawless world. By contrast, many of the Olympic gods and goddesses never marry; and the only marriage of Greek deities, that of Jupiter and Juno, is not only barren, but filled with dreadful quarrels. Thus, Jupiter suspends his chaste and jealous wife from a chain; while he himself gives birth to Minerva, who springs from his head. And finally, when Saturn begets children, he devours them.

Such examples are powerful examples of divinity; and they may even contain that complete esoteric wisdom which was desired in antiquity by Plato and in our own times by Francis Bacon in his *Wisdom of the Ancients*. But taken literally, they would debauch the most civilized peoples and incite them to indulge in the bestiality of Orpheus' beasts. So suitable and powerful are they in reducing bestial people to humanity! In reproving the pagan gods, St Augustine's *City of God* makes a small point regarding a scene in Terence's *The Eunuch*. In the play, the youth Chaerea is aroused by a painting of Jupiter copulating with Danae in a shower of gold: now finding the boldness he had lacked, he rapes the slave-girl who had inspired his mad and violent love.

[81] Yet we may avoid these dangerous reefs of mythology by applying the principles of my New Science. For they show that all such myths were in their beginnings true, severe, and worthy of their nations' founders. Yet later, as the years passed, their meanings were obscured, and human morality lapsed from severity into dissolution. To salve their consciences, people now sought to sin with the approval of the gods, and their myths developed the filthy meanings which they still have today.

The harsh tempests of chronology will in turn be calmed by our discovery of poetic archetypes. One of these is Orpheus, considered in his role as a theological poet. For in their original form, his myths founded and later confirmed the civilization of Greece. This role was particularly prominent in the contentions between the heroes and plebeians of the Greek cities. During this age, the theological poets distinguished themselves, among them Orpheus, Linus, Musaeus, and Amphion. With his song, Amphion moved the rocks – meaning the stupid plebeians – to build the walls of Thebes, which Cadmus had founded 300 years earlier. In precisely this way, about 300 years after the foundation of Rome, the Roman heroic state was reinforced when Appius Claudius, grandson of the decemvir, sang to the plebs about the divine power of the auspices, the science of which had previously been restricted to the patricians. It was from such heroic contentions that the heroic age took its name.

23 *Hercules, culmination of the Greek heroic age*

[82] We meet with the same difficulties if we regard Hercules as a real person who was Jason's shipmate in the expedition to Colchis. Instead, his Twelve Labours reveal him as a heroic archetype of the founder of peoples.

24 *Sanchuniathon writes history in vernacular letters*
Year of the World 2800 (1205 BC)

[83] Sanchuniathon, sometimes called Sancuniates, is characterized as the 'lover of truth' in the *Miscellanies* of Clement of Alexandria. He wrote a Phoenician history in vernacular letters at a time when the Egyptians and Scythians were still writing in hieroglyphics. (The Chinese write in the same fashion even today, and like the Egyptians and Scythians boast of their prodigious antiquity. For they too have had no contact with other nations, and in their obscure isolation cannot see the true light of chronology.) Indeed, when Sanchuniathon was using Phoenician vernacular letters, the Greek vernacular alphabet had not yet been invented.

25 *The Trojan War*
Year of the World 2820 (1185 BC)

[84] More cautious critics judge that the Trojan War never took place as it is described by Homer. And authors like Dictys of Crete and Dares of Phrygia, who wrote about the war in prose like later historians, are relegated by such critics to the Library of Impostures.

26 *Sesotris rules in Thebes*
Year of the World 2949 (1056 BC)

[85] Having subdued the other three dynasties in Egypt, Sesotris united them with his own empire. Sesotris proves to be the king Ramses described to Germanicus by the Egyptian priest in Tacitus' history.

27 *Greek colonies in Asia, Sicily, and Italy*
Year of the World 2949 (1056 BC)

[86] Here is a rare case in which powerful evidence compels me to disregard chronological authority. I date the first Greek colonies in Italy and Sicily about a century after the Trojan War. This is some three centuries before the time established by chronologers, who instead assign to this period the wanderings of heroes like Menelaus, Aeneas, Antenor, Diomedes, and Ulysses. (This should surprise no one, since the same chronologers disagree by 460 years in their dating of Homer, the author closest to these affairs of the Greeks.) For by the time of the Punic Wars, the Sicilian colony of Syracuse rivalled even Athens in magnificence and refinement, and we know that luxurious and grandiose lifestyles reach the islands later than the mainland. And in his day, Livy pitied the Greek colony of Croton for its few inhabitants, who had once numbered several million.

28 *The Olympic games, first established by Hercules and later*
suspended, are reinstated by Isiphilus [Iphitus]*
Year of the World 3223 (782 BC)

[87] Whereas Hercules numbered the years by harvests, Isiphilus instituted the solar year following the signs of the zodiac, which marks the
beginning of the certain chronology of Greek history.

29 *Founding of Rome*
Year of Rome 1 (753 BC)

[88] St Augustine's *City of God* cites a golden passage in Varro which,
like the sun clearing away the clouds, disperses all the exaggerated
notions ever held concerning the origins of Rome, and indeed of all
the famous capitals of various nations. Varro writes that under her kings,
who reigned for 250 years, Rome conquered more than twenty peoples,
but extended her dominion by no more than twenty miles.

30 *Homer, who lived before vernacular letters were invented and*
who never saw Egypt
Year of the World 3290; Year of Rome 35 (719/715 BC)

[89] Greek history has left this first light of Greece in the dark. For the
two principal parts of history, geography and chronology, tell us nothing
certain about his homeland or his age. Book 3 of my *New Science* will
describe a Homer completely at odds with previous interpretations.
Whoever he was, it is clear that he never saw Egypt. For in the *Odyssey*
he says that, even with a north wind filling its sails, an unladen ship
would take an entire day to sail from the mainland to the island where
the Alexandrian lighthouse now stands! Nor had he seen Phoenicia.
For in the *Odyssey* he says that Calypso's island Ogygia was so far away
that the winged god Hermes could reach it only with great difficulty.
Now since Homer's gods in the *Iliad* live on Mt Olympus in Greece,

---

* For Iphitus, traditional founder of the Olympic games, Vico mistakenly writes
'Isiphilus'.

he seems to imply that Ogygia is as far from Greece as, say, America is from Europe. We must conclude that if the Greeks of Homer's day had traded in Phoenicia and Egypt, none of them would have believed either of his epics.

31 *Psammeticus opens Egypt to the Ionian and Carian Greeks*
Year of the World 3334 (671 BC)

[90] Beginning with the reign of Psammeticus, Herodotus begins to recount Egyptian history with greater certainty. The late date of Psammeticus confirms the view that Homer never saw Egypt. In some cases, Homer's many statements about Egypt and other countries reflect Greek institutions and events, as we shall see in my Poetic Geography. In other cases, they are traditions which were modified over the years and brought to Greece by Phoenician, Egyptian, and Phrygian colonists. And in still others, they are the tales of Phoenician travellers who traded in Greek ports well before Homer's time.

32 *Aesop, popular moral philosopher*
Year of the World 3334 (671 BC)

[91] My section on Poetic Logic will show that Aesop was not a real individual, but an imagined category, or poetic archetype, representing the heroes' associates or family servants, who clearly lived before the Seven Sages of Greece.

33 *Seven Sages of Greece: Solon establishes popular freedom in*
Athens, and Thales of Miletus introduces philosophy by his study
of natural science
Year of the World 3406 (599 BC)

[92] Thales began with the insubstantial principle of water. Perhaps he had observed that water makes our gourds grow!

34 *Pythagoras, whose very name (Livy tells us) was unknown in*
Rome during his lifetime
Year of the World 3468; Year of Rome 225 (537/529 BC)

[93] Far from believing that Pythagoras was Numa Pompilius' teacher
in divinity, Livy places him in the age of Servius Tullius, nearly two
centuries later. Even in this age, inland Italy was so barbarous, Livy
says, that it was impossible not only for Pythagoras, but even for his
name, to reach Rome from Croton by passing through so many peoples
with different languages and customs. We may imagine, then, how
quickly and easily Pythagoras made those many long journeys to
Orpheus' disciples in Thrace, to the magi in Persia, to the Chaldaeans
in Babylon, and to the gymnosophists in India! And we may imagine
how, on his return trip, he visited the priests in Egypt, traversed the
breadth of Africa to see Atlas' disciples in Mauretania, and then crossed
the Mediterranean again to visit the Druids in Gaul! At last, Pythagoras
returned to his homeland, rich in what Van Heurn calls barbarian
wisdom from the barbarous nations to which, many years earlier, the
Theban Hercules had brought civilization as he travelled the world
slaying monsters and tyrants. These are the same nations which, many
years later, the Greeks claimed to have civilized, but with so little success
that they still remained barbarous. Such are the solemn and weighty
foundations of Van Heurn's succession of the schools of barbarian
philosophy, which I mentioned earlier and which the conceit of scholars
has so vigorously applauded!

[94] What shall we say to the incontrovertible authority of Lactantius,
who categorically denies that Pythagoras was a disciple of Isaiah? His
authority gains force from a passage in the *Jewish Antiquities* of Josephus,
which shows that in the ages of Homer and Pythagoras the Jews were
unknown to their inland neighbours, let alone to distant nations overseas.
In Josephus, when Ptolemy Philadelphus marvels that no poet or
historian ever mentioned the laws of Moses, Demetrius the Jew replies
that God had miraculously punished several men for trying to divulge
these laws to the gentiles: Theopompus lost his mind, and Theodectes
his sight. Commenting on this, Josephus himself generously confesses
that the Jews lived in obscurity, and cites the following reasons: 'We

do not inhabit the coast, and we take no pleasure in trade or in commercial dealings with foreigners.' Lactantius interprets the Jews' obscurity as a counsel of divine providence which prevented pagan commerce from profaning the religion of the true God. And in his *Commonwealth of the Jews*, Peter Cunaeus agrees with Lactantius' view.

All of this is confirmed by the Jews' own public confession. In atonement for the Septuagint, or Old Testament in Greek, they observed an annual fast on the eighth day of Tebet, which is our December. For when this translation was published, darkness covered the earth for three days, according to the rabbinical books cited in Isaac Casaubon's *Notes on Baronius' Annals*, Johann Buxtorf's *The Jewish Synagogue*, and Johannes Hottinger's *Philological Thesaurus*. And since the so-called Hellenists, or Hellenized Jews – including Aristeas, the supposed director of the translation – attributed divine authority to their work, they earned the mortal hatred of the Jews at Jerusalem.

[95] The very nature of their civil institutions made it impossible for the Jewish prophets to profane their sacred teaching to foreigners. And travel was nearly impossible. Even the civilized Egyptians closed their borders to the Jews. (The Egyptians were so inhospitable that, even after they opened their country to the Greeks, they were forbidden to use Greek pots, spits, and knives, and even to eat meat cut with a Greek knife.) The region was isolated by harsh and dangerous roads, peoples with no common language, and Jewish tribes whom the gentiles mocked, saying that they would not direct a thirsty stranger to a well. How then could the prophets reveal their sacred teaching to strange and unfamiliar foreigners, when in fact the priests of every nation kept their sacred teachings arcanely hidden from the masses of their plebeians? This is why all nations refer to their religious doctrine as sacred, which is synonymous with secret.

The secrecy of Jewish teaching offers us luminous proof of the truth of the Christian religion. For both Pythagoras and Plato, by virtue of their sublime human wisdom, raised themselves some of the way towards understanding those divine truths which the Jews learned from the true God. And conversely, it soundly refutes the error of recent mythologists, who think that myths are sacred stories which have been corrupted by pagan nations, and especially by the Greeks. (To be sure, the Egyptians had dealings with the Jews during their captivity. But it is the common custom of early peoples to regard the vanquished as godless men. So, instead of respecting the religion and history of the Jews, the Egyptians ridiculed them. Indeed, the holy book of Genesis relates that the scornful Egyptians often asked the Jews why the god they worshipped did not deliver them from captivity.)

35 King Servius Tullius
Year of the World 3468; Year of Rome 225 (537/529 BC)

[96] A common error previously led scholars to believe that Servius Tullius instituted the Roman census as the basis of popular liberty, but I shall show that it was the basis of aristocratic liberty. And a related error previously led them to believe that Tarquinius Priscus introduced all the badges of Roman office – the ensigns, togas, devices, ivory thrones, and even the triumphal chariots of gold. It was in such splendid trappings that Roman majesty supposedly shone forth in the age of its most glorious democracy. Yet during Priscus' reign, a sick debtor, when summoned before the praetor, had to appear on an ass or in a cart! As for the ivory thrones, they were obviously made from the tusks of elephants, which the Romans called Lucanian oxen, because they first saw them in Lucania during the war with Pyrrhus, two centuries later!

36 Hesiod
Year of the World 3500 (505 BC)

[97] According to the proofs by which I date the invention of the vernacular Greek alphabet, I place Hesiod in the time of Herodotus, or slightly earlier. Some chronologers were overly confident in placing Hesiod thirty years before Homer: we must bear in mind that authorities differ by 460 years in their dating of Homer. By contrast, Porphyry (who is cited in Suidas) and Velleius Paterculus maintain that Homer preceded Hesiod by many years. As for the tripod on Mt Helicon which Hesiod supposedly dedicated to Apollo, with the inscription that he had defeated Homer in song, despite Varro's endorsement in Aulus Gellius, we must store it in the Museum of Impostures. For it belongs

with the fakes perpetrated by today's counterfeiters of medals, who seek to reap a great profit from their deceptions.

37 *Herodotus and Hippocrates*
Year of the World 3500 (505 BC)

[98] Chronologers placed Hippocrates in the age of the Seven Sages of Greece. But his biography is heavily tinged with myths, one of which makes him the son of Aesculapius and the grandson of Apollo. By contrast, we know for certain that he wrote works in prose using the vernacular alphabet. For these two reasons, I date him to the age of Herodotus, who also wrote in prose using the vernacular alphabet, and who wove nearly all of his history from myths.

38 *Idanthyrsus, king of Scythia*
Year of the World 3530 (475 BC)

[99] When Darius the Great declared war on him, Idanthyrsus replied by sending him five objects: a frog, a mouse, a bird, a ploughshare, and an archer's bow. The earliest peoples used such physical words before they used spoken and, eventually, written words. Later, I shall explain the natural and appropriate meaning of these objects. For the moment, it would be pointless to repeat what St Cyril [Clement] of Alexandria relates of Darius' council, since he himself exposes how ludicrously they misinterpreted Idanthyrsus' message.* In any case, we should recall that Idanthyrsus is the king of the Scythians, who supposedly surpassed the Egyptians in antiquity, but who at this late date were still unable to write, even in hieroglyphics!

Now, Idanthyrsus must have resembled one of those Chinese kings who until a few centuries ago were isolated from the rest of the world, and therefore vainly boasted of their superior antiquity. Despite their great antiquity, the Chinese today still write in hieroglyphics. Because of their mild climate, they have the most refined sensibilities, and create the most amazingly delicate works of art. Yet their painters have not

---

* For Clement, Vico mistakenly writes 'Cyril'.

yet learned to highlight figures by shading them; and their paintings appear quite awkward because they lack relief and depth. Their porcelain statuettes, now commonly imported in Europe, reveal the same crudeness as the statues cast by the Egyptians, which suggests that the painting of the ancient Egyptians may have been as crude as that of today's Chinese.

[100] One of the ancient Scythians was Anacharsis [Abaris], who was reputed to be the author of Scythian oracles, as Zoroaster was of Chaldaean oracles.* At first, these must have been the oracles of soothsayers; but later, the conceit of scholars transformed them into the oracles of philosophers. Now, according to Herodotus, followed by Pindar, Pherenicus, and Cicero in his *On the Nature of the Gods*, the most famous oracles of pagan antiquity – those of Delphi and Dodona – came to Greece from the Hyperboreans of Scythia, which may mean either modern-day Scythia or a northern region within ancient Greece. As a result, Anacharsis was celebrated as the famous author of oracles and numbered among the most ancient diviners, as we shall see in my Poetic Geography.

For a moment, let us consider how learned the Scythians were in esoteric wisdom. We need only cite their practice of sticking a knife in the ground and worshipping it as a god – an act by which they justified the killings they were going to commit. And this savage religion was supposedly the origin of the many moral and civil virtues which are described by Diodorus Siculus, Justinus, and Pliny, and exalted by Horace! Later, when Anacharsis sought to establish civilization in Scythia by introducing Greek laws, he was killed by his brother Caduidas. So much did he profit from Van Heurn's barbarian philosophy that he was unable to conceive laws that could convert a barbarous people to humane civilization, and had to borrow them from the Greeks instead!

Thus, the relation of the Greeks to the Scythians is precisely the same as their relation to the Egyptians, which I described earlier. Indeed, for their vanity in tracing their wisdom from illustrious origins in foreign antiquity, the Greeks merited the reproach of being told they were always children – as they imagined that an Egyptian priest reproached

---

* For Abaris, Vico mistakenly writes 'Anacharsis'.

Solon, according to Critias in Plato's *Alcibiades*. We can only conclude that, by their conceited ties to the Scythians and Egyptians, the Greeks lost as much in true merit as they gained in vainglory.

39 *Peloponnesian War. Thucydides writes that he decided to recount it because in his father's day the Greeks knew nothing about their own antiquities*
Year of the World 3530 (475 BC)

[101] Thucydides was a youth when Herodotus, who could have been his father, was an old man. He lived in the most glorious age of Greece, that of the Peloponnesian War. As a contemporary witness, he wrote its history to record the truth about it. Thucydides notes that in his father's day, which was the age of Herodotus, the Greeks knew nothing about their own antiquities. If that is the case, what shall we think about Greek accounts of foreign affairs, which are our only source for the antiquities of the pagan barbarians? And if Thucydides says this is true of the Greeks, who developed philosophy so early, what shall we think of the antiquities of the Romans, who until the Punic Wars were occupied solely with agriculture and warfare? Unless perhaps we choose to say that the Romans enjoyed the special privilege of God.

40 *Socrates introduces rational moral philosophy. Plato excels in metaphysics. Athens radiant with all the arts of advanced civilization*
Year of the World 3553; Year of Rome 303 (452/451 BC)

[102] In this period, the Law of the Twelve Tables is supposedly brought to Rome from Athens. This was an uncivilized, crude, inhuman, cruel, and savage law, as my *Principles of Universal Law* demonstrated.

41 *Bearing Greek arms into the heart of Persia, Xenophon is the*
first to learn about Persian institutions with any certainty
Year of the World 3583; Year of Rome 333 (422/421 BC)

[103] Jerome notes this in his *Commentary on Daniel*. The commercial interests of the Greeks introduced them to Egyptian affairs during the reign of Psammeticus, which is why Herodotus writes more accurately about the Egyptians from that time onwards. From Xenophon onwards, the necessities of warfare introduced the Greeks to Persian affairs at first-hand. Aristotle too, who accompanied Alexander the Great into Persia, writes that the Greeks before him had merely told myths about the Persians, as my Notes on Chronology indicate. In this manner, the Greeks began to gain more certain knowledge of foreign institutions.

42 *Publilian Law*
Year of the World 3658; Year of Rome 416 (338 BC)

[104] Passed in the Year of Rome 416 (338 BC), this law marked a turning-point in Roman history, for it proclaimed the shift of the Roman constitution from aristocracy to democracy. This is why its framer, Publilius Philo, was called 'the people's dictator'. Yet the importance of this law has been neglected because no one knew how to interpret its language. Later, I shall clearly show this for a fact; suffice it here to give a hypothetical idea of this law.

[105] Both the Publilian Law and its equally important successor, the Poetelian Law, were not understood because three key terms were ill-defined: people, kingdom, and liberty. By a common error, many scholars believed that the Roman people from the time of Romulus included as citizens both patricians and plebeians; that the original Roman state was a monarchical kingdom; and that the liberty established by Brutus was a form of popular liberty. These ill-defined terms have misled all previous critics, historians, political thinkers, and jurists. For no present-day commonwealth can give us an adequate idea of the heroic ones, which were of a severely aristocratic form and thus completely different from those in our day.

[106] In his refuge in the clearing, Romulus founded Rome by

means of clientships, *clientelae*, based on the protection which Roman fathers offered to those who sought asylum there. Hired as day labourers, such refugees had none of the privileges of citizenship and hence no share in civil liberty. Since they had taken refuge to save their lives, the Roman patrician fathers guaranteed their natural liberty by assigning them in separate groups to cultivate their various fields. These fields formed the basis of the public lands of the Roman territory, just as the patrician fathers, assembled by Romulus, formed the basis of the Roman senate.

[107] Later, Servius Tullius instituted the census by granting the labourers bonitary ownership of the patricians' lands. The labourers were to cultivate the land for themselves, under the burden of the census and under the obligation of serving the patricians in wartime at their own expense – just as the plebeians in fact served the patricians in the period of imaginary popular liberty. Servius Tullius' law was the first agrarian law in the world, and it established the census as the basis of the heroic commonwealths, which were the most ancient aristocracies in all nations.

[108] Subsequently, Junius Brutus drove out the tyrannical Tarquins, and restored the Roman republic to its original principles. Instead of a single lifelong king, he created two consuls to be a sort of annual pair of aristocratic kings, as Cicero calls them in his *On Laws*. In this way, Brutus re-established the patricians' liberty from tyrannical rulers, but not the plebeians' liberty from the patricians. Then, when the patricians failed to respect Servius' agrarian law, the plebeians created two tribunes of the people, whom the patricians had to swear to recognize. The tribunes were created to defend the natural liberty which the plebeians enjoyed through their bonitary ownership of the fields. Next, the plebeians sought to obtain the right of civil ownership from the patricians; and when Coriolanus told the plebeians to go till the fields, the tribunes of the people drove him out of Rome. For he meant that, if the plebeians were dissatisfied with Servius' agrarian law and wanted a stronger, more complete law, they ought to be reduced to the status of Romulus' day labourers. If this was not his meaning, what foolish pride would have led these plebeians to disdain agriculture, when we know for certain that even the patricians considered it an honourable

profession? Or how could such a trivial motive have started such a cruel war? For to avenge his exile, Coriolanus marched on Rome, and would have destroyed it, if the pious tears of his mother and his wife had not dissuaded him from this impious enterprise.

[109] Still, the patricians continued to reclaim their fields after the plebeians had cultivated them, and the plebeians had no civil process for pressing their own claim. As a result, the tribunes of the people now demanded the passage of the Law of the Twelve Tables – which in fact only resolved this issue and no other, as I showed in my *Principles of Universal Law*. Under this law, the patricians now granted the plebeians 'quiritary' or citizen rights of ownership over their fields. Indeed, under the natural law of peoples, such civil ownership is granted even to foreigners. This was the second agrarian law of the nations of antiquity.

[110] But the plebeians realized that, despite their quiritary rights, they still could not bequeath the fields to their relations. For they could neither make intestate bequests, since without celebrating solemn marriages, they had none of the relations through which legitimate succession could pass. (At the time, these relations were limited to direct heirs, *sui heredes*; relatives on the father's side, *agnates*; and kinsmen through the clan, *gentiles*.) Nor could they dispose of fields by testament, since they lacked the rights of citizenship.

As a result, the plebeians asserted their claim to share the patricians' *connubium*, a term which meant the right to solemnized marriages. Now, the greatest solemnity of marriage was the auspices, which were both the exclusive domain of the patricians, and also the great source of all Roman law, both public and private. Hence, when the patricians granted solemnized marriage to the plebeians, they effectively granted them the rights of citizenship as well. (The jurist Modestinus defines marriage as the 'sharing of every divine and human right', *omnis divini et humani iuris communicatio*, which is tantamount to citizenship.) Then, following the natural progress of human desires, the plebeians secured from the patricians all those rights of private law which depended on the auspices: paternal authority, direct heirs, paternal kinsmen, and clan kinships. And by virtue of these rights, they further secured the rights to legitimate successions, testaments, and guardianships. Next, they claimed those rights of public law dependent on the auspices, first securing access to the consulship, with its attendant right to *imperium* or military command, and then to priesthoods and pontificates, with their attendant knowledge of the laws.

[111] In this manner, the tribunes of the people, who had been created as the basic defenders of their natural liberty, were gradually led to obtain for the plebeians all the rights of civil liberty. And the census instituted by Servius Tullius subsequently replaced the payments made privately to the patricians with taxes paid to the public treasury for disbursing monies to the plebeians in wartime. As a result, the census naturally developed from a basis of patrician liberty to a basis of popular liberty, as we shall later see in detail.

[112] With steady steps, the tribunes advanced in their power to make laws. Now, in fact the Horatian and Hortensian Laws had only made the plebeians' plebiscites binding on the whole people during two particular crises. The first was the secession of the plebs to the Aventine hill in the Year of Rome 304 (450 BC), at a time when the plebeians were not yet citizens, as I assume here hypothetically and later show in fact. The second was the secession of the plebs to the Janiculum hill in the Year of Rome 367 (287 BC), at a time when the plebeians were still struggling to make the patricians share the consulship with them.

On the basis of the Publilian and Poetelian Laws, the plebeians finally achieved the power to make laws that were universally binding. This must have led to great unrest and tumult in Rome, which necessitated the creation of Publilius Philo as dictator. For a dictator was created only in times of great danger to the republic, and such was the case here. The Roman republic had fallen into such great disorder that within the body politic it nourished two supreme legislative powers without any distinction between them of time, competence, or territory. As a result, the republic soon faced certain ruin.

As a remedy for this civil malady, Publilius Philo first ordained that whatever measures the plebeians approved by plebiscite in the tribal assemblies 'should be binding on all citizens', *omnes Quirites teneret*. By this, he meant all the people of the centuriate assemblies, in which all Roman citizens convened. (The Romans were termed *Quirites* only in public assemblies, and the singular form of the noun *Quiris* was never used in vernacular Latin conversation.) By this formula, Philo made clear that no laws could be passed that ran counter to the plebiscites. Now, the patricians themselves had already consented to laws that made the plebeians their equals in every possible respect. But by Philo's recent reform, which the patricians could not oppose without endangering the republic, the plebeians became superior to the patriciate: for, even without the senate's approval, they could enact general laws for all the people. In this way, the Roman republic had naturally become a government of popular liberty. And when Publilius Philo proclaimed the change by his law, he became known as the people's dictator.

[113] In keeping with this change, Philo added two ordinances which constitute the other two articles of his Publilian Law. The first of these concerned the authority of the senate. Until then, the authority of the senate lay with the authority of the nobles. In other words, the patricians had to ratify whatever measures the people had approved: this is the origin of the Roman formula 'Let the fathers give their authority', *deinde patres fierent auctores*. As a result, the popular election of consuls had merely been a public testimonial of the candidates' merit, and the popular enactment of laws merely a public call for legal action. But as dictator, Philo ordained that henceforth the patricians must grant authority to the people, now free and sovereign, before a vote was taken in the popular assembly, *in incertum comitiorum eventum*. In other words, the patriciate acted as the guardians of the people, who were the true lords of the Roman *imperium*, or supreme authority. If the people wished to enact laws, they could enact them using the wording offered them by the senate. If not, they could exercise their sovereign will and 'antiquate' the senate proposals, that is, declare that they wanted no new laws. This meant that all future decrees of the senate concerning public affairs would either be the senate's *instructions* to the people, or the people's *commissions* to the senate.

To conclude, Philo's last article concerned the census. In the past, the public treasury had been managed by the patricians, and only patricians could be made censors. But since this law made the treasury the property of the entire people, Philo's third article opened the censorship to the plebeians, the last magistracy in which they had not shared.

[114] If we adopt this hypothesis as the basis for our reading of Roman history, we shall find countless proofs that it underlies all the events narrated in that history. As long as the terms people, kingdom, and liberty are poorly defined, such events reveal no common foundation or particular connections. This alone would confirm the truth of my hypothesis. But on closer examination, my model proves to be not so much a hypothesis as a truth, contemplated in ideal form and proved factual by historical authorities. And if we further accept Livy's general statement that refuges were the ancient counsel of city founders – like Romulus' foundation of Rome in the refuge in the clearing – then my model reveals the histories of all the other cities of the world, which we previously despaired of knowing. This is a sample of the ideal eternal history, contemplated in my Science, through which the histories of all nations must in time pass.

43 Poetelian Law
Year of the World 3661; Year of Rome 419 (335 BC)

[115] The Poetelian Law on imprisonment for debt, de nexu, was enacted in the Year of Rome 419 (335 BC) by the consuls Gaius Poetelius and Lucius Papirius Mugillanus, just three years after the Publilian Law. It marks another turning-point in the history of Roman institutions. For it released the plebeians from feudal liability for debt, which previously had made them liege vassals of the patricians and compelled them to labour in their private prisons, often for life.

Even so, the senate retained its sovereign dominion over the lands under Roman authority, even though this authority itself had already passed to the people. And as long as the Roman republic was free, the senate could pass a declaration of public emergency – the 'senatorial decree of last resort', senatus consultum ultimum – to maintain their dominion by force of arms. Hence, when the people tried to reassign these lands under the agrarian laws of the Gracchi, the senate armed the consuls, who then declared the people's tribunes to be rebels and killed them as the instigators of this reform. Such a drastic measure was only possible because the rights of sovereign fiefs were subject to a higher sovereignty. This is confirmed by a passage in one of Cicero's

Speeches against Catiline, where he affirms that the agrarian law of Tiberius Gracchus was undermining the constitution of the republic. Hence, in putting him to death, Publius Scipio Nasica was justified by the right stated in the legal formula by which, as consul, he armed the people against the framers of this law: 'If anyone seeks to save the republic, let him follow the consul': *Qui rempublicam salvam velit, consulem sequatur.*

44 *War with Tarentum, in which the Greeks and Romans begin to know each other*
Year of the World 3708; Year of Rome 489 (282 BC)

[116] This war started when the people of Tarentum insulted both some Roman ships that had landed on their shores, and a subsequent Roman embassy. The people of Tarentum offered the excuse, cited by Florus, that 'they were unaware who these people were or whence they came'. So little did the earliest peoples know of each other, even when living on the same small peninsula!

45 *Second Punic War, the first certain part of the Roman history of Livy, who yet declares his ignorance of three important facts*
Year of the World 3849; Year of Rome 552 (218–202 BC)

[117] Livy declared that, beginning with the second Punic War, he would write his history of Rome with greater certainty, promising to narrate that war as the most memorable in Roman history. And the incomparable greatness of that war should have lent his annals the certainty that attends the most famous events. Yet Livy openly admits his ignorance of three important facts. First, he does not know in whose consulship Hannibal marched from Spain to Italy, after taking Saguntum. Second, he does not know where Hannibal crossed the Alps, whether in the Cottine or the Pennine range. Third, he does not know the size of Hannibal's army. For he found great variance in the ancient annals, in which some wrote 6,000 cavalry and 20,000 infantry, and others 20,000 cavalry and 80,000 infantry.

Conclusion

[118] All of these Notes make clear that everything we know about the ancient pagan nations, in the period shown on my Table, is completely uncertain. I have entered what is virtually unclaimed territory, in which the law grants rights to the occupant, *occupanti conceduntur*. Hence, I believe I am violating no one else's rights, if my account of the origins of national civilizations differs from and even contradicts those of previous scholars. For I am seeking scientific principles which will explain the origins of certain known historical facts, and give them a solid and coherent historical basis. For in previous studies, they have revealed no common foundation, no continuity of sequence, and no coherence among themselves.

SECTION 2
ELEMENTS

[119] To organize the material outlined in the Chronological Table, I propose here the following *axioms*, both philosophical and philological in nature, as well as some modest rational postulates and some elucidating definitions. Like the life-blood of a living creature, these principles run throughout my Science and enliven every part of my discussion of the common nature of nations.

I

[120] By its nature, the human mind is indeterminate; hence, when man is sunk in ignorance, he makes himself the measure of the universe.

[121] This axiom explains two common human customs: first, that rumour grows as it spreads, *fama crescit eundo*; and second, that presence diminishes rumour, *minuit praesentia famam*. Now, since the world began, rumour has travelled a very long way, and so has been the inexhaustible source of all the grandiose opinions which people have previously entertained about remote and unknown antiquities. This is due to that property of the human mind which Tacitus in his *Life of Agricola* describes in his aphorism 'Whatever is unknown is thought grandiose', *Omne ignotum pro magnifico est*.

2

[122] Another property of the human mind is that, when people can form no idea of distant and unfamiliar things, they judge them by what is present and familiar.

[123] This axiom indicates the inexhaustible source of all the erroneous views which entire nations and all scholars have entertained concerning the beginnings of civilization. For when nations first became aware of their origins, and scholars first studied them, they judged them according to the enlightenment, refinement, and magnificence of their age, when in fact by their very nature these origins must rather have been small, crude, and obscure.

[124] In this category, we may place the two kinds of conceit mentioned earlier: the conceit of nations, and the conceit of scholars.

3

[125] On the conceit of nations, we have seen the golden saying of Diodorus Siculus, who writes that all the nations, both Greek and barbarian, think they were the very first to invent the comforts of human life, and that they preserve memories of their history from the beginning of the world.

[126] This axiom instantly dispels the vainglory of the Chaldaeans, Scythians, Egyptians, and Chinese, who claim that they founded the first civilization of the ancient world. By contrast, the Jewish historian Flavius Josephus exonerates his own nation by generously admitting that the Jews lived hidden from all the pagan nations. Indeed, the Bible assures us that the world is quite young when compared to the hoary age with which it has been credited by the Chaldaeans, Scythians, Egyptians, and even today by the Chinese. This is an important proof of the truth of the Bible.

4

[127] In addition to the conceit of nations, there is the conceit of scholars, who assert that what they know is as old as the world.

[128] This axiom dispels the opinions of all the scholars who have praised the incomparable wisdom of the ancients. And it proves that the oracles of Zoroaster the Chaldaean, the lost oracles of Anacharsis the Scythian, the *Pimander* of Hermes Trismegistus, the *Orphica* (or *Hymns* of Orpheus), and the *Golden Verses* of Pythagoras were impostures, as all astute critics agree. It also exposes the absurdity of all the mystical senses which scholars have read into Egyptian hieroglyphics, and all the philosophical allegories they have read into Greek myths.

5

[129] If philosophy is to benefit humankind, it must raise and support us as frail and fallen beings, rather than strip us of our nature or abandon us in our corruption.

[130] This axiom expels two sects from the school of my New Science: the Stoics, who tell us to mortify our senses; and the Epicureans, who make them the rule of life. Both of them deny providence. The Stoics let themselves be dragged by fate; whereas the Epicureans abandon themselves to chance, and even affirm that the human soul perishes with the body. And so they both deserve to be called *monastic* or solitary philosophers.

By contrast, this axiom admits to our school the *political* philosophers, especially the Platonists. For they agree with all legislators on three principal points: that divine providence exists, that human emotions should be moderated to become human virtues, and that human souls are immortal. This axiom thus offers us the three central principles of my New Science: providence, marriage, and burial.

6

[131] Philosophy considers people as they should be, and hence is useful only to the very few who want to live in the republic of Plato, rather than to sink into the dregs of Romulus.

7

[132] Legislation considers people as they really are, in order to direct them to good purposes in society. Out of ferocity, avarice, and ambition, the three vices which plague the entire human race, it creates armies, trade, and courts, which form the might, affluence, and wisdom of commonwealths. Thus, from three great vices, which otherwise would certainly destroy all the people on the earth, legislation creates civil happiness.

[133] This axiom proves that divine providence exists and that it acts as a divine legislative mind. For out of the passions of people intent on their personal advantage, which might cause them to live as wild and solitary beasts, it makes civil institutions which keep them within human society.

8

[134] Outside their natural state, things can neither settle nor endure.

[135] Since from time immemorial the human race has lived harmoniously in society, this single axiom resolves the great question of whether law exists in nature, or whether human nature is sociable – which is the same thing. Our greatest philosophers and moral theologians are still debating the point against the sceptic Carneades and against Epicurus; and not even Grotius has resolved the question.

[136] Axioms 7–8 prove that man has free volition to turn his passions into virtues. But since his will is weak, he must be aided by God, who acts naturally as divine providence and supernaturally as divine grace.

9

[137] When people cannot know the truth, they strive to follow what is certain and defined. In this way, even if their intellect cannot be satisfied by abstract knowledge, *scienza*, at least their will may repose in common knowledge, *coscienza*.

10

[138] Philosophy contemplates reason, from which we derive our abstract knowledge of what is true. Philology observes the creative authorship and authority of human volition, from which we derive our common knowledge of what is certain.

[139] The second half of this axiom defines as philologists all the grammarians, historians, and critics who have contributed to our awareness of peoples' languages and deeds, including both their domestic customs and laws, and their foreign wars, peaces, pacts, travels, and trade.

[140] This axiom also shows how the philosophers and the philologists have failed each other. The philosophers should have used the philologists' authority to certify their reasoning, and the philologists should have used the philosophers' reasoning to verify their authorities. If they had done this, they would have done more good to our commonwealths, and they would have anticipated my conception of the New Science.

11

[141] Since human judgment is by nature uncertain, it gains certainty from our common sense about what is necessary and useful to humankind; and necessity and utility are the two sources of the natural law of nations.

12

[142] Common sense is an unreflecting judgment shared by an entire social order, people, nation, or even all humankind.

[143] Together with the following definition, this axiom establishes a new art of criticism concerning the founders of the nations, who lived more than a thousand years before those writers with whom previous criticism has dealt.

13

[144] When uniform ideas arise in entire nations which are unknown to each other, they must have a common basis in truth.

[145] This axiom is an important principle. For it establishes that mankind's common sense is a criterion which divine providence teaches peoples to aid them in defining what is certain in the natural law of nations. They arrive at this certainty by looking beyond local variations in this law to recognize its essential unities, on which they all agree. From these unities, we may derive a conceptual dictionary which traces the origins of all the various articulate languages. By using this dictionary, we may conceive the ideal eternal history which describes the histories of all nations through time. (See Axiom 22 below for this conceptual dictionary, and Axiom 68 for ideal eternal history.)

[146] This same axiom demolishes all previous ideas about the natural law of the nations, which was believed to have originated first in one nation, from which it was later adopted by others. This seductive error was promoted by the Egyptians and Greeks, who vainly boasted that they had sown the seeds of civilization throughout the world. And it was clearly the source of the myth that the Law of the Twelve Tables was brought to Rome from Greece. But in that case, it would have been a civil law which human provision then communicated to other peoples, rather than a law which divine providence established naturally in all nations, together with their civilized customs. One of the recurrent tasks of my Science is to show that the natural law of nations arose separately among various peoples who knew nothing of each other.

Only later, on occasions involving wars, embassies, pacts, and trade, was it recognized as common to all humankind.

14

[147] The *nature* of an institution is identical with its *nascence* at a certain time and in a certain manner. When these are the same, similar institutions will arise.

15

[148] The inherent properties of things are produced by the mode or manner in which they arise. Such properties therefore allow us to verify an institution's exact nature and nascence.

16

[149] Popular traditions always have a public basis in truth, which explains their birth and their preservation for many years by entire peoples.

[150] Another great task of my New Science is to discover these bases in truth, even when the passage of time and the subsequent changes in languages and customs have enveloped the truth in falsehood.

17

[151] Vernacular expressions are invaluable witnesses to the customs current among ancient peoples as their languages were forming.

18

[152] Any language of an ancient nation which has developed with complete autonomy provides an important witness to the customs of the world's earliest ages.

[153] This axiom assures us that Latin figures of speech afford the

weightiest philological proofs of the natural law of the nations. (And no one doubts that of all the nations the Romans were the wisest in that law.) For the same reason, scholars may use the German language in the same way, since it shares this property with Latin.

19

[154] Since the Law of the Twelve Tables reflects the customs of the peoples of Latium, it is an important witness to the ancient natural law of the Latin tribes. For while these customs, which arose in the age of Saturn, were variable elsewhere, at Rome they were inscribed on bronze tablets and religiously guarded by Roman jurists.

[155] Many years ago, I showed that this was true in my *Principles of Universal Law*; and my New Science will shed new light on the question.

20

[156] Since Homer's epics are civil histories of ancient Greek customs, they prove to be two great treasuries of the natural law of the Greek tribes.

[157] This axiom, simply posited here, will later be shown to be true in fact.

21

[158] The Greek philosophers accelerated the natural course of their nation's development. They appeared when the Greeks were still in a state of crude barbarism, and quickly led them to great sophistication, while preserving intact all their myths about the gods and heroes. By contrast, although the customs of the Romans progressed at a more reasonable pace, they completely lost sight of the history of their gods. (This is why what the Egyptians called the age of the gods is called by Varro the Romans' dark age.) But in their vernacular speech, the Romans preserved the heroic part of their history, which extends from Romulus to the Publilian and Poetelian Laws, and which is an unbroken historical mythology which parallels the Greek heroic age.

[159] This overlapping nature of human institutions is confirmed by the history of the French nation. The middle of the barbarous twelfth century witnessed the opening of the famous Parisian school where Peter Lombard, the famous Master of Sentences, set about teaching the subtleties of Scholastic theology. Yet the same age preserved the history written by Bishop Turpin of Paris – which, like a Homeric epic, is filled with myths about the paladins or heroes of France who were to figure in so many later romances and poems. This precocious transition from barbarism to the subtlest sciences made French a very refined language. Indeed, of all the living languages, French alone seems to have revived the Attic subtlety of the Greeks, and is the language best suited to scientific discourse. At the same time, like Greek, French retains many diphthongs, the mark of a barbarous language that is still unwieldy and combines consonants and vowels with difficulty.

An observation concerning young people will confirm these remarks about Greek and French. At the age when young people possess vigorous memory, vivid imagination, and ardent inspiration, they may profitably study languages and plane geometry without subduing that crudity, typical of minds governed by the body, which we may call the *barbarism* of the intellect. But if they advance, while still in this immature stage, to very subtle subjects like metaphysics and algebra, they become finicky in their mental habits, and so are rendered unfit for more important tasks.

[160] As I pondered my New Science, I discovered another reason, perhaps a more decisive one, for the peculiar development of Rome. When Romulus founded Rome in the midst of more ancient cities in Latium, he did so by opening a refuge, an act which Livy defines in a general way as 'the ancient counsel of city founders'. Since violence was still widespread, Romulus naturally established the city of Rome on the same basis as the world's earliest cities. Roman customs thus developed from primitive beginnings in an age when the vernacular dialects of Latium were already well advanced. As a result, the Romans used vernacular language to refer to their civil institutions, just as the Greeks had used heroic language to refer to theirs. Ancient Roman history thus offers us an unbroken mythology which parallels Greek heroic history. This explains why the Romans became the heroes of

the world. Rome subdued the other cities of Latium, then the entire Italian peninsula, and finally the world. For among the Romans, the heroic spirit was still young, whereas it was already in decline among the other Latin peoples, whose conquest prepared the way for Roman greatness.

22

[161] The nature of human institutions presupposes a conceptual language which is common to all nations. This language uniformly grasps the substance of all the elements of human society, but expresses them differently according to their different aspects. We witness the truth of this in proverbs, which are maxims of popular wisdom. For their meanings, while substantially the same, are expressed under as many different aspects as there are ancient and modern nations.

[162] This language is central to my New Science; and by studying it, language scholars will be able to compile a Conceptual Dictionary embracing all the different articulate languages, both living and dead. In the first edition of my *New Science*, I gave a specific example of this dictionary. Drawing on a large number of living and dead languages, I showed how the names given to family fathers reflected the different attributes they had in the earliest families and commonwealths, in the age when national languages were being formed. As far as my limited learning permits, I shall apply this dictionary to all the topics discussed in my *Science*.

[163] Let us review the preceding propositions. Axioms 1–4 offer us fundamental principles that refute all previous notions about the origins of civilization, exposing what is improbable, absurd, contradictory, and impossible in them. Axioms 5–15 offer fundamental principles of truth, which allow us to contemplate the world of nations in its eternal and ideal form. This is the essential property of every science, as Aristotle observed when he wrote that a science should treat what is universal and eternal, *scientia debet esse de universalibus et aeternis*. Axioms 16–22 offer fundamental principles of certainty, which we shall use to interpret the world of nations in its historical reality, just as we have contemplated it in its ideal form. This follows the rigorous philosophical

method of Francis Bacon, which I have transferred from the natural phenomena studied in his *Thoughts and Conclusions on Nature* to our human civil institutions.

[164] The preceding axioms are general and establish principles for my entire Science. The axioms which follow are specific and offer a basis for its discusssion of particular subjects.

23

[165] The sacred history of the Bible is more ancient than all the secular histories that survive. For it recounts, in great detail and over a period of more than 800 years, the state of nature under the patriarchs. This was the state of families, from which peoples and cities later developed, as all political thinkers agree. By contrast, secular history recounts little or nothing about this state, and what little it recounts is quite confused.

[166] This axiom proves the truth of biblical history, by contrast to the conceit of nations, as described by Diodorus Siculus. For the Jews have preserved their traditions in great detail from the beginning of the world.

24

[167] The true God founded Judaism on the prohibition of divination. By contrast, all the pagan nations sprang from the practice of divination.

[168] This axiom is one of the principal reasons why the world of ancient nations was divided into Jews and pagans.

25

[169] The fact of the universal flood is not proved by the philological and historical arguments of Martin Schoock, which are too flimsy. Nor is it proved by the astrological evidence of Pierre d'Ailly, who is followed by Giovanni Pico della Mirandola. This evidence is uncertain, and even false, since it relies on the *Alphonsine Tables*, which were later refuted by Jewish and then Christian scholars, who reject the calculations of Eusebius and Bede, and follow instead the Jewish historian Philo.

Instead, the fact of the flood can be proved by the references to natural history contained in myths, as the following axioms will make clear.

26

[170] The giants by nature had enormous bodies. They must have resembled the grotesque savages whom travellers at the foot of South America say they found in Patagonia, the land named for these *Patacones*, or Big Feet. In accounting for giants, we may dismiss as groundless, inappropriate, or simply false the causes cited by the philosophers, which have been assembled and approved by Jean Chassagnon in his treatise *On Giants*. We should instead cite the causes, both physical and moral, noted by Caesar and Tacitus in describing the gigantic stature of the ancient Germans. In my view, these causes derive from the brutish upbringing of their children.

27

[171] The flood and the giants are the starting-point of Greek history, which is our source for all pagan antiquity, with the exception of the Romans.

[172] Axioms 26 and 27 make it clear that humankind was at first divided into two kinds of people: the giants, or the pagans; and the people of normal build, or the Jews. This must reflect the difference between the brutish upbringing of the pagans and the human education of the Jews, which shows that the origin of the Jews was different from that of the pagans.

28

[173] Two great fragments of Egyptian antiquity have come down to us. First, the Egyptians divided the entire history of the world into three ages: the age of gods, the age of heroes, and the age of men. Second, during each of these three ages, a corresponding language was spoken: the hieroglyphic or sacred language; the symbolic or metaphorical language (which was heroic); and the epistolary or ver-

nacular language of men, using conventional signs to communicate the everyday needs of life.

29

[174] Homer clearly spoke a heroic language; but five passages in his two epics mention a more ancient language, which he calls the language of the gods.

30

[175] The diligent Varro collected 30,000 names of gods, for the Greeks counted that many. They referred to an equal number of needs in the natural, moral, economic, and civil life of the earliest ages.

[176] Axioms 28–30 establish the fact that the world of peoples began everywhere with religion. This is the first of the three basic principles of my New Science.

31

[177] Once warfare has made a people so fierce that human laws no longer have a place among them, religion is the only means powerful enough to subdue them.

[178] This axiom establishes that divine providence initiated the process by which fierce and violent men were led from their lawless condition to enter civilization and create nations. Providence did this by awaking in them a confused idea of divinity, which in their ignorance they ascribed to objects incompatible with the divine. Still, in their fear of this imaginary divinity, they began to create some order in their lives.

[179] In his own fierce and violent men, Thomas Hobbes failed to see this providential origin of human institutions. For in seeking his basic principles, he went astray, led by the chance of his admired Epicurus. As result, his conclusions were as unfortunate as his undertaking was noble. For Hobbes intended to add a great supplement to Greek philosophy by considering man within the whole society of the

human race – something which was certainly lacking, as George Pasch notes in *Learned Discoveries in this Century*. This would not have occurred to Hobbes if he had not been moved by the Christian religion, which commands us to practise not only justice but charity towards all human-kind. Here we may begin to refute Polybius' false dictum that 'if the world had philosophers, it would not need religions'. In fact, without religion there would be no commonwealths; and without common-wealths, the world would have no philosophers.

32

[180] When people are ignorant of the natural causes that produce things, and cannot even explain them in terms of similar things, they attribute their own nature to them. For example, the masses say that a magnet 'loves' iron.

[181] This axiom is a smaller part of Axiom 1: 'By its nature, the human mind is indeterminate; hence, whenever man is sunk in ignorance, he makes himself the measure of the universe.'

33

[182] The natural science of the ignorant is a sort of popular metaphysics, which explains the unknown in terms of God's will without considering the means he uses.

34

[183] Tacitus notes one of the true properties of human nature when he writes 'once struck with fear, minds are prone to superstition': *mobiles ad superstitionem perculsae semel mentes*. For once men are overcome by a fearful superstition, they associate it with all that they imagine, see, or even do.

35

[184] Wonder is the daughter of ignorance. The greater the cause inspiring it, the greater the wonder.

36

[185] The weaker its power of reasoning, the more vigorous the human imagination grows.

37

[186] The sublimest task of poetry is to attribute sense and emotion to insensate objects. It is characteristic of children to pick up inanimate objects and to talk to them in their play as if they were living persons.

[187] This philological and philosophical axiom shows us that people living in the world's childhood were by nature sublime poets.

38

[188] There is a golden passage in Lactantius which describes the origins of idolatry: 'At first, primitive men called their kings gods, either for their miraculous valour, which these primitive and simple folk truly believed miraculous; or, as is customary, in wonder at their manifest power; or else for those benefits which had united them in civilization.'

39

[189] Curiosity is an inborn human trait which is the daughter of ignorance and the mother of knowledge. Once wonder has opened our minds, curiosity has this habit: observing an extraordinary natural phenomenon – such as a comet, a parhelion, or a star at noon – our curiosity asks at once what it can mean or signify.

40

[190] Witches, who are full of fearful superstitions, are also extremely savage and monstrous. When the solemn rites of their witchcraft require it, they will heartlessly kill and dismember even darling and innocent babies.

[191] Axioms 28–38 reveal the origins of divine poetry, meaning poetic theology. Axioms 31–40 show us the origins of idolatry; Axioms 39–40, the origins of divination; and Axiom 40, the origins of sacrifice in bloody religions. Among the first crude and savage people, such sacrifices began with vows and human victims. From Plautus, we learn that the Romans called these Saturn's victims, *Saturni hostiae*. They correspond to the sacrifices made to Moloch by the Phoenicians, who consecrated children to their false deity and then cast them into the fire. Similar sacrifices are recorded in the Law of the Twelve Tables.

Such institutions point to the proper meaning of Statius' verse 'Fear created the world's first gods', *Primos in orbe deos fecit timor*. Indeed, false religions were born of people's own credulity, rather than the impostures of others. Yet despite Lucretius' impious exclamation – 'Such great evils could religion urge', *Tantum religio potuit suadere malorum* – Agamemnon's unfortunate vow and his sacrifice of his pious daughter Iphigenia yet reflect the counsel of providence. For it took obedience to such fearful religions to tame the descendants of the Cyclopes and to lead them to the humanity of men like Aristides, Socrates, Laelius, and Scipio Africanus.

41

[192] We may reasonably postulate that for several centuries the earth was drenched with the water of the universal flood, and thus could not send into the air any dry exhalations or flammable matter that might have generated lightning.

42

[193] Every pagan nation had a Jupiter, who hurled his lightning bolts and laid low the giants.

[194] This axiom contains the natural history, preserved in myths, that the universal flood covered the whole earth.

[195] Axioms 41 and 42 establish that the impious races who descended from Noah's three sons lived in a brutish state for many years. Wandering like beasts, they were scattered and dispersed throughout the earth's great forest. And because of their brutish upbringing, they produced giants in the age when the heavens thundered for the first time since the flood.

43

[196] Every pagan nation had its own Hercules, the son of Jupiter. Varro, the greatest scholar of antiquities, counted as many as forty of them.

[197] This axiom refers to the beginning of heroism among the first peoples, which was born of the false opinion that heroes were of divine origin.

[198] Axioms 42 and 43 explain the existence among the pagan nations of so many Jupiters, and later of so many Herculean heroes. And they prove that these nations could neither be founded without religion, nor grow without virtue. Now, at their origin these nations were savage and isolated, and therefore knew nothing of one another. But Axiom 13 states that when uniform ideas arise among peoples unknown to each other, they must have a common basis in truth. Hence, these axioms offer us this important principle: that the earliest myths must have contained civil truths, and therefore must have been the histories of the earliest peoples.

44

[199] The first wise men of the Greek world were theological poets, who clearly flourished before the heroic poets, just as divine Jupiter was the father of heroic Hercules.

[200] Axioms 42–44 establish that all the pagan nations were poetic in their origins, since each had its own Jupiter and its own Hercules. Among them, divine poetry arose first, and later heroic poetry.

45

[201] People tend naturally to preserve the memory of the laws and social orders that keep them within society.

46

[202] All the histories of barbarous peoples have mythical origins.

[203] Axioms 42–46 offer us the origin of our historical mythology.

47

[204] The human mind naturally tends to take delight in what is uniform.

[205] As regards myths, this axiom is confirmed by the custom of the masses. For when they consider famous people, noted for certain things and living in a certain context, they create myths which are appropriate to these conditions. These myths are *ideal truths*, since they truly conform to the merit of the figures they celebrate. And if they are sometimes false in fact, it is only to the extent that they inadequately recognize such merit. Indeed, if we consider the question carefully, poetic truth is metaphysical truth; and any physical truth which does not conform to it must be judged false. From this, we derive an important observation concerning poetic theory. Take Godfrey of Bouillon as Torquato Tasso imagines him. He is the true military commander, and all commanders who do not entirely conform to this Godfrey are not true ones.

48

[206] By nature, children retain the ideas and names of the people and things they have known first, and later apply them to others they meet who bear a resemblance or relation to the first.

49

[207] In a golden passage of *On the Mysteries of the Egyptians*, Iamblichus says that the Egyptians attributed to Hermes Trismegistus all the inventions that were useful or necessary to human life.

[208] Axioms 48 and 49 completely overturn all the senses of sublime natural theology which the divine Iamblichus ascribed to the mysteries of the Egyptians.

[209] Axioms 47–49 show us the origin of the poetic archetypes which constitute the essence of the myths. Axiom 47 describes the natural inclination of the masses to invent myths, and to invent them with the propriety of poetic decorum. Axiom 48 proves that the earliest men, as the children of the human race, were unable to conceive rational categories of things, and thus felt a natural need to invent poetic archetypes. These archetypes were imaginative categories or universals, to which (like ideal models or portraits) men could assign all the particular species that resembled them. And by virtue of this resemblance, ancient myths were invented with propriety. In precisely this way, the Egyptians assigned to the general category of the 'civil wise man' all the inventions useful or necessary to human life, which are the particular products of civil wisdom. But since they could not abstract the intelligible category of a civil wise man, let alone the idea of civil wisdom in which such Egyptians excelled, they imagined the figure of Hermes Trismegistus. Thus, in an age in which they enriched the world with inventions useful and necessary to mankind, we see how little the Egyptians as philosophers could grasp universals or intelligible categories!

[210] Axioms 47–49 also give us the principle of true poetic allegories. Such allegories gave myths meanings, based on identity rather than analogy, for various particulars comprised under poetic general categories. This is why in Latin allegories were called *diversiloquia*, different speeches: that is, expressions which reduce diverse species of men, deeds, and things to one general concept.

50

[211] Children possess a very vigorous memory, and thus have an excessively vivid imagination: for imagination is simply expanded or compounded memory.

[212] This axiom is the principle of the vividness of the poetic images which the world must have formed in its early childhood.

51

[213] In every endeavour but poetry, people with no natural gift can still succeed by diligent study of an art; but in poetry, no one who lacks the natural gift can possibly succeed through art.

[214] This axiom proves that the first poets were natural poets, for poetry laid the foundation of pagan civilization, which in turn was the sole source of all the arts.

52

[215] Children excel in imitation, and we see that they generally play by copying whatever they are capable of understanding.

[216] This axiom shows that the world in its childhood was made up of poetic nations, for poetry is simply imitation.

[217] This axiom gives us another principle. All the arts serving human need, advantage, comfort, and, to a great extent, even pleasure were invented in the poetic centuries, before philosophers appeared. For the arts are simply imitations of nature and are, in a certain sense, concrete poetry.

53

[218] People first feel things without noticing them, then notice them with inner distress and disturbance, and finally reflect on them with a clear mind.

[219] This axiom is the first principle of poetic statements, which are formed by feelings of passion and emotion. By contrast, philosophical

statements are formed by reflection and reasoning. Philosophical statements approach the truth as they ascend to universality. Poetic statements gain certainty as they descend to particulars.

54

[220] People naturally interpret doubtful or obscure matters affecting them according to their own nature, with its passions and customs.

[221] This axiom offers an important standard for our study of mythology. It means that all the myths invented by the first savage and crude people were interpreted severely, as befitted nations emerging from fierce and bestial freedom. Later, with the passage of many years and changes in customs, the myths lost their proper meaning, and were altered and obscured in the dissolute and corrupt age that preceded Homer. Yet religion still mattered to the Greeks, and they feared that the gods would prove contrary to their prayers if divine morals were contrary to their own. So the Greeks imputed their own customs to the gods, and thus gave foul, filthy, and obscene meanings to their myths.

55

[222] There is a golden passage in Eusebius, whose description of the Egyptians' wisdom may be generalized to apply to all pagan nations: 'The Egyptians' first theology was merely a history with interpolated myths. When later generations felt ashamed of these myths, they began gradually to supply them with invented mystical meanings.' This was also done by the Egyptian high priest Manetho, who converted all of Egyptian history into a sublime natural theology.

[223] Axioms 54 and 55 are two great proofs of my historical mythology. They are two mighty whirlwinds that dispel notions of the incomparable wisdom of the ancients. And at the same time, they are two great foundations of the truth of the Christian religion: for biblical history contains no stories which cause us to feel shame.

56

[224] Among the Near Eastern peoples, Egyptians, Greeks, and Romans, we find that the first authors were poets, as were the first writers of the new European languages during the medieval return of barbarism.

57

[225] Mute people express themselves by using gestures or objects which bear a natural relation to the ideas they wish to signify.

[226] This axiom is the principle of hieroglyphs, which we find that nations used in speaking during their early barbarism.

[227] This axiom is also the principle of the natural speech once spoken in the world, as Plato conjectured in his *Cratylus*, and after him Iamblichus in his *Mysteries of the Egyptians*. This view was shared by the Stoics and by Origen in his *Against Celsus*. But since it was merely a conjecture, it was rejected by Aristotle in his *On Interpretation* and by Galen in his *Doctrines of Hippocrates and Plato*. In Aulus Gellius, we find Publius Nigidius discussing the question. This natural speech was succeeded by the poetic style which used images, similes, comparisons, and the natural properties of things.

58

[228] Mute people can utter crude vowels by singing, just as by singing stammerers can overcome their impediment and articulate consonants.

59

[229] People vent strong passions by breaking into song, as we see in people who are overcome by grief or joy.

[230] Axioms 58 and 59 allow us to conjecture that the authors of the pagan nations must have formed their first languages by singing. For they had fallen into the brutish state of mute beasts, and in such dull-witted creatures only the stimulus of violent passions could have awakened consciousness.

60

[231] Languages must have begun with monosyllabic words. For even though children today are born amid a wealth of articulate languages, and they have very supple organs for articulating speech, they still begin with monosyllables.

61

[232] Heroic verse in hexameters is the oldest of all, and spondees are the slowest metre. Later I shall show that heroic verse was originally spondaic.

62

[233] Iambic verse is the closest to prose, and in Horace's definition the iamb is a 'swift foot'.

[234] Axioms 61 and 62 allow us to conjecture that ideas and languages grew more agile in step with each other.

[235] Together with the general principles stated in Axioms 1–22, Axioms 47–62 cover the full range of poetic theory in all its parts: namely, myth, character and decorum, statement, style and stylistic vividness, allegory, song, and finally verse. Axioms 56–62 also demonstrate that in all nations speech in verse preceded speech in prose.

63

[236] Because of the senses, the human mind naturally tends to view itself externally in the body, and it is only with great difficulty that it can understand itself by means of reflection.

[237] This axiom offers us this universal principle of etymology in all languages: words are transferred from physical objects and their properties to signify what is conceptual and spiritual.

64

[238] The order of ideas must follow the order of institutions.

65

[239] Here is the order of human institutions: first forests, then huts, next villages, later cities, and finally academies.

[240] This axiom is an important principle of etymology. In recounting the history of words in various native languages, we must follow the sequence of human institutions. Thus, we observe that nearly the entire lexicon of Latin had sylvan or rustic origins. For instance, the noun *lex*, law, must originally have meant the gathering of acorns. From this, I believe, came *ilex* or *illex*, holm-oak. For just as *aquilex* means someone who gathers water, the ilex produces acorns, which 'gather swine' [as if *hylex*, from Greek *hys*, swine, and Latin *lex*]. Later, *lex* meant the gathering of vegetables, which were therefore called 'legumes', *legumina*. Then, at a time when vernacular letters had not yet been invented for writing down laws, a necessity of civil nature caused *lex* to mean a gathering of citizens, or a public parliament. Hence, the presence of the people was the *lex*, law, that solemnized testaments, which was done 'when the assemblies were summoned', *calatis comitiis*. Finally, the act of 'gathering' letters into bundles forming single words was called *legere*, to read.

66

[241] People first sense what is necessary, then consider what is useful, next attend to comfort, later delight in pleasures, soon grow dissolute in luxury, and finally go mad squandering their estates.

67

[242] The nature of peoples is first crude, then severe, next generous, later fastidious, and finally dissolute.

68

[243] In the human race there first arise monstrous and grotesque beings, like Polyphemus and the Cyclopes; then great-spirited and proud heroes, like Achilles; next, courageous and just men, like Aristides and Scipio Africanus; closer to us, imposing figures in whom images of great virtues are linked to great vices, and whom the masses hail as men of true glory, like Alexander and Caesar; still later, gloomy and calculating men, like Tiberius; and finally dissolute and shameless madmen, like Caligula, Nero, and Domitian.

[244] As this axiom states, the first kind of people were needed to make individuals obey each other in the family state, and to prepare them to obey laws in the coming state of the city. The second kind, who by nature would not yield to their peers, were needed to establish aristocracies on the basis of the families. The third kind were needed to open the way towards popular liberty; the fourth, to introduce monarchies; the fifth, to consolidate them; and the sixth, to topple them.

[245] Axioms 65–68 offer us part of the principles of the *ideal eternal history* through which in time every nation passes in its birth, growth, maturity, decline, and fall.

69

[246] Governments must conform to the nature of the people governed.

[247] This axiom indicates that, by the nature of human civil institutions, the public school of rulers is the morality of the people.

70

[248] Let us make an assumption which does not contradict nature and which we shall later find true in fact. At first, a small number of the hardiest people withdrew from the abominable state of the lawless world and founded families, with whom and for whom they placed fields under cultivation. Much later, many other people likewise withdrew and took refuge on the cultivated lands of these fathers.

71

[249] Native customs, especially natural liberty, do not change all at once, but only gradually and over a long time.

72

[250] Since all nations began with the worship of some deity, fathers in the family state must have been (1) the wise men who interpreted divine auspices; (2) the priests who offered sacrifice to procure the auspices, meaning to interpret them properly; and (3) the kings who brought divine laws to their families.

73

[251] According to a popular tradition, the first to govern the world were kings.

74

[252] According to another popular tradition, the first kings created were by their nature the worthiest.

75

[253] According to yet another popular tradition, the first kings were wise men. This is why Plato vainly yearned for those most ancient times when philosophers reigned as kings, or when kings philosophized.

[254] Axioms 72–75 show that in their persons the first fathers united wisdom, priesthood, and kingship. Kingship and priesthood, moreover, were dependent on wisdom, which was the popular wisdom of legislators, not the esoteric wisdom of philosophers. As a result, the priests in all later nations were crowned.

76

[255] According to a popular tradition, the first form of government in the world was monarchy.

77

[256] Axioms 67–76, and particularly the corollary to 69, show us that fathers in the family state must have exercised monarchical power which was subject to God alone. This power extended over the persons and property of their children, and to a greater extent over those of the family servants, *famuli*, who had sought refuge on their lands. This made them the first monarchs of the world. (We must interpret the Bible as referring to such men when it calls them patriarchs, which means 'ruling fathers'.) Throughout the Roman republic, their monarchical rights were guaranteed by the Law of the Twelve Tables, which says 'The family father shall have the right of life and death over his children', *Patrifamilias ius vitae et necis in liberos esto*. And it adds that 'Whatever a son acquires, he acquires for his father', *Quicquid filius acquirit, patri acquirit*.

78

[257] According to their proper origin, the families can only have taken their name from the family servants, *famuli*, belonging to the fathers in the state of nature.

79

[258] Properly speaking, associates, *socii*, are people allied for their mutual advantage. The first associates in the world cannot be imagined or conceived before the appearance of the first refugees who fled to the first fathers in order to save their lives. These refugees were received by the fathers and, in exchange for their lives, were obliged to earn their living by cultivating the fathers' fields.

[259] Such refugees were the true associates of the heroes. Later they

became the plebeians of the heroic cities, and eventually the provincial people of sovereign nations.

80

[260] People naturally enter a feudal system of benefices, *benefizi*, when they see that it maintains or increases their personal advantages: for these are the benefits, *benefizi*, one hopes to derive from civil life.

81

[261] It is a characteristic of the strong that they do not relinquish through indolence what they have won by courage. Yet if it proves necessary or useful, they will gradually give up as little as they can.

[262] From Axioms 80–81 spring the perennial sources of fiefs, which Latin elegantly calls benefices, *beneficia*.

82

[263] Scattered throughout all the ancient nations we find clients and clientships, which are most aptly understood as vassals and fiefs. Indeed, erudite feudalists can find no apter Latin terms for the latter than *clientes* and *clientelae*.

[264] Axioms 70–82 reveal the origins of commonwealths, which were born of a crisis provoked by the family servants against the heroic fathers. This was a rebellion, described later in my Science, which caused the first commonwealths to be formed naturally as aristocracies. For when the servants rebelled, the fathers united themselves into orders to offer resistance; and then as a united order, the fathers sought to placate the servants and restore them to obedience by granting them a kind of rustic fief. At the same time, the fathers found that their own sovereign family powers – which can be understood only as a sort of noble fiefs – were now subjected to the sovereign civil power of the new ruling orders. And the leaders of these orders were called kings, for as the most courageous they had led the fathers during the servant rebellion.

Later, I shall prove that this was in fact the origin of cities. But even as a hypothesis, my account commands acceptance for its naturalness and simplicity, and because countless other civil phenomena derive from it as their proper cause. For in no other manner can we understand how civil power grew out of family powers, how the public patrimony emerged from private patrimonies, or how the foundations of commonwealths were laid by a social order which is made up of the few who command and the multitude of plebeians who obey – two elements which constitute the subject of political studies. Later, I shall show that civil states could not have arisen from simple nuclear families without servants.

83

[265] The law regarding the fields is established as the world's first agrarian law. By its nature, no law more restrictive can be imagined or conceived.

[266] This agrarian law distinguished the three kinds of domain or ownership which are possible in civil nature, and assigned them to three classes of persons. The bonitary domain was assigned to the plebeians. The quiritary domain was assigned to the fathers, since, being maintained by force of arms, it belonged to the nobility. And the eminent domain was assigned to the ruling order itself, which constitutes the lordship, or sovereign power, in aristocracies.

84

[267] There is a golden passage in Aristotle's *Politics* where, in his classification of commonwealths, he includes heroic kingdoms, in which kings administered laws at home, conducted wars abroad, and presided over the religion.

[268] This axiom tallies perfectly with the two heroic kingdoms of Theseus and Romulus, as the first is described in Plutarch's *Life of Theseus* and the second in Roman history. On such kings and the law, we may supplement Greek history with the Roman account of Tullus Hostilius administering the law in the prosecution of Horatius. As for

religion, the kings of Rome were also kings of sacred rites, and thus called *reges sacrorum*. Later, after the kings had been driven out of Rome, the need to authenticate the divine ceremonies led the Romans to create a priest called the king of sacred rites, *rex sacrorum*, who was the head of the herald-priests, or *fetiales*.

85

[269] There is another golden passage in Aristotle's *Politics*, which relates that ancient commonwealths had no laws for punishing private offences or righting private wrongs. He says that this custom is typical of barbarous peoples, since in their beginnings peoples are barbarous precisely because they are not yet civilized by laws.

[270] This axiom shows that duels and reprisals are necessary in barbarous ages, because they lack judicial laws.

86

[271] Golden as well is the passage in Aristotle's *Politics*, in which he says that in ancient commonwealths the nobles swore they would be the eternal enemies of the plebeians.

[272] This axiom explains the nobles' haughty, greedy, and cruel treatment of the plebeians, which is explicitly described in ancient Roman history. During this period, which was previously imagined to be an age of popular liberty, the patricians for many years overtaxed the plebeians, demanding military service paid at their own expense, and drowning them in a sea of usury. Then, when the wretched plebeians could not fulfil their obligations, the patricians locked them up for life in their private prisons, exacting payment from them in hard labour, and despotically stripping them to the waist and caning them like ignoble slaves.

87

[273] Aristocracies are quite reluctant to go to war, lest the plebeian masses grow warlike.

[274] This axiom is the principle of justice in the Roman army until the age of the Punic Wars.

88

[275] Aristocracies keep wealth within the order of the nobles, since it contributes to their power.

[276] This axiom is the principle of the Roman policy of clemency in victory. The Romans deprived conquered peoples of their arms alone, and granted them bonitary ownership of all else, only obliging them by law to pay a reasonable tribute. This axiom also explains why Roman patricians resisted the agrarian reforms of the Gracchi: they did not want the plebeians to grow wealthy.

89

[277] Honour is the noblest stimulus to military valour.

90

[278] Peoples will conduct themselves heroically in war, if in peacetime they contend with each other for honours, some to retain them, others to win merit by attaining them.

[279] This axiom is the principle of Roman heroism from the expulsion of the kings to the age of the Punic Wars. In this period, the patricians naturally sacrificed themselves to save their country, since it in turn safeguarded all the civil honours of their order. The plebeians in turn performed distinguished exploits to show that they merited patrician honours.

91

[280] The contentions between urban social orders seeking equal rights are the most effective means of making commonwealths great.

[281] This is the second principle of Roman heroism. Such heroism was attended by three public virtues: the plebeians' highmindedness in

seeking to gain civil rights by means of the patricians' laws; the patricians' fortitude in keeping the rights within their order; and the wisdom of the jurists in interpreting the laws and extending their benefits as new cases came to trial. These are the three intrinsic reasons by which Roman jurisprudence distinguished itself in the world.

[282] Axioms 84–91 place ancient Roman history in proper perspective. The next three are also partly relevant to this.

92

[283] The weak want laws; the powerful reject them. The ambitious promote laws to gain adherents. Rulers protect the laws in order to make the powerful equal to the weak.

[284] The first two clauses of this axiom are the torch that ignites heroic contentions in aristocracies. For the nobles wish to keep all the laws secret within their order, so that they are dependent on their will, and may be administered by their royal hand.

These three causes are cited by the jurist Pomponius when he relates that the Roman plebeians demanded the Law of the Twelve Tables because they were oppressed, in their phrase, by 'secret, uncertain law and regal might', *ius latens, incertum et manus regia*. And this axiom would also explain why the patricians were reluctant to grant the Twelve Tables to the plebs, and alleged that 'the customs of the fathers must be preserved, and no new laws enacted', *mores patrios servandos, leges ferri non oportere*. Now, this is recorded by Dionysius of Halicarnassus, who is better informed than Livy about Roman institutions. For he wrote his history with information supplied to him by Marcus Terentius Varro, who was hailed as the most learned of the Romans. And Dionysius is diametrically opposed to Livy, who relates that the nobles, in his words, 'did not spurn the plebeians' petitions', *desideria plebis non aspernari*.

In my *Principles of Universal Law*, I noted this and other greater contradictions, which reveal the sharp opposition between these two authors, who were the first to record this myth about the Twelve Tables – nearly 500 years after they were framed! The discrepancies are so great that it is better not to believe either of them – especially when in the same age this myth was not believed by Varro himself, who in his *Divine and Human Institutions* derives all of the Romans' divine and human institutions from native origins. Nor was it believed by Cicero in his dialogue *On the Orator*. In the presence of Quintus Mucius Scaevola, the foremost jurist of the age, Cicero has the orator Crassus say that the wisdom of the decemvirs far surpassed that of Draco and Solon, who gave laws to the Athenians, and that of Lycurgus, who gave them to the Spartans. This is tantamount to saying that the Law of the Twelve Tables was not brought to Rome from either Athens or Sparta.

I think my view is closer to the truth. Even in Cicero's day, this myth was all too widely accepted by learned men, born as it was of the conceit of scholars, who assign the wisest origins possible to their own wisdom. We may infer this from the words of Crassus himself, who says 'Let them all grumble; I shall say what I think', *Fremant omnes: dicam quod sentio*. We see that Cicero had a precise motive for having Scaevola speak only on the first day of the dialogue. He wished to forestall critics who might object to an orator discussing the history of Roman law, a subject which lay in the competence of jurists, whose profession was then distinct from that of orators. In this way, if Crassus had said anything wrong on the subject, Scaevola would certainly have reproached him. And Pomponius relates that Scaevola in fact reproached Servius Sulpicius, who also takes part in Cicero's discussion, telling him that 'it is disgraceful for a patrician to be ignorant of the law which it is his business to know', *turpe esse patricio viro ius, in quo versaretur, ignorare*.

[285] Even more than Cicero and Varro, Polybius offers irrefutable evidence for not believing either Dionysius or Livy. Without question, Polybius both knew more about politics than these two, and lived some 200 years closer to the decemvirs. Beginning in Book 6 of his *History* (I use Jakob Gronov's edition), Polybius pauses to examine the constitutions of the most famous free commonwealths of his day. He observes that the Roman constitution differs from those of Athens and Sparta, but more from the former. (Yet scholars who equate Attic and Roman law insist that the popular freedom established by Brutus was regulated by laws imported from Athens, not from Sparta!) By contrast, Polybius notes the similarity between the Roman and Carthaginian constitutions.

But no one has ever imagined that the freedom of Carthage derived from Greek laws. This was so far from true that a law at Carthage expressly forbade the Carthaginians to learn Greek! And how can it be that such an insightful writer on commonwealths does not even make a quite natural and obvious observation, or investigate the cause of this discrepancy? In other words, how can the Roman and Athenian states be different if they are ordered by the same laws? And how can the Roman and Carthaginian states be similar if they are ordered by different laws? To absolve him of such a gross oversight, we are forced to conclude that in Polybius' day no one at Rome had yet invented the myth that Greek laws were brought there from Athens to order the free popular government.

[286] The second part of this axiom opens the path by which ambitious men in popular states may rise to become monarchs. They do this by encouraging the natural desire of the plebeians who, in their ignorance of universal principles, seek laws for every particular case. Thus, when Sulla, head of the patrician party, had defeated Marius, head of the plebeian party, and was reorganizing the popular constitution with an aristocratic administration, he remedied the proliferation of laws by instituting the tribunals known as standing courts of inquiry, *quaestiones perpetuae*.

[287] The third part of this axiom reveals the hidden reason why Roman emperors beginning with Augustus made countless laws for private cases, and why sovereigns and powers everywhere in Europe adopted the corpus of Roman civil and canon law in their kingdoms and free republics.

93

[288] In democracies, the door to civil honours is by law open to the greedy masses who rule. Hence, in peacetime men can only contend for power by arms rather than by law, and will use their power to make laws that enrich them: witness the agrarian laws of the Gracchi at Rome. This results in civil wars at home and unjust wars abroad.

[289] Conversely, this axiom proves that the Romans were heroic in the period before the Gracchi.

94

[290] We defend our natural liberty most fiercely to preserve the goods most essential to our survival. By contrast, we submit to the chains of civil servitude to obtain external goods which are not necessary to life.

[291] The first part of this axiom is a principle basic to the natural heroism of the earliest peoples. The second part is a natural principle of monarchies.

95

[292] At first, people desire to throw off oppression and seek equality: witness the plebeians living in aristocracies, which eventually become democracies. Next, they strive to surpass their peers: witness the plebeians in democracies which are corrupted and become oligarchies. Finally, they seek to place themselves above the laws: witness the anarchy of uncontrolled democracies. These are in fact the worst form of tyranny, since there are as many tyrants as there are bold and dissolute persons in the cities. At this point, the plebeians become aware of their ills and as a remedy seek to save themselves under a monarchy. This is the 'natural royal law' which Tacitus invokes to legitimize the Roman monarchy of Augustus, 'who placed under his supreme authority a nation exhausted by civil wars, claiming the title of First Citizen'.

96

[293] When the first cities were formed from families, the lawless liberty of the nobles caused them to resist any checks and burdens: witness the aristocracies in which the nobles rule as lords. Later, when the plebeians had become numerous and grown warlike, the nobles were obliged to bear the same laws and burdens as the plebs: witness the nobility in democracies. Finally, to safeguard their easy lives, the nobles were naturally inclined to submit to a single ruler: witness the nobility under monarchies.

[294] Together with Axioms 66–94, Axioms 95 and 96 are principles of the ideal eternal history mentioned above.

97

[295] We may reasonably postulate the following. After the flood, people first lived in the mountains; somewhat later, they descended to the plains; and finally, after many years, they felt safe in migrating to the sea-coast.

98

[296] Strabo cites a golden passage from Plato, in which he describes humankind after the local floods of Ogyges and Deucalion. First, when people lived in mountain caves, Plato identifies them with the Cyclopes, whom he also regards as the world's first family fathers. Later, when they lived on the mountain slopes, he associates them with Dardanus, who built the city of Pergamum that later became the citadel of Troy. Finally, when they lived in the plains, he connects them with Ilus, by whom Troy was moved to the coastal plain and for whom it was renamed Ilium.

99

[297] According to an ancient tradition, Tyre was first founded inland and later moved to the coast of the Phoenician sea. And it is historically certain that the city was transferred from the shore to a nearby island, which Alexander the Great later reconnected to the mainland.

[298] Axioms 97-99 reveal that inland nations were founded first, and maritime nations later. They also offer us important proof of the antiquity of the Jewish people. For since the Jewish nation was founded by Noah in Mesopotamia, which is the region farthest inland of the early habitable world, it must have been the most ancient of all nations. This is confirmed by the fact that the first monarchy was also established in Mesopotamia, the kingdom of the Assyrians over the Chaldaean people, who produced the world's first wise men, and first among these Zoroaster.

100

[299] People will abandon for ever their native lands, which are naturally dear to them, only when driven by the ultimate necessity of survival. And they will leave them temporarily only from their greed to grow rich by trade, or from their jealousy in protecting their gains.

[300] This axiom is the principle of the migrations of peoples. It is based on the heroic maritime colonies, on the waves of invading barbarians (which are the only ones discussed by Wolfgang Lazius), on the last recorded Roman colonies, and on the European colonies in the Indies.

[301] This same axiom shows that the lost races of Noah's three sons must have been dispersed by their own bestial wandering. In this state, they fled from wild animals, which must have been very abundant in the world's great forest; they pursued shy and intractable women, whom this savage condition must have made extremely timid and fearful; and they searched for pastures and water. As a result, they found themselves scattered throughout the world at that moment when the heavens first thundered after the flood – an event which explains why every pagan nation began with its own Jupiter, the god of thunder. For if, by contrast, these lost races had remained civilized like God's chosen people, they too would have remained in Asia. Given the vastness of the continent and the scarcity of people in that age, they had no necessary reason for abandoning it: for people are not naturally accustomed to abandon their native lands from caprice.

101

[302] The Phoenicians were the first navigators of the ancient world.

102

[303] Nations in their barbarous stage are impenetrable. They must either be invaded from outside by wars, or they must voluntarily open themselves to foreigners from within, seeking the benefits of trade. For example, Psammeticus opened Egypt to the Ionian and Carian Greeks, who became famous as sea merchants after the Phoenicians. These same

Greeks used their great wealth to build two of the Seven Wonders of the Ancient World: the Temple of Samian Juno in Ionia, and the Mausoleum of Artemisia in Caria. And the glory of this trade later passed to the inhabitants of Rhodes, who built the Colossus of the Sun, another of the Seven Wonders, at the mouth of their harbour. In the same way, the Chinese have recently opened China to our European merchants, seeking the benefits of trade.

[304] Axioms 100–102 give us the principle for a new etymological dictionary which, by treating words with a clearly foreign origin, differs from the dictionary for native words which I mentioned earlier. Besides word origins, it can trace the history of nations which succeeded each other in colonizing foreign lands. For example, Naples was first called Sirena, siren, which is a Syriac word: this indicates that Syrians, meaning the Phoenicians, were the first to establish a colony there for commercial purposes. Later, Naples was called Parthenope, or virgin sight, in heroic Greek, and finally Neapolis, or new town, in vernacular Greek – names which prove that the Greeks arrived there subsequently to establish trading posts. This history produced a language mixing Phoenician and Greek elements, which it is said delighted the emperor Tiberius more than pure Greek. In precisely this way, on the Gulf of Tarentum there was a Syrian colony called Siris, whose inhabitants were called Sirites. Later, the Greeks called it Polieion, from which derived the epithet Polias given to the Minerva worshipped in the local temple.

[305] Axiom 102 also gives a scientific foundation to Pierfrancesco Giambullari's thesis that the Tuscan language derived from Syriac. This language could only have descended from the earliest Phoenicians, who were the ancient world's first navigators, as Axiom 101 states. Later, this honour belonged to the Carian and Ionian Greeks, and eventually it passed to the merchants of Rhodes.

103

[306] The Greeks must have founded an early colony on the coast of Latium, which was later conquered and destroyed by the Romans, so that it lies buried in the darkness of antiquity. This postulate must necessarily be granted.

[307] Without this postulate, anyone who studies and reflects on antiquity will be baffled by Roman history when it refers to the presence in Latium of Hercules, Evander, Arcadians, and Phrygians, and when it describes Servius Tullius as a Greek, Tarquinius Priscus as the son of Demaratus of Corinth, and Aeneas of Troy as the founder of the Roman people. Now, it is true that Tacitus notes a resemblance between Roman and Greek letters. But in Livy's opinion, the Romans in Servius Tullius' day had not yet heard the famous name of Pythagoras, who was then teaching in his renowned school at Croton. Instead, they only began to encounter the Greeks in Italy on the occasion of the war with Tarentum, which later led to the war with Pyrrhus and the Greeks across the sea.

104

[308] In a noteworthy simile, Dio Cassius [Dio Chrysostom] says that custom is like a king, and law like a tyrant. By which he must mean reasonable custom, and law which is not inspired by natural reason.*

[309] The implications of this axiom decide the great debate 'whether law exists in nature or in human opinion', which is the same question posed in the corollary to Axiom 8: 'whether human nature is sociable'. For the natural law of nations was established by custom, which Dio compares to a king commanding by pleasure – rather than by law, which Dio compares to a tyrant commanding by force. This natural law was born of human customs which sprang from the common nature of nations, which is the universal subject of my Science. And this natural law preserves human society: for there is nothing more natural, because more pleasing, than observing natural customs. Consequently, human nature, which is the source of human customs, is sociable.

[310] Taken together, Axioms 8 and 104 show that humankind is not unjust by its absolute nature, but only by its fallen and weak nature. Consequently, they prove the first principle of the Christian religion, which is Adam in the perfect image in which God created him. Hence, they also demonstrate the following Catholic principles of grace. Grace

* Vico mistakenly attributes this aphorism of Dio Chrysostom to Dio Cassius.

operates in man to remedy his privation, rather than negation, of good works: since man's potential for good works is ineffectual, grace must add its efficacy. But grace can act only in the presence of free will, which God's providence naturally aids, as Axiom 8 states; and in this, Christianity agrees with all other religions. It is on this foundation that Hugo Grotius, John Selden, and Samuel Pufendorf should have constructed their systems. In this way, they would have agreed with the Roman jurists, who define the natural law of nations as established by divine providence.

105

[311] The natural law of nations arose together with the customs of the nations. Such customs conform to a human common sense, which occurs without any reflection and without any imitation between nations.

[312] Together with Dio's simile, Axiom 105 establishes that providence, as the sovereign ruler of human affairs, ordains the natural law of nations.

[313] The same axiom establishes the distinctions between the natural law of the Jews, the natural law of nations, and the natural law of the philosophers. The pagan nations had only the ordinary help of providence. The Jews had also the extraordinary help of the true God, which is why they divided the world of nations into Jews and pagans. And the philosophers with their reason conceive a more perfect natural law than the nations practise in their customs. For philosophers only appeared some 2,000 years after the foundation of the pagan nations. The three systems of Grotius, Selden, and Pufendorf fail to note these three distinctions, and must therefore collapse.

106

[314] Sciences must begin at the point when their subject matter begins.

[315] This axiom is placed here as applying to one particular subject, the natural law of nations, but it applies universally to all the subjects treated in my Science. Although it properly belongs among the more

general Axioms 1–22, I place it here because its truth and importance are revealed by this particular subject more than any other.

107

[316] The earliest clans, *gentes*, originated before the cities, and were called by the Romans the greater clans, *gentes maiores*, meaning their ancient noble houses. From these, Romulus assembled the fathers of the senate, and with the senate, the city of Rome. By contrast, the new noble houses founded after the cities were called lesser clans, *gentes minores*. After the expulsion of the kings, Junius Brutus enrolled fathers from these new houses to replenish the senate, which had been nearly depleted by the deaths of senators executed by Tarquinius Superbus.

108

[317] Gods were divided accordingly into those of the greater clans and those of the lesser clans. The gods of the greater clans were those consecrated by the families before the founding of cities. Among the Greeks and Romans, they clearly numbered twelve; and I shall show later that the same number existed among the early Assyrians or Chaldaeans, Phoenicians, and Egyptians. Indeed, the number of the gods was so familiar to the Greeks that they were simply referred to by the word *dōdeka*, the Twelve. All twelve gods are named confusedly in a Latin distich of Lucilius, which I cited in my *Principles of Universal Law*. But in Book 2 of my *Science*, I follow the natural theogony, or genealogy of the gods, which naturally formed in the minds of the Greeks, and list them in this order: Jupiter, Juno, Diana, Apollo, Vulcan, Saturn, Vesta, Mars, Venus, Minerva, Mercury, and Neptune. By contrast, the gods of the lesser clans were those consecrated later by peoples living in cities: for example, Romulus, who after his death was called the god Quirinus by the Roman people.

[318] Axioms 106–8 show that the three systems of Grotius, Selden, and Pufendorf are based on faulty principles. For they begin with nations considered within the society of the entire human race. But I shall

show that the human race in all the first nations originated in the age of the families and under the gods of the greater clans.

109

[319] People with limited understanding regard the law as only what its words express.

110

[320] Ulpian gives a golden definition of civil equity. He calls it 'a kind of probable judgment, not naturally known to everyone' – and thus distinct from natural equity – 'but only to those few whose prudence, experience, and learning have taught them what things are necessary to preserve human society'. In good Italian, we call this *ragion di stato*, the reason of state.

111

[321] What is certain in laws is a dark area of legal reasoning which is enforced by authority alone. This is why we often find laws harsh in their application. Still, we are obliged to apply them because they are certain, for *certum* in good Latin means particularized, or individuated, as the Scholastics say. Hence, in extremely elegant Latin, *certum*, certain, and *commune*, common, are antonyms.

[322] Axioms 109–11 constitute the principle of *strict construction*. Its rule is civil equity, which relies on what is *certain*, meaning the limited particularity of legal wording. Hence, barbarous peoples, who can conceive only particular ideas, are naturally satisfied by civil equity, and consider it their due. In this context, Ulpian says, 'The law is harsh, but it is written.' But in better Latin and with greater legal elegance, we might say, 'The law is harsh, but it is *certain*.'

112

[323] Intelligent people regard the law as the principle of equal benefit to all parties.

113

[324] The truth in laws is a sort of light or splendour which illuminates their natural reason. This is why jurists often say 'it is true', *verum est*, for 'it is just', *aequum est*.

[325] The definitions of Axioms 111 and 113 derive from Axioms 9–10, which define what is true and certain in general terms. Because they apply general definitions to the particular subject of the natural law of nations, these axioms will prove useful throughout my New Science.

114

[326] Natural equity, as conceived by the fully developed human reason, is the practical application of wisdom to what is useful. For wisdom in the broadest sense is merely the science of making natural use of things.

[327] Axioms 112–14 constitute the principle of *generous construction*. Its rule is natural equity, which is a natural element of civilized nations. This is the public school from which philosophers emerged.

[328] Axioms 109–14 confirm that providence ordained the natural law of nations. For many centuries, nations had to live in ignorance of truth and natural equity, until the latter was explained by philosophers. During this time, providence allowed them to adhere to certainty and to civil equity, which scrupulously safeguards the wording of decrees and laws. In this way, the nations observed the letter of the law even when it proved harsh, and thus managed to preserve themselves.

[329] The three great proponents of the natural law of nations – Grotius, Selden, and Pufendorf – were ignorant of the principles stated in Axioms 109–14. As a result, all three of them erred together in laying the foundations of their systems. For they believed that natural equity in its perfect form was understood by the pagan nations from

the very beginning. But they failed to reflect that philosophers only appeared some 2,000 years after the founding of these nations. And they failed to give special consideration to the particular assistance which a single people, the Jews, received from the true God.

SECTION 3
PRINCIPLES

[330] Let us test the propositions enumerated as Elements of my New Science, and see whether they can give form to the matter outlined in the Chronological Table. I ask the reader to review what others have written about the principles in any field of pagan antiquity, whether human or divine, and to see whether it conflicts with any of my propositions, either singly or as a whole. (In fact, since all my propositions are in harmony, whatever conflicts with one of them will conflict with the rest.) I am certain that, on making this comparison, the reader will find that their writings are merely clichés based on confused and misplaced memories,* and the fancies of disordered imaginations, without any true understanding: since this has been impaired by the two conceits described in Axioms 3 and 4. Thus, the conceit of the nations, who each assert their primacy in the world, discourages our hopes of discovering the principles of this Science in the philologists. And the conceit of scholars, who claim that what they know was clearly understood at the beginning of the world, makes us despair of discovering these principles in the philosophers. In our inquiry, then, we must proceed as if there were no books in the world.

[331] Still, in the dense and dark night which envelops remotest antiquity, there shines an eternal and inextinguishable light. It is a truth which cannot be doubted: *The civil world is certainly the creation of humankind*. And consequently, the principles of the civil world can and

* Vico's expression *luoghi di confusa memoria* evokes the theory that the memory assigns ideas to certain places.

must be discovered *within the modifications of the human mind*. If we reflect on this, we can only wonder why all the philosophers have so earnestly pursued a knowledge of the world of nature, which only God can know as its creator, while they neglected to study the world of nations, or civil world, which people can in fact know because they created it. The cause of this paradox is that infirmity of the human mind noted in Axiom 63. Because it is buried deep within the body, the human mind naturally tends to notice what is corporeal, and must make a great and laborious effort to understand itself, just as the eye sees all external objects, but needs a mirror to see itself.

[332] Now, since the world of nations is the creation of humankind, let us see in what institutions all the human race agrees and has always agreed. From these, we may derive principles which, like those of every science, are universal and eternal, and on which all nations are founded and maintain themselves.

[333] We observe that the barbarous and civilized nations of the world, despite their great separation in space and time and their separate foundations, all share these three human customs: all have some *religion*, all contract *solemn marriages*, and all *bury their dead*. And in every nation, no matter how savage and crude, no rites are celebrated with more elaborate ceremonies or more sacred solemnities than those of religion, marriage, and burial. Now, according to Axiom 13, whenever uniform ideas originate among peoples unknown to each other, they must have a common basis in truth. Hence, all the nations must have grasped that these three institutions are the origin of all civilizations, and hence that they must be guarded religiously. For otherwise, the world would return to a brutish state and again become a wilderness. This is why I have adopted these three eternal and universal customs as the three first principles of my New Science.

[334] Let no present-day travellers denounce these principles as false. They may relate that tribes of Brazil, the Kaffir of Africa, and other peoples of the New World live in society without any knowledge of God; and Antoine Arnauld says the same of the inhabitants of the Antilles. It may have been such writers who induced Pierre Bayle to affirm in his treatise on comets that people can live in justice without the light of God. (Even Polybius dared not assert as much in his

acclaimed dictum that, if there were philosophers who lived in justice through reason rather than laws, the world would need no religions.) But these are tales told by travellers who hope that such exotica will help them peddle their books. Their view is shared by Andreas Rüdiger in his pompously titled *Divine Physics*, which he subtitled 'the only path between atheism and superstition'. But even in the free and popular Genevan republic, where writers enjoy greater freedom, Rüdiger was rebuked for this opinion by the censors of the University of Geneva, who charged that he wrote with too much assurance – in other words, with considerable audacity.

In fact, all nations believe in a provident deity. Yet in all of past history and the entire world of civilization, we can find only four primary religions. First is the religion of the Jews. Second is the religion of the Christians, which derives from the first. Both of these believe in a single deity which is a free and infinite spirit. Third is the religion of the pagans, who believe in the divinity of several gods, which they imagine as made up of body and free spirit. This is why pagans refer to the divine powers that rule and preserve the world as the immortal gods, *dei immortales*, in the plural. Fourth and last is the religion of the Mohammedans, who believe in the divinity of a god who is an infinite and free spirit in an infinite body. And as their reward in the next life, they expect pleasures of the senses.

[335] No nation has ever believed in a god which is purely body, or in a god which is purely spirit but not free. This is why the Epicureans, whose God is merely a body subject to chance, could not reason about commonwealths and laws; nor could the Stoics, who resemble the followers of Spinoza in making God an infinite spirit, subject to fate, in an infinite body. And Benedict Spinoza discusses the commonwealth as if it were a society of shopkeepers. Cicero was right, then, when he told his Epicurean friend Atticus that he could not discuss laws with him unless he granted the existence of divine providence. This shows us how compatible the Stoic and Epicurean sects are with Roman jurisprudence, which posits divine providence as its first principle!

[336] As for the principle of marriage, some believe that, when free men and women engage in sexual relations without solemn matrimony, as sometimes happens in fact, they commit no wrong under the law of

nature. But all the nations of the world reprove this opinion as false by their civilized customs. On the basis of these customs, they all celebrate marriage religiously, and thus define illicit relations as a bestial sin, if in a minor degree. The reason is simple. Parents in such unions are joined by no legal bond, and soon forsake their natural children. Since the parents may separate at any moment, the children find themselves abandoned by both of them, and are exposed to be devoured by dogs. Then, if they are not adopted and raised by the public or private charity of a humane society, such children will grow up with no one to teach them religion, language, or any other civilized custom. Left to themselves, such orphans will turn the world of nations, enriched and embellished by the many fine arts of humanity, into the great ancient forest where Orpheus' foul beasts, wandering in brutish and abominable error, practised the bestial intercourse of sons with mothers and of fathers with daughters. This incest is the execrable abomination of the lawless world. Socrates cited irrelevant biological arguments to prove that incest violates the law of nature. But incest in fact violates the law of *human nature*. For such relations are naturally considered abhorrent by all nations, and have only been practised by nations, like the Persians, in a state of advanced decadence.

[337] Finally, to appreciate the importance of my third principle, that of burial rites, let us imagine a brutish state in which human corpses are left unburied as carrion for crows and dogs. Such bestial behaviour clearly belongs to the world of uncultivated fields and uninhabited cities, in which people wandered like swine, eating acorns gathered amid the rotting corpses of their dead kin. This is why burials were rightly defined in a lofty Latin phrase as 'the covenants of the human race', *foedera humani generis*, and were characterized less grandly by Tacitus as 'exchanges of humanity', *humanitatis commercia*. Furthermore, all pagan nations clearly agree in the view that the souls of the unburied remain restless on the earth and wander around their corpses: which is to say, souls do not die with their bodies, but are immortal. We may regard this as the consensus of the barbarous nations of antiquity, for it is confirmed by what we read about today's barbarous nations in various authors: the tribes of Guinea in Hugo van Linschoten, the peoples of Peru and Mexico in José de Acosta, the Indians of Virginia in Thomas

Harriot, the Indians of New England in Richard Whitbourne, and the people of Siam in Joost Schouten. Hence, we may share Seneca's conclusion: 'When we discuss immortality, we must grant considerable importance to the consensus of humankind, who either fear or worship the spirits of the underworld. I follow this general belief.'

SECTION 4
METHOD

[338] To complete the establishment of the principles which I have adopted in my Science, it remains in this first book to discuss the method it should employ. And this Science must begin at the point when its subject matter began, as Axiom 106 states. Hence, if we heed the philologists, we must look backwards and seek it among the stones of Deucalion and Pyrrha, among the rocks of Amphion, and among the men born from the furrows of Cadmus or the hard oak of Virgil. And if we heed the philosophers, we must seek it among the frogs of Epicurus, among the cicadas of Hobbes, and among the simpletons of Grotius. Or we must look among those men described by Pufendorf who were cast into the world without God's aid or care, grotesque savages like the giants called 'Big Feet' reported in Patagonia near the Strait of Magellan – which is to say Homer's Cyclopes, in whom Plato sees the first fathers of the family state. Such are the scientific origins of humankind which philologists and philosophers have given us!

Furthermore, we must begin our discussion at the point when these creatures began to think humanly. There was only one means of taming the monstrous savagery and bridling the bestial freedom of such creatures. This was the terrifying thought of some deity, which is the only means powerful enough to reduce savage liberty to dutiful behaviour, as Axiom 31 states. Yet as I sought to discover the manner in which this first human thought arose in the pagan world, I met with arduous difficulties which have cost me a full twenty years of research to overcome. For I had to descend from today's civilized human nature to the savage and monstrous nature of these early people, which we can by no means imagine and can conceive only with great effort.

[339] For all these reasons, we must begin with some notion of God that is found in even the most wild, savage, and monstrous people. We may show that this notion is the following. When people fall into despairing of any natural assistance, they desire something higher to save them. But only God is higher than nature, and this is the light which God has shed on all people. We find confirmation of this in a common human custom: as libertines grow old and feel their natural powers failing, they naturally turn to religion.

[340] Now, before they became the founders of the pagan nations, the earliest men must have thought in powerful surges of violent passion, which is how beasts think. So we must begin with the popular metaphysics mentioned in Axiom 33, which proves to be the theology of the poets. From this, we must seek that terrifying thought of a deity which imposed form and measure on the bestial passions of these lost men and made them human passions. Such a thought must have given rise to the *moral effort, or conatus*, which is proper to the human will and which restrains the impulses that the body urges on the mind. By means of this effort, such impulses can be completely suppressed by the sage, and can be directed to better ends by the good citizen.

Our control of bodily impulses is undoubtedly due to the freedom of the human volition, and thus to free will, in which all the virtues reside, including justice. When justice informs it, the will is the source of all that is just and of all the laws that justice dictates. To assign such conscious efforts to the body would mean granting them the freedom to regulate their motions. But in nature all bodies are agents of necessity. What in mechanics are called power, force, and conatus are the insensate motions which cause bodies to approach their centres of gravity (as ancient mechanics taught) or to recede from their centres of motion (as modern mechanics teaches).

[341] Because of their corrupt nature, people are tyrannized by self-love, and so pursue their own advantage above all else. Seeking everything that is useful for themselves and nothing for their companions, they cannot subject their passions to the conscious impulse that directs them to just ends. This leads us to establish the following principle. In his bestial state, a man loves only his own well-being.

After he takes a wife and has children, he continues to love his own well-being, and comes to love the well-being of his family as well. After he enters civil life, he comes to love the well-being of his city. After his city extends its rule over other peoples, he comes to love the well-being of his nation. And after such nations are united through war, peace, alliances, and trade, he comes to love the well-being of the entire human race. In all these contexts, the individual continues to love his own advantage above all else. Hence, it is by divine providence alone that the individual remains within these social orders, observing justice in the society of the family, of the city, and finally of humankind. Within these orders, when an individual cannot obtain the advantages he wants, he will seek instead the advantages which are his due: this we call his just portion. In this way, all human justice is governed by the divine justice which divine providence administers to preserve human society.

[342] In its first principal aspect, then, my New Science must be a *rational civil theology of divine providence*, which was previously lacking in philosophy. For some philosophers were completely unaware of the existence of providence. The Epicureans said that human affairs are set in motion by the blind collision of atoms; and the Stoics said they are drawn along by an inexorable chain of causes and effects. And other philosophers merely considered providence within the order of natural things, calling their metaphysics a 'natural theology'. While contemplating the providential aspect of God, they confirmed its existence through the physical order of nature, which they observed in the motions of physical bodies like the spheres and the elements, as well as in the final cause revealed in lesser natural phenomena.

By contrast, the philosophers should have discussed providence as revealed in the economy of civil institutions. This is clear from the proper meaning of the word 'divinity', which was applied to providence. This noun derives from the Latin verb *divinari*, to divine: in other words, to understand either what is hidden from men, meaning the future, or what is hidden within them, meaning their conscience. Properly speaking, then, divinatory providence is the first and principal part of the subject of jurisprudence, or divine institutions; while the second and complementary part of jurisprudence, or human institutions,

126

must derive from divinatory institutions. My New Science is therefore a demonstration, as it were, of *providence as historical fact*. That is, it must provide a history of the orders and institutions which providence bestowed on the great polity of humankind without the knowledge or advice of humankind, and often contrary to human planning. For although by its creation our world is temporal and particular, the orders which providence establishes in it are universal and eternal.

[343] The contemplation of infinite and universal providence offers us three divine proofs to confirm and demonstrate my Science. (1) Since omnipotence is its minister, divine providence introduces its orders into the world through easy paths, such as our natural human customs. (2) Since infinite wisdom is its counsellor, there is order in whatever providence disposes. (3) And since its final purpose is its own infinite goodness, what is ordained by providence always tends towards a good higher than what humankind proposes.

[344] Faced with the lamentable obscurity of the origins of nations and the innumerable varieties of their customs, we can desire no sublimer proofs about this divine source of all human institutions than the three just mentioned: its naturalness, its order, and its final purpose, which is the preservation of the human race. And these proofs appear even more distinct and luminous when we ponder them further. (1) Let us reflect on the ease with which institutions arise, and consider under what diverse conditions, often remote from each other and contrary to human proposals, they come into being and gain acceptance. Such proofs are granted us by divine omnipotence. (2) Let us compare various institutions and their order. We shall find that some may arise now in their proper time and place, while others must wait to arise with that timelessness in which, according to Horace, all the beauty of order consists. Such proofs are offered us by eternal wisdom. (3) Finally, let us see whether it is conceivable that under the same circumstances different divine benefits could have arisen which, by relieving men's needs and ills, would have better guided and preserved human society. Such proofs are given us by God's eternal goodness.

[345] My Science proposes a central and unitary proof of providence. By comparing and analysing a wide range of possibilities – as many as are permitted and permissible – we shall see whether the human mind

can conceive of any other causes, different in number or in kind, which could have produced the effects seen in the civil world. By following this argument, the reader will experience a divine pleasure while still in his mortal body: for in their divine and ideal form, he will contemplate the world of nations in all their great variety and extent. And the reader will find that he has shown the Epicureans that their chance cannot madly wander about escaping in all directions, and shown the Stoics that the eternal chain of causes, which they say shackles the world, is dependent on the omnipotent, wise, and generous will of God the Best and Greatest.

[346] We shall find that these sublime proofs of natural theology are confirmed by the three kinds of logical proofs. First, by reasoning about the origins of divine and human institutions in the pagan world, we arrive at their first beginnings, beyond which only foolish curiosity would attempt to go – which is the hallmark of first principles. Second, we shall explain the particular manner in which they arose, or what I call their nascence or nature – which is the hallmark of a science. Finally, we shall find confirmation of these proofs in the eternal properties which are preserved by human institutions and determined by their 'nature', meaning the time, place, and manner of their origins, as Axioms 14 and 15 state.

[347] In exploring the origins of human institutions, my Science rigorously analyses our human notions about what is necessary or useful, which are the two perennial sources of the natural law of nations, as Axiom 11 states. Hence, in another principal aspect, my New Science is a *history of human ideas*, which forms the basis for constructing a metaphysics of the human mind. Axiom 106 states that sciences must begin at the point when their subject matter begins. Hence, the queen of the sciences, metaphysics, began when the first men began to think in human fashion, and not when philosophers began to reflect on human ideas. (The latter notion is found in Johann Jakob Brucker's recent *Philosophical History of the Theory of Ideas*, an erudite and scholarly little book which includes the latest controversies between the foremost geniuses of our age, Leibniz and Newton.)

[348] We must, then, determine the earliest times and places of this history: that is, when and where human thought arose. And we must

gain certainty for these times and places by applying the appropriate chronology and geography, which might be called *metaphysical*. To this end, my Science applies a new critical art, similarly metaphysical, to the founders of the nations: for they must have lived more than a thousand years before those writers with whom previous criticism has dealt. And as a criterion, I have adopted the common sense of the human race, which (as Axiom 11 states) is taught by divine providence and is common to all nations. This common sense is determined by the necessary harmony of human institutions, which is the source of all the beauty of the civil world. Hence, the predominant proofs of my Science follow this form: given the orders established by divine providence, human institutions *had to, have to, and will have to* develop in the way described by my Science. (Nor would this change even if infinite worlds were to arise from time to time throughout eternity, which is certainly false in fact.)

[349] Thus, my New Science also traces the *ideal eternal history* through which the history of every nation passes in time; and it follows each nation in its birth, growth, maturity, decline, and fall. Now, according to the first irrefutable principle stated above, the world of nations is clearly a human creation, and its nature reflected in the human mind. Hence, I would venture to say that anyone who studies my Science will retrace this ideal eternal history for himself, recreating it by the criterion that it *had to, has to, and will have to* be so. For there can be no more certain history than that which is recounted by its creator. In this way, my Science proceeds like geometry which, by constructing and contemplating its basic elements, creates its own world of measurable quantities. So does my Science, but with greater reality, just as the orders of human affairs are more real than points, lines, surfaces, and figures. This is an indication that my proofs are divine and should afford my reader something like divine pleasure. For in God knowledge and creation are the same thing.

[350] If we adopt the definitions of truth and certainty proposed in Axiom 10, we see that for a long time the pagan peoples lived in ignorance of truth and reason, which are the source of that inner justice by which the intellect is satisfied. By contrast, this justice was practised by the Jews, for they were illuminated by the true God. (Indeed, his

divine law even forbade the Jews from thinking unjust thoughts – something no mortal legislator ever bothered about. For the Jews believed in a purely spiritual God who can read human hearts, but the pagans believed in gods composed of bodies and minds who were incapable of this.) Eventually, the philosophers reasoned about this inner justice, but they only appeared some 2,000 years after the founding of the nations. Hence, in the meantime the nations were governed by the certitude of authority, which is the criterion adopted by my metaphysical criticism. (This is humankind's common sense, which is defined in Axiom 12, and on which the consciences of all nations repose.) Hence, in another principal aspect, my Science becomes a *philosophy of authority*, for this authority is the source of what moral theologians call outer justice. The three great proponents of natural law – Grotius, Selden, and Pufendorf – should have taken into account this authority, rather than the authority they drew from passages in early writers. For how could these writers have any awareness of the authority which reigned among nations more than a thousand years before they lived? Grotius, who is more learned and erudite than the others, attacks the Roman jurists on almost every particular point of this question. But he misses his mark, for the jurists established their principles of justice on the certainty of humankind's authority, not on the authority of learned scholars.

[351] These philosophical proofs form the basis of my Science and are consequently essential to its purpose. By contrast, philological–historical proofs have only secondary importance, and may be assigned to the following categories.

[352] (1) Without being forced or distorted, my mythological interpretations agree directly, easily, and naturally with the institutions I discuss. We shall see that myths are the civil histories of the earliest peoples, who everywhere were poets by nature.

[353] (2) Second, when explained by the complete truth of their sentiments and by the complete propriety of their expressions, heroic statements also agree with these institutions.

[354] (3) The etymologies of native languages also agree with these institutions, for they trace the histories of the words which denote them. Such etymological histories begin with the meanings proper to

their origins, and follow the natural progress of their metaphorical uses. This follows the order of ideas, along which the history of languages must proceed, as Axioms 17–18 and 64–5 state.

[355] (4) My Science illustrates the conceptual dictionary of human social institutions. As Axiom 22 states, all nations uniformly grasp the substance of the same institutions, but express them differently according to their different manifestations.

[356] (5) My Science attempts to sift the truth from falsehood in whatever popular tradition has preserved for many centuries. For as Axiom 16 states, popular traditions have been preserved for so many years by entire peoples because they have a public basis in truth.

[357] (6) The great fragments of antiquity were previously useless to science because they were squalid, mutilated, and dispersed. But once they have been cleaned, restored, and set in their proper place, they will shed new light on the past.

[358] (7) Finally, all the events we know from certain history may be traced to these institutions, which are their necessary cause.

[359] Such philological proofs concerning the world of nations allow us to see in reality the institutions we have contemplated as ideas. This follows the philosophical method of Bacon, which he calls 'contemplating and seeing', *cogitare videre*. In this way, the authority of my philological proofs is confirmed by the reason of my philosophical proofs; and the reason of my philosophical proofs is confirmed by the authority of my philological proofs.

[360] To summarize, I have defined the three principles of my New Science as *divine providence, the moderation of passions through marriage, and the immortality of human souls attested by burial.* And I have adopted the criterion that *whatever all or most people feel must be the rule of social life.* (These principles and criterion are agreed on both by the popular wisdom of all legislators and by the esoteric wisdom of the most renowned philosophers.) These are the boundaries of human reason, and transgressing them means abandoning our humanity.

BOOK 2
POETIC WISDOM

PROLEGOMENA

INTRODUCTION

[361] In the axioms, we established that all the histories of the pagan nations had mythical origins; that among the Greeks, who are the source of all our knowledge of pagan antiquity, the first wise men were theological poets; and that all temporal institutions by nature have crude origins. When we turn to poetic wisdom, we must regard its origins in the same light. Poetic wisdom has come down to us exalted by a supreme and sovereign esteem which springs both from the conceit of the nations and, to a greater extent, from the conceit of scholars. For it was the conceit of scholars that led the Egyptian high priest Manetho to convert all of Egypt's mythical history into a sublime natural theology, as Axiom 55 states, just as it led the Greeks to convert their myths into philosophy. These two peoples did this not only because they had both inherited extremely filthy stories, as Axiom 54 states, but also for the five following reasons.

[362] The first reason was their reverence for religion, for it was by their myths that the pagan nations were everywhere founded on the basis of religion. The second was the great effect of their religion, namely the civil world, which is so wisely ordered that it can only be the result of superhuman wisdom. The third reason was the opportunity which their myths, bolstered by a religious veneration and believed to contain great wisdom, offered the philosophers for investigating and pondering lofty philosophical topics, as we shall see later. The fourth reason was the facility with which philosophers could express their sublime philosophical meditations in language they happily inherited from the poets. The fifth and final reason, which stands for all the others,

was that the philosophers could confirm their theories by appealing to the authority of religion and the wisdom of the poets. Of these five reasons, the first two inspired the praise which the philosophers, even in their error, bestowed on divine providence for ordering the world of nations; while by the fifth they bore witness to this same providence. The third and fourth reasons are illusions which divine providence tolerated so that philosophers could understand and recognize providence for what it truly is, an attribute of the true God.

[363] Throughout this work, I shall show that everything that the poets sensed in their popular wisdom was later understood by the philosophers in their esoteric wisdom. We may say, then, that the poets were the *sense* of mankind, and the philosophers its *intellect*. Thus, what Aristotle said in particular about the individual is also true in general about humankind: 'Nothing is found in the intellect which was not found first in the senses', *Nihil est in intellectu quin prius fuerit in sensu*. This means that the human mind can only understand a thing after the senses have furnished an impression of it, which is what today's metaphysicians call an occasion. For the mind uses the intellect whenever it 'gathers' something insensible from a sense impression, and this act of gathering is the proper meaning of the Latin verb *intelligere*, to understand.

CHAPTER I

Wisdom in General

[364] Before discussing poetic wisdom, we must consider what wisdom is in general. Wisdom is the faculty governing all the disciplines that teach the arts and sciences which perfect our humanity. Plato defines wisdom as the perfecter of humankind. People essentially consist of mind and spirit, or (we may say) of intellect and will. Wisdom must perfect both these parts, beginning with the intellect. For once the mind is illuminated by a knowledge of what is highest, it will lead the spirit to choose what is best. The highest institutions in the universe are those we call divine, because they turn our reason and understanding

towards God. The best institutions are those we call human, because they serve the well-being of the entire human race. Hence, true wisdom must teach us the knowledge of divine institutions in order to direct human institutions towards the highest good. Indeed, I believe that Marcus Terentius Varro, who deserved to be called 'the most learned of the Romans', followed this two-part plan in constructing his *Divine and Human Institutions*, a great work which we have regrettably lost through the injustice of time. In my Science, I shall discuss these same topics as best I can, given the imperfections of my learning and the poverty of my erudition.

[365] Among the pagans, wisdom began with the Muse, whom Homer, in a golden passage of the *Odyssey*, defines as the knowledge of good and evil, or what was later called divination. (By contrast, God founded the true religion of the Jews – from which Christianity arose – on the natural prohibition of divination, which is naturally denied to people, as Axiom 24 states.) At first, the Muse must properly have been the science of divining by the auspices, which was the popular wisdom of all nations. This popular wisdom contemplated God in the attribute of His providence, so that from *divinari*, to divine, His essence was called divinity. And we shall soon see that the theological poets, who clearly founded the civilization of Greece, were experts in this wisdom, which is why the Romans called judicial astrologers 'professors of wisdom'. Next, wisdom was ascribed to people who were famous for the useful counsels they gave to humankind: hence the so-called Seven Sages, or Wise Men, of Greece. Later, wisdom was broadened to include people who wisely ordered and governed commonwealths for the good of their peoples and nations. Still later, the term was extended to the knowledge of divine things in nature, or metaphysics, which is accordingly called a divine science. (In seeking to know man's mind in God, metaphysics recognizes God as the source of all truth, and hence as the regulator of all good. Thus, metaphysics essentially serves the good of the human race, whose survival depends on its universal belief in the *provident* nature of divinity. Plato perhaps deserved to be called divine because he demonstrated this providence. By contrast, any doctrine which denies the providential aspect of God should be called folly rather than wisdom.) Finally, among the Jews and then

among us Christians, the knowledge of the eternal things revealed by God was called wisdom. Perhaps because they regarded such wisdom as the knowledge of true good and true evil, the early Tuscans called it 'science in divinity'.

[366] We must, then, distinguish three kinds of theology: (1) poetic theology, which was proper to the theological poets, and was the civil theology of all the pagan nations; (2) natural theology, which is proper to the metaphysicians; and (3) our Christian theology, which combines civil and natural theology with the highest revealed theology. (This division is truer than the one proposed by Varro, who regarded poetic theology as the third kind. In fact, the poetic theology of the pagans was the same as their civil theology. But since Varro was misled by the common error that the myths contained profound mysteries of sublime philosophy, he thought that poetic theology combined both the civil and natural kinds.) All three kinds of theology are connected by their contemplation of divine providence, and in fact divine providence directed human institutions so that poetic and natural theology prepared the nations for revealed theology. For poetic theology governed them through certain sensible signs, which they believed to be divine counsels sent by the gods to humankind; while natural theology demonstrates providence by eternal and insensible arguments. Hence, these two disposed the nations to accept revealed theology by virtue of a supernatural faith, which is superior not only to our senses but to human reason itself.

CHAPTER 2

Introduction to Poetic Wisdom and its Divisions

[367] Our discussion of poetic wisdom starts from the following three propositions. (1) Metaphysics is the sublime science which assigns specific subjects to the sciences we call subordinate. (2) The wisdom of the ancients was that of the theological poets, who were undoubtedly the first wise men of the pagan world, as Axiom 44 states. (3) And by nature all things must have crude origins. These three propositions lead

us to trace the beginnings of poetic wisdom to a crude metaphysics, from which various sciences branch out as if from a tree trunk. On one side, we find the branches of logic, ethics, economics, and politics, which are all poetic sciences. On the other, we find further poetic sciences: physics, with her daughters cosmography and astronomy; and astronomy's two daughters, chronology and geography, whom she endows with certainty.

With these sciences in mind, I shall trace clearly and distinctly how the founders of pagan civilization used their poetic wisdom. We shall see how they used their natural theology or metaphysics to imagine the gods; their logic to invent languages; their ethics to create heroes; their household economy to found families; and their politics to found cities. We shall see how they used their physics to establish the divine principles of all things; their human physiology to create themselves, in a certain sense; their cosmography to envision a universe of gods; and their astronomy to transfer planets and constellations from the earth to the heavens. And we shall see how they used their chronology to establish the starting-point of time reckoning; and how the Greeks, to cite one example, used their geography to describe the entire world within their own homeland.

[368] In this way, my New Science simultaneously offers a *history of the ideas, customs, and deeds of humankind*. From these three topics, we shall derive the principles of the history of human nature, which are the principles of universal history that we previously seemed to lack.

CHAPTER 3

The Universal Flood and the Giants

[369] The founders of pagan antiquity must have descended from the races of Ham, Japheth, and Shem, who one by one gradually renounced the true religion of their common father Noah. This religion was the only bond which kept them within human society, both in the union of marriage and hence in their family groups. When they renounced it and began to couple promiscuously, they dissolved their marriages

and dispersed their families. In this way, they began to wander like brutes through the earth's great forest. (The race of Ham wandered through southern Asia into Egypt and the rest of Africa; that of Japheth through northern Asia, or Scythia, into Europe; and that of Shem through central Asia to the Near East.) They were scattered widely as they fled from the wild beasts which abounded in the great forest, and as they pursued women who in that state were wild, timid, and intractable. And they were further separated as they sought pasture and water.

Since mothers abandoned their children, they grew up without hearing any human speech, or learning any human behaviour, and sank to an utterly bestial and brutish state. In this state, mothers merely nursed their infants and let them wallow naked in their own faeces, abandoning them for ever once they were weaned. Wallowing in their faeces (whose nitrous salts wondrously enriched the soil), these children struggled to make their way through the great forest, now grown dense after the recent flood. And as their muscles expanded and contracted in this struggle, the children absorbed more and more nitrous salts. At the same time, these children lacked that fear of gods, fathers, and teachers which tempers the most exuberant phase of childhood. As a result, their flesh and bones must have grown inordinately large, and they became so vigorous and robust that they turned out to be giants.

(This upbringing was even more brutish than that to which Caesar and Tacitus attribute the gigantic stature of the Germans, as Axiom 26 states. This upbringing also explains the gigantic stature of the Goths reported by Procopius, and that of the Patagonians, who are said to live near the Strait of Magellan. On this subject, natural scientists have written numerous absurdities, which have been assembled by Jean Chassagnon in his treatise *On Giants*. Great skulls and bones of an enormous size have been found and are still being found today, for the most part in the mountains – which is an important fact to which I shall return. The size of these remains is further exaggerated by popular traditions, for reasons I shall discuss in their place.)

[370] After the flood, these giants were scattered throughout the earth. We have seen that such giants are found in Greek mythology; and Latin historians unwittingly confirm their existence in ancient Italy.

For they write that the most ancient peoples of Italy, known as the Aborigines, called themselves 'autochthonous', which is synonymous with 'sons of Earth', which to the Greeks and Romans meant nobles. Appropriately, the Greeks called the sons of Earth 'giants', just as their myths called the Earth the mother of giants. Hence, we should translate the Greek *autochthones* in Latin as *indigenae*, indigenous people, which properly means the native sons of a land. For in Latin the native gods of a people or nation were called *dii indigetes*, as if to say *inde geniti*, born there, or as we now say more succinctly *ingeniti*, inborn. (The syllable *de* is one of the redundancies of the early languages which I shall discuss later. Thus, the early Latins said *induperator* for *imperator*, commander; and the Law of the Twelve Tables reads *endoiacito* for *iniicito*, to lay hands on. This may be why armistices came to be called *induciae*, truces, as if from *iniiciae*: for to make a peace treaty was *icere foedus*, to strike an agreement.) To return to my point, from *indigena* the Romans derived *ingenuus*, whose first and proper meaning was noble – as in the *artes ingenuae*, noble arts. Eventually, the adjective came to mean free. (Still, the phrase *artes liberales*, liberal arts, retained the sense of noble arts.) For the nobles alone made up the free populations of the first cities; whereas the plebeians in them were slaves or the precursors of slaves.

[371] The same Latin historians observe that all ancient peoples were called Aborigines. And the Bible mentions entire peoples called the Emim and Zamzummim, names which Hebrew scholars interpret as meaning giants, one of whom was Nimrod. The Bible also describes the giants who lived before the flood as 'mighty men which were of old, men of renown'. By contrast to the giants, the Jews were taught cleanliness and feared God and their fathers, and therefore kept the normal stature with which Adam was created by God and with which Noah's sons were begotten. Indeed, it was perhaps in abomination of giantism that the Jews observed numerous ceremonial laws regarding the cleanliness of the body.

The Romans preserved an important vestige of such laws in the public rite of purification which they celebrated with *water* and *fire* to purge their city of all the citizens' sins. They used these two elements to celebrate solemn nuptials. And they even considered the sharing of these elements a mark of citizenship, so that banishment was called the interdict of water and fire, *interdictum aqua et igni*. The Romans' purification rite was called a *lustrum*; and since the rite was repeated every five years, a lustrum meant a five-year period, as the Greeks called a four-year period an Olympiad after their Olympic games.

The Latin noun *lustrum* also meant a beast's lair. Hence, the verb *lustrare*, to seek out or to purge, must initially have meant to seek out lairs and purge them of the beasts lurking inside; and the water needed for these sacrifices came to be called lustral water, *aqua lustralis*. Now, the Greeks had begun to reckon their years from the burning of the Nemean forest by Hercules to clear it for sowing grain, which the hero celebrated by founding the Olympic games. By contrast, the Romans, with perhaps greater insight, began to reckon their years in *lustra* after the water of sacred ablutions. For civilization had begun with water, the necessity of which people understood before that of fire, just as the formulas of marriage and interdict mention *aqua* before *igni*. This is the origin of the sacred ablutions which must precede sacrifices, a custom which was and still is common to all nations. It was the cleansing of their bodies, together with their fear of the gods and their fathers – fears quite terrifying in a primitive age – which caused the giants to shrink to our normal stature. This is perhaps why the Latin adjective *politus*, cleansed or neat, derives from Greek *politeía*, civil government.

[372] This reduction of the giants' stature must have continued until the civilized age of the nations. This is shown by the enormous weapons of ancient heroes which, according to Suetonius, Augustus assembled in his museum, together with the bones and skulls of ancient giants. All of the world's early people must be divided into two kinds: the people of normal build, meaning only the Jews; and the giants who were the founders of the pagan nations, as Axiom 27 states. The giants in turn should be divided into two kinds. The first were the sons of the Earth or nobles, who gave their name to the age of giants. Indeed, they were giants in the proper sense, described in the Bible as 'mighty men which were of old, men of renown'. The second kind, who are less properly called giants, were the giants ruled by the first kind.

[373] When did the founders of the pagan nations reach this gigantic condition? In my Notes on Chronology, I assign this change to 100 years

after the flood for the race of Shem, and 200 years after it for the races of Japheth and Ham. (We shall later trace the natural history of the giants, which is factually recorded in Greek myths but has previously been neglected. This will also offer us a new natural history of the universal flood.)

SECTION I
POETIC METAPHYSICS

CHAPTER I

Poetic Metaphysics as the Origin of Poetry, Idolatry, Divination, and Sacrifices

[374] In reasoning about the wisdom of the ancient pagans, all the philosophers and philologists should have begun with these first men, who were stupid, insensate, and horrid beasts, that is, giants in the proper sense I have just described. (In *The Church Before the Law*, Father Jacques Boulduc says that the biblical term giants means 'pious, venerable, and illustrious men'. But this can be true only of the noble giants who established pagan religions by divination and gave their name to the age of giants.) And these scholars should have begun with metaphysics, since it finds its proofs not in the external world, but within the modifications of the reflective mind. The world of nations was clearly a human creation, and hence its principles should have been sought within the human mind. And to the extent that human nature coincides with that of animals, it must rely on the senses as the sole means of knowing things.

[375] As the first wisdom of the pagan world, poetic wisdom must have begun with a metaphysics which, unlike the rational and abstract metaphysics of today's scholars, sprang from the senses and imagination of the first people. For they lacked the power of reason, and were entirely guided by their vigorous sensations and vivid imaginations, as Axiom 36 states. This metaphysics was their own poetry, which sprang from an innate poetic faculty: for they were naturally endowed with sense and imagination. Their poetry also sprang naturally from their ignorance of causes. For, as Axiom 35 states, ignorance is the mother of wonder; and being ignorant of all things, the first people were amazed by everything. In them, poetry began as literally *divine*. For whenever

something aroused their feelings of wonder, they imagined its cause as a god. And at the same time, whatever aroused their wonder they endowed with a substantial being based on their own ideas. This is the nature of children, whom we see picking up inanimate objects in play and talking with them as if they were living persons, as Axiom 37 states.

Lactantius observed how early people saw gods in the objects of their wonder, as Axiom 38 states. This is now confirmed by the behaviour of the American Indians, who call gods all the things that exceed their limited understanding. To them, we may add the ancient Germans who lived near the Arctic Ocean. According to Tacitus, they said they could *hear* the sun at night as it passed by sea from west to east, and they claimed to *see* the gods. Such crude and simple nations give us a clearer understanding of the founders of the pagan world who are discussed here.

[376] In this manner, the earliest people of the pagan nations created things according to their own ideas: for they were the children of the nascent human race, as Axiom 37 states. Yet their act of creation was infinitely removed from the creation of God, who by his perfect understanding knows things and creates them in this knowledge. In their robust ignorance, the earliest people could create only by using their imagination, which was grossly physical. Yet this very physicality made their creation wonderfully sublime, and this sublimity was so great and powerful that it excited their imaginations to ecstasy. By virtue of this imaginative creation, they were called poets, which in Greek means creators. Great poetry has three tasks: (1) *to invent sublime myths* which are suited to the popular understanding; (2) *to excite to ecstasy** so that poetry attains its purpose; and this purpose is (3) *to teach the masses to act virtuously*, just as the poets have taught themselves. The natural origin of this human institution gave rise to that invariable property, nobly expressed by Tacitus, that frightened people vainly 'imagine a thing and at once believe it', *fingunt simul creduntque*.

[377] Now, this was clearly the nature of the first founders of pagan civilization when the heavens thundered for the first time since the flood. This happened in Mesopotamia a century after the flood, and in

---

* Vico uses *eccesso* in the Latin sense of *excessus mentis*, 'ecstasy'.

the rest of the world two centuries after it. For that much time was necessary for the moisture of the universal flood to dry out, so that the earth could send into the air any dry exhalations or flammable matter that might have generated lightning. As was inevitable when such a violent phenomenon filled the sky for the first time, the heavens now produced the most frightening thunderclaps and lightning bolts. At this time, a few giants, who must have been the most robust, were living scattered through the forests of the mountain heights, which is where the most robust animals have their lairs. Suddenly frightened and thunderstruck by this inexplicably great phenomenon, they raised their eyes and observed the heavens. In this state, such people by nature possessed only robust physical strength and expressed their violent passions by shouting and grunting. So they imagined the heavens as a great living body, and in this manifestation, they called the sky Jupiter. (The nature of the human mind in such cases leads it to attribute its own nature to an external phenomenon, as Axiom 32 states.) And they thought that Jupiter, the first god of the so-called greater clans, was trying to speak to them through the whistling of his bolts and the crashing of his thunder.

The giants now began to exercise that natural curiosity which is the daughter of ignorance and the mother of knowledge, and which is born when wonder arouses the human mind, as Axiom 39 states. This natural trait still persists tenaciously among the common people. When they see a comet, parhelion, or any unusual natural phenomenon, especially in the heavens, they grow curious and then quite anxious to learn its significance, as Axiom 39 states. And when they wonder at the marvellous effect of a magnet on iron, they arrive at the conclusion that the magnet has a secret sympathy for iron – and this in the present age, when our minds are keener and even enlightened by philosophy. Indeed, they view all of nature as a vast living body that feels passions and emotions, as Axiom 32 states.

[378] The countless abstract expressions which permeate our languages today have divorced our civilized thought from the senses, even among the common people. The art of writing has greatly refined the nature of our thought; and the use of numbers has intellectualized it, so to speak, even among the masses, who know how to count and

reckon. As a result, we are by nature incapable of forming the vast image of that mistress which some call 'Sympathetic Nature'. (In fact, people who mouth this expression have literally nothing in mind; for a mental falsehood is nothing, and the imagination is powerless to form vast images of falsity.) We are likewise incapable of entering into the vast imaginative powers of the earliest people. Their minds were in no way abstract, refined, or intellectualized; rather, they were completely sunk in their senses, numbed by their passions, and buried in their bodies. This is why I said earlier that we can barely understand, and by no means imagine, the thinking of the early people who founded pagan antiquity.

[379] In this manner, the first theological poets invented the first divine myth, which was the greatest myth ever invented: Jupiter, the king and father of gods and men, in the act of hurling a thunderbolt. The figure of Jupiter was so poetic – that is, popular, exciting, and instructive – that its inventors at once believed it, and they feared, revered, and worshipped Jupiter in frightful religions, which I shall discuss later. These people now believed that everything they saw, imagined, or even did themselves was Jupiter – which illustrates the trait of the human mind noted by Tacitus in Axiom 34. And they endowed all the universe and its parts with the being of an animate substance. This is the civil and historical meaning of the poetic tag 'all things are full of Jupiter', *Iovis omnia plena*. Later, Plato interpreted this to mean the ether that permeates and fills everything in the universe. But in fact, the theological poets thought that Jupiter was no higher than the mountain tops. And since these early people communicated by signs, they naturally believed that lightning bolts and thunderclaps were signs made to them by Jupiter. (Later, from Latin *nuo*, to make a sign by nodding, they derived *numen*, divine will, by an idea which is utterly sublime and worthy to express divine majesty.) They believed that Jupiter commanded by signs, that these signs were physical words, and that nature was Jupiter's language.

The science of this language the pagans universally believed to be divination, which the Greeks called theology, meaning the science of the gods' speech. This is how Jupiter was assigned to the fearful kingdom of lightning, which made him the king of gods and men. He acquired two titles: *optimus*, best, meaning *fortissimus*, strongest (in early Latin *fortus* meant the same as classical *bonus*, good); and *maximus*, greatest, alluding to his body, which was as vast as the heavens. Because he did not destroy the human race with his bolts, he acquired the title Soter or Saviour. (This first beneficent act gave rise to religion, which is the first of the three basic principles of my New Science.) And because he stayed the giants from their brutish wandering, so that they became the rulers of the nations, he acquired the title Stator, or Stayer. (Latin historians give too restricted a meaning to this title when they cite a single historical event, and observe that, during a battle with the Sabines, Jupiter was invoked by Romulus and 'stayed' the Romans from flight.)

[380] This is the origin of those many Jupiters, whose existence amazes the philologists. Each pagan nation had its own Jupiter, and the Egyptians in their conceit said that their Jupiter Ammon was the oldest of all, as Axiom 3 states. In fact, all these Jupiters are mythical references to natural history, which show that the flood was universal, as Axiom 42 states.

[381] Thus, if we bear in mind the principles of poetic archetypes formulated in Axioms 47–49, we see that Jupiter was born naturally in poetry as a *divine archetype* or *imaginative universal*, to whom the ancient pagans with their poetic nature referred every aspect of divination. In this way, their poetic wisdom began with the poetic metaphysics of contemplating God in his attribute of providence. And they called themselves theological poets, meaning wise men or sages who understood the speech of the gods expressed in Jupiter's auspices. They were also properly called divines in the sense of diviners, from the Latin verb *divinari*, which properly means to divine or predict. Their science was called the Muse, which Homer defines as the knowledge of good and evil. (This meant divination, which God prohibited to Adam when he established the true religion, as Axiom 24 states.) And for their mystical theology, the poets were in Greek called *mystae*, initiates, a term which Horace learnedly translates as 'interpreters of the gods', for they explained the divine mysteries of the auspices and oracles. In this science, every pagan nation had its own sibyl, and we find mention of twelve of them. Sibyls and oracles are the most ancient institutions of the pagan world.

[382] All these remarks tally with the passage from Lactantius, cited in Axiom 38, who describes the origins of idolatry by saying that the earliest people, being simple and uncouth, invented gods 'in terror of their manifest power'. Thus, it was fear that invented gods in the world; and not fear inspired by other people, but fear born within their own minds, as Axiom 40 states. This origin of idolatry also reveals the origin of divination, since they were born as twins. In turn, these institutions were followed by sacrifices, which were offered to 'procure' the auspices, that is, to interpret them correctly.

[383] We find confirmation of this origin of poetry in this invariable property: the proper subject of poetry is a believable impossibility. Thus, while it is impossible that physical objects have intelligence, people believed that the thundering heavens were Jupiter. This is why poets are so fond of singing the wonders created by the spells of sorceresses. To explain this, we must posit a hidden sense that nations have of God's omnipotence. This sense in turn engenders another by which all peoples are naturally led to offer infinite honours to divinity. This was the manner in which the poets founded religions among the pagans.

[384] These remarks overturn all the previous theories about the origins of poetry, from Plato and Aristotle in antiquity to our own Francesco Patrizi, Julius Caesar Scaliger, and Ludovico Castelvetro. Unlike them, we have discovered that poetry was born sublime precisely because it lacked rationality. This is why no later discipline – philosophy, poetics, or criticism – ever equalled or surpassed the sublimity of poetry. Hence, it is Homer's privilege to be the foremost of all the sublime or heroic poets, in terms of both merit and age. My discovery of the true origins of poetry dispels the common belief in the *incomparable wisdom* of the ancients, which scholars have eagerly sought to discover, from Plato to Bacon in his *Wisdom of the Ancients*. For this wisdom was in fact the *popular wisdom* of the lawgivers who founded mankind, rather than the *esoteric wisdom* of a few lofty philosophers. Hence, as in the case of Jupiter, we shall judge absurd all the *mystical senses* of profound philosophy which scholars have given to Greek myths and Egyptian hieroglyphics. By contrast, we shall judge natural the *historical sense* which they naturally preserved.

CHAPTER 2

Corollaries on the Principal Aspects of the New Science

I

[385] The preceding remarks indicate that divine providence allowed humankind to be deceived into fearing Jupiter as a false deity who could strike them with lightning. (These crude, savage, and brutish people possessed enough human sense that in their despair of nature's aid they longed to be saved by a supernatural agent – which is the first principle enumerated in my section on Method.) In this way, in the clouds of the first storms and in the flash of lightning, they beheld the great truth that divine providence watches over the well-being of the entire human race. Viewed in this first principal aspect, my Science becomes a *rational civil theology of providence*. This theology originated in the popular wisdom of the lawgivers who founded nations by contemplating God in his aspect of providence. Later, it culminated in the esoteric wisdom of the philosophers who demonstrated it rationally in their natural theology.

2

[386] Here begins the *philosophy of authority*, which is the second aspect of my Science. I take the word authority in its primary sense of property, in which sense it is always used in the Law of the Twelve Tables. Thus, in Roman civil law, people who grant rights of ownership were called *auctores*. The noun *auctor* undoubtedly derives from Greek *autós*, oneself, which in Latin would be *proprius* or *suus ipsius*, one's own. In fact, many scholars write the words as *autor* and *autoritas*, rather than *author* and *authoritas*.

[387] Originally, authority was divine. By it, the deity 'appropriated' those few giants mentioned above, by 'properly' casting them down into cavernous depths and recesses beneath the mountains. In myth, this is represented by the iron links which chained these giants to the earth. Scattered on the mountains, these giants were transfixed by their

fear of heaven and of Jupiter when the heavens first thundered. Thus, Tityus and Prometheus were chained to a high cliff and had their hearts devoured by an eagle, which symbolizes the religion of Jupiter's auspices. In a heroic phrase, the Romans said they were 'transfixed by terror', *terrore defixi*, which is how painters depict them, with such links chaining their hands and feet to the mountains. These links formed the great chain of Jupiter, which Longinus admires as the greatest sublimity in all the Homeric myths. To prove that he is the king of gods and men, Jupiter claims that if all the gods and men held one end of this chain, he alone could drag all the others by the other end. The Stoics choose to interpret this chain as the eternal series of causes with which their Fate encircles and binds the world. But let them beware its entanglements: for if the gods and men are dragged by this chain whenever Jupiter so wills, then he cannot be subject to Fate as they maintain.

[388] This divine authority led to human authority. In the purest philosophical sense, this authority is the essential property of human nature which not even God can take from man without destroying him. (This sense of property is expressed by Terence when he describes 'the pleasures proper to the gods', *voluptates proprias deorum*, because God's happiness does not depend on others. Likewise, Horace speaks of his 'proper laurel of virtue', *propriam virtutis laurum*, because envy cannot detract from the triumph of virtue. When Caesar refers to his 'proper victory', *propriam victoriam*, Denis Petau [Denis Voss] mistakenly brands this as bad Latin;* but in fact the fine Latin elegance of Caesar's phrase denotes a victory which the enemy could not take from him.)

Now, human authority lies in the *free use of the will*, for the intellect is merely a passive power subject to truth. Hence, the starting-point of all human affairs dates from the time when people began to exercise the freedom of their human will and so to control their bodily impulses, either by suppressing them altogether or by directing them to better ends. (This is the conscious effort, or conatus, which is proper to free agents, as we saw in the section on Method.) By such an effort, the giants gave up their bestial custom of wandering through the earth's

* For Denis Voss, Vico mistakenly writes 'Denis Petau'.

great forest. Instead, they grew accustomed to remaining hidden and settled in their caves for a long time.

[389] The authority of human nature was followed by the authority of natural law. Now, the giants had occupied the lands where they chanced to be at the time of the first thunder, and became lords of these lands after a long period of settlement. For occupation and longstanding possession are the source of all ownership in the world. These giants are described by Virgil as 'those few whom just Jupiter has loved', *pauci quos aequus amavit Jupiter*. Later philosophers wrongly transformed them into persons whom God has endowed with a natural aptitude for sciences and virtues. But the historical meaning of this poetic tag is that the giants, settled in the hidden depths of their caves, became the founders of the so-called greater clans, who counted Jupiter as the first god, as Axiom 108 states. We shall later see that these clans were the ancient noble houses which, branching out into many families, made up the first kingdoms and cities. Their memory is preserved in the fine phrases of heroic Latin – 'to found clans, kingdoms, and cities', *condere gentes, regna, urbes* and *fundare gentes, regna, urbes* – which recall the hidden depths (*nascondigli, fondi*) of their underground caves.

[390] This philosophy of authority is intimately connected to the rational civil theology of providence. For by using providence's theological proofs, authority's philosophical proofs can clarify and distinguish our philological proofs. (These are the three kinds of proofs outlined in my section on Method.) Hence, as we study the institutions of nations during their darkest antiquity, the philosophy of authority renders our human judgment certain, even though it is by nature most uncertain, as Axiom 11 states. In other words, it reduces philology to the form of a science.

3

[391] The third principal aspect of my New Science is the *history of human ideas*. As we have seen, human ideas sprang from the divine ideas formed by early people when they contemplated the heavens with the 'eyes of the body', as we say, rather than the eyes of the mind. In their science of augury, the Romans used the verb *contemplari* for observing

the parts of the heavens whence auguries came or the auspices were taken. This verb referred to the precincts of the heavens, *templa coeli*, which was the Latin name for the regions marked out by augurs with their divining wands. Similar rites must have given the Greeks their early *theōrēmata* and *mathēmata*, things divine and sublime to contemplate, which ultimately became metaphysical and mathematical abstractions.

This is the civil and historical meaning of the poetic tag 'From Jupiter the Muse began', *A Iove principium Musae*. For, as we have just seen, Jupiter's lightning bolts were the origin of the first Muse, which Homer calls the knowledge of good and evil. Later, philosophers found it all too easy to impose their interpretation of the phrase as the biblical maxim, 'The beginning of wisdom is piety.' The first Muse must have been Urania, who contemplates the heavens for the taking of auguries, and who later came to symbolize astronomy, as we shall see. Earlier, we divided poetic metaphysics into subordinate sciences, which all share the poetic nature of their mother. Just so, my history of ideas will trace the crude origins which gave rise both to the practical sciences, which are customarily used by various nations, and to the speculative sciences, which are perfected and pursued by scholars.

4

[392] The fourth aspect of my Science is a *philosophical criticism* which springs from the history of ideas just described. Such criticism will offer us true judgments about the founders of the nations, who lived more than a thousand years before those writers who have been the subject of philological criticism. Beginning with Jupiter, this philosophical criticism will trace a natural theogony, meaning the genealogy of the gods as it was naturally created by the founders of the pagan world, who were by nature theological poets. We shall see that these founders imagined the twelve gods of the greater clans on certain occasions associated with institutions necessary or useful to humankind. And we shall assign these twelve gods to twelve shorter epochs, into which we may divide the age in which myths were born. In this way, our natural theogony will provide us with a rational chronology of poetic history

during the heroic period, which lasted at least 900 years before it was succeeded by vernacular history.

5

[393] The fifth aspect of my Science is the *ideal eternal history* through which the history of all nations must in time pass. For whenever nations emerge from their savage, ferocious, and brutish ages, and are civilized by religion, they begin, develop, and end in the same stages. After discussing these stages theoretically in Book 2, we shall find them confirmed both in Book 4 on the Course of Nations, and in Book 5 on the Recurrence of Human Institutions.

6

[394] The sixth aspect of this Science is the *system of the natural law of nations*. In expounding this doctrine, its three great proponents – Grotius, Selden, and Pufendorf – should have begun with the beginning of the nations, since this is when their subject begins, as Axiom 106 states. But all three of them made the same mistake of beginning in the middle, that is, with the recent ages of civilized nations, in which people are enlightened by fully developed reason. And this soon led to an age in which philosophers emerge to ascend to the contemplation of justice in its ideal perfection.

[395] First, there is Grotius, who in his passion for the truth discards the notions of divine providence, claiming that his system will stand even if we rule out any knowledge of God. As a result, all the objections he makes to the Roman jurists on numerous topics miss their mark. For by making divine providence their first principle, the Roman jurists intended to examine the natural law of nations, rather than the law of philosophers or moral theologians.

[396] Next, there is Selden, who assumes that providence exists. But he disregards the inhospitable character of the earliest peoples, and God's original division of the world of nations into Jews and pagans. He disregards the fact that God had to give Moses his Law on Mt Sinai, in order to restore to the Jews that natural law which they had lost

during their Egyptian slavery. He disregards the fact that God's law even forbade the Jews from thinking unjust thoughts – something no mortal legislator ever bothered about. And he disregards the bestial origins of all the pagan nations, which are discussed here. Although he claims that the Jews later taught their natural law to the pagans, the fact is impossible to prove. For we have seen that Josephus generously confesses that the Jews lived in obscurity, and that Lactantius solemnly confirms the point. And we recall the hostility with which the Jews have always regarded the pagans, and which they maintain even now when dispersed among all the nations.

[397] Finally, there is Pufendorf, who begins with the Epicurean hypothesis that man was cast into the world without God's aid or care. In fact, he was reproached for this, and therefore justified himself in a separate tract. But without providence as a first principle, he cannot even begin to reason about law, as Cicero tells his Epicurean friend Atticus in the dialogue *On Laws*.

[398] For all these reasons, I begin my discussion of law from the most ancient point in history, the moment when the idea of Jupiter was born in the minds of the nation founders. The Latin word for law is *ius*, which is a contraction of the ancient *Ious*, Jove or Jupiter. This coincides wonderfully with the Greek derivation, which we happily find in the dialogue *Cratylus* by Plato, who notes that the Greeks at first called law *diaïon*, but later for the sake of euphony pronounced it *dikaion*, just. Plato says that *diaïon* means 'running through' or 'permeating'. He thus imposes a philosophical etymology on the word because his intellectual mythology interprets Jupiter as the ether which pervades and penetrates the universe. In fact, *diaïon* derives historically from the name of Jupiter, who is also called *Dios* in Greek. From this form, the Latins derived the phrases *sub dio* or *sub Iove* to mean 'under the open sky'.

I therefore begin my discussion of law by considering its divine origins and its first properties, which were expressed by divination, meaning the science of Jupiter's auspices. For these divine institutions regulated all the nations' human institutions; and together, both kinds of institution constitute the universal subject of jurisprudence. My discussion of natural law in turn begins with the idea of divine providence, which was conceived together with the idea of law. Law began to be observed naturally by the founders of the most ancient clans, the so-called greater clans whose first god was Jupiter.

7

[399] The seventh and last of the principal aspects of my New Science is that of the *origins of universal history*. From the first moment of all the human institutions in the pagan world, this history begins with the first of the world's three ages which the Egyptians said had elapsed before them. This is the age of the gods, in which Heaven began to reign on earth and to bestow great benefits on humankind. And it is the Golden Age of the Greeks, in which the gods mingled on earth with people, as we have seen Jupiter begin to do. From this first age of the world, the Greeks in their myths have faithfully recorded the universal flood and the existence of giants in nature, and thus have truthfully narrated the origins of secular universal history.

But later people could not enter into the imaginations of the first founders of the pagan world, who truly thought they saw the gods. Thus, in myths about the giants, the verb *atterrare*, to lay low, was no longer understood in its proper sense of *mandar sotterra*, to send underground. By the later traditions of overcredulous peoples, the giants, who had in fact lived hidden in their mountain caves, were radically transformed into Titans who piled Olympus, Pelion, and Ossa on top of each other to drive the gods from heaven. (In fact, the first impious giants, far from fighting the gods, were unaware of their existence until Jupiter hurled his lightning bolts.) And the later Greeks, with their highly developed minds, raised heaven itself to an inordinate height, whereas the first giants thought heaven was only the summit of the mountains. Hence, the myth of the Titans storming heaven must have been invented after Homer and tacked onto the *Odyssey* by a later poet. In Homer's day, the collapse of Olympus alone would have sufficed to cause the gods' downfall, for the *Iliad* always portrays them as residing on the summit of Mt Olympus. All of this shows that secular universal history has previously lacked a beginning and that, for lack of this rational chronology of poetic history, it has lacked continuity as well.

SECTION 2
POETIC LOGIC

CHAPTER I
Poetic Logic

[400] Metaphysics contemplates things in all the categories of their being, but it becomes logic when it considers them in the categories by which they are signified. Hence, now that we have considered poetry as a poetic metaphysics, by which the theological poets imagined most physical objects to be divine substances, we may consider it as a *poetic logic*, by which it signifies those substances.

[401] The word logic comes from Greek *logos*, which at first properly meant fable, or *fabula* in Latin, which later changed into Italian *favella*, speech. In Greek, a fable was also called *mythos*, myth, from which is derived Latin *mutus*, mute. For speech was born in the mute age as a mental language, which Strabo in a golden passage says existed before any spoken or articulated language: this is why in Greek *logos* means both word and idea. Appropriately, divine providence ordained that this language arose in a religious age, for it is the invariable property of religion that meditation is more important than speech. As Axiom 57 states, the first language employed by the nations in their mute age must have originated with signs, gestures, or physical objects which had a natural relation to the ideas expressed. Hence, Greek *logos* also meant thing, and the Hebrew word for word (translated by Greek *logos* and Latin *verbum*) also meant deed, as Thomas Gataker observes in *The Style of the New Testament*. We find that *mythos* was also defined as *vera narratio*, or true narration. According to Plato and later Iamblichus, this is the natural speech which was once spoken in the world; but as Axiom 57 notes, this was mere conjecture on their part. Hence, Plato's effort to discover this speech in his dialogue *Cratylus* proved vain, and he was

criticized for it by Aristotle and Galen. In fact, the earliest speech, that of the theological poets, did not use words which suited the nature of the things they expressed. (This was the sacred language invented by Adam, on whom God bestowed divine *onomatothesia*, nomenclature, which is the art of assigning names to things according to their nature.) Rather, their first speech was a *fantastic speech based on animate substances*, most of which they imagined to be divine.

[402] For example, the theological poets understood Jupiter, Cybele or Berecynthia, and Neptune in this way. At first, pointing mutely, they interpreted them as the substances of the sky, earth, and sea, which they imagined to be animate deities; and, trusting the truth of their senses, they believed they were gods. In this way, they used these three deities to explain everything related to the sky, earth, and sea, which is the function of poetic archetypes explained in Axioms 47–9. And they used other deities to signify various subspecies of each major god: for example, Flora for flowers and Pomona for fruits. Today we reverse this mental process when we deal with intellectual notions, such as the faculties of the human mind, the emotions, virtues, vices, sciences, and arts. For we generally imagine them as feminine personifications, to which we refer their various properties, causes, and effects. And when we wish to express our understanding of intellectual notions, our imagination must assist us in explaining them and in giving them human form, as painters of allegories do. By contrast, the theological poets could not use their understanding, and so performed the contrary operation, which is far more sublime. They attributed senses and emotions to physical bodies, even bodies as vast as the sky, earth, and sea, as we have just seen. Later, as their vast imaginations diminished and their powers of abstraction increased, these deities shrank to diminutive symbols of themselves. Since the origins of these human institutions were buried in obscurity, metonymy dressed these symbols in the learned guise of allegory. Jupiter grew so small and light that an eagle now carries him in its flight. Neptune rides the sea in a dainty coach. And Cybele is seated on a lion.

[403] Mythologies were *expressions proper to myths*, which is what the word means literally. And since myths are imaginative categories, as we have seen, mythologies were their allegories. The term allegory was

defined in Latin as *diversiloquium*, different speech, as Axiom 49 states. By an identity not of proportion but of predicability (to use a Scholastic term), allegories signify the various species and individuals comprised under the general categories of myths. Allegories thus have a single, unambiguous meaning based on common semantic elements. For example, Achilles represents the idea of valour common to all strong men; and Ulysses the idea of prudence common to all wise men. In this way, allegories offer us the etymologies of poetic languages. And we shall find that the origins of poetic languages are all unambiguous, whereas those of vernacular languages are generally analogous. Indeed, the term etymology is defined in Latin as *veriloquium*, true speech, just as myth is defined as *vera narratio*, true narration.

CHAPTER 2

Corollaries on Poetic Figures of Speech, Monsters, and Metamorphoses

[404] All the primary figures of speech are corollaries of poetic logic. The most luminous figure, and hence the most basic and common, is metaphor. Metaphor is especially prized when, by the metaphysics just described, it confers sense and emotion on insensate objects. The first poets attributed to physical bodies the being of animate substances, endowed with limited powers of sense and emotion like their own. In this way, they created myths about them; and every such metaphor is a miniature myth. This gives us a criterion for dating the origin of metaphors in various languages. For example, all metaphors based on analogies between physical objects and the products of abstract thought must date from an age in which philosophies were just beginning to take shape. We find proof of this in the fact that in every language the terms used in the fine arts and advanced sciences are of rustic origin.

[405] Noteworthy too is the fact that in all languages most expressions for inanimate objects employ metaphors derived from the human body and its parts, or from human senses and emotions. Thus, we say *head* for top or beginning; *front* or *brow*, and *shoulders* or *back*, for before and

behind; *eyes* of vines [Latin *oculi*, buds]; *lights* [Italian *lumi*] for entrances
to a house; *mouth* for any opening; *lip* for the rim of a pitcher or other
container. We speak of the *tooth* of a plough, rake, saw, or comb; the
beards of plants and their roots; a *tongue* of the sea; the *throat* of rivers
and mountains [French *gorge*]; a *neck* of land; and the *arm* of a river. We
say *hand* for a small number; *lap* of the sea for a gulf [Latin *sinus*, bay];
and *flanks* and *sides* for lateral portions. We speak of the *coast* [Italian
costiera, rib] of the sea, and the *leg* or *foot* of countries. We say *heart* for
the centre (as the Romans said *umbilicus*, navel); *foot* for end, and *plan*
[Latin *planta*, footprint] for base or foundation. We speak of the *flesh*
and the *bones* [English *stones*] of fruit; a *vein* of water, rock, or ore; the
blood of the vine, meaning wine; and the *bowels* of the earth. Similarly,
the sky or sea *smiles* on us; the wind *whistles*; the waves *murmur*; and a
body *groans* under a great weight. In antiquity, the farmers in Latium
used to say that the fields were *thirsty*, the crops were *distressed*, and
grains *ran riot*. Even today farmers say that plants *fall in love*, vines *go
mad*, and fir-trees *weep* with sap. And countless other examples can be
cited in any language.

All this follows from Axiom 1: 'In his ignorance, man makes himself
the measure of the universe.' And in the examples cited, man has
reduced the entire world to his own body. Now, rational metaphysics
teaches us that man becomes all things through understanding, *homo
intelligendo fit omnia*. But with perhaps greater truth, this imaginative
metaphysics shows that man becomes all things by not understanding,
homo non intelligendo fit omnia. For when man understands, he extends
his mind to comprehend things; but when he does not understand, he
makes them out of himself and, by transforming himself, becomes them.

2

[406] Using their poetic logic, which was a product of poetic metaphysics, the early poetic peoples named things in two ways: (1) by using
sensible ideas, which are the source of metonymy; and (2) by using
particular ideas, which are the source of synecdoche.

(1) Metonymy which substitutes the author for the work originated
because authors were more often named than their works. Metonymy

which substitutes the object for its form and accidents originated because they could not abstract forms and qualities, as Axiom 49 states. And metonymy of cause for effect created miniature myths, in which causes were imagined as feminine personifications clothed in their effects, such as ugly Poverty, sad Old Age, and pale Death.

3

[407] (2) Synecdoche became metaphor when people raised particulars to universals or united parts to form wholes. At first, only human beings were properly called mortals, since they were the only ones who sensed their mortality. The use of 'head' for man or person, so common in vernacular Latin, reflects the age when people lived in woodlands and only a man's head could be seen at a distance. (By contrast, the word 'man' is an abstraction, a sort of philosophical category comprising the body and its parts, the mind and its faculties, and the heart and its feelings.) Similarly, Latin *tignum*, beam, and *culmen*, stalk of straw, must have properly meant rafter and straw when houses were thatched. Later, as cities became more ornate, *tignum* came to mean all construction materials, and *culmen* the completion of a building. Thus, *tectum*, roof, came to mean the entire house, because in the earliest times a covering overhead was all that was needed to make a house. And *puppis*, poop, came to mean a ship, because its height made it the first part visible to people ashore; just as people said 'sail' for ship during the medieval return of barbarism. Thus, *mucro*, point, came to mean a sword, since it was the point which early people felt and which aroused their fright. (By contrast, the word 'sword' is an abstraction, a general category comprising pommel, hilt, edge, and point.) Similarly, the material meant the whole thing formed from it – witness 'iron' for sword – because they could not abstract the form from its material.

In Ovid, we find the poetic phrase, 'It was the third harvest', *Tertia messis erat*, which combines synecdoche and metonymy. This combination was doubtless born of natural necessity, since it must have taken more than a thousand years for this astronomical idea to arise among the nations. Even today, farmers outside Florence say 'We have reaped so many times' to indicate a number of years. Likewise, Virgil joins two synecdoches and a metonymy in his verse, 'After several ears of grain I shall marvel seeing my kingdoms', *Post aliquot, mea regna videns, mirabor aristas*. This phrase exposes the awkward way in which people of the early rustic age expressed themselves. They signified years by saying 'ears of grain', *aristas*, which is more particular than 'harvest'. But because the phrase is so awkward, textbooks have judged it a rhetorical extravagance.

4

[408] Irony could clearly arise only in an age capable of reflection, because it consists of a falsehood which reflection disguises in a mask of truth. From this emerges an important principle of human institutions, which confirms the origin of poetry discovered in my Science. Since the pagan world's earliest people were as simple as children, who are by nature truthful, they could invent nothing false in their early myths. These myths must therefore have been *true narratives*, as we have defined them.

5

[409] All figures of speech may be reduced to these four types – metaphor, metonymy, synecdoche, and irony – which were previously thought to be the ingenious inventions of writers. But my discussion of them proves that they were in fact necessary modes of expression in all the early poetic nations, and originally had natural and proper meanings. These expressions became figurative only later, as the human mind developed and invented words which signified abstract forms, that is, generic categories comprising various species, or relating parts to a whole. Knowing this, we may begin to demolish two common errors of the grammarians: that prose is the proper form of speech, and poetic speech improper; and that men spoke first in prose and later in verse.

6

[410] Poetic monsters and metamorphoses were necessary products of early human nature, since people were incapable of abstracting forms and properties from objects, as Axiom 49 states. Using poetic logic, they had either (1) to combine objects in order to combine their underlying forms, or (2) to destroy an object in order to distinguish its proper form from any contrary forms imposed on it.

(1) Poetic monsters sprang from combinations of form and ideas. As Antoine Favre observes in *The Jurisprudence of Papinianus*, children born to prostitutes are in Roman law called monsters, because they combine human nature with the bestial characteristic of being born of erratic or uncertain unions. These are the monsters, children born to noble women without solemn nuptials, which the Law of the Twelve Tables ordered thrown into the Tiber.

7

[411] (2) Metamorphoses in turn sprang from distinctions between ideas. Among the various instances preserved by ancient jurisprudence is the heroic Latin phrase *fundum fieri*, to be the ground, which meant *auctorem fieri*, to be author or sponsor of a bill. For just as the ground supports a farm and everything built or planted in its soil, so the mover of a bill must support it to prevent its failing. In this expression, the mover is transformed into the opposite idea, that of an unmoved property.

CHAPTER 3

Corollaries on the Speech in Poetic Archetypes of the First Nations

[412] Poetic speech, which we have studied as a product of poetic logic, continued to run its course well into the historical period, just as large and rapid rivers, flowing far out to sea, continue to carry fresh water in their powerful course. In Axiom 49, I cited a passage in which Iamblichus says that the Egyptians attributed to Hermes Trismegistus

all the inventions that were useful to human life. This is confirmed by Axiom 48: 'Children retain their ideas and names of the people and things they have known first, and later apply them to others they meet who bear a resemblance or relation to the first.' This was the great source of poetic archetypes with which the earliest peoples naturally thought and spoke. If Iamblichus had pondered this human aspect of human nature and related it to the Egyptians' custom he himself describes, he could never have violently imposed the sublime mysteries of his own Platonic wisdom on the popular wisdom of the Egyptian mysteries.

[413] In the light of the nature of children and the customs of the early Egyptians, I maintain that the notion of poetic speech, with its poetic archetypes, offers us many important discoveries about the ancient world. I describe ten poetic archetypes in the following corollaries.

I

[414] Solon must have been a sage of popular wisdom who led the plebeian party during the early period, when Athens was an aristocracy. This period is in fact attested in Greek history, which relates that Athens was at first controlled by the oligarchs. Thus, Athens was what I call a heroic commonwealth, and it followed the universal pattern which is described in my Science. The heroes, meaning the nobles, claimed to have a nature of divine origin, by virtue of which they said that the gods, and hence the divine auspices, belonged to them. And by virtue of the auspices, the nobles of the heroic cities kept control of all public and private rights within their social orders. By contrast, the plebeians were considered of bestial origin, and hence people with no gods and thus without divine auspices, so that they were granted only the benefits of natural liberty. (This is an important principle of the institutions discussed throughout my Science.) It was Solon who urged the plebeians to reflect on themselves and to conclude that they were equal to the nobles in their human nature, and consequently should be equal in civil rights. Indeed, Solon may well be a poetic archetype of the Athenian plebeians in their call for equality.

[415] The ancient Romans must likewise have had such a Solon.

Roman history explicitly relates how, in their heroic contentions with the nobility, the plebeians at Rome protested that the fathers chosen for the senate by Romulus 'had not descended from heaven', *non esse coelo demissos*. In other words, the founders of the patriciate did not have the divine origin of which the patricians boasted. Instead, Jupiter was equal for all. This is the civil and historical sense of the Virgilian tag *Iupiter omnibus aequus*, Jupiter is equal for all. (Later, scholars imposed on this verse the doctrine that all minds are initially equal, but that differences in their physical constitution and civil education make them different.) Reflecting on this equality, the plebeians began to seek equality with the patricians in civil liberty, and eventually changed the Roman state from an aristocracy to a democracy.

In my Notes on Chronology, I proposed this as a hypothesis in the discussion of the Publilian Law. I shall later show that it happened in fact, not only in Rome but in all the other ancient commonwealths. On the basis of both reason and authority, I shall prove that the plebeians of all ancient peoples took Solon's reflection literally, and so changed the commonwealths from aristocracies to democracies.

[416] Solon was therefore considered the author of the famous phrase 'Know thyself', which was inscribed in all the public places of Athens because of the civil benefits it offered the Athenian people. Later, scholars chose to interpret it as a profound counsel in metaphysics and ethics, which in fact it is. And Solon was considered a sage of esoteric wisdom and the foremost of the Seven Sages of Greece. In this manner, all the laws and social orders of Athenian democracy that began with this reflection were attributed to Solon, because early peoples were accustomed to thinking in poetic archetypes, just as the Egyptians attributed to Hermes Trismegistus all the inventions useful in civil life.

2

[417] In the same way, the Romans attributed to Romulus all their laws about social orders.

3

[418] The Romans attributed to Numa Pompilius all their laws about sacred institutions and divine rites, which made Roman religion so prominent in the age of Rome's greatest pomp.

4

[419] The Romans attributed to Tullius Hostilius all the laws and organizations of their military discipline.

5

[420] The Romans attributed to Servius Tullius both the census, which was the foundation of democracy, and numerous laws about popular liberty, so that Tacitus acclaimed him as the supreme lawgiver, *praecipuus sanctor legum*. The census of Servius Tullius was initially the basic institution of aristocracy, by which the plebeians obtained from the patricians the bonitary ownership of the fields. In Rome, the tribunes of the people were created to defend this part of their natural liberty, and later helped the plebeians gradually achieve full civil liberty. In this way, the census of Servius Tullius prepared opportunities for change by which it became a census which was the basis of Roman democracy. (This hypothesis, proposed in my notes on the Publilian Law, will later be shown to be true in fact.)

6

[421] The Romans attributed to Tarquinius Priscus all the insignia and regalia which later made the majesty of the Roman Empire so resplendent during Rome's most glorious age.

7

[422] In the same way, numerous laws which we find enacted in later times were grafted onto the Twelve Tables. The law by which the patricians extended quiritary ownership to the plebeians was the first law inscribed on a public tablet, and was the sole reason for the creation of the decemvirs. Hence, as I showed in my *Principles of Universal Law*, all later laws which promoted popular liberty and were inscribed on public tablets were likewise attributed to the decemvirs. As a proof of this, we may cite the law forbidding sumptuous funerals 'in the Greek manner', which was attributed to the decemvirs. Now, sumptuous funerals could scarcely have been introduced at Rome by the decemvirs' prohibition, but must already have been adopted by the Romans. But this could only have happened two centuries later, after the wars with Tarentum and with Pyrrhus, which is when the Romans began to learn about the Greeks. Indeed, this later dating would account for Cicero's observation that this law translated into Latin the exact wording of the original in Athens.

8

[423] In the same way, Draco, author of the laws 'written in blood', lived in the age when according to Greek history Athens was controlled by the oligarchs, which is the age of the heroic aristocracies. As my Notes on Chronology indicate, Greek history further relates that in this age the Heraclids were scattered through all of Greece, even Attica. Eventually, they settled in the Peloponnese and established their kingdom in Sparta, which was clearly an aristocracy. The name Draco means dragon, and so Draco must represent one of the Gorgon's serpents that were nailed to the shield of Perseus, a symbol of the authority of the laws. Indeed, by its frightful penalties, this shield petrified all who beheld it; and its laws, like those mentioned in the Bible, were called laws of blood, *leges sanguinis*, because of their exemplary punishments. Minerva, who armed herself with such a shield, was called Athena in Greek, and gave her name to the aristocracy at Athens, as we shall see. (Today, the dragon is likewise the emblem of civil rule among the

Chinese, who still write in hieroglyphics. That two nations so distant in time and place should share this poetic mode of thought and expression is truly amazing.) And this is all that Greek history records about this poetic Dragon.

9

[424] This discovery of poetic archetypes confirms my dating of Aesop to a period well before the Seven Sages of Greece. And the historical truth of this date is confirmed by the following history of human ideas. The Seven Sages were admired when they began to express moral and civil precepts in the form of maxims. The first of these sages was Solon, whose famous 'Know thyself' began as a civil precept, as we have seen, and was later transferred to metaphysics and ethics. But even before Solon, Aesop expressed such counsels in the form of extended *similes*, which poets had already used as a means of expression. Now, according to the order in which human ideas evolve, we first observe similarities to express ourselves, and later employ them for purposes of proof. Proofs in turn are made at first by example, which requires only one similarity; and are eventually made by induction, which requires several. (The father of all the philosophical sects, Socrates, used induction to establish dialectic. Later, Aristotle perfected it in the syllogism, which requires universals for its validity.) But if we seek to persuade people of limited understanding, we need only cite a single example of similarity. Thus, by a single fable in the style of Aesop, the worthy Menenius Agrippa reduced the insurgent Roman plebeians to obedience.

[425] In a prologue to one of his verse fables, the polite poet Phaedrus reveals with prophetic inspiration that Aesop was a *poetic archetype of the associates, meaning the family servants of the heroes*:

> Now, why the *genre* of fables was invented
> I shall in brief explain. The fearful slave
> Dared not express himself as he desired,
> And so transferred his feelings into fables.
> Fam'd Aesop made a path; I've built a road.

(Nunc fabularum cur sit inventum genus,
brevi docebo. Servitus obnoxia,
quia, quae volebat, non audebat dicere,
affectus proprios in fabellas transtulit.
Aesopi illius semitam feci viam.)

Phaedrus' point is clearly proved by Aesop's fable 'The Lion's Share', in which a lion shares no part of the kill with his hunting partners. In the heroic cities, the plebeians were called the heroes' associates, *socii*, as Axiom 79 states. With the heroes, they shared the hardships and dangers of war, but not the spoils and conquests.

Aesop was said to be a slave because the plebeians were the family servants of the heroes. And he was described as ugly because 'civil beauty' was considered the product of solemn marriages, which only heroes could contract. A similar figure of ugliness is Thersites, who must be an archetype of the plebeians who served the heroes of the Trojan War. Indeed, Thersites is beaten by Ulysses with Agamemnon's sceptre, just as the ancient Roman plebeians, stripped to the waist, were caned by the patricians. (Augustine in his *City of God* cites Sallust as calling this punishment 'in royal fashion', *in regium morem*. Eventually, the Porcian Law forbade the caning of Roman citizens.)

[426] The plebeians of the heroic cities must have nurtured such counsels for a life of civil liberty as the dictates of natural reason. Aesop became the poetic archetype of the plebeians under this aspect. Later, fables concerning moral philosophy were ascribed to him, and he became the first moral philosopher, just as Solon became the first sage because his laws ordered the free state of Athens. Since Aesop offered his counsels in the form of fables, he was regarded as living before Solon, who offered his counsels in the form of maxims. At first, Aesop's fables must have been conceived in heroic metre, or hexameter verse. A later tradition says that they were conceived in iambic verse, which (as we shall see) the Greek peoples spoke between heroic verse and later prose. Eventually, Aesop's fables were written down in prose, which is the form in which they survive.

[427] In this manner, the first authors of popular wisdom were credited with the later discoveries of esoteric wisdom. Lawgivers like Zoroaster in the Near East, Hermes Trismegistus in Egypt, Orpheus in Greece, and Pythagoras in Italy were eventually believed to be philosophers, just as Confucius is today in China.

To cite one example, the so-called Pythagoreans of Magna Graecia were in fact nobles who were killed for attempting to change their governments from democracies to aristocracies. I showed earlier that the *Golden Verses* of Pythagoras were a forgery, as were the Oracles of Zoroaster, the *Pimander* of Hermes Trismegistus, and the *Orphica* or verses of Orpheus. Indeed, no work of philosophy by Pythagoras survived in antiquity; and the first Pythagorean to write such a work was Philolaus, as Johannes Scheffer observed in his book *Pythagorean Philosophy*.

CHAPTER 4

Corollaries on the Origins of Languages and Letters; Including the Origins of Hieroglyphics, Laws, Names, Family Arms, Medals, and Money; and the Origins of the First Language and Literature of the Natural Law of Nations

[428] Now, departing from the theology of the poets, which was the first metaphysics, and proceeding by their poetic logic, we seek to discover the origin of languages and letters. On this topic, we find as many opinions as there are scholars who have written about it. For example, Gerard Jan Voss writes in his treatise *On Grammar*: 'Many authors have written about the origin of letters with such profusion and confusion that the reader goes away more ignorant than before.' And Herman Hugo observes in his *Origin of Writing*: 'No subject arouses as many contradictory opinions as the origin of letters and writing. How many conflicting opinions! What should one believe, and what not believe?' Bernard von Mallinckrodt wrote in his *Origin of Printing*

that, since no one can fathom the origin of letters, they must be a divine invention. And Ingewald Eling in his *History of the Greek Language* agreed with him.

[429] In fact, such difficulties were created by the scholars themselves. They regarded the origin of letters as distinct from the origin of languages, when they are in fact inseparable by nature. The words 'grammar' and 'characters' should have alerted them to this. For grammar is defined as the art of speaking; but since *grammata* in Greek means letters, grammar should be defined as the art of writing, which is how Aristotle defines it. In fact, this was its origin, for all the nations were at first mute, and only began to speak by writing. Character in turn means idea, form, or model; and it is clear that poetic archetypes or characters preceded the characters representing articulate sounds. Hence, Josephus vigorously maintains against the Greek grammarian Apion that in Homer's age the so-called vernacular letters had not yet been invented. Furthermore, if these letters had been the forms of articulate sounds, rather than arbitrary signs, they would have been uniform in all nations, just as articulate sounds are uniform in them all. But since scholars despaired of learning the origins of letters, they failed to realize that the first nations thought in poetic archetypes, spoke in myths, and wrote in hieroglyphics. These principles, which are by nature most certain, should have formed the foundation both of philosophy in its study of human ideas and of philology in its study of human words.

[430] Before discussing the origin of letters and languages, I should give a small sample of the many opinions scholars have held on the subject – opinions so unclear, frivolous, inept, conceited, and ridiculous, not to mention so numerous, that there is no point in reviewing all of them. Here is a sample, then.

During the medieval return of barbarism, the conceit of nations caused Scandinavia to be called the womb of nations, *vagina gentium*, and to be considered the mother of all the other nations in the world. In their conceit as scholars, Johannes and Olaus Magnus fancied that the letters divinely invented by Adam had been preserved by the Goths since the beginning of the world. This illusion was derided by scholars everywhere. But that did not prevent Jan van Gorp from following and even surpassing their example. He claimed that his Dutch language, which is similar to the Low German of the Saxons, came from the earthly paradise of Eden and was the mother of all other tongues. Van Gorp's opinion was mocked by Joseph Justus Scaliger, Philip Camerarius, Christian Becman, and Martin Schoock. Yet this conceit puffed itself up and burst in the *Atlantica* of Olof Rudbeck, who maintained that the letters of the Greek alphabet were derived from Norse runes. Supposedly, these runes were simply the Phoenician letters inverted, to which Cadmus later assigned an order and pronunciation similar to that of Hebrew letters, and which the Greeks eventually straightened and rounded out using a rule and compass. And since the Scandinavians call the inventor of letters Merkurssman, Rudbeck insists that the Mercury who invented the letters of the Egyptians was a Goth!

Such far-fetched speculations about the origins of letters should prepare the reader to hear my ideas on the subject, not only weighing their novelty impartially, but giving them due attention and accepting them for what they offer, namely, principles basic to all our human and divine knowledge of the pagan world.

[431] All the philosophers and philologists ought to have begun their discussion of the origins of languages and letters with the following three principles. (1) The first pagan people conceived ideas of things using imaginative archetypes of animate beings, or personifications. (2) In their mute condition, they expressed themselves by using gestures and objects naturally related to their ideas, such as three ears of grain or three scythe strokes to mean three years. (3) And they expressed themselves using language with natural meanings. This language, which Plato and Iamblichus said was once spoken in the world, must have been the most ancient language of Atlantis, which according to scholars expressed ideas using the nature of things, or their natural properties.

The origins of languages and letters are inseparable. But the philosophers and philologists treated them as separate, and so the inquiry proved too difficult. For while both questions involved equal difficulties, they paid little or no attention to the origins of languages.

[432] In beginning our discussion, then, let us posit as our first principle my Axiom 28. The Egyptians related that the entire history of the world was divided into three ages: the ages of gods, heroes,

and men. And people in these ages spoke three languages: first, the *hieroglyphic*, or sacred and divine, language; second, the *symbolic* language, which used signs and heroic emblems; and third, the *epistolary* language, by which people at a distance communicated their current needs. Two golden passages in Homer's *Iliad* make clear that the Greeks shared the Egyptians' view. The first passage relates that Nestor lived through three ages of men speaking different languages. Thus, Nestor must have been a heroic archetype representing the Egyptian chronology of languages; and the proverbial phrase 'to live as long as Nestor' meant to grow as old as the world. In the second passage, Aeneas tells Achilles that, after Troy was moved to the seashore and Pergamum became its citadel, Ilium was inhabited by people speaking different languages. To this first principle, we may join another Egyptian tradition, which said that their god Thoth, or Mercury, invented both laws and letters.

[433] With these truths, we may group the following ones concerning the first human institutions, beginning with names and laws. In Greek, the nouns 'name' and 'character' were synonymous, so that the Church Fathers use both interchangeably in their writings about divine names and divine characters. In Latin, the nouns 'name' and 'definition' are likewise synonymous. Hence, in rhetoric, the *definition of the fact* is called the question of name, *quaestio nominis*. And *nomenclature* is the area of medicine which defines the *nature* of diseases. In Roman personal names, the *nomen* or surname primarily and properly referred to a person's extended clan of families. The names of the early Greeks shared this meaning, as is shown by their patronymics, meaning the names of the fathers, which are often cited by the poets, especially by the first poet Homer. (In Livy, a tribune of the people likewise defines the Roman patricians as those 'who can cite their fathers by name', *qui possunt nomine ciere patrem*.) With the rise of democracy throughout Greece, these patronymics eventually disappeared; but in the aristocracy at Sparta, they were preserved by the Heraclids. In Roman law, the word *nomen*, name, means one's right to something. In Greek, the phonetically similar *nomos* means law. From this noun, comes *nomisma*, meaning coin, as Aristotle observes; and some etymologists also derive Latin *nummus*, coin, from it. (Similarly, in French, *loi* means law, and *aloi* means coin. During the medieval return of barbarism, the term

'canon' meant both an ecclesiastical law and the feudal rent paid to the owner of a fief.)

This same way of thinking is found among the Romans, and perhaps explains why the Romans used the word *ius* to mean both justice and the fat of sacrifices, which was Jupiter's due. For Jupiter was originally called *Ious*, with the genitive *Iouis* or *Iuris*. Similarly, the Jews divided the animal sacrificed as a peace offering into three parts, of which the fat was considered God's due and burned on the altar.

To turn to property, the Latin term *praedia* initially meant rustic estates, and only later urban ones. These were so called because the first cultivated fields were the world's first *booty*, *praeda*, as we shall see later. Such fields were the first to be tamed, and thus in early Roman law were called *manuceptae*, taken in hand; and a person under real-estate bond to the public treasury was called a *manceps*, bondsman. In Roman laws, the term *iura praediorum* came to mean so-called real servitudes, which are attached to real estate. Lands called *manuceptae* must originally have been called *mancipia*. This is the evident meaning of that article in the Law of the Twelve Tables which reads 'Whoever shall make bond or conveyance', *Qui nexum faciet mancipiumque*. Using a similar concept, Italians called estates *poderi*, because they were acquired by force, *podere*.

There are later examples of such origins. During the medieval return of barbarism, fields and their boundaries were called *presas terrarum*. The Spanish call daring enterprises *prendas*. The Italians call family coats of arms *imprese*, and they use the word *termini*, boundaries, for key words or terms, as Scholastic logicians still do. Likewise, Italians call family coats of arms *insegne*, insignia, from which they derive the verb *insegnare*, to teach. In the same way, before the invention of vernacular letters, Homer says that Proetus' letter to Eureia, with instructions to kill Bellerophon, was written in *sēmata*, signs.

[434] Let me conclude these observations with the following three indisputable truths. (1) Since all the first pagan nations were at first mute, they must have expressed themselves by gestures or objects naturally related to their ideas. (2) They must have used signs to secure the boundaries of their estates and to provide lasting witnesses of their rights. (3) They all used some form of money. All these truths indicate

the origins of languages and letters, and in turn the origins of hieroglyphics, laws, names, family coats of arms, medals, and coins, as well
as those of the language and writing used by the first natural law of the
nations.

[435] To establish our principles more firmly, we must eradicate the
false belief that philosophers invented hieroglyphics to conceal the
mysteries of their esoteric wisdom, as many have believed the Egyptians
did. In fact, all the first nations everywhere shared a natural need to
speak by means of hieroglyphic symbols, as Axiom 57 states. Thus, in
Africa we find not only the Egyptians, but also the Ethiopians, who
used workmen's tools as hieroglyphs, according to Heliodorus' *Ethiopian
Romance* [Diodorus' *History*].* In the Near East, the Chaldaeans' magic
symbols must also have been hieroglyphs.

In northern Asia, we have already seen how the Scythian king
Idanthyrsus used five physical objects as words to reply to Darius the
Great, who had declared war on him. (This was relatively late in the
Scythians' supposedly boundless history, which surpassed even that of
the Egyptians, who claimed to be the oldest nation of all.) The five
objects were a frog, a mouse, a bird, a plough, and a bow. The frog
meant that Idanthyrsus had been born of the Scythian earth, just as
frogs are born of the earth after summer rainstorms. The mouse meant
that he had made his home where he was born, that is, had founded a
nation. The bird meant that the auspices were his, and hence that he
was subject only to God. The plough meant that he had placed his
lands under cultivation, that is, conquered and claimed them by force.
And finally the bow meant that he was supreme commander of the
arms of Scythia, and thus was bound and able to defend his country.
Contrast this explanation, so natural and inevitable, with the ludicrous
ones which St Cyril [St Clement] says that Darius' counsellors proposed.† Then compare their interpretations of the Scythian symbols
with the far-fetched, distorted, and contorted ones which scholars have
proposed for Egyptian hieroglyphics. The comparison will clearly reveal

---

* For Diodorus' universal history, Vico mistakenly writes 'Heliodorus' *Ethiopian
Romance*'.
† For Clement of Alexandria, Vico mistakenly writes 'Cyril'.

that scholars previously misunderstood the true and proper use of the hieroglyphs employed by early peoples.

As for the Latin peoples, Roman history has preserved something of this tradition in the wordless heroic reply which Tarquinius Superbus sends to his son in Gabii. As a messenger watched, he wielded a stick and cut the heads off some poppies. Some have interpreted this gesture as an act of pride, but it was in fact dictated by the need for confidentiality. In northern Europe, as Tacitus observes in describing their customs, the ancient Germans knew nothing of the 'secrets of letters', *litterarum secreta*, meaning that they could not write in hieroglyphs. This must have been the case as late as the age of Frederick II, or even that of Rudolph I, when official documents began to be written in vernacular German script. In northern France, there existed a hieroglyphic speech known as the rebus of Picardy, which as in Germany must have been speech using objects, like the symbols of Idanthyrsus. Even in Scotland, the remotest part of remote Britain, or Ultima Thule, people in olden times wrote in hieroglyphics, as Hector Boece notes in his *History of Scotland*. In the West Indies, the Mexicans were found to have written using hieroglyphs. In his *Description of the New Indies*, Jan van Laet describes how the Indians' hieroglyphs depict various animal heads, plants, flowers, and fruits, and how the symbols on their totem poles distinguish their families, like those in our coats of arms. In the East Indies, the Chinese still write in hieroglyphs.

[436] In asserting that the Egyptians taught all the world's sages how to conceal their wisdom in hieroglyphics, the conceit of later scholars even surpassed the overblown conceit of the Egyptians themselves. But their exaggerations are now deflated.

[437] Now that we have established the principles of poetic logic, and dispelled the conceit of the scholars, let us return to the three languages of the Egyptians. The first of these, the language of the gods, is attested among the Greeks in Homer, as Axiom 29 states. In five passages of his two epics, Homer mentions a language older than his own heroic speech, which he calls the 'language of the gods'. Three of these passages are in the *Iliad*. The first says that the giant called Briareus by the gods is called Aegaeon by men. The second speaks of a bird called *chalcis* by the gods, and *cymindis* by men. And the third says that

the river near Troy is called Xanthus by the gods, and Scamander by men. The other two passages are in the *Odyssey*. In one, he says that what men call Scylla and Charybdis the gods call *Planctae Petrae*, moving rocks. In the other, as a secret remedy against Circe's spells, Mercury gives Ulysses a herb which men are forbidden to know but which the gods call *moly*.

Plato comments on these passages at length, but makes little sense. And Dio Chrysostom later maligns Homer as an impostor for claiming to understand the language of the gods, which is by nature denied to men. Yet we may doubt whether in these Homeric passages we shouldn't perhaps interpret 'gods' to mean 'heroes'. In fact, the heroes assumed the title of 'gods' to distinguish themselves from the plebeians of their cities, whom they simply called 'men'. (During the medieval return of barbarism, vassals were likewise simply called *homines*, men, as François Hotman notes with amazement.) And both in antiquity and the Middle Ages, great lords boasted that they possessed wondrous medical secrets. Such expressions merely reflect the distinctions between noble and vernacular speech.

At any rate, we cannot doubt that the Roman Varro devoted himself to studying this language of the gods, and diligently collected the names of 30,000 gods, as Axiom 30 states. These names must have furnished a copious divine lexicon, sufficient for expressing all the needs of the peoples of Latium, which in that simple and frugal age must have been limited to the few necessities of life. The Greeks too reckoned 30,000 gods, as Axiom 30 states: for they saw deities in every rock, spring, brook, plant, and reef, including the nature spirits called dryads, hamadryads, oreads, and napeas. In precisely this way, the American Indians regard as gods everything that is beyond their limited grasp. Hence, the divine myths of the Greeks and Romans must have been the first true hieroglyphs, meaning sacred and divine archetypes, like those of the Egyptians.

[438] The Egyptians said that the second kind of speech, which corresponds to the age of heroes, was spoken by using symbols. These must have included heroic emblems like those *mute similes* which Homer calls *sēmata*, the signs written by the heroes. Later, when language had become articulate, these symbols must have become the metaphors,

images, similes, or comparisons which furnished the materials of poetic style. Hence, there is a connection between heroic speech and poetry. And Homer is certainly the first author in the Greek language. (Indeed, Josephus resolutely denies that any more ancient author survives.) In fact, since all we know about pagan antiquity comes from the Greeks, Homer is the first author of the entire pagan world. As for the Romans, the earliest specimens of the Latin language are the fragments of the Saliar verses, or hymns of the Salii; and the earliest author mentioned by historians is the poet Livius Andronicus. Later, as different languages arose during the medieval return of barbarism, the first language of the Spanish was called *el romance*, which denotes *heroic poetry*, since the authors of romances were the heroic poets of the Middle Ages. In France, the first writer in vernacular French was Arnaut Daniel, who flourished in the eleventh century and was the earliest of the Provençal poets. In Italy, to conclude, the first writers were the Florentine and Sicilian rhymers.

[439] The third kind of speech, which the Egyptians called epistolary, was a conventional language which distant persons used to discuss the common needs of everyday life. It must have arisen among the common people of a ruling class in Egypt. (This can only be the people of Thebes, whose king Ramses extended his dominion over all that great nation.) For in the Egyptians' view this language corresponded to the age of men, the heroic term used for the plebeians to distinguish them from the heroes. We must imagine that this language was created by the free agreement of the common people. For it is a universal principle that vernacular speech and writing are the right of the people. When the emperor Claudius invented three letters which he thought necessary to the Latin language, the Roman people refused to adopt them. And the Italians have not adopted the supplementary vowels invented by Gian Giorgio Trissino, even though the Italian language could use them.

[440] The epistolary languages of Egypt, which we may call vernacular or demotic, were appropriately written with vernacular letters. Since these Egyptian letters resemble those of the Phoenicians, we must presume that one nation borrowed from the other. Some believe that the Egyptians were the first to invent all the institutions that are necessary or useful to human society, and therefore conclude that the Egyptians

taught the Phoenicians their letters. But Clement of Alexandria, who is better informed about Egypt than anyone else, relates that the Phoenician historian Sanchuniathon – dated in my Chronological Table to the Greek heroic age – wrote his Phoenician history in vernacular letters. Indeed, Clement cites him as the first pagan author to write in vernacular characters. Since the Phoenicians were clearly the world's first merchant nation, we must conclude that they introduced their vernacular letters to Egypt when they travelled there to trade.

But even without such arguments and conjectures, we know from popular tradition that the Phoenicians introduced their alphabet to Greece. Commenting on this tradition, Tacitus supposes that the Phoenicians presented as their own invention letters which others had invented, meaning the hieroglyphics of the Egyptians. If we maintain that this popular tradition had a basis in truth, as all such traditions do everywhere, the Phoenicians must have introduced into Greece hieroglyphics which they had adopted from other nations. These can only have been the mathematical characters and geometric figures which they had learned from the Chaldaeans. For the Chaldaeans were clearly the first mathematicians and, more importantly, the first astronomers of the nations. And the Chaldaean Zoroaster, whose name Bochart takes to mean 'star-gazer', was the first sage of the pagan world. Hence, the Phoenicians must have adopted the Chaldaeans' characters as a notation of the numbers they used in their commercial transactions. The epics of Homer, and the *Odyssey* in particular, make it clear that Phoenician merchants were trading in the ports of Greece long before his own day. (At this time, the Greeks had not yet invented vernacular letters, as Josephus vigorously maintains against the Greek grammarian Apion.)

Then the Greeks, using the extraordinary genius in which they clearly surpassed all other nations, transferred the Phoenicians' geometrical figures to represent different articulate sounds; and with their extraordinary sense of beauty shaped them into the vernacular characters of their letters. The Greek alphabet was later adopted by the Romans, and Tacitus observes that Latin letters resemble the most ancient Greek ones. We find persuasive evidence of this origin in the fact that the Greeks used letters to write numbers for many centuries, and Latin capitals were used as numerals until recently. These must be the letters which the Latins learned from Demaratus of Corinth and from Carmenta, the wife of Evander of Arcadia. (We shall see that the early Greeks founded maritime and inland colonies in Latium.)

[441] We must reject as worthless the view of many scholars who contend that the Greeks adopted their vernacular alphabet from the Jews, merely because the names of the letters in both languages are nearly the same. It is more reasonable to suppose that the Jews borrowed their names from the Greeks, rather than the other way round. For everyone agrees that the Greek language was diffused throughout the Near East and Egypt by Alexander the Great's conquest of his Eastern empire, which was divided between his generals after his death. And all agree that Hebrew grammar developed quite late, so that Jewish scholars must have named their letters after the Greek ones.

Furthermore, since basic elements are by nature very simple, the Greeks must at first have called their letters by their simplest phonetic sounds, which is why they called them 'elements'. The Romans followed the Greeks in naming their letters with similar austerity, and did the same in retaining the simple forms of the earliest Greek ones. Hence, we must conclude that the complex names for the Greek letters, such as alpha and beta, developed at a late date, and were transmitted to the Jews of the Near East even later as aleph, beth, and so on.

[442] These observations dispel the opinion of those who assert that Cecrops the Egyptian introduced vernacular letters into Greece. And another such opinion says that these letters were brought from Egypt to Greece by Cadmus the Phoenician, who founded the Greek city of Thebes and named it after the capital of the greatest Egyptian dynasty. But I shall soon dispel this notion, for the principles of my Poetic Geography reveal that the Egyptian capital was called Thebes by Greek travellers who noted its resemblance to their own city. And we may now understand why cautious scholars, cited by the anonymous English author [Thomas Baker] of the treatise *The Uncertainty of the Sciences* [*Reflections upon Learning*, 1699],* conclude from the exaggerated

---

* Vico read Baker in an Italian translation (Venice, 1735) which was titled *Trattato dell'incertezza delle scienze* (*Treatise on the Uncertainty of the Sciences*).

antiquity of Sanchuniathon that he never existed at all. Yet rather than discount Sanchuniathon entirely, I think we must date him to a later period, certainly after Homer. And if we maintain that the Phoenicians invented vernacular letters before the Greeks – bearing in mind that the Greeks were more ingenious – we must conclude that Sanchuniathon lived just before Herodotus. For the latter was called the father of Greek history, and wrote in the vernacular tongue; and Sanchuniathon was called the historian of truth, which places him in what Varro calls the historic period. (In their division of history into three ages and languages, the Egyptians said that in the third age people spoke the epistolary language and wrote in vernacular characters.)

[443] Now, just as heroic or poetic language was created by the heroes, vernacular or popular language was created by the populace, who were the plebeians of the heroic nations. In Latin, such languages were properly called vernaculars, but they could not have been introduced by the *vernae*, whom grammarians define as 'servants born in a household from slaves captured in war'. For such servants naturally learn the native language of their masters. Rather, we shall see that the first *vernae*, properly speaking, were the family servants, *famuli*, in the state of the heroic family. These servants came to form the plebeian masses of the heroic cities, and were the precursors of the slaves who were later taken by cities in wartime. All of this is confirmed by Homer's distinction between the languages of gods and men, which I have identified as the heroic and vernacular languages.

[444] Philologists have all shown too much credulity by embracing the view that the meaning of words in vernacular languages was purely arbitrary and conventional. In fact, they possessed natural meanings by virtue of their natural origins. This is easy to observe in vernacular Latin, which is more heroic than vernacular Greek, and therefore has more vigour, as Greek has more delicacy. For almost all Latin words derive from metaphors based on natural objects, natural properties, or sensible effects. Generally speaking, metaphor makes up the bulk of vocabulary in all languages. But when classical grammarians encountered numerous words with confused or vague meanings, their ignorance of word origins led them to establish the universal principle that articulate words have merely arbitrary and conventional meanings. In defence of

this view, they called up Aristotle, Galen, and other philosophers; and armed them against Plato and Iamblichus, as we have seen.

[445] Yet a great difficulty still remains. Why are there as many vernacular languages as there are different peoples? To solve this problem, we may establish the following great truth. Different climates clearly produce peoples with different natures and different customs, and these in turn produce different languages. Nations with different natures view what is necessary and useful to human life under different aspects. This produces different and even opposite customs, and at the same time different languages, which therefore vary according to their origins. Proverbs offer us distinct proof of this. For their meanings, while substantially the same, are expressed under as many different aspects as there are ancient and modern nations, as Axiom 22 states.

These same heroic origins, preserved in condensed form by vernacular languages, have caused biblical scholars to marvel. For the names of the same kings have one form in scripture and another in secular history. The reason for this is that the Bible describes kings in terms of their appearance or might; whereas secular historians describe them in terms of their customs, deeds, or something of the sort. Even today, we see that the cities of Hungary are given different names by the Hungarians, Greeks, Germans, and Turks. The German language is a living heroic language, and therefore changes nearly all foreign names into its own native forms. We may conjecture that the heroic Greeks and Romans did the same when they spoke about barbarian institutions in their refined Greek and Latin. This would account for the obscurity that we encounter in reading ancient geography and the natural history of fossils, plants, and animals.

The first edition of my *New Science* contains a section called the 'Idea of a Conceptual Dictionary for Assigning Meanings to All the Different Articulate Languages'. This dictionary reduces these meanings to certain underlying ideas which peoples have considered from various viewpoints and hence expressed with different words. I continue to use it in developing the theory of my Science. And my first edition cites a lengthy excerpt from this dictionary, which shows how family fathers, during the formative period of languages in the family state and the early commonwealths, were considered under fifteen different aspects, and hence were called by fifteen names in fifteen separate nations, both ancient and modern. (The original meanings of words in this formative period offer us important insights into early institutions, as Axiom 65 states. This is the third of the three passages in my first edition which cause me no regret.) My dictionary offers a different interpretation of topics discussed by Thomas Hayne in his treatise *The Kinship of Languages, or On Languages in General and The Affinities of Different Languages*.

These observations suggest the following corollary. Languages are more beautiful as they are richer in condensed heroic figures of speech. They are more beautiful as they are vivid; and they are more vivid as they are truer and more faithful to their origins. By contrast, the more crowded they are with words of obscure origin, the less delightful they are, and the more obscure and confused, and hence the more likely to deceive and mislead. Such confusion is characteristic of those languages which have been formed by the mixture of many barbarous languages, for the history of their origins and of their metaphors remains unclear.

[446] Turning now to the very difficult question of how the three kinds of languages and letters were formed, we must establish the following principle. The gods, heroes, and men all originated at the same time, for it was after all men who imagined the gods and who believed that their own heroes were a mixture of divine and human natures. And their three languages also originated at the same time, each with its own letters. The language of the gods was almost entirely mute, or wordless, and only slightly articulate. The language of heroes was an equal mixture of mute and articulate speech; which means that it mixed vernacular speech with the heroic characters which Homer calls signs, *sēmata*. The language of men was almost entirely articulate and only slightly mute, since no vernacular language is so copious that it has words for all things.

Because of its mixture, heroic language must originally have been extremely confused, which is the main reason why ancient myths are so obscure. We may regard the myth of Cadmus as a notable example of this obscurity. Cadmus slays a great serpent and sows its teeth. When armed men spring from the furrows of the fields, Cadmus throws a boulder among them. They fight to the death, and Cadmus finally changes into a serpent. So great was the ingenuity of Cadmus in bringing letters to the Greeks that this myth contains several centuries of poetic history!

[447] To resume my argument, just as the divine character of Jupiter was taking shape as the first human thought of the pagan world, articulate language began to take shape in onomatopoeia, which children still happily use to express themselves. In Latin, Jupiter was initially called *Ious* after the sound of crashing thunder; and in Greek, he was called *Zeus* after the whistling sound of lightning. In the Near East, he was called *Ur*, after the sound of burning fire, from which derived *Urim*, the power of fire; and this must be the etymology of Greek *ouranos*, heaven, and Latin *urere*, to burn. The whistling sound of lightning also produced Latin *celum*, heaven, and the poetic monosyllable, *cel*. Indeed, if we pronounce the word with a Spanish cedilla as *çelo*, it points up the wit of Ausonius' punning verse which describes Venus as *Nata salo, suscepta solo, patre edita celo*: 'Born in the sea, raised on the soil, and borne to the sky by her father'. Within this origin of language, we see that the sublimity of invention which I noted in the myth of Jupiter also marks the beginning of poetic diction in onomatopoeia. Indeed, Longinus counts onomatopoeia as one of the sources of sublimity, citing the passage in Homer when the fiery stake thrust by Ulysses into Polyphemus' eye makes the sizzling noise *sidz*.

[448] Next, human words were formed by interjections or exclamations, which are articulate sounds caused by the stimulus of violent emotion, and which are monosyllabic in all languages. It seems likely that, when the first lightning bolts had awakened the wonder of humankind, Jupiter's exclamations called forth the first human exclamation, the syllable *pa*. Later, the syllable was doubled and became the exclamation of astonishment *pape*, from which was derived Jupiter's title of father, *pater*, of gods and men. Eventually all the gods were called father, and all the goddesses mother. Thus, in Latin we find father Jupiter, *Iupiter* or *Diespiter*, father Mars, *Marspiter*, and mother Juno, *Juno genetrix*, even though the myths relate that Juno was barren. Many of the gods and goddesses in heaven never married, which is why Venus was called the concubine of Mars, rather than his wife. Nevertheless, all these gods were called fathers, as is shown by the verses of Lucilius cited in my *Principles of Universal Law*.

This divine title *patres* is related to the verb *patrare*, which originally meant 'to make', as in the creation proper to God the Father. We find this confirmed in the Bible's account of the Creation, which says that on the seventh day God rested 'from the work he had made', *ab opere quod patrarat*. The verb *impetrare*, to achieve, is clearly derived from the same root, as if from *impatrare*. The science of augury used the related verb *impetrire*, to obtain a good omen, although Latin scholars have written a good deal of nonsense about its origin. All this proves that the first interpretation was that of divine laws ordained by taking auspices, which was called *interpretatio*, as if from *interpatratio*.

[449] From the natural ambition of their human pride, powerful men in the state of families usurped this divine title and called themselves fathers. (This may account for the popular tradition that the first powerful men caused others to worship them as gods.) But with the sense of the piety they owed the deities, they called them gods. Later, when the powerful men of the first cities assumed the title of gods, the same piety moved them to call the heavenly deities 'the immortal gods', to distinguish them from the mortal gods of mankind. From this we see how grotesque these early giants were, like the Big Feet reported by travellers in Patagonia. We find a striking trace of this in the early Latin words *pipulum*, complaint, and *pipare*, to complain, which must derive from the exclamation of lament, *pi, pi*. Scholars of Plautus interpret his word *pipulum* as synonymous with the noun *obvagulatio*, hue and cry, which is found in the Twelve Tables, and which must be derived from *vagire*, to wail, which properly describes the crying of babies.

The exclamation of fear *pai* must also have given rise to the Greek exclamation *paian*. A golden tradition of great antiquity relates that, when the great serpent known as Python frightened the Greeks, they called on Apollo to aid them by crying *iō paian*. At first, numb with fear, they uttered these words slowly three times, thus forming six spondees. But when Apollo had slain the Python, they rejoiced and shouted the words another three times more quickly. In so doing, they divided the omega of *iō* into two omicrons and separated the diphthong *ai* of *paian* into two syllables, thus forming six dactyls. This was the natural origin of the heroic verse called the hexameter, which began with spondees and developed into dactyls. Evidence of this origin remains in the invariable property of hexameters that dactyls tend to replace spondees in any foot but the last. In this metre of heroic verse, song arose naturally from the stimulus of violent emotions. Even today we see that people break into song when they are moved by strong emotions, especially powerful grief or joy, as Axiom 59 states. We shall soon find these observations useful to our discussion of the origins of song and verse.

[450] Next, people proceeded to form pronouns. Exclamations give vent to personal emotions, which can be expressed in solitude. By contrast, pronouns serve to signify things whose proper names we do not know or others cannot understand. Like exclamations, nearly all pronouns are monosyllabic in every language. In Latin, the first pronoun, or one of the first, must have been the pronoun *hoc*, which occurs in Ennius' golden verse, *Aspice hoc sublime cadens, quem omnes invocant Iovem*: 'Look at this which falls from above, which all invoke as Jupiter'. Ennius says *hoc*, this, instead of *coelum*, heaven. And in vernacular Latin, Plautus writes *lucescit hoc iam*, it's dawning now, rather than *albescit coelum*, the sky is growing bright. This is why articles from the beginning have had the invariable property of being placed before the nouns they modify.

[451] Later, they formed particles. In most languages, these consist largely of prepositions, and are monosyllabic. The name preposition indicates their invariable property of preceding the nouns and verbs which they modify.

[452] Nouns began to be formed gradually. In the first edition of my *New Science*, the chapter on the 'Origins of the Latin Language' listed many nouns which originated among the inhabitants of Latium, from the period of their savage life through their rural and early urban societies. All these nouns were formed as monosyllables; and none of them reveals any trace of foreign origin, not even Greek, with the exception of *bous*, ox, *sus*, pig, *mus*, mouse, and *sēps*, which means hedge in Latin and serpent in Greek. (This chapter is the second of those passages in my first *New Science* which I judge valuable, for it may serve as an example to scholars of other languages and encourage them to investigate the origins of those languages, which will benefit the community of literary scholars. For example, German is a mother language, and since that nation was never ruled by foreign ones, the

roots of all German words are monosyllabic.) And that nouns originated before verbs is shown by the invariable property that there can be no sentence without a noun as its subject, whether expressed or understood.

[453] Finally, the authors of languages formed verbs. In just this way, we observe that children often express nouns and particles, but leave the verbs to be understood. For nouns awaken ideas and images which leave clear mental imprints, and particles do the same by signifying modifications of these ideas. But verbs signify motion, which implies past and future moments measured against an indivisible present, a concept which even the philosophers find difficult to grasp. This scientific observation is confirmed by the following case. There is living in Naples a gentleman who has suffered a severe stroke, and can only utter nouns, having completely forgotten the verbs.

Let us consider the verbs which are the generic categories of other verbs: *sum*, I am, of *being*, which comprises all existence and all metaphysical categories; *sto*, I stand, of *rest*, and *eo*, I go, of *motion*, which comprise all physical objects; and *do*, I give, *dico*, I say, and *facio*, I do, which comprise all human activities, whether moral, economic, or civil. All these verbs must have originated in imperatives. For in the state of families, which was extremely poor in language, the fathers alone must have spoken and given commands. And in their terror of patriarchal authority, the children and servants must have been obliged to carry out the fathers' commands with blind obedience and in silence. In Latin, such imperatives still preserve their monosyllabic form, *es*, *sta*, *i*, *da*, *dic*, *fac*: be, stand, go, give, say, do.

[454] This monosyllabic genesis of languages conforms to the principle of universal nature which says that the elements which make up larger, divisible entities must themselves be indivisible. And it conforms to the principles of human nature, specifically my Axiom 60, which states that 'even though children today are born amid a wealth of articulate languages, and they have very supple organs for articulating speech, they still begin with monosyllables'. This must have been even truer of the first men of the nations, whose vocal organs were very rigid and who had not yet heard human speech. My account also prescribes the order in which the parts of speech originated, and hence the natural origins of syntax.

[455] All of this seems more reasonable than the theories of the Latin language advanced by Julius Caesar Scaliger and Francisco Sanchez. For their arguments derive from Aristotle, as if the peoples who invented language must first have studied with him!

CHAPTER 5

Corollaries on the Origins of Poetic Style, Digressions, Inversions, Prose Rhythm, Song, and Verse

[456] In this manner the nations formed poetic language, which was first composed of divine and heroic symbols, then expressed in vernacular languages, and finally written in vernacular characters. It arose entirely from the first peoples' poverty of language and their need for expression, as the basic ornaments of poetic style indicate. These include vivid depictions, images, similes, comparisons, metaphors, and periphrases; as well as phrases explaining things by their natural properties, descriptions of things drawn from their most particular and important effects, and, finally, emphatic and even redundant pleonasms.

[457] *Digressions* were born of the coarseness of heroic minds, which were incapable of sticking to the principal subject at hand. This is why we find that simpletons and women in particular naturally digress when they speak.

[458] *Inversions* in word order arose from the difficulty of completing sentences with verbs, which were the last words to be invented, as we have just seen. The Greeks, who were a clever people, inverted their word order less than the Romans; and the Romans inverted theirs less than the Germans do now.

[459] *Prose rhythm* was only understood quite late by writers, in Greek by Gorgias of Leontini and in Latin by Cicero. Before them, writers had used poetic metres to make their sentences rhythmical, as Cicero himself tells us. We shall find his observation quite useful in our discussion of the origins of song and verse.

[460] All these observations prove that human nature determined the creation of poetic style before prose style, just as human nature

determined the creation of mythical and imaginative universals before rational and philosophical universals, which were the product of discourse in prose. For after the poets had formed poetic speech by combining universal ideas, the nations formed prose speech by contracting these poetic combinations into single words, as if into general categories. Take for example the poetic sentence 'My blood boils in my heart', which expresses a natural, eternal, and universal property of humankind. They took the notions of blood, boiling, and heart, and formed them into a single word, or general category: anger, which is called *stomachos* in Greek, *ira* in Latin, and *collera* in Italian. By the same steps, hieroglyphs and heroic emblems were reduced to a few vernacular letters, as general types to which countless different articulate sounds could be assigned. This process required the utmost ingenuity; and the use of such general words and letters rendered people's minds more agile and more capable of abstraction. This in turn prepared the way for the philosophers, who formulated intelligible general categories. This offers us a small piece of the history of human thought, from which we see that the origin of letters could only be traced in the same breath with the origin of languages!

[461] Concerning *song* and *verse*, we have shown that people were originally mute. Hence, like mute people, they must have uttered crude vowels by singing; and like stammerers, they must have articulated consonants by singing, as Axiom 58 states. We find important proof of this first song in the diphthongs preserved by various languages. These must initially have been more numerous: for the Greeks and the French, who passed abruptly from the poetic to the vernacular age, have preserved many examples, as Axiom 21 states. The reason for this is that vowels are easy to pronounce, and consonants difficult. The first people, being dull-witted, were only moved to utter sounds when they felt violent emotions, which they naturally expressed in a very loud voice. And by nature, when people raise their voices, they utter diphthongs and produce song, as Axiom 59 states. Thus, in their age of the gods, the early Greeks formed the first heroic verse of spondees with the diphthong *pai*, composed of two vowels and a single consonant.

[462] The first song of various peoples also sprang naturally from the difficulty they had in pronouncing sounds. We find evidence of this

difficulty both in its causes and its effects. Its causes were physical, for the earliest people had rigid vocal organs, and knew very few words. Even today, when children have supple vocal organs, and are born amid a wealth of words, they still find consonants hard to pronounce, as Axiom 60 states. We may note that the Chinese have no more than 300 distinct syllables; but by modulating their inflection and duration, they express the 120,000 ideograms of their vernacular language. Thus, they truly speak by singing!

The effects of such phonetic difficulties are evident in word contractions, which are nearly innumerable in Italian poetry. (In the first edition of my *Science*, my chapter on the Origins of the Latin Language lists a large number of words which must have originated as contractions that were later expanded.) They are also evident in verbal repetitions and reduplications. For example, when stammerers have trouble with a syllable, they replace it by one which they can sing easily, as Axiom 58 states. In my time, there lived in Naples an excellent tenor with a speech impediment who, in stumbling on a word, would break into sweet song and thereby succeed in pronouncing it. We see that the Arabs begin nearly all their words with the syllable *al*, and it is said that the Huns were so called because they began all their words with *hun*. To conclude, the origin of language in song is also demonstrated by the fact that the Greek and Latin orators before Gorgias and Cicero used almost poetic metres. During the medieval return of barbarism, the Fathers of the Roman Church did the same, as did the Greek Fathers, so that their prose seems like a sort of singsong.

[463] As we have seen, the first verse must have originated in a form appropriate to the age and language of heroes, that is, as heroic verse. Born of violent emotions of fear and joy, this grandiose verse is proper to heroic poetry, which deals only with the most turbulent passions. Yet popular tradition is mistaken in attributing its spondaic origin to the Greeks' fear of the Python. Such turbulent passion, instead of slowing one's ideas and words, accelerates them; which is why Latin *festinans*, hastening, and *solicitus*, restless, connote trepidation. Rather, heroic verse was originally spondaic because the founders of the nations possessed slow minds and sluggish tongues; and from this origin it retains the use of a spondee in the last foot. Later, as men's minds and

tongues grew more agile, dactyls were allowed in the rest of the verse. Then, as they developed far greater agility, the iamb was born, which Horace calls the 'swift foot', as Axiom 62 states. Eventually, when people's minds and tongues were both very agile, prose arrived, which speaks, as it were, using intelligible categories. Now, iambic verse so closely resembles prose that ancient writers often lapsed into it inadvertently. In this way, song passed into verse, and moved more quickly in step with ideas and languages, as Axiom 62 states.

[464] This philosophical theory is confirmed by history, which records oracles and sibyls as the most ancient institutions. Indeed, the expression 'It's older than the sibyl' meant that a thing was very ancient. Of the sibyls, who were scattered throughout all the earliest nations, we find mention of twelve; and popular tradition relates that they sang in heroic verse. The oracles of all nations likewise gave their responses in heroic verse, so that the Greeks called this metre Pythian after the famous oracle of Pythian Apollo. (This oracle took its name from the god's slaying of the serpent Python, which was the origin of the first spondaic verse, as we have seen.) In Latin, heroic verse was called Saturnian, as Festus informs us. This means that it originated in the age of Saturn, which corresponds to the Greeks' Golden Age, when Apollo and other gods mingled with men. And according to Festus, Ennius says it was in Saturnian verse that the fauns of Italy delivered their prophecies or oracles, just as the Greek oracles spoke in hexameters. Later, the term Saturnian metre was used for the iambic trimeter, or *senarius*, perhaps because poets then spoke in Saturnian iambics as naturally as their ancestors had in Saturnian hexameters.

[465] Although contemporary scholars of biblical Hebrew disagree whether the poetry of the Jews is metrical or merely rhythmical, Josephus, Philo, Origen, and Eusebius clearly favour metre. Even more important for my argument, St Jerome maintains that chapters 3–42 of the Book of Job, which is even older than the books of Moses, were composed in heroic verse.

[466] The author [Thomas Baker] of *The Uncertainty of the Sciences* relates that, until the time when the Arabs overran the eastern provinces of the Byzantine empire, they had no form of writing and hence preserved their language by memorizing poems.

[467] The Egyptians inscribed verse memorials of their dead in burial shafts called *syrinxes*, from *sir*, meaning song, which is also the source of the name Siren, a goddess principally renowned for her song. And Ovid mentions a nymph named Syrinx, who was equally renowned for her song and her beauty. By the same etymology, we must conclude that the Syrians and Assyrians initially spoke in verse.

[468] The founders of Greek civilization were clearly the theological poets, who were heroes who sang in heroic verse.

[469] We have seen that the first authors in the Latin language were the Salii, who were sacred poets. Extant fragments of their Saliar verses, which resemble heroic hexameters, are the most ancient specimens of the Latin language. When the ancient Romans celebrated a triumph, they recorded their victories in what sound like heroic hexameters. For example, Lucius Aemilius Regillus is celebrated for 'Concluding the great combat and subjugating kings', *Duello magno dirimendo, regibus subiugandis*. Similarly, Acilius Glabrio 'Routs, disperses, and destroys mighty legions', *Fundit, fugat, prosternit maximas legiones*. And there are verses about other victors as well. If we examine closely the fragments of the Law of the Twelve Tables, we find that most of its articles end in the Adonic metre, which forms the last feet of heroic hexameters. Cicero clearly imitated this rhythm when he framed his ideal laws, which begin with the metrical phrases *Deos caste adeunto, pietatem adhibento*: 'Let all approach the gods chastely; let them show piety.' This explains the Roman custom, described by Cicero, that children learned the Twelve Tables by singing them as essential poetry, *tanquam necessarium carmen*. (Aelian relates that children in Crete did the same.)

We have seen that, like Gorgias among the Greeks, Cicero was famous for inventing Latin prose rhythm. Even when he writes on the grave subject of law, his prose avoids not only solemn poetic metres, but even iambics, which closely resemble prose and which he shuns even in his *Letters to Friends*. Hence, Cicero's use of verse in *On Laws* must confirm the truth of the following four popular traditions concerning laws. (1) Plato tells us that the laws of the Egyptians were poems of the goddess Isis. (2) Plutarch relates that Lycurgus gave laws to the Spartans in verse, including one prohibiting them from learning to read and write. (3) Maximus of Tyre tells us that Jupiter gave laws to Minos in verse. (4) Suidas informs us that Draco laid down his laws to the Athenians in verse, although another popular tradition relates that he wrote them in blood.

[470] From ancient laws, let us return to history. In describing the customs of the ancient Germans, Tacitus relates that they preserved the origins of their history in verse. And Lipsius in his notes on this passage says the same about the American Indians. Now, the Germans were unknown to other peoples and only known to the Romans quite late, and the Indians were only discovered by Europeans two centuries ago. So the example of these two nations gives us good reason to infer the same for all the other barbarous nations, both ancient and modern. As for the ancient Persians and the modern Chinese, there is no need for conjecture, for authorities tell us that they wrote their earliest histories in verse. This leads us to an important observation. If both the laws by which the nations were founded, and their first institutions were everywhere recorded in verse, we can conclude only that all the earliest peoples were poetic.

[471] Let us return to our topic, the origins of verse. Festus informs us that, even before Ennius, Naevius recounted the Punic Wars in heroic verse. And Livius Andronicus, the earliest Latin writer, wrote a heroic poem called the *Epic of Rome*, which contains the annals of the ancient Romans. Similarly, in the medieval return of barbarism, the Latin historians were heroic poets, like Gunther, William of Apulia, and others. We have seen that the first writers in the new European vernaculars wrote verses; and that in Silesia, a province inhabited almost exclusively by peasants, most of the people are born poets. Indeed, if Greek compound words, especially poetic ones, can be felicitously translated into German, the reason is that the German language preserves its heroic origins quite intact. Adam Rechenberg observed this fact without understanding its cause. And Matthias Bernegger compiled a catalogue of such compounds, which Georg Christoph Peisker studiously expanded in his *Parallels between the Greek and German Languages*. Early Latin likewise offers many examples of such compounds which later poets continued to use as the privilege of their art. All early languages clearly shared the property of forming nouns first, and only later verbs, as we have seen; hence, they made up for their lack of

verbs by forming compound nouns. These principles underlie Daniel Georg Morhof's *Introduction to German Language and Poetry*, and confirm my Axiom 18, which says that scholars of the German language will make marvellous discoveries if they trace its origins by my New Science.

[472] From this discussion, it seems clear that we have refuted the common error of grammarians, who say that speech in prose preceded speech in verse. For by discovering the origins of poetry, we have found the origins of languages and letters.

CHAPTER 6

Further Corollaries

I

[473] The birth of symbols and languages was accompanied by the birth of *law*, which the Romans called *ius* and the Greeks *diaïon*. (The latter was later pronounced *dikaion* for the sake of euphony, according to Plato's *Cratylus*.) In Greek, *diaïon* was derived from *Dios*, the genitive of Zeus, and meant 'heavenly'. And from it were derived the Latin phrases *sub dio* and *sub Iove*, meaning 'under the open heavens'. This is because pagan nations everywhere observed the heavens as an aspect of Jupiter, and sought to frame their laws by the auspices, which they believed were his divine warnings or commands. This etymology thus proves that all the nations were founded on their belief in divine providence.

[474] Let us review the Jupiters of various nations. (1) For the Chaldaeans, Jupiter was the heavens, for they thought he presaged the future in the aspects and movements of the stars. They had two sciences concerning the stars: astronomy, which dealt with the laws of their motion; and astrology, which dealt with their language, in the restricted sense of judicial astrology. (This is why Chaldaean came to be the term for a judicial astrologer in Roman law.)

[475] (2) For the Persians, Jupiter was likewise the heavens, which

they thought held occult meanings hidden from mankind. Sages in this science were called magi, and their science was called magic. There were two kinds of magic: the licit 'white magic' of nature's marvellous occult powers, and the forbidden 'black magic' of supernatural powers, whose magi were considered sorcerers. The magi used a wand, like the lituus of Roman augurs, to describe astronomical circles; and the sorcerers later adopted both the wand and the circle in their spells. To the Persians, the heavens were Jupiter's temple: it was this religious scruple which moved Cyrus, king of the Persians, to destroy the temples built by the Greeks.

[476] (3) For the Egyptians as well, Jupiter was the heavens, which they thought influenced sublunar affairs and presaged the future. Hence they believed they could harness the influence of the heavens by casting statues of their gods at prescribed times. Even today, the Egyptians, or gypsies, practise a popular form of divination.

[477] (4) For the Greeks also, Jupiter was the heavens, in which they pondered their *theōrēmata* and *mathēmata*, divine and sublime things, which they contemplated with the 'eyes of the body', and which they observed, or carried out, as Jupiter's laws. In Roman law, judicial astrologers were also called mathematicians, after these *mathēmata*.

[478] (5) As for the Romans, we have seen Ennius' famous verse, 'Look at this which falls from above, which all invoke as Jupiter', *Aspice hoc sublime cadens, quem omnes invocant Iovem*, in which *hoc* means heaven, *coelum*. The Romans called precincts of heaven *templa coeli*, those heavenly regions marked out by the augurs for taking auspices. Later, *templum* came to mean any space that is open on all sides and has an unobstructed view; which gave rise to the adverb *extemplo*, meaning straightaway. And Virgil strikes an archaic note when he calls the sea the precincts of Neptune, *Neptunia templa*.

[479] (6) As for the ancient Germans, Tacitus relates that they worshipped their gods in holy places which he calls sacred groves and woods, *luci et nemora*, meaning areas cleared in the thick of the forest. Later, the Church had great trouble in getting them to abandon this custom, as we gather from the Councils of Arles and Braga in Burchard's collection of *Decrees*. Even today traces of such worship survive in Lapland and Livonia.

[480] (7) As for the Peruvian Indians, explorers have found that they simply call their god 'the Sublime'. Their temples are open-air mounds, which they ascend by steep stairways on two sides. They consider the great height of these mounds to form all their magnificence, just as the magnificence of temples everywhere is measured by their extraordinary height. As proof of this point, we may cite Pausanias, who says that the gable of a Greek temple was called an *aetos*, which means eagle. (Presumably, the Greeks cleared the forests to open a view for observing the auspices of eagles, which fly higher than all other birds.) This may explain the Latin phrase 'temple pinnacles', *pinnae templorum*, and by analogy the phrase *pinnae murorum*, wings of walls, meaning parapets. For the walls of the first cities rose along the boundary lines of the world's first temples, as we shall see. Finally, we may note that in architecture *aquilae*, eagles or gables, came to mean battlements, which we now call 'merlons', or blackbirds.

[481] (8) By contrast, the Jews worshipped the true God, the Most High who is above the heavens, within the enclosure of their tabernacle, not in a wooded precinct. And wherever the people of God extended their conquests over others, Moses commanded them to 'burn their groves, *lucos*, with fire', meaning those enclosing the sacred clearings, *luci*, described by Tacitus.

[482] From this survey of nations, we gather that the first laws everywhere were the divine laws of Jupiter, god of the heavens. This ancient origin must account for the use of 'heaven' for 'God' in the language of many Christian nations. Thus, when we Italians say 'may heaven grant', *voglia il cielo*, and 'I hope to heaven', *spero al cielo*, we actually mean God; and the Spanish express themselves in the same way. In French, *bleu* means blue, and as a physical phenomenon implies 'heaven'. So, just as the pagan nations said 'heaven' for 'Jupiter', the French uttered the impious oath *morbleu* for 'God's death' and still say *parbleu* for 'by God'. This is a sample of the conceptual dictionary outlined in Axiom 22.

2

[483] To a great extent, the invention of characters and names was the result of the need for certainty of ownership. (As we have seen, 'names' retains its original Latin sense of extended clans of families; and these clans were properly called *gentes*.) Hermes Trismegistus was the poetic archetype of the first founders of the Egyptians, and the inventor of both their laws and letters. As Mercury, he was also considered the god of mercantile trade. From his name, the Italians derive the verb *mercare*, to mark, which means to countersign a letter and to brand cattle or other *merchandise* in order to certify ownership. The persistence even today of this uniformity between thought and expression is truly amazing.

3

[484] Such were the origins of family coats of arms, and hence of medals and coins. From these emblems, which were devised first for private and later for public needs, came the learned emblems devised as a pastime. Scholars intuitively called these emblems heroic, but in fact they require mottoes to make their analogies come alive; whereas the natural emblems were heroic precisely because they lacked mottoes and thus spoke mutely. Hence, these were in their own right the best emblems because they contained their own meanings. For example, three ears of grain, or three strokes of a scythe, naturally meant three years. This is why the terms 'names' and 'characters' became interchangeable, and 'name' and 'nature' became synonymous.

[485] Let us go back now to family emblems. During the medieval return of barbarism, the nations again fell mute, unable to write their vernacular speech. We have no early record of the language of the Italians, French, Spanish, or the other nations. Latin and Greek, in turn, were learned only by the clergy. This is why French *clerc*, cleric, meant a literate person; and Italian *laico*, layman, meant an illiterate, as is clear from a valuable passage in Dante. Among the priests, such great ignorance prevailed that we find documents signed with a cross by bishops who couldn't write their own names. Even learned prelates

were scarcely able to write, as we see from Father Jean Mabillon's *Study of Official Documents*. In this work, the indefatigable author presents engraved facsimiles to show how bishops and archibishops signed the conciliar acts of those barbarous ages – signatures written in letters more ugly and misshapen than those of the most ignorant simpletons today. Many such prelates were also chancellors of the European courts. Indeed, the Holy Roman Empire had three chancellor archbishops, one each for German, French, and Italian. The irregular forms of their letters later became known as chancery script. Because literacy was so scarce, the English passed a law which said that, if he knew how to write, a criminal under sentence of death would be spared as distinguished by his learning. This may explain why the Italian adjective 'literate', *letterato*, later came to mean erudite.

[486] Because writing was so rare, we do not find a single wall in medieval houses without an emblem, *impresa*, inscribed on it. We find a related term in medieval Latin, in which *terrae presa*, taking of land, meant a farm and its boundaries. In Italian, a farm is called a *podere*, power, which connotes the same forceful seizure as Latin *praedium*, farm, which reflects the fact that the world's earliest booty, *praeda*, consisted of lands placed under cultivation. By the same token, in the Law of the Twelve Tables estates are called *mancipia*, holdings; persons under real-estate bond, especially to the public treasury, are called *praedes*, guarantors, or *mancipes*, tenants; and what we call 'real' servitudes are *iura praediorum*, rights of the farms.

Among the modern languages, Spanish *prenda*, estate, can also mean a bold enterprise, just as the Italian *impresa forte* means a heroic emblem. For the world's first bold enterprises were the taming and cultivation of the land, which proves to be the greatest of all Hercules' labours. In Italian, an emblem used to be called an ensign, *insegna*, which implies the notion of signifying, as in the verb *insegnare*, to teach. Today, an emblem is still called *divisa*, device, because they were invented as signs to mark the first 'division' of the fields, which had previously been used in common by all humankind. The *real* terminations, or physical boundaries, of these fields later became what Scholastic logicians call *verbal* terms, which are the significant words known as the 'extreme terms' of a proposition. The American Indians use their totemic hieroglyphs as such 'real terms' in order to distinguish their families.

[487] To conclude, in an age when nations were mute, the certification of ownership made necessary the private ensigns, or coats of arms, that could signify it. In peacetime, these became public ensigns, from which medals were struck. Later, as wars arose, these emblems were adopted as military insignia, for wars are generally fought by nations who speak distinct languages and are therefore 'mute' in relation to each other. We find a marvellous confirmation of this in the symbol of the eagle on a sceptre. By a uniformity of ideas, this device was used by the Egyptians, Etruscans, and Romans, and later by the English, whose royal arms it still graces. The presence of this uniform symbol in so many nations separated by vast expanses of land and sea signifies that all these realms originated in the first divine kingdoms sanctioned by Jupiter's auspices.

Eventually, with the introduction of trade using money, medals lent themselves to use as coins, which in Latin were called *monetae* from *monere*, to remind – a parallel to Italian *insegnare*, to teach, from *insegna*, ensign. In this way, from Greek *nomos*, law, was derived *nomisma*, coin, as Aristotle notes; and perhaps also Latin *nummus*, coin, which in fact the best scholars write as *numus*. In French, law is called *loi*, and a coin *aloi*. All these terms must derive from the law or right which is the proper use of medals and which was represented by a hieroglyph on coins. The names of Italian coins offer marvellous confirmation of this origin. The ducat comes from *ducere*, to command, which is the duty of a captain; *soldo* gives us the word soldier, *soldato*; and *scudo* means shield, the defensive weapon which formerly represented the ground of family arms. (This meant the land cultivated by a father in the age of families.) This sheds new light on ancient medals. For many of them depict an altar; a *lituus*, which was the augur's wand for taking the auspices; or a tripod, from which an oracle prophesied, whence the Latin phrase *dictum ex tripode*, meaning an oracular utterance.

[488] Such medals must have featured wings. In Greek myths, we find wings associated with objects symbolizing the heroes' rights based on the auspices. Thus, we have seen that Idanthyrsus included a bird among the concrete symbols which he sent as his reply to Darius. And in their heroic contentions with the plebeians, the Roman patricians

sought to defend their heroic rights by claiming that the auspices belonged to them, *auspicia esse sua*, as Roman history explicitly tells us. In precisely this sense, we find that noble coats of arms during the medieval return of barbarism are surmounted by plumed helmets. And in the West Indies only the nobles may adorn themselves with feathers.

4

[489] The Latin name of Jupiter was *Ious*. Contracted to *ius*, it must have meant the fat of the victims sacrificed as his due. We find a similar combination of ideal and real in the medieval return of barbarism, when the term canon meant both an ecclesiastical law and the payment which a fief holder made directly to his lord. (For the first fiefs may have been instituted by ecclesiastics who could not themselves cultivate the Church's fields, and therefore leased them to others.) These two examples tally with the terms for law and coin cited above in Greek, *nomos* and *nomisma*, and in French, *loi* and *aloi*. In precisely the same way, the Latin phrase *Ious optimus* meant strongest Jupiter. For it was the strength of his thunderbolt that established divine authority in its earliest sense, which was that of ownership, so that all things literally belonged to Jupiter.

[490] This is why the poets said that 'All things are full of Jupiter', *Iovis omnia plena*. Although this was misinterpreted as a statement of poetic metaphysics, it was in fact a truth of rational metaphysics, which conferred human authority (in the sense of domain or ownership) on the giants who had occupied the world's first vacant lands. In Roman law, such domain or ownership was called *ius optimum*, supreme right. Cicero gives us the original meaning of this phrase, which is quite different from its later interpretations. In a golden passage in an oration, he defines *ius optimum* as 'ownership of real estate subject to no private or public encumbrance'. This right, *ius*, was called the strongest, *optimum*, because it was not weakened by any outside encumbrance, and because right was measured by power in the world's early ages. Such ownership must have belonged to the fathers in the family state, and thus was the natural ownership which preceded civil ownership. Later, when cities were formed by uniting families on the basis of this supreme ownership,

they were called aristocracies, because this 'best' ownership is called *dikaion ariston* in Greek. Among the Romans, the commonwealth of optimates, or 'best men', had the same origin. It was also called the commonwealth of the few, since it was formed of those 'few whom just Jupiter loved,' *pauci quos aequus amavit Iupiter*.

[In their heroic contentions with the plebeians, the heroes maintained their rights by controlling the divine auspices. In the mute language of symbols, these heroic rights were represented by the bird of Idanthyrsus, and by the wings in Greek myths. In articulate language, they were later expressed by the Roman patricians who claimed that the auspices belonged to them, *auspicia esse sua*.]★

[491] Now, with his lightning bolts, which were the source of the greater auspices, Jupiter had laid low the giants, driving them underground to live in mountain caves. By laying them low, he brought them good fortune: for they became the lords of the ground in which they dwelt hidden, and so emerged as the lords of the first common-wealths. And because of this land ownership, any giant proposing a law said he was the ground, *fundus*, rather than the author, *auctor*, of the measure – a usage preserved in heroic Latin. As we shall see, the giants' private and familial authorities were later united, and grew into the public and civil authority of their heroic ruling senates.

On medals and coins, these senates were represented by three human legs whose thighs meet in the middle and whose feet rest on the outer rim. This symbol is quite common on the Greek coins reproduced by Hubert Goltz, and signifies the ownership of the ground in each region, territory, or district of a commonwealth. (Such owner-ship, now called eminent domain, is represented by the symbol of an apple supported by crowns representing the civil powers, as we shall see.) The three-legged symbol derives its full power from the num-ber three. For the Greeks used to create superlatives by adding the prefix *tris*, thrice, just as the French today use *très* to mean 'very'. By the same manner of speaking, Jupiter's thunderbolt was called *thrice-furrowed*, *trisulcus*, because of its great power in furrowing the air. (The notion of furrowing may first have applied to air, then to earth, and

---

★ The bracketed material repeats paragraph 488 and seems out of place here.

finally to water.) In the same way, Neptune's *three-pronged* spear or *trident* was named after a powerful hook designed to grip or grapple ships; and Cerberus was called *triple-throated*, *trifaux*, because of his huge gullet.

[492] This account of the origins of family coats of arms will serve as an introduction to my discussion of the topic in the first edition of my *New Science*, which is the third of the three passages in that work which I do not regret having published.

5

[493] We may now see that the three princes of the law of nations – Grotius, Selden, and Pufendorf – should have founded their doctrine on three things: the letters and laws which Hermes Trismegistus invented for the Egyptians, the symbols and names of the ancient Greeks, and the names of the Romans which signify both their clans and laws. They should have offered an intelligent account of their doctrine based on the early symbols and myths, which are emblematic medals of the age when the pagan nations were founded. And they should have traced the customs of the pagan founders by applying a metaphysical criticism. (This would in turn shed light on our philological criticism, which has dealt only with writers who lived more than a thousand years after the founding of the nations.)

CHAPTER 7

Final Corollaries on Logic in Educated People

I

[494] The notion of poetic logic has aided us in tracing the origins of language and in doing justice to their first authors, whom later ages considered sages because they had assigned natural and proper names to things. Accordingly, we have seen that the words name and nature were synonymous in Greek and Latin.

2

[495] The first founders of civilization strove to devise an art of *sensory topics*. This allowed them to combine what might be termed the concrete properties, qualities, and relations of individual objects and their species. These combinations in turn created their poetic *genres*.

3

[496] We may truly say that in the world's first age people employed the primary function of the human mind.

4

[497] First of all, these people created a crude form of topics. For this art regulates our mind's primary function by showing us all the commonplaces which we must review in order to know a subject well and completely.

5

[498] Providence directed human affairs wisely by causing the human mind to conceive the art of topics before that of criticism, for we must be familiar with things before we can judge them. Topics makes the mind more inventive, just as criticism makes it more exact. In that early age, the institutions necessary to human life had to be invented, and invention is the proper task of ingenuity. In fact, on closer consideration, we find that, even before philosophers existed, the Greeks had invented not only the things necessary to life, but also many useful, comfortable, and pleasant things, including non-essential luxuries, as we shall see later in discussing Homer's age. As Axiom 52 states: 'Children excel in imitation; poetry is simply imitation; and the arts are simply imitations of nature and are, in a certain sense, concrete poetry.' In other words, the first peoples were the children of the human race, and founded the world of the arts. Coming much later, the philosophers were the old

men of the nations and founded the world of the sciences, by which civilization was completed.

6

[499] This historical development of human ideas finds wonderful confirmation in the history of philosophy. When men first began to philosophize crudely, they used the evidence of their senses, which the Greeks call *autopsía*, seeing for oneself. (Later, this was used by Epicurus who, being a philosopher of the senses, was content to base his judgments on sensory evidence.) Indeed, my 'Origins of Poetry' has shown that the first poetic nations possessed the most vigorous senses. Next came Aesop, symbol of the so-called popular moralists, who preceded the Seven Sages of Greece. Aesop reasoned by example; and since he lived in an age of poetry, he created his examples by inventing similes. (One of these, the fable of the belly and the limbs, was used by the worthy Menenius Agrippa to reduce the rebellious Roman plebeians to obedience.) Even today an example of this sort, especially a true one, convinces the ignorant masses more effectively than the irrefutable logic of maxims.

Then came Socrates, who introduced dialectic, which resolves doubtful questions by induction from what is more certain. Even before Socrates, medicine had used induction from observations. And it had produced Hippocrates, the prince of physicians both for his achievements and for his antiquity, who earned the immortal eulogy 'He neither deceives anyone, nor is deceived by anyone', *Nec fallit quenquam, nec falsus ab ullo est*. In Plato's day, as we learn from the *Timaeus*, the mathematics of the Italian school of Pythagoras had reached great heights by employing the unitive or so-called synthetic method. By virtue of this unitive method, Athens in the age of Socrates and Plato shone forth in all the arts for which human genius is admired – poetry, eloquence, and history, as well as music, statuary, painting, sculpture, and architecture. Then came Aristotle, who taught the syllogism, a method for deducing particulars from universals, rather than by uniting particulars to obtain universals. And Zeno, who taught the sorites, or cumulative syllogism, which, like the method of our modern philosophers, teaches us subtlety rather than acumen. These were their greatest contributions to human advancement. Hence the great philosopher and statesman Bacon justly proposes, recommends, and demonstrates the inductive method in his *Novum Organum*; and still enjoys a following among the English with great advances in experimental science.

7

[500] This historical progression of human ideas clearly demonstrates the common error of everyone who has laboured under the false notion of the wisdom of the ancients. Such scholars believed that Minos was the first lawgiver of the pagan nations, and that universal laws were established by Theseus at Athens, by Lycurgus at Sparta, and by Romulus and the other kings at Rome. In fact, we find that the most ancient laws were framed as *injunctions or prohibitions directed at an individual*, and only later were applied to others. For not only were the earliest people incapable of grasping universals; they could not conceive laws until events had made them necessary. In the prosecution of Horatius, for example, the 'law' of Tullus Hostilius was simply the penalty decreed against the renowned defendant by the duumvirs, the two officials appointed by the king for that purpose. Livy pronounces it a law with a fearful formula, *lex horrendi carminis*, which would make it one of the laws written in blood by Draco, or what scripture calls blood laws, *leges sanguinis*. But when Livy writes that the king refused to proclaim the law and thus to claim responsibility for a harsh and unpopular verdict, his interpretation becomes utterly ridiculous. For the king himself imposed the formula of condemnation on the duumvirs, so that they could not have acquitted Horatius even if he had been found innocent. Livy's account is quite unintelligible at this point. For he failed to see that, since heroic senates were aristocratic, the king's only power was to create duumvirs as commissioners to judge criminal trials; and that the 'people' in heroic cities was composed solely of nobles, to whom the condemned could appeal.

[501] To return to my point, the law of Tullus is in fact one of the so-called *exempla*, meaning exemplary punishments, which were the first examples employed by human reason. (This tallies with Aristotle's observation, cited in Axiom 85, that in heroic common-

wealths there were no laws concerning private wrongs or injuries.) In this manner, concrete examples preceded the rational examples used by logic and rhetoric. At length, when intelligible universals had been understood, the essential property of law, its universality, was recognized. Thus was established the celebrated maxim of jurisprudence that 'we must judge by laws, not examples', *legibus, non exemplis, est iudicandum.*

SECTION 3
POETIC MORALITY

CHAPTER I

Poetic Morality and the Origins of the Common Virtues Taught by Religion through the Institution of Matrimony

[502] It is through the idea of God that the rational metaphysics of the philosophers accomplishes its principal task of clarifying the human mind. For the human mind needs logic in order to form clear and distinct ideas which may reach the heart and cleanse it with morality. In just this way, the poetic metaphysics of the first giants, based on their idea of Jupiter and their sensory logic, created a poetic morality. In their atheism, these giants had warred with heaven. But when they beheld Jupiter's lightning bolts, terror subdued them, laying low not only their bodies, but also their minds, in which they imagined the frightful idea of Jupiter. (Being incapable of reasoning, the giants conceived this idea through their sense impressions which were formally true, but materially false: for this logic suited their natures.) And this frightful idea of Jupiter in turn inspired their piety, and thus planted in them a poetic morality. From this natural origin of human institutions arose the invariable property that minds must be laid low and humbled if they are to profit fully from the knowledge of God. By contrast, pride leads minds into atheism, so that atheists become giants in spirit, who in Horace's words declare 'In our folly we assail the very heavens', *Caelum ipsum petimus stultitia.*

[503] Plato clearly identified Homer's Polyphemus with such pious giants, an interpretation which we may confirm by citing the words which Homer himself assigns to this giant. Polyphemus tells his fellows that the misfortune he has suffered at Ulysses' hands was foretold by an augur who once lived among them; and clearly augurs cannot live among atheists. Thus, poetic morality originated in the piety which

divine providence ordained as the foundation of the nations. (Indeed, among all nations, piety is popularly called the mother of all the moral virtues – personal, domestic, and civil. And if philosophy is useful in discussing virtuous behaviour, religion alone is capable of inspiring it.) And piety originated in religion, which properly consists in the *fear of divinity*. The heroic origin of the word 'religion' was preserved among the Romans, according to the scholars who derive it from *religare*, to bind. For this verb refers to the chains which bound Tityus and Prometheus to mountain cliffs, where their heart and organs were devoured by an eagle, the symbol of the frightful religion of Jupiter's auspices. This was the source of that invariable property of all nations, that piety is instilled in children by their fear of some divinity.

[504] Moral virtue began, as it must, from a conscious *effort*. Chained under the mountains by their frightful religion of thunderbolts, the giants checked their bestial habit of wandering wild through the earth's great forest. Completely reversing their customs, they now settled down, hidden away in their lands (*fondi*), so that that they later became the founders (*fondatori*) of the nations and lords of the first common-wealths. According to popular tradition, this was the first great benefit which Heaven bestowed on humankind during the age when he reigned on earth through the religion of the auspices. And it was the source of Jupiter's title of Stator, stayer or settler. With this conscious effort, the virtue of the spirit began to grow, and kept them from satisfying their bestial lust in the sight of Heaven, which now inspired their mortal fear. Instead, each giant would drag a woman into his cave and keep her there as his lifelong mate. In this way, they practised human intercourse secretly in private, which is to say, with modesty and shame. Hence, they began to feel a sense of shame, which Socrates called virtue's outward aspect. After religion, shame is the second bond that keeps nations united, just as shamelessness and impiety cause their ruin.

[505] In this manner, marriage was introduced, which we may define as a *carnal union modestly consummated in fear of some divinity*. Marriage is the second principle basic to my New Science, and derives from the first principle, which is divine providence. From its origin, marriage involved three solemn rites.

[506] (1) The first marriage rite was the auspices of Jupiter, which

were taken from the lightning bolts which had led the giants to celebrate marriages. From this divinatory *lot*, called *sors* in Latin, the Romans defined marriage as *omnis vitae consortium*, a lifelong sharing of one's lot; and husband and wife were called consorts. Even today, Italian girls are commonly said to choose their lot, *prendere sorte*, when they marry. In this precise manner, we may trace to the world's first age that law of nations by which a wife adopts the public religion of her husband. For when husbands shared their first civilized ideas with their wives, they began with the idea of that divinity which had forced them to drag the women into their caves. Thus, even their crude metaphysics began by knowing the human mind through God. From this first origin of all human institutions, all pagan people must have begun to *praise*, *laudare*, the gods, in the ancient Roman legal sense of citing or calling by name. From this, they derived the phrase *laudare auctores*, which meant to cite the gods as the authors of all human deeds. These were the praises which people could rightly offer to the gods.

[507] This primitive origin of marriage established the custom that a woman enters the household and family of the man she marries. This natural custom of the nations was preserved by the Romans: in their families, wives held the same legal status as their husbands' daughters or as their sons' sisters. By virtue of this origin, marriage meant a union with one woman, a practice preserved by the Romans. (Tacitus admires the same custom in the ancient Germans, who like the Romans preserved their national origins, and whose example allows us to infer the same for all other nations.) And by virtue of its origin, marriage also meant a lifelong union, as in fact it remains among many peoples. Because of this property, the Roman jurists defined marriage as an inseparable companionship for life, *individua vitae consuetudo*; and divorce was only introduced quite late.

[508] The importance of the auspices taken from lightning has left traces in Greek myth. For example, Hercules, an archetype of the founders of nations, was born to Alcmena in a thunderclap. And another great Greek hero, Bacchus, was born when Semele was struck by lightning. This was the primary reason why heroes called themselves sons of Jupiter; indeed, they spoke with the truth of their senses because they were convinced that the gods determined everything. (In Roman

history, we read about this in the heroic contentions between the patricians and plebeians. When the patricians claimed that the auspices were theirs, the plebeians countered that the patricians' ancestors, whom Romulus had made senators, had not descended from heaven. If this reply is to make sense, it can only mean that the patricians were not heroes.)

To signify that only the nobles had the right of contracting solemn nuptials, or Roman *connubium*, which depended on the major solemnity of the auspices, they represented the god of love, Amor, as a winged noble with a blindfold signifying modesty. The Greek heroes called him Eros, using a name like their own title of *heros*, hero; and they also depicted the god of marriage, Hymen, with wings.

Hymen was the son of the muse Urania, who was so called because she contemplated the heavens, *ouranos*, in order to take the auspices. Urania, the first-born of the Muses, was defined by Homer as the knowledge of good and evil; and, like the other Muses, she was depicted with wings because she belonged to the heroes. Earlier, we saw the historical meaning of the poetic tag *A Iove principium Musae*, 'Jupiter the origin of the Muses'. We may now add that Urania and all the other Muses were believed to be Jupiter's daughters, since all the civilized arts sprang from religion. The presiding deity of these arts was Apollo, who was chiefly worshipped as the god of divination. When the Muses are said to sing, it is in the sense of the Latin verbs *canere* and *cantare*, which mean 'to foretell'.

[509] (2) The second solemn rite of marriage was the veil worn by brides. Symbolizing the origin of the first marriages in a sense of shame, this custom has been preserved in all nations. In Latin, weddings are called nuptials, *nuptiae*, which derives from *nubere*, to cover. In the medieval return of barbarism, unmarried *maidens* were called virgins *in capillo*, with unbound hair, in contrast to *married women*, who were veiled.

[510] (3) The third solemn rite of marriage was the ritual abduction of the bride by mock force, or *deductio*. Practised by the Romans, this ritual evoked the real violence with which the giants dragged the first wives into their caves. Originally applied to the lands physically occupied by the giants, the Latin term *manucaptae*, seized with the hands, was later extended to solemnly wedded wives.

[511] After Jupiter, the theological poets created Juno as the second divine archetype to represent solemn matrimony. The second deity of the so-called greater clans, Juno is both Jupiter's *sister* and *wife*, because the first *lawful or just* solemn marriages – so called for the solemn auspices of just Jupiter – were celebrated between brothers and sisters. Juno is also the *queen (regina) of gods and men*, because kingdoms (*regna*) sprang from such legitimate marriages. And statues and medals portray her *fully clothed* as a token of her modesty.

[512] (Heroic Venus was also regarded as a goddess of solemn marriages. Called *pronuba*, bridesmaid, she covered her private parts with her famed girdle, which lascivious poets later embroidered with all sorts of aphrodisiac charms. At that point, the severe historical truth of the auspices had been corrupted, and people believed that Venus lay with men, as Jupiter lay with women. Hence, Aeneas, who was conceived under Venus' auspices, was said to be Venus' son by Anchises. This Venus is accompanied by swans, which she shares with prophetic Apollo and which sing in the sense that the Latin verbs *canere* and *cantare* mean *divinari*, to foretell. When the myth relates that Jupiter took the form of a swan in mating with Leda, it means that Leda conceived the egg-born Castor, Pollux, and Helen under Jupiter's auspices.)

[513] Juno's Roman title *iugalis*, goddess of the yoke, alludes to the yoke of solemn matrimony, which in Latin was called *coniugium*, as a husband and wife were called *coniuges*, conjugal partners. She was also called Lucina, goddess of light, because she brings offspring into the light. But this refers not to the natural light of day, which is shared by the offspring of slaves, but rather to the 'civil light', for which nobles are said to be illustrious. The epithet *jealous* refers to Juno's political jealousy in guarding solemn matrimony. This jealousy explains why, until Rome's 309th year (445 B C), the patricians excluded the plebeians from nuptial rights. In Greece, Juno was called Hera, for whom the heroes must have been named. For they were born of solemn nuptials, of which Juno was the presiding deity; and they were conceived by *noble Love*, the similarly named Greek god Eros, who is the same as Hymen.

(The word 'hero' must also have meant the lord of a family, as opposed to the *famuli* or family servants, who were essentially slaves.

This was the sense of the Latin noun *herus*, master, from which was derived *hereditas*, inheritance, which originally was called *familia*, estate. This very origin shows that *hereditas* meant a despotic lordship, like the sovereign power of testamentary disposition which the Law of the Twelve Tables confers on the family father: 'As a family father disposes concerning his possessions and the guardianship of his estate, it shall be legally binding', *Uti paterfamilias super pecunia tutelave suae rei legassit, ita ius esto*. This disposing was generally called *legare*, to bind, which is proper to sovereigns; and thus an heir became a 'legatee', or person delegated through the inheritance to represent the deceased family father. (By contrast, both children and slaves alike were included under the terms 'estate', *res*, and 'possessions', *pecunia*.) All this is incontrovertible proof of the monarchical power which fathers exercised over their families in the state of nature. They must have retained this power in the state of heroic cities, as in fact we shall soon see. The heroic cities, in turn, must have begun as aristocracies, meaning commonwealths of lords: for even under the later democracies, the fathers still retained their power. All this will be discussed later.)

[514] The goddess Juno imposed great labours on the Theban or Greek Hercules. (As Axiom 43 states, every ancient pagan nation had as a founder its own Hercules.) In other words, marriage, with its origins in piety, is the school in which we learn the rudiments of all the great virtues. With the favour of Jupiter, under whose auspices he had been conceived, Hercules accomplished all twelve labours; and so was called Herakles, meaning *Hēras kleos*, Hera's glory. If we adopt Cicero's apt definition of glory as 'widespread fame for services to mankind', imagine how much glory is due to the Herculean figures who by their labours founded the various nations! Nevertheless, as time passed, the original sense of these severe myths was obscured, and human morals grew dissolute. People thought that Juno's sterility was a natural condition, and that her jealousy was provoked by the adulteries of Jupiter, whose bastard son was Hercules. Contrary to the meaning of his name, Hercules accomplished his labours with Jupiter's favour, and triumphed despite Juno. Rather than Hera's glory, he became her utter disgrace; and Juno was regarded as the sworn enemy of virtue.

In myth, Juno was depicted as hanging in the air with a rope around her neck, with her hands tied by another rope, and with two heavy stones tied to her feet. This symbol, which until now has greatly perplexed the mythologists, in fact represented the sanctity of marriage. She hangs *in the air* to signify the heavenly auspices required for solemn nuptials. (For this reason, Iris, goddess of the rainbow, became Juno's handmaiden; and the peacock with its rainbow tail was thought sacred to her.) The *rope around her neck* signifies the violent seizure of the first wives by the giants. The *rope binding her hands* betokens the subjection of wives to their husbands, which was later represented in all nations by the more civilized symbol of the wedding ring. The *heavy stones tied to her feet* denote the stability of marriage, which Virgil appropriately calls *coniugium stabile*. But later ages with their corrupt morals perverted the original meaning of the myth, and Juno's suspension was viewed as a cruel punishment devised by the adulterous Jupiter.

[515] For precisely such reasons, Plato interpreted the Greek myths just as Manetho had the Egyptian hieroglyphs. In the myths, he observed that the gods' customs were entirely inappropriate to their divinity, but quite appropriate to his own ideas. Take, for example, the poetic tag 'All things are full of Jupiter', *Iovis omnia plena*. Plato imposed on the mythical Jupiter his own idea of ether, which pervades and penetrates everything. But in fact the Jupiter of the theological poets was no higher than the mountain tops and the region of the atmosphere which generates lightning. And Plato imposed the idea of breathable air, *aer* in Greek, on the mythical Juno, since her Greek name is *Hera*. But in fact Juno has no offspring by Jupiter, whereas air and ether produce everything. By this poetic tag, the theological poets intended neither the truth of physics that ether fills the universe, nor that truth of metaphysics which demonstrates what natural theologians call God's omnipresence!

On the basis of poetic heroism, Plato constructed his philosophical heroism, which places the hero above both man and beast. For Plato, the beast is a slave to its passions; man, placed in the middle, struggles with his passions; but the hero commands his passions as he chooses. In this way, the heroic nature lies midway between human and divine nature. So Plato found that the poets had depicted two kinds of Love quite appropriately. Noble Love, whose name Eros is related to *herōs*, was represented with a blindfold and wings: for he was blind to things of the senses, and flew upwards to contemplate intelligible things. By contrast, plebeian Love, having no blindfold, was always intent on things of the senses; and lacking wings, constantly falls back on them.

In the severe interpretation of the early poets, Ganymede snatched up to heaven by Jupiter's eagle symbolized a *contemplator of Jupiter's auspices*. Later, corrupt ages made him Jupiter's abominable paramour. Quite appropriately, Plato regarded Ganymede as a *metaphysical contemplative* who, by contemplating the highest being in the so-called unitive way, achieves union with Jupiter.

[516] In this manner, piety and religion created the four cardinal virtues. (1) The first people became naturally *prudent* because they consulted Jupiter's auspices. (2) They became *just* both towards Jupiter, from whose name *Ious* justice is derived, and towards others, in whose affairs they did not meddle. (In speaking to Ulysses, this is how Polyphemus describes the giants scattered in their Sicilian caves; but this apparent justice was in fact mere savagery.) (3) They became *temperate* because they were content with one spouse for their entire lifetime. (4) And they became *courageous, industrious, and magnanimous*, all virtues of the Golden Age.

Now, the Golden Age was not an age in which pleasure was law, as dissolute poets later imagined it. In the true Golden Age of the theological poets, people were indifferent to the tastes created by sick imaginations, and only took pleasure in what was accepted and useful, as peasants do today. (The heroic origin of the Latin verb *iuvare*, to be useful, is preserved in the use of *iuvat* to mean 'it is pleasant'.) Nor was the Golden Age, as the philosophers imagined it, an age in which men read the eternal laws of justice in Jupiter's bosom. Rather, it was in the heavens that men first read the laws dictated by lightning bolts. In fine, the virtues of this primitive age resembled those praised by the Scythians, who would stick a knife in the ground and worship it as a god, and so justify their murders. In other words, they were virtues of the senses which combined religion and cruel savagery, qualities which today we find in witches, as Axiom 40 states.

[517] The primitive morality of the savage and superstitious pagans gave rise to the custom of sacrificing human victims to the gods.

Philo of Byblus relates that, whenever the ancient Phoenicians were threatened by some great disaster like war, famine, or plague, the kings sacrificed their own children to placate the anger of heaven. Quintus Curtius reports that such sacrifices of children were regularly offered to Saturn. And Justin records that the Carthaginians, who undoubtedly came from Phoenicia, continued this custom and practised it quite late in their history. This is confirmed by Ennius' celebrated verse, 'And the Phoenicians, used to sacrifice their small sons': *Et Poinei solitei sos sacrificare puellos*. In fact, after their defeat by Agathocles of Syracuse, the Carthaginians sacrificed 200 noble children to placate their gods. Agamemnon's votive sacrifice of his daughter Iphigeneia shows that the Greeks shared this impious piety with the Phoenicians and Carthaginians. This will surprise no one who considers the Cyclopean paternal power of the first fathers of the pagan world, which was practised by the Greeks, who were the most learned nation of antiquity, and by the Romans, who were the wisest. In both nations, fathers had the right to kill their new-born children, even in the later age of their advanced civilization.

Such considerations should certainly reduce the horror which, in this gentler age, we feel when we read that Brutus beheaded his two sons for plotting to restore Tarquinius as king of Rome, or that Manlius Torquatus, nicknamed the Imperious, beheaded his valiant son for fighting and winning a battle against his father's orders. Caesar reports that the Gauls too made such human sacrifices. And in his *Annals*, Tacitus relates that the Britons used the entrails of human victims to foretell the future according to the divine science of their Druid priests, whom the conceit of scholars has supposed so rich in esoteric wisdom. According to Suetonius in his *Life of Claudius*, this savage and monstrous religion was forbidden by Augustus to Romans living in Gaul, and later prohibited by Claudius among the Gauls themselves.

Scholars of Near Eastern languages maintain that the Phoenicians spread throughout the world their custom of burning a man alive, which was their sacrifice to Moloch – a god which Mornay, Van Driesche, and Selden identify with Saturn. Such was the civilization which the Phoenicians, who brought the Greeks their alphabet, taught to the early nations of the most barbarous pagans! It is said that Hercules purged Latium of another monstrous custom – the sacrifice of live victims thrown into the Tiber – by substituting victims made of straw. Tacitus relates that solemn sacrifices of human victims were made by the ancient Germans, who from time immemorial were so closed to foreigners that not even the all-powerful Romans could penetrate their society. And the Spanish found such sacrifices in America, which until two centuries ago was unknown to us. In his *History of New France*, Marc Lescarbot observes that barbarians there ate human flesh, presumably that of victims slain in rituals like those described in Oviedo's *History of the Indies*.

In short, in an age when the ancient Germans were seeing the gods on earth, and the American tribes were too, and when the most ancient Scythians abounded in the many golden virtues we have heard praised by various authors – in this age, I say, they all practised such inhuman humanity! Plautus calls all such sacrifices 'Saturn's victims', *Saturni hostiae*, because they date from the age of Saturn, which our writers regard as the *Golden Age of Latium*. What a gentle, benign, moderate, tolerant, and moral age it was!

[518] The only conclusion to draw from all this is the extreme vanity with which conceited scholars have previously affirmed the innocence of the Golden Age in the first pagan nations. In fact, it was their *fanatical superstition* which, by means of the powerful terror their imagined deity inspired, held in moral check the savage, proud, and ferocious men of the early pagan world. Reflecting on such superstition, Plutarch posed this question: which is the lesser evil for men, to worship the gods in such an impious manner, or not to believe in them at all? But his antithesis is unfair. For even the most brilliant nations arose from such primitive worship, while no nation in the world has ever been founded on atheism.

[519] Let these remarks suffice concerning the *divine morality* of the first peoples of the lost human race. I shall discuss their *heroic morality* later, in the appropriate place.

SECTION 4
POETIC ECONOMICS, OR
HOUSEHOLD MANAGEMENT

CHAPTER I
Household Management in Nuclear Families

[520] With their merely human senses, the heroes sensed two truths which constitute the whole science of household management. These truths are preserved in the two Latin verbs *educere*, to bring forth, and *educare*, to bring up. With supreme elegance, *educere* refers to the education of the mind, while *educare* refers to the education of the body. Later, by a learned metaphor, physicists transferred *educere* to the bringing forth of forms from matter. For heroic education had begun in a way to bring forth the form of the human soul, which had lain buried by matter in the giants' huge bodies. And it likewise began to bring forth the form of the human body in its just dimensions from the disproportionate bodies of the giants.

[521] Let us first consider the education of the mind. Axiom 72 showed us the threefold role played by heroic fathers in what is called the state of nature. (1) They were sages in the wisdom of the auspices, which was a popular wisdom. (2) By virtue of their wisdom, they were priests whose dignity made it their duty to offer sacrifices, both to procure the auspices and to interpret them correctly. (3) Finally, they were kings whose duty was to bring the laws from the gods to their families; that is, they were legislators in the proper sense of the word, which means bearers of laws. Later, the kings of the heroic cities were legislators as well, for they brought the laws of the governing senates to their people in the two kinds of heroic assemblies described by Homer, the *boulē* and *agora*. As we saw in my Notes on Chronology, the heroes framed their laws *orally* in the *boulē*, and then promulgated them *orally* in the *agora*: for letters had not yet been invented. At Rome,

the heroic kings had their laws brought from the governing senates to the people by the duumvirs, who had been created for this very purpose, and thus came to be living, speaking laws. (We have seen that Tullus Hostilius used the duumvirs to proclaim his law in the trial of Horatius. But since Livy did not understand this, we cannot understand his account of the trial.)

[522] Plato was seduced by this popular tradition about wise father-kings, as well as by his false belief in the incomparable wisdom of the ancients. This is why he vainly yearned for an age in which philosophers would rule or rulers philosophize. Now, it is clear that fathers were *monarchical family kings*, superior to everyone else in their families and subject to God alone, as Axiom 75 states. And they possessed an authority which was enforced by terrifying religion and sanctioned by brutal punishments, like that of the Cyclopes, whom Plato regards as the world's first family fathers. But since this popular tradition was later misunderstood, it gave rise to the serious misconception, later shared by political thinkers, that the world's first form of civil government was monarchy. And this in turn gave rise to those unjust principles of bad politics which say that civil governments were created either by *open violence* or by *deceit* which erupted into violence. But let us consider that early age, when proud and fierce people, having just abandoned their bestial wanderings, led a crudely simple life, eating nature's freely offered fruits, drinking water from springs, and sleeping in caves. In the natural equality of this state, all the fathers were sovereign in their own families, which makes it inconceivable that one father could, by fraud or violence, have subjected the others to a monarchical state, as we shall see.

[523] At this point, we may contemplate the long time which must have passed before the pagan peoples, developing from a state of bestial native freedom through a long period of Cyclopean family discipline, were civilized enough to obey naturally the laws of their emerging civil states. From this, we may deduce the invariable property that a commonwealth will be happier than Plato's ideal republic, if its fathers teach their children religious piety, and if its children admire their fathers as sages, revere them as priests, and fear them as kings. Such great divine force was necessary to reduce these grotesque and savage

giants to civilized behaviour! Since these early people could not express this force abstractly, they represented it concretely as a physical object, a cord. In Greek, this was called *chorda*, and in early Latin *fides*, whose primary and proper meaning is implied in the phrase *fides deorum*, the force or faith of the gods.

This chord was the earliest lyre or monochord; and by adding others, they fashioned the lyre of Orpheus. By playing this lyre, Orpheus sang the divine force of the auspices, and reduced the bestial Greeks to civilization. And Amphion too played the lyre as he raised the walls of Thebes with stones that moved at his song. Just such stones are found in the myth of Deucalion and Pyrrha, who found them at their feet and threw them over their shoulders, causing people to spring up. The couple stood in front of the temple of Themis to show their fear of divine justice, and veiled their heads as a symbol of marital modesty. The stones lying before their feet were the stupid people who had come before them; indeed, in Latin *lapis*, stone, means stupid. And by throwing these stones over their shoulders – that is, by introducing family order through household teaching – they changed them into people, as my Notes on Chronology explain.

[524] The second part of household teaching was the physical education of their human bodies. Through their frightful religion, their Cyclopean authority, and their sacred ablutions, the heroic fathers began to educe or bring forth the proper human proportions from their children's giant bodies, as we have seen. How admirably providence endowed this lost race with giant bodies before they learned householding! For in their bestial wandering, they needed a robust constitution to endure harsh climates and seasons. Their enormous strength helped them penetrate the world's great forest, which was densely overgrown as a result of the recent flood. As they fled from wild beasts and pursued timid women, these giants became isolated; and their search for pasture and water scattered them throughout the earth, so that eventually the whole world became inhabited. It was only after the giants had begun to settle in one place with their wives – first in caves, then in huts near perennial springs, and near fields which they cultivated for food – that they shrank to the proper stature of today's men, for the reasons explained earlier.

[525] At its very birth, they brought household management to its ideal form, in which fathers by their toil and industry acquire a patrimony that insures their children's easy, comfortable, and secure subsistence. The ideal patrimony guarantees the survival of the family and offers hope that nations will rise again, even if foreign trade, civil products, or the cities themselves should fail. And this patrimony should be located in a healthful climate near perennial water sources; should occupy a naturally strong site as a possible refuge when people despair of defending their cities in wartime; and should include fields large enough to sustain any poor peasants who, fleeing the ruined cities, may till them to support their lords.

In the words of Dio cited in Axiom 104, providence did not order the family state by decree, like a tyrant; but instead followed human customs, since she is the queen of human institutions. We find that the strong men chose lands on the mountain heights, where the air is breezy and salubrious. They chose lands in naturally strong sites, which became the world's first citadels, *arces* in Latin. (Later, military engineers systematically fortified them, which is why the Italian word for fortress, *rocca*, derives from the word for a steep, rugged mountain, *roccia*.) And they chose lands near perennial springs, which are most commonly found in the mountains.

Near such springs, birds of prey make their nests, and hunters set their nets. This may explain why the ancient Romans called any bird of prey *aquila*, eagle, from *aquilega*, water seeker. (The noun *aquilex* means a diviner or bearer of water.) Now, Roman history clearly tells us that the birds which Romulus used to take the auspices for his new city were vultures. But they came to be identified as eagles, which were the guardian symbols of the Roman armies. For the first people, being simple and uncouth, believed that eagles were the birds of Jupiter because they flew high in the heavens. And when they followed the eagles' flight, they discovered perennial springs. Hence, they venerated the eagles for revealing these springs, which were the second great benefit, after Jupiter's fearful lightning, which Heaven bestowed on them during his earthly reign. And so they regarded the auspices taken from eagle flights as the most august after those taken from lightning. These are the auspices, called major or public auspices by Messalla and

Corvinus, which the Roman patricians meant when, in their heroic contentions with the plebeians, they said that the auspices belonged to them.

All these institutions, ordained by providence as the foundation of pagan civilization, were interpreted by Plato as the ingenious provisions of the first city founders. Yet during the medieval return of barbarism, when cities everywhere were destroyed, it was in this same manner that the families were preserved from which the new European nations arose. The new Italian signories created in the medieval period were called *castella*, castles; and we find that the oldest cities and most capitals lie high in the mountains, whereas villages are scattered throughout the plains. This is why in Latin nobles were said to be 'born in a high or illustrious place', *summo loco, illustri loco nati*; and plebeians 'born in a low or obscure place', *imo loco, obscuro loco nati*. For the heroes inhabited the cities, and their servants the fields.

[526] Political thinkers had these perennial springs in mind when they wrote that the communal sharing of water was the occasion for the first families uniting. Hence, the Greeks called their first communities *phratríai*, clans, from *phrear*, well, or *phreatía*, cistern. In Latin, an early village was called *pagus*, and the Doric Greeks called a spring *paga*. For a spring gives water, the first of the two principal solemnities of marriage. The Romans celebrated marriages by water and fire, *aqua et igni*, because the first marriages were naturally contracted between men and women who shared common water and fire. This meant that they were of the same family, and that marriage originated with brothers and sisters, as we have seen.

The Romans called the god of this fire the household *lar*; and the *focus laris* (Italian *focolare*) was the hearthplace on which the family father sacrificed to the household gods. In Jacob Raewaerd's edition of the Law of the Twelve Tables, we find in the article on parricide that these household gods are called *deivei parentum*, gods of the fathers. Similar expressions are common in Holy Scripture: *Deus parentum nostrorum*, God of our fathers, and, more specifically, *Deus Abraham, Deus Isaac, Deus Iacob*, the God of Abraham, Isaac, and Jacob. Referring to such household worship, Cicero proposes a law which reads 'Let family rites be perpetually observed', *Sacra familiaria perpetua manento*. In Roman law, we often find a son defined as being *in sacris paternis*, within paternal rites. And since in the earliest times all rights were considered to be rites, as my New Science shows, paternal power was itself called *sacra patria*, the father's rites.

I should add that this custom was observed by the barbarians of the Middle Ages. In his *Genealogy of the Gods*, Boccaccio attests that every New Year each Florentine father would sit at the hearth, and would sprinkle incense and wine on a burning log. In Naples today, we find the same ritual observed on Christmas eve by families of the lower classes, in which the father must solemnly light such a log on the hearth. Indeed, in the present Kingdom of Naples, families are counted by the number of hearthfires.

When the first cities were founded, people adopted the universal custom of contracting marriages between couples from the same city. Later, when marriages were also contracted with outsiders, the rule remained that the couple must share a common religion.

[527] From fire, let us return to water. All the gods swore by the river Styx, which was the source of all springs. These 'gods' must be the nobles of the heroic cities, whose reign over the plebeian 'men' was based on the communal sharing of water. (Until 445 BC, Roman patricians excluded the plebeians from marriage solemnities of water and fire.) By the same token, the Bible often mentions Beersheba, whose name means the well of the oath, or the oath of the well. And the name of the Italian city of Pozzuoli preserves its great antiquity: in Latin, it was called Puteoli because it united many small wells, *putei*. Based on my conceptual dictionary, we may reasonably conjecture that the many cities with plural names scattered throughout the ancient nations took their name from such a cluster of wells – an idea which was *one in substance*, but was expressed differently in various articulated languages.

[528] At this point, people imagined the third major deity, which is *Diana*. She represents the primary human need for water, which the giants felt once they had settled on certain lands and united in marriage with certain women. The theological poets described the history of these institutions in two myths about Diana. In the first, Diana lies with the sleeping Endymion in complete silence and darkness, which signifies

the modest shame of matrimony. Diana's chaste behaviour manifests the chastity enjoined by Cicero's law *Caste deos adeunto*, 'Let all approach the gods chastely': sacred ablutions must precede a sacrifice.

The second myth describes the fearful religion of the water springs, which are invariably qualified by the epithet 'sacred'. In this myth, Actaeon sees Diana naked, a symbol of the living spring. Diana sprinkles him with water, which means that the goddess casts great terror over him. (In Latin, persons like Actaeon who were driven mad by their superstitious terror were called *lymphati*, which properly means sprinkled with *lympha*, pure water.) Actaeon is then changed into a stag, the most timid animal of all, and is torn to pieces by his own dogs, that is, by the remorse of his own conscience for violating religious taboo. This poetic history was preserved in the Latin noun *latices*, waters – derived from *latere*, to hide – which is invariably modified by the epithet *puri*, pure, and which means the water that gushes from a spring. These pure waters are symbolized by the Greek nymphs who were Diana's companions, for in Greek *nymphai* means the same as Latin *lymphae*. These water nymphs were named in an age when all things were perceived as animate, often human substances, as my Poetic Metaphysics shows.

[529] Later, the pious giants who settled in the mountains must have noticed the stench which arose from the corpses of their dead as they rotted on the ground nearby, and must have begun to bury their dead. For it is principally in the mountains that huge skulls and bones have been found and are still being found. By contrast, this evidence strongly suggests that the impious giants, who lived scattered through the plains and valleys, let their corpses rot unburied, so that their skulls and bones were swept into the sea by torrents or were dissolved by rains.

The pious giants imbued their tombs with such great religious awe, or fear of the divine, that the Latin expression *locus religiosus*, hallowed ground, came primarily to mean a cemetery. This was the origin of the universal belief in the immortality of human souls, which is the third principle on which my New Science is based. [The Latin word for civilization, *humanitas*, derives from the verb *humare*, to bury, which is why burial is the third principle of my New Science. The Athenians were the most humane and civilized of nations and hence, by Cicero's account, the first to bury their dead.]*

In Latin, these souls were called *Dii Manes*; while in the Law of the Twelve Tables, under the article on parricide, they are termed *deivei parentum*, the gods of our fathers. To mark each grave, the giants must have fixed a slab (Italian *ceppo*) in the ground above or next to each burial mound, or tumulus. In Latin, the noun *cippus*, tombstone, came to mean the grave, while in Italian *ceppo* also means the trunk of a genealogical tree. The first graves were only a mound of slightly raised earth. Tacitus relates that the ancient Germans, whose example allows us to infer the same for all primitive barbarians, took care not to burden their dead with too much earth, which explains the classical prayer for the dead *Sit tibi terra levis*, 'May the earth be light upon you!'

In Greek, the grave marker was called *phylax*, or guardian, because they believed in their simplicity that it would guard the grave. From it must derive the Greek noun *phylē*, tribe or clan. We find a related word in the rows (*fili*) in which the Romans placed their ancestors' statues throughout the house to display their genealogies, which were called *stemmata*, family trees. *Stemmata* must derive from *temen*, woven thread (*filo*), which is found in the noun *subtemen*, the weft or the thread 'carried under' when cloth is woven. Later, jurists called these genealogical strands *lineae*, lines, and today the term *stemmata* still means family arms.

It is highly probable that these first lands with their gravesites formed the first family shields. This shows us that the famous phrase of the Spartan mother, handing a shield to her son as he goes to war, 'Come back with this, or on it', *aut cum hoc, aut in hoc*, must mean 'Return with this, or on a bier.' Even today, a bier in Naples is called a shield, *scudo*. And since these early graves lay in the ground of the fields which had been previously cultivated, the shield or escutcheon in heraldry is defined as the 'ground of the field', or what was later called the ground of arms.

[530] Derived from these genealogical threads (*fili*) is the Latin noun *filius*, son, which meant noble, when distinguished by the father's surname or lineage. In precisely this way, we have seen that a Roman patrician is defined as someone 'who can cite his father by name'. And

* I have moved the bracketed material here from the end of 537.

we saw that Roman names corresponded to the patronymics which the early Greeks so often used. Homer calls his heroes the sons of the Achaeans, *filii Achivorum*, just as the nobles of the Jewish people are in the Bible called the sons of Israel, *filii Israel*. We must conclude that, since the tribes were at first made up of nobles, the first cities were composed of nobles alone.

[531] By the burial sites of their dead, the giants indicated their dominion over their lands; and under Roman law burying the dead in the proper place made it hallowed ground. The giants spoke truly when they uttered heroic sentences such as 'We are sons of this earth' or 'We were born of these oaks.' In Latin, a family head called himself *stirps*, stem, and *stipes*, stock, and his descendants were called *propagines*, offshoots or offspring. In Italian, such families are called lineages, *legnaggi*, as if from *legno*, wood.

The noblest houses in Europe, and nearly all the European sovereigns, take their surnames from their domains. In both Latin and Greek, the expression 'sons of the Earth' means nobles. In Latin, nobles were called *ingenui*, well-born, as if from *indegeniti*, indigenous, which was then shortened to *ingeniti*, inborn. Indigenous clearly meant the natives of a land, and *dii indigetes* its native gods, which meant the noblemen of the heroic cities: for they were called gods, and the Earth was their mother, as we have seen. From the beginning, the Latin adjectives *ingenuus* and *patricius* meant noble, since the first cities were composed of nobles alone. These *ingenui* must have been the same as the aborigines, so called because they had no origin, or because they were 'born of themselves', which is the precise meaning of the Greek *autochthones*. These aborigines were called giants, a term which properly means sons of Earth. This is why the ancient myths faithfully relate that Earth was the mother of the gods and the giants.

[532] I have repeated some of my previous observations here, because they reveal how Livy misattributes the phrase 'the sons of this earth'. For when he portrays Romulus and the Roman fathers as addressing the refugees in the refuge in the clearing, he has Romulus call them 'the sons of this earth'. By applying this title to the refugees, Livy makes Romulus utter a shameless lie, which would have been a heroic truth if he had applied it to these first founders of nations. For Romulus was

Alban royalty, and hence a noble son of Earth; and his patrician companions had a mother, the Earth, so unjust that she bore men only, forcing them to abduct the Sabine women as their wives. One can only conclude that, since early people thought in poetic archetypes, Romulus as the founder of Rome was invested with the properties of the founders of the first Latin cities, even though Rome was only one of many cities in Latium. Livy commits a related error when he defines the refuge as the 'ancient counsel of city founders'. For in the first city founders, who were simple folk, it was not counsel but nature which served the ends of providence.

[533] At this point, early people imagined the fourth deity of the so-called greater clans, *Apollo*, the god of civil light. By virtue of this light, heroes were called *kleitoi*, illustrious, in Greek, from *kleos*, glory. And in Latin, they were called *incluti*, celebrated, from *cluor*, splendour of arms. (For the heroes shone with that light into which Juno Lucina brought noble offspring.)

Apollo was also the leader of the Muses. The first Muse was Urania, whom Homer defines as the knowledge of good and evil, meaning divination, for which Apollo is the god of poetic wisdom, or divine science. After Urania, the second Muse imagined by early people was Clio, who narrates heroic history and the nobles' *cluor*. This history clearly began with the genealogies of the heroes, just as sacred scripture begins with the descendants of the patriarchs.

The first episode in this heroic history is Apollo's pursuit of Daphne. In the myth, Daphne is a nomadic maiden who wanders through the forests living an abominable life. Pursued, she implores the aid of the gods, whose auspices are required for solemn nuptials. They stop her wandering and change her into a laurel, a plant which, as an evergreen with clear and acknowledged offshoots, symbolizes the family's stock which is called *stipes* in Latin. (During the medieval return of barbarism, this terminology was revived. Genealogies were called family trees; founders were called stocks or stems; descendants, branches; and families, lineages, *legnaggi* as if from *legno*, wood.) In the original myth, Apollo was a pursuing deity, and Daphne a fleeing beast. But later, when the severe language of this history had been forgotten, the roles were reversed: Apollo became a libertine, and Daphne a goddess like Diana.

[534] Apollo is the brother of Diana, whose perennial springs encouraged the founding of the first nations high in the mountains. Hence, Apollo's seat is on Mt Parnassus, the dwelling of the Muses, who are the arts of civilization. And it is near the spring called Hippocrene, whose waters are drunk by the swans whose song is prophetic, as in the Latin verbs *canere* and *cantare*. It was under the auspices of swans that Leda conceived two eggs, from which were born Helen of Troy and the twins Castor and Pollux.

[535] Apollo and Diana are the children of Latona, whose name derives from *latere*, to hide, which was the original sense of *condere*, to found, in the phrases *condere gentes, condere regna, condere urbes*, to found peoples, kingdoms, or cities. Also derived from *latere* is the name of Latium. In myth, Latona bore Apollo and Diana near the waters of the perennial springs; and their birth changed men into frogs, which are born of the earth after summer rains. Hence, frogs symbolized the heroic giants: for the Earth is the mother of giants, and the name giants properly means the sons of Earth. This explains the frog that Idanthyrsus sent to Darius. And it explains the three frogs which appear on the royal arms of France, which some have taken for toads, and which were later changed to lilies. Since superlatives are expressed by the number three – which gave the French their adverb *très* – the three frogs signify one great frog, that is, a very great son of earth, and hence a very great lord.

[536] Both Apollo and Diana are hunters who uproot trees and use them as clubs, like the club of Hercules, to kill wild beasts. They hunt first of all to defend themselves and their families, since they may no longer seek refuge in flight like the lawless nomads. And they hunt to provide food for themselves and their families. Virgil describes his heroes feasting on such hunted game, and Tacitus relates that the ancient Germans and their wives went hunting for wild beasts.

[537] Apollo is also the divine founder of civilization and its arts, which are represented by the Muses. In Latin, these arts are called liberal, which means noble. One of these arts is riding. This is why Pegasus flies over Mt Parnassus on wings symbolizing the nobility. During the medieval return of barbarism, the Spanish called their nobles cavaliers, meaning horsemen, because they alone could afford to arm themselves and their horses.

[538] Finally, Apollo is always young, just as Daphne, changed to a laurel, is always alive and verdant: for he immortalizes great houses through their family names. Apollo wears his hair long as a sign of his nobility, a custom which is still observed by nobles in many nations. We read that the Persians and the American Indians punished their nobles by pulling out some of their hair. In Latin, Transalpine Gaul was called *Gallia comata*, long-haired, probably because it was founded by nobles. And we find that slaves in every nation have their heads shaved.

[539] After the heroes had settled in well-defined lands, their families began to grow in number, and the fruits freely offered by nature no longer sufficed to feed them. Yet they were afraid to seek more food beyond their boundaries, for these were marked off by the same chains of religious fear that had chained the giants beneath the mountains. But this same religion inspired them to burn away the forests so that they could view the open sky for taking the auspices. Thus they undertook the great and difficult labour of placing lands under cultivation and sowing them with grain. As they cleared land, they chanced to toast some grain amid the burning thorns and briars, and found that it was pleasant and nutritious. So, using a natural and necessary metaphor, they called the ears of grain 'golden apples', transferring the idea of apples, which are fruits of nature gathered in the summer, to ears of grain, which human industry also harvests in the summer.

[540] The archetypal Hercules was most illustrious for this labour, the greatest and most glorious of all, which was truly the glory of Hera, who had commanded him to nourish families. Early people used three apt and essential metaphors to imagine Hercules' labour in taming the earth. (1) They imagined the earth in the form of a great *dragon*. This dragon was completely covered with scales and thorns, which symbolized the earth's briars and thorns. He had wings, which symbolized the heroes' ownership of the earth. And he was always vigilant, that is, always dense with vegetation. This dragon guarded the golden apples in the orchards of the Hesperides, and was believed to have been born of water, because of the moisture of the universal flood. (2) Under a different aspect, they imagined the earth as the *hydra*, also born of water, *hydōr* in Greek. The hydra had several heads which grew back when cut off. And the hydra was three different colours, matching the

skin sloughed off as a snake grows: black for the scorched earth; green for its blossoming leaves; and gold for its ripening grain. (3) Finally, under the aspect of the earth's fierce resistance to cultivation, they imagined it as a *mighty beast*, the Nemean lion. Later, the name lion was given to this mighty beast, but many philologists interpret the Nemean lion as an enormous serpent. All three of these beasts spew forth fire, which represents the fire with which Hercules burned off the forest.

[541] These three different myths originated in three different parts of Greece, but they signify what is substantially the same thing. A myth from another part of Greece relates that the child Hercules kills serpents while still in his cradle, meaning the infancy of the heroic age. Another myth says that Bellerophon kills the monster called the Chimaera, which had the tail of a serpent, the body of a goat (symbolizing the shaggy and wooded earth), and the head of a lion spewing forth fire. In Thebes, it is Cadmus who kills the great serpent and sows its teeth. (Using an apt metaphor, they called serpent's teeth the hardwood blades which were used to till the earth before iron was discovered.) The mythical Cadmus himself becomes a serpent; the ancient Romans would have said he became a ground, *fundus factus est*.

We shall see that the serpents on Medusa's head and on Mercury's staff signified the dominion of lands. This is why land rent, which was also called the tithe of Hercules, was in Greek called *ōpheleia* from *ophis*, serpent. This meaning of serpents is found in Homer. When the soothsayer Calchas sees a serpent devour eight sparrows and their mother, he interprets this to mean that the land of Troy will fall under the Greeks' dominion in nine years. And in the midst of a battle with the Trojans, an eagle drops a serpent it has killed, which the Greeks, by Calchas' divinatory science, consider a good omen. This is why Proserpine, who is identical with Ceres, is depicted in sculpture as borne aloft in a chariot drawn by serpents; and why we so often find serpents on coins of the Greek republics.

[542] Here are some noteworthy contributions to my conceptual dictionary. In his poem *Syphilis*, Girolamo Fracastoro relates that the chiefs of the American Indians carry dried snakeskins as their sceptres. The Chinese charge their royal arms with a dragon, and they carry a

dragon as an emblem of their civil authority. This dragon is clearly identical with the Draco, or Dragon, who wrote the Athenian laws in blood. As we have seen, this Draco was one of the serpents of the Gorgon Medusa, whom Perseus nailed to his shield. Later, this shield became the shield of Minerva, goddess of the Athenians, and its gaze turned to stone the people who beheld it, which symbolizes the civil authority of Athens. In the book of Ezekiel, the Bible calls the king of Egypt 'the great dragon that lieth in the midst of his rivers'. This title corresponds precisely to the mythical dragons that were born in the water, and to the hydra, which takes its name from water. And the emperor of Japan created an order of knights who bear the dragon as their device.

In the medieval return of barbarism, history tells us that the house of the Visconti was summoned to the duchy of Milan by virtue of their great nobility. On their arms, the Visconti bear a dragon devouring a child, which corresponds precisely to the ancient Python, which devoured the men of Greece until it was slain by Apollo, the god of the nobility. This uniformity of heroic thought in ancient and medieval emblems is truly amazing. We find another example in the two winged dragons which are the guardians of the order of the Golden Fleece. They hold up a necklace made of flintstones, which kindles the fire they spew forth. But this symbol was not understood by Jean-Jacques Chiflet, who wrote the history of the order, and Silvestro da Pietrasanta declares its history obscure.

[543] In various regions of Greece, Hercules killed the serpents, lion, hydra and dragon. In another, Bellerophon slew the Chimaera. In still another, Bacchus tamed tigers, which must have been lands clothed in various colours like a tiger's pelt. (This is why the name tiger later passed to the animals of this mighty species.) By contrast, the myth that Bacchus tamed tigers with wine appeals to natural history, which made little sense to the heroic rustics who founded the nations. Nor did heroic myth relate that Bacchus went to Hyrcania and Africa to tame tigers. As we shall see in my Poetic Geography, the Greeks could not have known about Hyrcania, much less Africa, to say nothing of tigers in Hyrcanian forests or the African desert.

[544] The early peoples called ears of grain 'golden apples'. This was

in fact the world's first gold: for the metal gold was still unmined, and
no one knew how to refine it, much less burnish it. How could they
value gold and its use when people still drank water from springs? It
was only later that the metal was called gold, because its colour and
value resembled that of their staple grain. This is why Plautus has to
specify 'a treasury of gold', *thesaurum auri*, to distinguish a hoard of
metal from a granary. In the Bible, when Job is lamenting the great
luxuries he has lost, he mentions eating bread made of grain. Even
today, in the rural districts of our remote provinces, when people are
sick, they are fed bread from grain. (In the cities, we administer potions
of ground pearls to our patients.) Indeed, when we say a sick man is
eating bread from grain, we mean that he is nearly dead.

[545] Later, the same idea of value and scarcity must have been
extended to fine wool, which was called 'golden'. In Homer, for
example, Atreus complains that Thyestes stole his 'golden' sheep; and
the Argonauts steal the Golden Fleece from Pontus. This is why Homer
describes his kings and heroes with the invariable epithet *polymēlos*,
which we translate as 'rich in flocks'. By a uniformity of ideas, the
Romans called a patrimony *pecunia*, which Latin grammarians derive
from *pecus*, herd or flock. By Tacitus' account, the ancient Germans
considered their flocks and herds their 'most valuable, indeed their only
wealth': *solae et gratissimae opes sunt*. The ancient Romans must have
shared this custom, for the article on testaments in the Twelve Tables
attests the use of *pecunia* to mean patrimony. In Greek, the noun *mēlon*
means both apple (or pome) and sheep; and in Italian, the word for
apple is *mela*. (Perhaps because honey is regarded as a precious fruit, it
is called *meli* in Greek.)

[546] These ears of grain must thus have been the golden apples
which Hercules first brought back from Hesperia, or harvested there.
In one myth, the Gallic Hercules binds men's ears with chains of gold
that issue from his mouth. Later, we shall see that this symbolizes
humankind cultivating the fields.

Hercules became the tutelar deity of treasure troves, of which Dis
was the god. Dis is identified with Pluto, who abducts Proserpine,
identified with Ceres or grain, and carries her into the underworld.
Poets divide the underworld into three parts: (1) the banks of the river

Styx; (2) the burial place of the dead; and (3) the bottom of the furrows. From the god Dis (genitive, Ditis), the Latins called rich people *dites*. They were the nobles, who are called rich men, *ricos hombres*, in Spanish; and who were once called *benestanti*, well-off, in Italian. In Latin, the noun *ditio* meant what we now call the dominion of a state, for the true wealth of a state consists in its cultivated fields. By the same token, the Romans called the extent of such dominion *ager*, field, which is properly land that is worked with a plough, *aratro agitur*.

In Greek, the Nile was truly called Chrysorrhoes, streaming with gold: for by flooding Egypt's vast fields, its waters produce great and abundant harvests. The Pactolus, Ganges, Hydaspes, and Tagus were likewise called rivers of gold, because they fertilize the adjacent fields of grain. It was clearly by extending the metaphor of the golden apples that Virgil, a poet learned in heroic antiquities, invented the golden bough carried by Aeneas into the underworld, as we shall see.

In fact, gold in the heroic age was no more highly valued than iron. For example, when the ambassadors of king Cambyses presented many golden vessels to the Ethiopian king Etearchus, he said that he found them neither useful nor necessary, and refused them out of natural magnanimity. Tacitus relates precisely the same thing about the ancient Germans, who in his day were the kind of ancient heroes we are discussing. 'In their society,' he writes, 'you will see that the silver vessels, given as gifts to their envoys and chieftains, are held as cheap as those made of clay.' Hence, we read in Homer that the heroes' armouries indifferently mixed arms of iron or gold. For, like newly discovered America, the ancient world must have abounded in such metals, which were only later exhausted by human avarice.

[547] All this suggests an important corollary. The division of world history into the four ages of gold, silver, copper, and iron was invented by the poets in more recent times. For it was the poetic gold, or grain, which gave its name to the Greeks' Golden Age. As we have seen, the so-called innocence of this age was in fact the utter savagery of the Cyclopes, in whom Plato sees the first family fathers. As Polyphemus tells Ulysses in Homer's *Odyssey*, the Cyclopes lived apart and alone in their caves, with only their wives and children, and never meddled in the affairs of others.

[548] As confirmation of this theory, we may cite two customs, still in use today, which can only be explained in terms of these principles. The first involves the golden pome, or globe, which is handed to a king during his coronation ceremony, and which is clearly the same pome that surmounts the crown in royal coats of arms. Now, the pome handed to the king must originally have been one of the golden pomes of grain we are discussing as a symbol of the heroic ownership of lands. And this symbol was apparently introduced when the barbarians invaded the nations of the Roman Empire. (The priests of Egypt may have symbolized the same thing by having their god Kneph hold a pome in his mouth, but it is perhaps an egg.)

The second custom involves the gold coins which kings give their brides as part of the wedding solemnities. These coins must likewise derive from the poetic gold or grain we are discussing as a symbol of heroic nuptials. The ancient Romans celebrated such nuptials with a symbolic purchase and with an offering of spelt-cakes, *coemptione et farre*. And Homer describes how heroes purchased their wives with a wedding gift. When Jupiter changes himself into a shower of gold to couple with Danae locked in a tower, meaning a granary, he symbolizes the abundance of wedding solemnities. This Greek myth corresponds strikingly to the Hebrew phrase found in the psalms: 'and abundance in thy towers', *et abundantia in turribus tuis*. We find confirmation of this theory in the wedding ceremonies of the ancient Britons, in which the grooms gave flatbread cakes to their brides.

[549] As these human institutions emerged, three new deities of the greater clans arose in the Greek imagination, following a sequence of ideas matching the institutions they symbolized. First was *Vulcan*. Second was *Saturn*, who takes his name from Latin *sata*, sown crops. (The Roman age of Saturn corresponds to the Greek Golden Age.) Third was *Cybele*, or *Berecynthia*, who symbolizes cultivated land. This is why she is shown seated on a lion, which represents the forested earth placed under cultivation by the heroes.

Cybele is called the great mother of the gods, and also the mother of the giants. (As we have seen, the name giants properly meant sons of Earth, so that Cybele is mother of the 'gods', meaning the giants who claimed to be gods in the first cities.) Sacred to Cybele is the pine tree, which symbolizes the stability by which the nation founders established fixed settlements and founded the cities over which the goddess presides. The Romans called her Vesta, the goddess of divine rites: for the first lands ploughed, *arate*, were the world's first altars, *arae*, as we shall see in my Poetic Geography. Armed with fierce religious taboos, the goddess Vesta watched over fire and spelt, which was the grain of the primitive Romans. This is why the Romans celebrated marriages with water and fire, *aqua et igni*, and with spelt, *far*. (Nuptials consecrated with spelt-cakes were called *nuptiae confarreatae*, and were later restricted to priests. For the first families consisted entirely of priests, like the kingdoms of Buddhist monks found in the Far East.) Water, fire, and spelt were thus the principal elements used in the Romans' divine rites.

On these lands, Vesta sacrificed to Jupiter the impious people who were abominably sharing their women and property and who had violated the first altars, meaning the first fields of grain. These first sacrificial victims, *hostiae*, were the first victims of the pagan religions, whom Plautus calls Saturn's victims. They were called victims from Latin *victus*, vanquished, because they were isolated and weak; and the adjective *victus* later retained this sense of weakness. They were called *hostiae* because such impious folk were justly deemed the enemies, *hostes*, of the entire human race. Later, the Romans preserved the custom of sprinkling the brow and horns of their sacrificial victims with spelt.

After their goddess Vesta, the Romans named the Vestal virgins who watched over the eternal fire. If any mishap caused this fire to go out, they had to relight it using the sun's rays. For humankind's first fire was stolen from the sun by Prometheus and brought down to earth, where the Greeks used it to burn away forests and cultivate the land. Thus, Vesta became the goddess of the Romans' divine rites for two reasons: (1) because the first cult of the pagans was their cultivation of the land; and (2) because this cult raised field-altars, set fire to them, and on them sacrificed impious men, as we have seen.

[550] This is the manner in which the first boundaries of the fields were set and safeguarded. The jurist Hermogenianus describes this division in too ideal a fashion. He fancies that it was established by deliberate agreement, executed with complete justice, and observed in

perfect faith – this in an age when, without any public coercive power, laws had no civil authority! In fact, among people of utter savagery, we can only understand such division of lands as inspired by their fearful religion, which kept them settled within well-defined lands. Indeed, it was the bloody rites of this religion which consecrated the first city walls.

Historians say that the city founders traced the first walls using a plough. According to my theory of the origins of language, the plough's mouldboard must first have been called *urbs* (Latin for city), from which derives the early Latin adjective *urbum*, which means curved. The noun *orbis*, orb, may share this origin, in which case the expression *orbis terrae*, circle of earth, initially meant any enclosure of land bounded by a fence. The first fences were quite low, so that Remus could leap over the wall at Rome. For this, he was killed by Romulus; and Roman historians relate that this blood consecrated the first walls of Rome. The earliest fence must have been a hedge, *saeps* in Latin; and the Greek noun *sēps* means serpent, which is a heroic symbol of cultivated land. This must be the origin of the Latin phrase *munire viam*, to build a road, which is done by reinforcing the hedge bounding the fields: for the Latin word for walls is *moenia*, a variant of *munia*; and the verb *munire* kept the meaning 'to fortify'.

Hedges were planted with bloodwort or elder, Latin *sagmina*, plants which are still used and named in the same way. Later, *sagmina* came to mean the herbs which adorned altars. This name must derive from the blood, *sanguis*, of people who, like Remus, were killed for transgressing city boundaries. The sanctity of city walls likewise derives from blood, *sanguis*. And heralds enjoyed sanctity because they crowned themselves with these herbs, or *sagmina*. We know that ambassadors in early Rome did just this with herbs they picked on the Capitoline hill. Finally, this established the sanctity of the laws of war and peace, which were carried by heralds. This is why the term 'sanction' refers to any clause in a law which imposes penalties on transgressors.

The sanctity of the Roman heralds confirms the thesis of my New Science, which is that divine providence ordained the natural law of nations separately for each people, who recognized its universality only after they came into contact with other peoples. For if the other peoples of Latium regarded as inviolate the Roman heralds consecrated with ritual herbs, it must have been because they themselves, though ignorant of Roman ways, observed the same custom.

[551] It was thus by religion that the family fathers supported their heroic families, whose structure was likewise preserved by religion. Hence, it was invariably the custom for nobles to be religious, as Julius Caesar Scaliger observes in his *Poetics*. And when the nobility scorn their native religion, it is a clear indication that their nation is in decline.

CHAPTER 2

Extended Families of Family Servants as Essential to the Founding of Cities

[552] Both philologists and philosophers commonly supposed that families in what is called the state of nature included children only; but in fact they included the *household servants* or *famuli*, which is the principal reason why they were called families. On this flawed economics, they constructed a false politics, as my Science shows. By contrast, I address the topic of the family servants, *famuli*, which pertains to domestic economics, as an introduction to politics.*

[553] Eventually, the abominable sharing of property and women by the impious giants provoked continuous quarrels among them. As a result, Grotius' simpletons and Pufendorf's abandoned men took refuge from Hobbes' violent men, to borrow the language of the jurists. So they fled to the altars of the strong, just as we see that wild beasts, when driven by intense cold, take refuge in populated areas. The strong men, who were already united in a family society, now fiercely slew the violent men who had violated their lands, and took under their protection the wretches who had fled from them. As men 'born of Jupiter', that is, conceived under his auspices, the strong possessed natural heroism, but now it was the *heroism of virtue* which they principally displayed. In this kind of virtue, the Romans later surpassed all other

---

* I have advanced paragraph 552 from Chapter 1 to Chapter 2.

nations, practising the two aspects described by Virgil as 'sparing the humble and conquering the proud'.

[554] Here is a matter worthy of reflection. What caused these fierce and untamed people, living in a brutish state, to advance from their bestial liberty to human society? When the first, pious giants entered the first stage of society, which is marriage, it was the keen stimulus of bestial lust that urged them, and the powerful restraint of fearful religions that kept them within its bounds. Such was the origin of marriage, which was the world's first form of friendship. Thus, when Homer describes Jupiter and Juno engaging in intercourse, he says with heroic gravity that they 'celebrated their friendship'. In Greek, the word for friendship, *philía*, has the same root as the verb *phileo*, to love, from which is also derived Latin *filius*, son. In Ionic Greek, *philios* means friend, and a slight change of vowel formed the noun *phylē*, tribe. (We have seen that genealogical strands, *fili*, were called *stemmata* in Greek, and *lineae* in Roman law.) The nature of this human institution determined this invariable property: that marriage is the true natural form of friendship, and that spouses naturally share all three kinds of ultimate good, the honourable, the useful, and the pleasant. Husband and wife by nature share the same lot in all of life's prosperity and adversity. In precisely the way friends hold all things in common, the jurist Modestinus defines marriage as the lifelong sharing of one's lot.

[555] Next, the second, impious giants, being driven by utmost necessity, joined the second stage of 'society', which was so called because they became 'associates'. Here is another matter worthy of reflection. The first giants advanced to human society, moved by religion, which is a *pious* motive, and by a natural instinct for procreation, which is properly a *gentle* or noble motive, thus laying the basis for noble and lordly friendship. By contrast, the second giants acted from the need to save their lives, and created what is properly termed an 'association', which by serving one's self-interest takes the form of a base and servile friendship. The refugees were thus received by the heroes under the just law of protection, which obliged them to serve the heroes as journeymen in order to stay alive.

The refugees were called *famuli* after two kinds of fame: (1) the fame that the heroes chiefly acquired through the heroic virtue of sparing the humble and conquering the proud; and (2) the worldly renown which is called *kleos* and *phēmē* in Greek, and *fama* in Latin. And the extended families now took their name from these *famuli*. We find a clear allusion to this fame in the Bible, which describes the giants who lived before the flood as famous men, *viri famosi*. And Virgil describes the goddess Fama in the following way. She is seated on a high tower, which represents the heroes' highland territories. Her head reaches the heavens, which originally meant the mountain tops. She has wings, which are the mark of heroes. (In Homer, Fame flies among the Greek heroes camped before Troy, but not through the ranks of the common soldiers.) She holds a trumpet, which belongs to Clio, the Muse of heroic history. And she celebrates great names, which means the founders of nations.

[556] Before the founding of cities, these servants lived like slaves in their families. (They were the precursors of the slaves who were captured in the wars fought after the cities were founded. In Latin, such slaves were called *vernae*, and their languages vernaculars.) The children of the heroes were called *liberi*, free, to distinguish them from their slaves' children, but in actual fact they were indistinguishable. Tacitus relates that among the ancient Germans 'No refinements of education distinguished the master from his slave', and their example allows us to infer the same of all primitive barbarians. Among the ancient Romans, moreover, family fathers clearly exercised both sovereign power over their children's life and death, and despotic dominion over all their possessions, including slaves. Hence, until the Roman empire there was no legal distinction between sons and slaves as owners of private property.

In the same way, in Roman law all the children and slaves of a family father were counted under his person or 'head' (which meant his mask, as we shall see) or under his 'name' (which we would now call his coat of arms). And the term *clypea*, shields, came to mean the half-bust portraits of their ancestors which the Romans placed in their courtyard niches. In recent architecture, quite in keeping with the origins of medals traced earlier, these are called 'medallions'.*

Originally, Latin *liberi* also meant nobles, so that the *artes liberales* are noble arts; and the adjective *liberalis* retained the sense of well-born,

* I have moved this paragraph here from 559.

and *liberalitas* that of gentility. (This ancient root is also found in *gentes*, clans or noble houses; as we shall see, the first *gentes* comprised nobles alone, and in the first cities only nobles were free.) By contrast, the family servants were called clients, originally *cluentes*, a form derived from the ancient verb *cluere*, to shine under arms. For the splendour of arms was called *cluor*, and the family servants reflected the shining armour of the heroes, who were also called *incluti*, renowned, and later *inclyti*. Without this reflected glory, the family servants went unnoticed, as if they were not even human.

[557] This was the origin of clientships and of the first crude forms of fiefdoms, which I shall discuss later. Ancient history records that such clients and clientships were scattered throughout all the nations, as Axiom 82 states. Thucydides relates that even in his day all the dynasties of Tanis in Egypt were divided among the family fathers, who were shepherd princes of such families. In Homer, all the heroes are kings, and are characterized as 'shepherds of the peoples'. (We shall see that such shepherds preceded the more familiar shepherds of flocks.) Today there are many such shepherd-rulers in Arabia, as there once were in Egypt. In the West Indies, most of the people were found living in a state of nature governed by such families, and attended by so many slaves that Charles V, king of Spain, was moved to regulate and restrict them. Abraham must have had such a family when he waged war against the gentile kings. Biblical scholars nicely confirm my point when they call Abraham's servants *vernaculi*, which links them to the Roman *vernae*, or captured slaves, mentioned above.

[558] The birth of these institutions gave rise to the famous *Herculean knot*, the actual bond by which clients were bound, *nexi*, to the lands they had to cultivate for the heroes. Later, in the Law of the Twelve Tables this became a symbolic knot which embodied civil mancipation, which was the formal conveyance by which all Roman legal acts were solemnized. Now, since it is impossible to conceive a more limited and necessary association – more limited for the affluent partners, and more necessary for the indigent partners – the world's first associates must have played a completely subservient role. These associates were the refugees who were received by the heroes and who literally placed their lives in the heroes' hands, as Axiom 79 states.

This accounts for Ulysses' behaviour when he takes offence at an innocent remark, and nearly beheads Antinous, the chief of his associates. It also explains why Aeneas kills his associate Misenus when a sacrifice is required. This episode was related by popular tradition; but Virgil, who celebrates Aeneas for his piety, could scarcely describe such cruelty to the gentle people of Rome. Instead, the poet wisely invented the story that Misenus was killed by Triton for daring to compete with him on the trumpet. All the same, Virgil provides obvious clues for our true understanding of the myth. For he recounts Misenus' death when describing the solemn rites which the Sibyl imposes on Aeneas. Before he can descend to the underworld, Aeneas has to bury Misenus, whose death had been predicted to him by the Sibyl, as Virgil explicitly tells us.

[559] Now, the associates shared the labours of the heroes, but not their gains, let alone their glory. (We have seen that only the heroes shone with glory, which is why they were called *kleitoi* in Greek, and *inclyti* in Latin.) This is why the provinces which the Romans later called their allies or associates had the same subordinate status. And we recall that Aesop complains of such unequal partnerships in his fable 'The Lion's Share'. Among the ancient Germans, Tacitus tells us, the principal oath of the Germans' family servants, who were their clients or vassals, was to 'defend and protect their chieftain, and to dedicate all their own valorous deeds to his glory'. The example of the Germans allows us to infer the same for all other barbarian peoples; and later, such an oath was one of the most deeply felt rituals of feudalism.

During the Greeks' heroic age, Homer could say with perfect truth that Ajax, the 'tower of the Greeks', battled alone against whole battalions of Trojans. And in the Romans' heroic age, Horatius, alone on the bridge, could withstand an army of Etruscans. In heroic language, this meant that Ajax and Horatius fought alone *with their vassals*. In precisely this way, during the medieval return of barbarism, forty Norman heroes, returning from the Holy Land, routed an army of Saracens besieging Salerno.

We may conclude, then, that the world's fiefs originated from the first protection offered by the heroes to the refugees on their lands. The first fiefs were personal rural fiefs, whose vassals were the first *vades*, bondsmen who were personally obliged to follow the heroes wherever they led them to till the fields. (Later, the term was applied to defendants who were obliged to appear in court with their attorneys.) And a vassal, called *vas* in Latin and *bas* in Greek, came to be called *was* or *wassus* by the medieval feudalists. Next, there arose real rural fiefs, by which the vassals must have been the first *praedes* or *mancipes*, bondsmen under real-estate obligation; and *mancipes* became the proper term for persons under bond to the treasury.

[560] This period also saw the origin of the first heroic inland colonies, so called in distinction to the later maritime colonies, which were bands of refugees who went to sea and found safety in other lands, as Axiom 100 states. The term colony properly denotes a large gang of journeymen who till the fields for their daily wage. Two myths preserve the history of both kinds of colony. (1) The inland colonies are represented by the famous Gallic Hercules. A chain of poetic gold, symbol of grain, stretches forth from his mouth, and he binds the ears of the masses, whom he leads wherever he chooses. This myth was previously interpreted as a symbol of eloquence, but in fact it dates from the age when the heroes lacked articulate speech. (2) The maritime colonies were represented by the heroic Vulcan, who catches the plebeian gods Venus and Mars in his net. (We shall discuss this social distinction later.) He drags the couple out of the sea, and the Sun discovers them naked, that is, not clothed in the civil light which makes heroes shine. The other gods, who symbolize the nobility of the heroic cities, ridicule them, just as ancient Roman patricians ridiculed the poor plebeians.

[561] Finally, it was during this period that refuges originated. Cadmus founded Thebes, the oldest city in Greece, on a refuge. Theseus founded Athens on the Altar of the Unfortunates. (The impious nomads were justly called unfortunate, because they lacked all the divine and human blessings which human society confers on the pious.) Romulus founded Rome by opening a refuge in a clearing. As the archetype of a city founder, Romulus and his companions established Rome according to the plan of the refuges that gave rise to the ancient cities of Latium. Livy defines this as the 'ancient counsel of city founders', but this anachronistic notion causes him to misattribute Romulus' assertion that he and his companions are sons of the earth. Yet Livy's phrase is relevant here because it proves that refuges were the origin of cities, whose

invariable property is to protect their residents from violence. In this manner, from the multitude of impious nomads who found refuge and safety in the lands of the pious heroes, there derived Jupiter's graceful title, the Hospitable. For such refuges were the world's first hospices, and the first people received there were the first guests or strangers, *hospites* in Latin, of the early cities.

[562] At this point, the poetic pagans imagined two more major divinities, *Mars* and *Venus*. Mars was a symbol of the heroes whose primary and proper task was to fight to defend their altars and hearths, *pro aris et focis*, as if *pro Ares et focis*. This kind of fighting was always heroic, since it means fighting for one's own religion, which is the first principle of my New Science. (We have seen that humankind turns to religion when there is no hope of nature's help; that religious wars are extremely bloody; and that libertines become religious when they grow old and feel their natural powers failing.) Now, Mars combats on true and real fields, and bearing true and real shields, which the Romans at first called *clupei* and later *clypei*, from *cluor*, splendour of arms. (By the same token, during the medieval return of barbarism, pastures and enclosed woods were called defences.)

The shields of Mars were charged with true arms. At first, before iron was in use, these arms were simply wooden poles, one end of which was burned, tapered, and honed to a sharp point for inflicting wounds. Such were the *purae hastae*, spears unadorned with iron, which Roman soldiers received as military prizes for their wartime heroism. Among the Greeks, the goddesses Minerva, Bellona, and Pallas Athena are armed with a spear. Among the Romans, Juno is called Quirina, and Mars Quirinus, from the noun *quiris*, spear. And Romulus, who excelled with the spear in life, was likewise called Quirinus after his death. Similarly, when they met in solemn assembly, the Roman people were called Quirites, because they were armed with javelins; just as in Greece, the heroic Spartans were armed with spears. According to Roman historians, barbarian nations wielded such primitive spears, which they describe as *praeustae sudes*, burned-tip spears, and which resemble those used by the American Indians. Today, our nobles, who once used spears in war, only use them in tournaments. The invention of such weapons, *arma*, reflects a just notion of strength: for a combatant stretches forth his arm to keep injury at a distance, as in Latin *arcere*, to defend. By contrast, arms held close to the body make combat more like that of beasts.

[563] We have seen that the world's first shields were the grounds of the burial fields, which is why in heraldry the shield is called the 'ground' of arms. The colours of these fields were actual colours. (1) Black was the colour of the scorched earth to which Hercules had set fire. (2) Green was the colour of the unripe grain. (3) Gold was the colour of ripe and yellowing grain, and thus the third colour derived from the earth. (Only later was it mistaken for the metal gold.) As one of their heroic military prizes, the Romans charged with grain the shields of soldiers who had distinguished themselves in battle. Military glory was called *adorea*, from *ador*, the toasted grain which was their primitive food. The ancient Latins called it *adur*, from the verb *urere*, to burn, and the first 'adoration' in their religious age was perhaps made by burning grain. (4) Blue was the colour of the heavens which were the roof of the early clearings; which is why French *bleu* means blue, heaven, and God, as we have seen. (5) Red was the blood of the impious thieves killed by the heroes for trespassing in their fields.

We find that the noble arms of the medieval barbarians are charged with many lions in these five colours: black, green, gold, blue, and red. Since the early fields of grain later became fields of arms, these lions symbolize cultivated lands, which are depicted as the lion slain by Hercules in all five colours. Many medieval arms are charged with vairs, or variegated furs. These symbolize the furrows from which the armed men of Cadmus sprang, after he had sown the teeth of the slain dragon. Others are charged with pales, which must be the spears which the heroes wielded. And still others are charged with rakes, which are clearly agricultural tools rather than symbols. All this leads us to conclude that agriculture was the basis of the first nobility of nations, both in the first age of barbarism, as represented by the Romans, and in the second age of medieval barbarism.

[564] The shields of the ancients were covered with leather, and the poets describe the ancient heroes as dressed in leather made from the hides of the wild beasts which they had hunted and killed. In a fine passage, Pausanias relates that the inventor of leather garments was

Pelasgus. (After this very ancient hero of Greece, the people of that nation were first called Pelasgians. In his *Origin of the Gods*, Apollodorus calls him autochthonous, meaning a son of the Earth, which simply means a giant.) This ancient use of leather finds a striking parallel in the medieval return of barbarism. Dante says that the great men of old dressed 'in leather and bone', and Boccaccio relates that they went about in cumbersome leatherwear. This must be why leather was used to cover family coats of arms, and why the ends of the pelt were scrolled to form suitable ornaments. Such shields were round because the cleared and cultivated lands were the world's first *orbes terrarum*, circles of lands, as we have seen. This feature was preserved in the round Latin *clypeus*, as distinguished from the angular *scutum*. Every clearing was called a grove, *lucus*, which meant that it admitted light, *lux*, like an eye. Even today, we still call eyes those openings that admit light in houses. The heroic sentence 'Every giant has his own grove (*lucus*)' was originally true, but later it was misunderstood, altered, and corrupted. By the age of Homer, it was falsely interpreted as meaning that every giant had an eye in the middle of his forehead.

Such one-eyed giants helped Vulcan as he worked in the first forges, which were the forests cleared by fire, and where he fashioned the burned-tip spears that were the world's first arms. Later, by an extension of the idea of arms, Vulcan forged Jupiter's thunderbolts: for it was to observe these that Vulcan had burned the forests.

[565] The second divinity born amid these ancient human institutions was *Venus*, who was an archetype of civil beauty. The Latin word for civil beauty is *honestas*, which means nobility, beauty, and virtue. These three ideas were understood in the following order: (1) civil beauty, which belonged to the heroes; (2) natural beauty, which is apparent to our human senses; and finally (3) the beauty of virtue, which is the *honestas* understood by philosophers alone. Civil beauty was an attribute of Apollo, Bacchus, Ganymede, Bellerophon, Theseus, and other heroes. Perhaps by analogy with them, Venus was sometimes imagined as having male attributes.

(As for natural beauty, it is in fact evident only to people with acute and perceptive minds, who can distinguish the parts of the body and thus grasp that harmony of the whole which is the essence of beauty.

By contrast, peasants and the urban rabble understand little or nothing about beauty. This reveals the error of those historians who claim that, in the simple and dull-witted age we are discussing, kings were chosen for their beauty and fine build. Rather, this tradition must be understood as referring to civil beauty, which is the nobility of the heroes.)

[566] The idea of civil beauty was conceived by the theological poets when they saw that the impious refugees had a human appearance, but the ugly customs of brute beasts. (In this regard, the poetic history of Greek myth records as two of Hercules' many labours that he travelled the world slaying monsters, who were human in appearance and bestial in their behaviour, and that he cleaned the filthy Augean stables.)★ Because they cherished this beauty alone, the Spartans, who were the most heroic of the Greeks, cast down from Mt Taygetus ugly and deformed babies, that is, the offspring of noble women conceived without nuptial solemnities.

It was clearly such offspring which the Law of the Twelve Tables called monsters and ordered thrown into the Tiber. For since early commonwealths pass laws sparingly, it is highly unlikely that the Roman decemvirs would have given any thought to natural monsters, which occur so rarely that the term refers to anything rare in nature. Even today, amid an overwhelming abundance of laws, legislators leave such rare cases to the discretion of judges. Hence, the Twelve Tables must refer to those monsters which were originally and properly called civil. (In Terence's *Lady of Andros*, this is what Pamphilus means when, falsely suspecting that the unwed Philomena is pregnant, he says that 'something monstrous is being nurtured': *aliquid monstri alunt*.) The term was retained in later Roman laws, which had to be formulated with great precision, as Antoine Favre observes in his *Jurisprudence of Papinianus* and as we have seen.

[567] This must be the meaning of a passage in Livy, who writes about Roman antiquities with his usual blend of good faith and incomprehension. If the patricians had shared nuptial rights with the plebeians, Livy says, any offspring would have been born 'at odds with itself', *secum ipsa discors*. By this, Livy clearly meant a 'monster with two

★ I have moved the parenthesis on Hercules here from the end of 561.

natures', combining the heroic nature of the patricians, and the bestial nature of the plebeians, who (in his words) practised intermarriage like wild beasts, *agitabant connubia more ferarum*. Livy evidently borrowed the phrase *secum ipsa discors* from some ancient annalist; and in his ignorance, he cited it as if it meant that patricians could intermarry with plebeians. But in their wretched condition of near-slavery, the plebeians could not have demanded such a thing of the patricians. Rather, they asked for the right of contracting solemn nuptials – this is the true meaning of *connubium* – which only the patricians enjoyed. As for Livy's 'wild beasts', since no species intermarries with another, we can only conclude that the phrase was the patricians' way of insulting the plebeians in that heroic contention. Since the plebeians were denied the public auspices which solemnized legitimate marriages, none of them had a legally certain father. By the familiar definition, in Roman law 'marriage rites identify the father', *nuptiae demonstrant patrem*. So the patricians were referring to this uncertain paternity when they said that the plebeians had intercourse with their mothers and daughters, like wild beasts.

[568] There were two Venuses. (1) Plebeian Venus had doves as her attributes, not as symbols of amorous passion, but because they were ignoble birds, which Horaces characterizes as *degeneres*, debased, in contrast to eagles, which he characterizes as *feroces*, fierce. This meant that the plebeian auspices were minor or private auspices, as distinguished from the patrician auspices, based on thunderbolts and eagles, which Varro and Messala call the major or public auspices. As Roman history clearly proves, the major auspices were the basis of all the patricians' heroic rights. (2) By contrast, heroic Venus, or Venus *pronuba*, had swans as her attributes. Swans are also associated with Apollo, the god of the nobility; and it is under the auspices of Jupiter as a swan that Leda conceives her eggs.

[569] Plebeian Venus was described as naked, whereas Venus *pronuba* was covered by a girdle, as we have seen. This shows us what distorted notions we inherit about poetic antiquities. For Venus' nudity, which was later imagined as an aphrodisiac, was in truth invented to signify the natural modesty and the scrupulous good faith with which the plebeians fulfilled their natural obligations. As we shall see, plebeians were excluded from citizenship in heroic cities, and therefore the

obligations they contracted were not enforced by any bonds of civil law. Among her attributes, Venus was accompanied by the Graces, who were naked as well. Since *causa*, legal action, and *gratia*, grace, are synonymous, the naked Graces in poetic Latin signified the simple agreements, *pacta nuda*, involving only natural obligations.

(By contrast, those agreements which the Roman jurists called *pacta stipulata* were later called 'vested' or 'clothed' by medieval commentators. Since the Romans jurists understood 'stipulated' as the opposite of 'naked', they clearly did not derive *stipulatio* from Latin *stipes*, stock or pole, in the forced sense of 'supporting an agreement'. (Besides, this etymology would have formed the noun *stipatio*.) Instead, they derived it from *stipula*, stalk, which the peasants of Latium described as 'clothing' the grain. The original term of the feudalists, 'vested', in turn shares its etymology with the 'investiture' of fiefs. It must be from this notion of stipulation that the verb *exfestucare*, de-stalk, derives its sense 'to divest of rank'.)

For all these reasons, then, the poetic Latins understood *gratia* and *causa* as meaning the same in contracts made by the plebeians of the heroic cities. Later, when contracts were introduced according to the natural law of nations – which the jurist Ulpian calls the natural law of *human* nations, *ius naturale gentium humanarum* – the terms *causa* and *negotium* were synonymous. For in such contracts, the transactions, *negotia*, are nearly always *caussae* (originally, *cavissae* or precautions) which serve as stipulations to secure the agreement.

CHAPTER 3

Corollaries on Contracts Sealed by Simple Consent

[570] Heroic peoples were entirely occupied with obtaining the necessities of life and gathering the fruits of natures; and being all body, as it were, they could not understand the use of money. So their most ancient law did not recognize those contracts which we now say are sealed by simple consent. Since they were uncouth, moreover, heroic people were suspicious: for crudeness springs from ignorance, and it is

a property of human nature that we always doubt when we cannot know. As a result, they did not recognize good faith, and guaranteed all their obligations by a real or symbolic handing-over, which was further certified by solemn stipulations made during the transaction. From this derived the celebrated article in the Law of the Twelve Tables, 'Whoever shall make bond or conveyance, as he has declared with his tongue, so shall it be binding', *Qui nexum faciet mancipiumque, uti lingua nuncupassit, ita ius esto*. The following eight truths derive from this natural origin of human civil institutions.

I

[571] As is commonly said, the earliest buying and selling took the form of barter. But in the case of real estate, such barter must have been what was called *libellus*, or feudal leasehold, during the medieval return of barbarism. Its utility became evident when one man's fields produced abundant crops which another man lacked, and vice versa.

2

[572] As long as cities were small and dwellings cramped, it was impractical to rent houses. Hence, proprietors must have only rented lands for others to build on, so that the sole rent was ground rent.

3

[573] The renting of lands must have taken the form of a long-term or perpetual farm lease, called *emphyteusis*, which the Romans called *clientela*, clientship. This is why some Latin scholars have conjectured that *clientes* is derived from *colentes*, cultivators.

4

[574] This must be the reason why the only contracts we find in medieval archives are leases for dwellings or farms, whether in perpetuity or for a set term.

5

[575] This may be the reason that a long-term farm lease, or *emphyteusis*, constitutes a contract in civil law, *de iure civili*, which by the principles set forth here proves to be identical to a contract in the heroic law of the Romans, *de iure heroico Romanorum*. To this law, the jurist Ulpian contrasts the natural law of human nations. He distinguishes the humanity of such law from the barbarity of the early nations that preceded Rome, rather than from the barbarous nations which in his day lived outside the Roman empire: for their law was of no interest to Roman jurists.

6

[576] Partnerships and associations were unknown among heroic peoples. For it was the Cyclopean custom that each family father only took care of his own affairs and did not meddle in those of others, as Polyphemus tells Ulysses in the passage from Homer cited earlier.

7

[577] For the same reason, mandates, or contracts appointing agents, were unknown. The famous rule of ancient civil law stated that 'No one may acquire property through an outside agent', *Per extraneam personam acquiri nemini*.

8

[578] After heroic law was succeeded by what Ulpian defines as the law of human nations, great institutional changes took place. In early ages, contracts of sale and purchase did not guarantee recovery unless double compensation, known as *dupla*, was stipulated during the transaction. But today such transactions reign supreme among what are called contracts of good faith, *bonae fidei*; and recovery is guaranteed even when it is not stipulated.

CHAPTER 4

A Principle of Mythology

[579] To return now to the three poetic archetypes Vulcan, Mars, and Venus, I note the following important principle of my mythology. In myth, these three divine archetypes symbolized the plebeians, in contrast to Jupiter, Juno, and Minerva, who symbolized the heroes. Consider Vulcan. He splits Jupiter's head open with an axe, giving birth to Minerva. And when Vulcan intercedes in the quarrel between Jupiter and Juno, he is literally kicked out of heaven by Jupiter and remains crippled from the fall. As for Mars, Homer's Jupiter harshly rebukes him by calling him 'the vilest of all the gods'. And during Homer's battle of the gods, Minerva throws a rock and wounds Mars. If in these myths Vulcan and Mars represent the plebeians who served the heroes in war, Venus in turn represents the natural wives of the plebeians. Together with plebeian Mars, plebeian Venus is caught in the net of heroic Vulcan; and when the Sun discovers them naked, they are ridiculed by the other gods. Because of this myth, Venus was later mistakenly believed to be Vulcan's wife. But we have just seen that there was only one marriage in heaven, that of Jupiter and Juno, which was in fact sterile. Indeed, the myth did not say that Mars was an adulterer, but rather that Venus was his concubine. For plebeians could only enter into natural marriages, which in Latin were called concubinages.

[580] Later, we shall have occasion to explain other archetypes like these three. Among them, we shall find the plebeian Tantalus, who can neither lay hold of the apples which dangle beyond his grasp, nor touch the water which recedes from his lips. We shall find the plebeian Midas, who starves because everything he touches becomes gold; and the plebeian Linus, who competes in song with Apollo and is defeated and slain by him.

[581] Such myths, with their double archetypes (noble and plebeian), were clearly necessary in the heroic state, when the plebeians, having no names of their own, adopted those of the heroes. In addition, the

early ages faced an extreme poverty of expressions, which is all the more striking when we consider that even in today's abundance of languages, a single word often has different and even contrary meanings.

SECTION 5
POETIC POLITICS

CHAPTER I

Poetic Politics: The Severely Aristocratic Form of the First Commonwealths

[582] In this manner, the first families were founded when the heroes received the family servants into their trust, power, and protection. These servants were the world's first associates, who entrusted to their lords both their lives and their possessions. By their paternal Cyclopean authority, the heroes held the right of life and death over the persons of their own children, and consequently also held a despotic right over their possessions. This is what Aristotle meant when he defined the children in a family as 'animate instruments of their fathers'. In Rome, too, well into an age of extensive popular liberty, the Law of the Twelve Tables perpetuated these two monarchical prerogatives of Roman family fathers over their children: power over their persons, and ownership of their possessions. Until the Roman empire, both sons and slaves alike had only one kind of private property, which was called *peculium profecticium*, possession 'proceeding' from the family father. In fact, in the earliest times Roman fathers even had the power to sell any of their children as many as three times. Later, when gentler customs prevailed, fathers who chose to free their children from paternal power did so through a series of three symbolic sales.

Among the Gauls and Celts, fathers held equivalent power over their slaves and children. In the West Indies, it was found that fathers actually held the right of selling their children. And in Europe, the Muscovites and Tartars can sell their children as many as four times. Consider, then, the truth of the jurists' assertion that barbarous nations have no paternal power exactly like that of Roman citizens, *talem qualem habent cives Romani*! This is patently false when it is misinterpreted, as scholars have commonly done, as referring to all barbarous nations. In fact, the ancient jurists were referring to nations conquered by the Roman people. For by the law of victory, such nations were deprived of all civil rights, and merely retained their natural rights: paternal powers, blood ties of any sort (the 'cognation' of Roman law), and bonitary rights of ownership. In other words, conquered nations retained only the natural obligations said to be part of the natural law of nations – a law which Ulpian further qualified as the law of *human* nations. By contrast, all the peoples living outside of the Roman empire must have enjoyed civil rights precisely like those of Roman citizens.

[583] To return to our topic, when the sons in a family were freed by the father's death from his private monarchical power, each son assumed this power entire for himself. Hence, in Roman law every citizen free of paternal power is called a family father, *paterfamilias*. By contrast, the family servants continued to live in their servile state, so that at length they must have grown weary of it. For subject people naturally yearn to escape their servitude, as Axiom 95 states. In myth, these family servants are symbolized by Tantalus, Ixion, and Sisyphus. The plebeian Tantalus can neither eat the apples above him – which are the golden apples of grain grown on the heroes' land – nor quench his burning thirst with even a sip of the water below, which rises to his lips only to recede. Ixion must forever turn his wheel. And Sisyphus pushes his rock uphill. (Like the teeth cast by Cadmus, this rock symbolizes the hard earth, and rolls back when it reaches the top. This gave rise to the Latin expressions *vertere terram*, to turn the earth, and *saxum volvere*, to roll a rock, meaning to perform a long and arduous labour.) Under such conditions, the family servants finally rebelled against the heroes. This was the crisis provoked by the family servants against the heroic fathers, which marked the birth of commonwealths from the family state, as I conjectured generally in Axiom 82.

[584] Faced with this emergency, the heroes were naturally impelled to unite themselves into orders as a means of resisting the masses of rebellious family servants. And they must have chosen as their leader a father who had a fiercer and more resolute spirit than the others. In Latin, such leaders were called *reges*, kings, from the verb *regere*, whose proper meaning is to sustain and direct. In this manner, to cite

the jurist Pomponius' insightful phrase, 'kingdoms were founded as circumstances dictated', which tallies with the doctrine of Roman law which declares that 'the natural law of nations was established by divine providence'. Such was the generation of the heroic kingdoms.

Now, the fathers were already the sovereign kings of their own families; and their equality in that state, combined with their Cyclopean ferocity, meant that none of them would naturally yield to another. Instead, there spontaneously emerged ruling senates, composed of as many kings as there were families. These rulers found that, even without any human insight or planning, they had united their private interests in a common concern. They called this their *patria*, which is shortened from *patria res*, meaning 'the concern of the fathers'. The nobles were accordingly called patricians, *patricii*, and must have been the only citizens of the first *patriae*, fatherlands. In this sense, there may be some truth in the tradition which informs us that the first kings were elected by nature. This tradition survives in two golden passages in Tacitus' *Germany*, which allows us to infer the same for all primitive barbarians. The first says that 'The Germans' squadrons and divisions are not formed by chance or random assembly, but drawn from their households and relatives.' The second says that 'Their generals command more by example than authority, winning admiration by their prominence and courage in the front lines.'

[585] The nature of the world's first kings is shown by the poets' image of Jupiter as king of the gods and men. In a golden passage in Homer, Jupiter explains to Thetis that he cannot act contrary to what the gods have decided in their great celestial council – which is language worthy of a true aristocratic king. This passage was later used by the Stoics as the basis of their dogma that Jupiter is subject to the fates. But in fact Jupiter and the other gods deliberated about human affairs, and decided them using their free will. This passage also explains two others in Homer which political thinkers have misinterpreted as proof that Homer knew about monarchy. In the first, Agamemnon rebukes Achilles for his contumacy; while in the second, Ulysses persuades the rebellious Greeks to continue the siege of Troy, although they wish to return home. In both passages, Homer says that 'only one man is king'. But both refer to wartime, when there can be only one commander-in-

chief, as Tacitus observed aphoristically: 'The prerequisite of command is that all must account to one person alone.' Moreover, whenever Homer mentions his heroes by name, he invariably gives them the title 'king'. There is a wonderful parallel to this in a golden passage of Genesis, in which Moses lists the descendants of Esau, whom he calls kings, or as the Vulgate says, *duces*, generals. Similarly, the ambassadors of Pyrrhus report having seen in Rome a senate of many kings.

Now, politically speaking, there is no conceivable reason why the fathers, forced by the plebeians to reform the state, would have made any changes from the state of nature, except to subordinate their sovereign family powers to the new ruling orders. For the strong by nature will surrender as little as possible of what their valour has acquired, and only as much as is necessary to preserve their possessions, as Axiom 81 states. This is why we read so often in Roman history about the heroic disdain of the strong, who cannot stand 'to lose through shameful deeds what was won by valour', as the phrase has it. Now, we have seen that civil governments were not created by the fraud or force of a single person. So, of all the various human possibilities, only the manner I have described can explain how civil power grew out of family authority, and how the eminent domain of civil states grew out of the natural domains of paternal authority. (These last were exercised *ex iure optimo*, by supreme right, which means free of every private and public encumbrance, as we have seen.)

[586] My theory of this process finds wonderful confirmation in etymology. Since the fathers' supreme domain was called *dikaion ariston* in Greek and *dominium optimum* in Latin, the commonwealths founded on it were called 'aristocracies' by the Greeks, and 'commonwealths of optimates' by the Romans. The commonwealths of optimates thus took their name from Ops, the goddess of power, from whose name they derived *op-timus*, meaning most powerful or best: *aristos* in Greek and *optimus* in Latin. Ops was said to be the wife of Jupiter, symbol of the ruling orders established by the heroes. (By contrast, Juno was the wife of Jupiter in his auspicial aspect as the thundering sky.) Now, the heroes had claimed the title of gods; and their mother was Cybele, the Earth goddess with whom Ops is sometimes identified. Cybele was called the 'mother of giants', which properly meant 'mother of the

nobles'; and my Poetic Cosmography will show that she was regarded as the queen of cities.

Ops thus gave her name to the optimates, whose commonwealths were established to preserve the power of the nobles, so that all aristocracies retain two invariable properties, namely, their guarding of social *orders* and of social *boundaries*.

The guarding of social orders involved four different institutions: (1) the guarding of *kinships*, by which the Romans excluded the plebeians from solemnized marriage, *connubium*, until 445 BC; (2) the guarding of *magistracies*, by which the patricians opposed the plebeians who aspired to the consulship; (3) the guarding of *priesthoods*; and hence (4) the guarding of *laws*, which all early nations held sacred. Before the Law of the Twelve Tables the patricians governed Rome by custom, as we are informed by Dionysius of Halicarnassus, cited in Axiom 92. And for a century afterwards, according to the jurist Pomponius, the interpretation of the Law was kept within the college of pontiffs, to which only patricians were admitted.

Aristocracies also guarded social boundaries. This is why the Romans, until they destroyed Corinth in 146 BC, observed incomparable justice in their wars, and the utmost clemency in their victories. For this kept the plebeians from becoming either warlike or wealthy, as Axioms 87 and 88 state.

[587] This great and important period in poetic history is described in the myth which relates how Saturn tries to devour the infant Jupiter, and the priests of Cybele hide him and drown out his crying by the clash of their arms. In this myth, Saturn is an archetype of the family servants, or day labourers, who till the fields of their heroic masters, and burn with a desire of obtaining their own fields to live on. Hence, Saturn is also the father of Jupiter because he is the source and occasion of the fathers' civil reign, which is symbolized by Jupiter's marriage to Ops.

(As the god of the most solemn auspices of the thunderbolt and eagle, Jupiter is the husband of Juno. As god of the auspices in general, Jupiter is also the father of the 'gods', that is, of the heroes who believed they were his sons, because they were conceived under Jupiter's auspices and by the solemn nuptials sacred to Juno. This is why the heroes assumed the title of gods, whose mother is Earth, identified with Ops, another wife of Jupiter.)

Jupiter was also called the king of 'men', that is, of the family servants in the state of families, and of the plebeians in the state of heroic cities. Ignorance of this poetic history later led people to confuse the two titles of father and king, as if Jupiter were also the 'father of men'. But well into the age of the Roman republic, Livy tells us, neither the family servants nor the plebeians could name their fathers, because they were born of natural marriages rather than solemn nuptials. This was the origin of the judicial dictum 'Marriage rites identify the father.'

[588] The myth further relates that Jupiter is hidden by the priests of Cybele or Ops, which means that all the earliest kingdoms were composed of priests, as I said earlier and shall later show in detail. Latin philologists have conjectured that the name Latium derived from this 'latent' or hidden Jupiter, and this historical fact is preserved in the Latin expression for founding kingdoms, *condere regna*, since *condere* also means 'to hide'. For when the servants rebelled, the fathers formed a closed order, whose secrets gave rise to what political thinkers call secrets of state, *arcana imperii*. Then, by the clash of their arms, the priests keep Saturn from hearing the crying of Jupiter, newly born from the union of the orders, and thereby save him. In this manner, the myth explains clearly what Plato expressed obscurely when he wrote that commonwealths arose on the basis of arms. To this we may add Aristotle's observation, cited in Axiom 86, that in the heroic commonwealths the nobles swore eternal enmity against the plebeians. We recognize this invariable property when we say that servants are the paid enemies of their masters. And this piece of history is preserved in the Greek etymology by which *polemos*, war, is derived from *polis*, city.

[589] At this point, the Greek nations imagined the tenth deity of the major clans, *Minerva*, whose birth they imagined in a savage and grotesque fashion. Vulcan splits Jupiter's head with an axe, and Minerva springs forth. The myth signified that the masses of family servants, whose servile arts belonged to the poetic category of plebeian Vulcan, 'broke' Jupiter's reign, that is, weakened or diminished it. (The Latin expression *minuere caput* meant 'to break the head', for since they lacked

the abstract noun 'reign', they used the concrete word 'head'.) In the family state, Jupiter's reign had been monarchical, but in the new city state it became aristocratic. We are not wrong, then, to conjecture that the name Minerva is derived from the Latin verb *minuere*, to diminish; and that the Roman legal phrase *capitis deminutio*, diminution of the head, descended from the remotest age of poetic antiquity, since its meaning of 'change in status' recalls how Minerva changed the state of families to that of cities.

[590] On the myth of Minerva's birth, the philosophers later imposed their sublimest metaphysical meditation: that God *generates* the eternal idea in himself, whereas he *produces* created ideas in us. But the theological poets only contemplated Minerva through the idea of civil order, so that order, *ordo*, became the Latin term *par excellence* for the senate. This may be the reason why the philosophers considered it an eternal idea of God, who is eternal order. This established the invariable principle that the order of the 'best' holds the wisdom of cities.

In Homer, Minerva is always characterized by the invariable epithets of Warrior and Despoiler; whereas I can recall only two passages in which she is called Counsellor. The owl and the olive were sacred to her, but the reason is not that she meditates at night, or reads and writes by lamplight. Instead, these symbols signify the darkness of the hidden depths (Italian *nascondigli*) in which civilization was founded. Perhaps more specifically, they signify the fact that the senates of the heroic cities framed their laws in secret. We know for certain that at Athens, which was the city of Athena, the Greek Minerva, the council of the Areopagus customarily voted in darkness. This heroic custom is preserved in the Latin expression for framing laws, *condere leges*, since *condere* also means 'to hide'. Thus, *legum conditores* properly meant the senates that *decreed* the laws, and *legum latores* meant those who *carried* the laws from the senates to the plebeians of various peoples, as we have seen in the trial of Horatius. Clearly, Minerva was scarcely considered the goddess of wisdom by the theological poets. For we find that statues and medals depict her as armed, and the goddess called Minerva in the curia was known as Bellona in warfare. This goddess was called Pallas in the plebeian assemblies, and Homer tells us that it is Pallas who leads Telemachus, about to depart in search of his father

Ulysses, into the assembly of the plebeians, whom he calls the 'other people'.

[591] The erroneous belief that the theological poets regarded Minerva as the symbol of wisdom goes hand in hand with another error, namely, that Latin *curia*, assembly, was derived from *curanda respublica*, managing the government. But in fact, in this early age the nations were quite dull and dim-witted. The word must rather reflect early Greek *kyria*, from *cheir*, hand, which then passed into Latin as *curia*. We may infer this from the two great fragments of antiquity mentioned in my Notes on Chronology. Denis Petau found these fragments, which fortunately bolster my argument, embedded in the history of Greece before its heroic age, and consequently during what the Egyptians called the age of the gods, which is our topic here.

[592] The first fragment of antiquity is that the Heraclids or descendants of Hercules, who had been scattered throughout Greece, including Attica, the site of Athens, later retired to the Peloponnesus, the site of Sparta. Now, the government of Sparta was an aristocracy, or rather an aristocratic kingdom. In it, two kings, supposedly descended from Hercules and called Heraclids or nobles, administered laws and conducted wars under the supervision of the ephors. These officials were the guardians of a liberty which was aristocratic rather than popular. Thus, the ephors had king Agis strangled for attempting to offer the people two laws. The first would have cancelled all debts, and was characterized by Livy as a torch meant to inflame the masses against the oligarchs: *facem ad accendendum adversus optimates plebem*. The second was a testamentary law which would have legalized inheritances outside the order of the nobility; whereas the law of legitimate succession had previously restricted legacies to the nobles, who alone could claim proper heirs, or heirs through the males or the clan. Similar laws also existed in Rome before the Twelve Tables. And just as the senate executed as traitors men like Spurius Cassius, Manlius Capitolinus, the Gracchi, and other prominent Romans for seeking to pass laws aiding the poor oppressed plebeians, so the ephors condemned Agis to be strangled. We see, then, how little the Spartan ephors were guardians of the popular liberty of Lacedaemon, as Polybius paints them!

Athens, which was named for Athena, the Greek Minerva, must also have had an aristocratic government in its earliest age. Greek history faithfully records this by saying that Draco ruled in Athens in the period when the oligarchs occupied the city. And it is confirmed by Thucydides [Isocrates], who relates that, while Athens was governed by the severe councillors of the Areopagus, it was resplendent with the finest heroic virtues and accomplished the noblest undertakings, precisely like Rome in its aristocratic period.* From this glory, Athens was later plunged into popular liberty by Pericles and Aristides, precisely as Rome began to decline under the tribunes Canuleius and Sextius. (Juvenal translates the name Areopagites as 'judges of Mars', meaning armed judges. Since the name comes from *Ares*, Mars, and *pēgē*, spring – which corresponds to Latin *pagus*, country district – he might better have rendered it as 'the people of Mars'. The early Romans were called just that, since newly founded peoples were composed solely of nobles, who alone had the right to bear arms.)

[593] The second great fragment of antiquity relates that in their travels the Greeks found the Curetes, or priests of Cybele, scattered throughout Saturnia or ancient Italy, Crete, and Asia. This means that there were kingdoms of Curetes throughout the first barbarous nations, corresponding to the Heraclid kingdoms scattered through ancient Greece. These Curetes appear in the myth we have just examined as the armed priests whose clashing arms muffled the cries of the infant Jupiter, whom Saturn wished to devour.

[594] This discussion of the heroic senates shows the manner in which the first Comitia Curiata arose in remote antiquity. These curial assemblies are the oldest recorded in Roman history. They initially met under arms, and later assembled to discuss sacred institutions: for in that early age all profane institutions were viewed as sacred. Livy marvels that such assemblies were common in Gaul when Hannibal passed through it. But in his *Germany* Tacitus relates that such assemblies, held by priests to decree punishments, gathered in the midst of arms as if in the presence of their gods. They did so with a just sense of purpose, for heroic assemblies which mete out punishments are armed because the supreme authority of laws follows the supreme authority of arms.

---

* Vico has confused the Athenian orator Isocrates with the historian Thucydides.

Tacitus also notes that the Germans generally conducted all their public affairs under arms and with priests presiding. In the customs of the ancient Germans, whose example allows us to infer the same for all primitive barbarians, we rediscover three institutions: (1) the kingdom of Egyptian priests, (2) the kingdoms of the Curetes or armed priests which the Greeks observed in ancient Italy, Crete, and Asia, and (3) the Quirites of ancient Latium.

[595] We may conclude, then, that the law of the Quirites was the natural law of the heroic peoples of Italy, which was called the *ius Quiritium Romanorum* to distinguish it from the law of other peoples. Now, the Quirites did not derive their name, as some maintain, from a pact between the Romans and the Sabines, whose capital city was Cures. If that had been the case, they would have been called Curetes, which was rather the name of the priests observed by the Greeks in Saturnia. And if the Sabine capital had been named Caere, as some Latinists maintain, they would instead have been known as Caerites. But this distorts the facts. The term Caerites applied to those Roman citizens whom the censors had condemned to bear civil burdens without enjoying suffrage or public office – precisely like the plebeians who later became family servants when the heroic cities arose. In fact, rather than joining the heroic Romans, the Sabines were in fact merged with the Roman plebeians. For in that barbarous age, conquered cities were levelled, and their inhabitants dispersed over the plains and forced to cultivate fields for the victors – a fate that the Romans did not even spare their mother city of Alba.

Such conquered cities were the first provinces, *provinciae*, so called as if from *prope victae*, conquered nearby. (One of these was Corioli, whose conqueror took the name Marcius Coriolanus.) Conversely, the farthest provinces were so called as being *procul victae*, conquered far off. The first inland colonies were settled on these conquered plains, and were thus properly called *coloniae deductae*, colonies led down, because teams of peasant labourers were moved down to the lowlands. (Later, the term meant the opposite when applied to the farthest colonies. For in these, plebeians who lived in the low and cramped areas of Rome were moved up to the fortified highlands of the provinces, where they became the lords who kept order, reducing the former landlords to poor labourers.) In this manner, according to Livy, who only witnessed the effects of the process, Rome grew on the ruins of Alba. And the Sabines brought the wealth of Caere to their Roman sons-in-law as a 'dowry' for their abducted daughters, as Florus vainly comments. These first inland colonies differed from the later colonies established after the agrarian reforms of the Gracchi. And Livy relates that in their heroic contentions with the patricians, the Roman plebeians disdained, or rather resented, the earlier colonies. For unlike the later ones, they did nothing to improve the plebeians' condition. Yet when Livy finds that the struggles persisted even despite the later colonies, he offers his vain reflections about them.

[596] To conclude, two passages in Homer prove that Minerva signified the armed aristocratic orders. (1) In the contest of the gods, Minerva hurls a stone and wounds Mars, who is an archetype of the plebeians who serve the heroes in war. (2) Later, she seeks to conspire against Jupiter. This is typically aristocratic behaviour, since in aristocracies lords often plan in secret to eliminate rulers who aspire to tyranny. It is only in aristocratic ages that we read of statues erected to tyrannicides, who would have been thought traitors, if they had lived under monarchical kings.

[597] The first cities, then, were composed solely of the nobles who governed them. But these nobles also needed others to serve them, so that their common sense of advantage forced them to appease the multitude of their rebellious clients. To their clients they sent the first embassies – as sovereigns do under the law of nations – bearing the world's first agrarian law. Under this law, the nobles, as the stronger party, conceded as little as possible to their clients, namely, the bonitary ownership of only such fields as the heroes chose to assign them. In this sense, it seems true that Ceres discovered both grain and laws. This agrarian law was dictated by a natural law of nations. Since ownership follows power, and since the servants' lives depended on the heroes who had given them safety and refuge, it was lawful and right that their ownership should be dependent and 'precarious'. In other words, they would remain as owners of assigned fields only at the pleasure of the heroes. Under this law, the servants merged to form the first plebeians of the heroic cities, in which they had none of the privileges of

citizenship. This is precisely the way Achilles says that Agamemnon has treated him by wrongfully seizing Briseis. He claims that no one would dare commit such an outrage against even a labourer with no rights as a citizen.

[598] Such was the primitive condition of the Roman plebeians down to the age of their contention for solemnized marriage. Then, in the Law of the Twelve Tables, the patricians had granted them a second agrarian law, by which they gained quiritary ownership of their fields. (Many years ago, I showed this in my *Principles of Universal Law*; which is one of two passages which has caused me no regret.) Yet since they were not yet citizens, the plebeians were still denied civil ownership, from which aliens are excluded by the law of nations. When plebeians died, they could not leave their fields intestate to their kin. For they had no direct heirs and no relatives on either the father's or mother's side, since all these relations depend on solemn nuptials. Nor could they dispose of their fields by testament, since they lacked citizenship. Hence the lands assigned to them reverted to the patricians who had given them the title of ownership. But the plebeians soon noticed this; and three years after the Law of the Twelve Tables was enacted, they demanded the right to solemnized marriage. Yet in their state of miserable servitude, which is described in Roman history, they did not demand the right of intermarriage with the nobles, which in Latin would have been called 'connubia *cum patribus*'. Instead, they asked the right to contract the solemn nuptials of the patricians, 'connubia *patrum*'. (These rights were solemnized principally by the public auspices, which Varro and Messala called the major auspices, and which the patricians said belonged to them.) The plebeians' demand was thus a request for Roman citizenship, of which marriage was the natural principle. This is why the jurist Modestinus defines marriage as the 'sharing of every divine and human right', which is also the most proper definition that can be formulated for citizenship itself.

CHAPTER 2

All Commonwealths Arise from Invariable Principles
of Fiefs

[599] As Axioms 80–81 state, the invariable principles of fiefs are based on two natural characteristics of human institutions, namely, that the strong naturally safeguard their possessions, and that people naturally seek benefits from civil life. In the manner described above, commonwealths arose in the world with three kinds of ownership for three kinds of fiefs, which were held by three kinds of persons over three kinds of things.

[600] (1) The first kind was the bonitary ownership of rural or human fiefs enjoyed by the plebeians over the products of the heroes' farms. The phrase 'human fief' refers to the plebeians simply as 'men', a term which, to François Hotman's amazement, meant vassals in the feudal laws of medieval barbarism.

[601] (2) The second kind was the quiritary ownership of noble fiefs, which are also called heroic, armed, or (nowadays) military fiefs; for by uniting in armed orders, the heroes safeguarded their sovereignty over their farms. In the state of nature, this was the supreme ownership, *ius optimum*, which Cicero mentions in his speech *On the Soothsayers' Prophecies*. In reference to some old Roman houses surviving in his day, Cicero defines this as 'the ownership of real estate free of any real encumbrance either public or private'. In a golden passage in Genesis, Moses writes that in Joseph's day the priests of Egypt did not pay Pharaoh tribute on their fields. We have seen that all the heroic kingdoms were priestly, and shall soon see that at first the Roman patricians did not pay the public treasury any tribute even on their own fields. When the heroic commonwealths were formed, these sovereign private fiefs naturally became subject to the higher sovereignty of the ruling heroic orders. (Each ruling community was called a *patria*, which is shortened from *patria res*, meaning 'the concern of the fathers'.) The heroes were bound to defend and maintain the sovereignty of the ruling orders, because it preserved their sovereign family powers equally

among all of them. This is a unique feature of aristocratic liberty.

[602] (3) The third kind was properly called civil ownership or eminent domain, which the heroic cities, originally composed solely of heroes, had over the lands. This ownership was based on certain divine fiefs, which the family fathers had received from the provident deity, by which they became sovereign in the state of families, and formed ruling orders in the state of cities. The heroic cities thus became sovereign civil kingdoms subject only to the supreme sovereign God, whose providence is recognized by all sovereign civil powers. This is manifestly acknowledged by the sovereigns themselves, who append to their majestic titles such phrases as 'by divine providence' or 'by the grace of God', because it is from these that they must profess having received their kingdoms. Indeed, if they were to forbid the worship of providence, they would naturally lose their sovereignty. For no nation composed of fatalists, casualists, or atheists has ever existed in the world.* And we saw earlier that all the nations of the world believe in a provident deity, and have thus embraced only four principal religions: paganism, Judaism, Christianity, and Islam.

In recognition of their providential sovereignty, the plebeians swore by the heroes. Latin preserves oaths such as *mehercules*, by Hercules; *mecastor*, by Castor; *edepol*, by Pollux; and *mediusfidius*, by the god Fidius, which was the Roman Hercules, as we shall see. For the plebeians were at first in the power of the heroes, and until 335 BC, Roman patricians exercised the right of private incarceration over plebeian debtors. By contrast, the heroes swore by Jupiter, since as members of the ruling orders they were in Jupiter's power by reason of the auspices. When the auspices seemed favourable, the heroes appointed magistrates, enacted laws, and exercised their other sovereign rights; when they were unfavourable, the heroes took no action.

All these relations are in Latin called *fides deorum et hominum*, the faith of gods and men, as in the expressions *implorare fidem*, to implore help and aid, and *recipere in fidem*, to receive under protection or authority. The exclamation *proh deum atque hominum fidem imploro* was used by the

---

* Vico again alludes to the Stoics' belief in destiny (fatalism) and the Epicurean doctrine of chance (casualism).

oppressed to implore 'the force of gods and men', a notion which the Italians render in more human terms as 'the power of the world'. All these expressions denote the force which sustains and rules our civil world: the 'power' from which civil powers take their name; the 'force' of gods and men; the 'faith' in the oaths just cited, which attest the obeisance of the weak; and the 'protection' which the powerful must offer the weak. (The last two groups are essential elements of feudalism.) The centre of this force was sensed, if not fully understood, by ancient nations as the ground of every civil sphere; the civic medals of the Greeks and the heroic expressions of the Romans show us this. Even today the crowns of sovereigns support an orb on which is planted the divine symbol of the cross. We have seen that this orb is the golden apple which symbolizes their lofty dominion as sovereign lords of the lands they rule. This is why a new sovereign, during the high solemnities of coronation rites, holds an orb in his left hand.

Civil powers are thus the lords of the 'substance' or patrimony of their peoples, which sustains, contains, and maintains all that is above it and rests on it. Considered as one part of this substance (the Scholastic term is *pro indiviso*), the patrimony of each family father is in Roman law called the father's substance, *patris substantia* or *paterna substantia*. This is the underlying reason why sovereign civil powers may dispose of whatever belongs to their subjects – including their persons, possessions, works, and labours – and can impose on them tributes and taxes, whenever they need to exercise dominion over their lands. Viewed differently but meaning substantially the same thing, this dominion is now called eminent domain by moral theologians and by specialists in public law, who also speak of laws concerning this domain as 'fundamental' laws of the realm. Since this dominion is over the lands themselves, sovereigns may naturally exercise it only to preserve the 'substance' of their states. For the preservation or destruction of this substance entails the preservation or destruction of all the private concerns of their peoples.

[603] That commonwealths are based on the invariable principles of fiefs was sensed, if not fully understood, by the Romans. This is clear from their ancient legal formula for claiming property: 'I declare this ground mine by quiritary right', *Aio hunc fundum meum esse ex iure Quiritium*. This formula links the civil action of vindication to the

ownership of the land, which belongs to the state and which proceeds from what I have called the central power. By this power, every Roman citizen is the recognized lord of his estate, which he owns *pro indiviso* (to repeat the Scholastic term), and therefore by quiritary right, *ex iure Quiritium*. (The original Quirites were those Romans who, armed with spears in public assembly, were the only citizens.) This is the underlying reason why, in default of an owner, lands and all goods deriving from them revert to the public treasury. Every private patrimony *pro indiviso* is public patrimony, so that, in the absence of a private owner, it loses its designation as a part and retains that of the whole. This accounts for the elegant legal expression by which inheritances, especially those termed 'legitimate', are said to return, *redire*, to the heirs, even though in truth they come to them but once. For in founding the Roman republic, the founders of Roman law established all private patrimonies as fiefs of the kind which feudalists call *ex pacto et providentia*, by pact and provision. In other words, they all derive from the public patrimony and, by pact and provision of the civil laws, are transferred with certain formalities from one private owner to another; and in default of any owners, they must revert to their public source.

All of this is clearly confirmed by the Lex Papia Poppaea, a Roman law on lapsed legacies. This law penalized celibates in an appropriate fashion. For since they had neglected to perpetuate their Roman names through marriage, their wills were to be declared invalid; and if they died intestate, none of their relatives could inherit from them. In either case, they had no heirs to preserve their names. And their patrimonies reverted to the public treasury, not in the form of a legacy but as property which returned to the people, in Tacitus' phrase, 'as to the parent of all citizens', *tamquam omnium parentem*. In these words, this profound author evokes the reason for all penalties on lapsed legacies, which date from the earliest ages when the first fathers of humankind occupied the first vacant lands. This occupation was the original source of all the ownership in the world. Later, when the fathers united in cities, from their paternal powers they created the civil power, and from their private patrimonies they created the public patrimony, which they called the public treasury. This is why the patrimonies of citizens pass from one private owner to another as inheritances; but when they revert to the public treasury, they resume their original, ancient status as *peculium*, or managed assets.

[604] As the heroic commonwealths were being created, the heroic poets imagined their eleventh major deity, *Mercury*. He uses his divine wand, the physical symbol of the auspices, to carry the law to the rebellious servants. And, as Virgil tells us, he uses his wand to call souls back from Orcus, which means that he called back to society those clients who had left the heroes' protection and were again dispersed in the lawless state which the poets called Orcus and described as devouring men whole. Mercury's wand is depicted with one or two serpents wound around it. These were originally snakeskins, which signified both the bonitary ownership which the heroes granted to their servants, and the quiritary ownership which they reserved for themselves.

There were two wings at the top of Mercury's wand, signifying the eminent domain of the ruling orders. There were wings on Mercury's cap as well, in confirmation of the heroes' lofty and free sovereignty; and this cap remained a symbol of liberty. Mercury also has wings on his heels, to signify that the ownership of lands was held by the ruling senates. Except for this, Mercury is naked, for he offered the family servants ownership barren of civil solemnity, and based entirely on the heroes' sense of shame. (In precisely this sense, Venus and the Graces were depicted naked.) To return to Mercury's wings, we recall that Idanthyrsus used a bird to tell Darius that he was the sovereign lord of Scythia through the auspices. Later, the Greeks adopted the symbol of a bird's wings to signify heroic institutions. Finally, in articulate language the Roman patricians made the abstract statement that 'The auspices belong to us', which showed the plebeians that they controlled all heroic laws and rights.

Without its serpents, Mercury's winged wand is the same as the eagle-headed sceptre of the Egyptians, Etruscans, Romans, and eventually the English. In Greek, this wand was called a *kērykeion*, herald's staff, because it was used to carry the agrarian law to the heroes' servants, whom Homer calls *kērykes*, heralds. It also carried Servius Tullius' agrarian law establishing the census, so that peasants subject to it were called *censiti* in Roman law. Its serpents carried bonitary ownership of the fields, so that the land rent paid by the plebeians to the heroes was called *ōpheleia*, from *ophis*, serpent. Finally, it carried the famous Herculean knot, by which men paid the tithe of Hercules to the heroes, and by which plebeian debtors in Rome were the 'bound' or liege vassals of the patricians until the passage of the Poetelian Law. I shall have more to say on this subject later.

[605] I should note here that the Greek Hermes is the same as the Mercury figure Thoth, who gives laws to the Egyptians and who is represented by the hieroglyph of Kneph. He is depicted as a serpent, which denotes the cultivated earth. He has the head of a hawk or eagle, just as the hawks of Romulus later became the Roman eagles, symbol of the heroic auspices. He is girded by a belt, which is a sign of the Herculean knot. In his hand, he holds a sceptre, which signifies the kingdom of the Egyptian priests; and he wears a winged cap, which alludes to their eminent domain over the lands. Finally, he has an egg in his mouth, which represents the world of Egypt, unless it is a golden pome, signifying the priests' eminent domain over the lands of Egypt. Into this hieroglyph, Manetho read the generation of the whole world; and the conceit of scholars led to such madness that in *The Obelisk of Innocent X* Athanasius Kircher says that it signifies the Holy Trinity.

[606] This was the origin of the world's first commerce, for which Mercury was named and later regarded as the god of mercantile trade. From his first embassy as law-bearer, moreover, he was considered the god of ambassadors. And it was said with palpable truth that 'the gods', meaning the heroes of first cities, had sent Mercury to 'men', meaning the servants. (Just so, during the medieval return of barbarism, vassals were simply called 'men', to Hotman's amazement.) Since Mercury had wings, which signified heroic rights, people later thought that he flew between heaven and earth. To return to commerce, we find that it originated with real-estate transactions; and that the first wages were perforce the simplest and most natural, namely, the produce of the land. Such wages, paid in labour or goods, are still customary in commercial dealings between peasants.

[607] This entire historical process is recorded in the Greek noun *nomos*, which means both law and pasture. For the first law was the agrarian law, and the heroic kings were accordingly called the shepherds of the people, as we have seen.

[608] In the barbarous nations of antiquity, the heroes must have settled the plebeians across the countryside, living in houses by their assigned fields and contributing what produce was needed to sustain their masters. This is precisely how Tacitus describes the plebeians of the ancient Germans, although he mistakenly considers them slaves, when they were in fact the heroes' associates. To these living conditions, we should add the oath cited by Tacitus, which bound them to defend and protect their masters and to serve their glory. If we look for a legal term to define such rights, we shall clearly see that none fits them better than feudalism.

[609] In this fashion, the first cities were founded on the basis of orders of nobles and work-gangs of plebeians. These two groups are characterized by two invariable and opposite principles which spring from the nature of human civil institutions. (1) The plebeians always wish to change the form of government, and are in fact the ones who change it. (2) By contrast, the nobles always wish to maintain the *status quo*. During civil disturbances, anyone who strives to preserve the state is called an optimate, or aristocrat. And 'states' are so called because it is their property to 'stand' firm and upright.

[610] Two social divisions arose at this time. The first division distinguished the *wise men* from the *vulgar masses*. The former arose because the heroes founded their kingdoms on the wisdom of the auspices, as Axiom 72 states. By contrast, the vulgar masses acquired the invariable epithet 'profane', in distinction to the heroes or nobles, who were the priests of the heroic cities. (Even a full century after the Law of the Twelve Tables, the Roman patricians still monopolized the priesthoods.) Hence, when the earliest peoples deprived someone of citizenship, they observed a sort of religious excommunication, like the Roman interdict of water and fire. For the first plebeians of the nations were regarded as foreigners, and their status established the invariable principle that citizenship is denied to any person of an alien religion. And since the early plebeians could not participate in sacred and divine institutions, and for many centuries could not contract solemn marriages, children born out of wedlock came to be known as 'drawn from the vulgar masses', *vulgo quaesiti*.

[611] The second division was that between *civis*, citizen, and *hostis*,

which meant guest, foreigner, or enemy. It reflects the fact that the first cities comprised both the heroes and those protected in their refuges. These refuges may all be considered heroic hospices. In the medieval return of barbarism, Latin *hostis* became Italian *oste*, which means innkeeper and soldiers' quarters, and *ostello*, inn. In Greek myth, Paris was both the guest and the enemy of the royal house of Argos, because he abducted the noble Argive maidens symbolized by the archetype of Helen. In the same sense, Theseus was the guest of Ariadne, and Jason the guest of Medea, for both heroes later abandoned these women without marrying them. Such deeds were once considered heroic, but to our modern sensibilities they appear villainous, as indeed they are. This is the only way to defend the so-called piety of Aeneas. Even though Dido shows him great kindness and generously offers him the kingdom of Carthage as her dowry, Aeneas rapes and abandons her, and instead obeys the fates, who have destined another foreigner, Lavinia, to be his wife. Homer illustrates this heroic custom in the person of Achilles, the greatest Greek hero. When Agamemnon offers him one of his three daughters in marriage, and includes a royal dowry of seven towns inhabited by many ploughmen and shepherds, Achilles refuses, saying that he will marry the bride chosen by his father Peleus in his fatherland.

In sum, the plebeians were the 'guests' of the heroic cities, against whom the heroes swore eternal enmity, as Aristotle observes. The same division is expressed by the Latin antonyms *civis*, citizen, and *peregrinus*, stranger. In its original and proper sense, *peregrinus* means a person who wanders through the countryside, as if *per-agrinus*, from *ager*, meaning territory or district. (For example, the lands around Naples and Nola are in Latin called *ager neapolitanus* and *ager nolanus*.) By contrast, a true foreigner who travels through the world does not wander through the countryside, but stays on the directer public roads.

[612] This account of the original heroic 'guests' sheds great light on those passages in Greek history which tell us that 'foreigners' changed the aristocratic states to democracies in Samos, Sybaris, Troezen, Amphipolis, Chalcedon, Cnidos, and Chios. And it adds a crowning touch to my argument, published years ago in *Principles of Universal Law*, which refutes the myth that the Law of the Twelve Tables came from Athens

to Rome. (This is one of two passages in that work which I still regard as valuable.) In that passage, I showed that the entire contention between the Roman patricians and plebeians was summarized in the article of the Twelve Tables called 'The valorous man, restored to allegiance, is freed from bond', *De forti sanate nexo soluto*. Now, Latin historians had interpreted the phrase 'valorous man restored to allegiance' to mean any foreigner reduced by Rome to obedience. But in fact it meant the Roman plebeians who had rebelled because the patricians would not grant them the certain ownership of their fields. Such ownership could be made certain and lasting only by a law, permanently fixed on a public tablet, which both specified the rights that had been uncertain and published the rights that had been secret, thus preventing the patricians from reclaiming them by royal privilege. This is the truth behind the account given by Pomponius in the *Digest*. And this is why the plebeians caused such turmoil that it was necessary to create decemvirs. By this article, the decemvirs reformed the constitution and reduced the rebellious plebeians to obedience. For this article declared the plebeians free from the veritable bond of bonitary ownership, by which they had previously been bound to the soil, *glebae addicti, adscriptitii*, or assessed, *censiti*, by the census of Servius Tullius. Henceforth, they were only bound by the symbolic knot of quiritary ownership. Nevertheless, until the Poetelian Law was enacted, a vestige of the old bond persisted in the patricians' right to privately imprison plebeian debtors. These plebeians were the 'foreigners' who, with the aid of what Livy elegantly calls the enticements of the tribunes, finally changed the Roman state from an aristocracy to a democracy. (In my Notes on Chronology, I review these measures in discussing the Poetelian Law.)

[613] The fact that Rome was not founded on the first agrarian revolts shows us that it was in fact a new city, as it is celebrated in history. Rome was founded on the refuge where, as violence still raged everywhere, Romulus and his companions first consolidated their strength, and then received the refugees who formed the first clientships. Now, some 200 years must have passed before the clients grew weary of their condition, for this is precisely the time that elapsed before the king Servius Tullius introduced the first agrarian law. In other ancient cities, this process must have taken some 500 years: for their citizens

were simpler folk, whereas the Romans were shrewder. Their sudden maturity made the Romans more youthfully heroic than the other Latin peoples, which is why Rome soon subjugated Latium, Italy, and finally all of the known world. This also explains why the Romans wrote their heroic history in their own vernacular language, whereas the Greeks had written theirs in myths, as Axiom 21 states.

[614] The principles of poetic politics which we have analysed and observed in Roman history find marvellous confirmation in four heroic archetypes: (1) the lyre of Orpheus or Apollo; (2) the head of Medusa; (3) the Roman fasces; and (4) Hercules wrestling with Antaeus.

[615] (1) The lyre was invented by the Greek Mercury, just as law was invented by the Egyptian Mercury. This lyre was given to him by Apollo, god of civil light, or the nobility, since in heroic commonwealths laws were dictated by the nobles. Orpheus, Amphion, and other theological poets, who professed the science of laws, used this lyre to found and establish the civilization of Greece, as we shall see later in greater detail. The lyre symbolized the union of the cords or forces of the fathers that composed the public force known as the civil power, which finally put an end to all private force and violence. Hence, with great propriety the law came to be defined by the poets as 'the lyre of kingdoms', *lyra regnorum*. It brought into one accord the family kingdoms of the fathers, which had previously been at odds because in the state of families they lived alone and separate from each other, as Polyphemus tells Ulysses. The glorious history of the lyre was then outlined in the heavens by the stars of the constellation Lyra. On the English royal arms, the kingdom of Ireland charges its shield with a harp. Later, the philosophers interpreted the lyre as symbolizing the harmony of the spheres attuned by the sun. Yet it was on earth that Apollo played the lyre which Pythagoras must have heard, indeed must have played himself, if we consider him a theological poet and nation founder, rather than an impostor, as some have charged.

[616] (2) The snakes which spring from Medusa's winged head represent the fathers' sovereign dominion in the state of families, which later constituted the civil eminent domain. Medusa's head was nailed to the shield of Perseus, which is the same as the shield of Minerva. Bearing this shield among the armed assemblies of the first nations,

such as Rome, Minerva dictates terrifying punishments which turn to stone all those who behold it. One of these snakes was Draco the dragon. Tradition said that he wrote his laws in blood, which meant that Athens, the city of Athena, the Greek Minerva, had armed itself with these laws when it was ruled by the oligarchs. And the Chinese, who still write in hieroglyphics, regard the dragon as an emblem of civil authority.

[617] (3) The Roman fasces represent the fathers' divining wands or *litui* in the state of families. Describing the shield of Achilles, on which is depicted the history of the world, Homer mentions such a wand, which he significantly calls a sceptre. And Homer calls the father who holds it a king: in other words, he places the epoch of families before that of cities. With such divining wands, the fathers took the auspices and dictated punishments to their children. One such punishment for an impious son became the article on parricide in the Law of the Twelve Tables. The union of these wands or *litui* in the Roman fasces signifies the birth of the civil authority in the united orders of the heroic fathers.

[618] (4) Finally, Hercules wrestles with Antaeus. In other words, the archetype of the Heraclids or nobles of the heroic cities wrestles with the archetype of the rebellious servants. By lifting him into the air, that is, by leading the servants back to the first highland cities, Hercules conquers Antaeus and ties him to the earth. This was the source of the game which the Greeks called the 'knot', after the Herculean knot by which Hercules founded the heroic nations. By virtue of this knot, the plebeians paid the heroes the tithe of Hercules, which was the census or assessment on which aristocracies were based. Hence, under the census of Servius Tullius the Roman plebeians became the bondsmen, *nexi*, of the patricians. And by the oath described in Tacitus, the ancient Germans swore to serve their chieftains as vassals obliged to offer military service at their own expense, a burden of which the Roman plebeians still complained even in the period of supposed popular liberty. These plebeians were the first tribute-payers, *assidui*, so called because they fought at their own expense, *suis assibus militabant*. Yet rather than soldiers of fortune, they were soldiers of harsh necessity.

CHAPTER 3

Origins of the Census and Public Treasury

[619] For many years, the patricians continued to oppress the plebeians through burdensome usury and the frequent usurpation of their fields. At last, the tribune of the plebeians Lucius Marcus Philippus publicly denounced the fact that a mere 2,000 patricians owned fields which should have been divided among the 300,000 citizens which Rome then numbered. Now, some forty years after Tarquinius Superbus had been driven out, the Roman patricians, made bold by his death, had resumed their insolent treatment of the poor plebeians; and the senate was then obliged to introduce a new regulation. The plebeians were now to pay into the public treasury the tax they had hitherto paid privately to the patricians, so that the treasury could eventually provide for their expenses in wartime. From this point, the census assumed a new prominence in Roman history. According to Livy, the patricians disdained the administration of the census as unworthy of their dignity. But he is mistaken, for clearly no Roman magistracy had greater dignity than the censorship: witness the fact that from its inception it was administered by former consuls. (Livy failed to see that the patricians rejected it because it differed from the census established by Servius Tullius which, being paid privately to the patricians, formed the basis of aristocratic liberty. And this misled Livy and all the other historians into thinking that the census of Servius Tullius had formed the basis of popular liberty.)

In fact, it was the patricians themselves who by their own greedy devices instituted the census, which eventually formed the basis of popular liberty. By the time of the tribune Philippus, when all the fields had fallen into their hands, these 2,000 patricians had to pay tribute for the 300,000 other citizens which Rome then counted. (In precisely this way, all the land at Sparta came to be owned by a few.) For the public treasury held a register of the census taxes which the patricians had privately imposed on the fields when they had of old assigned these untilled lands to the plebeians to farm. This huge inequality provoked great tumults and rebellions among the plebeians. But they were soon quelled by the censor Quintus Fabius, whose prudent measures earned him the nickname Maximus, the Greatest. He ordered that the whole Roman people be divided into three classes – senators, knights, and plebeians – and that the citizens be assigned to a class according to their means. This consoled the plebeians. For now plebeians of sufficient wealth could enter the senatorial order, which had previously been open only to patricians and which held all the magistracies, so that the plebeians now found open to them the regular path to all civil honours.

[620] It is only in this manner that we may regard as true the tradition that the census of Servius Tullius formed the basis of popular liberty, since it provided the material and prepared the opportunities for this liberty. In my Notes on Chronology, I advanced this hypothesis concerning the Publilian Law. In fact, it was this ordinance, created in Rome itself, which established the democratic commonwealth there, rather than the Law of the Twelve Tables supposedly brought from Athens. Indeed, what Aristotle calls a democratic commonwealth is translated into Tuscan by Bernardo Segni as a commonwealth by census, meaning a free popular commonwealth. This is clear even from Livy who, despite his ignorance of the early Roman constitution, relates how the patricians complained that, under the Publilian Law, they had lost more at home than their armies had gained abroad in that year, when the Romans had won numerous great victories. For this reason, Publilius, as author of the law, was called the people's dictator.

[621] Under this popular liberty, the whole Roman people now constituted the city. As a result, civil ownership lost its proper meaning of public ownership, which had been called civil from the word city, and was instead divided and distributed among the private ownerships of all the Roman citizens now making up the city of Rome. Supreme ownership, *dominium optimum*, gradually lost its original sense of strongest ownership, not weakened by any real encumbrance, private or public; but it retained the limited meaning of ownership of property free of any private encumbrance. And quiritary ownership no longer signified the ownership of land by which, if the client or plebeian lost possession, the patrician granting ownership was required to defend him. Quiritary ownership now came to mean that kind of private civil ownership

which can be defended by 'revendication' or a suit for recovery of property. As such, it was distinguished from bonitary ownership, which is maintained by possession alone.

In early Roman law, quiritary ownership meant that the patricians were the first legal authorities, *auctores iuris*, who under the clientships founded by Romulus were obliged to teach the plebeians these laws and no others. For what other laws were the patricians obliged to teach the plebeians, when the latter had none of the privileges of citizenship until 445 BC, and when the patricians kept the laws secret in the pontifical college for a century after the Law of the Twelve Tables? Hence, the patricians at this time were *auctores iuris* of the kind which survives today when the owners of purchased lands are summoned by others in a suit for recovery of property, they 'cite the authors' of their title to assist and defend them.

[622] In exactly the same manner, the invariable nature of fiefs caused the recurrence of these institutions during the medieval return of barbarism. Let us consider the kingdom of France, for example. The many provinces which make up the modern French nation were once sovereign lordships of various princes who were subject to the king, but whose property was subject to no public encumbrance. Later, as a result of succession, rebellion, or default of heirs, they were gradually incorporated into the kingdom; and all the property which the princes formerly held by supreme right, *ex iure optimo*, became subject to public taxes. Even the lands and houses of the kings, including their royal Chambers, which had passed by marriage or concession to their vassals, are nowadays subject to tax and tribute. Thus, in hereditary kingdoms ownership by supreme right came to be confused with private ownership subject to public charges. In the same way, the Roman fisc, which was originally the emperor's patrimony, was later confused with the public treasury.

[623] Of all my research into Roman institutions, the study of the census and treasury has proved the most difficult, as I remarked in the Idea of this Work.

CHAPTER 4

The Origin of Roman Assemblies

[624] We have seen that Homer mentions two heroic Greek assemblies, the *boulē* and the *agora*. (1) The *boulē* corresponds to the Roman *comitia curiata*, or curiate assembly, which is the oldest recorded under the kings. (2) The *agora* in turn corresponds to the *comitia tributa*, or tribal assembly.

(1) The curiate assembly was so called from *quir*, spear. (Later, the genitive *quiris* became the nominative, as I explained in the first edition of my *New Science* under the 'Origins of the Latin Language'.) In the same way, from Greek *cheir*, hand, the symbol of power in all nations, was derived *kyría*, authority or power, which was synonymous with Latin *curia*. This was the origin of the Curetes, the priests armed with spears whom the Greeks found in Saturnia or ancient Italy, Crete, and Asia. (We have seen that all heroic peoples consisted of priests, and that only the nobles had the right to bear arms.) The ancient meaning of *kyría* was lordship, even as aristocracies today are called lordships. From the *kyría* of the heroic senates came the word for authority, *kyros*, which meant the authority of ownership. This etymology is shared by the Greek titles *kyrios*, lord, and *kyria*, lady. And just as the Greeks named the Curetes for *cheir*, so the Roman Quirites took their name from *quir*. Quirites was the title of Roman majesty given to the people in their public assembly. Earlier I compared the assemblies of the Curetes with those of the ancient Gauls and Germans, and concluded that all primitive barbarians held their public assemblies under arms.

[625] This shows that the majestic title of Quirites dates from the age when the Roman people consisted solely of patricians, who alone had the right to bear arms. Later, after Rome had become a democracy, the title was extended to the people, who now included the plebeians.

(2) The assembly of the plebeians, who at first had no right to arms, was called the *comitia tributa*, from *tribus*, tribe. Just as in the state of families the Romans named families for the *famuli*, in the state of cities they derived the word tribute from the tribes of plebeians. For these

tribes, which assembled to receive the orders of the ruling senate, were mainly and most often ordered to contribute to the public treasury.

[626] Later, Quintus Fabius Maximus introduced the new census which divided all the Roman people into three classes according to the citizens' patrimony. Until then, only senators had been knights, since in the heroic age only nobles had the right to bear arms. This is why historians divide the ancient Roman state into patrician 'fathers' and plebeians: for at that time the terms senator and patrician were synonymous, as were plebeian and base-born. Since there were only two classes of the Roman people, there were only two kinds of assembly: the curiate assembly comprising fathers, meaning patricians or senators; and the tribal assembly comprising plebeians, meaning base-born persons. But after Fabius divided the citizens according to their means into the three classes of senators, knights, and plebeians, the patricians ceased to be a separate order within the city and were assigned to one of the classes according to their means. From that time on, patricians were distinct from senators and knights, and plebeians from the base-born; and the plebeians were no longer differentiated from patricians, but from knights and senators. The term plebeian no longer meant a base-born person, but rather a citizen with a small patrimony, who might even be noble. On the other hand, the title of senator no longer meant a patrician, but a citizen of substantial patrimony, who might be base-born.

[627] From that time on, the centuriate assemblies, *comitia centuriata*, were the body in which all three classes of the Roman people met to enact consular laws among other business. By contrast, the term tribal assemblies, *comitia tributa*, was still used for the assemblies in which the plebeians alone enacted tribunitial laws, now called plebiscites, which originally meant what Cicero calls 'laws made known to the plebeians', *plebi nota*. (The jurist Pomponius cites the example of Junius Brutus announcing to the plebeians that the kings had been expelled from Rome for ever.) Accordingly, in monarchies the royal laws might with similar propriety be termed laws made known to the people, *populo nota*. The jurist Baldus, who was as discerning as he was lacking in erudition, expressed amazement that the word *plebiscitum* was written with one *s*: for it signifies *plebis-scitum*, decree of the plebs, from *sciscere*,

to decree, rather than *plebi-scitum*, known to the plebs, from *scire*, to know.

[628] Finally, the curiate assemblies, *comitia curiata*, in which only the heads of the curias met to discuss sacred institutions, continued as the body that certified divine rites. In the age of the kings, all secular institutions were considered sacred, and heroes everywhere were Curetes or armed priests, as noted above. Hence, down to the last days of Rome, since paternal power retained its sacred aspect, and its rules were called paternal rites, *sacra patria* in Roman law, it was by the laws of the curiate assemblies that solemn adoptions were sanctioned.

CHAPTER 5

Corollary: Divine Providence Ordains both Commonwealths and the Natural Law of Nations

[629] We have found that commonwealths were born in the age of the gods, when governments were theocratic, meaning divine. Later they developed into the first heroic governments, which I call human to distinguish them from the divine ones. Yet within these human governments, the age of the gods continued to run its course, just as the mighty current of a majestic river drives its surging flow of fresh water far out to sea. In this way, there persisted the religious way of thinking that the gods were responsible for human actions. (Thus they created Jupiter from the ruling fathers of the family state, Minerva from their closed orders in the nascent cities, Mercury from the ambassadors sent to rebellious clients, and Neptune from the heroic corsairs, as we shall see.) Here we must greatly admire divine providence: for while people were occupied with other matters, it instilled in them a fear of divinity, which is the first and most fundamental basis of a commonwealth. Religion in turn moved them to settle on the first vacant lands, which they became the first to occupy, an action which was the source of all later property rights. The most robust giants occupied lands on the mountain heights near perennial springs. There providence ordained that they would cease wandering and settle in places that were health-

ful, naturally secure, and abounding in water – the three qualities which make land suitable for building cities. Then, through religion providence induced them to unite with chosen women as their constant companions for life, thus creating the institution of marriage, which is the recognized source of all authority. Later, with these women they were moved to found families, which are the seed-bed of all commonwealths. Finally, with the opening of refuges they were moved to found clientships.

This process prepared the matter from which, by the first agrarian law, cities were born, composed of two communities: the nobles who command and the plebeians who obey. (When in a speech Homer's Telemachus calls the plebeians 'the other people', he means a subject people in distinction to the ruling heroes.) This furnishes the subject matter of political science, which is merely the science of commanding and obeying in civil states. At their birth, providence causes commonwealths to emerge aristocratic in form, as befits the savage and solitary nature of the first people. As political thinkers point out, this form of state consists entirely in safeguarding its boundaries and orders. In this way, the very form of government induces newly civilized peoples to continue to live within these restrictions, and thus to forget the infamous and abominable promiscuity of their bestial and brutish state. Now, such people had only very particular concepts and could not understand any general good, so that they habitually ignored the affairs of others, as Homer's Polyphemus tells Ulysses. (In this giant, Plato recognizes the family fathers of the so-called state of nature, which preceded that of the cities.) But providence used this aristocratic form of government to lead people to unite with their fatherlands. Hence, by seeking to preserve the great private interests of their family monarchies, which were their only absolute concept, these early peoples unintentionally joined together in the universal civil good we call a commonwealth.

[630] Let us now return to the 'divine proofs' outlined in my section on Method, and consider how simply and naturally providence ordained these human institutions, so that the first people unwittingly spoke the truth when they said that the gods made them. And let us reflect on the immense number of civil effects which may all be traced to the four causes which constitute the four elements of the civil universe:

religion, marriage, refuges, and the first agrarian law. Then let us consider all the human possibilities, and ponder whether such numerous, various, and diverse institutions could have arisen so simply and naturally in any other manner. (Epicurus calls people the products of chance, but chance did not make them swerve from their place in the natural order; and Zeno calls them creatures of necessity, but fate did not drag them from this natural order.) At the point when commonwealths were emerging, the civil matter was already prepared and ready to receive its form, and produced the format of commonwealths composed of both mind and body. The civil matter prepared to receive this form consisted of the people's own proper religions, languages, lands, nuptials, names (meaning clans and houses), arms, dominions, magistracies, and laws. Since all these elements were the people's own, they provided matter which was completely free and therefore constitutive of true commonwealths.

All of this was possible only because these institutions had already belonged to the family fathers when they were monarchs in the state of nature. So, when they now united in a social order, they created a sovereign civil power, formed of those sovereign family powers which in the state of nature had been subject to none but God. This sovereign civil power was a sort of person formed of mind and body. Its mind was an order of sages, who were as wise as was possible in that extremely crude and simple age. This established the first invariable property of commonwealths: that without an order of wise men, a state may outwardly appear to be a commonwealth, but is in fact a dead and soulless body. Its body in turn was formed of the head and lesser members. This established the second invariable property of commonwealths: that some citizens must apply their minds to the tasks of civil wisdom, while others must employ their bodies in the useful arts and crafts of peace and war. And the distinction between the two established a third invariable property of commonwealths: that the mind must always command, and the body always obey.

[631] Even more astonishing is the manner in which providence created natural law at the same time it created families. Now, all the families were born with some awareness of divinity, even if in their ignorance and disorder none knew the true one. As a result, each family

had its own religion, language, land, nuptials, name, arms, government, and laws. So, together with the families, providence created the natural law of the major clans which shared the same institutions, and the family fathers now extended this law over their clients. Then, when providence created commonwealths in an aristocratic form, it transformed the natural law of the major clans or families, as observed in the state of nature, into the natural law of the minor clans or nations, which they now observed in the age of the cities. For when the family fathers founded their natural order against the rebellious clients, they kept all the rights they had held over their clients within the civil orders, from which the plebeians were now excluded. This was the essence of the severely aristocratic form of the heroic commonwealths.

[632] In this manner, the natural law of nations, as now observed among peoples and nations, was born as a property of the sovereign civil powers of the nascent commonwealths. Accordingly, whenever a people or nation lacks this sovereign civil power with such properties, it is not properly a people or nation; nor can it exercise the natural law of nations with any foreign people or nation. Rather, both the law and its exercise will fall to another people or nation superior to it.

[633] These observations, together with the fact that the heroes of the first cities called themselves gods, explain the meaning of the proverbial phrase 'laws laid down by the gods', *iura a diis posita*, which is how the dictates of the natural law of nations were defined. This law was later replaced by what Ulpian called the natural law of human nations, on which philosophers and moral theologians based their concept of a natural law based on fully developed eternal reason. And so 'laws laid down by the gods' appropriately came to mean the natural law of nations as ordained by the true God.

CHAPTER 6

Heroic Politics Continued

[634] As all historians agree, the heroic age began with the corsair raids of Minos and with Jason's naval expedition to Pontus; it continued through the Trojan War; and it ended with the wanderings of heroes which concluded with Ulysses' return to Ithaca. It must have been in such a sea-going age that the last of the major deities, *Neptune*, was born. The authority of the historians can be confirmed both by a philosophical argument, and by a philological argument based on several golden passages in Homer. The philosophical argument is that the naval and nautical arts were the last inventions of the nations, since their invention required the greatest ingenuity. Thus, Daedalus, who invented these arts, became a symbol of ingenuity; and Lucretius uses the phrase *daedala tellus* to mean the creative earth. As to the philological argument, we find several passages in Homer's *Odyssey* in which Ulysses, going ashore or driven ashore by a storm, climbs a hill to look for smoke as a sign of human habitation. These Homeric passages are in turn confirmed by the golden passage in which Plato, cited by Strabo in Axiom 98, describes the horror the first nations long felt towards the sea. The reason for this was noted by Thucydides, who writes that in their fear of corsair raids the Greek nations were slow to move down to coastal dwellings. This is why Neptune is portrayed as armed with the trident he used to make the earth quake. This must have been a large hook for grappling ships, which by an apt metaphor was called a tooth, *dent*, intensified by the superlative prefix 'three', *tri*. With this trident, Neptune made people's cities, *terre*, quake in fear of his raids. Later, by Homer's day he was believed to cause the very earth, *terra*, to quake. In this belief, Homer was followed by Plato, who places a watery abyss in the bowels of the earth.

[635] Corsair raids were symbolized by bulls: witness Jupiter abducting Europa, and the Minotaur or bull of Minos abducting youths and maidens from the coast of Attica. (By the same token, sails came to be called 'the horns of ships', an expression used by Virgil.) Landsmen

thus spoke truly when they said that the Minotaur had devoured their children, for they would watch with fright and grief as ships swallowed them up. In just this way, the Orc seeks to devour Andromeda, who is chained to the rock and turned to stone by her fright, whence Latin retains the phrase 'immobilized with terror', *terrore defixus*. And the winged horse which Perseus rides to her rescue must likewise have been a corsair ship, for sails came to be called the 'wings' of ships. As one versed in heroic antiquities, Virgil in speaking of Daedalus, the inventor of the sailship, calls his flying machine a 'rowing of wings', *alarum remigium*. Daedalus was said to be the brother of Theseus. Thus, Theseus must be an archetype of the Athenian youths who, under the law of force practised on them by Minos, are devoured by his Minotaur, the bull symbolizing a pirate ship. And Ariadne, who represents the art of seafaring, teaches Theseus to use the thread of navigation to escape from the labyrinth of Daedalus. For although labyrinths later became elegant playgrounds in royal villas, the first labyrinth represented the Aegean Sea as it winds among its many islands. After Theseus learns the labyrinthine art of the Cretans, he abandons Ariadne and returns home with her sister Phaedra, who must symbolize an art related to seafaring. Then he kills the Minotaur and frees Athens from the cruel tribute which Minos had imposed: in other words, the Athenians now become corsairs. As Phaedra was Ariadne's sister, Theseus was Daedalus' brother.

[636] In his life of Theseus, Plutarch says that the heroes considered it a great honour and a military distinction to be called brigands. (Later, in the medieval return of barbarism 'corsair' was considered a title of nobility.) About the same time, the laws of Solon are said to have allowed associations for purposes of piracy, which shows how well Solon understood the perfect civilization which we now enjoy, in which pirates are not even protected by the natural law of nations! What is even more astonishing, Plato and Aristotle regarded brigandage as a form of hunting. For all their barbarity, the ancient Germans agreed with these great philosophers. According to Caesar, the Germans did not consider brigandage disgraceful, but counted it among the valorous pursuits by which persons with no particular trade could avoid idleness. This barbarous custom persisted for a long time even among the most

enlightened nations. According to Polybius, when the Romans imposed peace terms on the Carthaginians, they prohibited them from sailing beyond Cape Pelorum in Sicily 'either for piracy or for trade'. The example of the Romans and Carthaginians is less significant, since they themselves acknowledged their own barbarism in that age. (This is clear from several passages in Plautus, who says that he has translated Greek comedies into a barbarous tongue, meaning Latin.) What is more significant is that the highly civilized Greeks, even in their age of advanced civilization, continued to practise this barbarous custom, which furnishes nearly all the plots of their comedies. It is perhaps for this same custom that the northern coast of Africa, where it is still practised against Christians, is called Barbary.

[637] The basic principle of the ancient law of war is the inhospitality of heroic peoples. They looked on foreigners as their perpetual enemies, and based the reputation of their dominions on keeping them as far as possible from their borders. (This is how Tacitus describes the Suevi, who were the most highly regarded nation of the ancient Germans.) And heroic peoples regarded foreigners as brigands. In a golden passage, Thucydides relates that even in his day when travellers met on land or sea they would ask each other if they were pirates, meaning foreigners. Yet the Greeks rapidly grew more civilized, and soon cast off this barbarous custom, reserving the name 'barbarian' for all the nations that continued to practise it. This sense was preserved in the name Barbary, the land of the Troglodytes, who were supposed to kill foreigners who crossed their borders. There are barbarous nations today which still practise this custom. Even civilized nations clearly admit no foreigners who have not obtained their permission.

[638] The Romans were one of the nations which the Greeks called barbarians for this reason. This is clear from two golden passages in the Law of the Twelve Tables. The first reads 'Against any foreigner title of ownership holds good for ever', *Adversus hostem aeterna auctoritas esto*. The second is cited by Cicero: 'When a day has been appointed, let him appear with a foreigner', *Si status dies sit, cum hoste venito*. In this passage, many have conjectured from general terms that the noun *hostis* is a metaphor for the adversary in a lawsuit. But Cicero observes that in early Latin *hostis* meant the same as the later *peregrinus*, which proves

my point. Taken together, these two passages suggest that the Romans originally regarded foreigners as perpetual wartime foes.

But we may rather interpret these passages as referring to the world's first *hostes*, who were the foreigners received in the refuges, who later became the plebeians of the emerging heroic cities. In this way, the passage cited by Cicero means that on the appointed day 'the noble shall appear with the plebeian to claim his farm for him'. And the 'eternal authority' mentioned in the same law was that held over the plebeians. We recall that Aristotle was cited as saying that the heroes swore eternal enmity against the plebeians, as Axiom 86 states. Under this heroic law, no matter how long a plebeian possessed Roman land, he could not gain ownership through usucaption, for title to such property could only pass between patricians. This is a major reason why the Law of the Twelve Tables did not recognize simple possession.

Later, as heroic law sank into disuse and human law gained force, the Roman praetors treated simple possession as an 'extraordinary' case. For they could neither cite nor construe any passage in the Law of the Twelve Tables as a basis for ordinary judgments, whether strict or equitable. The reason for this was that the law regarded simple possession by plebeians as subject in every case to the pleasure of the patricians. Nor did it deal with acts of theft or violence by the patricians. For it is an invariable property of the first commonwealths that they had no laws concerning private wrongs or offences, as Aristotle said in Axiom 85. Instead, individuals were left to settle such wrongs by force of arms, as we shall see in Book 4. As a solemn act of property claims, this real force survived in the symbolic force which Aulus Gellius calls 'festucary', sanctioned with a stalk. All this is confirmed by the interdict 'Against violence', *Unde vi*, which a praetor issued in an extraordinary ruling, because the Law of the Twelve Tables did not envision, much less mention, private acts of violence. And it is confirmed by two actions which were also late praetorian rulings: 'On violent robbery of property', *De vi bonorum raptorum*, and 'What was done in fear', *Quod metus causa*.

[639] Such was the heroic custom of regarding foreigners as perpetual enemies, which each people observed privately during peacetime. Extended abroad, it became the recognized and common custom that all heroic nations perpetually waged war on each other and continually

carried out raids by land and sea. We recall that Plato says that cities were founded on the basis of arms. And even before they waged war on one another, they were initially governed by wartime measures. Hence, in Greek the word for war, *polemos*, is derived from *polis*, city.

[640] As proof of these assertions, I offer an important observation. The Romans extended their conquests and gained their victories over the world on the basis of four laws which they had already used to govern the plebeians at home. (1) In the more barbaric provinces, they employed the clientships of Romulus which sent Roman colonists to make day labourers of the owners of the fields. (2) In the more civilized provinces, they employed the agrarian law of Servius Tullius which granted them bonitary ownership of the fields. (3) In Italy, they employed the agrarian law of the Twelve Tables which granted its inhabitants the quiritary ownership enjoyed on the lands known as Italian soil, *solum italicum*. (4) To free municipalities and meritorious towns, they granted the right to solemn marriage and the share in the consulship which had been extended to the Roman plebeians.

[641] The perpetual enmity between the first cities meant that declarations of war were unnecessary, and that brigand raids were considered lawful. By contrast, after the nations ceased to practise such customs, undeclared wars came to be considered a sort of brigandage, so that they were no longer recognized by what Ulpian called the natural law of human nations. This perpetual enmity explains the long years of war waged by Rome and Alba as in fact a long period of mutual raids. In this light, it makes more sense that Horatius' sister, who was killed for mourning the Alban Curiatius, had been abducted by him rather than married to him. (Romulus himself could not marry a woman from Alba, even though he was of the royal house of Alba and had done Rome the great service of expelling the tyrant Amulius and restoring the legitimate king Numitor.) It is important to note that victory in such wars was determined by the outcome of heroic combat fought by the most interested parties. In Rome's war with Alba, these were the three Horatii and the three Curiatii. In the Trojan War, they were Paris and Menelaus; but when their combat proved indecisive, the Greeks and Trojans continued fighting to end the war. Later, during the medieval return of barbarism, princes resolved the disputes of their

realms by personal combat, to whose outcome their peoples were subject. We see, then, that Alba was the Latin Troy, and Horatia the Roman Helen. (Indeed, in his *Rhetoric*, Gerard Jan Voss mentions a parallel to Horatia in Greek legend.) And the ten years of the Greek siege of Troy must correspond to the years of the Roman siege of Veii. In both cases, this precise figure stands for an undetermined number of years in which cities waged perpetual hostilities on one another.

[642] For the rational system of numbers was highly abstract, and therefore was the last thing to be grasped by the ancient nations, as we shall see. Later, when their reason was more developed, the Romans said six hundred, *sexcenta*, for any number beyond reckoning; just as the Italians used to say a hundred, *cento*, and then a hundred thousand, *centomila*, with the same meaning. For only the minds of philosophers can grasp the idea of infinity. This may explain why early peoples used twelve to mean a large number. Witness the twelve gods of the greater tribes, which in fact Varro and the Greeks reckoned as 30,000; or the twelve labours of Hercules, which must have been innumerable. So too the Romans said there were twelve parts to the farthing, *as*, which can in fact be divided infinitesimally. Another example must be the Twelve Tables, because of the countless laws which were later inscribed on tables at various times.

[643] At the time of the Trojan War, the name Achaeans must have referred to the Greeks who lived near the site of the conflict. (Earlier, they had been called Pelasgians after Pelasgus, one of Greece's most ancient heroes.) Later, the name Achaeans must have gradually spread throughout Greece. According to Pliny, it lasted to the conquest of Greece by Lucius Mummius in 146 BC; thereafter the Greeks were called Hellenes. It must have been this diffusion of the name Achaeans which led people in Homer's day to believe that all the Greeks had been allies in the Trojan War. In precisely this way, Tacitus relates that the name Germany eventually spread over a large part of Europe, when it derived from the tribes who, having crossed the Rhine and expelled the Gauls, began to call themselves Germans. Thus, the glory of this people extended their name throughout Germany, just as the fame of the Trojan War spread the name Achaeans throughout Greece. Yet in

their barbarism, early peoples knew so little about alliances that not even the subjects of offended kings bothered to take up arms to avenge them, as the beginning of the Trojan War shows us.

[644] Only this aspect of heroic nature can solve the remarkable problem of Spain. This land was the mother of many nations which Cicero hails as courageous and warlike, and whose valour Caesar experienced at first hand. In other regions of the world, which he conquered without exception, Caesar fought for empire; in Spain alone did he fight for survival. Saguntum collapsed thunderously, but it cost Hannibal eight months of strain to take it by siege, even though his African forces were still fresh and complete. (Later, when those forces were tired and much reduced, he won at Cannae and nearly held a triumph over Rome on its own Capitoline.) Numantia fell with a crash which shook the glory of Rome, despite her recent triumph over Carthage; and it fell only after it had put to the test the valour and wisdom of Scipio, conqueror of Africa. Why was it, then, that Spain never united all her peoples and established a world empire on the banks of the Tagus? Instead, she occasioned the pathetic eulogy of Lucius Florus, who wrote that Spain only discovered her strength after she had been conquered little by little. (In his life of Agricola, Tacitus notes the same custom among the Britons, who in his day were known as fierce warriors, and characterizes them with this equally apt expression: 'As long as they fight singly, they are defeated as a nation', *dum singuli pugnant, universi vincuntur*). For until they were attacked, the Spanish stayed like beasts in the dens of their boundaries, and continued to live the savage and solitary life of the Cyclopes.

[645] Now, historians were inspired and even blinded by the fame of heroic naval warfare, and so paid little notice to heroic land warfare, and even less to the heroic politics by which the Greeks must have governed themselves in that age. But the insightful and learned Thucydides has left us an important piece of information, when he relates that all the heroic cities were built without walls, like the later cities of Sparta and Numantia, which was the Spanish Sparta. And given their proud and violent nature, the heroes were continually driving each other from power. In the kingdom of Alba, for example, Amulius drove out Numitor, and Romulus drove out Amulius and restored Numitor.

We see, then, how much certainty chronologers may derive for their timelines from the heroic genealogies of Greek royal houses and from the unbroken succession of the fourteen Latin kings! During the medieval return of barbarism, especially in its most primitive period, we read of nothing more varying and inconstant than the fortunes of kingdoms, as my Notes on Chronology indicate. Indeed, Tacitus most prudently refers to this fact in the opening sentence of his *Annals*: 'In the beginning kings had the city of Rome', *Urbem Romam principio reges habuere*. He uses the verb *habere*, which signifies the weakest of the three degrees of possession distinguished by the jurists, *habere, tenere, possidere*, 'to have, hold, and possess'.

[646] The political events of such unstable kingdoms are narrated by poetic history in the many myths which feature singing contests. Like the Latin verbs for singing, *canere* and *cantare*, which mean 'to predict', such myths refer to heroic contentions concerning the auspices.

[647] For example, when the satyr Marsyas – the sort of monstrous hybrid Livy calls of discordant nature – is defeated by Apollo in a contest of song, he is flayed alive by the god. Behold the savagery of heroic punishments! In a similar contest of song, Apollo slays Linus, who must be a symbol of the plebeians. (There was another Linus, who was clearly a heroic poet since he was associated with Amphion, Orpheus, Musaeus, and others.) In both myths, the contests are with Apollo, the god of divinity, meaning the science of divination or of the auspices. We saw earlier that Apollo was also the god of the nobility, since the science of the auspices belonged to the nobles alone.

[648] There are similar myths. The Sirens put sailors to sleep with their song and then slit their throats. The Sphinx poses enigmas to travellers and kills them when they find no solution. Circe uses incantations to turn Ulysses' comrades into swine. (From such incantations or enchantments, the verb *cantare*, to sing, was later interpreted as meaning 'to practise witchcraft': witness Virgil's phrase *cantando rumpitur anguis*, 'the serpent is destroyed by the spell'. Magic must originally have been the astrological wisdom of auspicial divination in Persia; only later did it come to mean the art of sorcerers, whose spells were called incantations.) In such myths, the sailors, travellers, and wanderers represent the foreigners of the heroic cities. In other words, they are

plebeians who contend with the heroes to share in the auspices, are defeated in the attempt, and are cruelly punished.

[649] In the same fashion, Pan tries to seize the nymph Syrinx, who is famed for her song, but finds himself embracing reeds. Similarly, the enamoured Ixion reaches towards Juno, the goddess of solemn nuptials, but instead embraces a cloud. In these myths, reeds signify the inconstancy of natural marriages, and the cloud their emptiness. From this cloud, it is said, were born the centaurs, meaning the plebeians, who are Livy's monsters with discordant natures, and who abduct the brides of the Lapiths during their wedding ceremony. Likewise, Midas, who is a plebeian, hides his ass's ears, only to have them revealed by Pan's reeds, that is, by natural marriage. In precisely this way, the Roman patricians argued that the plebeians were all monsters because 'they practised marriages like wild beasts'.

[650] Vulcan must also be a plebeian. When he attempts to interfere in a contention between Jupiter and Juno, he is literally kicked out of heaven by Jupiter, falls headlong to earth, and is left crippled. This symbolizes the plebeians' contention with the heroes to share in Jupiter's auspices and Juno's solemnized marriage. Defeated in this contention, they were left crippled, which is to say humiliated.

[651] Similarly, Phaethon, who as part of Apollo's family is regarded as a child of the Sun, attempts to drive his father's golden chariot, which is the chariot of poetic gold, or grain. But he swerves from the regular course that leads to the family father's granary; and when he lays claim to ownership of the fields, he is cast down headlong from heaven.

[652] The most significant symbol is the apple of discord that falls from heaven. (The apple signifies ownership of the fields, and the first discord on earth arose when the plebeians sought to cultivate fields for themselves.) In this myth, the plebeian Venus contends with Juno for solemn nuptials, and with Minerva for dominion. As for the Judgment of Paris, our good fortune preserves Plutarch's essay on Homer, in which he notes that the two verses at the end of the *Iliad* which mention it are not by Homer, but by a later hand.

[653] Similarly, Atalanta throws golden apples to defeat her suitors in a footrace, precisely as Hercules wrestles with Antaeus and defeats him. In other words, Atalanta grants the plebeians first bonitary, and

then quiritary ownership of the fields, but reserves solemnized marriage for herself. Precisely so, the Roman patricians granted the first agrarian law of Servius Tullius and the second agrarian law in the Twelve Tables, but still kept solemn marriage rights within their order. For the article which reads 'Solemnized marriages shall not be shared with plebeians', *Connubia incommunicata plebi sunto*, is the direct consequence of the earlier article 'The auspices shall not be shared with plebeians', *Auspicia incommunicata plebi sunto*. This is why the plebeians began to claim solemnized marriage three years after the Twelve Tables, a right which they won after another three years of heroic contention.

[654] In the *Odyssey*, the suitors of Penelope invaded Ulysses' palace, which symbolized the kingdom of the heroes. They called themselves kings, devoured the royal estate by appropriating ownership of the fields, and claimed Penelope for a wife, that is, laid claim to solemnized marriage. In some versions, Penelope preserved her chastity, and Ulysses hung the suitors like thrushes from a net, like the net heroic Vulcan used to catch the plebeian Mars and Venus. (In other words, Ulysses bound the suitors to cultivating the fields like Achilles' day labourers, just as Coriolanus sought to reduce to Romulus' labourers the plebeians who were not content with Servius Tullius' agrarian law.) Ulysses also fought with the pauper Irus and killed him, which must refer to an agrarian contention in which plebeians were devouring Ulysses' estate. In other versions, Penelope prostituted herself to the suitors: in other words, she shared solemnized marriage with plebeians. From this union was born Pan, a monster with two discordant natures, human and bestial, precisely like the monstrous hybrid mentioned by Livy. For the Roman patricians said that if the plebeians shared in the nobility's solemnized marriage, their offspring would resemble Pan, that monster of two discordant natures which Penelope bore after prostituting herself to the plebs.

[655] From her union with a bull, Pasiphae gave birth to the Minotaur, another monster with two discordant natures. This mythical history must mean that the Cretans shared solemnized marriage with foreigners who arrived aboard a ship which was called a 'bull'. The bull symbolized the pirate ship in which Minos abducted youths and maidens from Attica, and Jupiter abducted Europa.

[656] The myth of Io also related to this kind of civil history. Jupiter fell in love with her, that is, he favoured her with his auspices. Juno was jealous with the civil jealousy of the heroes who guarded solemn nuptials; and she placed Io under the watch of hundred-eyed Argus, that is, of the many Argive fathers, each with his clearing, or cultivated land. But by playing his pipe, which must mean his song, Mercury put Argus to sleep. In other words, Mercury, the archetype of the mercenary plebeians, defeated the Argive fathers in a contention for the auspices, which sang the future in solemn nuptial rites. Io was then changed into a cow, mated with the same bull as Pasiphae, and went wandering in Egypt, that is, among those Egyptian foreigners who helped Danaus drive the Inachids from the kingdom of Argos.

[657] As Hercules aged, he grew effeminate and had to spin at the bidding of Iole and Omphale. In other words, the heroic right to the fields was subjected to the womanly plebeians. By contrast, the heroes called themselves 'men', *viri* in Latin, which is synonymous with 'heroes' in Greek. Virgil uses the word emphatically at the beginning of his *Aeneid*: *Arma virumque cano*, 'Arms and the man I sing'. And Horace translates the first verse of the *Odyssey* as *Dic mihi, Musa, virum*, 'Tell me, Muse, of the man.' Later, the Romans continued to use the noun *viri* to mean magistrates, priests, judges, and husbands by solemn matrimony. For in poetic aristocracies, magistracies, priesthoods, judge-ships, and solemn marriages were restricted to the heroic orders. In this myth, the heroic right to the fields was shared with the plebeians of Greece, just as the Roman patricians shared the quiritary right with the plebeians under the second agrarian law, which they fought for and won in the Law of the Twelve Tables.

In precisely the same way, fiefs in the medieval return of barbarism were called goods of the lance, whereas allodial goods were called goods of the distaff, as we read in the Law of the Angles. In allusion to the Salic law, which bars women from succeeding to the kingdom of France, the French royal arms are supported by two angels wearing dalmatics and bearing spears, and are adorned by the heroic motto *Lilia non nent*, 'Lilies do not spin'. To our good fortune, we find that Baldus called the Salic law 'the law of the clans of France', *ius gentium Gallorum*. By the same token, we may speak of 'the law of the clans of Rome', *ius gentium Romanorum*, after the Law of the Twelve Tables, inasmuch as it severely restricted intestate succession to direct heirs and relatives through the males. Later, I shall show how little truth there is in the belief that it was customary in early Rome for daughters to succeed intestate to their fathers, and that this custom passed into law in the Twelve Tables!

[658] Finally, Hercules burst into a fury when he was stained with the blood of the centaur Nessus, who was precisely the sort of plebeian monster which Livy describes as having two discordant natures. In other words, during a time of civil fury Hercules shared solemnized marriage with the plebeians, and died contaminated with plebeian blood. The Roman Hercules called Fidius died in this way under the Poetelian Law *de nexu*, by which in Livy's phrase 'the bond of faith came unbound', *vinculum fidei victum est*.

Now, Livy applies this phrase to an event which, some ten years later, was substantially the same as that which occasioned the Poetelian Law. In any case, it would have required action rather than mere words to 'unbind the bond of faith'. Clearly, this must be the phrase of some ancient annalist, which Livy cites with his usual blend of good faith and incomprehension. After plebeian debtors had been freed from private imprisonment by patrician creditors, they were still compelled by judicial laws to pay their debts. But they were now released from feudal bond, the law of the Herculean knot, which originated in the world's first refuges and which Romulus had used to found Rome in his refuge. Hence, we may well conjecture that the annalist wrote *vinculum Fidii*, the bond of the god Fidius, whom Varro identifies as the Hercules of the Romans. But when later historians failed to understand the name Fidius, they mistakenly substituted the word *fides*, faith. This same heroic natural law is found among the American Indians. In our own hemisphere, it persists among the Abyssinians in Africa, the Muscovites in Europe, and the Tartars in Asia. The Jews practised it with greater clemency, for among them debtors faced no more than seven years of servitude.

[659] To cite one last myth, Orpheus founded Greece with his lyre, which is a cord or force, which symbolizes the bond of the Herculean knot, the *nexus* of the Poetelian Law. He was killed by bacchants, or

frenzied plebeians, who smashed to pieces his lyre, a symbol of the law. In other words, the heroes in Homer's day were already taking foreign women as their wives, and bastards became royal successors, which indicates that Greece had begun to enjoy popular liberty.

[660] All these myths lead us to conclude that the heroic age took its name from such heroic contentions. Many of the leaders of these struggles were defeated and oppressed, and so put to sea with their followers, wandering in search of new lands. Some of them, like Menelaus and Ulysses, eventually returned to their homelands. Others settled in foreign lands, among them Cecrops, Cadmus, Danaus, and Pelops, who settled in Greece. (In Phoenicia, Egypt, and Phrygia, heroic contentions took place many centuries before those in Greece, since their civilizations had begun earlier.) One such refugee must have been Dido, who fled Phoenicia to escape the persecution of her brother-in-law's faction, and settled in Carthage, which from its Phoenician origin was called a Punic city. After the destruction of Troy, several Trojan refugees fled to Italy: Capys settled in Capua, Aeneas landed in Latium, and Antenor journeyed inland to Padua.

[661] In this manner, there ended the age of the theological poets, who were the wise men and statesmen of the Greeks' poetic age, men like Orpheus, Amphion, Linus, Musaeus, and others. It was the duty of such poets to sing hymns of praise to the gods, that is, to praise divine providence. And by singing the power of the gods revealed in the auspices, they kept the plebeians in subjection to their heroic orders. In precisely this way, some three centuries after the foundation of Rome, Appius Claudius, grandson of the decemvir, ensured the plebeians' obedience by singing about the divine power of the auspices, which could only be interpreted by the patricians' science. And in precisely the same way, by singing to his lyre, Amphion caused the stones to move and raise the walls of Thebes, which Cadmus had founded three centuries earlier; in other words, he confirmed its heroic state.

CHAPTER 7

*Corollaries on Roman Antiquities, Particularly the
Imaginary Monarchy at Rome and the Imaginary
Popular Liberty Established by Junius Brutus*

[662] The many parallels I have drawn between the civil institutions of
the Greeks and Romans show that ancient Roman history is an
unbroken historical mythology, containing elements of many various
and diverse Greek myths. These parallels will force the reader who
possesses true intelligence, rather than mere memory or imagination,
to recognize the following fact: that from the age of kings to the sharing
of solemnized marriage with the plebeians, the Roman people, the
people of Mars, was composed only of patricians. During the trial of
Horatius, King Tullus Hostilius as ruler of these nobles granted the
right of anyone condemned by the duumvirs or quaestors to appeal to
the entire order. The only orders were made up of the heroes, and the
plebeians were mere accessions to them, in the same way that provinces
later were accessions to conquering nations, as Grotius rightly observed.
Hence, the plebeians were the 'other people', as Telemachus called
them in a public assembly. By applying the irrefutable force of our
metaphysical critique to the founders of nations, we may refute the
following error: that, after the death of Romulus, work-gangs of base-
born labourers were treated as slaves, but had the right to elect kings
subject to the patricians' approval. This anachronistic view dates from
a later age, when the plebeians were Roman citizens and, having
obtained solemnized marriage by the patricians, shared in the creation
of consuls. But it was mistakenly dated back three centuries to the
interregnum which followed the death of Romulus.

[663] Since neither the philosophers nor the philologists could
imagine such severe aristocracies, they extended our modern sense of
the word 'people' to the early age of the first cities. This also entailed
misconceptions about the words 'king' and 'liberty', so that everyone
believed that the Roman kingship was a monarchy and that the liberty
established by Junius Brutus was popular. Even Jean Bodin fell into

the common error of previous political thinkers, and assumed that monarchies came first, then tyrannies, next democracies, and finally aristocracies. (This shows us how what distortions of human ideas can and do occur when true principles are lacking!) Then, when Bodin observed the effects of aristocracy within the imagined popular liberty of Rome, he propped up his theory by making the distinction that ancient Rome had a popular constitution, but was governed aristocratically. Even so, the facts still contradicted him, and this prop could not keep his political fabrication from collapsing. At last, the force of truth compelled Bodin to confess with gross inconsistency that both the constitution and administration of the ancient Romans were aristocratic.

[664] All this is confirmed by Livy, who explicitly affirms that there was no change whatsoever in the form of the Roman constitution when Junius Brutus instituted the office of two annual consuls. This was in fact the course which Brutus, as a wise man, was obliged to follow in restoring the corrupt state to its original principles. With the creation of the consuls, Livy writes, 'the royal power suffered no diminution', *nihil quicquam de regia potestate deminutum*. Indeed, the two consuls became annual aristocratic kings. In his *Laws* Cicero calls them 'annual kings', just as the kings reigned for life at Sparta, which was unquestionably an aristocracy. And, as everyone knows, the consuls were subject to recall during their reign, just as the Spartan kings were subject to censure by the ephors. And after their year's reign, they could be put on trial, just as the Spartan kings could be condemned to death by the ephors.

This passage in Livy shows us two things. First, the Roman kingship was aristocratic. Second, the liberty established by Brutus, rather than being popular because it secured the people's freedom from their lords, was lordly and aristocratic because it secured the patricians' freedom from the Tarquins. Brutus could clearly not have achieved this liberty without the pretext offered him by the rape of Lucretia, which he shrewdly exploited. This scandal abounded in circumstances sublime enough to arouse the plebeians' feelings against the tyrant Tarquinius. As for the patricians, Tarquinius had treated them so badly that Brutus found it necessary to rebuild the senate, which had been so depleted by Tarquinius' execution of many senators. By shrewd planning, Brutus benefited the Roman people in two ways: he strengthened the order of the patricians, which was declining; and he won the favour of the plebeians by choosing many of them, no doubt including the most militant opponents of his reform of the patriciate, and enrolling them in the patricians' order. In this way, he unified the city of Rome, which until then had been completely divided, in Livy's phrase, between patricians and plebeians, *inter patres et plebem*.

[665] We have examined the many various and diverse causes which preceded the kingship at Rome, beginning with the age of Saturn. Bodin in turn has traced the many varied effects of this kingship on the ancient Roman republic. And Livy has described the unbroken continuity which links historical causes to their effects. Now, if all these arguments do not suffice to prove my thesis – that the Roman kingship was aristocratic, and that Brutus established the liberty of the patricians – we can conclude only that the Romans, a barbarous and rude people, enjoyed a special privilege from God. (By contrast, this privilege was denied the Greeks, who were a shrewd and highly civilized people. According to Thucydides they knew nothing about their own antiquity before the Peloponnesian War, the most brilliant age of Greece, as I remarked in my Notes on Chronology. In these Notes, I showed that the same was true of the Romans until the second Punic War, from which point Livy professes to write Roman history with greater certitude, even though he openly confesses his ignorance of three important circumstances of that war.) Yet, even if we grant such a privilege to the Romans, the surviving record would without my Science remain an obscure recollection of confused images, so that no rational mind can reject the arguments I have made about Roman antiquities.

CHAPTER 8

Corollary on the Heroism of the First Peoples

[666] The topic of the early world's heroic age inevitably leads us to a discussion of the heroism of the first peoples. The relevant axioms and principles of my Poetic Politics show that this heroism was utterly different from the heroism which the philosophers imagined was produced by the incomparable wisdom of the ancients. For the philosophers were misled by the historians about the meaning of those three ill-defined terms – people, king, and liberty – and thought that heroic peoples included plebeians, that their kings were monarchs, and that their liberty was popular. Moreover, the philosophers applied to heroic peoples three ideas proper to their own refined and educated minds: first, a sense of justice rationally derived from tenets of Socratic morality; second, a notion of glory conceived as fame won by beneficial service to humankind; and third, the desire for immortality. These errors and mistaken ideas led the philosophers to believe that the kings and other great individuals of antiquity devoted themselves, their families, and their entire patrimonies and estates to ensuring the happiness of the poor, who always form the majority of cities and nations.

[667] Yet in describing Achilles, the greatest of the Greek heroes, Homer records three qualities which run contrary to the philosophers' three ideas. Consider first his sense of justice. When Hector asks to be buried if he is killed, Achilles disregards both their equal rank and their common lot – two considerations which naturally induce people to recognize justice – and savagely replies: 'When did men ever come to terms with lions? When were wolves and lambs of one mind?' What's more, he adds: 'If I kill you, I shall drag you around the walls of Troy, naked and bound to my chariot, for three days' (which he does), 'and at last I shall throw you as food to my hunting dogs.' This he would have done too, if Hector's wretched father Priam had not come to ransom the corpse from him.

Consider next Achilles' idea of glory. When he is personally aggrieved by Agamemnon's wrongful seizure of Briseis, Achilles considers himself affronted by both the gods and men, and complains to Jupiter that his honour must be restored. Then he withdraws his men from the allied army and his ships from the fleet, and allows Hector to slaughter the Greeks. Against the dictates of that devotion which all owe to their homeland, he stubbornly avenges a personal affront by ruining his entire nation. What's more, he shamelessly rejoices with Patroclus at Hector's slaughter of his fellow Greeks. And even worse, this hero who carries Troy's fate in his heel expresses the disgraceful wish that all the Greeks and Trojans may die in the war, leaving only Patroclus and himself alive.

Consider the third idea, the desire for immortality. When Ulysses asks Achilles in the underworld if he is happy there, he replies that he would rather be the ignoblest slave among the living. This is the hero whom Homer sings as a model of heroic virtue to the peoples of Greece and to whom he gives the invariable epithet 'blameless'! If, as poets should, Homer benefits us by offering delightful instruction, this epithet can be interpreted only to mean a man so arrogant that he won't let a fly buzz past the tip of his nose, as we say in Italian. In fact, Homer is preaching the virtue of punctiliousness on which medieval duellists based their entire morality, and which inspired the haughty laws, pompous ceremonies, and vindictive satisfactions of the knights errant celebrated in romance.

[668] In this light, let us ponder the oath of eternal enmity which Aristotle says the heroes swore against the plebeians. And let us further ponder Roman history in the age of Roman virtue. Livy identifies this period as the time of the war with Pyrrhus, which he hails in the phrase: 'No age was more fruitful in virtues', *nulla aetas virtutum feracior*. Following Sallust, who is cited in Augustine's *City of God*, we may expand this period from the expulsion of the kings down to the second Punic War. In this age, Brutus sacrifices two sons of his house to the cause of liberty. Scaevola places his right hand in the fire for failing to kill Porsena, which so unnerves the Etruscan king that he is put to flight. Manlius, nicknamed the Imperious, has his son beheaded for a breach of military discipline, even though he was driven by his passion for valour and glory, and won a victory. Men like Marcus Curtius throw themselves, mounted and armed, into fatal chasms. The Decii,

father and son, sacrifice themselves to save their armies. Gaius Fabricius refuses the piles of gold offered him by the Samnites. Manius Curius refuses to share in Pyrrhus' kingdoms. And Atilius Regulus returns to certain and cruel death in Carthage in order to preserve the sanctity of Roman oaths.

Yet what did any of these men do for the poor and wretched plebeians of Rome? Did they not increase their wartime burdens, plunge them deeper into seas of usury, and bury them deeper in the patricians' private prisons, where they were stripped to the waist and caned like ignoble slaves? And if anyone sought to offer the plebs some small relief through agrarian or grain laws, he was accused of treason and executed. To cite one example, such was the fate of Manlius Capitolinus, even though he had prevented the fierce Senones of Gaul from burning the Capitoline. In Sparta, which was the city of Greek heroes as Rome was the city of the world's heroes, the magnanimous king Agis shared this fate. When Agis attempted to free the poor plebeians from the nobles' oppressive usury by a law cancelling debts, and tried to aid them by a testamentary law, the ephors had him strangled. The valorous Agis was thus the Manlius Capitolinus of Sparta. And Manlius, who was the Agis of Rome, was thrown to his death from the Tarpeian rock because he was suspected of aiding the poor and oppressed plebeians of Rome.

The early nobles misgoverned the poor masses of their nations precisely because they believed that as heroes they were naturally superior to the plebeians. Clearly, Roman history will baffle any discerning student who attempts to find any Roman virtue in such great arrogance, any moderation in such avarice, any mercy in such cruelty, or any justice in such inequality.

[669] Such astonishing contradictions can only be resolved by the following principles of heroic society.

I

[670] The brutish upbringing of the giants was replaced by the severe, harsh, and cruel education of the young. Witness the illiterate Spartans, who were the heroes of Greece: in order to teach their sons to fear neither pain nor death, the Spartans caned them in the temple of Diana,

often so severely that they fell dead, convulsed with pain under their fathers' blows. Both the Greeks and Romans retained this Cyclopean kind of paternal authority, which even allowed them to kill innocent newborns. By contrast, the delicacy, *delicatezza*, of our modern natures arises from the delight, *delizie*, we feel for our young children.

2

[671] Wives were bought with heroic dowries, which survived in the nuptial solemnities of Roman priests, who contracted marriages by symbolic purchase and by an offering of spelt-cakes. (According to Tacitus, this was also the custom of the ancient Germans, whose example allows us to infer the same for all early barbarian peoples.) Wives were maintained as a necessity of nature for bearing children. In other respects, they were treated as slaves; and this is still the practice in many parts of the Old World and nearly everywhere in the New World. Later, a woman's dowry purchased the freedom of her husband, and was his public acknowledgement that he could not bear the expense of the marriage. This may account for the many privileges by which Roman emperors encouraged dowries.

3

[672] Whatever children acquired or wives saved went to their fathers and husbands. Today, our practice is just the opposite.

4

[673] Heroic games and pastimes were arduous activities, like wrestling and footraces: for example, Homer gives Achilles the invariable epithet 'swift-footed'. They were also dangerous, like jousting and hunting wild beasts, which accustomed men to toughen their minds and bodies, and to disdain and risk their lives.

5

[674] Luxury, sumptuousness, and comforts were completely unknown.

6

[675] Wars like the ancient heroic ones were based on religion, which is a basic principle of my Science, and which made such wars bloody and ruthless.

7

[676] Heroic slavery was the result of heroic wars. In this period, defeated peoples were considered godless, and so lost both their civil and natural liberty. Relevant here is my Axiom 94: 'We defend our natural liberty most fiercely to preserve the goods most essential to our survival. By contrast, we submit to the chains of civil servitude to obtain external goods which are not necessary to life.'

8

[677] For all these reasons, heroic commonwealths were by nature aristocratic, that is, composed of those who were by nature the strongest. Civil honours were open only to the few noble fathers, and the public good consisted in the family monarchies preserved by the fatherland. The true fatherland, *patria*, was literally the concern of a few fathers, and its citizens were naturally patricians. Where these natures, customs, commonwealths, social orders, and laws prevail, the heroism of the first peoples will flourish.

By contrast, such heroism is impossible today. Our civil nature springs from causes contrary to the heroism which I have just described. It thus produces the two kinds of civil states which are human rather than heroic: free democracies, and monarchies, which are even more human. Throughout the age of Roman popular liberty, the only person reputed to be a hero was Cato of Utica, whose reputation reflected his aristocratic spirit. The death of Pompey left Cato to head the party of the nobility;

and when he could not bear to see it humiliated by Caesar, he killed himself. By contrast, heroes in monarchies are men who sacrifice themselves for the glory and greatness of their sovereigns. Hence, we must conclude that such an ideal hero is desired by afflicted peoples, theorized by philosophers, and imagined by poets. But such virtues are not among the benefits which civil nature provides, as Axiom 80 states.

[678] Axioms 84–91 on Roman heroism provide illumination and illustration of these remarks about the heroism of early peoples. They also apply to the heroism of the ancient Athenians in the age when Thucydides [Isocrates] says they were ruled by the severe Areopagites, who formed an aristocratic state.★ And they apply to the heroism of the Spartans, who formed a commonwealth of Heraclids or nobles, as I have repeatedly shown.

★ As in 592, Vico confuses Thucydides with Isocrates.

SECTION 6
EPITOMES OF POETIC
HISTORY

CHAPTER I

Epitomes of Poetic History

I

[679] Earlier I promised to elucidate the myth of Cadmus, which narrates the entire divine and heroic history of the theological poets with great obscurity. In the myth, Cadmus first kills the great serpent, and sows its teeth. In other words, he clears the earth's vast ancient forest, and ploughs the world's first fields using curved pieces of hardwood which, before the use of iron was invented, must have formed the teeth of ploughs. (This fine metaphor is still in use.) Cadmus hurls a large stone, which symbolizes the hard earth which the heroes' clients or servants sought to till for themselves. From the furrows, armed men spring to life. In other words, during the heroic contention over the first agrarian law, the heroes emerge from their estates to assert their dominion. They fight now with each other, as the myth relates, but unite in arms against the rebellious plebeians. The furrows signify the orders in which they unite and by which they form and confirm the earliest cities on the basis of arms. Finally, Cadmus is changed into a serpent, which symbolizes the origin of aristocratic senates. The ancient Latins would have said 'Cadmus became the ground', *Cadmus fundus factus est*. And the Greeks said that Cadmus had changed into Draco, the dragon who wrote laws in blood.

As I promised to show earlier, the myth of Cadmus contains several centuries of poetic history, and offers a notable example of the inarticulateness of the human race in its infancy. (As we shall see, this is one of seven reasons why ancient myths are so difficult.) And it shows how clearly Cadmus wrote out his own story using the vernacular letters he supposedly brought the Greeks from Phoenicia! Even Erasmus, who has been called the Christian Varro, utters countless absurdities when he argues that this myth recounts Cadmus' invention of letters. Now, clearly the glorious story of such a great contribution, the invention of an alphabet for the nations, would have become celebrated far and wide. But our humanist believes that when Cadmus arrived in Greece he concealed it from mankind by veiling it in this myth, so that until the age of Erasmus, the vulgar masses were unaware of the greatest invention of popular wisdom, the vernacular letters which are named for them!

2

[680] By contrast to this myth, Homer relates the same history with marvellous brevity and propriety by reducing it to the symbol of the sceptre which Agamemnon inherits. The sceptre is fashioned by Vulcan for Jupiter. This refers to the thunderbolts by which Jupiter after the flood founded his kingdom over gods and men, meaning the divine kingdoms of the state of families. Jupiter then gives Mercury a sceptre. This is the caduceus which Mercury used to bring the first agrarian law to the plebeians, thus creating the heroic kingdoms of the first cities. Mercury then gave it to Pelops, who gave it to Thyestes, who gave it to Atreus, who gave it to Agamemnon – which is the entire dynasty of the royal house of Argos.

3

[681] We find a fuller and more detailed account of the history of the world on the shield of Achilles as described by Homer.

[682] (1) In the beginning, the shield showed the sky, earth, sea, sun, moon, and stars, which symbolize the epoch of the world's creation.

[683] (2) Next, the shield showed two cities. In the first were songs, wedding-songs, and nuptials, which represent the age of the heroic families, whose children are born of solemn nuptials. In the second, there were no such rites: this represents the age of the heroic families with their family servants, who contracted only natural marriages without the solemnities of heroic nuptials. Together, these two cities represent the

state of nature, which is the state of families. In the *Odyssey*, Ulysses' swineherd Eumaeus describes two such cities in his fatherland. They were both ruled by his father, he says; and in them the citizens' goods were all distinctly divided, meaning that they shared no part of citizenship in common. Thus, Homer's city without wedding-songs must be inhabited by the 'other people', as Telemachus calls the plebeians of Ithaca during an assembly. And Achilles has such a place in mind when, complaining of Agamemnon's affront to him, he says he has been treated like a common labourer with no part in the government.

[684] (3) Then, in the city celebrating nuptials, the shield showed parliaments, laws, legal judgments, and punishments. This is a precise parallel to the response of the Roman patricians to the plebeians during their heroic contentions. For by claiming the auspices and nuptial solemnities as their own, the patricians asserted that they alone held rights over nuptials and military commands, as well as over priesthoods, which were the basis of legal science and judgments. This is why the Latin word for men, *viri*, which was synonymous with the Greek word heroes, also meant husbands in solemn marriage, magistrates, priests, and judges. This Homeric city thus represents the epoch of heroic cities which, on the basis of families including servants, emerged in a severely aristocratic form.

[685] (4) The other city is under armed siege, and both cities raid each other for booty. In other words, the city without nuptials, symbolizing the plebeians of the heroic cities, becomes independent from and hostile to the city of the heroes. This offers us striking proof that the first foreigners, *hostes*, were the plebeians of heroic peoples, against whom the heroes swore eternal enmity, according to Aristotle. Since they regarded each other as foreign, these two cities waged unceasing hostilities against each other in the form of heroic raids.

[686] (5) Finally, the shield depicted the history of the arts of civilization, beginning with the epoch of the families. First of all, it showed a father-king who holds a sceptre and orders the division of a roasted ox among his harvesters. Next, it showed planted vineyards; then, flocks, shepherds, and huts; and finally, dances. This image fairly and truly depicted the order of human institutions: first, the invention of

the necessary arts, like agriculture, which produced bread and then wine; next, the useful trades, like herding; then, the arts of comfort, like urban architecture; and finally, the arts of pleasure, like dancing.

SECTION 7
POETIC PHYSICS

CHAPTER I

Poetic Physics

[687] In Book 2, we saw that the trunk of poetic metaphysics splits into two branches. Having examined the topics of the first branch – poetic logic, morals, economics, and politics – we may now pass to the other branch, which is that of physics. It branches into cosmography, then into astronomy, which in turn yields chronology and geography. Let us begin with physics.

[688] The theological poets contemplated physics within the world of nations. At first, they defined Chaos as the confusion of human seeds in the abominable age when women were shared promiscuously. (Later, when physicists were moved to contemplate the confusion of the universal seeds of nature, they expressed it by using the name Chaos, which had been invented by the poets and was thus suitable.) Poetic Chaos was confused because it had no civilizing order, and it was obscure because it lacked the civil light which made heroes illustrious. The poets also imagined it as Orcus, a formless monster that devoured all things. For people born in this abominable promiscuity lacked the proper form of human beings; and without any certain offspring, they were 'swallowed up' by the void, leaving no trace of themselves. (Later, physicists interpreted this as the prime matter of natural things which, being formless, is greedy for forms and devours everything.) The poets also assigned Chaos the monstrous form of the silvan god Pan. As the protecting spirit of all satyrs, who inhabit forests rather than cities, Pan became a symbol of the impious wanderers of the earth's great forest, who had the appearance of men but the habits of abominable beasts. (Later, misled by the name Pan, which in Greek means All, philosophers

used forced allegories to interpret this god as a symbol for the formed universe.) Scholars also believed that the poets had signified prime matter by their myth of Proteus. In this myth set in Egypt, Ulysses on the shore wrestles with Proteus in the water, but cannot hold on to the monster, which keeps changing shape. What the scholars mistook for sublime learning was in fact the extreme coarseness and ignorance of early people. For just as children try to grasp their own reflections when they look in a mirror, so primitive people thought they saw an ever-changing person in the water when they beheld how it altered their own features and movements.

[689] When the heavens finally thundered, Jupiter created the world of men by waking in them the moral effort or *conatus*. The human civil world originated in this effort, which is proper to the mind and its freedom. By the same token, the world of nature originated in motion, which is proper to physical bodies, which are not free agents but are subject to necessity. (What appears to be 'effort' in bodies is in fact merely insensate motion, as we saw in my section on Method.) From this conscious effort came the civil light symbolized by Apollo, whose light revealed the civil beauty, or nobility, which made the heroes beautiful. Venus was the symbol of this civil beauty, and was later interpreted by physicists as the beauty of nature, and even as the whole of formed nature, which is beautifully arrayed with all sensible forms.

[690] The theological poets viewed the world as composed of four sacred elements: (1) the air in which Jupiter thunders, (2) the water of the perennial springs sacred to Diana, (3) the fire with which Vulcan cleared the forests, and (4) the cultivated earth of Cybele or Berecynthia. All four elements are elements of divine rites: the auspices, water, fire, and spelt. These rites are watched over by Vesta, who is identified with Cybele or Berecynthia, the goddess of cultivated lands protected by hedges and surmounted by tower-like towns in the highlands. (From such towers came the Latin *extorris*, exiled, as if *exterris*, driven from the land.) Cybele goes about crowned, and her crown encloses what was called the *orbis terrarum*, or circle of lands, which is properly the world of mankind. These elements of the world of men later moved physicists to contemplate the world of nature as composed of four elements.

[691] The theological poets assigned living, sensate, and often human

forms to these elements and to the countless natural species arising from them. In this way, they imagined many various deities, on which Plato easily imposed his doctrine of minds and intelligences: Jupiter as the mind of ether, Vulcan as the mind of fire, and so on. But the theological poets had so little conception of such intelligent substances that even in Homer's day they did not even understand the human mind's capacity for opposing the senses by reflection. In two golden passages in the *Odyssey*, Homer calls the human mind a sacred force and a mysterious power, which are synonymous terms.

CHAPTER 2

Poetic Physics of the Human Body: Heroic Nature

[692] The greatest and most important part of physics is the contemplation of human nature. We have seen how the founders of pagan civilization used their frightful religions and terrifying paternal powers to generate and produce our properly human forms, both physical and mental. By means of sacred ablutions, they 'educed' our proper human proportions from gigantic bodies; and by means of the discipline of household economy, they educated our human minds from bestial minds. This is the proper place to review this development, which is described in my Poetic Economy.

[693] With their crude physics, the theological poets beheld in humankind two metaphysical ideas: being and substance. Being was clearly apprehended by the Latin heroes in a very coarse manner. Thus, the Latin verb *esse*, 'to be', originally meant 'to eat'. Even today, when our peasants say that a sick man is still alive, they say he is still eating. The verb *esse* in the sense of being is highly abstract because it transcends all particular beings; it is very fluid because it pervades all beings; and it is completely pure because it is not limited by any other beings. Substance, in turn, was apprehended as something that stands beneath and sustains. Since a person stands on his feet, the heroes located his substance in the heels. This is why Achilles' fate was in his heel, which held his fated allotment of life and death.

[694] The theological poets viewed the human body as made up of solids and liquids.

Bodily solids were divided into four kinds. (1) First were the viscera, or flesh. In Latin, *visceratio* refers to the act of Roman priests when they distribute the flesh of sacrificial victims to the people; and the verb *vesci*, to feed, implies nourishment by eating meat. (2) Second were the bones and joints. In Latin, the word for joint is *artus*, so called from *ars*, which in early Latin meant bodily force, and from which was derived *artitus*, robust. Later, the noun *ars*, art, came to mean a body of precepts which serves as a framework for some intellectual skill. (3) Third were the sinews. When the theological poets were still mute and spoke using physical objects, sinews were taken to mean forces. (In Latin, one word for sinew, *fides*, meant a cord, and was used to denote the force or faith of the gods; later, Orpheus' lyre was imagined as made of such sinews, cords, or forces.) They correctly located force in the sinews, since it is the tendons which extend muscles to exert a force. (4) Fourth was the marrow, in which with equal propriety they located the vital essence. In Latin, a lover called his beloved *medulla*, marrow. The adverb *medullitus*, from the marrow, means the same as our phrase 'from the heart'; and intense love was said to melt one's marrow.

The body's liquids, in turn, were reduced to the one category of blood. They correctly called the neural and spermatic fluids 'blood', since they are the essence of the blood. This gave rise to the poetic phrase *sanguine cretus*, born of the blood, which means engendered. And they correctly regarded the blood as the juice of the tissues which make up the flesh. In Latin, the adjective *succiplenus*, filled with juice, means fleshy or steeped in good blood.

[695] As for the soul, Latin *anima*, the theological poets located it in the air, which is also called *anima*, and conceived it as the vehicle of life. (This was the proper meaning of the Latin expression 'we live and breathe', *anima vivimus*. In poetic Latin, we find used phrases such as *ferri ad vitales auras*, to bring to life's breath, or be born; *ducere vitales auras*, to draw life's breath, or live; and *vitam referri in auras*, to return one's life to the air, or die. In everyday Latin, *animam ducere*, to draw breath, meant to live; *animam trahere*, to draw one's last breath, meant to suffer the throes of death; and *animam efflare*, *animam emittere*, to

breathe forth one's soul, meant to die.) This may have led the physicists to locate the world-soul in the air. The theological poets correctly located the course of life in the course of the blood, since our life consists in its flowing properly.

[696] The poets also correctly sensed that the spirit is the vehicle of sensation. This was the proper meaning of the Latin expression 'we feel in our hearts', *animo sentimus*. And they correctly made *spirit* masculine (*animus*) and *soul* feminine (*anima*), for the spirit acts on the soul, like Virgil's fiery force, *igneus vigor*. The spirit acts through the nerves and neural matter, and the soul acts through the veins and the blood. Since the spirit's vehicle is the ether, and the soul's vehicle is the air, the animal spirits are swift in relation to the slower vital spirits. The spirit is the agent and therefore the principle of the conscious effort, like Virgil's fiery force; while the soul is the agent of motion. The theological poets sensed this, but did not fully understand it. This is why Homer speaks of a sacred force, a mysterious power, or an unknown god. When the Greeks and Romans felt that their words or deeds came from a higher principle within themselves, they said that a god had willed it: for in their crude way, they understood the sublime truth that ideas come to men from God. Accordingly, the natural theology of the metaphysicians proved irrefutably that the Epicureans erred when they said that ideas spring from the body.

[697] The poets understood generation in a manner which seems superior to that of later scholars. Their notion is epitomized by the Latin verb *concipere*, to conceive, which derives from *con-capere*, to take in. This verb expresses the natural activity of all physical forms – including atmospheric pressure, discovered in our time – which take in surrounding objects, overcome their resistance, and adapt and assimilate them to their own form.

[698] Physical decay was quite wisely expressed by the verb *corrumpere*, to break down, which means the breakdown of all the body's components. Its opposite was *sanum*, whole, since life depends on the sound condition of all the body's parts; and they believed that disease caused death by destroying the body's solid parts.

[699] The poets reduced all the internal functions of the spirit to three parts of the body: the head, the breast, and the heart.

To the head they assigned all cognitive functions. Since all of these involved the imagination, they located memory in the head: for the Greek word for imagination, *phantasía*, corresponds to Latin *memoria*. During the medieval return of barbarism, *fantasía* meant ingenuity, and an ingenious person was said to be fantastical. This is how Cola di Rienzo is described in the barbarous Italian of his contemporary biographer. The similarity of such characters and customs to those of the ancient heroes offers a strong argument for their recurrence in various nations.

Now imagination is simply the resurfacing of recollections, and ingenuity is simply the elaboration of things remembered. As my Poetic Metaphysics showed, during the heroic age the human mind was neither refined by the art of writing, nor intellectualized by the arts of reckoning and reasoning, nor rendered capable of abstraction by the many abstractions which abound in modern languages. The primitive mind thus applied all its force to the three noble faculties derived from the head, breast, and heart. As my Poetic Logic shows, these faculties belong to the mind's primary function, which is regulated by the art of topics, or the art of invention, just as the mind's secondary function is regulated by the art of criticism, which is the art of judging. As invention naturally precedes judgment, the people of the world's childhood exercised the primary function of the human mind. For their world still needed to invent all the institutions that are necessary and useful to human life. As I shall show more fully in my Discovery of the True Homer, all these needs were satisfied before the appearance of the philosophers. The theological poets were correct, then, in calling Memory the mother of the Muses, because they symbolized the arts of civilization.

[700] At this point, I must clarify my earlier statement that we can by no means imagine and can conceive only with great effort how the first founders of pagan civilization thought. Their minds were so limited to particulars that they viewed every change in facial expression as a new face, as the myth of Proteus indicates. And they viewed every new passion as a new heart, a new breast, or a new spirit. It was this nature of human institutions, rather than an urge to count, which created the poetic plurals used for the singular: *ora*, faces; *vultus*, visages; *animi*, spirits; *pectora*, breasts; *corda*, hearts.

[701] The poets made the breast the seat of all passions, and fittingly

placed beneath it two stimuli. (1) They placed the irascible principle, or stimulus of anger, in the stomach. For when we react against the threat of danger, it is there that we feel bile rise in response to the stomach's increased peristaltic action on the biliary vessels. (2) And they placed the appetitive principle, or stimulus of desire, principally in the liver, since it is defined as the factory of the blood. The poets called these *praecordia*, organs in front of the heart; and in them Prometheus the Titan implanted the most prominent passions found in each species of animal. Thus the poets understood in crude fashion that desire is the mother of all passions, and that the passions reside in our bodily humours.

[702] The theological poets assigned all volition to the heart. Thus, heroes in Latin poetry 'shook, turned, and revolved their cares in their heart', *agitabant, versabant, volutabant corde curas*. For being stupid and insensible, they considered a course of action only when they were shaken by passions. In Latin, wise men were called *cordati*, strong-hearted; and dolts by contrast were *vecordes*, senseless. Their resolutions were called *sententiae*, sentiments, because they judged as they felt, which is why heroic judgments were always true in form, even when false in substance.

CHAPTER 3

Corollary on Heroic Statements

[703] The minds of the early pagans perceived all phenomena singly. In this respect, they were almost like animals, in which each new sensation completely erases any previous sensations, which makes them incapable of rational comparison and discourse. Thus, all heroic statements were particularized expressions of single sensations. In the ode of Sappho which Catullus translated into Latin, Longinus admired the sublimity of the simile with which the beloved describes her lover: 'He seems equal to a god', *Ille mi par esse deo videtur*. Yet this simile lacks the highest degree of sublimity because it does not make the statement particular to the lover. By contrast, Terence does this when he writes 'We have attained the life of the gods', *Vitam deorum adepti sumus*. This

sentiment is proper to the speaker, but it has a generalized tone because the first-person plural replaces the singular. In another of Terence's comedies, this sentiment is raised to the highest degree of sublimity by being made singular and particular to the character who says 'I have become a god', *Deus factus sum*.

[704] Philosophers make abstract statements which contain universals. By contrast, only false and frigid poets offer reflections on their passions.

CHAPTER 4

Corollary on Heroic Descriptions

[705] To conclude, the poets reduced the spirit's external functions to the body's five senses, which were keen, vivid, and strong, while their minds served only as a vigorous imagination with very little or no reason. The Latin words for the five senses may serve as proof of this.

[706] The verb for hearing was *audire*, as if from *haurire*, to draw in: for the ears drink in air which has been set vibrating by other physical bodies. Seeing distinctly was called 'separating with the eyes', *cernere oculis*. This may be the origin of the Tuscan verb *scernere*, to sift: for the eyes are like a sieve, and the pupils are like two holes. And just as rods of dust issue from a sieve and touch the earth, so rods of light issue from the pupils and touch those objects which we see distinctly. (This is the visual rod or ray, which the Stoics theorized and whose existence Descartes has successfully demonstrated.) Seeing in general was called *usurpare oculis*, to occupy with the eyes, as if one's vision actually took possession of the things it sees. The verb *tangere*, to touch, also meant to steal: for when we touch an object we take something away from it, as our most astute physicists are beginning to understand. Smelling was called *olfacere*, as if to smell an odour is to make it, *ol-facere*. (In careful experiments, scientists later discovered that the senses truly create what are called sensible qualities.) Finally, tasting was called *sapere*: properly, the verb refers to things which have a taste, and then to the testing of things for their proper taste. Later, by a fine metaphor wisdom

was called *sapientia*, tastefulness, because it puts things to their natural uses, rather than to artificial ones.

[707] Here too we must admire divine providence for endowing us with senses to protect our bodies. Since in that early age primitive people had fallen into the condition of beasts, whose senses are astonishingly keener than human senses, providence ensured that they had the acutest senses for their survival. Later, when people entered the age of reflection, and could take counsel for their own defence, human senses grew less keen. As a result, Homer's heroic descriptions radiate a brilliance and splendour which no later poets could imitate, much less equal.

CHAPTER 5

Corollary on Heroic Customs

[708] The heroic nature of such people, endowed with heroic senses, led to the formation of similarly heroic customs. Newly descended from giants, the heroes were extremely grotesque and savage – as the Patagonians are described – possessing limited intelligence, but endowed with vast imaginations and violent passions. As a result, they were boorish, crude, harsh, savage, and arrogant. They were difficult and obstinate in pursuing an end, and yet at the same time inconstant and easily diverted when confronted by something new and contrary. Today we often find such behaviour in stubborn peasants. They yield to any reasonable argument they are offered; but having weak powers of reflection, they soon forget the argument that convinced them, and go back to what they originally wanted. This very lack of reflective power made heroic people frank, sensitive, magnanimous, and generous – which is how Homer describes Achilles, the greatest of the Greek heroes. In his *Poetics*, Aristotle has such heroic customs in mind when he formulates his precept that heroes who form the subject of tragedies should not be very good or very bad, but exhibit a mixture of great vices and great virtues. For the heroism which attains its ideal form through virtue belongs to philosophy rather than poetry; and gallant heroism was invented after Homer.

Later poets either invented entirely new myths, or they adapted early myths – which had originally been serious and severe, as befits the founders of nations – by altering and eventually corrupting them to suit the effeminate customs of later times. We find signal proof of this in the example of Achilles, who provides an important example of this historical mythology. After Agamemnon has seized his captive Briseis, Achilles makes outcries which both fill heaven and earth, and provide the entire plot of the *Iliad*. Yet nowhere in all the epic does he show the slightest feeling of amorous passion at losing her. Likewise, Menelaus mobilizes all of Greece against Troy on Helen's account. Yet through all that long and great war, he does not show even the smallest sign of a lover's anguish or jealousy of Paris, who has stolen Helen and enjoys her.

[709] These corollaries on heroic statements, descriptions, and customs will prove relevant to the Discovery of the True Homer found in Book 3.

SECTION 8
POETIC COSMOGRAPHY

CHAPTER I
Poetic Cosmography

[710] As the principles of their physics, the theological poets posited what they imagined as divine substances. And in their description of the cosmography corresponding to this physics, they posited a world formed of gods in three realms: (1) gods of the heavens, the Latin *dii superi*; (2) gods of the underworld, *dii inferi*; and (3) gods intermediate between heaven and earth, *dii medioxumi*.

[711] The first object of their contemplation in the world was the heavens, which the Greeks called *mathēmata*, or sublime things, and the *theōrēmata*, or divine objects of contemplation. In Latin, the act of contemplating took its name from the regions of the heavens, *templa coeli*, which augurs marked off to take the auspices by observing the paths of falling stars. In the Near East, these heavenly regions gave their name to the Zoroastrians, a name which Bochart interprets as meaning 'star-gazers'.

[712] The theological poets thought that the first heaven was no higher than the mountain heights, where Jupiter's thunderbolts had stayed the giants from their brutish wandering. This is the Heaven which reigned on earth and which began to confer great benefits on mankind. They clearly thought that the heavens were the mountain peaks. From the mountains' sharp edge, the Latin noun *coelum* also came to mean a burin, which is a tool for engraving stone and metal. In precisely this way, children imagine that mountains are columns supporting the upper storey of the heavens; and the Arabs gave similar principles of cosmography to their Koran. (Two of these columns came to be called the Pillars of Hercules. The original word in Latin, *columen*,

meant a prop or stay, which architects later made rounded in form.) It was from such a roof on Olympus, as Thetis tells Achilles in Homer, that Jupiter and the other gods went to feast on Mt Atlas. Hence, we must regard as post-Homeric the passage in the *Odyssey*, in which the Titans war against heaven by piling up high mountains – Ossa on Pelion and Olympus on Ossa – in order to climb up and expel the gods. For everywhere in the *Iliad*, Homer clearly describes the gods as residing on top of Mt Olympus, so that the collapse of Olympus alone would have sufficed to cause the gods' downfall. Even in the later epic, the *Odyssey*, the myth of the Titans seems inappropriate: for in that poem, the underworld in which Ulysses sees and speaks with deceased heroes is no deeper than a ditch. Now, if in the *Odyssey* Homer had such a limited idea of the underworld, the heavens must have had similar dimensions, which would correspond to those in the *Iliad*. Thus, the myth cannot be Homeric.

[713] It was in this heaven that the gods first reigned on earth and mingled with the heroes, beginning with Jupiter and following the order of the natural theogony outlined above. And it was from this heaven that Astraea dispensed justice on earth. Astraea was crowned with ears of grain, since the first human justice was administered by the heroes through the first agrarian law. And she held a balance, since people perceived weight first of all. (Later, they perceived measure, and gradually number, which came to constitute the basis of reason. This is why Pythagoras conceived the essence of the human soul as numbers, which were the greatest abstraction from physical objects which he could conceive.) Through this heaven heroes galloped on horseback, like Bellerophon on Pegasus; and in Latin *volitare equo*, to fly on a horse, later meant to gallop on horseback. In this heaven, Juno whitened the Milky Way with milk. (Juno was barren, and this milk, rather than her own, was the milk of family mothers who suckled their legitimate children, born of the heroic nuptials which Juno protected.) Over this heaven, the gods were borne in chariots of poetic gold, meaning the grain for which the golden age was named. In this heaven, wings were not used for flight or to signify the swiftness of intelligence, but symbolized the heroic laws based on the auspices. Various gods wore such wings, including Hymen or heroic Love, Astraea, the Muses,

Pegasus, Saturn, and Fame. Mercury has wings on his temples and heels, as well as on his caduceus, which uses them to bring the first agrarian law down from heaven to the rebellious plebeians in the valleys. (Winged too was the dragon, one of the serpents on the winged temples of the gorgon Medusa, who cannot signify intelligence or flight.) In this heaven, Prometheus steals fire from the sun: in other words, the heroes used flints to set fire to thorn bushes dried by the burning sun on the mountain heights. In this sense, the torch of Hymen is truly made of thorns. From this heaven, Vulcan is cast down headlong by Jupiter's kick; from this heaven, Phaethon plunges headlong in the chariot of the sun; and from this heaven, the apple of Discord drops. Finally, from this heaven fell the *ancilia* or sacred shields of the Romans.

[714] The first underworld deities imagined by the theological poets were the water deities. And the first underworld was the source of perennial springs, which they called the river Styx and by which the gods swore. (This may be why Plato supposed that the abyss of waters was found in the centre of the earth. Yet in his contest of the gods, Homer describes how Pluto fears lest Neptune's earthquakes open the earth and expose the underworld to men and the gods. Now, if the abyss had been located in the deepest bowels of the earth, Neptune's earthquakes would have had the opposite effect, and would have submerged and covered the underworld with water. This shows that Plato's allegory is ill suited to Homer's myth, and that the first underworld must have been no deeper than the source of the springs.) The foremost deity of springs was Diana, who is described in poetic history as having three forms: Diana in heaven; the huntress Cynthia on earth, with her brother Apollo; and Proserpine in the underworld.

[715] The second idea of the underworld was then extended to include graves. This is why the poets referred to the grave as the underworld, *infernum*, an expression we also find in the Bible. This underworld is no deeper than a ditch, like that where Homer's Ulysses sees the underworld and the souls of deceased heroes. In this underworld, they imagined the Elysian Fields, where through burial the souls of the dead enjoy eternal peace. The Elysian Fields are the happy abode of the Latin *Dei Manes*, or kind souls of the dead.

[716] Later, the third idea of the underworld was also quite shallow

and still only as deep as a furrow. Abducted here by Pluto, Proserpine (or Ceres, the seed of the grain) spent six months before returning to see the light of heaven. We shall see that the golden bough, with which Aeneas descends into the underworld, was a Virgilian invention continuing the heroic metaphor of the golden apples, which were ears of grain.

[717] Finally, the underworld was interpreted to mean the plains and valleys, in contrast to the heavenly heights of the mountains. In these valleys, the impious peoples lived dispersed in their abominable promiscuity. The god of this underworld was Erebus, who was said to be the son of Chaos, that is, of the confusion of human seed. Erebus is the father of civil night, or the obscurity of family names, in contrast to the civil light of the heroes' splendour, which illuminates the heavens. Through this underworld runs the river Lethe, which is the river of oblivion: for such men left no name of themselves to their posterity, whereas the glory of heaven immortalizes the names of illustrious heroes. It is from this underworld that Mercury, who bears the agrarian law in his wand, recalls souls from all-devouring Orcus. This piece of civil history is recorded in Virgil's verse: 'With this wand he summons souls from Orcus,' *hac ille animas evocat Orco*. In other words, Mercury summons the lives of lawless and bestial men from their brutish state, which completely devours men who leave no name to posterity. (Later, magicians used such a wand in the vain belief that it would help them revive the dead. And Roman praetors used such a rod to free slaves, striking them on the back, as if restoring them from death to life.) In their witchcraft, sorcerer-magicians used the same wand which the wise magi of Persia used for the divination of the auspices. Hence, divine properties were attributed to this wand; and nations regarded it as a god that would work miracles, as we learn from Justin's epitome of Pompeius Trogus.

[718] This underworld is guarded by Cerberus, who shows doglike immodesty by copulating shamelessly in public. He is triple-throated, which means that he has an enormous gullet, since the prefix *tri-* is a superlative, and like Orcus he devours everything. When he comes up to the earth, the sun moves backward: that is, when he enters heroic cities, the heroes' civil light reverts to civil night.

[719] At the bottom of this underworld flows the river Tartarus, where the damned are tormented. Ixion turns his wheel, Sisyphus rolls his stone, and Tantalus dies of hunger and thirst. Here, the river Phlegethon, which in Greek means that they 'burn' with thirst, flows into Acheron, the river 'without gladness'. Through their ignorance, later mythographers later cast Tityus and Prometheus into this underworld. But in fact it was in the sky that they were chained to the rocky crags, where their entrails were devoured by an eagle flying in the mountains, which represents the tormenting superstition of the auspices.

[720] Later philosophers found all these myths quite useful in pondering and explaining their moral and metaphysical theories. These myths prompted Plato to conceive of three divine punishments which can only be imposed by the gods, and not by men: oblivion, infamy, and the remorse that torments a guilty conscience. Plato interpreted the underworld of the theological poets as meaning the way of purgation, *via purgativa*, which cleanses the human spirit of the passions tormenting it. This way leads to the way of unity, *via unitiva*, which unites the human mind with God through the contemplation of eternal and divine things, which is how Plato interprets the Elysian Fields of the theological poets.

[721] All the founders of pagan nations descended into this underworld, but with ideas quite different from the moral and metaphysical ones of the philosophers. For the theological poets described the underworld with political ideas, as was both natural and necessary for men founding nations. Thus, Orpheus, who founded the Greek nation, descends to the underworld. Forbidden to look back on his return, he looks back and loses his wife Eurydice: that is, he reverts to the abominable promiscuity of women. Hercules, whom every nation calls its founder, descends to the underworld, where he frees Theseus, who founded Athens. Theseus descends to the underworld to bring back Proserpine, meaning Ceres. In other words, he descends to bring back sown seed as ripened grain.

Later, Virgil's *Aeneid* described the descent to the underworld of Aeneas, who is sung as a political hero in the first six books, and as a military hero in the last six books. With his profound knowledge of heroic antiquity, Virgil relates this descent in the greatest detail. First,

Aeneas obtains the instructions and safe-conduct of the Cumaean Sibyl. (We have seen that all pagan nations had a Sibyl, twelve of whom we know by name.) In other words, Aeneas descends by divination, which was the popular wisdom of the pagans. Next, he sacrifices his associate Misenus, exercising that cruel right which the heroes had over their first associates. For Aeneas has the piety of a bloodthirsty religion, which is the piety which the heroes professed in the ferocity and cruelty of their recent bestial origin. He now enters the ancient forest, which represents the primitive earth in its uncultivated and wooded state. There he throws a drugged scrap of meat to Cerberus, which puts him to sleep. (Orpheus puts beasts to sleep with his lyre, which symbolizes the law; and Hercules chained Cerberus using the knot with which he bound Antaeus in Greece, that is, with the first agrarian law; and his insatiable hunger caused Cerberus to be imagined as triple-throated, or having an immense gullet.) Aeneas descends into the underworld — originally no deeper than a furrow — and meets Dis, the god of heroic wealth, meaning poetic gold or the grain. (Dis is identified with Pluto, who abducted Proserpine or Ceres, goddess of grain.) Aeneas offers the golden bough to Dis. Thus, the great poet Virgil adapts the metaphor of the golden apple, or the ear of grain, and extends it to the golden bough, symbol of the harvest. When the golden bough is torn from the tree, another grows in its place, because there can be no second harvest until the first has been gathered. When it pleases the gods, the bough yields easily to the hand that grasps it; but otherwise no force in the world can pluck it. For grain springs forth naturally when God is willing; but without God's will, no human effort can harvest it. Next, Aeneas passes through the middle of the underworld to the Elysian Fields. In other words, the heroes settled in cultivated fields, and after death they enjoyed eternal peace through burial. Here Aeneas sees his ancestors and his future descendants. For the first genealogies, with which history began, were founded on the religion of burial sites, which the poets called the underworld.

[722] The theological poets felt the earth to be the guardian of boundaries, which is why it was called *terra*. The heroic origin of the word is preserved in the Latin noun *territorium*, territory, meaning a district over which dominion is exercised. The Latin grammarians

mistakenly derived territory from *terrere*, to frighten, because the lictors used the terror of the fasces to disperse crowds and make way for Roman magistrates. But in the age when the word territory arose, there were no great crowds in Rome. Indeed, I have cited Varro as saying that in her first 250 years of rule Rome subjugated more than twenty peoples without extending her dominion more than twenty miles! Rather, the true origin of the verb *terrere*, to frighten, derives from the bloody rites by which Vesta guarded the boundaries of the cultivated fields, in which civil dominions were to arise. The Latin goddess Vesta is the same as the Greek Cybele or Berecynthia, who is crowned with towers, *torres*, or strongly situated lands, *terrae*. From her crown there began to take shape the so-called *orbis terrarum*, or world of nations, which cosmographers later expanded and called the *orbis mundanus*, mundane world, or simply *mundus*, world, which is the world of nature.

[723] The world of the theological poets was thus divided into three kingdoms or regions: (1) Jupiter's realm in heaven, (2) Saturn's realm on earth, and (3) Pluto's realm in the underworld. (This Pluto was called Dis as the god of heroic wealth, meaning the first gold, or grain: for the true wealth of peoples consists in their cultivated fields.)

[724] This world was formed of four elements, which physicists later considered natural elements: (1) Jupiter's air, (2) Vulcan's fire, (3) Cybele's earth, and (4) Diana's water. This last deity is the underworld Diana of the springs. By contrast, Neptune became known to the poets only later, since nations were slow to descend to the sea-coasts. Likewise, any sea reaching beyond the horizon was called Ocean, and any land girt by it was called an island: thus Homer describes the island of Aeolia as surrounded by the Ocean. From this Ocean came the mares of Rhesus, who were pregnant by Zephyrus, the west wind of Greece. And on the shores of this Ocean were born the horses of Achilles, which were also sired by Zephyrus. Later, when geographers observed that the whole earth was girt by the sea like a vast island, they gave the name Ocean to the sea which girds the whole earth.

[725] To conclude, in early Latin *mundus* meant a slight slope, which is why *in mundo est* and *in proclivi est* both mean 'it is easy'. Later, everything that trims (*monda*), cleans, and adorns a woman was called *mundus muliebris*, feminine ornament. Eventually, the poets understood

that heaven and earth are spherical; that each point of their circumference slopes in all directions; and that the ocean washes the earth on all sides. So when they saw that the whole is adorned with countless various and diverse sensible forms, the poets called the universe *mundus* as a beautiful and sublime metaphor for the ornament with which nature adorns herself.

SECTION 9
POETIC ASTRONOMY

CHAPTER I

Poetic Astronomy

[726] In somewhat more developed form, this world system lasted until the age of Homer, who in the *Iliad* always describes the gods as dwelling on Mt Olympus. We have heard Thetis tell her son Achilles that the gods have left Olympus to feast on Mt Atlas. Clearly, in Homer's day the highest mountains in the world were believed to be columns supporting the heavens. Later, Abila and Calpe on the Straits of Gibraltar came to be called the Pillars of Hercules, named for the hero who had replaced Atlas when he grew weary of supporting the heavens on his shoulders.

CHAPTER 2

Astronomical, Physical, and Historical Proof that All Ancient Pagan Nations Shared Uniform Astronomical Principles

[727] As human minds continued to develop their unlimited power, and as the contemplation of the heavens for taking the auspices obliged people to observe them constantly, in the minds of the nations the heavens rose higher, and with them the gods and heroes. In attempting to rediscover poetic astronomy, we may make use of three points of historical erudition. (1) Astronomy was introduced into the world by the Chaldaeans. (2) The use of the quadrant to measure latitude was taught by the Chaldaeans to the Phoenicians, who then taught it to the

Egyptians. (3) The notion of gods dwelling in the stars was taught by the Chaldaeans to the Phoenicians, who then taught it to the Greeks. We may supplement these philological points with two philosophical truths. (1) It is a truth of civil societies that nations are naturally reluctant to embrace foreign deities, unless they are liberated by an extreme freedom of religion, which only occurs in the late stages of their decadence. (2) It is a truth of physics that the planets appear larger than the fixed stars because of an optical illusion.

[728] Having posited these principles, we may assert that astronomy sprang from popular origins which were uniform in the Near East, in Egypt, in Greece, and even in Latium. Since planets appear much larger than fixed stars, these peoples uniformly assigned gods to the planets, and heroes to the constellations. Thus, among the Greeks the Phoenicians found gods ready to move with the planets and heroes to form constellations, just as easily as the Greeks later found them among the Romans. And these examples allow us to conclude that the Phoenicians found the same readiness among the Egyptians as among the Greeks. In this manner, the heroes and the symbols of their rights and exploits, together with a good number of the major gods, were raised to the heavens. And they readily served the learned astronomers, who could now assign names to the previously nameless stars, constellations, and planets, thus giving form to matter, as it were.

[729] Using their popular astronomy, the first peoples wrote the history of their gods and heroes in the heavens. This established an invariable principle of history: the principal matter worthy of record consists of the memory of people with divine or heroic qualities, that is, persons divine for their ingenious works and esoteric wisdom, or heroic for their virtuous works and popular wisdom. Thus, poetic history gave learned astronomers reasons for envisioning heroes and symbols in certain groups of stars and certain regions of the sky, and for assigning the major gods to those planets whose names they still bear.

[730] Let us describe the planets in more detail than the constellations. Diana is the goddess of the chastity of solemn nuptials who lies silently all night with sleeping Endymion; she is therefore assigned to the moon, which illuminates the night. Venus is the goddess of civil beauty, and

therefore is assigned to the brightest and fairest planet of all. Mercury is a divine herald, clothed in civil light and adorned with the symbolic wings of nobility, who bears the agrarian law to rebelling clients; hence he is lodged in the planet which is so covered with the rays of the sun that it is rarely seen. Apollo is the god of the civil light which makes heroes illustrious; hence he is assigned to the sun, the source of natural light. Mars is the bloody war-god, and so is assigned to the blood-red planet. Jupiter is the king and father of gods and men, superior to the other planets, but inferior to Saturn. (For Saturn is the father both of Jupiter and of Time, and the period of his revolution is longer than those of all the other planets. If Saturn's wings are taken as an awkward allegory for the swiftness of time, they ill suit him, for he moves through the year more slowly than the other planets. Rather, when winged Saturn bears his scythe into heaven, it means that he reaps grain, rather than human lives. For the heroes reckoned years by grain harvests, and Saturn's wings symbolize the heroes' cultivated fields.) We see then that the planetary gods who once rode through heaven on earth in their chariots of gold, or grain, now revolve in their celestial orbits.

[731] From such observations, we may conclude that the predominant influence which the stars and planets were thought to exercise on sublunary objects were in fact transferred to them from the deeds of gods and heroes once on earth. So little do they depend on natural causes!

SECTION 10
POETIC CHRONOLOGY

CHAPTER I
Poetic Chronology

[732] The theological poets based their chronology on their astronomy. Since Saturn was in Latin named for *sata*, sown crops, and was in Greek called Chronos, meaning Time, we may assume that the first nations, being composed of peasants, initially reckoned years by their harvests of grain, which were the sole or principal object of their yearly labours. In their muteness, the early nations must have signified a number of years by holding up as many ears or straws, or by making as many reaping motions. This helps explain two passages in Virgil, whose knowledge of heroic antiquities was unrivalled. The first is that infelicitous phrase which by its infelicitous word order artfully expresses the infelicity of the first people in expressing themselves: 'After several ears of grain I shall marvel to see my kingdoms', *Post aliquot, mea regna videns, mirabor aristas*, which means 'after several years', *post aliquot annos*. The second is rather more clear: 'It was the third harvest', *Tertia messis erat*. Even today the peasants in Tuscany, the region of Italy most esteemed for its speech, say 'We have harvested three times' rather than 'Three years ago'. The ancient Romans preserved this heroic custom of poetically counting years by harvests in the Latin noun *annona* which, derived from *annus*, year, signified the administration of the yearly surplus, principally of grain.

[733] As the founder of the Olympiads, Hercules was the founder of the chronological epochs of the Greeks, who are the source for all we know of pagan antiquity. For Hercules set fire to the forests to prepare lands for sowing, thus preparing the harvests by which people later reckoned their years. And Greek athletic games were clearly

instituted by the people of Nemea to celebrate Hercules' victory over the fire-breathing lion. We have seen that this beast symbolized the earth's great forest, which was conceived as a powerful animal and called a lion because taming it required such great effort. Later, this name was applied to the most powerful animal, especially in heraldry; and astronomers assigned to Leo the house of the zodiac which is next to that of Libra, or Astraea crowned with ears of grain. This is why the Romans' oval circuses often featured images of lions and the sun; why their turning-posts, originally made of grain, were surmounted by eggs; and why these circuses were shaped like the clearings or deforested 'eyes' of the giants. Later, astronomers identified the oval with the ellipse described by the yearly course of the sun on its path through the ecliptic. Surely this interpretation is better suited to the egg which Kneph holds in his mouth than Manetho's view that this egg signifies the generation of the universe!

[734] The natural theogony which I outlined earlier helps establish the succession of the epochs which arose within the age of the gods. These epochs were associated with institutions necessary or useful to the human race, whose origins were always religious in nature. In each pagan nation, this divine age lasted at least 900 years after the appearance of Jupiter – that is, from the time when the heavens first began to thunder after the universal flood – and may be divided into twelve shorter epochs, corresponding to the twelve major gods imagined from Jupiter onwards. From this succession, our poetic history gains greater chronological certainty. Take Deucalion, for example. In traditional mythology, Deucalion appears immediately after the flood and the giants. Yet since he founds families by his marriage to Pyrrha, he must be a creation of the Greek imagination in the epoch of Juno, who is the goddess of solemn nuptials. Similarly, Hellen, who founds the Greek language and whose sons divide it into dialects, is born in the epoch of Apollo, the god of song, in whose age poetic verse must have originated. Hercules achieves the great labour of killing the Hydra and the Nemean lion: that is, he reduces the lands to cultivated fields. And from Hesperia he brings back four golden apples, meaning the first harvests. (This is a feat worthy of recording; whereas to bring back pomegranates, as some interpret these apples, would be the act of a gourmand.) Thus,

Hercules attains distinction in the epoch of Saturn, god of the sown fields. By contrast, Perseus achieves his fame in the epoch of Minerva, or epoch of civil authority, because he shares with her a shield bearing the head of Medusa. To conclude, Orpheus is born after the epoch of Mercury. For he sings to the beasts of Greece about the power of the auspices; and since auspicial science belonged to the heroes, he re-establishes the heroic nations of Greece, and thus names the heroic age, in which heroic contentions took place. Contemporary with Orpheus there flourished Linus, Amphion, Musaeus, and other heroic poets. Some 300 years after Cadmus founded Thebes, Amphion raised the city walls by using 'stones', an expression which, like Latin *lapis*, dolt, means the simple-minded plebeians. Precisely so, some 300 years after Rome was founded, Appius Claudius reduced the plebs to obedience and established the heroic Roman state by singing of the divine power of the patrician auspices to the plebeians who, like Orpheus' beasts, 'practised marriages in the manner of brutes'.

[735] At this point, we must note four kinds of anachronisms, or errors in chronology, which fall under the familiar heading of events dated *too early* or *too late*. The first error regards as *uneventful* periods which were actually full of events. For example, Varro regards as a dark age that age of the gods in which we have found nearly all the origins of civilized institutions. Conversely, a second error regards as *eventful* those periods which were actually uneventful. The age of heroes only lasted some 200 years, but people filled it with events from the age of the gods, because they mistakenly believed that myths were invented all at once by the heroic poets, and especially by Homer. (In fact, these events should be pushed back to the earlier age.) A third error *unites* periods which should be separated. During the lifetime of Orpheus, the people of Greece were supposed to have passed from a bestial existence to the illustrious deeds of the Trojan War. (This chronological monstrosity is exposed in my Notes on Chronology.) Conversely, a fourth error *divides* periods which should be united. Greek colonies were supposed to arrive in Sicily and Italy over 300 years after the wanderings of the heroes of Troy, when in fact they arrived there with the heroes' wanderings.

CHAPTER 2

*Canon of Chronology for Determining the Origins of
Universal History, Which Must Antedate the
Monarchy of Ninus, its Traditional Starting Point*

[736] We have traced a natural genealogy of the gods which gives us a rational poetic chronology, and we have exposed the kinds of anachronistic errors which distort poetic history. In order to determine the origins of universal history, which must antedate the kingdom of Ninus, I propose the following principle of chronology.

(1) After the Fall, the dispersion of humankind through the earth's great forest began in Mesopotamia, as Axiom 99 states. (2) This was followed by a relatively brief period of brutish wandering: 100 years for the impious descendants of Shem in eastern Asia, and 200 years for the descendants of Ham and Japheth in the rest of the world. This period came to an end when the leaders of the nations were moved by their religious awe of Jupiter – whose many manifestations among the early pagan nations are proof of the universal flood – and began to settle in the various lands to which fortune had led them. (3) There followed the age of the gods, which lasted 900 years. At first, all the nations were founded inland as scattered peoples searched for food and fresh water, which are not found on the seashore. Then, as the age of the gods came to an end, the nations descended to the coasts, where the Greeks conceived the idea of Neptune, who is the last of the twelve major deities, as we have seen. In the same way, 900 years passed between the Latin age of Saturn, which was the golden age of Latium, and Ancus Marcius' descent to the sea to capture Ostia. (4) Finally, there followed a period of 200 years, which the Greeks reckon as their heroic age. This age began with the corsair raids of King Minos, continued with Jason's naval expedition to Pontus, extended through the Trojan War, and ended with the wanderings of the heroes, including Ulysses' return to Ithaca.

Thus, it must have been more than a thousand years after the flood that the Phoenician capital Tyre was moved first from an inland site to the shore, and later to a nearby island in the Phoenician Sea. Even before the Greek heroic age, Tyre was celebrated for both its navigation and its colonies, which were scattered throughout the Mediterranean and the Ocean. This proves conclusively that the entire human race had its origins in the Near East. And it proves that the earliest nations were scattered through the rest of the world in three stages: first, during their brutish wanderings through the earth's inland regions; then under heroic law on both land and sea, and finally through the Phoenicians' maritime trading. These principles of the migration of peoples, formulated in Axiom 100, appear more reasonable than those imagined by Wolfgang Lazius.

[737] We have seen that the uniformity of the gods raised to the stars, which the Phoenicians brought from the Near East to Egypt and Greece, demonstrates the uniform course run by all early nations. On the basis of this uniformity, we may conclude that the Eastern kingdom of the Chaldaeans lasted for an equivalent period of some thousand years, from Zoroaster to Ninus' founding of the world's first monarchy in Assyria. And we may conclude that in Egypt a similar period of a thousand years extends from Hermes Trismegistus to the foundation of an equally great monarchy by Sesotris, whom Tacitus calls Ramses. Both the Chaldaeans and the Egyptians were isolated inland nations. As a result, they must have arrived at monarchy, which is the last form of human government, by passing through the three forms into which the Egyptians divided all their previous history: divine rule, heroic rule, and popular liberty. (We shall see later that monarchy can only spring from the people's unbridled liberty, to which in time of civil war the aristocracy subjects its power. For when power is divided into smaller units among the people, the whole of it is more easily seized by those leaders who, by championing popular liberty, eventually emerge as monarchs.) By contrast, Phoenicia as a maritime nation had grown wealthy through trade, and thus remained in the stage of popular liberty, which is the first form of human government.

[738] Thus, aided by reason alone, we have reconstructed the origins of universal history, both in ancient Egypt and in the more ancient Near East; and we have shed light on the origins of the Assyrian monarchy. (This reconstruction could not be based on historical

memory, which cannot exist unless it is supplied with facts by the senses.) Until now, no one had understood the many diverse causes which lead to the formation of a monarchy as the last of the three forms of civil government; so that the Assyrian kingdom sprang abruptly on the historical scene, like a frog born of a summer shower.

[739] In this manner, our chronology acquires greater certainty by retracing the progression of customs and deeds through which mankind has passed. Our science of chronology begins at the same point as its subject matter, as Axiom 106 states. It begins with Chronos (the Greek word for time) or Saturn, who reckoned the years by harvests; with Urania, who contemplates the heavens for taking auspices; and with Zoroaster, the 'star-gazer' who prophesies from falling stars. (We have seen that these were the first *mathēmata* and the first *theōrēmata*, the first sublime or divine phenomena that the nations contemplated and observed.) Later, Saturn ascended to the seventh sphere, and Urania became the contemplator of stars and planets. And from the vantage point of their immense plains, the Chaldaeans became astronomers and astrologers. For they measured the stars' motions, observed their aspects, and imagined their influence on sublunary bodies and (in their folly) on human free will. These sciences retained the original names given them, with great propriety, by the Greeks. Astronomy was the science of the 'laws of the stars', and astrology was the science of 'the language of the stars'. Since both of these implied divination, their *theōrēmata* or observations gave rise to the term theology, which meant the science of the gods' language as revealed in their oracles, auspices, and auguries. Then, from these heavenly sciences, mathematics descended to measure the earth, using measurements whose validity derived from heavenly measurements. This primary and principal branch of mathematics took its proper name from the earth, so that the Greeks called it geometry, or earth measurement.

[740] We are impressed by the stupendous erudition displayed by those two marvellous geniuses, Joseph Justus Scaliger in his *Critique of Chronology* and Denis Petau in his *Science of Chronology*. Yet they fail to begin their science at the point where its subject matter begins. For they base their chronology on the astronomical year, which the nations developed only after a thousand years of their history. And while the

astronomical year helps us calculate celestial conjuctions and oppositions between constellations and planets, it teaches us nothing about earthly events and their consequences. (The noble efforts of Cardinal Pierre d'Ailly to predict these were wasted.) Hence, Scaliger and Petau have done little to advance our knowledge of the origins and development of universal history.

SECTION II
POETIC GEOGRAPHY

CHAPTER I

Poetic Geography

[741] I have said that we view poetic history through two eyes, poetic chronology and poetic geography. Now that we have cleansed the former, we may proceed to the latter. It is a property of human nature that 'when men try to explain something distant and unfamiliar without having a true idea of it, they describe it in terms of what is present and familiar', as Axiom 2 states. It was in accordance with this property that the limited ideas of the early Greeks gave birth to poetic geography in all its parts and as a whole. Later, as the Greeks travelled through the world, this geography was gradually enlarged until it reached the extensive form in which it has survived. Although they did not draw the proper conclusions, ancient geographers agree on this truth. They maintain that, when ancient nations migrated to strange and distant lands, they gave their own native names to the places they found: cities, mountains, rivers, hills, straits, islands, and promontories.

[742] Within Greece itself, then, the East was called Asia or India; the West, Europe or Hesperia; the North, Thrace or Scythia; and the South, Libya or Mauretania. Later, these names from the Greek microcosm were extended to places in the outside world which resembled them. We find clear proof of this in the four cardinal winds, for in later geography they retain the names they initially had within Greece itself. In Homer, for example, it is on the shores of the Ocean that Rhesus' mares were impregnated by Zephyrus, the west wind of Greece, and that the horses of Achilles were likewise sired by Zephyrus. (As we shall see, Homer's Ocean originally meant any sea with a boundless horizon.) Similarly, Aeneas tells Achilles that the

338

mares of Erichthonius were impregnated by Boreas, which was the north wind of Greece. This truth about the cardinal winds is confirmed by another immense projection: as the minds of the Greeks expanded, they extended the name of the mountain where the Homeric gods lived to the starry heaven, which thereafter was called Olympus.

[743] By the same principles, the great peninsula east of Greece came to be called Asia Minor when the name of Asia passed to the great eastern part of the world which is now simply called Asia. Conversely, Greece itself was at first called Europe, as lying west of Asia, and was the Europa abducted by Jupiter in the form of a bull. But later the name Europe was extended to include the whole of the continent as far as the Atlantic Ocean. The Greeks called the western part of their country Hesperia after the planet Hesperus, or evening star, which rises there in the lower quarter of the horizon. Later, they saw Italy in the same direction, but much larger than in Greece, and they called it Hesperia Magna, the greater west. Finally, when they reached Spain in the same direction, they called it Hesperia Ultima, the far west. Conversely, the Greeks in Italy must have called Ionia their lands across the sea to the east, so that the sea between ancient Greece and Greater Greece came to be called the Ionia Sea. Later, the similar positions of their native Greece and its Asiatic colonies led the native Greeks to call Ionia the coast of Asia Minor to the east. Hence, when we read that Pythagoras arrived in Italy from Samos, it is reasonable to assume this means an island in the early Ionia, the Samos or Cephallenia ruled by Ulysses, rather than the Aegean island Samos, which is located in the later Ionia.

[744] From the Thrace within Greece came Mars or Ares, who was clearly a Greek deity; and from this same Thrace came Orpheus, who was one of the first Greek theological poets.

[745] From the Scythia within Greece came Anacharsis [Abaris], who left Scythian oracles in Greece.* These must have resembled those of Zoroaster, which were originally a history written in oracles. For his oracles, Anacharsis was regarded as one of the most ancient gods of

---

* For Abaris, Vico again mistakenly writes 'Anacharsis'.

prophecy, but later impostors converted his oracles into philosophical doctrines. The same thing happened to the *Orphic Hymns*, which, like Zoroaster's oracles, lack any poetic flavour and are instead redolent of the schools of Plato and Pythagoras. It was likewise from this Scythia, by way of the native Hyperboreans, that the two famous oracles at Delphi and Dodona must have come to Greece, as I conjectured in my Notes on Chronology. In this Scythia, or among the Hyperboreans of northern Greece, Anacharsis sought to establish civilization with Greek laws, and was killed by his brother Caduidas. So much did he profit from the barbarous philosophy imagined by Van Heurn that he was unable to frame laws by himself! For similar reasons, Abaris must have been a Scythian: for it is said that he wrote Scythian oracles, which must be the same as those introduced by Anacharsis. Now if Abaris wrote in the same Scythia where many years later Idanthyrsus was still writing using physical objects, we can only conclude that his oracles were in fact written by an impostor well after the introduction of Greek philosophy. Thus, the oracles of Anacharsis were regarded by the conceit of scholars to be oracles of esoteric wisdom, even though they do not survive.

[746] Zalmoxis, whom Herodotus credits with introducing the doctrine of the soul's immortality to the Greeks, was a Getan, just as Mars was from Getan Thrace.

[747] In the same way, it must have been from an India within Greece that triumphant Bacchus arrived from the Indian East, which means a Greek region rich in poetic gold. He celebrates his triumph in a golden chariot, which means a cart of grain. Bacchus is a tamer of serpents and tigers, just as we have seen that Hercules was a tamer of hydras and lions.

[748] Even today, the name Morea means the Peloponnese, which clearly proves that Perseus, who was a Greek hero, accomplished his feats in the Mauretania within Greece. (The Peloponnese lies south of Achaea, as Africa lies south of Europe.) We see how little Herodotus understood Greek antiquities – for which he was reproved by Thucydides – when he relates that the Moors were once white. Yet this was certainly true of the 'Moors' of his own Greece, which is still called White Morea.

[749] When we read that Aesculapius used his medical skill to protect his native island of Cos from a 'Moorish' pestilence, it must have come from this Mauretania within Greece. For protecting Cos from a Moroccan pestilence would have meant protecting it from all the pestilences in the world.

[750] In the same Mauretania, Hercules submitted to the burden of heaven which old Atlas had grown weary of supporting. The name Atlas must originally have meant Mt Athos, which rises on the neck of land, later cut through by Xerxes, that divides Macedonia and Thrace. In fact, between Greece and Thrace there was also a river named Atlas. (Later, the Greeks observed that Mt Abila and Mt Calpe divide Africa from Europe at the straits of Gibraltar. So they said that these were two pillars erected by Hercules to support the heavens, and the name Atlas was given to a nearby mountain in Africa.) The identification of Atlas with Athos renders more plausible that passage in Homer in which Thetis tells her son Achilles that she cannot bear his complaint to Jupiter, because the gods have left Olympus to feast on Mt Atlas. (The Homeric gods were thought to dwell on the tops of the highest mountains.) It would be hard to believe that Homer meant the Mt Atlas in Africa. For he himself says that even Mercury, with his wings, could barely reach Calypso's island, which lay in the Phoenician sea, much closer to Greece than the kingdom now called Morocco.

[751] In this way, it was from the Hesperia within Greece that Hercules brought the golden apples to Attica, which was the home of the Hesperides, or daughters of Atlas, who guarded them.

[752] In this way, the river Eridanus, into which Phaethon plunged, must have been the Danube in Greek Thrace, which flows into the Black Sea. Later, when the Greeks In Italy found that the river Po runs from west to east like the Danube, they called it the Eridanus. The later mythographers accordingly placed Phaethon's fall in Italy, but they were mistaken. For Greek constellations, including Eridanus, only represent figures from Greek heroic history, and not those of other nations.

[753] Finally, when the Greeks reached the Atlantic Ocean, they extended their limited idea of an ocean. (Previously, an ocean was any sea with a boundless horizon, which explains why Homer described

the island of Aeolia as girt by the Ocean.) By this larger idea, they extended the name to the sea which girds the entire earth, which they thought was an immense island. The powers of Neptune were thus immeasurably enlarged, so that with his trident he could shake the whole world from the abyss of the waters. According to the crude physics described earlier, Plato located this abyss of water deep in the bowels of the earth.

[754] These principles of poetic geography acquit Homer of three serious errors which have been wrongfully imputed to him.

[755] (1) Homer's Lotus Eaters, who ate the bark of a plant called the lotus, lived closer to Greece than some have thought. Homer says that Ulysses' voyage from Cape Malea to the Lotus Eaters took nine days. But if they lived beyond the straits of Gibraltar, as many thought, this nine-day voyage would have been not only implausible, but impossible. This is an error imputed to Homer by Eratosthenes.

[756] (2) In Homer's day, the Laestrygons must have been a people in Greece. When Homer says that they have the longest days, he must mean within Greece rather than in the whole world. This passage led the scholiast on Aratus to locate the Laestrygons under the head of Draco, which is a polar constellation. But the authoritative and exact historian Thucydides places the Laestrygons in Sicily, where they must have been the northernmost people.

[757] (3) Similarly, the land of the Cimmerians was in the northernmost region of Greece, where the nights were the longest, which is why the Cimmerians were said to live near the underworld. The people of Cumae, who lived near the cave of the Sibyl which led to the underworld, came to be called Cimmerians because of the apparent similarity of the sites. Later, the name Cimmerian was applied to the distant inhabitants of the Sea of Azov. But it is scarcely credible that in a single day Ulysses could travel to these remoter Cimmerians, visit the underworld there, and then return to Circeii, the present-day Mt Circello near Cumae. We should note that Ulysses made this journey without using any magic, for he was protected against Circe's spells by a secret herb given to him by Mercury.

[758] These principles of poetic geography also allow us to resolve many difficulties in the ancient history of the East. For peoples originally

found in the Near East, especially in the north and south, have been taken for inhabitants of the distant Orient.

[759] We may apply the principles of Greek poetic geography to the ancient geography of the Latin people. Originally, Latium must have been very limited in size. We have seen that Rome, during the first 250 years of its kingship, subdued some twenty peoples but only extended its dominion by twenty miles. And early Italy was clearly confined to the area between Cisalpine Gaul and Greater Greece. Only later did Roman conquests extend the name Italy to the entire peninsula, which is its present meaning. By the same token, the Etruscan or Tyrrhenian sea must have been quite small when Horatius Cocles alone withstood the entire Etruscan nation at the bridge. But later Roman victories extended the name to mean the entire western coast of Italy.

[760] In exactly the same way, the Pontus to which Jason sailed with the Argonauts must originally have been the land closest to Europe, from which it is divided by the strait called Propontis. From this land, the name passed to the Sea of Pontus, and then was extended further into Asia, where Mithridates had his kingdom. According to the myth of the Argonauts, Medea's father Aeëtes was born in Chalcis [Colchis], a city on the island of Euboea.* Today, this island is called Negropont, and it must have given its name to what is still called the Black Sea. The original Crete must have been an island in the Greek archipelago within the labyrinth of Cycladic islands mentioned earlier, from which Minos must have raided Athens. Only later was the name Crete transferred to the large island in the Mediterranean.

[761] To turn from the Romans to the Greeks, we note how they travelled the world and in their conceit spread the fame of the Trojan War and of the wandering heroes – both Trojans like Antenor, Capys, and Aeneas, and Greeks like Menelaus, Diomedes, and Ulysses. Everywhere in the world, they found a poetic archetype of nation founder like their Theban Hercules, and therefore spread his name far and wide. (Varro reckoned forty such Herculean founders among the ancient nations, including the Latin god Fidius.) We have seen that the Egyptians claimed that their god Ammon was the world's oldest Jupiter, and that

---

* For Colchis, Vico mistakenly writes 'Chalcis'.

every Hercules in the world derived from their Egyptian one. But with equal conceit, the Greeks had their Hercules wander through every region in the world, cleansing it of monsters and bringing home nothing but glory.

[762] The Greeks also found everywhere a poetic archetype of a shepherd speaking in verse, like their Evander the Arcadian. Evander had migrated from Arcadia to Latium, where he received his countryman Hercules and wed Carmenta, who was named for *carmina*, verses. She invented the Latin letters, meaning the forms of the articulate sounds of which verses are composed. In sum, the Greeks found their poetic archetypes in Latium, just as they found their own Curetes scattered in Saturnia or ancient Italy, in Crete, and in Asia.

[763] Now, these Greek names and ideas arrived in Latium in an utterly savage age, when nations were closed to foreigners. In the age of Servius Tullius, for example, Livy says that it was impossible for even the name of Pythagoras, much less the philosopher himself, to reach Rome from Croton, since the way was blocked by so many nations with different languages and customs. Precisely this difficulty of communication caused me to formulate Axiom 103: 'The Greeks must have founded an early colony on the coast of Latium, which was later conquered and destroyed by the Romans, so that it lies buried in the darkness of antiquity.' Such a colony could have taught the Latins their letters, which according to Tacitus originally resembled the earliest Greek ones. This strongly suggests that the Latins got their alphabet from Greeks living in Latium, and not from the inhabitants of Greater Greece, much less those of Greece proper. For the Romans only encountered these Greeks during their wars with Tarentum and Pyrrhus; and from them the Romans would have adopted the latest Greek letters, rather than retaining the earlier Greek alphabet.

[764] In this way, the names of Hercules, Evander, and Aeneas arrived in Latium from Greece. This illustrates the following four customs of the nations.

[765] (1) Barbarous nations cherish their native customs. But when they begin to grow more refined, they take delight in foreign languages as well as in foreign merchandise and fashions. For example, the Romans exchanged their god Fidius for the Greek Hercules. Instead of their

native oath *mediusfidius*, by Fidius, they introduced new oaths like *mehercule*, by Hercules; *mecastor*, by Castor; and *edepol*, by Pollux.

[766] (2) The conceit of nations causes them to boast of illustrious foreign origins, particularly when their own barbarous traditions offer them some motive. For example, the Latins gladly disavowed their true founder Fidius in favour of the Greek founder Hercules, and exchanged their own shepherd poets for Evander the Arcadian. (Similarly, in the medieval return of barbarism, Giovanni Villani wrote that Atlas had founded Fiesole and that a Trojan king named Priam had reigned in Germany.)

[767] (3) When people of one nation observe foreign things which they cannot express clearly in their native language, they must perforce make use of foreign words.

[768] (4) Finally, since early peoples cannot abstract the qualities inherent in objects, they name the objects themselves to signify their qualities. (This property is discussed in my Poetic Logic.) The following Latin idioms offer us striking examples of this usage.

[769] The early Romans had no idea of luxury; but when they observed the luxuries of the Greeks in Tarentum, they called anyone wearing perfume a Tarentine. The Romans had no conception of military stratagems; but when they observed how the Carthaginians used them, they called them Punic tricks. They had no notion of pomposity; but when they observed it in the Capuans, they used the expression 'Campanian haughtiness' to mean pompous or proud behaviour. Similarly, Numa Pompilius and Ancus Marcius were said to be Sabines, because there was no Latin word to describe notable piety like that of the Sabines. Servius Tullius was said to be Greek, because there was no word for 'cunning'. (The Romans had no such word until they had conquered Tarentum and encountered its Greek inhabitants.) Servius Tullius was also said to be a slave, because they had no word for 'weakling'. For by his first agrarian law, Servius granted bonitary ownership of the fields to the plebeians, an act for which the patricians may have had him killed. We may note that cunning often accompanies weakness, and both qualities were foreign to Roman candour and bravery. Indeed, it is a great insult to early Rome and an affront to her founder Romulus to assert, as some have, that Rome

could produce no heroes worthy to be kings, and had to endure the reign of an ignoble slave. Such a compliment is paid her by critics who have only consulted literary sources. And it was succeeded by a similar compliment, intended to salvage the myth that the Law of the Twelve Tables came to Rome from Athens. In this view, the Romans, after having founded a powerful empire in Latium and defended it from the massed forces of Etruria, were supposed to roam like lawless barbarians through Italy, Greater Greece, and Greece itself to find laws establishing their liberty.

CHAPTER 2

Corollary on Aeneas' Arrival in Italy

[770] The preceding remarks reveal the actual manner in which Aeneas arrived in Italy and founded the Roman nation in Alba, the city from which the Romans trace their origin. There must have been a Greek city on the coast of Latium which was founded by Greeks from Phrygia in Asia Minor, the site of Troy. This city was unknown to the Romans until their conquests led them down to the nearby coast. This happened under the third Roman king, Ancus Marcius, who began by colonizing the nearby coastal city of Ostia, which as Rome expanded later became its port. In this manner, the Romans first received the Arcadians as inland refugees in Latium. Later, they offered their protection to the Trojans who had fled Phrygia by sea, and by the heroic right of war destroyed their coastal city. But two anachronisms distorted the sequence in which these two peoples reached safety in the refuge of Romulus. The arrival of the Arcadians on land was dated too late, and arrival of the Trojans by sea too early.

[771] If we reject this sequence of events, we must be perplexed and confused by Aeneas' role in the origin of Rome, as Axiom 103 states. Scholars from Livy onwards have sought to avoid this perplexity and confusion by regarding Rome's origin as a myth. But in so doing, they ignore the fact that myths have a public basis in truth, as Axiom 16

346

states. In the traditional view, Evander is so powerful in Latium that he offers Hercules hospitality 500 years before the founding of Rome. Aeneas in turn founds the royal house of Alba, which grows to such distinction under its fourteen kings that it becomes the capital of Latium. And after living many years as nomads, the Arcadians and Trojans at last flee to the refuge of Romulus!

Yet how could people from Arcadia, deep in the Greek interior, shepherds who by nature knew nothing of the sea, have crossed such a large expanse of it and journeyed deep into Latium, when Ancus Marcius, the third king after Romulus, was the first Roman to lead colonists to the nearby sea? How could the Arcadians, together with the dispersed Trojans from Phrygia, have arrived there 200 years before the age when, in Livy's judgment, not even the name of Pythagoras, so renowned in Greater Greece, could have travelled from Croton to Rome, because the way was blocked by so many nations of diverse languages and customs? And how could they have arrived 400 years before the Greeks of Tarentum had even heard of the Romans although they were already a power in central Italy?

[772] Such popular traditions must originally have had a firm public basis in truth, as Axiom 16 states, which is why the entire nation of Rome preserved them for such a long period of time. What then? Clearly, we must presume that there was a Greek city on the coast of Latium, just as there were many others that long remained on the shores of the Tyrrhenian Sea. The Romans must have conquered this city before the Law of the Twelve Tables existed, destroyed it by the heroic right of barbaric victory, and adopted its defeated people as their heroic associates. Using poetic archetypes, the Greeks must have called Arcadians those inland nomads who wandered the forests, and Trojans or Phrygians those who wandered by sea.

(In the same way, the Romans said that people subdued by conquest and capitulation had been received into Romulus' refuge. This simply meant that they were employed as day labourers, like the clients created by Romulus when he opened his refuge in the clearing. Such conquered and capitulating peoples evidently became Roman clients between the expulsion of the kings in 509 BC and the adoption of the Law of the Twelve Tables in 451 BC. From them there emerged those Roman plebeians who gained bonitary ownership of their fields under Servius Tullius' agrarian law. When they demanded more than this, Coriolanus sought to reduce them to their former status as Romulus' labourers.)

Later, as the Greeks everywhere trumpeted the Trojan War and the wanderings of its heroes, they celebrated those of Aeneas in Italy, where they had already discovered their Hercules, their Evander, and their Curetes. Over the years these traditions were altered and eventually corrupted by the barbarous people who inherited them. In this manner, Aeneas became the founder of the Roman people in Latium, even though Samuel Bochart insists that he never set foot in Italy, even though Strabo says he never left Troy, and even though the weightier authority of Homer relates that he died in Troy and left a kingdom to his descendants. Thus was Aeneas transformed by the contrary conceits of two nations. By proclaiming the fame of the Trojan War, the Greeks imposed Aeneas on the Roman people. And by vaunting their illustrious foreign origin, the Romans eventually adopted him as their national founder.

[773] In fact, this myth must have arisen late, around the time of the war with Pyrrhus, when the Romans began to take delight in Greek things. For we find that nations develop such tastes only after they have had long and extensive contact with foreigners.

CHAPTER 3

Names and Descriptions of Heroic Cities

[774] To complete our discussion of Poetic Wisdom, it only remains to discuss the two principal parts of geography. These are nomenclature and chorography, which denote respectively the naming and the description of places and of cities in particular.

[775] We have seen that divine providence caused heroic cities to be built in fortified sites, to which in their divine age the ancient Latins gave the sacred name *arae*, altars. They were also called *arces*, citadels, just as lordships during the medieval return of barbarism were in Italian called *rocche*, from *rocce*, steep and sheer cliffs, and later called *castella*,

castles or fortresses. Similarly, the meaning of the noun *ara* must have been extended to the entire district of a heroic city. (In terms of its borders with foreigners, a city was called *ager*, field; whereas in terms of jurisdiction over its citizens, it was called *territorium*, territory.) On this, there is a golden passage in Tacitus describing the great altar of Hercules in Rome, which I cite here at length as weighty proof of my principles: 'The furrow marking the city boundary began at the cattle market, where we now see the bronze statue of an ox, which is the animal commonly yoked to the plough; and it was drawn to include the great altar of Hercules.' A similar golden passage in Sallust describes the famous altar of the Philaenus brothers which marked the boundary between the dominions of Carthage and Cyrene.

[776] All of ancient geography was strewn with such altars. To begin with Asia, Christoph Cellarius says in his *Geography of the Ancient World* that all the names of the cities in Syria begin or end with Ara(m), altar, and that Syria itself was called Aramea or Aramia. In Greece, Theseus founded the city of Athens on the famous Altar of the Unfortunates. (He justly regarded as unfortunate the lawless and godless men who had fled the quarrels caused by their abominable promiscuity and had taken refuge in the strongholds of strong men. These refugees arrived alone, weak, and in need of all the benefits which the pious men derived from civilization.) In Greek, the noun *ara* also means vow: for the first victims were consecrated to Vesta and then killed on the altars of the early pagan world. These early sacrifices were in Latin called Saturn's victims, and in Greek *anathēmata*, accursed, a term the Romans translated as 'victims consecrated to the Furies', *diris devoti*. And the sacrificial victims were the violent and impious people who dared trespass on the heroes' tilled fields, *campi*, to which the weak fled for safety. (This may explain why the Italian verb *campare* means to survive.) From this slaying, the Latin noun *supplicium*, prayer, came to mean both punishment and sacrifice, senses in which it is used by Sallust and other authors. These meanings are wonderfully matched by those of the Greek noun *ara*, which means not only a vow, but also an offending party (Latin *noxa*) and the Furies (Latin *dirae*) as well. In Book 4, we shall see that the first victims were consecrated, or devoted, to the Furies and then sacrificed on the altars of the early pagan world.

By the same token, the Latin noun *hara*, which survived in the sense of a sty or pen, must originally have meant victim; and from it clearly derives *haruspex*, seer, so called for consulting the entrails of victims slain at the altars.

[777] Tacitus' account of the great altar of Hercules makes it clear that, when Romulus founded Rome in his refuge in the clearing, he based it on an altar like that of Theseus. Indeed, the later Romans never spoke of a clearing or sacred grove without mentioning an altar raised there to some divinity. Thus, when Livy characterizes refuges as the ancient counsel of city founders, he reveals why we read in ancient geography of so many cities named Arae, altars. This also shows that Cicero spoke as an expert in antiquities when he called the Roman senate an 'altar of associates', *ara sociorum*. For it was to the senate that Roman provinces referred their fiscal grievances against the mismanagement of greedy governors.

[778] I have shown that heroic cities in both Asia and Europe, particularly in Greece and Italy, were called altars, Arae. And in Africa, Sallust describes the famous altar of the Philaenus brothers. To return to Europe, the northern cities of Transylvania are called Altars of the Sicilians, or Székelyek. (Besides the Hungarians and Saxons, the inhabitants of this region descend from the ancient nation of Huns, a nation of noble peasants and shepherds.) In Germany, Tacitus mentions a town called the Altar of the Ubians, *Ara Ubiorum*. In Spain, the word *ara* is still part of the names of many cities, such as Aranjuez. In the Syrian language, the word *ari* means lion. Similarly, we saw in our natural genealogy of the twelve major divinities that the Greeks derived their notion of Mars, called Ares, from the defence of their altars, *pro aris*. And in the medieval return of barbarism, the same idea of strength led many cities and noble houses to charge their coats of arms with lions. This word *ara*, so uniform in sound and meaning in various nations separated by distance, time, and customs, must be the root of the Latin noun *aratrum*, plough, the curved part of which was called *urbs*, city. Also from *ara* must derive the Latin noun *arx*, citadel, and the verb *arcere*, to defend; as well as the cognate expression *ager arcifinius*, buffer land, used by writers on the subject of fields and their boundaries. From this same root must derive the nouns *arma*, arms, and *arcus*, bow.

For the ancient Latins had a just idea of strength, which they conceived as driving back harm and keeping it at a distance.

CONCLUSION

[779] We have seen that poetic wisdom justly deserves supreme and sovereign praise on two counts. (1) As is clearly and consistently recognized, poetic wisdom founded pagan civilization. Even while striving to affirm this, the conceits of nations and scholars have in fact denied it. For the nations have imagined poetic wisdom as a vain magnificence, while scholars have distorted it with incongruous philosophical wisdom. (2) As popular tradition relates, poetic wisdom created sages who were equally great as philosophers, lawmakers, generals, historians, orators, and poets. But in creating them, this wisdom formed them only roughly: this is how we see them in their myths, in which we perceive the embryonic outlines, as it were, of all esoteric wisdom. We may conclude that in their myths the nations used crude and physical language to describe the principles of the world of sciences. Later, this was elucidated by the specialized researches of scholars who used rational argument and general rules. All this confirms the thesis of my second book, that the theological poets were the sense of human wisdom, as the philosophers were its intellect.

BOOK 3
DISCOVERY OF THE
TRUE HOMER

SECTION I
THE SEARCH FOR THE
TRUE HOMER

INTRODUCTION

[780] In Book 2, I showed that poetic wisdom was the popular wisdom of the peoples of Greece, who were first theological and later heroic poets. It follows necessarily that Homer's wisdom was no different in kind. But Plato's belief in Homer's sublime and esoteric wisdom became so firmly embedded that all the other philosophers eagerly followed his view, especially Plutarch, who dedicated an entire book to the subject. In response to them, I propose to examine *whether Homer was in fact a philosopher*. According to Diogenes Laertius in his life of Pyrrhon, Longinus devoted an entire book to this question.

CHAPTER I
The Esoteric Wisdom Attributed to Homer

[781] If we are to judge this question, we must concede that Homer shared the popular feelings and customs of the barbarous Greeks of his time: for such feelings and customs constitute the proper materials of all poets. And we must concede that Homer means what he says when he asserts that the gods are ranked by their physical strength. Homer illustrates this in his myth of the great chain, in which Jupiter cites his supreme strength to prove that he alone is the king of gods and men. Only such a belief makes it credible that Minerva first helps the mortal Diomedes wound Venus and Mars, and then in the battle of the gods disarms Venus and strikes Mars with a rock. (This shows how little

Minerva was popularly regarded as the goddess of philosophy, and how well she uses arms befitting Jupiter's wisdom!) And let us concede that Homer describes the fearful customs current among the barbarous people of Greece. (Even though many think that the Greeks spread civilization throughout the world, these customs run contrary to what theorists have called the 'eternal' practices of the natural law of nations.) First, the Greeks poisoned their arrows, which is why Ulysses goes to Ephyra in search of poisonous herbs. And second, they denied burial to enemies killed in battle, whose bodies were left as carrion for crows and dogs. This is why Priam paid so much to ransom his son Hector, even after Achilles had bound his corpse to a chariot and dragged it around the walls of Troy for three days.

[782] Poets are the teachers of the masses, and the aim of poetry is to tame their savagery. So it was unworthy of a wise man, versed in savage feelings and customs, to arouse such admiration of them that the masses found pleasure and hence encouragement from his myths. And it was unworthy of a wise man to arouse the pleasure of the knavish masses by describing the knaveries of the gods, to say nothing of the heroes. In the battle of the gods, we find Mars insulting Minerva as a 'dog-fly', and Minerva striking Diana in the chest. Even the two kings, Agamemnon, commander of the Greek allies, and Achilles, the greatest of the Greek heroes, call each other dogs – an insult which the servants in our comedies would scarcely utter today.

[783] As for Agamemnon's supposed wisdom, good heavens, what can we call it but folly? When Apollo sends a deadly plague and decimates the Greek army for the seizing of Chryseis, this commander of the Greeks has to be compelled by Achilles to do his duty and restore Chryseis to her father Chryses, who is the priest of Apollo. Then, considering his dignity slighted, Agamemnon decides to regain his honour by observing a justice commensurate with his great wisdom: he wrongfully seizes Briseis from Achilles. In response, the hero who carries Troy's fate in his heel withdraws in disgust, taking with him his men and ships, and allows Hector to kill any Greeks who have survived the plague.

This is the Homer who was previously regarded as the founder of Greek polity or civilization! From this incident, he weaves the whole fabric of the entire *Iliad*, whose principal characters are two Greek leaders: the commander Agamemnon, and the hero Achilles, whose character we discussed in the Heroism of Early Peoples. This is Homer, the incomparable creator of poetic archetypes, whose greatest characters are completely unsuited to our present civilized and social nature, but are perfectly suited to the heroic nature of punctilious nobles!

[784] What shall we say, then, when Homer relates that his heroes take so much pleasure in wine, and that in their greatest afflictions they take comfort in drunkenness, especially the wise Ulysses? Such precepts of consolation are truly worthy of a philosopher!

[785] Julius Caesar Scaliger takes offence because nearly all of Homer's similes are based on wild animals and other savage things. But even if we concede that Homer thought them necessary to making himself understood by the wild and savage masses, it is clear that no mind civilized and refined by philosophy could have succeeded in inventing such similes, which are truly incomparable. And no mind rendered humane and compassionate by philosophy could have created the truculent and ferocious style which Homer uses in describing the great variety of bloody battles, and the great variety of extravagantly cruel kinds of slaughter, which constitute the particular sublimity of the *Iliad*.

[786] Furthermore, Homer's capricious gods and heroes could scarcely have been created by a mind in which the study of the philosophers' wisdom has instilled consistency. Some Homeric characters, at first disturbed or distressed, are suddenly silenced and subdued when moved by a contrary whim. Others, seething with violent anger, collapse in tears when they remember a sad event. (We find precise parallels to this during the later part of the medieval return of barbarism in Italy. In this age, Dante, the Tuscan Homer, sang historical events. The anonymous biography of Cola di Rienzo vividly expresses the morals of Homeric heroes. As Cola publicly decries the oppression of the wretched Roman state by haughty nobles, both he and his audience burst into uncontrollable sobbing.) Still other Homeric heroes, who are afflicted by overwhelming grief, meet with cheerful circumstances, and so completely forget their woes that they abandon themselves to gaiety, like Ulysses at the banquet of Alcinous.

Other Homeric heroes, who at first seem calm and quiet, suddenly take offence at an innocent remark and fly into such a blind fury that they threaten the speaker with a terrible death. This is how Achilles threatens Priam. With Mercury as his guide, Priam enters the Greek camp at night to ransom Hector's corpse. There Achilles receives him and invites him to dinner. But when this wretched father, out of pity for his valorous son, inadvertently lets slip a single remark that displeases Achilles, the hero flies into a rage. Oblivious of the sacred laws of hospitality, unmindful of Priam's good faith in coming alone and placing complete trust in him, unmoved by the many great misfortunes of such a king, by pity for such a father, or by the veneration due such an old man, and disregarding their common lot, which is the strongest motive for compassion – Achilles flies into a bestial rage and thunders that he will cut off Priam's head!

Furthermore, Achilles refuses with impious obstinacy to forgive Agamemnon's personal affront which, though serious in nature, could not be avenged justly by the ruin of their homeland and the entire Greek nation. Instead, this hero who carries Troy's fate in his heel takes pleasure in letting all the Greeks suffer miserable defeat and destruction at the hands of Hector. Nor is he moved by devotion to his homeland or the glory of his nation to offer them any aid. When he finally aids the Greeks, it is only to assuage his personal grief because Hector has killed his friend Patroclus! Even in death, his wrath at the loss of Briseis is not yet placated. The beautiful princess Polyxena, who is the daughter of the once rich and powerful Priam, and is now a miserable slave despite her royal birth, must be sacrificed on Achilles' tomb, so that his ashes, thirsty for vengeance, may soak up the last drop of her blood! To say nothing of what defies comprehension: how a poet with any philosophical gravity or decorum could have spent his time inventing the many old wives' tales, suitable for children, which fill his second epic, the *Odyssey*.

[787] In Book 2, I described the morals of early peoples as crude, boorish, fierce, cruel, volatile, unreasonable and unreasonably headstrong, capricious, and foolish. Since such behaviour can only be found in people who have the mental weakness of children, the vigorous imagination of women, and the seething passions of violent youths, we must deny that Homer possessed any esoteric wisdom. These are the reasons which first occasioned the doubts that inevitably led to my search for the *true Homer*.

CHAPTER 2

Homer's Native Land

[788] So much for the esoteric wisdom previously attributed to Homer. Let us now consider his native land. Nearly all the cities of Greece vied for the honour of being his birthplace, and there were even some who maintained that he was a Greek from Italy. In his essay *On Homer's Native Land*, Leone Allacci labours in vain to resolve the question. Now, since no author older than Homer survives, as Josephus stoutly maintains against the grammarian Apion, and since all other authors wrote long after his age, we are obliged to consider Homer the founder of his nation. Hence, we must apply our metaphysical criticism to discover in Homer's text the truth about his age and his native land.

[789] A golden passage in the *Odyssey* offers us certain proof that the Homer who wrote that work came from southwestern Greece. When Ulysses is eager to depart from Phaeacia, or present-day Corfu, the king Alcinous offers him a well-fitted ship manned by his vassals. He says they are expert sailors who can, if necessary, take Ulysses even as far as Euboea, or present-day Negropont. The latter is named as a sort of Ultima Thule of the Greek world, which is described as very distant by those who have chanced to see it. This passage shows clearly that the Homer of the *Odyssey* is different from the author of the *Iliad*, for Euboea was not far from Troy. (Troy was located in Asia Minor by the shore of the Hellespont, the narrow strait where the two fortresses called the Dardanelles now stand. Even today their name preserves its origin in Dardania, which was the ancient territory of Troy.) Indeed, Seneca tells us that there was a celebrated debate among Greek scholars on the question of whether the *Iliad* and the *Odyssey* were by the same author.

[790] The Greek cities vied for the honour of claiming Homer as their own because in his epics they found words, phrases, and dialectal forms which belonged to their own vernaculars.

[791] These observations will aid us in our discovery of the true Homer.

CHAPTER 3

Homer's Age

[792] The following passages in Homer's epics offer us certain proof about his true age.

I

[793] During Patroclus' funeral, Achilles organizes nearly all the kinds of games which were later celebrated in the Olympics of civilized Greece.

2

[794] Among other things, the shield of Achilles indicates that the arts of low-relief casting and of metal engraving had already been invented. By contrast, painting had not yet been invented. Casting abstracts a surface with some relief, and engraving abstracts it with some depth. But painting completely abstracts the surfaces it depicts, which requires considerable ingenuity. The fact that neither Homer nor Moses mentions paintings is one indication of their antiquity.

3

[795] The delights of the gardens of Alcinous, the magnificence of his palace, and the sumptuousness of his banquets prove that the Greeks already admired luxury and pomp.

4

[796] To the ports of Homer's Greece, the Phoenicians had already introduced wares such as ivory, purple dye, Arabian incense (the scent of Venus' cave), cotton gauze finer than onionskin, and garments with embroidery. One of the suitors' gifts to Penelope was a robe woven

with brooches which made the fabric fit the contours of the body –
truly an invention worthy of today's effeminate refinements!

5

[797] The coach in which Priam rides to see Achilles is made of cedar,
and its fragrance fills the cave of Calypso. Such sensual refinements
were still unknown in the Rome of Nero and Heliogabalus, when
voluptuaries madly squandered their estates on luxuries.

6

[798] Homer describes luxurious baths on Circe's island.

7

[799] In the *Odyssey*, the suitors' young servants are handsome, graceful,
and blond boys, precisely like those required by today's amenities.

8

[800] Some Homeric men wear their hair long like women. Hector
and Diomedes reproach the effeminate Paris for this.

9

[801] Homer consistently portrays his heroes eating roast meat, which
is the simplest and plainest kind of food, since it can be prepared just
using coals. Later, sacrificial meals retained this simple custom. At first,
the Romans roasted the meat of victims on the altar, and then carved
and served its slices, *prosicia*, to the guests. Later, they roasted it on spits
just like unconsecrated meat. When Achilles prepares a dinner for
Priam, he chops up a lamb, which Patroclus then roasts, setting the
table with bread in baskets. All the banquets celebrated by the heroes
were sacrifices, in which they acted as priests. In Latin, such sacrifices
survived as the *epulae*, sumptuous banquets usually given by the great;

as the *epulum*, a public feast for the people; and as the sacred banquet celebrated by the priests known as *epulones*. Agamemnon slaughters two lambs as a sacrifice to ratify his treaty with Priam. Such was the magnificence in that age of something we now associate with a butcher!

Only later were meats boiled. Besides a fire, such cooking requires water, a cauldron, and a tripod. Virgil describes his heroes as eating such boiled meat, as well as roasting it on spits. Finally, as seasonings were discovered, people learned how to prepare seasoned food. To return to Homeric banquets, the greatest delicacy of the Greek heroes is simply a mixture of meal with cheese and honey. And two Homeric similes refer to fishing. Indeed, in the *Odyssey* Ulysses, disguised as a pauper begging alms, tells one of the suitors that hospitable kings, who are generous to poor travellers, are rewarded by the gods with seas abounding in fish, which are the greatest delicacy of a banquet.

10

[802] Finally, and more important for my argument, Homer apparently lived in an age when heroic law had lapsed in Greece, and was being replaced by an era of popular liberty. In Homer, heroes contract marriages with foreign women, and bastards succeed to kingdoms. This must reflect historical reality. Many years earlier, Hercules had died in a furious agony because he was tainted by the blood of the bestial centaur Nessus, which marked the end of heroic law.

[803] In discussing Homer's age, we cannot afford to overlook textual authority altogether. I have cited the *Iliad* less often than the *Odyssey*, which Longinus regards as a work of his old age. In Homer's epics, we noted many passages which confirm the opinion of those who date Homer long after the Trojan War – after an interval of some 460 years, which brings us down to the age of Numa Pompilius. Indeed, I think we are indulging these scholars by not dating Homer later. For we are told that Psammeticus only opened Egypt to the Greeks after the age of Numa. And countless Homeric passages, especially in the *Odyssey*, indicate that the Greeks had long since opened their country to trade with the Phoenicians, and thus delighted in their stories no less than in

their merchandise, just as Europeans now delight in those of the Indies. Hence, we may reconcile two facts: that Homer never saw Egypt, but that he describes many things about Egypt and Libya, Phoenicia and Asia, and especially Italy and Sicily; for the Greeks learned about such things from Phoenician merchants.

[804] Yet I do not see how to reconcile so many refined customs with the many wild and savage ones Homer ascribes to his heroes, especially in the *Iliad*. In other words, to avoid mingling barbarous ways with milder ones – *ne placidis coeant immitia*, as Horace puts it – it would appear that the Homeric epics were composed and revised by several hands in several ages.

[805] These observations about the native land and age of the *traditional Homer* create various doubts as we search for the *true Homer*.

CHAPTER 4

Homer's Incomparable Gift for Heroic Poetry

[806] We have seen that Homer knew nothing about philosophy, and we have discovered little about his native land and age. This leads us to suspect that Homer was simply a commoner. Horace's *Art of Poetry* confirms this suspicion. For Horace notes that all the poets writing after Homer find a desperate difficulty in inventing original tragic characters. He therefore counsels them to adopt characters from the Homeric epics. To this desperate difficulty, we must add the fact that all the characters of New Comedy are completely original: indeed, a law at Athens required that such comedies be staged solely with original characters. And the Greeks managed this so successfully that even the Romans in their pride despaired of rivalling them. As Quintilian observes, 'In comedy we cannot compete with the Greeks.'

[807] To this difficulty noted by Horace, we may in a broader context add two others. (1) Although Homer came first, he was inimitable as a heroic poet. By contrast, tragedy, which arose later, began quite crudely, as everyone is aware and as we shall soon see. (2) Even though he came before philosophy and the arts of poetry and criticism, Homer

was the most sublime of all the sublime heroic poets. By contrast, no poet who lived in an age of philosophy and the arts even came close to rivalling Homer. Even if we don't pose these questions, Horace's difficulty and the general problem of New Comedy should have moved our distinguished scholars of poetics – Patrizi, Scaliger, Castelvetro, and others – to investigate the reasons for this discrepancy.

[808] The solution can only lie in the origins of poetry discovered in my Poetic Wisdom, that is, in the poetic archetypes which alone constitute the very essence of poetry. (1) New Comedy offers portraits of our modern civilized customs. Since Greek poets were well versed in the teachings of Socratic philosophy, they could use general maxims of civil ethics to create notable exemplars of ideal people. (Such a poet was Menander, whose Roman imitator Terence was merely styled 'half a Menander' by his countrymen.) The lustre and splendour of their characters could inspire the masses, who are as quick to learn from striking examples as they are slow to profit from rational precepts. (2) Old Comedy took its plots or subjects from real life, and wrote plays about people as they were. In *The Clouds*, the malicious Aristophanes wrote a play about the good Socrates, and thereby caused his downfall. (3) By contrast, tragedy places on the stage passions like heroic hatred, scorn, anger, and revenge, which are clothed with marvellous elements. All of tragedy's fierce emotions, crude speeches, and horrible deeds – passions naturally produced by sublime natures – display a remarkable conformity and uniformity: for they are the product of the Greeks' heroic age, whose later phase is represented by Homer.

The following argument of metaphysical criticism shows this. Myths which had originally been direct and proper reached Homer in a corrupt and indecorous form. As we saw under Poetic Wisdom, all these myths were initially true stories which, gradually altered and corrupted, reached the age of Homer, who belongs to the third age of heroic poets. (The first heroic age invented myths as true narratives, which is the primary and proper meaning of the Greek word *mythos*. The second age altered and corrupted these myths; and the third and final age, Homer's age, received them in this corrupt form.)

[809] To return to the topic of heroic poetry, we now understand why Aristotle in his *Poetics* says that Homer alone knew how to invent

poetic falsehoods. For Homer's poetic archetypes, which Horace so greatly admires for their incomparable sublimity, were imaginative universals. In my Poetic Metaphysics, we saw that the heroic Greeks assigned to such archetypes all the particular qualities belonging to each genus. Thus, the Greeks assigned to Achilles, who is the principal subject of the *Iliad*, all the qualities of heroic virtue, and all the emotions and behaviour which spring from these qualities. (Describing Achilles, Horace summarizes these qualities as a quick temper, fastidiousness, irascibility, implacability, violence, and the judging of right by might.) And the Greeks assigned to Ulysses, the principal subject of the *Odyssey*, all the properties of heroic wisdom, namely, caution, patience, dissimulation, duplicity, deception, and a combination of regard for words with an indifference to deeds which leads others into error and self-deception. Thus, the Greeks assigned to both archetypes the deeds appropriate to each particular hero; and these so aroused the dull and dim-witted Greeks that by observing them they conceived general categories. Since these two archetypes were formed by an entire nation, they were necessarily imagined in a uniform way. (The decorum, or graceful beauty, of a myth consists solely in such uniformity, which is appropriate to the common sense of an entire nation.) And since they were created by powerful imaginations, they could only be imagined as sublime. This origin determined two eternal properties of poetry. First, poetic sublimity always contains popular elements. Second, once a people has created heroic archetypes, they can imagine human behaviour only in terms of the striking archetypes of their illustrious exemplars.

CHAPTER 5

Philosophical Proofs for the Discovery of the True Homer

[810] To these observations, we may add the following philosophical proofs.

I

[811] People tend naturally to preserve the memory of the laws and social orders that keep them within society, as Axiom 45 states.

2

[812] Ludovico Castelvetro understood this truth: that history was born first, and poetry later. For history is a direct expression of the truth, while poetry is an imitation of the truth. Yet despite his insight, Castelvetro failed to use this truth to discover the true principles of poetry by adding to it the following philosophical proof.

3

[813] Since poets clearly preceded vernacular historians, the first history must have been poetic.

4

[814] Myths were born as true and severe narratives, which is why the Greek word *mythos* has been defined as a true narrative. Since most of them at first seemed indecorous, they soon lost their proper meanings, and were then altered; later they became improbable, afterwards obscure, then scandalous, and finally incredible. These are the seven sources of the difficulty of myths, as described in Book 2.

5

[815] As we have seen, Homer inherited myths in this debased and corrupt form.

6

[816] Poetic archetypes, which are the essence of myths, were created by primitive people because their nature was incapable of abstracting forms and properties. As a result, they represent the *manner of thinking of entire peoples* as expressed within the natural limits of their barbarism. It is an invariable property of such poetic myths that they magnify the ideas of particular things. In a golden passage in his *Rhetoric*, Aristotle observes that people with limited ideas generalize particulars into maxims. The reason for this must be that, when the human mind, with its infinite powers, is constricted by the vigour of the senses, it can only express its nearly divine nature by enlarging particulars in the imagination. This may explain why the gods and heroes are imagined as superhumanly large in both Greek and Latin poetry. And in the medieval return of barbarism, the paintings of God the Father, Jesus Christ, and the Virgin Mary portray them as extraordinarily large.

7

[817] When they are misused, our human powers of reflection can give birth to falsehood. But barbarous people have no such powers, which is why the first heroic poets in Latin sang true histories, namely, the wars of the Romans. In the medieval return of barbarism, with the same barbarous nature, Latin poets like Gunther, William of Apulia, and others sang only of historical events; and the medieval authors of romances believed that they were writing true histories. Even Boiardo and Ariosto, who lived in an age enlightened by philosophy, still took the subjects of their epics from the history written by Bishop Turpin of Paris. Dante possessed this same barbarous nature which, being incapable of reflection, cannot feign, and is therefore naturally truthful, open, faithful, generous, and magnanimous. For all his erudition and

esoteric knowledge, Dante in his *Comedy* portrayed real persons and represented real events in the lives of the dead. And he titled his poem the *Comedy* because the Old Comedy of the Greeks portrayed real persons on the stage. In this respect, Dante resembled the Homer of the *Iliad*, which Longinus describes as entirely dramatic, or representational, just as the *Odyssey* is all narrative. Even Francis Petrarch, for all his learning, undertook a Latin poem about the second Punic War, and wrote his Italian *Triumphs* in a heroic style as a collection of histories. Here we find a striking proof of the fact that the first myths were histories. Satire poked fun at persons who were not only real but also well known. Tragedy based its plots on characters in poetic history. Old Comedy made plays about famous living persons. Finally, New Comedy, which sprang from philosophical reflection, invented completely original characters. (In the same way, in Italian literature the New Comedy arose during the early Cinquecento, which was a century of marvellous learning.) Neither the Greeks nor the Romans ever invented a completely original character as the protagonist of a tragedy. This is strikingly confirmed by our popular taste. For our public today only tolerates historical subjects in musical dramas, in which the plots are always tragic. But since the plots of comedies are private and hence unfamiliar, the public accepts their invented plots as if they were true.

8

[818] Since poetic archetypes were historical in nature, their poetic allegories must contain historical references to the earliest ages of Greece.

9

[819] Early peoples must have preserved their histories in their collective memory, as Axiom 45 states. They were the children of the first nations, and thus had marvellously strong memories. Divine providence must have played a part in this, for vernacular script was not invented until after Homer's day, as Josephus maintained against Apion. Primitive people lived an entirely physical existence, and had practically no

capacity for mental reflection in meeting their human needs. But their vivid sensations helped them perceive particulars; their powerful imagination grasped and enlarged them; their keen wits assigned them to general categories of the imagination; and their vigorous memories retained them.

While such faculties belong to the mind, they are rooted in the body and derive their power from it. This is why memory is the same as imagination, and in Latin both are called *memoria*. (For example, in Terence we find *memorabile* meaning imaginable. In everyday Latin, *comminisci* means feigning or inventing, which is proper to the imagination; and *commentum* means a fiction or invention.) Imagination, *fantasía*, also connotes ingenuity. During the medieval return of barbarism, an ingenious man was in Italian called fantastical: this is how Cola di Rienzo was described by his contemporary biographer. Thus, memory has three distinct aspects: memory when it recalls things; imagination when it alters or recreates them; and ingenuity or invention when it orders them in a suitable arrangement or context. For these reasons, the theological poets called Memory the mother of the Muses.

10

[820] Poets were thus the first historians of their nations. Unfortunately, Castelvetro failed to use his insight about history to find the true origins of poetry. Indeed, like all the others who have discussed the topic since Plato and Aristotle, he could easily have observed that all pagan histories have their origins in myth, as Axiom 46 states and as my Poetic Wisdom shows.

11

[821] By the very nature of poetry, it is impossible for anyone to be both a sublime poet and a sublime metaphysician. For metaphysics draws the mind away from the senses, while the poetic faculty sinks the whole mind into them. Metaphysics rises above universals, while the poetic faculty plunges deep into particulars.

12

[822] Axiom 51 states: 'In every endeavour but poetry, people with no natural gift can still succeed by their industry; but in poetry, no one who lacks the natural gift can possibly succeed in this way.' This is why the arts of poetry and criticism may refine a talent, but not make it great. For delicacy is a minute virtue, but greatness naturally disdains all small things. Just as a great rushing torrent carries muddy water and sweeps rocks and trunks along in its violent course, so we often find base elements swept along in the flow of Homer's poetry.

13

[823] Yet despite these elements, Homer remains the supreme father of all sublime poets.

14

[824] Aristotle judged Homer's falsehoods incomparable, and Horace judged his characters inimitable, which is the same thing.

15

[825] Homer is celestially sublime in his poetic statements. Such statements spring from real passions and are deeply felt by an excited imagination, so that they are particular to those who feel them, as we saw in Book 2. By contrast, we defined maxims about life, which are more general, as philosophical statements; and reflections about our emotions are the work of false and frigid poets.

16

[826] Homer's poetic similes taken from wild and savage things are clearly incomparable.

17

[827] The gruesome atrocity of Homeric battles and deaths is the source of all the astonishing power of the *Iliad*.

18

[828] No placid, refined, or meek philosopher could have naturally produced Homer's statements, similes, and descriptions.

19

[829] In their behaviour, Homer's heroes exhibit the capriciousness of children, the vigorous imagination of women, and the seething passion of violent youths. It is clearly impossible that a philosopher could have invented them so naturally and felicitously.

20

[830] Homer's clumsy and indecorous passages reflect the awkwardness under which the Greeks laboured to express themselves while their language was still taking shape and was extremely poor.

21

[831] The Homeric epics clearly contain no sublime mysteries of esoteric wisdom, as my Poetic Wisdom has shown. Even if they did, their tone could not have been conceived by the direct, orderly, and serious thought required in a philosopher.

22

[832] Heroic speech used resemblances, images, and similes, because it lacked the categories of genus and species which are required in proper definitions. Hence, it sprang from a necessity of nature which is common to all peoples.

23

[833] By a necessity of nature, the first nations spoke in heroic verse. Here too we must admire divine providence. In an age when popular letters had not yet been invented for writing, the nations expressed themselves in verses; and their metre and rhythm, by aiding the memory, helped preserve the histories of their families and cities.

24

[834] Such myths, statements, behaviour, speech, and verse were all called heroic, and were used in the age to which history has assigned the heroes, as we saw under Poetic Wisdom.

25

[835] All these properties were common to entire heroic peoples, and therefore were common to all the individuals of those peoples.

26

[836] Since Homer's supreme greatness as a poet was the product of his heroic nature, we must deny that he was a philosopher.

27

[837] All the notions of esoteric wisdom imposed on the Homeric myths were the inventions of later philosophers, as we saw under Poetic Wisdom.

28

[838] Just as esoteric wisdom is denied to all but a very few, so the essence of heroic myths – the decorum of poetic archetypes – is beyond the grasp of our most outstanding philosophers, poets, and critics. It is for this poetic decorum that Aristotle calls Homer's similes incomparable, and that Horace calls his characters inimitable, which is the same thing.

CHAPTER 6

Philological Proofs for the Discovery of the True Homer

[839] By applying our metaphysical criticism to the founders of the pagan nations – including Homer, whom Josephus regards as the earliest secular author – we have formulated the preceding philosophical proofs, to which we may now add the following philological or historical proofs.

I

[840] All ancient secular histories have their origin in myth.

2

[841] Barbarous peoples who live isolated from other nations, such as the Germans and the American Indians, preserve the origins of their history in verse.

3

[842] The earliest Roman history was written by poets.

4

[843] The history of the medieval return of barbarism was written by Latin poets.

5

[844] The Egyptian high priest Manetho transformed the ancient history of Egypt, which he found written in hieroglyphics, into a sublime natural theology.

6

[845] In the same way, Greek philosophers transformed the ancient history of Greece which they found related in their myths, as we saw under Poetic Wisdom.

7

[846] This is why my Poetic Wisdom had to retrace the steps taken by Manetho, discarding his mystical meanings and restoring the original historical meanings to the early myths. The natural ease with which we did this, which involved no violence, duplicity, or distortion, confirms the aptness of the historical allegories these myths contained.

8

[847] All these observations clearly confirm the golden passage in which Strabo asserts that before Herodotus, and indeed before Hecataeus of Miletus, all the history of the Greek peoples was written by poets.

9

[848] In Book 2, we saw that the first writers of both the ancient and modern nations were poets.

10

[849] There are two golden passages in the *Odyssey* in which someone is praised for telling a story well, and is said to have told it like a musician or singer. Just such were the Homeric rhapsodes, who were simple commoners who memorized various books of the Homeric epics and thus preserved them.

11

[850] Homer did not write down his epics, a fact which Josephus stoutly maintains against the Greek grammarian Apion.

12

[851] The rhapsodes travelled throughout the cities of Greece, singing the various books of Homer's epics at fairs and festivals.

13

[852] Etymologically, the noun rhapsode means a stitcher of songs, and the rhapsodes clearly must have collected the songs of their own people. Similarly, some derive the Greek noun *homēros*, guarantor, from *homou*, together, and *eirein*, to connect, because a guarantor binds a creditor and debtor together. This etymology is far-fetched and forced when applied to a guarantor, as it is proper and plausible when applied to Homer, the binder or 'composer' of myths.

14

[853] The division and arrangement of Homer's books into the *Iliad* and *Odyssey* was made or commissioned by Pisistratus and his sons, the tyrants of Athens. Before this, Homer's poems were evidently a confused aggregation of material, for we see that his two epics differ immeasurably in style.

15

[854] Pisistratus and his sons decreed that rhapsodes should sing these epics in all future Panathenaic festivals, as we learn from Cicero's *Nature of the Gods*, and from Aelian's *Miscellany*, in a passage noted with approval by his editor Johannes Scheffer.

16

[855] Yet Pisistratus and his sons were driven out of Athens only a few years after the Tarquins were driven from Rome. So, if we consider Homer a contemporary of Numa Pompilius, his epics must have been transmitted orally by the rhapsodes for several centuries. This tradition completely discredits a different tradition which said that Aristarchus emended, divided, and arranged the books of Homer's epics in Pisistratus' day. For such a revision would have been impossible without vernacular writing; and if writing existed, why were rhapsodes needed to sing parts of Homer from memory?

17

[856] By contrast, Hesiod left his works in writing; and we have no authority for believing that his works were preserved like Homer's by the memory of the rhapsodes' singing. So, despite the vain effort of chronologers to place him thirty years before Homer, we must place Hesiod after the sons of Pisistratus. Similar to the Homeric rhapsodes, in turn, were the so-called cyclic poets who preserved all of Greek mythical history from the origin of the gods to Ulysses' return to Ithaca. Taking their name from Greek *kyklos*, circle, the cyclic poets must have been uneducated folk who sang myths to commoners gathered in a circle on holidays. In his *Art of Poetry*, Horace mentions precisely such a circle in the phrase *vilem patulumque orbem*, a base and ample circle. Some commentators believe that Horace is referring to long episodes, but André Dacier disagrees with them, apparently because a long episode in a poem is not necessarily base. We may cite two examples from Tasso's *Jerusalem Delivered*: the episode of the dalliance of Rinaldo and Armida in the enchanted garden, and the speech of the old shepherd to Erminia. Both are quite long; but rather than base, they are noble – the former refined and delicate, and the latter ornate.

To return to the *Art of Poetry*: after Horace advises tragic poets to take their plots from Homer's epics, he foresees the objection that poets who adopt myths of Homer's invention cannot be true poets. But Horace counters that poets can make Homer's epic myths into their own tragic plots by observing three rules. (1) They must not add superfluous paraphrases to their model. Even today we find people who read *Orlando Furioso*, *Orlando Innamorato*, or some other rhymed romance to the 'base and ample circles' of idle folk on holidays; and after reading each stanza, they explain it at length in prose. (2) They must not be literal translators. (3) Most important, they must not be slavish imitators. While preserving the characters of Homer's heroes, they must develop them to produce new emotions, speeches, and actions. For it is by treating the Homeric subjects in this way that they become poets different from Homer.

By the same token, Horace also uses the term 'cyclical poet' in the *Art of Poetry* to mean a street-corner or carnival poet. In Greek, authors of this kind are ordinarily called *kyklioi* and *enkyklioi*, cyclic. Their collective works were called cyclic epics, *kyklos epikos*, *kylika epē*, *poiēma enkyklikon*, and sometimes merely *kyklos*, cycle, with no modifier, as Gerard Langbaine notes in his preface to Longinus. Hence, in this sense Hesiod may have preceded Homer, because his poems contain all the myths of the gods.

18

[857] These arguments concerning Hesiod lead us to similar conclusions about Hippocrates. He left many great works which are written not in verse but in prose, and which therefore could not naturally be transmitted orally. Hence, we may consider him a contemporary of Herodotus.

19

[858] With too much good faith, Gerard Voss thought he had proved Josephus wrong by citing three heroic inscriptions which Herodotus attributes to Amphitryo, Hippocoön, and Laodamas. But in fact these were ancient forgeries, not unlike those produced by counterfeiters today. And Martin Schoock rightly takes Josephus' side against Voss.

20

[859] We should add that Homer never refers to vernacular Greek letters. Rather, when he describes the famous letter which Proetus wrote to Eureia as a trap for Bellerophon, he says it was written in signs, *sēmata*.

21

[860] Despite the emendations of Aristarchus, Homer's epics retain such a great variety of dialectal forms, so many irregularities of expression, and such metrical liberties that they must reflect the local idioms of various peoples of Greece.

22

[861] Homer's native land is unknown.

23

[862] Nearly all the peoples of Greece claimed Homer as one of their own.

24

[863] We have seen strong arguments that the Homer of the *Odyssey* was from southwestern Greece, and the Homer of the *Iliad* from northeastern Greece.

25

[864] Even Homer's age is unknown.

26

[865] Among the many opinions about Homer's age, the most extreme differ by some 460 years, placing him as early as the Trojan War, and as late as Numa Pompilius.

27

[866] Longinus was unable to gloss over the great stylistic difference between the Homeric epics, and therefore wrote that Homer composed the *Iliad* in his youth, but the *Odyssey* in his old age. This is truly a nice distinction to make about this greatest luminary of Greece, when we are in the dark about the two essential facts of his history, namely, when and where he lived!

28

[867] This observation should undermine all our faith in Herodotus or whoever else was the author of the *Life of Homer*, which contains so many charming details that it fills an entire volume. And the same is true of the life written by Plutarch, even though as a philosopher he wrote with greater seriousness.

29

[868] Of course, it is possible that Longinus based his conjecture on the fact that in the *Iliad* Homer depicts Achilles' pride and anger, which are the qualities of a young man, whereas in the *Odyssey* he recounts Ulysses' deceptions and precautions, which are characteristic of an old man.

30

[869] According to tradition, Homer was blind, and this blindness gave him the name *Homēros*, which in the Ionic dialect means unseeing.

31

[870] In the *Odyssey*, Homer himself describes two blind poets who sing at the banquets of the great: Demodocus at Alcinous' banquet for Ulysses, and Phemius at the suitors' banquet.

32

[871] By a property of human nature, blind people have astonishingly powerful memories.

33

[872] To conclude, tradition says that Homer was poor and wandered the marketplaces of Greece singing his own epics.

SECTION 2
DISCOVERY OF THE TRUE
HOMER

INTRODUCTION

[873] When some of my friends, men remarkable for their acumen and
scholarly learning, read my *New Science* in its less methodical first edition,
they began to suspect that the traditional Homer had never existed, a
thesis I had not yet conceived or formulated. In this light, the traditional
accounts of Homer and his epics, combined with my own analysis of
them, compel me to assert that the same thing happened to Homer as
to the Trojan War. That is, it defines an important historical era, but
the most perceptive critics agree that it never really took place. And
like the Trojan War, if Homer had not left behind great and certain
vestiges in the form of his epics, so many difficulties would lead us to
conclude that Homer was a purely ideal poet who in fact never existed
as an individual. Faced with these difficulties on the one hand, and the
extant poems on the other hand, we seem compelled to posit a sort of
halfway existence and to say that Homer was an idea or *heroic archetype
of the Greeks who recounted their history in song.*

CHAPTER I

Inconsistencies and Improbabilities in the Traditional Homer Become Consistent and Necessary in the Homer Discovered Here

[874] In light of this discovery, all the inconsistencies and improbabilities of the traditional Homer become consistent and necessary facts about the true Homer revealed here. As a first step, the great unresolved questions about Homer compel us to note the following points:

1

[875] The peoples of Greece so vigorously contested Homer's native land, and nearly all of them claimed him as their own, because these Greek peoples were themselves Homer.

2

[876] Opinions about his age vary so greatly because the true Homer lived in the oral memory of the Greeks from the Trojan War down to the age of Numa Pompilius, a span of 460 years.

3

[877] Homer's blindness

4

[878] and his poverty were characteristic of the rhapsodes. For as blind men, each called *homēros*, unseeing, they possessed extraordinary memories. And as poor men, they sustained themselves by wandering through the cities of Greece, singing the Homeric epics. In fact, the rhapsodes were themselves the authors of these epics, since they were part of the peoples who recorded their history in these epics.

5

[879] In this sense, Homer composed the *Iliad* in his youth, when Greece was young and therefore burning with sublime passions, like pride, anger, and thirst for revenge. Such passions brook no dissembling, but love magnanimity; and this youthful Greece admired Achilles, the hero of violence. In turn, Homer wrote the *Odyssey* in old age, when the spirits of Greece had been somewhat cooled by reflection, which is the mother of prudence. This older Greece admired Ulysses, the hero of wisdom. In the time of Homer's youth, the peoples of Greece took pleasure in coarseness, boorishness, ferocity, savagery, and atrocity. In the time of his old age, they delighted in the luxuries of Alcinous, the sensuality of Calypso, the pleasures of Circe, the songs of the Sirens, the recreations of the suitors, and their attempts (or rather, their siege and assaults) on Penelope's chastity. Earlier, when we considered such customs as contemporaneous, we judged them incompatible. This difficulty so troubled the divine Plato that he attempted to resolve it by saying that only Homer's inspiration allowed him to foresee the sickening, morbid, and dissolute morality of the *Odyssey*. But in so doing, Plato made Homer a dull-witted founder of Greek civilization who, despite all his censures, taught the corrupt and decadent behaviour that was destined to befall the Greeks long after their nations had been founded. Thus, Homer accelerated the natural course of human institutions, so that the Greeks hastened towards their own corruption.

6

[880] In this manner, we may show that the Homer of the *Iliad* is considerably older than the Homer of the *Odyssey*.

7

[881] We may further show that the Homer of the *Iliad* was from northeastern Greece, since he sang the Trojan War as fought in his country. And the Homer of the *Odyssey* was from southwestern Greece, since he sang of Ulysses, whose kingdom was in that region.

8

[882] Since the true Homer is lost in the multitude of the Greek peoples, we may acquit him of all the charges which critics have brought against him, particularly the following:

9

[883] base and uninspired statements,

10

[884] boorish manners,

11

[885] crude similes,

12

[886] local idioms,

13

[887] metrical liberties,

14

[888] dialectal inconsistencies,

15

[889] and his portrayal of men as gods, and gods as men.

[890] In defending Homer's myths, Longinus has recourse to the props of philosophical allegory. In effect, he argues that, as they sounded when first sung to the Greeks, these myths cannot justify Homer's glory

as the founder of Greek civilization. Thus, Homer incurs the same objection as that raised against Orpheus as a founder of Greek civilization. Now, the Greeks of Homer's day had all the characteristics listed above, and particularly their fusion of things human and divine. As my natural theogony shows, the earliest Greeks made their gods precisely as pious, religious, chaste, courageous, just, and magnanimous as they were themselves. (Just so, people naturally bend doubtful or obscure laws to suit their passions or their advantage, as Axiom 54 states.) Later, after the passage of time had made their myths obscure and their own morality corrupt, they believed that the gods were as dissolute as themselves, as we saw under Poetic Wisdom. For the Greeks feared that the gods would prove contrary to their prayers if divine morals were contrary to their own.

16

[891] In all fairness, we must grant Homer two great distinctions which are in fact a single one: his unique ability to create what Aristotle calls his poetic falsehoods and what Horace calls his heroic characters. Horace even declares himself to be no poet because he is ignorant or incapable of observing what he calls artistic conventions, *colores operum*. This expression is synonymous with Aristotle's poetic untruths. In Plautus we find the parallel expression *obtinere colorem*, to put on a good appearance, in the sense of telling a lie that appears truthful in every respect – which is what a good fiction must be.

[892] Besides these things, Homer possesses all the special qualities which the masters of the poetic art have bestowed on him. They declare him incomparable

17

[893] for his wild and savage similes,

18

[894] for his bloody and gruesome descriptions of combat and carnage,

19

[895] for his statements filled with sublime emotions,

20

[896] and for his vivid and luminous style. All these were qualities of the heroic age of the Greeks. Thus, Homer lived in a time which made him an incomparable poet, precisely because in that age of vigorous memory, robust imagination, and sublime invention, he could in no way have been a philosopher.

21

[897] As a result, none of the philosophies, the arts of poetry, or the arts of criticism that arose later could create a poet who could even approach Homer.

[898] What is more, Homer lays certain claim to the three immortal eulogies which have been bestowed on him:

22

[899] First, he was the founder of Greek polity or civilization.

23

[900] Second, he was the father of all other poets.

24

[901] Third, he was the source of all Greek philosophies. Yet none of these eulogies could have been bestowed on the traditional Homer. Not the first: for if we reckon from the time of Deucalion and Pyrrha, Homer appears 1,800 years after Greek civilization was established by the institution of marriage, as we saw under Poetic Wisdom. Not the second: for it was certainly before Homer's day that the theological

poets flourished, including Orpheus, Amphion, Linus, Musaeus, and others, among whom chronologers place Hesiod, dating him some thirty years before Homer. (In his *Brutus*, Cicero asserts that there were other heroic poets before Homer. And in his *Preparation for the Gospel*, Eusebius specifically names Philammon, Thamyris, Demodocus, Epimenides, Aristaeus, and others.) And not the third: for my Poetic Wisdom showed in great detail that the philosophers did not discover their philosophy in Homer's myths, but rather imposed them on his epics. Still, Homer's poetic wisdom offered occasions for philosophers to ponder their profound truths, and at the same time gave them a means of expounding them, as we saw in Book 2.

CHAPTER 2

Homer's Epics: Two Great Repositories of the Natural Law of the Greeks

[902] Above all, our discovery of the true Homer allows us to crown him with another resplendent glory:

25

[903] Homer is the first historian of pagan antiquity whose works survive.

26

[904] In the future, then, we should highly esteem the Homeric epics as two great repositories of the customs of early Greece. Unfortunately, Homer's epics met with the same fate as the Laws of the Twelve Tables. For as long as people thought that the Twelve Tables were first given by Solon to the Athenians, and later brought to the Romans, the history of the natural law of the heroic nations of Latium remained hidden. By the same token, as long as people thought that the Homeric epics were composed at once by a single individual, the history of the natural law of the Greek nations remained hidden.

APPENDIX

A Rational History of the Dramatic and Lyric Poets

[905] We have seen that there were three ages of poets up to Homer's day: (1) the age of the theological poets, heroes who sang true and severe myths; (2) the age of the heroic poets, who altered and corrupted these myths; and (3) the age of Homer, who received them in this altered and corrupted form. Our metaphysical criticism of the history of darkest antiquity, which helped explain the ideas that were naturally formed by the earliest nations, will now elucidate and define the history of the lyric and dramatic poets, which was previously treated by philologists in an obscure and confused manner.

[906] Among the lyric poets, these scholars include Arion of Methymna, a very ancient poet of the heroic age, who invented the dithyramb, which led to choral poetry. Arion introduced satyrs singing in verse, and the dithyramb was a chorus of dancers who, like satyrs, sang the praises of Bacchus. These scholars say that celebrated tragic poets flourished at the same time as the lyric poets; and Diogenes Laertius asserts that in tragedy the chorus was at first the only actor. They also say that the first tragic poet was Aeschylus, who was commanded by Bacchus to write tragedies, as Pausanias tells us. (By contrast, Horace says that Thespis was the inventor of tragedy. In his *Art of Poetry*, Horace traces the origins of tragedy to satire, and says that Thespis introduced satyr plays which were acted on carts during the wine harvest.) Later came Sophocles, whom Palaemon [Polemon] called the Homer of tragic poets.* Finally, tragedy reached its zenith with Euripides, whom Aristotle called the most tragic poet, *tragikōtatos*. Contemporary with Euripides was Aristophanes, the inventor of Old Comedy, whose comedy *The Clouds* led to Socrates' death and opened the way towards New Comedy, which was developed by Menander.

Now, some scholars date Hippocrates to the age of the tragic poets,

---

* For the Greek philosopher Polemon, Vico has substituted the Roman grammarian Palaemon.

while others date him to that of the lyric poets. But Sophocles and Euripides lived some years before the Law of the Twelve Tables, and the lyric poets lived after it. So any chronology dating Hippocrates to the age of the Seven Sages of Greece must appear seriously flawed.

[907] To resolve this difficulty, we must assert that there were two kinds of lyric poets and two kinds of tragic poets.

[908] The ancient lyric poets were at first the authors of hymns praising the gods, like the so-called Homeric hymns written in heroic hexameters. Later, like Homer's Achilles, they used lyric to praise deceased heroes.

In the same way, the first poets in Latin were the authors of the Saliar verses, which were hymns sung on divine festivals by the priests called Salii. (They may have been so called from the Latin verb *salire*, to leap, just as the first Greek choruses began with dancers leaping in a circle.) Fragments of these verses are the oldest surviving specimens of the Latin language, and they sound like heroic verse. All of this confirms the origins of pagan civilization, since during its earliest religious stage such lyric hymns can only have praised the gods. (During the medieval return of barbarism, this religious custom recurred. In that age, priests, who alone were literate, wrote only sacred poems and hymns.) In the later heroic ages, the lyric poets admired and celebrated only the courageous deeds of the heroes, like those sung by Achilles. Arion of Methymna was this kind of sacred lyric poet. He was also the originator of the dithyramb, the first rough form of tragedy, which was written in heroic hexameters, the earliest kind of verse in Greek poetry, as noted above. Arion's dithyramb was thus the earliest satire or satyr play, with which Horace begins his outline of tragedy.

[909] The later lyric poets were the so-called melic poets, whose greatest proponent was Pindar. These poets wrote in verse what we Italians call airs set to music, *arie per musica*. Their metres developed after iambics, which were the popular metre which the Greeks used after heroic hexameters. Pindar lived in an age when all the pomp of the Greeks was displayed at their Olympic games, which thus furnished the subjects of lyric poetry. By the same token, Horace lived in the age of Augustus, the most sumptuous age of Rome. In Italian, melic poetry flourished in the Baroque era, which was a highly refined and delicate age.

[910] Tragic and lyric poetry developed in the following stages. In different parts of Greece, Thespis and Arion invented the satyr play, which was the primitive form of tragedy with satyrs for its characters. In such a crude and simple age, people invented the first costumes and masks in the following way. Around their feet, legs, and thighs, they wrapped goatskins, which must have been readily available. They dyed their chests and faces with wine lees, and fitted horns on their foreheads. This may explain why today Italian grape harvesters are still called *cornuti*, horned men. It is perhaps in this sense that Bacchus, the god of the wine harvest, is said to have commanded Aeschylus to compose tragedies. This symbol is appropriate to an age when heroes regarded plebeians as monsters with a dual nature, half human and half goat.

We are thus justified in conjecturing that the word tragedy derives from the goatlike costume and mask of such rites, rather than from the supposed award of a goat, *tragos*, to the victor of a poetry contest – a prize which Horace dismisses as ignoble without further comment. Since tragedy began with this early chorus of satyrs, from its origin later satire retained as an invariable property the use of invective and insult. Wearing crude masks and riding in their harvest carts, ancient peasants were at liberty to hurl abuse at their masters, like wine harvesters today in our own fertile Campania, which in fact was once called the dwelling of Bacchus. From this we see how truthfully scholars later interpreted the myth of Pan. Since *pan* in Greek means 'all', they saddled him with their philosophical mythology, saying that he signifies the universe: his shaggy lower half means the earth, his ruddy chest and face denote the element of fire, and his horns represent the moon. By contrast, the Romans preserved the historical mythology of Pan in their word *satyra*. According to Festus, a *satyra* was a dish made of various ingredients, from which derived the later expression *lex per satyram* for a law containing miscellaneous provisions. To return to the topic of dramatic satire, not a single one survives in Greek or Latin; but Horace relates that in such satire there appeared various kinds of characters, such as gods, heroes, kings, craftsmen, and slaves. But the verse satire which survived among the Romans does not discuss various subjects; instead, each single satire deals with a particular subject.

[911] Later, Aeschylus transformed Old Tragedy, meaning the satyr

play, into Middle Tragedy by introducing human masks. In other words, he converted Arion's dithyramb, or satyr chorus, into a human chorus. Middle Tragedy was thus the origin of Old Comedy, whose plots were based on famous people, and the appearance of a chorus was appropriate in this public context. Later came Sophocles, and then Euripides, who left us tragedy in its final form. Old Comedy ended with Aristophanes after the scandal over his portrayal of Socrates. And Menander left us New Comedy which was based on private and invented characters. (As we have seen, these characters were private persons, who could be invented and made believable.) As a result, there was no longer any need for a chorus: for a chorus represents the public, which can only speak about what is public knowledge.

[912] Since the earliest peoples spoke in heroic metre, satire came to be composed in heroic hexameters, as it survives in Latin. Later, when they spoke in iambic verse, tragedy was naturally composed in iambics. When people already spoke in prose, they still wrote comedy in iambic verse, vainly imitating the model of tragedy. Iambic verse was clearly suited to tragedy, since its metre was created to vent anger and its rhythm is what Horace calls the 'swift foot', as Axiom 62 states. According to popular tradition, Archilochus invented iambs to vent his anger against Lycambes, who had refused to give him his daughter in marriage; and the harshness of his verses drove both the father and daughter to hang themselves in desperation. This must symbolize the history of the heroic contention for marriage rights, in which rebellious plebeians hanged noblemen and their daughters.

[913] Hence was born that poetic monstrosity, that the same violent, rapid, and excited verse is suited both to the lofty poetry of tragedy, considered by Plato as loftier than epic, and to the delicate poetry of comedy. And the same metre, which (as noted) appropriately vents the wrath and rage that horrendously erupt in tragedy, is equally good at conveying the jests, games, and tender loves that lend comedy all its grace and charm.

[914] Because the terms lyric and tragic were so poorly defined, Hippocrates was placed in the age of the Seven Sages. But in fact he was a contemporary of Herodotus, for he lived in an age when people still spoke for the most part using myths. Thus, his biography has a mythical tinge, and the stories Herodotus relates are in large part myths.

Yet this same age witnessed the introduction of prose speech, and vernacular writing as well. Both are used by Herodotus in his histories and by Hippocrates in his numerous medical treatises.

BOOK 4
THE COURSE OF NATIONS

INTRODUCTION

[915] In Book 1, we established the first principles of my New Science. In Book 2, we sought and discovered the origins of all the human and divine institutions of pagan antiquity, under the heading Poetic Wisdom. And in Book 3, we revealed Homer's epics as two great storehouses of the natural law of nations in Greece, corresponding to the Law of the Twelve Tables, the greatest imposing monument of the law of nations in Latium. Now, in the light shed by philosophy and philology, and by Axioms 66–96 on ideal eternal history, we shall in Book 4 discuss the *course that nations run*. For in all their various and diverse customs, nations proceed with constant uniformity through the three distinct ages which the Egyptians noted in their earliest history: the ages of *gods, heroes, and men*. Corresponding to these three ages are a number of threefold stages through which nations must pass. Since every nation is governed by the same constant and unbroken process of causes and effects, it must pass through (1) three kinds of *natures*. From these natures spring (2) three kinds of *customs*; and springing from these customs we observe (3) three kinds of *natural laws of nations*. As a result of these laws, men establish (4) three kinds of *governments* or *commonwealths*. In a civilized society, men seek to communicate these three kinds of essential institutions – customs, laws, and states – by employing (5) three kinds of *languages* and (6) three kinds of *symbols* or *characters*. And they seek to justify these same institutions by applying (7) three kinds of *jurisprudence*, each accompanied by (8) three kinds of *authorities* and (9) three kinds of *reasons* in (10) three kinds of *judgments*. Finally, the three kinds of jurisprudence are practised according to (11) three *schools*

of thought, which people profess throughout the course of their life as nations.

These particular groups of three in turn engender many others which I shall discuss in this book. Together all of them lead to a general unity: the religion of a *provident deity*, which is the unity of the spirit that gives form and life to the world of nations. In the previous books, I discussed these topics separately, but here I shall show how they develop together.

SECTION I
THREE KINDS OF
HUMAN NATURE

[916] The first human nature was a poetic or creative nature produced by the powerful illusions of the imagination, which is most vigorous in people whose powers of reasoning are weakest. Indeed, we might call it a divine nature, since it endowed physical objects with the animate substance of real gods, each of which represented an idea. This was the nature of the theological poets, who were the earliest sages of the pagan nations founded on their belief in certain gods. This nature was utterly cruel and dreadful, for the errors of the human imagination inspired in people a terrible fear of the very gods they had created. This established two invariable properties. First, religion is the only means powerful enough to restrain the savagery of entire peoples. Second, religions prosper when they are deeply revered by the religious leaders themselves.

[917] The second human nature was a heroic nature, based on the heroes' belief in their own divine origin. Since they considered the gods responsible for all things, the heroes regarded themselves as sons of Jupiter, under whose auspices they had been begotten. Although they were born human, they justly thought that their heroic status gave them a natural nobility which made them the rulers of the human race. This natural nobility caused them to boast of their superiority over the people who lived in abominable and bestial promiscuity. As we have seen, these people fled to the heroes' refuges to escape the quarrels caused by their promiscuity, and were regarded as beasts by the heroes, because they arrived without gods.

[918] The third nature was the truly human or civilized nature, which is intelligent, and hence moderate, benign, and reasonable. This nature is guided by the laws of conscience, reason, and duty.

SECTION 2
THREE KINDS OF
CUSTOMS

[919] The first customs were imbued with religion and piety, like those of Deucalion and Pyrrha just after the flood.

[920] The second were short-tempered and punctilious, like those described in Achilles.

[921] The third are dutiful, taught to us by our sense of civil duty.

SECTION 3
THREE KINDS OF
NATURAL LAW

[922] The first natural law was divine, by which people believed that their lives and affairs depended on the gods, whom they regarded as responsible for all things.

[923] The second was heroic law, or the law of force. This law was tempered by religion, for only religion can keep force within the bounds of duty, even when there are no human laws or none strong enough to restrain it. This is why providence ordained that the naturally fierce early peoples should obey religion. In this way, they naturally acceded to force; and while still lacking power to reason, they measured right by fortune, and practised divination by the auspices. This law of force is the law of Achilles, who judges everything by the point of his spear.

[924] The third is the human law which is dictated by fully developed human reason.

SECTION 4
THREE KINDS OF
GOVERNMENT

[925] The first governments were divine, or what the Greeks would call theocracies. Under them, people believed that the gods ordained all things. It was an age of oracles, which are the most ancient institutions recorded by history.

[926] The second were heroic or aristocratic governments, which is to say governments of 'optimates', meaning the most powerful. In Greek, they were also called governments of the Heraclids, meaning the descendants of Hercules, or the nobles. In remote antiquity, such governments were scattered throughout Greece; but in the historical period, only the one at Sparta survived. The Greeks also called them governments of Curetes, the priests whom the Greeks found scattered through Saturnia or ancient Italy, Crete, and Asia. The Romans called them governments of Quirites, who were the armed priests of their public assembly. In such governments, civil rights were all restricted to the ruling orders of the heroes, because their birth, regarded as divine in origin, gave them a noble nature. By contrast, the plebeians were considered of bestial origin, and thus were only allowed to enjoy life and natural liberty.

[927] The third are the human or civilized governments. Under these, the equality of our intelligent human nature makes everyone equal under the law, so that we are born free whether in a democracy or in a monarchy. In the former, the whole population or the majority constitutes the civil powers of the state, which make them sovereign over their own democracy. In the latter, all the subjects are made equal under the monarch's laws. By contrast, monarchs have a superior civil nature, because they alone possess the force of arms.

SECTION 5
THREE KINDS OF
LANGUAGE

[928] There are three kinds of language.

[929] The first was the divine and conceptual language expressed by wordless religious acts, or divine ceremonies. Roman civil law preserves these in the 'legal acts', which they used in transacting all their civil business. The suitability of this language reflects this property, that reverence is more essential to religion than is reasoning. This language was necessary in the early ages when pagan peoples were still incapable of articulate speech.

[930] The second language used heroic emblems, in which arms are expressive. This symbolic language survives in military disciplines.

[931] The third language uses articulate speech, which is employed by all of today's nations.

SECTION 6
THREE KINDS OF
SYMBOLS

[932] There are three kinds of symbols or characters.

[933] The first were the divine symbols which in Greek are appropriately called 'hieroglyphics', or sacred signs, and which all nations originally used. They consisted of certain imaginative universals conceived by the human mind, which naturally takes pleasure in uniformity, as Axiom 47 states. For since early people were unable to conceive general categories using abstract thought, they formed images by using their imagination. To these poetic universals, they reduced all the particular species belonging to each general category. Thus, under Jupiter they subsumed everything involved in the auspices, under Juno everything concerning marriage, and so on.

[934] The second were heroic symbols. These too were imaginative universals, under which heroic peoples subsumed specific varieties of heroic things. Thus, all the exploits of valiant warriors were subsumed under Achilles, and all the counsels of wise men under Ulysses. Later, as the human mind learned to abstract the forms and properties of things, these imaginative general categories became intelligible categories, from which philosophy emerged. Later, in Greece's most civilized age, the authors of the New Comedy used the philosophers' intelligible categories of human behaviour for the portraits of their comedies.

[935] Finally, men invented vernacular symbols or characters, together with their vernacular languages. In vernacular languages, words offered what we may call general categories to replace the particulars previously used by the heroic languages. (Thus, we saw that the sentence 'I get angry' replaced the heroic sentence 'The blood boils in my heart'.)

In the same way, vernacular symbols used a small number of letters to signify a large number of words. (By contrast, the 120,000 words of vernacular Chinese are still expressed by 120,000 ideograms, or hieroglyphic symbols.)

The invention of vernacular symbols or letters was clearly not the work of a merely human mind. Indeed, we have seen that Bernard von Mallinkrodt and Ingewald Eling regard it as a divine invention. Various nations were moved by their common feeling of wonder to attribute the invention of their alphabet to prominent divines: witness St Jerome among the Illyrians, St Cyril among the Slavs, and others. (These are noted by Angelo Rocca in his *Curiosities of the Vatican Library*, a volume containing illustrations of the inventors of the so-called vernacular letters and their alphabets.)★ Yet this popular opinion proves manifestly false when we pose the following question: Why didn't these divine men simply teach their own alphabets? I already noted this objection in my discussion of Cadmus. For it is said that Cadmus brought letters from Phoenicia to the Greeks, but afterwards the Greeks used letters quite different from those of the Phoenician alphabet.

[936] Such languages and letters were under the sovereignty of the common masses of their peoples, which is why they are called vernacular or popular. This sovereignty over their languages and letters makes free peoples equally sovereign over their laws. For the people give the laws interpretations which the powerful are compelled to observe even against their will, as Axiom 92 states. It is naturally impossible for monarchs to deprive the people of this sovereignty. Yet by virtue of this negative nature of human civil institutions, this sovereignty which is inseparable from the people contributes largely to the power of monarchs. For monarchs may issue royal laws which are binding even on the powerful, according to the interpretation given them by the people. According to the order of civil nature, this sovereignty over vernacular letters and languages determined that free democracies preceded monarchies.

★ The frescos of the Salone Sistino in the Vatican portray various alphabets and their inventors; Rocca's 1591 guide to the Vatican reproduces only the alphabets.

SECTION 7
THREE KINDS OF
JURISPRUDENCE

[937] There are three kinds of jurisprudence or legal wisdom.

[938] The first kind was the 'divine' wisdom which was called mystical theology, which means the science of divine speech or the understanding of the divine mysteries of divination. This science of auspicial divinity was the popular wisdom whose sages were the theological poets, the first sages of the pagan world. From their mystical theology, they were called *mystai*, initiates, a word which Horace knowingly translates as interpreters of the gods. Part of this first jurisprudence was the first act of 'interpretation', which properly speaking derived from *inter-patrari*, to enter into the 'fathers', as the gods were at first called. (In Italian, Dante calls this *indiarsi*, to enter into the mind of God.) By this jurisprudence, justice depended entirely on the solemn rites of divine ceremonies. This explains why the Romans later observed their legal acts so superstitiously, and why in Roman law solemn nuptials and testaments were called 'just'.

[939] The second kind was heroic jurisprudence, or taking precautions by the use of certain proper words. This is the wisdom of Homer's Ulysses, who always speaks so cleverly that he gets what he wants without breaking his word. Hence, the entire reputation of ancient Roman jurists rested on the counsels and precautions implied by the Latin verb *cavere*. The legal counsel given by jurists was called *de iure respondere*, which meant that they instructed their clients how to present the relevant facts which the judge, or praetor, had to admit. The reputation of medieval jurists depended on their ability to safeguard contracts and wills, and on their knowing how to formulate legal pleas

and arguments. These are precisely the same skills which Roman jurists called *cavere* and *de iure respondere*.

[940] The third is human jurisprudence, which examines the truth of the bare facts and which generously bends the strict principles of laws as equity dictates. This kind of jurisprudence is practised by humane governments, namely democracies, and especially monarchies.

[941] Thus, in primitive nations, divine and heroic jurisprudence are based on certainty. By contrast, in enlightened nations human jurisprudence is based on truth. (These terms are defined in Axioms 9–10 and 111–13.)

SECTION 8
THREE KINDS OF
AUTHORITY

[942] There are three kinds of authority. The first is divine authority, by which providence cannot be called to account. The second kind is heroic, and is entirely based on the solemn formulas of the law. The third is human authority, which is based on the trust placed in experienced persons, who are noted for their remarkable prudence in practical matters and for their sublime wisdom in intellectual matters.

[943] Corresponding to the three kinds of authority cited by jurisprudence as nations develop, there are three kinds of senatorial or legislative authority, which follow the same development.

[944] Let us review the three kinds of senatorial authority. (1) The first was the authority of ownership. By virtue of this authority, persons granting title to property were called *auctores*. Indeed, the Law of the Twelve Tables always calls ownership *auctoritas*. This authority had its roots in the divine governments of the age of the family state, when divine authority must have belonged to the gods. For in that age people rightly believed that everything belonged to the gods. Later, in heroic aristocracies – as in today's aristocracies – senates were the seat of sovereignty; and heroic authority appropriately belonged to the ruling senates. This is why heroic senates had to ratify proposals made by the people. In Livy's words, 'what the people had ordained was then authorized by the fathers': *eius, quod populus iussisset, deinde patres fierent auctores*. Yet this process dates not from Romulus' interregnum, as the historians tell us, but from the late period of the aristocracy, when citizenship had already been extended to the plebeians. This arrangement, as Livy himself says, often threatened to lead to rebellion, *saepe*

spectabat ad vim. Indeed, if the people wanted to prevail, they had to nominate consuls acceptable to the senate, in precisely the way the people nominate magistrates under today's monarchies.

[945] (2) After the Publilian law had declared the Roman people free and absolute master of the political power, the authority of the senate became that of a guardianship. (In Roman law, the approval which guardians give to business dealings of their wards, who are masters of their patrimonies, is similarly termed the guardians' authority, *auctoritas tutorum*.) This authority was conferred on the people by the senators when they presented a law drafted earlier in the senate; and it was conveyed in a formula like that by which guardians confer their authority on their wards. By this formula, the senate was to be *present* among the people, *present* in the great assemblies, and *present* when the law was promulgated, if the people chose to approve it. (If not, the people would reject the law and 'approve the old ways', *probaret antiqua*: they were said to 'antiquate' the proposed changes.) This process prevented the people, whose judgment was imperfect, from enacting laws harmful to the state: for it subjected popular legislation to senatorial regulation. The formulas of the laws which the senate presented to the people for promulgation are knowingly defined by Cicero as written-out authorities, *perscriptae auctoritates*. These were not *personal* authorizations, like those of guardians, whose presence is required to approve the actions of their wards. And Cicero's verb *perscribere* means that they were authorities *written out at length*. (By contrast, the formulas of legal actions were written using abbreviations, *per notas*, which the people did not understand.) This was the import of the Publilian law: that henceforth the authority of the senate, to borrow Livy's expression, would prevail before a vote was taken in the popular assembly, *valeret in incertum comitiorum eventum*.

[946] (3) Finally, after the state had passed from democracy to monarchy, there developed the third kind of authority, which was based on the trust placed in people with a reputation for wisdom. This is an authority of counsel, which is why jurists under the emperors were called *auctores*, authorities. This is the authority of those senates which convene under monarchs, who have full and absolute freedom to follow or disregard their senatorial advice.

SECTION 9
THREE KINDS OF
REASON

CHAPTER I

Divine Reason and Reason of State

[947] There were three kinds of reason.

[948] (1) The first is divine reason, which is only understood by God, and which is only known to people through his revelation. The Jews and later the Christians received this revelation in two forms: the internal speech of God the spirit to human minds, and the external speech of the prophets and Jesus Christ to the apostles, who proclaimed it to the Church. By contrast, God revealed his divine reason to the pagans through auspices, oracles, and other physical signs. (Since the pagans believed that the gods existed physically, they regarded these physical signs as their divine messages.) Now, since God is pure reason, divine reason and authority are the same thing; and good theology places divine authority on a level with reason.

Yet the earliest pagans did not understand reason, especially in the family state. So providence, which once again deserves our admiration, allowed the pagans to err by substituting the authority of the auspices for divine reason. In this way, the pagans governed themselves according to the divine counsels which they perceived in the auspices. For it is an invariable property that, when human affairs appear to lack reason and even to contradict it, people resign themselves to the inscrutable counsels hidden in the abyss of divine providence.

[949] (2) The second kind was reason of state, which the Romans called civil equity, *civilis aequitas*. The jurist Ulpian defines this equity as something which is not naturally known to all men, but only to those few experienced men who can discern what is necessary to preserve human society, as Axiom 110 states. This reason of state was

the basis of the wisdom of heroic senates. In particular, the Roman senate demonstrated its greatest wisdom both in the aristocratic period, when the plebeians had no say in public matters, and in the democratic period as long as the people's role in public affairs was subject to senatorial regulation, which is to say until the age of the Gracchi.

CHAPTER 2

Corollary on the Ancient Romans' Wisdom of State

[950] All this raises a question which appears quite difficult to resolve. How could the Romans have been so wise in statecraft during their crudest age, when in their most enlightened age Ulpian said that reason of state was understood by only a few people experienced in governing? The answer lies in the same natural causes which produced the heroism of the first peoples. As the heroes of their world, the Romans naturally observed civil equity, and therefore paid scrupulous attention to the wording of laws. By their superstitious observance of legal wording, the Romans framed laws which cut straight through all the facts of any case, even when that made the laws severe, harsh, and cruel, just as today we apply reason of state. Thus, civil equity naturally subordinated everything to the public safety. For the public safety is the queen of all laws, and Cicero described it with appropriate gravity: 'The supreme law shall be the safety of the people', *Suprema lex populi salus esto*.

Since the states of the heroic age were aristocratic, as I have just shown, each hero privately possessed a large share of the public interest, which consisted of the family monarchies protected by the commonwealth. And since the state protected the heroes' greater private interests, they naturally subordinated to it their lesser private interests. Being magnanimous, the heroes naturally defended the public good, which is that of the state; and being wise, they offered their advice in state affairs. This reflects the profound counsel of divine providence. For if the Cyclopean fathers described by Homer and Plato had not identified their private interest with the public interest, they would not have been moved to abandon their savage life for civilization.

[951] The situation is quite different in the more civilized states of democracy and monarchy. In a democracy, the citizens control the public wealth, which is divided into small shares according to the number of citizens. In a monarchy, the subjects are commanded to look to their own private interests, and to leave public matters to the sovereign ruler. We must also bear in mind that both democracy and monarchy spring naturally from causes which are quite unheroic: a love of comfort, affection for one's wife and children, and the desire for survival. As a result, people today naturally pay most attention to those minor details that ensure equal benefit to all.

(3) This criterion of an equitable good, *aequum bonum*, which is contemplated by our third kind of reason, or natural reason, gives rise to what the jurists call natural equity, *aequitas naturalis*. This is the only kind of reason of which the masses are capable. For the masses can only appreciate those precise points of law which are applicable to the specific facts of their case. Given these two kinds of equity, monarchies need only a very few expert ministers who can apply civil equity in decisions regarding public emergencies. But they need a great many jurists of private law who can apply natural equity in administering justice to the people.

CHAPTER 3

Corollary: The Fundamental History of Roman Law

[952] These observations about the three kinds of reason offer a foundation on which to construct the history of Roman law. Governments must conform to the nature of the people they govern, since they arise from that very nature, as Axiom 69 states. And laws in turn must be administered in conformity with the government, and consequently must be interpreted according to the form of the government. Yet no jurists or legal scholars seem to have done this, since they fell into the same error as the historians of Roman institutions. These historians describe the history of the laws promulgated at various times in the Roman republic, but they fail to note the inevitable correlation between

the laws and the stages of government through which the republic passed. In this way, the naked facts are divorced from the particular causes which naturally produced them. Consider Jean Bodin's discussion of the institutions created by the ancient Romans in their age of liberty, which historians have falsely described as popular. Equally learned as a jurist and as a statesman, Bodin argues that these institutions were the product of a popular commonwealth with an aristocratic administration, which is only half true, as we shall see.

In this context, let us ask the embellishers of the history of Roman law the following questions. Why was ancient republican jurisprudence so rigorous in applying the Law of the Twelve Tables? Why did early imperial jurisprudence, with its praetorian edicts, begin to practise a rational clemency while still respecting the terms of that Law? And why did later imperial jurisprudence generously profess natural equity without any pretence of observing that Law? The answer given by these historians seriously insults the generosity of the Romans. For they say that all the severity and solemnity of Roman law, all its scrupulous and subtle wording, and finally all its secrecy, were merely deceptions perpetrated by the patricians in order to exercise control over the laws, which in any state constitute a great part of the civil power.

[953] Yet far from being deceptions, such practices were customs arising from human nature. For customs determined states, and states determined precise practices. For example, in the first age of humankind, only religion was powerful enough to tame people's utter savagery. So providence ordained that people should live under divine governments, and be ruled everywhere by sacred laws, which is to say arcane laws kept secret from the masses. In the state of families, laws were naturally kept secret. They were transmitted through the wordless language of consecrated solemnities, such as were later preserved in Roman legal acts. The dull-witted minds of early people regarded such rites as necessary to assure one person of another's effective will in providing goods or services. By contrast, in today's age of natural intelligence, a few simple words or even mere gestures are sufficient assurance of a contract.

(1) Divine governments were succeeded by the human governments of civil aristocratic states. Under these, people naturally continued to

observe their religious customs, by virtue of which they persisted in keeping their laws arcane and secret. Such secrecy is the vital soul of an aristocracy, and the religious observance of the law is the rigorous principle of civil equity, which is the principal mainstay of aristocracies. (2) Later, there emerged democracies, which are by nature open, generous, and magnanimous. They are governed by the masses, who naturally understand natural equity. Together with these governments, there emerged the so-called vernacular languages and letters, over which the masses exercise sovereign control. People now used these to frame and write down laws, and thus naturally published what had been secret. This is the hidden law, *ius latens*, described by Pomponius, who says that it so rankled the Roman plebeians that they insisted that the laws be inscribed on tablets, after the Greeks had brought vernacular letters to Rome. (3) Finally, this order of human civil institutions prepared the way for monarchies. In these, monarchs seek to administer the laws according to natural equity, and hence as the masses understand them. This renders both the powerful and the weak equal before the law, a condition which can only be found in a monarchy. By contrast, civil equity, or reason of state, is understood only by a few wise men versed in public policy. By virtue of this invariable property, reason of state is kept secret within royal cabinets.

SECTION 10
THREE KINDS OF
JUDGMENTS

CHAPTER I

First Kind: Divine Judgments

[954] There were three kinds of judgments.

[955] The first was divine judgment. In what we call the state of nature, which was the state of families, there was no civil authority of law. Hence, whenever they suffered any wrongs, the family fathers appealed to the gods. This was the primary and proper meaning of the Latin phrase *implorare deorum fidem*, to implore the faith of the gods. And they summoned the gods as witnesses of the justice of their cause, which was the primary and proper meaning of *deos obtestari*, to call the gods to witness. These defences and accusations were with native propriety called the world's first *orations*. In later Latin, the noun *oratio* was still used for a defence or accusation, as is shown by several passages in Plautus and Terence. And the Law of the Twelve Tables preserves two golden passages in which the verb 'to plead' is *orare*. (Lipsius mistakenly reads *adorare*, to accuse.) In the first, *furto orare*, to plead concerning theft, is used for *agere*, to bring suit; and in the second, *pacto orare*, to plead after agreement, is used for *excipere*, to stipulate. From such orations, the Romans continued to call *oratores* those who plead cases in court. Originally, these appeals to the gods were made by simple and rude people who credulously believed that they were literally heard by the gods, whom they imagined as living on the mountaintops. This is how Homer describes the gods atop Olympus. And Tacitus relates that the tribes of the Hermunduri and Chatti fought a war over a territory where they superstitiously believed that 'the gods were closest to hear human prayers'.

[956] Since in that age the pagans imagined all their institutions as

gods, the rights granted by divine judgments were themselves considered gods. Among the Romans, for example, a Lar stood for the ownership of a household; Dii Hospitales, the right to shelter; Dii Penates, paternal power; Deus Genius, the right of marriage; Deus Terminus, ownership of a farm; and Dii Manes, the right of burial. (Of the last, the Law of the Twelve Tables preserves a golden remnant in the *ius deorum manium*, the law of the deceased.)

[957] Once the gods had been summoned by orations (also called obsecrations or implorations) and by obtestations, early peoples invoked them to the execration of criminals. Among the Greeks, there were temples of execration, such as the famous one at Argos. The people execrated there were called *anathēmata*, which meant accursed, or what we would now call excommunicated. They were first execrated – the Latin *nuncupare vota* referred to solemn vows made against such persons with consecrated formulas – and then consecrated to the Furies, or literally vowed to the Dire Ones, *diris devoti*. Then they were killed, just as the Scythians fixed a knife in the ground, worshipped it as a god, and then killed a man with it. In Latin, this ritual slaying was called *mactare*, to kill; and this verb remained a sacred term used in sacrifices. From this derive both the Spanish *matar* and the Italian *ammazzare*, to kill. The site of this ritual slaying, the altar, is preserved in the Greek noun *ara*, which means harmful object, vow, and fury; and in Latin *ara*, which means both altar and victim. Some form of this primitive excommunication remained among all nations. Julius Caesar has left us a detailed description of such a rite among the Gauls, and the Romans observed the interdict of fire and water. Many of these consecrations passed into the Law of the Twelve Tables. For example, anyone who had violated a tribune of the people was consecrated to Jupiter, and an impious son was consecrated to the paternal gods. Further, anyone who had set fire to another's crops was consecrated to Ceres, and then burned alive. Such persons must have been those whom Plautus calls Saturn's victims. All this shows us that the punishments of divine judgments rivalled the cruelty of bloodthirsty witches, as Axiom 40 states.

[958] From such judgments rendered in their private affairs, peoples went forth to fight what they called pure and pious wars, *pura et pia*

bella. Such wars were waged for their altars and hearths, *pro aris et focis*, that is, for both their public and private institutions. They considered all human institutions as manifestations of the divine, and all heroic wars were wars of religion. When heralds delivered a declaration of war to an enemy city, they summoned the gods to leave, and consecrated the foe to the gods. In the triumphs of the early Romans, defeated kings were presented to Jupiter Feretrius on the Capitoline, and then killed there. This followed the example of the impious and violent men who were the first victims sacrificed by Vesta on the world's first altars. Likewise, surrendering peoples were considered people without gods, after the example of the first family servants. This is why the Romans called slaves *mancipia*, possessions, like inanimate objects; and why Roman jurisprudence treated them like things, *loco rerum.*

CHAPTER 2

Corollary on Duels and Reprisals

[959] In barbarous nations, another kind of divine judgment took the form of duels, which must have originated under the ancient government of the gods and continued for a long time in heroic commonwealths. In a golden passage from his *Politics*, Aristotle says that heroic commonwealths had no judicial laws for punishing private wrongs and rectifying private acts of violence, as Axiom 85 states. But until now no one believed this, since the conceit of scholars falsely opined that early peoples had a heroic philosophy, supposedly derived from the incomparable wisdom of the ancients.

[960] Yet retributive laws were clearly introduced quite late by the Romans: witness the praetorian interdict 'On violence', and the actions 'On violent robbery of property', and 'What was done in fear'. And during the medieval return of barbarism, private reprisals persisted until the age of Bartolus. Such reprisals must have been what the ancient Romans called 'condictions', which are claims of restitution also known as 'personal actions'. According to Festus, *condicere* means to denounce, or to serve formal notice. Hence, before seeking reprisal, a family father

had first to serve formal notice to claim restitution from the person who had unjustly taken his possessions. This kind of denunciation remained a solemn formality of personal actions, as Ulrich Zasius acutely discerned.

[961] By contrast, duels involved real judgments; and since they took place at the site of the dispute, *in re praesenti*, they required no formal denunciation. These early duels were replaced by the claim of ownership, *vindiciae*, vindication, which must originally have been so called from the real force, *vi*, used to enforce the claim. Later, the claimant merely took a clod of earth from the wrongful possessor, making a feigned show of force, which Gellius describes as *festucaria*, made of straw. He then brought it to the judge, and swore over it: 'I declare this ground mine by quiritary right.' Jurists are thus wrong when they say that duels were introduced for lack of proofs; the real reason was the lack of *judiciary laws*. It is certain that the Danish king Frotho ordered all disputes settled by combat, and forbade resolutions by legal judgments. Indeed, to avoid resolution by legal judgments, the laws of the Lombards, Salians, English, Burgundians, Normans, Danes, and Germans are filled with duelling procedures. In his treatise *On Fiefs*, Jacques Cujas writes: 'Christians have long used this way of clearing up both civil and criminal cases, and have settled all their disputes by duelling.' This custom persists in Germany, where the men called knights, *Ritter*, who profess the art of duelling, compel all duellists to tell the truth. For if witnesses were admitted and judges had consequently to intervene, duels would become either criminal or civil judgments.

[962] No one previously believed that the earliest barbarous people practised duelling, since there are no extant records. But let us consider Homer's Cyclopes, in whom Plato recognizes the earliest family fathers in the state of nature. When wronged, how could they have reacted with patience, let alone humanity? In Axiom 85, Aristotle clearly states that in the earliest commonwealths – not to mention the state of the family – there were no laws to right wrongs and punish offences suffered by private citizens. We have confirmed this for ancient Roman law. And Aristotle calls this the custom of barbarous peoples, for primitive peoples are barbarous until they have been tamed by laws.

[963] Greek and Roman history preserve two great traces of such

ancient duels. These show that among early peoples wars, which were called *duella* in early Latin, began with single combats fought by the interested parties. The combatants could even be kings, and their peoples looked on, eager to see the offences publicly justified or avenged. In Greek history, the Trojan War clearly began when Menelaus challenged Paris for abducting his wife Helen; and it was only when their duel was indecisive that the Greeks and Trojans declared war. In Roman history, we find the same custom observed in the war between the Romans and the Albans. Their conflict was definitively decided by the combat between the three Horatii and the three Curiatii, one of whom had abducted Horatia.

In these armed judgments, right was determined by the fortune of victory, in which we see the counsel of divine providence. In this way, the barbarous nations, with their limited powers of reason, were prevented from spreading their wars everywhere. And they learned a crude idea of human justice and injustice, which they measured by the favour or disfavour of the gods. Thus, we see how saintly Job, fallen from his royal estate, is scorned by the gentiles when they see that God is against him. During the medieval return of barbarism, the losing party had his hand barbarously cut off, no matter how just his cause.

[964] This custom, privately observed by early peoples, gave rise to what moral theologians call external justice, which allows nations to rest secure in their dominions. In the same way, the auspices first founded the paternal monarchical authority of fathers in the family state; then they prepared and preserved the fathers' aristocratic rule in the heroic cities; next, by extension to the plebeians, they produced the free democracies explicitly described by Roman historians; and finally, through the fortune of armed combat, they legitimized the conquests of successful conquerors. This can be explained only by the notion of providence, which is innate and universal in all nations and to which all people turn when they see the just afflicted and the wicked prospering.

CHAPTER 3

Second Kind: Ordinary Judgments

[965] The second kind of judgments, called ordinary, followed close on divine judgments, and were therefore practised with the rigidly scrupulous attention to words which, as a survival of divine judgments, was called the religious observance of wording, *religio verborum*. This is the order by which divine things are universally couched in sacred formulas, in which not a single letter can be altered. A Roman proverb described these ancient legal formulas: 'If you lose a comma, you lose the case.' This natural law of heroic nations was naturally observed by ancient Roman jurisprudence. The praetor's ruling was an unalterable utterance, *fari*, and the days on which he dispensed justice were *dies fasti*, or legal court-days. In the heroic aristocracies, only the heroes enjoyed this justice, which was called *fas deorum*, divine law, because in that age the heroes claimed the title of gods. Later, the ineluctable order which creates things in nature was called *fatum*, fate, because it was thought to be the utterance of God. This may explain why in Italian *ordinare*, to order, means to give commands which must perforce be executed, especially with reference to laws.

[966] In terms of Roman judgments, *order* meant the solemn formula of a legal action. This order dictated the cruel and shameful punishment of the renowned defendant Horatius from which the duumvirs themselves could not have absolved him, even if he had been proved innocent. (Yet when he appealed to the people, they absolved him, in Livy's words, more in admiration of his valour than from the justice of his cause.) This order of judgments was necessary in the age of Achilles, who measured all questions of right by force. With his usual wit, Plautus described this trait of the powerful, for whom 'An agreement is no agreement, and no agreement is an agreement', *pactum non pactum, non pactum pactum*. For powerful men may find others' promises contrary to their haughty desires, or may choose not to fulfil their own promises.

The counsel of divine providence sought to prevent the proliferation of lawsuits, quarrels, and even murders. So it moved people to interpret justice 'naturally', that is, as meaning only such rights as were expressed in solemn verbal formulas. This is why jurists both in ancient Rome and in medieval Italy staked their reputations on the verbal precautions they could offer their clients. This natural law of the heroic nations supplied the plots for several of Plautus' comedies. In these plays, young men in love cheat pimps of their slave girls, using deceptions which make the pimps seem guilty under some legal formula. Despite their innocence, the pimps cannot file suit for fraud, but must pay those who have cheated them. One of them repays the lover the full price of the girl; another, facing a charge for alleged theft, begs a youth to accept half the penalty; and a third leaves town fearing a conviction for rape. This is the extent to which natural equity determined legal judgments in Plautus' age!

[967] Not only did people naturally observe such strictly construed law; but judging by their own nature, they believed that even the gods observed it in their divine oaths. In Homer's *Iliad*, for example, Juno swears to Jupiter that she did not urge Neptune to send a tempest against the Trojans: for she did so through the god Sleep as her agent. And Jupiter, who is both witness and judge of oaths, is satisfied by her oath! In Plautus' *Amphitryon*, when Mercury is disguised as Sosia, he swears to the true Sosia: 'If I deceive you, may Mercury turn against Sosia.' It is scarcely credible that Plautus wanted the gods to teach the spectators to swear false oaths. And it is even less credible in the case of Scipio Africanus and Laelius (called the Roman Socrates), the two wisest leaders of the Roman republic, who are said to have helped Terence write his comedies. Yet in Terence's *Lady of Andros*, the slave Davus has the servant girl Mysis place the baby on Simo's doorstep. In this way, if his master should ask him, he can in good conscience deny having placed it there himself.

[968] An important proof of this comes from ancient Athens, a city whose people were astute and intelligent. A play by Euripides contains the line 'I swore with my tongue, but kept my mind unsworn', a verse which Cicero translated as *Iuravi lingua, mentem iniuratam habui*. When the Athenian spectators first heard this, they grumbled in disgust. For they naturally shared the view enjoined in the Law of the Twelve Tables that 'As a person has declared with his tongue, so shall it be

binding'. This is why the wretched Agamemnon could not escape his rash vow to sacrifice Iphigenia, his pious and innocent daughter! (Yet Lucretius, ignoring providence, was so shocked by Agamemnon's deed that he impiously exclaimed: 'So great were the evils religion could urge!')

[969] As final confirmation of my point, I note two late measures which are clearly recorded by the history of Roman jurisprudence: (1) the action for fraud, *de dolo*, which Aquilius Gallus introduced in the last years of the republic; and (2) the discretion which Augustus granted a jury to pardon defendants who had been victims of misunderstanding or misrepresentation.

[970] Since they were accustomed to such judgments in peacetime, heroic nations which had been defeated in war either suffered miserable oppression under the terms of surrender, or were fortunate enough to mock the anger of the victors.

[971] Miserable oppression was the fate of the Carthaginians. In defeat, they accepted the Roman peace with the provision that they could keep their life, their city, and their substance. By city, they understood the actual buildings, which the Romans called *urbs*. But the Roman treaty used the word *civitas*, which means a community of citizens. When the treaty was put into effect, they were ordered to abandon their city on the sea and to move inland. When they refused these terms and again armed themselves in self-defence, the Romans declared them rebels and, according to the heroic right of war, occupied Carthage and barbarously burned it to the ground. The Carthaginians repudiated the terms of peace because they had misunderstood the Romans' negotiations. For their intelligence had developed much earlier, as the result of their native African shrewdness and their practice of maritime trading, which teaches nations to be clever. For their part, the Romans did not regard this war as unjust, since most historians agree that their unjust wars began with the later destruction of Corinth. (Some mistakenly believe that such wars began with the campaign against Numantia, which was concluded by Scipio Africanus.)

[972] Medieval history offers a clear example of a defeated nation which mocked its conquerors. The emperor Conrad III had subdued the city of Weinsberg for supporting a rival claimant of the empire. In

the terms of surrender, he stipulated that only the women would be allowed to leave the city in safety, carrying with them whatever they could. The loyal women of Weinsberg came out carrying their sons, husbands, and fathers. The victorious emperor stood at the gates of the city, ready to enjoy the fruits of victory, which often make men insolent. But even though great rulers are subject to frightful anger, which is most deadly when they find their sovereignty threatened or challenged, Conrad restrained his feelings. As he stood before his army, which waited with swords drawn and lances poised to slaughter the men of Weinsberg, Conrad simply looked on and let pass in safety all those whom he had intended to put to the sword. To such an extent the natural law of advanced human reason, touted by Grotius, Selden, and Pufendorf, naturally pervades all nations in all ages!

[973] Axioms 111–14, which define truth and certainty in laws and agreements, offer the basis for this entire discusssion of ordinary judgments. We must also note that, just as the strict construction of legal wording is natural in barbarous ages, so generous construction – measured by the principle of equal benefit to all parties – is natural in civilized ages. Strict construction is properly called *fas gentium*, the right of nations. Generous construction, in turn, may properly be called *fas naturae*, the right of nature: for it is the immutable law of that rational humanity which is the true and proper nature of mankind.

CHAPTER 4

Third Kind: Human Judgments

[974] The third kind of judgments are all 'extraordinary', or rendered outside the strict order. While they are governed by the truth of the facts involved, the law is construed generously, following the dictates of conscience, and ensures that the principle of equal benefit to all parties is applied. Such judgments are imbued with the natural moderation produced by intelligence, and are guaranteed by the good faith engendered by civilization. Extraordinary judgments are characteristic of the open spirit of democracies, and even more to the generosity of

monarchies. For by their extraordinary judgments, monarchs show that, being above the laws, they are subject only to their conscience and to God. This kind of judgment, practised in our modern age of peace, forms the basis of the three political systems of Grotius, Selden, and Pufendorf. Yet my colleague Father Niccolò Concina, having observed many errors and defects in these systems, devised one more in keeping with sound philosophy and more useful to human society. To Italy's glory, he still teaches this system in the renowned university of Padua, where he is also the principal professor of metaphysics.

SECTION II

THREE SCHOOLS OF
THOUGHT

CHAPTER I

Schools of Thought in Religious, Punctilious, and
Civil Ages

[975] All the preceding institutions were practised during the ages of
three schools of thought.

[976] The first was the religious school of thought, which was
observed under divine governments.

[977] The second was the school of thought of punctilious men, like
Achilles. During the medieval return of barbarism, this was the age of
duellists.

[978] The third was the school of thought of civility or moderation,
which was practised under the natural law of the nations which Ulpian
specifically calls human or civilized. (This is why Latin authors of the
Roman empire call the duty of Roman subjects *officium civile*, and call
any legal violation of natural equity *incivile*, uncivil or unjust.) This is
the last of the schools of Roman jurisprudence, which began with the
age of popular liberty. Later, as the character, customs, and government
of the Romans changed, the Roman praetors reduced the severity, and
relaxed the rigour of the Law of the Twelve Tables, which had been
enacted in the spirit of Rome's heroic age. Finally, the emperors stripped
this Law of all the veils in which the praetors had cloaked it, thus
revealing all the openness and generosity of natural equity, as befitted
the civility now customary in the nations.

[979] The jurists appeal to these schools of thought in justifying their
views on justice. And while they are proper to Roman jurisprudence,
these schools of thought are the source of the agreement between the
Romans and the other nations of the world. For they were taught by
divine providence, which Roman jurists establish as a principle basic

to the natural law of nations. (These schools of thought are not the same as the philosophers' sects, even though some learned interpreters of Roman law have violently thrust them into legal matters, as Axioms 104 and 114 state.) The emperors themselves, when seeking to justify their laws or decrees, say that they were moved by the current school of thought, as we see from the passages assembled by Barnabé Brisson in his *Legal Formulas and Solemn Oaths of the Roman People*. For the school of princes is the morality of the age, or *saeculum*, as Tacitus calls the degenerate moral code of his age when he writes that 'To corrupt and be corrupted passes for the spirit of our age', *corrumpere et corrumpi saeculum vocatur*. Today we would call it the fashion.

SECTION 12
FURTHER PROOFS DRAWN
FROM THE PROPERTIES OF
HEROIC ARISTOCRACIES

INTRODUCTION

[980] A powerful concatenation of diverse causes and effects determines the constant, continuous, and ordered progression of human civil institutions. As we have observed it in the course the nations run, this progression must force us to accept the truth of my principles. But since I wish to leave no room for doubt, I now offer an account of other civil institutions, which can only be explained in terms of the heroic commonwealths which we have discovered.

CHAPTER I

The Guarding of Boundaries

[981] The two greatest invariable properties of aristocracies are (1) the guarding of boundaries, and (2) the guarding of social orders.

[982] (1) As we have seen, the guarding of boundaries began under divine governments with the bloody religious rites by which people set boundary-lines around their fields, thus putting an end to the abominable promiscuity of possessions in the bestial state. These boundary-lines formed the basis for all the boundaries of later social groups: first, families; then, clans or houses; later, peoples; and finally, entire nations. In the *Odyssey*, Polyphemus tells Ulysses that each giant lived in his own cave with his wife and children. Retaining the habits of their recent savagery, the giants never meddled in the affairs of others, and they brutally killed anyone who entered within their boundaries –

426

just as Polyphemus sought to kill Ulysses and his shipmates. From this practice of the Cyclopes, whom Plato regards as the fathers of the family state, there derived the longstanding custom that cities regarded each other as enemies. So much for the peaceable division of the fields described by the jurist Hermogenianus and accepted in good faith by every interpreter of Roman law! Now, since sciences should begin at the point where their subject matter began, the jurists' discussion of the 'Division of Property and the Acquisition of Ownership' should have begun with the most ancient origin of this human institution. The guarding of boundaries is most naturally observed in aristocracies, which is why they are not made for conquest, as political thinkers have observed. Later, once the abominable promiscuity of property had been completely eliminated by the establishment of boundaries between peoples, democracies arose, which are made for the expansion of empires; and eventually monarchies arose, which are even better suited for expansion.

[983] This must be the reason why the Law of the Twelve Tables did not recognize simple possession. Instead, natural transfers of property were in heroic ages solemnized by usucaption, which was defined by the best jurists as *dominii adiectio*, or the addition of civil ownership to previously acquired natural ownership. Later, in the age of popular liberty, the praetors supported simple possession by their interdicts, so that usucaption became known as *dominii adeptio*, or the direct acquisition of civil ownership. And whereas cases of possession were initially not heard in court – the praetors decided them by extrajudicial rulings – today the most certain judgments are those called possessory, as regarding the right of possession alone.

[984] As a result, the Romans' distinction between four kinds of ownership – bonitary, quiritary, optimal, and civil – was largely lost under their popular liberty; and it completely disappeared under the monarchy. Originally these terms had meanings quite different from their present ones. Bonitary meant natural ownership, which was upheld by continuous physical possession. Quiritary meant ownership that one could legally vindicate. (This ownership was current among the plebeians, since the patricians extended it to them in the Law of the Twelve Tables. But plebeians could legally claim it only by summoning

427

the patrician who had authorized their title.) Optimal meant ownership free of any encumbrance either public or private. (This was held by the patricians alone until they established the census, which was the basis of popular liberty.) Finally, civil ownership meant that of the cities, which we now call eminent domain.

During the age of liberty, the distinction between optimal and quiritary ownership had become so blurred that later imperial jurists took no account of it. (Under the monarchy even bonitary ownership, which is created by mere natural delivery, and quiritary ownership, which is created by mancipation or civil conveyance, were utterly confused in Justinian's Code, as in the constitutions titled 'The abolition of mere quiritary rights' and 'The transfer of usucaption'.) And the famous distinction between conveyable property, *res mancipi*, and non-conveyable property, *res nec mancipi*, was completely abolished. As a result, civil ownership came to mean ownership which could be legally claimed; and optimal ownership came to mean ownership subject to no private encumbrance.

CHAPTER 2

The Guarding of Social Orders

[985] (2) The guarding of social orders originated in the divine age with acts of jealousy – symbolized by Juno, the goddess of solemn matrimony – which protected the certain offspring of families against the abominable promiscuity of women. This jealous guarding is naturally characteristic of aristocracies, in which the nobility seek to keep the bonds of kinship and succession, with their attendant wealth and power, within their own orders. This is why nations were slow to adopt testamentary laws; and Tacitus relates that the ancient Germans had no wills at all. Hence, when King Agis tried to introduce such laws in Sparta, he was strangled by command of the ephors, who were the guardians of the liberty of the Lacedaemonian nobility.

This shows us the wisdom of those embellishers of the Twelve Tables who assigned to Table XI the article 'The auspices shall be withheld from the plebeians'. In early Rome, all civil institutions, public and private, depended on the auspices. (These included solemn matrimony, paternal power, legitimate succession, testaments, guardianships, and legal kinships, including proper heirs, and relatives through the males or the clan.) Now, in the first Ten Tables, the patricians had extended all these rights to the plebeians, especially the testamentary law, and had thus established laws suited to a democracy. Yet we are to suppose that one year later, by a single article in Table XI restricting the auspices to the patriciate, they changed the entire Roman state back into an aristocracy! Still, for all the confusion of these institutions, the same scholars managed by a happy guess to note the historical truth that Tables XI and XII codified several ancient Roman customs as law – which verifies my point that the ancient Roman state was aristocratic.

[986] To return to our subject, once the human race had been firmly settled through solemnized marriage, democracies arose, and much later monarchies. In these, the orders of the nobility were shaken by marriages with plebeians and by the resulting successions, and the wealth was gradually drained from their noble houses. As we have seen, Roman plebeians contracted only natural marriages until 445 BC, when they finally prevailed on the patricians to grant them *connubium*, or the right of contracting solemn nuptials. Indeed, as Roman history records, in their wretched state, like abject slaves the plebeians could not aspire to marriage with the patricians. As I wrote in the first edition of my *New Science*, unless we establish these principles as the basis of Roman jurisprudence, Roman history as previously related will seem more incredible than the mythological history of the Greeks. For while we do not know how to interpret Greek myths, we are aware that the facts of Roman history run completely contrary to the normal pattern of human desires. For it describes how the neediest men first sought nobility in their struggle for solemn marriage, then honours in their struggle for the consulate, and finally wealth by aspiring to the priest-hoods. Yet their invariable social nature causes people to desire wealth first, then honours, and nobility last of all.

[987] There is only one way to explain this. Under the Law of the Twelve Tables, which was the world's second agrarian law, the plebeians won from the patricians the right to certain ownership of the fields;

but they still remained aliens, since such ownership was open even to aliens. Experience soon taught the plebeians that they could not bequeath their fields intestate to their kin, since without solemn marriage they had no legal kinship, whether proper heirs, or relatives through the males or the clan; much less by testament, since they were not citizens. (Their status is scarcely surprising, for the plebeians had little or no understanding: witness the fact that it took three later plebiscites – the Furian, Voconian, and Falcidian laws – for them to achieve their goal of preventing bequests from exhausting estates.) Hence, the first three years of the Law of the Twelve Tables taught the plebeians that, when they died, the fields assigned to them soon reverted to the patricians. They now laid claim to solemn marriage and thereby to citizenship. At this point, all the historians were misled by all the political thinkers who imagined that Rome was founded by Romulus with the form of government which cities now have. As a result, they were unaware that for centuries plebeians in heroic cities were considered aliens, and therefore contracted only natural marriages among themselves. Hence, they were unaware that their reading of Livy did violence both to the facts and to the Latin language. They read the statement that the plebeians sought to obtain the marriage rights 'of the patricians', *plebei tentarunt connubia patrum*, as if it said that they sought marriage rights 'with the patricians', *cum patribus*. (The latter is the usage of marriage laws: witness 'An uncle shall not marry his brother's daughter', *patruus non habet cum fratris filia connubium*.) Had the historians seen this, they would have grasped that the plebeians claimed not the right of intermarriage with the patricians, but the right of contracting solemn nuptials, which belonged to the patricians.

[988] Concerning legitimate successions, the Law of the Twelve Tables prescribes that the deceased father of a family is succeeded first by his proper heirs; if there are none, by his male relatives; and if there are none, by his clan relatives. In this light, the Law of the Twelve Tables seems precisely like a Roman version of the Salic law. Although the Salic law eventually survived only in France and Savoy, during its earliest period it was observed in Germany as well, which allows us to infer the same for other medieval nations. In a way that suits our purpose here, Baldus calls this law of succession the law of the Gallic peoples,

ius gentium Gallorum. Along these lines, we may justly call the Roman law of male and clan successions the law of the Roman peoples, *ius gentium Romanarum.* When we add the adjective 'heroic', and more properly the adjective 'Roman', this Roman law of the heroic clans corresponds precisely to the law of the Roman citizens, *ius Quiritium Romanorum,* which earlier I showed to be the natural law common to all heroic peoples.

[989] The tradition that the Roman kingdom was ruled by Tanaquil, a woman, does not contradict the exclusion of women from royal succession under the Salic law. This was merely a heroic way of describing a weak-willed king who let himself be guided by the crafty Servius Tullius. As we have seen, Servius Tullius invaded the Roman kingdom with the support of the plebeians, for whom he passed the first agrarian law. And we find a parallel to Tanaquil in the medieval return of barbarism, when the same heroic way of speaking caused Pope John VIII to be called a woman. The myth of Pope Joan, exposed in a book by Leo Allacci, in fact alludes to John's great weakness in yielding to Photius, patriarch of Constantinople, as Cesare Baronio and his editor Henri de Sponde agree.

[990] Having resolved this difficulty, we return to the law of nations. We have seen that the early law of the Roman citizens, *ius Quiritium Romanorum,* meant the natural law of the heroic Roman peoples, *ius naturale gentium heroicarum Romanarum.* And with carefully chosen words, the imperial jurist Ulpian defines this law as the natural law of human nations, *ius naturale gentium humanarum,* which is current in free commonwealths and especially in monarchies. (Hence, we must apparently correct the title in Justinian's *Institutes* which reads 'Of natural law, the law of nations, and civil law', *De iure naturali, gentium, et civili.* By removing the first comma with Hermann Vulteius, adding 'human' with Ulpian, and eliminating 'and', we read 'Of the natural civil law of human nations', *De iure naturali gentium humanarum civili.*) For the Romans studied their own law with the same care with which, from its introduction in the age of Saturn, they preserved it first in their customs and later in their laws. This is why Varro in his great *Divine and Human Institutions* derives Roman institutions from purely native origins without any foreign elements.

[991] To return to heroic Roman successions, we have many substantial grounds for doubting that daughters in ancient Rome were an exception to the exclusion of women. Indeed, there is no reason to believe that heroic fathers felt any familial affection, since all the evidence points to the contrary. For example, under the Law of the Twelve Tables a male heir, even seven times removed, was called to exclude the succession of an emancipated son. Family fathers held the sovereign right of life and death over their children, and hence despotic dominion over their possessions. They arranged their sons' marriages so that only women deemed worthy would enter their house. (This historical practice is preserved in the Latin verb *spondere*, which properly means to promise on another's behalf, and from which derives *sponsalia*, a betrothal ceremony.) They considered adoptions as useful as marriages: for by choosing prolific male heirs of noble houses, they could reinvigorate their own declining families. They regarded emancipation as a form of penalty or punishment, and they were ignorant of legitimation. (The only concubines were freedwomen or foreigners, with whom solemn marriages were forbidden in the heroic age, lest the offspring degenerate from their forebears' nobility.) They had their wills nullified, cancelled, broken, or rendered ineffectual under the most frivolous pretexts, if they wished to reinstate a legitimate succession. So naturally bedazzled were these Roman fathers by the private splendour of their names, and so naturally inflamed by the common glory of Roman renown! All these customs are proper to aristocracies like the heroic commonwealths, and all these properties tally with the heroism of early peoples.

[992] Here we must reflect on another incongruous error made by the embellishers of the Law of the Twelve Tables, who insist that it was brought to Rome from Athens. During all the time before the Tables established testamentary and legitimate successions, they say that estates left intestate by Roman fathers were assigned to the category called no one's property, *res nullius*. But to prevent the world from relapsing into the abominable promiscuity of property, divine providence ordained that the very form of aristocracies would preserve certainty of ownership. Hence, all the early nations observed legitimate successions even before they understood the idea of testaments, which are proper to democracies and even more to monarchies. Tacitus

explicitly relates this about the ancient Germans, whose example allows us to infer the same for other early barbarian peoples. This is the basis of my conjecture that the Salic law, which clearly obtained in Germany, was universally observed by the nations during the medieval return of barbarism.

[993] Roman jurists of the imperial school judged the institutions of obscure antiquity in terms of more recent ones – an approach which is a source of countless errors. They thought that the Law of the Twelve Tables called daughters to inherit the estates of fathers who died intestate. As proof, they noted that in the phrase *suus heres*, direct heir, the masculine *suus* implied the feminine as well by the rules of Latin grammar. But heroic jurisprudence interpreted the wording of laws in their strictest meaning, and *suus* can only refer to the son of a family. This is clearly proved by the formula for the education for posthumous children, which Gallus Aquilius introduced many centuries after the Twelve Tables. It specifies that 'If a son or daughter be born', *Si quis natus natave erit*, because the masculine form *natus*, child, alone might not imply a daughter. Justinian was unaware of this when he wrote in his *Institutes* that the noun *adgnatus*, relative on the father's side, was used in the Law of the Twelve Tables to call both male and female agnates, but that jurists of the middle period later made the law more rigid by restricting it to sisters of the same blood. In fact, just the opposite must have happened. First the pronoun *suus* must have been extended to include family daughters, and later the noun *adgnatus* extended to include sisters of the same blood. (Quite aptly, this period came to be called 'middle' jurisprudence: for in judging such cases, it moderated the rigours of the Twelve Tables, whereas ancient jurisprudence had guarded this law with the utmost scrupulosity.)

[994] Once sovereignty had passed from the nobles to the people, the plebeians began to measure their strength, wealth, and power by the number of their offspring, and so began to feel affection for their own blood. By contrast, the plebeians of the heroic cities had not felt such affection. Plebeian fathers had only begotten children into slavery; indeed, the nobles forced them to mate so that the offspring were born in the springtime, when they would be more healthy and even robust. (Latin etymologists view this as the origin of the noun *vernae*, family

433

slaves, from which derives the expression 'vernacular languages'.) Plebeian mothers in turn must have hated rather than loved children who occasioned the pains of childbirth and the inconveniences of nursing without offering them any joy or benefit in life. In this early age, the large number of plebeians posed a threat to the aristocracies, which are based on and named after the minority. But later they contributed much to the greatness of democracies and even more of monarchies, which is why imperial laws compensate women so generously for the dangers and pains of childbirth. In the age of popular liberty, praetors began to recognize the rights of blood relations by granting them the inheritances called possessions of property, *bonorum possessiones*. And they began to offer remedies for faulty or defective testaments in order to promote the diffusion of wealth, which the masses value above all else.

[995] Finally, when the emperors took power, they felt themselves in the shadow of the patriciate's splendour and therefore devoted themselves to promoting the rights of human nature, which are common to both plebeians and patricians. This began with Augustus, who undertook to protect trusteeships, and succeeded so well that in his lifetime they gained the power of compelling heirs to fulfil them. (Before this, property could pass by trusteeship to persons incapable of inheritance, but only when the fiduciary heirs acted in good conscience.) There followed a great number of senatorial decrees which placed cognates, or relatives on the mother's side, on a par with agnates, those on the father's side. At last, Justinian abolished the distinction between legacies and trusteeships, fused the minimum inheritance of the Falcidian and Trebellian laws, eliminated nearly all distinctions between testaments and codicils, and made agnates and cognates virtually equivalent in intestate cases. These late Roman laws so lavishly favoured last wills that, whereas in ancient times the slightest reason invalidated them, today they must always be interpreted in a way which supports their validity.

[996] These later ages were more humane. Democracies love children, and monarchies encourage parents to love them. Since family fathers no longer had Cyclopean authority over the persons of their children, the humane Roman emperors acted to abolish paternal authority over

their possessions as well. They did this by granting sons three kinds of inheritable private property. First, to attract sons to the army, they introduced military assets, *peculium castrense*. Next, to attract them to the imperial service, they extended such property to quasi-military assets, *peculium quasi castrense*. Finally, to content sons who were neither soldiers nor clerks, they introduced 'outside' assets, *peculium adventicium*, which derived from the mother rather than the father. They also deprived the paternal power of its authority in adoption cases, which were no longer restricted to a few close relations. They everywhere favoured formal adoptions, *arrogationes*, which proved complicated when citizens who were family fathers became sons subject to other families. They regarded emancipations as beneficial acts, and gave the legal force of solemn nuptials to legitimations made under a subsequent marriage. Above all, since the supreme power of fathers, *imperium paternum*, seemed to diminish their own imperial majesty, they renamed it the paternal power, *patria potestas*.

This followed the example of their own title, which Augustus had shrewdly introduced. To avoid arousing the jealousy of the people, who might seek to reduce his supreme power, *imperium*, Augustus assumed the title of tribunal power, *tribunicia potestas*, meaning a protector of Roman liberty. In the tribunes of the people, this had been a *de facto* power, since they never held supreme power, *imperium*, in the republic. In Augustus' day, a tribune of the people ordered Marcus Antistius Labeo to appear before him. Labeo, who founded one of the two schools of Roman jurists, refused to obey on the reasonable ground that the tribunes of the people had no supreme power. Oddly, no philologists, jurists, or historians have grasped the patricians' tactics during the plebeians' struggle to share in the consulship. To satisfy the plebeians without surrendering any of their own supreme power, the patricians found the expedient of creating military tribunes. Part noble and part base-born, these officers were endowed with consular power, *cum consulari potestate*, as historians consistently describe it, but not with consular supreme power, *cum consulari imperio*, which is nowhere mentioned in history.

[997] The free Roman republic was conceived on the basis of the threefold formula 'the authority of the senate, the supreme power of

the people, and the power of the people's tribunes': *senatus auctoritas, populi imperium, tribunorum plebis potestas*. In Roman laws, the two terms *imperium* and *potestas* preserved their original elegance and precision. *Imperium* applied to major magistrates, like consuls and praetors, and included those who could impose the death penalty. *Potestas* applied to minor magistrates, like aediles, and involved limited means of coercion, *modica coercitione continetur*.

[998] Finally, as the Roman emperors extended their clemency towards all mankind, they began to show favour to slaves by restraining the cruelty of their masters against these wretches. They increased the legal effects of manumission while reducing its solemn formalities. Citizenship, which had previously been awarded only to distinguished foreigners for their services to the Roman people, was now granted to anyone born in Rome, even of a slave father, as long as the mother was free by birth or enfranchisement. The law proper to the aristocracies of the heroic age had been called the law of clans or noble houses, *lex gentium*. But later there arose democracies, in which entire nations are sovereigns over their domain; and then monarchies, in which monarchs represent their entire subject nations. Under these governments, the more inclusive notion of free birth in the state gave rise to what is called 'the natural law of nations'.

CHAPTER 3

The Guarding of the Laws

[999] The guarding of social orders entails the guarding of magistracies and priesthoods, and thus the guarding of laws and their interpretation. In the aristocratic period of Roman history, we read that marriage rights, consulships, and priesthoods were all restricted to the senatorial order, which was entirely composed of nobles. And as in all other heroic nations, the science of the laws was kept sacred or secret – the terms are synonymous – within the college of pontiffs, to which only patricians were admitted. According to the jurist Pomponius, this lasted for about a century after the Law of the Twelve Tables. (During this

age, legal husbands, magistrates, priests, and judges were in Latin simply called *viri*, men, which was synonymous with Greek *heroes*.) We must now discuss the guarding of the laws, for as an essential property of heroic aristocracies it was the last thing which the patricians shared with the plebeians.

[1000] In the divine age, the guarding of the laws was scrupulously observed; and this observance of divine laws was simply called religion. This was perpetuated by all later governments, under which the divine laws had to be observed with certain inalterable formulas of consecrated words and solemn ceremonies. There is nothing so essential to aristocracies as the guarding of the laws. By contrast, Athens rapidly became a democracy, and nearly all the other Greek cities followed her example. This moved the Spartans, who lived in an aristocracy, to observe that in Athens many laws were written, but in Sparta the few laws were obeyed.

[1001] In their aristocratic phase, the Romans were the severest guardians of the Law of the Twelve Tables. Tacitus called these Tables the culmination of all equitable law, *finis omnis aequi iuris*. Indeed, under this Law equal liberty seemed to be guaranteed, and consular decrees of private law all but disappeared. (We must remember that the Twelve Tables were enacted after the decemvirs, but were named for them because ancient peoples thought in poetic archetypes.) For the same reason, Livy called them the source of all equitable law, *fons omnis aequi iuris*, because they were the source of all legal interpretation.

Like the Athenian populace, the Roman plebeians daily passed special laws because they could not grasp universal categories. This chaos was in part reduced by the creation of standing boards of inquiry, *quaestiones perpetuae*, which were instituted by the patrician leader Sulla after he had defeated the plebeian leader Marius. But as Tacitus relates, after Sulla had renounced the dictatorship, special laws again began to multiply just as before. As political thinkers observe, nothing paves the way to monarchy so much as a multitude of laws. When Augustus was establishing his reign, he decreed a great number of laws; and later emperors used the senate above all to issue senatorial decrees concerning private law.

But even in the age of popular liberty, legal formulas were so severely observed that it took all the eloquence of Crassus (whom Cicero called the Roman Demosthenes) to show that the express naming of an orphan's heir implied an unexpressed but common substitution. And it took all the eloquence of Cicero to prevent Sextus Aebutius from claiming the farm of Aulus Caecina, because a single letter was missing from a legal formula! Eventually, after Constantine had completely abolished legal formulas, things reached the point where any particular motive of equity took precedence over the laws. At first, the Roman aristocracy observed the article in the Law of the Twelve Tables which says 'Private laws shall not be proposed', *Privilegia ne irroganto*. Later, under the age of popular liberty, numerous special laws were enacted. Finally, the monarchy brought things to the point where the emperors did nothing but grant privileges – which, if they reflect merit, are in perfect harmony with natural equity. Indeed, all the exceptions which today are made to the laws can be truly called privileges dictated by the particular merit of the facts, which places them beyond the general provisions of the laws.

[1002] The return of barbarism in the early Middle Ages caused nations to forget Roman laws. Indeed, anyone citing a Roman law in court was severely punished in France, and could even be put to death in Spain. In Italy, noblemen clearly thought it shameful to regulate their affairs by Roman laws, and instead professed their allegiance to Lombard laws. Only the commoners, who were slow to abandon their customs, still observed some Roman laws by dint of habit. This is why the corpus of Justinian and other Western jurists were lost to the Latins, and the *Basilica* and other Eastern jurists were forgotten by the Greeks. Later, after monarchies again arose and popular liberty was reintroduced, the Roman law contained in Justinian's books was so universally embraced that Grotius even asserted that it now constitutes the natural law of European nations.

[1003] Clearly, we have good reason to admire the gravity and wisdom of the Romans. Despite changes in the state, praetors and jurists did everything in their power to see that the words of the Law of the Twelve Tables shifted in meaning as little and as slowly as possible. Indeed, this may be the principal reason for the great growth and endurance of the Roman empire. Throughout the changes in its state,

Rome did everything in its power to stand firm on its principles, which are those that govern this world of nations. Indeed, all political thinkers agree that there is no better counsel for the growth and endurance of states. The same cause which gave the Romans the wisest jurisprudence in the world also made the Roman empire the greatest in the world. It was also the cause of Rome's greatness, which Polybius vaguely attributes to the religion of the patricians, and Machiavelli by contrast to the magnanimity of the plebeians. Plutarch, who is envious of Roman virtue and wisdom, in his book *On the Fortune of the Romans* attributes this greatness to their good fortune. But he was reproved, if rather indirectly, by Torquato Tasso in his noble *Reply of Rome to Plutarch*.

SECTION 13

CHAPTER I

Further Proofs Drawn from Mixed Commonwealths Which Combine Earlier Governments with Later States

[1004] In Book 4, I have offered further evidence to prove that the lives of nations pass through three kinds of commonwealths or civil states. In other words, after their origins in the first divine governments, all nations proceed through the same sequence of human institutions, according to the principles of ideal eternal history outlined in Axioms 65–68. First, they are ruled by aristocracies, next by free democracies, and finally by monarchies. Tacitus names these as the forms of government ordained by the nature of nations, even if he does not specify this order. Apart from these, he notes, constitutions blended by human design are more desirable than feasible, and short-lived when they happen to arise. To eliminate any doubts about this, I shall show how within the natural sequence of civil constitutions, some mixtures occur. Clearly, one form cannot mix with another to produce monstrous hybrids. But sometimes an earlier form of government, or administration, persists and mixes with a later form of state, or constitution. Such a mixture illustrates Axiom 71, which says that, even as people change, they still follow for some time in the tracks of their earlier habits.

[1005] In this way, even after their transition from bestial to human life, the earliest pagan fathers during the religious state of nature retained much of the savagery and cruelty of their recent origin – traits which caused Plato to recognize in Homer's Cyclopes the world's first family fathers. In the same way, even as the first aristocracies were formed, family fathers retained intact the private sovereignty which they had held in the earlier state of nature. Then, since they were all equal and none in his pride yielded to any other, the family fathers submitted only to the public sovereignty of their own ruling orders, which they had created in this aristocratic form of state. In this state, their private dominions united to form the higher public dominion of their senates, just as in the state of nature the private sovereign powers they held over their families had joined to form the sovereign civil power of their social orders. This is the only possible manner in which cities could have been formed, namely, as aristocracies in which the sovereign families were preserved.

[1006] Early commonwealths remained aristocratic as long as the fathers retained their authority of ownership within their ruling orders. But then the laws of the heroic fathers granted the plebeians the certain ownership of fields, marriage rights, sovereign powers, and priesthoods with the attendant knowledge of laws. The plebeians of the heroic cities now grew numerous and warlike besides, which frightened the fathers, who must have been very few in a commonwealth comprising so few citizens. By the force of their numbers, the plebeians began to enact laws without senate authority, so that the commonwealths changed from aristocratic to democratic.

But two supreme legislative powers could not coexist for a moment when there was no distinction between the subjects, times, or territories involved in their legislation. This is why the Publilian law of the dictator Philo declared that the Roman republic had by its nature become democratic. In this change, authority of ownership tended to retain what it could of its changing form, and was naturally transformed into the authority of guardianship. (In the same way, when a father dies, paternal power over minor children becomes the authority of those appointed as guardians.) The newly free peoples now found themselves masters of their own sovereign powers; but like wards attempting to rule, they proved weak in public counsel. In view of the fathers' authority, they naturally let themselves be governed by their guardians, the senates. Hence, these republics were by nature free in their form, but were governed aristocratically. Eventually, the powerful persons in the democracy directed public counsel towards the private interests of their power. By pursuing their own private interests, free peoples let themselves be seduced by the powerful into subjecting their own public freedom to the ambition of others. This led to factions, acts of sedition, and civil wars, which proved ruinous to their nations and introduced the monarchical form into the state.

CHAPTER 2

An Eternal and Natural 'Royal Law' By Which Nations Come to Rest in Monarchies

[1007] The monarchical form was introduced in keeping with the eternal and natural 'royal law', which all nations sensed when they recognized Augustus as the founder of the Roman monarchy. The interpreters of Roman law failed to see this law because they were all engrossed with the myth of the 'royal law' of Tribonian, a law which Tribonian explicitly claims as his own in the *Institutes* but ascribes to Ulpian in the *Digest*. But Roman jurists, who were versed in the natural law of nations, clearly understood this law. Thus, in his brief history of Roman law, Pomponius described this royal law with the insightful phrase, 'when circumstances dictated, kingdoms were founded'.

[1008] This natural royal law is conceived under the following natural and invariable formula of self-interest. In free commonwealths, all citizens are so intent on their private interests that they use public arms to serve them, which leads to the ruin of the nation. To preserve the nation, a single ruler must arise who, like Augustus in Rome, assumes command of the army and thus takes control of all public concerns. At the same time, such a monarch allows his subjects to manage both their private affairs and any part of public affairs he may grant them. This ensures the survival of a people which would otherwise destroy itself.

Professors of law agree on this truth when they say that 'corporations under a king are treated like private persons', since the majority of citizens take no part in the public welfare. In his *Annals*, Tacitus, who was an expert in the law of nations, describes the family succession of the Caesars in terms of the following sequence of political ideas. As

Augustus neared the end of his life, he writes, 'a few vainly discoursed on the benefits of liberty'. On Tiberius' succession, 'everyone awaited the ruler's commands'. Under the next three Caesars, the Romans at first displayed 'indifference', *incuria*, and finally 'an ignorance of the state as of something foreign to them'. Thus, as citizens become a sort of foreigners in their own nations, it proves necessary for monarchs to rule and represent them in their own persons.

In a free commonwealth, a powerful man can become monarch only when the people support his party. This is why monarchies must by nature be popularly governed through the following measures. First, monarchs use laws to establish the equality of all their subjects. Then, by a property of all monarchies, sovereigns humble the powerful in order to keep the masses free and secure from oppression. Next, by a similar property, they see that their subjects' needs are satisfied and their enjoyment of natural liberty assured. Finally, they grant privileges to entire classes, which are called privileges of liberty; and they confer extraordinary civil honours on individuals of exceptional merit by means of special decrees dictated by natural equity. This is why monarchy is the form of government best suited to human nature when it possesses the most developed reason.

CHAPTER 3

A Refutation of the Principles of Political Theory Based on the System of Jean Bodin

[1009] We are now in a position to judge the validity of the principles underlying Jean Bodin's political theory. Bodin places the forms of civil states in the following sequence: first, monarchy; then, after a tyrannical phase, democracy; and finally, aristocracy. This view is thoroughly refuted by the natural sequence of political forms, as demonstrated by countless proofs in my Science. But I would like to go even further and point out what is impossible and absurd in his theory.

[1010] Now, Bodin admits the truth that the first cities were made up of families. But by the common error I noted earlier, he believes that such families included children only. Let us ask him, then: how could monarchies have arisen from such families?

[1011] There are two possible means: either by force or by fraud.

[1012] Was it by force? How could one family father have possibly subdued all the others? For in Bodin's view, democracies came after tyrannies, in which the family fathers had grown accustomed to monarchy, and in which they had vowed themselves and their families to the fatherland as protecting them. Is it not more probable that the family fathers – still Cyclopes recently used to bestial and savage freedom – would have chosen death for themselves and their families, rather than suffer any inequality?

[1013] Was it by fraud? Fraud is the instrument of those who seek kingship in a democracy by seducing others with promises of liberty or power or wealth. But what liberty could anyone promise in the family state, when all the fathers were already sovereigns? What power could be promised, when the Cyclopes by nature lived alone in their caves and, in keeping with their monstrous origin, cared only for their own families with no concern for others? What wealth, when no one in the simplicity and frugality of that early age could conceive such a thing?

[1014] The difficulty grows out of all proportion when we recall that there were no fortresses in early barbarous ages. Indeed, as Thucydides informs us, for many centuries the heroic cities, composed of families, had no walls. In the heroic aristocracies I have described, any violation of this rule was jealously punished as treason to the state. When the Roman consul Valerius Publicola built a house on high ground, he was suspected of attempting to create a tyranny. To acquit himself of these charges, he had the house torn down overnight; and the next morning, before an assembly of the people, he had the lictors throw his consular fasces at their feet. The custom of building cities without walls persisted longest among the fiercest nations. In medieval Germany, we read that Henry the Fowler was the first to gather people who lived in scattered villages into walled cities. So much for the theory that the first founders of cities marked off walls and gates with a plough – whence Latin etymologists derive the word 'portal' from *portando aratro*, 'lifting the plough' where a gate was to open! In the savagery of early medieval Spain, the security of the royal palaces was so inadequate that within a period of sixty years more than eighty members of the royal family were killed. Such crimes were so frequent that the fathers of the Council of Elvira, one of the earliest in the Latin Church, condemned them under pain of excommunication.

[1015] The difficulty becomes infinite when one posits that families included children only. If that were the case, the children must have served the ambitions of others by force or fraud, that is, by betraying or killing their own fathers. And the first cities would have been impious and criminal tyrannies rather than monarchies. Yet when the young Roman patricians conspired against their own fathers in favour of the tyrant Tarquin, they did so out of hatred for the severity of the laws. (Severe laws are proper to aristocracies, just as benign laws are proper to democracies, clement laws to legitimate kingdoms, and corrupt laws to tyrannies.) The young conspirators challenged the laws at the cost of their own lives, including both of Brutus' sons, who were beheaded because their own father imposed the severest penalty on them. This shows us how monarchical the Roman kingdom was, and how democratic its liberty as established by Brutus!

[1016] In the light of such great difficulties, Bodin and all other political thinkers must recognize the family monarchies which existed in the family state. And they must recognize that families included not only children but also family servants, or *famuli*, from which the word family derives. These family servants were the forerunners of the slaves later taken in wars after cities were founded. In this manner, free men and slaves in fact furnished the material of commonwealths, as Bodin correctly says, but not in the way implied by his theory.

[1017] Because free men and slaves are confused in his theory, Bodin is amazed that the people of his own nation were called the Franks, or freemen, when he notes that in their earliest period they were treated like ignoble slaves. For his theory blinded him to the fact that the founding of the nations was only complete when they incorporated the people freed from bondage by the Poetelian Law. The Franks who amaze Bodin are the same as the rustic vassals who, to Hotman's amazement, are called men, *homines*, meaning the plebeians who made up the earliest heroic peoples. It was these masses who transformed aristocracies into democracies and eventually into monarchies. And they did so through their use of vernacular language, in which they conceived the laws of democracy and monarchy. This is why the Romans called their popular language a vernacular, naming it for slaves born in the household – the meaning of *verna* – rather than those taken in war.

We have seen that such family slaves existed in all ancient nations from the age of the family state. This is why the Greeks were no longer called Achaeans, as in Homer's phrase 'sons of the Achaeans', but called themselves Hellenes after Hellen, who first spoke vernacular Greek. In the same way, the Jews were no longer called by their early name 'the sons of Israel', but were now called the Hebrew nation after Heber, whom our Church Fathers regard as the originator of the sacred language. So clearly did Bodin and all the political theorists behold the luminous truth which my Science so vividly demonstrates, especially in Roman history! In every age and in every nation, it is the plebeians who have changed the government from aristocracy to democracy, and from democracy to monarchy. And it is they who, by establishing vernacular languages, have given their names to the nations, as I showed under the Origin of Languages. This why the ancient Franks, to Bodin's amazement, gave their name to France.

[1018] Finally, to consider our own experience, we see that very few aristocracies survive from the medieval age of barbarism: Venice, Genoa, and Lucca in Italy; Ragusa in Dalmatia; and Nuremberg in Germany. (The others cited by Bodin are in fact democratic states with aristocratic administrations.) Now, according to Bodin's theory, the Roman kingdom was a monarchy, and the expulsion of the tyrants introduced democratic liberty in Rome. Hence, Bodin cannot discover in the early period of Roman liberty the effects which should follow from his principles, since they were the effects of an aristocracy. To be sure, Bodin tries to acquit himself honourably by saying that at first the Roman state was democratic but had an aristocratic administration. But in another passage, the force of truth compels him to confess, with shameful inconsistency, that both the state and the government were aristocratic.

[1019] Such errors in political theory were the result of the failure to define three crucial terms: (1) people, (2) liberty, and (3) kingdom.

(1) Everyone thought that the first peoples comprised both plebeians and nobles, but I have shown a thousand times over that only the nobles were included. (2) They thought that the liberty of ancient Rome was popular in nature because it ensured the people's freedom from the patricians. Yet we have seen that it was an aristocratic liberty which ensured the patricians' freedom from the Tarquin tyrants. This is why statues were erected to the slayers of tyrants, who had acted by order of the ruling senates. (3) The kings, living in unprotected palaces amid savage peoples, were aristocrats rather than monarchs. Witness the two lifelong kings at Sparta, which was clearly an aristocracy; and later the two yearly consuls at Rome, whom Cicero in his *Laws* calls annual kings. Livy explicitly declares that the creation of the consulship by Junius Brutus did nothing to change the royal power within the Roman kingdom. Indeed, we observed earlier that appeal could be made to the people during the reign of these yearly kings, and that when their reign had expired they had to give the people an account of their administration. We also observed how kings in the heroic age were dethroned almost every day, as Thucydides tells us. And we compared this with the medieval return of barbarism, in which we read that nothing was more uncertain and variable than the fortune of kingdoms. We pondered the words which open the *Annals* of Tacitus, who often conveys his message by the propriety and force of the words he chooses: 'In the beginning kings had the city of Rome', *Urbem Romam principio reges habuere.* He uses the verb which signifies the weakest of the three degrees of possession distinguished by the jurists, *habere, tenere, possidere*, 'to have, hold, and possess'. And he uses the noun *urbs*, city, which properly means buildings, to denote a possession held by the body rather than *civitas*, the community of citizens who, as a whole or as a majority, established the public law by their minds.

447

SECTION 14
FINAL PROOFS CONFIRMING
THE COURSE OF NATIONS

CHAPTER I
Punishments, Wars, and the Order of Numbers

[1020] In passing, I have mentioned other causes and effects which derive from the principles of my New Science, and thus confirm the natural course of the nations. But since I have touched on them only randomly, I assemble them here, showing how they fit into the natural sequence of human civil institutions.

[1021] Take punishments, for example. In the age of families, punishments displayed a Cyclopean cruelty: thus, for example, Apollo flays Marsyas alive. Such punishments continued under the aristocracies, as when the shield of Perseus turned its beholders to stone. In Greek, such punishments were called *paradeigmata*, examples, just as in Latin they were called *exempla*, exemplary chastisements. (Similarly, during the medieval return of barbarism, the death penalty was called ordinary punishment.) Under the laws of aristocratic Sparta, which Plato and Aristotle deemed savage and cruel, the ephors had to strangle their illustrious king Agis. Under the laws of aristocratic Rome, the celebrated victor Horatius was nearly stripped, caned, and crucified on a barren tree. Under the Law of the Twelve Tables, a person who set fire to another's crops was condemned to be burned alive; false witnesses were hurled from the Tarpeian Rock; and debtors in default were torn limb from limb. Tullus Hostilius did not hesitate to inflict this last punishment on Mettius Fufetius, the king of Alba and his equal, for breaking the terms of their alliance. Even earlier, the patrician fathers had Romulus torn to pieces on the mere suspicion of treason to the state. Let this suffice for those who assert that such punishments were unknown in Rome.

[1022] By contrast, punishments are milder in democracies, because they are ruled by the masses who, being weak, are naturally inclined to compassion. For example, when the great Horatius killed his sister in heroic rage because she wept during the city's rejoicing, he was condemned by the duumvirs, but absolved by the Roman people, in Livy's elegant phrase, more in admiration of his valour than from the justice of his cause. During the age of Athenian liberty, Plato and Aristotle censured the laws of Sparta, as we have seen. And when in the milder age of Rome's democratic freedom Gaius Rabirius was found guilty of treason, Cicero decried the inhuman cruelty of assigning the death penalty to a Roman knight and private citizen. Finally, monarchies arose, in which the rulers are pleased to be called by the gracious title 'Clement'.

[1023] Take wars, for example. These were likewise barbarous during the heroic period. Conquered cities faced ruin, and defeated peoples were converted to herds of day labourers scattered across the countryside to cultivate the fields of the victorious peoples – thus forming the heroic inland colonies. Later, democracies were more magnanimous: while ruled by their senates, they only deprived conquered peoples of the law of heroic nations, but allowed them to enjoy natural law of what Ulpian calls the human nations. (As Rome's conquests expanded, she restricted to Roman citizens all the rights which came to be called 'proper' to them, *propriae civium Romanorum*. These included nuptials, paternal power, proper heirs, heirs through the males or the clan, quiritary or civil ownership, mancipation, usucaption, stipulation, testaments, guardianship, and inheritance. Before they became subject to Rome, free nations must have had all these rights as their own.) Finally, monarchies arose, which seek to make one Rome of the entire Roman world, as did the edict of Antoninus Pius [Caracalla].* It is the hope of great monarchs to make a single city of the entire world. Thus, Alexander the Great used to say that the entire world was for him a single city in which his phalanx was the citadel. As the monarchs sought to make all the subjects equal before the law, the natural law of the nations, as

* The edict extending Roman citizenship in 212 was issued by Caracalla (officially, Marcus Aurelius Antoninus), rather than Antoninus Pius.

formulated in the provinces by Roman praetors, finally became the law of Rome; and the heroic law which had governed her provinces disappeared.

Take jurisprudence. The Roman jurisprudence which in heroic times was entirely based on the Law of the Twelve Tables, had by Cicero's day (as he informs us in his dialogue *On Laws*) begun to follow the edicts of Roman praetors; and from the emperor Hadrian onwards, it dealt exclusively with the Perpetual Edict, which was assembled and arranged by Salvius Julianus almost entirely from provincial edicts.

[1024] Take territories. Beginning from small districts which are governed well by aristocracies, nations expand to the larger provinces which democracies tend to conquer, and finally arrive at monarchies, which derive their beauty and magnificence from their great size.

[1025] Take political passions. Nations pass from the deadly suspicions of aristocracies, through the feverish turmoil of democracies, and finally come to rest under monarchies.

[1026] Take numbers, as a last example. The progression of numbers, which are abstract and simple, corresponds to the order of human civil institutions, which are concrete and complex. Governments began with the one in the unit of the family monarchies; passed to the few of heroic aristocracies; advanced to the many and the all in democracies, in which all the citizens or the majority make up the body politic; and finally returned to the one in civil monarchies. By the very nature of numbers, we cannot conceive a more comprehensive division or a different order than one, few, many, and all. Yet in this progression, each quantity retains unity as its basic principle, since numbers consist of indivisible units, as Aristotle says. And after we have passed through the totality of the All, we must return to the unity of the One. Thus, all of human civilization is contained between the family monarchies and the civil monarchies.

CHAPTER 2

Corollary: Ancient Roman Law as Serious Epic Poem,
and Ancient Jurisprudence as Severe Poetry Containing
the First Rough Outlines of Legal Metaphysics; also,
the Legal Origins of Greek Philosophy

[1027] There are many other great effects, especially in Roman jurisprudence, whose causes must be traced to the same principles. We know, for example, that people are naturally inclined to seek what is true, and when the truth eludes them, they hold to what is certain, as Axiom 9 states. This is why mancipations were originally performed by an *actual hand*, *vera manu*, which meant real force: since force is abstract, and hand is concrete. In all nations, the hand signified power. Thus, the Greeks spoke of the 'laying on of hands', *cheirothesiai*, by which persons elected to power were confirmed by having hands laid on their heads. And they spoke of the 'raising of hands', *cheirotoniai*, by which powers already confirmed were acclaimed by raising hands in the air. Such solemnities are proper to wordless ages. In the medieval return of barbarism, newly elected kings were acclaimed in this way. Actual mancipation was an act of occupation, the first great natural source of all ownership. The Romans preserved this notion in their wars, in which slaves taken were called *mancipia*, mancipated. Booty and conquests passed to the Romans as *res mancipi*, or legal possessions; but to the vanquished, Roman victory made them *res nec mancipi*, or precarious possessions. We see, then, how true it is that mancipation began exclusively within Rome's city walls as a means of acquiring civil ownership in the private transactions of Romans!

[1028] Actual mancipation was followed by a similar act of physical 'usucaption', that is, the acquisition of ownership through actual use. (In Latin, *usus*, use, can mean possession; and *capio*, taking, means acquisition.) For possession was initially exercised when the things possessed were physically occupied. Indeed, Latin *possessio* must derive from *porro sessio*, continued sitting, just as Romans later called a domicile *sedes*, seat, from the continuous act of sitting or staying put. Latin

451

etymologists err in deriving possession from *pedum positio*, placing the feet. For it was possession by settlement, *sedes*, rather than by standing, *pedes*, which Roman praetors defended and upheld in their interdicts. The name Theseus must derive from the Greek *thesis*, in the sense of settlement, rather than handsome posture, as Greek etymologists say: for the people of Attica founded Athens by remaining settled there for a long time. In all nations, such usucaption is the act which legitimates all the forms of social status of all nations.

[1029] Furthermore, Aristotle describes heroic commonwealths which had no laws to right private wrongs. In them, property claims, *rei vindicationes*, were asserted with real force, which were the world's first duels or private wars. And the claims of restitution known as condictions were in fact private reprisals, which persisted until the age of Bartolus during the medieval return of barbarism.

[1030] Later, the ferocity of the age diminished, and judicial laws began to prohibit private acts of violence, so that all private forces were united in the public force called civil sovereignty. But by their poetic nature, the first peoples naturally continuted to imitate the real forces which they had formerly used earlier to preserve their rights and authority. So they created a myth of natural mancipation, and from it derived the solemn act of civil transfer, which they symbolized by handing over a symbolic knot. This knot represented the chain with which Jupiter had bound the giants to the first vacant lands, and with which the first peoples had chained their clients, or family servants, to the land. By this myth-based mancipation, they performed all their civil business using what were called 'legal acts', which must have originated as the solemn ceremonies of mute peoples.

Later, when articulate speech had been formed, and both parties to a contract wished to make certain of the other's will, they decided that agreements should be clothed in solemn words uttered as the knot was handed over. These solemn words declared certain and precise stipulations, and later in wartime they declared the terms under which conquered cities surrendered. These terms were called peaces, *paci* in Italian, from Latin *pacio*, covenant, which is synonymous with *pactum*, agreement. An important trace of this survived in the formula declaring the surrender of Collatia. As Livy describes it, the formula is a contract of receiving under one's power, in the form of solemn questions and answers. With great propriety, those surrendering were said to be received, *recepti*. When he received the embassy from Collatia, the Roman herald responded 'And I receive them', *Et ego recipio*. So much for the notion that in the heroic age only Roman citizens could make stipulations! And so much for the commonsense of those who believed that Tarquinius Priscus used the surrender formula of Collatia to instruct the nations in the conduct of surrenders!

[1031] The law of the heroic Latin peoples thus became fixed in the famous article of the Law of the Twelve Tables: 'Whoever shall make bond or conveyance, as he has declared with his tongue, so shall it be binding.' This is the great source of all ancient Roman law, and even those who equate Roman and Attic law confess that it was not brought to Rome from Athens.

[1032] At first, usucaption was effected through physical possession. Later, it was merely feigned, and possession was assured by a mental agreement. In the same way, property claims came to be symbolized by a feigned use of force. And heroic reprisals later turned into personal actions, or claims of restitution, which still retained the solemn formality of declaring the claim to the debtor. This was the only means available in the childhood of the world. For children excel in imitating the truth they can understand; and poetry, which is simply a form of imitation, depends on this ability, as Axiom 52 states.

[1033] In the public square, there were as many masks as there were persons, for in Latin *persona* properly means a mask. And there were as many names: for in the age of wordless speech, which used physical objects for words, names must have been the family coats-of-arms. (We have seen that American Indians distinguish their families by using such totemic symbols.) The person, or mask, of a family father stood for all his children and family servants. And the physical object, or emblem, of a house stood for all the relatives through the males or the clan. For example, we have seen that Ajax was the tower of the Greeks, and that Horatius alone on the bridge withstood the entire Etruscan nation. Then, in the medieval return of barbarism, we read of forty Norman heroes who drove an entire Saracen army out of Salerno. This accounts for the belief in the astounding strength of the paladins of France –

sovereign rulers whose name survived in the counts palatine of Germany – and especially of Count Roland, later called Orlando. The reason for this lies in the poetic principles by which the founders of Roman law, living in an age which could not grasp intelligible universals, created imaginative universals. Where poets by *art* later brought characters and masks onto the stage, these men by *nature* had already brought names and persons to the public forum.

[1034] Clearly, the noun *persona*, mask, cannot derive from the verb *personare*, to resound everywhere. As Horace tells us, early cities had quite small theatres in which the few spectators were easily counted; so that such masks were not needed to make the actors' voices resound enough to fill a large theatre. (Besides, the length of the second syllable argues against this root: the *o* in *persona* is long, but the *o* in *personare* is short.) Instead, *persona* must derive from the verb *per-sonari*, which we may conjecture meant to wear the skins of wild beasts, something only heroes were allowed to do. From this root, the related verb *ob-sonari* is attested, which must originally have meant to feed on the meat of hunted game. Such game must have provided the heroes' 'first rich feasts' which Virgil describes. And the skins of slain beasts must have been the 'first rich spoils' brought back by the heroes from the first wars they fought against wild beasts to defend themselves and their families. Indeed, the poets clothe their heroes in such skins, and above all others Hercules, who wears a lionskin. We may conjecture that this origin of the verb *personari*, with its primary sense restored, gave rise to the Italian use of *personaggi*, personages, to denote persons of high station and great prominence.

[1035] By the same principles, since early people could not grasp abstract forms, they imagined corporeal forms, which they endowed with their own animate nature. For example, they imagined Inheritance as the mistress of hereditary property, and perceived her complete presence in every single article of a legacy. In precisely this way, they would take a lump or clod from a farm and present it to the judge, calling it 'this land', *hunc fundum*, in their formula for claiming restitution. Thus, even if they did not understand, they at least crudely sensed that rights were indivisible.

[1036] In conformity with this nature, ancient jurisprudence was thoroughly poetic. It imagined the real as unreal, the unreal as real, the living as dead, and (in cases of pending legacies) the dead as still alive. It introduced many empty masks without subjects, *iura imaginaria*, rights invented by the imagination. Its entire reputation depended on the invention of myths which could preserve the dignity of the laws and administer justice to the facts. Thus all the fictions of ancient jurisprudence were masked truths. And since their strict measures used exactly so many words, the formulas in which the laws spoke were called songs, *carmina*, which is Livy's term for the formula condemning Horatius to death. This is confirmed by a golden passage in Plautus' *Comedy of Asses*, in which the youth Diabolus calls the parasite a great *poet* because he excels in devising formulas and clauses, which were also called songs, *carmina*.

[1037] In this way, all of Roman law was a serious poem, acted out by the Romans in their forum; and ancient jurisprudence was a severe kind of poetry. Quite aptly for my point, Justinian in the preface to his Institutes speaks of the 'myths of ancient law', *antiqui iuris fabulae*. The phrase must be taken from some ancient jurist who understood what we are discussing, even if Justinian cites it derisively. Roman jurisprudence based its principles on such ancient myths. And the doctrine of personal rights, *de iure personarum*, traces its origins to the masks called *personae* that were used in the true and severe mythical dramas.

[1038] When the civilized age of democracies arrived, human intellect began to play a role in civic assemblies. The universal concepts abstracted by the intellect were now said to 'exist in the understanding of the law'. This meant the understanding of the intention, or *ius*, expressed by the lawmaker in his law, which in turn reflected the intention of the citizens who agreed on a rational notion of their common advantage. They must have understood such advantage as spiritual in nature, for all the rights unattached to physical objects (called *nuda iura*, rights without materiality) were said to exist in the understanding of the law. Such rights are spiritual in substance, and are therefore indivisible and also eternal: for corruption is simply the division and breakdown of elements.

[1039] Now, interpreters of Roman law have based the entire reputation of legal metaphysics on the notion of indivisible rights: witness the famous legal question On Divisibles and Indivisibles. But they have neglected another principle of Roman law, its eternity, which is no less important and which should have been obvious from two rules of law. The first rule states that 'If the purpose of a law ceases, the law ceases', *cessante fine legis, cessat lex*. (Note that this rule does not say 'if the reason of the law ceases', *cessante ratione*, because this reason is the conformity of the law to the facts as clothed in certain circumstances; and when the facts are so clothed, the reason of the law lives and governs them. Instead, it specifies the 'purpose of the law', which being defined as the equal benefit to all causes, may not always be attained.)

The second rule states that 'Time is not a restriction which creates or destroys a right.' Time can neither begin nor end what is eternal. In cases of usucaption and prescription, time neither creates nor abolishes rights, but merely indicates that the holder of these rights intends to relinquish them. For example, when we say that usufruct terminates, we do not mean that the right terminates, but simply that it returns from servitude to its original freedom. Two important corollaries follow from these rules. First, since rights exist eternally in the understanding as an idea, but men have their being in time, rights can only come to mankind from God. Second, all the diverse and countless rights that have been, are now, or ever will be in the world, are diverse modifications of the power of the first man, who was the ruler of the human race, and of the dominion he held over the entire earth.

[1040] We know for certain that laws existed before philosophers. In order for Socrates to sketch his intelligible general categories or abstract universals, he must have observed how the citizens of Athens passed laws by agreeing on a common notion of equal benefit to all. Socrates did this by means of induction, which means assembling uniform particulars to make up a general category characterized by this uniformity.

[1041] In civic assemblies, individuals passionately pursue their own private advantage, but they all dispassionately agree on a notion of their common advantage. (This is the source of the saying 'Separately men are led by their private interests, but collectively they seek justice.') It was by observing this that Plato raised himself to contemplate the highest intelligible ideas of created minds. These ideas are distinct from the created minds, and can reside only in God. In this way, Plato arrived at his lofty conception of a philosophical hero who commands his passions at will.

[1042] Next, Aristotle formulated his divine definition of a good law as a will free of passions, which means the will of a hero. And he understood justice as a queen of the virtues, residing in the hero's soul and commanding all the others. For he had observed how legal justice, residing in the soul of sovereign civil power, commands prudence in the legislature, fortitude in the army, and moderation in festival celebrations. And he saw that justice commands two particular kinds of justice: distributive justice in the public treasury, based on geometrical proportion; and commutative justice in the forum, based on arithmetical proportion. He must have observed distributive justice in the census, which is the basis of democracies and which distributes honours and taxes using the geometrical proportions of citizens' estates.

Before Aristotle's day, people only understood arithmetical proportion. This is why Astraea, goddess of heroic justice, is depicted with a balance. And it is why we read that the Law of the Twelve Tables punished financial crimes by twice the damages, *duplio*, and physical harm by injury in kind, *talio*. As the inventor of the law of retaliation, Rhadamanthus was made a judge in the underworld, where punishments are clearly assigned. When Aristotle in his *Ethics* calls retaliation 'Pythagorean justice', he is referring to the mythical Pythagoras who founded a nation in Magna Graecia whose nobles were called Pythagoreans. For such an invention would be a disgrace if attributed to the Pythagoras who became a sublime philosopher and mathematician.

[1043] We may therefore conclude that all the principles of metaphysics, logic, and ethics originated in the public square in Athens. As we said in a corollary of Poetic Logic, Solon's advice to the Athenians, 'Know thyself', gave rise to democracies, which gave rise to laws, which in turn gave rise to philosophy. And Solon, a sage of vernacular wisdom, was believed to be a sage of esoteric wisdom. This may be viewed as a fragment of the history of philosophy recounted philosophically, and as the last of many confutations presented in this work against the remark of Polybius that, if there were philosophers in the world, there would be no need for religions. But if in fact there had been no religions, and hence no commonwealths, there would have been no philosophers in the world. And if providence had not guided human affairs, there would have been no notion of either science or virtue.

[1044] To conclude this argument, it was during the humane ages of democracy and then monarchy that people first understood the nature of legal causes, *causae*. At first, these causes were precautionary formulas with proper and precise wording. From taking precautions, *cavere*, they were called *cavissae*, a form later shortened to *caussae*. In consensual contracts, such causes were found to be identical with the affairs or transactions themselves. Today such affairs or transactions are solemnized by pacts, which are agreed upon in the act of contract in order to produce actions. In contracts which constitute valid titles for the transfer of ownership, these agreements solemnized the natural delivery in order to effect the transfer. Only in those contracts said to be completed by verbal agreement, or stipulations, did precautionary formulas remain causes in the strict original sense. This should shed more light on my earlier discussion of the obligations arising from contracts and agreements.

[1045] To sum up, a human being properly consists only of mind, body, and speech, with the last as a sort of intermediate between mind and body. In questions of justice, *certainty* in wordless ages was at first understood in bodily terms. Later, when articulate speech had been invented, it passed to certain ideas expressed by verbal formulas. Finally, when the human mind had fully developed its reason, it reached its final stage in the *truth* of ideas about justice, which were determined by the particular factual circumstances of a case. This truth is a formless formula, which the learned Varro calls the formula of nature, *formula naturae*. When this truth is diffused over the external aspects of a case, it acts like light in giving form to their minutest details, as Axiom 113 states.

BOOK 5
THE RESURGENCE OF NATIONS AND THE RECURRENCE OF HUMAN INSTITUTIONS

INTRODUCTION

[1046] Countless passages in my *New Science* have shown us the astonishing correspondence between the barbarism of antiquity and its medieval return. For the resurgence of nations entails the recurrence of human institutions. In order to offer the reader more thorough proof of this point, I have chosen to devote this last book of my *Science* to this particular subject. This will shed greater light on the second barbarism of the medieval period, which has remained even more obscure than that of the first barbarism, called the 'dark age' by Varro, the greatest scholar of early antiquities. And it will show how God, the Best and Greatest, has used the counsels of his providence, which guides the human institutions of all nations, to serve the ineffable decrees of his grace.

CHAPTER I

Medieval Barbaric History Illuminated by Ancient Barbaric History

[1047] In late antiquity, providence acted in superhuman ways. It revealed and confirmed the truth of the Christian religion by setting the virtue of martyrs against the power of Rome, and the teaching of the Fathers and the holy miracles of saints against the vain wisdom of Greece. But later, when armed nations rose up to combat the true divinity of their Creator, providence allowed the birth of a new order of human civilization among the nations, by which the true religion was firmly established within the natural course of human institutions.

[1048] By this eternal counsel, providence restored the truly divine ages of antiquity: for Catholic kings everywhere, like heroic priests, swore to defend the Christian religion as its protectors. They put on the dalmatics of church deacons. They consecrated their royal persons, which is why they still retain the title Sacred Royal Majesty. They took ecclesiastical orders. (In his *Genealogy of the Kings of France*, Symphorien Champier writes that Hugh Capet took the title of Count and Abbot of Paris. In his *Annals of Burgundy*, Guillaume Paradin cites ancient documents in which the rulers of France bore joint titles such as Duke and Abbot or Count and Abbot.) And these first Christian kings founded military religious orders. In this way, they re-established the Catholic religion in their realms against the Arians, who had polluted nearly all the world, according to St Jerome; against the Saracens; and against numerous other infidels.

[1049] This marked the true return of what heroic peoples had called pure and pious wars; which is why the crowns of all Christian powers still bear the cross raised on a globe, an emblem which they once displayed on their banners in fighting the wars they called crusades, or wars of the cross.

[1050] The recurrence of civil human institutions during the medieval return of barbarism is truly astonishing. We recall that, when ancient heralds declared war on an enemy city, they literally 'called out their gods', to cite the elegant and splendid formula which Macrobius has preserved. For they believed that this would deprive conquered peoples of gods, and thus of the auspices which are an essential principle of civilization. Indeed, under the heroic law of victory, conquered peoples were left without civil rights, public or private, which depended on the auspices. This was entirely encompassed by the heroic formula of surrender, such as that used by Tarquinius Priscus at Collatia, by which the conquered people relinquished all their sacred and secular institutions to the victors.

In just this way, whenever medieval barbarians had captured a city, their first concern was to find and carry away any famous remains or relics of saints. This is why people in that age took such great care in burying or hiding these remains, and why we find such repositories in the innermost and deepest recesses of churches everywhere. And it is why nearly all the removals of saints' bodies took place during the medieval period. A trace of this custom persists today, when conquered townspeople must pay the victors ransom for the bells of their city.

[1051] By the fifth century, moreover, many barbaric nations had begun to inundate Europe, Africa, and Asia; and neither conquerors nor conquered could understand each other's language. In their barbarism, the invaders, as enemies of the Christian religion, destroyed all written trace of the vernacular languages of this new Iron Age – whether Italian, French, Spanish, or German. (In his *Annals of Bavaria*, Johannes Aventinus says that the Germans only began to write documents in their own language during the age of the emperor Frederick II; and others date this from the age of Rudolph I.) In all these nations, we find writings solely in barbarous Latin, which was understood by only a handful of nobles who were also clerics. During those unfortunate centuries, we may surmise that the nations reverted to wordless speech, using mute signs. And since vernacular writing was rare, they must have reverted to the symbolic writing of hieroglyphics: witness their family coats of arms, which proved ownership by signifying the rights acquired by a lord over such things as houses, graves, fields, and flocks.

[1052] Certain kinds of divine judgments returned, which were called 'canonical purgations'. By contrast, medieval canon law did not recognize duels, which were the divine judgments of heroic antiquity.

[1053] Heroic raids returned, and it became a title of nobility to be a corsair, just as ancient heroes considered it an honour to be called brigands.

[1054] Heroic reprisals returned, and persisted until the age of Bartolus.

[1055] Heroic slavery returned and persisted for many years, even among Christian nations. All the wars of the medieval barbarism were religious in nature, like those of heroic antiquity. When heroic duels were customary, conquerors believed that the conquered had no God, and so considered them no better than beasts. This nationalistic feeling persists even today between Christians and Turks. To a Christian, the name Turk means a dog; and the Turks call Christians swine. (Christians who want or have to treat Turks politely call them Moslems, which means true believers.) In their wars, both nations practise heroic slavery, although the Christians do so more humanely.

[1056] The most astonishing recurrence among human institutions is the medieval return of the world's first refuges, on which Livy writes that all the first cities were founded. In the utter savagery and ferocity of these barbarous centuries, violence, robbery, and murder were rampant everywhere. So there was no effective means of restraining such people, bound by no human laws, except the divine laws dictated by religion, as Axiom 31 states. Since in the barbarous violence of those centuries the only relatively humane people were bishops and abbots, it was to them that people appealed when they feared oppression or destruction. They placed themselves, their families, and their property in the care of these prelates, who in turn offered them refuge and protection. This exchange of submission and protection is the principal element which constitutes a fief. In Germany, which was clearly the most savage and ferocious of the European nations, there came to be almost more clerical sovereigns – bishops or abbots – than there were secular ones. In France, all the sovereign rulers took the title of Count and *Abbot* or Duke and *Abbot*.

An immense number of cities, towns, and castles in Europe take their names from saints. For people who wished to hear mass and the other holy offices of our religion built little churches on elevated or protected sites, which we may define as the Christians' natural refuges in that age. Then they built their dwellings nearby. Everywhere in Europe, the most ancient traces of medieval barbarism are the little churches built on such sites, now for the most part in ruins. A notable example of this is our local abbey of San Lorenzo of Aversa, with which the abbey of San Lorenzo of Capua was united. Either directly or through dependent abbots and monks, the abbey of San Lorenzo once governed 110 churches between the Volturno river and the gulf of Taranto, in an area covering the ancient regions of Campania, Samnium, Apulia, and Calabria. And the abbots of San Lorenzo were the barons of nearly all these places.

CHAPTER 2

The Recurrence of the Invariable Nature of Fiefs, and the Recurrence of Ancient Roman Law in Feudal Law

[1057] As in antiquity, this divine age was succeeded by a heroic age, marked by the return of a clear distinction between the heroic and the human, which were nearly opposite in nature. This contrast explains why in feudal language rustic vassals are simply called men, *homines*, an expression that amazed Hotman. And from *homines* were derived the two feudal synonyms for vassalage, *hominium* and *homagium*. *Hominium* stands for *hominis dominium*, the ownership of a vassal by a baron. Jacques Cujas notes that Helmodius thought this noun more elegant than *hominagium*, which stands for *hominis agium*, the baron's right to 'lead the vassal' wherever he chooses. Learned feudalists translate the barbarous term *hominagium* by the elegant Latin noun *obsequium*, allegiance: for the two are interchangeable, and the latter originally meant the readiness of a man to follow, *obsequi*, a hero anywhere to till his fields. The principal sense of this allegiance is the loyalty which a vassal owes his baron; and the Latin noun *obsequium* means both the homage and the loyalty which must be sworn when a fief is invested.

Among the ancient Romans, such allegiance was inseparable from military service, which they called *opera militaris* and which our feudalists call *militare servitium*. As Roman history shows, this was the service which for many years the Roman plebeians furnished at their own expense to the patricians during wartime. Even freedmen, *liberti*, continued to owe their patrons this allegiance and its attendant services. As we have seen, this duty dates from Romulus' foundation of Rome on the basis of clientships, the form of protection he offered to the peasant day labourers when he offered them refuge. As Axiom 82 indicates, the clientships of ancient history cannot be explained more properly than as fiefs. Indeed, learned feudalists translate the barbarous term *feudum* by the elegant Latin noun *clientela*, clientship.

[1058] The etymologies of the Latin nouns *opera*, labour, and *servitium*, service, offer cogent proof of the origins of these institutions. In its original sense, *opera* is the day's labour of a peasant, whom the Romans called *operarius*, labourer, and Italians call *giornaliere*, day labourer. When Agamemnon wrongfully seizes Briseis, Achilles protests that he has been treated like a day labourer with no rights as a citizen. In Latin, these workers came to be called herds of labourers, *greges operarum*, and even herds of slaves, *greges servorum*. For the heroes regarded them, like slaves later, as beasts, which are said to graze in herds, *pasci gregatim*. In fact, herds of men must have preceded herds of beasts; since these herds were interchangeable, shepherds of men must have preceded shepherds of flocks and herds. This is why Homer always gives his heroes the invariable epithet 'shepherd of the people'. We find confirmation of this in the Greek noun *nomos*, which means both law and pasturage. For the first agrarian law granted the rebellious family servants sustenance on the lands assigned them by the heroes. And this sustenance was called *nomos*, or pasturage, which is the word proper to beasts, just as food is proper to human beings.

[1059] The task of pasturing the world's first herds must properly have belonged to Apollo, who was the god of civil light, meaning the nobility. Mythical history depicts him as a shepherd on the banks of the Amphrysus. Another such shepherd was Paris, who was clearly a royal prince of Troy. A shepherd as well was the family father portrayed on the shield of Achilles. Homer calls him a king, and he uses a sceptre to command his harvesters as they divide a roasted ox. In the history of the world depicted on the shield of Achilles, this scene records the age of families. It is the task of our shepherds today not only to feed their flocks and herds, but also to guide and to guard them. But since raids were prevalent in the heroic age, this pastoral art must have been introduced after the boundaries of the first cities had been secured. This explains why bucolic or pastoral poetry only arose in ages of advanced civilization: with Theocritus among the Greeks, with Virgil among the Romans, and with Sannazaro among the Italians.

[1060] The Latin word for service, *servitium*, shows that these heroic institutions recurred during the medieval age of barbarism. By contrast to his vassals, the baron was called an elder, *senior*, which meant lord, *signore*. The ancient Franks who surprised Bodin must have been servants born in the house, who were generally the same as the family servants called *vernae* by the ancient Romans. The latter gave their name to the vernacular languages introduced by the masses, which were originally the plebeians of the heroic cities. By contrast, poetic language was introduced by the heroes or nobles of the early commonwealths.

[1061] Later, civil wars, which render the mighty dependent on the people, caused the power of the barons to be dispersed and dissipated. This power was easily absorbed by monarchical kings; and the fealty of freedmen developed into allegiance to the ruler, *obsequium principis*, which in Tacitus' view constitutes the entire duty of subjects in a monarchy. But feudal titles continued to reflect a belief in the difference between two natures, one heroic and one human. Feudal lords were called 'barons', a term which, like the heroes of the poetic Greeks and the *viri* of the ancient Romans, simply meant men, a sense preserved in Spanish *varón*, man. By contrast, vassals, being weak, were called women, in the heroic sense we discussed earlier.

[1062] Furthermore, the Italian word for barons, *signori*, is clearly derived from Latin *seniores*, elders, who must have made up the first public parliaments in the new European kingdoms. In precisely this way, Romulus called his public council the senate because he naturally filled it with the senior members of the patriciate. Just as the senate fathers were called *patres*, owners who freed their slaves were called *patroni*, patrons, from which is derived Italian *padroni*, which means protectors with all the propriety and elegance of its Latin original. Conversely, the term *clientes*, clients, was used with equal elegance and propriety to mean the rustic vassals to whom Servius Tullius granted fiefs: for in decreeing the census, he changed as little as possible the 'clientships' of Romulus. These clients correspond precisely to the freedmen, *affranchiti*, who gave their name to the nation of the Franks, as noted in my reply to Bodin.

[1063] In this manner, fiefs returned, springing from the eternal sources of fiefs described in Axioms 80–81. (We saw that fiefs offer all the 'benefits' we hope to gain from civil society, and hence are properly and elegantly called *beneficia* by learned feudalists. This is noted without further comment by Hotman, who observes that in conquered lands the victors kept the cultivated fields for themselves, but allowed the poor conquered people to sustain themselves on the uncultivated fields.)

When the world's first fiefs returned, they had by nature to originate in personal rural fiefs like the clientships of Romulus. (These were scattered throughout the ancient world of nations, as Axiom 82 states.) Later, when Rome was resplendent with popular liberty, these heroic clientships developed flocks of plebeians, who practised the custom of daily salutations. Dressed in togas, the plebeians each morning went to pay court to their great lords, whom they saluted with the title of ancient heroes 'Hail, king!', *Ave rex*. By day, they accompanied them to the forum, and in the evening returned home with them. Here, their lordly patrons gave them dinner, just as the 'shepherds of the people' fed their flocks in heroic antiquity.

[1064] Among the ancient Romans, the first bondsmen, *vades*, must have been just such personal vassals. Later, the term came to mean the defendants who were obliged to appear in courts with the plaintiffs; and this obligation was called a *vadimonium*. The plural form *vades* must derive from a nominative *vas*, which the Greeks called *bas*, and the barbarians *was*, from which were derived *wassus* and eventually *vassalus*. (This is noted in the Origins of the Latin Language found in the first edition of my *New Science*.) Today, such vassals are found in great numbers in the realms of the cold North, which still retain many features of barbarism. This is especially true in Poland, where a vassal is called *kmiets* and is a kind of slave. Indeed, Polish counts gamble away entire families of these vassals, who are obliged to pass to the service of new masters. In the ancient myth, these vassals are represented by the people whose ears are linked to the Gallic Hercules by a chain of poetic gold, or grain, which stretches forth from his mouth and with which he leads them wherever he chooses.

[1065] Personal rural fiefs developed into 'real' rural fiefs with the first agrarian law. This was the law by which Servius Tullius decreed the first Roman census, and by which the plebeians were granted bonitary ownership of fields, which the patricians now assigned them under both personal and real burdens. These plebeians must have been the first lessees, *mancipes*, a term which came to be applied to those with real estate debts to the public treasury. Of the same kind, no doubt, were those conquered people described by Hotman, to whom the victors granted uncultivated fields which they could till for their own sustenance. Thus returned the Antaeuses, bound to the soil by the Greek Hercules, and the bondsmen, *nexi*, of the god Fidius, the Roman Hercules, who were eventually released by the Poetelian law.

[1066] The bondsmen freed by the Poetelian Law correspond exactly to medieval vassals, who were initially called 'lieges' because they were bound, *legati*, by such a knot. Our feudalists define them as men who must recognize their lord's friends and enemies as their own, which is precisely the oath which Tacitus says the ancient Germans swore, pledging themselves to serve the glory of their chieftains. Later, when fiefs had attained the splendour of political sovereignty, liege vassals included the conquered kings to whom the Roman people gave kingdoms as a gift, *regna dono dabat*: for this solemn formula, recorded in Roman history, means they gave them in fief, *dabat beneficio*. Later, such kings were allied to Rome by a so-called unequal league, *foedus inaequale*, and were called 'royal friends' of the Roman people, just as later emperors called noble courtiers their friends. This kind of unequal alliance was merely the investiture of a sovereign fief expressed by the formula that Livy cites, that the allied king must 'preserve the majesty of the Roman people'. (In the same way, the jurist Paulus [Proculus] says that the praetor renders justice while 'preserving the majesty of the Roman people'.* In other words, he renders justice to those to whom the laws grant it, and withholds it from those to whom the law denies it.) Such allied kings were thus lords of sovereign fiefs subject to a greater sovereignty. This restored to Europe a common notion of the title Majesty, which is reserved for the great kings who are lords of large kingdoms with numerous provinces.

[1067] Together with the rural fief, which gave rise to other institutions, there returned the *emphyteusis*, a long-term or perpetual farm lease, by which in antiquity the earth's great forests had been cultivated. From such contracts, the lease premium, Italian *laudemio*, came to mean both the vassal's payment to his lord and the rural tenant's rent to his landlord.

[1068] There returned the ancient Roman clientships, now called commendations. Hence, with Latin elegance and propriety, learned

---

* For Proculus, Vico mistakenly writes 'Paulus'.

feudalists call vassals clients, *clientes*, and their fiefs clientships, *clientelae*.

[1069] There returned the census of the kind instituted by Servius Tullius, under which for many years the Roman plebeians offered the patricians wartime service at their own expense. These medieval vassals were known as *angarii* or *perangarii*, men who rendered required services. They were the equivalent of the ancient Roman *assidui*, tribute-payers, so called because they fought at their own expense, *suis assibus militabant*. For until the Poetelian Law released the plebeians from the feudal law of obligation, *nexum*, Roman patricians had a similar right of private imprisonment over plebeian debtors.

[1070] There returned the *precaria*, or 'provisional tenancies'. Originally, these were lands granted by lords in response to the entreaties, *preces*, of the poor, who wished to sustain themselves by cultivating them. Precisely this kind of simple possession is nowhere recognized in the Law of the Twelve Tables.

[1071] The violence inherent in barbarous society destroys the trust on which commerce depends, and forces people to think only of the bare necessities of life. All medieval rents had to be paid in what are called natural products, which gave rise to the *libellus*, or annual deed of lease, for the exchange of real estate. This offered obvious advantages. When people owned fields producing crops which others lacked, they would simply exchange some of their property.

[1072] There returned mancipations, by which a vassal placed his hands in those of his lord as a token of his fealty and submission. The rural vassals created by the census of Servius Tullius were the Romans' first *mancipes*. With mancipation there returned the division of property into conveyable, *res mancipi*, and non-conveyable, *res nec mancipi*. Thus, feudal estates were *nec mancipi* for the vassal, who cannot alienate them, but *mancipi* for their lord; precisely as estates in the Roman provinces were non-conveyable for the provincials, but conveyable for Roman citizens. With the act of mancipation there returned stipulations, also called infestucations or investitures, which are synonymous, as we have seen. With stipulations there returned precautionary clauses. (In ancient jurisprudence, these were originally called *cavissae*, a form later shortened to *caussae*. In the medieval return of barbarism, they were called *cautelae* from the same Latin root.) Since all contracts in that age were feudal, the use of these clauses to solemnize pacts and contracts was called *homologare* after the *homines*, vassals, from which *hominium* and *hominagium* also derived. With these clauses, there returned pacts which were guaranteed in the act of mancipation. Roman jurists called these stipulated pacts *pacta stipulata*, after the *stipula* or stalk which clothes the grain. In the same sense, medieval doctors of law named vested pacts *pacta vestita*, for their investitures, which were also called infestucations. Using the same expression in the same sense, jurists of both periods called pacts without safeguards 'naked pacts', *pacta nuda*.

[1073] There returned two kinds of ownership, direct and useful – *dominium directum* and *dominium utile* – which correspond exactly to the quiritary and bonitary ownership of the ancient Romans. Direct ownership originated in the same way as the Romans' quiritary ownership, which was the ownership of lands granted by the patricians to the plebeians. When the plebeians' possession lapsed, they had recourse to the claim for restitution, expressed in the formula 'I declare this ground mine by quiritary right.' This claim was in fact a citation of the patrician order – the only true citizens of Rome under the aristocracy – as the authority from which the plebeians derived the civil ownership entitling them to claim lands. The Law of the Twelve Tables always calls this sort of ownership *auctoritas*, meaning the authority of ownership held by the ruling senate over the Roman territory at large. Later, with the advent of popular liberty, the sovereign command, or *imperium*, over this territory passed to the Roman people.

[1074] Here, as with countless other institutions, my New Science uses the antiquities of the first barbarism to shed light on the 'authority' of the second barbarism. (Indeed, the later medieval period proves more obscure than the earlier classical one!) Medieval authority has left three conspicuous traces in three feudal terms: *directus, laudemio, laudo*. (1) The Latin adjective *directus* proves that the claim for restitution was at first authorized directly by the immediate overlord. (2) The Italian *laudemio*, lease premium, refers to the vassal's payment when he takes possession of a fief by the citation, *laudatio*, of his lord's authority. (3) The Italian *laudo*, ruling, originally a judge's ruling, later came to mean what is called an arbitrated decision. For such feudal cases apparently ended in friendly terms, in contrast to the judgments concerning allodia, or freeholds, which the contending lords originally decided by armed duels. (In Budé's view, the medieval Latin *allodium* derives from *allaudium*, just as Italian *lode* derives from *laude*.) This custom persists even today in the Kingdom of Naples, where barons use duels rather than civil suits to avenge the incursions of rival barons into their feudal territories. Like the quiritary ownership of the ancient Romans, the direct ownership of medieval barbarians eventually came to mean an ownership which produces a real civil suit.

[1075] Here is another shining example of the recurrence of national institutions, namely, the recurrent fate of Roman law at the hands of the later Roman jurists and the more recent medieval doctors of law. We have seen countless times that the jurists of late antiquity lost sight of ancient Roman law. Just so, we find that the medieval legal doctors lost sight of ancient feudal law. For the learned interpreters of Roman law stoutly deny that their jurisprudence recognizes the barbarous kinds of ownership called direct and useful. But they were so blinded by the difference in terminology that they completely failed to see that the principles were equivalent.

[1076] There returned those goods said to be held by supreme right, *ex iure optimo*. Learned feudalists define these as allodial goods free of every encumbrance, public or private, and they compare them to the few houses remaining at Rome which Cicero says were still held *ex iure optimo*. But just as any mention of such goods was lost in late imperial Roman legislation, so in our day we cannot find a single instance of these allodial freeholds. Like the Roman estates held by perfect right, the later allodia developed into real estate free from any real private encumbrance but subject to real public encumbrances. This repeated the manner in which the census of Servius Tullius developed into the census which was the basis of the Roman treasury. The two great categories of property in feudal law, allodia and fiefs, were originally distinguished in this way: feudal goods were protected by a citation of the lord's authority, but allodial goods were not.

Since they fail to grasp these principles, all the learned feudalists are at a loss to explain why allodia, which they translate by Cicero's phrase *bona ex iure optimo*, came to be called goods of the spindle. As we have seen, these goods in their proper sense were held by a strong title which was not weakened by any public encumbrance. Such were the goods acquired by fathers in the family state and held by them for many years in the state of the first cities. Now, the fathers had acquired their property through the labours of Hercules, and this mythical origin aids us in solving the riddle. For we recall that in myth Hercules took to spinning when he became the slave of Iole and Omphale. This means that the heroes, who had previously called themselves men, grew effeminate and yielded their heroic rights to the plebeians, whom they regarded as women. And they allowed their goods – now 'goods of the spindle' – to be subjected to the public treasury under the census, which was first the basis of democracies, and later a suitable foundation for monarchies.

[1077] This ancient feudal law was forgotten by later ages, but it returned in the medieval estates held *ex iure Quiritium*. Originally, this meant the right of the Romans in public assembly, armed with the lances called *quires*. And from these Quirites was derived the formula in a claim for restitution – 'I declare this ground mine by quiritary right' – which cited as authority the heroic citizens of Rome. In the medieval return of barbarism, these fiefs were called 'goods of the lance', which implied a citation of a feudal lord as authority. By contrast, allodial freeholds were called 'goods of the spindle', with reference to the spinning of Hercules, now demeaned and enslaved by women. In similar fashion, the motto on the royal arms of France – 'Lilies do not spin', *Lilia non nent* – means in heroic language that women may not succeed to that kingdom. For the medieval period witnessed the return of the laws of successions found in the Law of the Twelve Tables, which were called the law of the clans of Rome, *ius gentium Romanorum*. And its counterpart, the Salic law, is termed by Baldus the law of the clans of France, *ius gentium Gallorum*. Since the Salic law was observed in Germany, it must have been observed in all the early medieval nations of Europe. Later, it was limited to France and Savoy.

[1078] Finally there returned armed courts, which resembled the heroic assemblies convened under arms by the Greek Curetes and the Roman Quirites. The first parliaments of the European realms must have been formed of barons, just as the French parliament was in fact formed of peers. French history explicitly relates that the original heads of the parliament were the French kings, who created the peers of the court in the capacity of commissioners for judging cases: whence their later title of Dukes and Peers of France. This is a precise parallel to the first Roman trial in which Cicero says that a citizen's life was at stake. For the king Tullus Hostilius created the duumvirs in the capacity of commissioners whose task it was, in Livy's legal phrase, to 'charge Horatius with treason', *in Horatium perduellionem dicerent* – for killing his sister!

[1079] Horatius was so charged because in that severe age, when only heroes made up a city, the killing of a citizen was regarded as an act of hostility against the fatherland, which is the precise meaning of *perduellio*, high treason. Any such killing was called a *parricidium*, as if *patricidium*. For a slain citizen was necessarily a father or patrician, since Rome in that age consisted only of patricians and plebeians. From Romulus to Tullus Hostilius, there were no trials for the murder of a patrician. Evidently, the patricians were careful to avoid committing such crimes, and instead practised duels. But in Horatius' case, there was no relative left to take private revenge for Horatia's death, and Tullus Hostilius called for a trial, which was the first of its kind. By contrast, when plebeians were slain, it was either by their masters, who could not be accused of any crime, or by others who could pay the master for his loss. This is still the custom today in Poland, Lithuania, Sweden, Denmark, and Norway.

The learned interpreters of Roman law failed to see this objection, because they trusted their vain belief in the innocence of Rome's golden age. By the same token, political thinkers trusted Aristotle's statement that ancient republics had no laws concerning private wrongs and offences. Thus, when Tacitus, Sallust, and other perceptive authors speak of the origin of commonwealths and laws, they describe men in the primitive state before cities as if they had lived in a state of innocence like Adam. Yet after the cities had admitted those plebeians simply called *homines* – the name amazed Hotman and gave rise to the natural law of Ulpian's 'human' nations – the killing of any man was henceforth called homicide, *homicidium*, rather than parricide.

[1080] Such parliaments must have discussed feudal cases concerning questions such as rights, successions, or fiefs devolving through felony or default of heirs. Through their repeated judicial rulings in these cases, they established the customs of feudalism, which are the oldest customs in Europe. This proves that the natural law of nations sprang from the human customs of fiefs.

[1081] To conclude, after Horatius had been condemned, the king Tullus Hostilius granted him an appeal to the 'people', who in fact consisted entirely of patricians. (For where a senate rules, it is the only body to which a condemned man may appeal.) During the medieval return of barbarism, nobles made just such appeals to the kings in their parliaments, such as the kings of France who were originally heads of parliament.

[1082] The Sacred Council of Naples preserves important traces of such heroic parliaments. Its president bears the title of Sacred Royal Majesty. Its councillors are called soldiers, *milites*, and act as commissioners. (In the medieval age of barbarism, only nobles were soldiers, and the plebeian vassals were merely their wartime servants. Homer and Roman history show that this was also the case in the ancient age of barbarism.) And its rulings admit no appeal before any other judge, but only a request for revision by the Council itself.

[1083] From all this, we may conclude that medieval realms everywhere were aristocratic in government, if not in constitution. In the cold North, Poland is still such a realm, as Sweden and Denmark were until 150 years ago; and unless extraordinary events change its natural course, Poland will eventually become a perfect monarchy.

[1084] In the light of this truth, Bodin goes so far as to say that, under the Merovingian and Carolingian dynasties, the kingdom of France was aristocratic in constitution, if not in government, as I maintain. Here I must ask Bodin: 'How then did the kingdom of France become perfectly monarchical, as it is now? Was it perhaps through some royal law by which the paladins of France divested themselves of their power and conferred it on the kings of the Capetian line?' Suppose Bodin has recourse to Tribonian's fiction of the 'royal law', by which the Roman people divested themselves of their free sovereignty and conferred it on Augustus. To prove this a myth, we need only read the opening pages of Tacitus' *Annals*. He recounts how by his last acts Augustus legitimized in his own person the origin of the Roman monarchy – an origin which was observed by all the nations. 'Was it perhaps because one of the Capetian kings conquered France by force of arms?' None of the histories even hint at such a disaster.

Bodin and all the other political thinkers and jurists who have written on public law must therefore recognize the following eternal and natural 'royal law', by which the free power of a state, because it is free, must be realized. As the nobles cede power, the people acquire it, and so become free; and as free people cede power, kings acquire it, and so become monarchs. Hence, just as the natural law of philosophers and moral theologians is a law of reason, so the natural law of nations is a law of self-interest and force. As the jurists observe, nations observe this law 'as use requires and human necessities demand', *usu exigente humanisque necessitatibus expostulantibus.*

[1085] Learned feudalists have tried to temper the barbarity of feudal doctrine by adapting many fine and elegant expressions used by ancient Roman jurists. But I have shown that such Roman terms in fact match feudal concepts with great propriety. So let Johann Oldendorp and his colleagues explain just how 'feudal law was born from the sparks of the fire set by the barbarians to Roman law'! In fact, Roman law arose from the sparks of ancient fiefs, which were established during Latium's early barbarism, and from which all the world's commonwealths arose. I showed this in my Poetic Politics; and, as promised in my Idea of the Work, I have shown that the key to the origins of modern European kingdoms is found in the invariable nature of fiefs.

[1086] Eventually, the universities of Italy created faculties to teach the Roman laws contained in the books of Justinian, which are based on the natural law of human nations. Since human minds were now more developed and intelligent, they strove to elaborate a jurisprudence based on natural equity, which makes commoners and nobles equal in civil rights, as they are equal in human nature. In Rome, when Tiberius Coruncanius began to teach laws publicly, legal secrets began to slip from the hands of the patricians, and their power began gradually to weaken. Precisely the same thing happened to the European nobility when their kingdoms of Europe ceased to be ruled by aristocracies and developed into democracies and later into perfect monarchies.

[1087] Since both democracies and monarchies are human governments, they are readily interchangeable; but our civil nature makes a reversion to aristocracy nearly impossible. This is why Dion of Syracuse was barbarously murdered when he attempted to restore the aristocracy, even though he was part of the royal family, had exiled the monstrous tyrant Dionysius II, and had won Plato's friendship by the splendour of his civic virtues. And in the same attempt, the so-called Pythagoreans, or nobility of Magna Graecia, were nearly all cut to pieces; and the few people who took refuge in strongholds were burned alive by the mob. For once the plebeians perceive that they are equal in nature with the nobles, they naturally cannot tolerate inequality in civil law, especially when they can obtain equality in democracies or monarchies. This is why in the present civilized state of nations the few aristocracies that survive must take infinite pains and prudent measures to see that the masses are at once both dutiful and happy.

CHAPTER 3

Description of the Ancient and Modern Worlds in the Light of the New Science

[1088] Carthage, Capua, and Numantia, the three cities which made Rome fear for her world empire, did not follow this course of human civil institutions. The Carthaginians developed too rapidly because of their native African shrewdness, which was sharpened by their maritime trading. The Capuans likewise developed too rapidly because of their mild climate and the abundance of fertile Campania. And the people of Numantia were still in the first flower of their heroic age, when they were subjugated by the full power of Rome under the great Scipio Africanus, the conqueror of Carthage, assisted by the forces of a world empire. By contrast, the Romans' progress was accelerated by none of these factors. They proceeded at a just pace, letting themselves be governed by providence, which worked through vernacular wisdom. Hence, they passed through all three forms of civil state, following the natural order which my New Science has demonstrated by so many proofs, and remaining in each form until it was naturally replaced by the next. They safeguarded aristocracy until the passage of the Publilian and Poetelian Laws. They safeguarded democracy until the time of Augustus. And they safeguarded the monarchy as long as it was humanly possible to resist the internal and external causes which destroy it.

[1089] Today a perfect form of civilization seems to have spread itself throughout the nations, for a few great monarchs rule this world of peoples. If barbarism survives, the reason is that their monarchies still persist in the popular wisdom of fantastic and fierce religions, whose effects are sometimes compounded by the ill-balanced climate of their subject nations.

[1090] To begin with the cold North, the czar of Moscovy is a Christian, but he rules over people with sluggish minds. In Tartary, the khan or knyaz ('prince' in Russian) governs a people as dissolute as the ancient Seres, who formed the original bulk of his great empire, which he has now united with China. In the torrid zone, the negus of Ethiopia and the powerful kings of Fez and Morocco rule over very weak and sparse peoples.

[1091] By contrast, in the middle of the temperate zone, people are born with a more balanced nature. To begin with the Far East, the emperor of Japan acts with a civility similar to that of the Romans during the Punic wars. When at war, he imitates Roman ferocity; and many travellers find that his speech has a Latin ring to it. At the same time, because of his fantastic religion of fierce and terrible gods, all armed with deadly weapons, he retains much of the heroic nature. Missionaries report that the greatest obstacle to converting the Japanese to Christianity is that their nobles cannot be persuaded that the plebeians share their human nature. By contrast, the Emperor of China rules with a mild religion, is devoted to literary studies, and is very humane. The Emperor of the Indies is generally humane, and on the whole cultivates the arts of peace. The Persians and the Turks combine the luxury of their Asian domains with the harsh doctrine of their religion. The Turks in particular temper their pride with magnificence, pomp, liberality, and gratitude.

[1092] In Europe, people everywhere observe the Christian religion, which teaches the idea of an infinitely pure and perfect God, and enjoins all mankind to practise charity. Europe has great monarchies with very humane customs. To be sure, the European nations found in the cold North seem to be governed aristocratically, even if they have monarchical constitutions: witness Sweden and Denmark 150 years ago, and Poland and England today. But unless extraordinary events change the natural course of human civil institutions, they too will attain perfect monarchies. This part of the world cultivates the sciences, and therefore has far more democracies than are found in the others. Indeed, the recurrence of the same public benefits and needs has revived the form of the Aetolian and Achaean leagues. The Greeks established such alliances out of necessity, since they had to protect themselves against the enormous power of the Romans. In just this way, both the Swiss cantons and the United Provinces or States of Holland have organized several free and democratic cities into aristocracies, which unite them in a perpetual league in both peace and war. The body of the German empire is likewise a system of many free cities and sovereign rulers, whose head is the emperor. In affairs concerning the constitution of the empire, it is governed aristocratically.

[1093] Here we should note that when sovereign powers unite in leagues, whether perpetual or temporary, they proceed by themselves to form aristocratic states, which are troubled by the anxious suspicions characteristic of aristocracies. Now, in civil nature we cannot conceive of a state superior to aristocracies. Hence, since confederation is the final form of civil states, it must also have been the first form, namely, that of the aristocracies of the fathers, or sovereign kings of the families, who united to form the ruling orders of the first cities. For it is the nature of principles that institutions begin and end in them.

[1094] To return to our topic, there are only five aristocracies in Europe today: Venice, Genoa, and Lucca in Italy; Ragusa in Dalmatia; and Nuremberg in Germany. All of them have limited territory. But Christian Europe is everywhere so radiant with civilization that it abounds in all the goods which render human life happy, including both physical comforts and mental and spiritual pleasures. All this is due to the Christian religion, which teaches truths so sublime it receives into its service the most learned philosophies of the pagans, and cultivates three languages as its own: Hebrew, the most ancient in the world; Greek, the most delicate; and Latin, the most monumental. Considered from a human point of view, Christianity is the best of all the world's religions. For it unites the wisdom enjoined by God with the wisdom of human reason, as found in the choicest doctrine of the philosophers and in the most refined erudition of the philologists and historians.

[1095] Finally, across the Atlantic, we see that the American Indians in the New World would have followed this course of human institutions, if they had not been discovered by the Europeans.

[1096] My Book 5 has examined the recurrence of civil human institutions. In summary, we may review the parallels I have drawn throughout my *New Science* between the first and final ages of nations, both ancient and modern. This will not merely explain the particular chronological history of the Greeks and Romans. Instead, by finding the substantial identity of meaning amid the diversity of manifestations, we shall provide an ideal history of eternal laws which all nations follow in the course of their birth, growth, maturity, decline, and fall. (They would follow this course even if there were infinite worlds, which is not true.) This is why I could not refrain from giving this work the invidious title of *New Science*. It would have been too gross an injustice to defraud it of its rightful claim when it dealt with so universal a topic as that *concerning the common nature of nations*. For every perfect science must be based on an idea. Seneca expresses this in a portentous phrase: 'The world is a paltry thing unless the whole world finds in it what it seeks', *Pusilla res hic mundus est, nisi id, quod quaerat, omnis mundus habeat.*

CONCLUSION OF THE WORK

On the Eternal Natural Commonwealth, Best in its Kind, Ordained by Divine Providence

[1097] My *New Science* fittingly concludes with Plato's proposal of a fourth kind of commonwealth, in which good and honourable men would be supreme lords, and which would literally be a true and natural aristocracy. This Platonic republic was brought forth by providence from the earliest origins of the nations. For providence ordained that the people with gigantic proportions and the greatest strength would wander the mountain heights like beasts with natural strength. Then, on hearing the first thunder after the universal flood, they entered the earth in its mountain caves, and subjected themselves to the superior force which they imagined as Jupiter. All their pride and ferocity was converted to astonishment, and they humbled themselves before this divinity. Given the order of human institutions, divine providence could not conceivably have acted otherwise to end their bestial wandering through the earth's forests, and to establish the order of human civil institutions.

[1098] The first societies were monastic, or ruled by solitary sovereigns under the government of a Greatest and Best deity, which the family fathers had imagined and embraced in the thunderbolts, as showing that God's true light governs humankind. People now imagined as gods all the benefits they enjoyed, and all the assistance provided for their necessities were gods. But in their fear and reverence for such divine gods, they found themselves torn between the powerful restraints of fearful superstitions and the sharp goading of bestial lust, passions which must have been extremely violent in such people. Terrified by the aspect of the heavens, they checked their urge to sexual intercourse, and instead subjected their lustful impulses to a conscious effort. In this way, they began to enjoy human liberty, which consists in restraining the impulses of physical desire, and giving them a new direction. (Since the body is the source of desire, this liberty must come from the mind, and thus is proper to humankind.)

Following this direction, the giants forcibly seized women, who were by nature shy and intractable, and dragged them into their caves where they mated with them and kept them as permanent companions for life. In this way, the giants instituted matrimony by the first civilized acts of coition, which were modest and religious. Through such marriages, they became the *certain* fathers of *certain* children by *certain* women. Having thus founded families, they governed their wives and children with a Cyclopean authority appropriate to their proud and savage natures, so that later, when cities arose, men were disposed to fear civil authority. In this way, providence ordained certain household commonwealths, in the form of monarchies under the fathers, who as rulers in that state were best suited by their sex, age, and virtue. In the state of families, which we would call the state of nature, they must have formed the first natural social orders. Such pious, chaste, and strong men naturally settled on lands where they defended themselves and their families. No longer able to survive by fleeing, as they had done before in their brutish wandering, they now had to kill the wild beasts that threatened them. No longer foraging for food, they now had to tame the land and sow grain in order to provide sustenance for themselves and their families. All this preserved the human race.

[1099] Meanwhile, a great number of impious men remained scattered across the plains and valleys. They feared no gods, shamelessly engaged in open intercourse, and nefariously coupled with their own mothers and daughters. Their abominable promiscuity of women and possessions caused problems which drove them apart; and the violence of the stronger threatened their lives. So after many years, these weak, drifting, and solitary people fled to the refuges of the family fathers, who received them under their protection, and thus expanded their family kingdoms through the clientships of these family servants. The commonwealths that emerged were based on social orders, whose superiority was guaranteed by the following heroic virtues. (1) They showed *piety* in their worship of divinity; although as unenlightened people they multiplied and divided the gods, whom they shaped according to their various apprehensions. (We find proof of this in Diodorus Siculus and even more in Eusebius' *Preparation for the Gospel* and Cyril's *Against Julian the Apostate*.) (2) This piety endowed them with *prudence*, so that they took counsel from the auspices of the gods. (3) It endowed them with *temperance*, for each man chastely mated with a single woman whom he took as his perpetual companion for life, sanctioned by the divine auspices. (4) It endowed them with *fortitude*, by which they killed wild beasts and tamed the land. (5) And it endowed them with *magnanimity* for aiding the weak and helping those in danger. This was the nature of the Herculean commonwealths, in which the pious, wise, chaste, strong, and magnanimous cast down the proud and defended the weak – which is the most excellent form of civil governments.

[1100] But although the family fathers owed their greatness to their ancestors' piety and virtue and to their clients' labours, they eventually began to abuse the laws of protection and to subject their clients to harsh treatment. When they had abandoned the natural order, which is that of justice, their clients rebelled against them. But without order, which is to say without God, human society cannot endure for even a moment. So providence led the family fathers naturally to unite with their relations in social orders formed against their clients. In the world's first agrarian law, they appeased the clients by granting them bonitary ownership of the fields, while retaining for themselves supreme ownership as family sovereigns. In this way, the first cities sprang from the ruling orders of nobles.

In the state of nature, the natural order had been based on kinship, sex, age, and virtue. But as the natural order now declined, providence created a new civil order together with the cities, beginning with the orders closest to nature. Because of their heroic nature, and their nobility in the human race, the nobles ruled over the plebeians. (In this state, nobility was defined by children born in human wedlock to wives taken under divine auspices; whereas the plebeians did not contract marriages by such solemnities.) Divine rule now ended, under which the families had been governed by the divine auspices, and the heroes ruled by virtue of the form of their heroic governments. The principal basis of their commonwealths was the guardianship of religion within the heroic orders, since religion alone guaranteed all the civil rights and laws of the nobility. But as noble birth had become a mere gift of fortune, providence caused the emergence among the nobles of a new order based on those family fathers whose age naturally made them worthiest. And providence saw that the most spirited and robust fathers became kings, who would keep the others within their orders and lead them in opposing and intimidating any rebellious clients.

[1101] As many years passed and the human mind advanced, the plebeians eventually had second thoughts about the vain claims of nobility. Realizing that they had a human nature equal to that of the nobles, they resolved to enter the civil orders of the cities. Since the people were eventually to become sovereign, providence allowed the plebeians, well before their time, to compete with this nobility founded on piety and religion. In heroic contentions, the plebeians strove to force the nobles to share the auspices, since they saw that all civil rights, public and private, were dependent on them. Thus, by their concern for piety and love of religion, the people attained sovereignty in their cities. And as the Roman people surpassed all other nations in this regard, they became masters of the world. In this manner, the natural order increasingly combined with the civil orders, and democracies were born. Everything in them was decided by lot or balance, which would have allowed chance or fate to rule them. So providence ordained the census as the measure of fitness for public honours. Under the census, the persons judged best qualified to govern were the industrious rather than the indolent, the frugal rather than the prodigal, the provident rather than the idle, the magnanimous rather than the petty-minded: in a word, the rich who had some virtues or semblance of virtue, rather than the poor with their many shameless vices.

In such commonwealths, the entire people seek justice in common and thus enact laws which are just because they are universally good. In a divine definition, Aristotle calls such laws 'will without passions', which means a heroic will in control of its passions. In such commonwealths, philosophy was born, inspired by the form of the government to form the ideal hero and, in forming him, to concern itself with the truth. This was ordained by providence. For since virtuous actions no longer sprang from religious feelings, philosophy had to make virtues intelligible in ideal form. Thus, even if people lacked virtues, by reflecting on virtuous ideals, they would at least be ashamed of their vices. This is the only way in which people who tend to act badly can be reminded of their duty. Providence allowed philosophy to give birth to eloquence. From the very form of democracy, which enacts good laws, eloquence took its passion for justice; and from the ideals of virtue, it inflamed the people to enact good laws. Such eloquence we find flourishing in Rome in the time of Scipio Africanus. In that age, civil wisdom and military valour fortunately established Rome's world empire on the ruins of Carthage, and therefore produced eloquence filled with vigour and prudence.

[1102] Yet when democracy grew corrupt, so did philosophy, which sank into scepticism. Learned fools took to maligning the truth. And false eloquence arose, prepared to argue opposite sides of a cause with equal force. People now misused eloquence, as did the plebeian tribunes at Rome. And the citizens, being no longer content with wealth as a source of order, resolved to use it as a source of power. Like furious winds lashing the sea, they stirred up civil wars in their republics and reduced them to utter chaos. The state fell from its perfect liberty to the perfect tyranny of anarchy, or the unbridled liberty of free peoples, which is the worst of all.

[1103] Against such great civil maladies, providence must administer one of three great remedies in the order of human civil institutions.

[1104] (1) Providence may arrange that the people discover a leader like Augustus, who rises up and establishes himself as their monarch. When all the orders and laws devised to safeguard liberty are now powerless to regulate it and hold it in check, this leader takes control of them all by force of arms. Yet the very form of monarchy confines the will of the monarch, whose authority is infinite, within the natural order. The monarch must keep the people content and satisfied with their religion and natural liberty. For without the people's universal satisfaction and contentment, monarchies are neither long-lived nor secure.

[1105] (2) If providence finds no such remedy within, it seeks one outside the commonwealth. When people are corrupt, they are natural slaves to unbridled passions such as luxury, fastidiousness, avarice, envy, pride, and ostentation. And in seeking the pleasures of their dissolute life, they relapse into all the vices characteristic of ignoble slaves: lying, trickery, slander, theft, cowardice, and hypocrisy. Hence, providence causes them to become real slaves under that natural law which derives from the nature of nations. Such peoples are subjected to superior nations which conquer them by arms and then protect them as subject provinces. In this process, two great lights of natural order shine forth. First, when people cannot govern themselves, they must be governed by another. Second, the people who govern the world must by nature be superior.

[1106] (3) But if people are rotting in this fatal civil malady, and can neither accept a native monarch, nor tolerate the conquest and protection of a superior nation, then providence may administer an extreme remedy to their extreme illness. Like beasts, such people are accustomed to think of nothing but their own personal advantage, and in their extreme fastidiousness, or rather pride, they are filled with bestial rage and resentment at the least provocation. Although their bodies are densely crowded together, they live like monstrous beasts in the utter solitude of their private wills and desires. Not even two of them can agree, because each pursues his own pleasure or caprice. Seeing all this, providence causes their obstinate factional strife and desperate civil wars to turn their cities into forests and their forests into human lairs.

In this way, long centuries of barbarism corrode the ignoble subtleties of malicious wits. (This barbarism of reflection turns such people into beasts even more savage than did the primitive barbarism of the senses.★ For early peoples displayed a generous savagery, from which others could guard or defend themselves or flee. But decadent peoples practise an ignoble savagery, and use flattery and embraces to plot against the life and fortunes of their intimates and friends.) When providence administers this extreme remedy to people who practise the malice of reflection, they are stunned and stupefied, and are no longer sensible to comforts, luxuries, pleasures, and ostentation, but only to the basic necessities of life.

★ Vico's expression 'barbarism of reflection', *barbarie della riflessione*, is an implicit attack on Cartesian rationality.

Eventually, the few survivors, finding themselves amid an abundance of life's necessities, naturally become sociable. Returning to the primitive simplicity of the early world of peoples, they naturally become religious, truthful, and faithful. Thus, providence renews the piety, faith, and truth which are both the natural foundations of justice, and the grace and beauty of God's eternal order.

[1107] Even if we learned nothing else from the philosophers, historians, philologists, and jurists, this pure and simple analysis of the institutions of the entire human race would lead us to affirm that this is the great city of the nations founded and governed by God. Now, men like Lycurgus, Solon, and the Roman decemvirs have been eternally praised to the heavens as wise lawmakers. For it was previously thought that, by establishing good social orders and good laws, they had founded the three cities which outshone all others in the finest and greatest civil virtues: Sparta, Athens, and Rome. Yet these cities were of short duration and limited extent in comparison to the universe of peoples. This universe was ordered by such institutions and secured by such laws that, even when it is corrupted, it takes on forms of states which uniquely ensure its widespread survival and its perpetual existence. Must we not declare this a counsel of superhuman wisdom? For this wisdom divinely rules and guides the universe of peoples, not by the force of laws, which resemble a tyrant in using force, as Dio remarked in Axiom 104, but by exploiting human customs, which people practise as freely as their own nature, so that Dio compares them to a king, commanding by pleasure.

[1108] The world of nations is in fact a human creation. (Having despaired of discovering this truth in the philosophers and philologists, I adopted it as the first incontestable principle of my New Science.) Yet without doubt this world was created by the mind of providence, which is often different, sometimes contrary, and always superior to the particular goals which people have set for themselves. Instead, to preserve the human race on the earth, providence uses people's limited goals as a means of attaining greater ones. Thus, people seek to satisfy their bestial lust and abandon their offspring, but they establish the chastity of marriage, from which families arise. Fathers seek to exercise immoderate paternal authority over their clients, but they subject them to the civil powers which create cities. The ruling orders of the nobility seek to abuse their lordly freedom over the plebeians, but they become slaves to the laws which create popular liberty. Free peoples seek to free themselves of laws, but become the subjects of monarchs. Monarchs seek to strengthen their rule by debasing their subjects in every kind of dissolution and vice, but they prepare them to endure slavery under stronger nations. Nations seek to disband, but their fragmented peoples take refuge in isolated regions from which nations rise again, like the phoenix. In all these cases, the agent is mind, since people have acted with intelligence. It was not fate, for they acted by choice. It was not chance, for the results of such consistent actions are always the same.

[1109] The facts therefore refute Epicurus and his disciples Hobbes and Machiavelli, who believe in chance. And they refute Zeno and Spinoza, who believe in fate. Instead, they speak in favour of the political philosophers who are led by the divine Plato. For Plato established the fact that human institutions are guided by providence. This is why Cicero was right to say that he could not discuss laws with Atticus unless he renounced Epicurus and granted that human institutions are guided by providence. In recent political theories, Pufendorf refused to recognize providence; Selden took it for granted; and Grotius ignored it. But the Roman jurists established it as the first principle of their natural law of nations.

My *New Science* has shown in detail how providence caused the world's first governments to base themselves on religion, which alone made the state of families possible. Next, as they developed into heroic civil governments, or aristocracies, religion clearly provided the principal stable foundation. Then, as they advanced to popular governments, religion likewise served as the people's means of attaining democracies. Finally, as they come to rest in monarchical governments, this same religion must be the shield of rulers. If peoples lose their religion, nothing remains to keep them living in society. They have no shield for their defence, no basis for their decisions, no foundation for their stability, and no form by which they exist in the world.

[1110] Now let Bayle explain how nations can in fact exist without any knowledge of God! And let Polybius examine the truth of his statement that if there were philosophers in the world it would need no religions! Only religion can make people perform virtuous works by appealing to their feelings, which effectively move people to action. By contrast, the logical maxims of the philosophers about virtue only assist moral eloquence in inciting the feelings to fulfil the obligations of virtue. There is an essential difference between our true Christian religion and all the other religions, which are false. In Christianity, divine grace inspires virtuous works for the sake of an infinite and eternal good. And since this good lies beyond the feelings, the mind must move the feelings to virtuous actions. By contrast, false religions have as their goal the finite and transient goods both of this life and the next; and in both they expect to find blessedness in physical pleasures. Hence, their feelings must drag the mind to perform virtuous works.

[1111] Within the order of civil institutions outlined in my *New Science*, providence makes itself clearly felt through three feelings: first, *wonder*, second, *veneration*, which scholars felt towards the incomparable wisdom of the ancients; and third, ardent *desire*, with which scholars burned to seek and attain this wisdom. For the three stages of human institutions are in fact three lights of providential divinity, which inspired these three lofty and righteous feelings in people. (Later, these feelings were distorted by the conceit of scholars and the conceit of nations, described in Axioms 3 and 4, and repeatedly reproved throughout my *New Science*.) These feelings are shared by all scholars, who *wonder at, venerate, and desire* unity with the infinite wisdom of God.

[1112] In sum, all the observations contained in this work lead to one conclusion. My *New Science* is indissolubly linked to the study of piety; and unless one is pious, one cannot be truly wise.

INDEX AND GLOSSARY

The numbers refer to paragraphs

confuses with Dionysius the
Areopagite, 45

CHALCEDON, Greek city near
Byzantium, 612

CHALCIS, city confused by Vico with
Colchis, 760

CHALDAEANS, 32, 43, 49, 50, 54–5,
57, 59, 60, 93, 100, 126, 128, 298,
317, 435, 440, 474, 727, 737, 739

CHAMPIER, SYMPHORIEN, French
royal physician and chronicler
(1472–1559), author of a Latin
Genealogy of the Kings of France
(1507), 1048

CHAOS, 688, 717

CHARLES V, Holy Roman Emperor
(1500–1558), 557

CHASSAGNON, JEAN, French
Protestant scholar (1531–98),
author of the Latin treatise *On
Giants* (1580), 170, 369

CHATTI, ancient Germanic tribe, 955

CHIFLET, JEAN JACQUES, French
physician and antiquary (1588–
1660), author of the Latin *Coats of
Arms of the Order of the Golden
Fleece* (1632), 542

CHIMAERA, 541, 543

CHINA, CHINESE, 32, 48, 50, 54, 83,
99, 126, 303, 423, 427, 435, 462,
470, 542, 616, 935, 1090–91

CHIOS, Aegean island, 612

CHRISTIANITY, CHRISTIANS, 68, 95,
169, 179, 223, 310, 334, 365, 602,
636, 948, 961, 1047–9, 1051,
1055–6, 1091–2, 1094, 1110

CHRONOS, Greek god often identified
with Cronus (Saturn), 3, 73, 732

CHRYSEIS, 783

CHRYSES, 783

CHURCH (ROMAN CATHOLIC), 479,
948, 1014, 1051

CHURCH FATHERS, 62, 433, 462,
1047

CICERO, Roman statesman and author
(106–43 BC), 39, 52, 66, 79, 100,
108, 115, 284–5, 335, 397, 422,
459, 462, 469, 490, 514, 526, 528,
537, 601, 627, 638, 644, 664, 777,
854, 901, 945, 950, 968, 1001,
1019, 1022–3, 1076, 1078, 1109

CIMMERIANS, ancient people
originally from southern Russia,
757

CIRCE, 437, 648, 757, 798, 879

CIRCEII, 757

CIRCELLO, MT, 757

CLAUDIUS, Roman emperor (41–54),
439, 517, 1008

CLAUDIUS, APPIUS, Roman
magistrate (consul 312 BC), 81,
661, 734

CLEMENT OF ALEXANDRIA, Greek
theologian (ca. 150–216), 45, 83,
99, 432, 435, 440

CLIO, 533, 555

CNIDOS, ancient Spartan colony in
Asia Minor, 612

COLA DI RIENZO, medieval Roman
patriot (1313–54), 699, 786, 819

COLCHIS, ancient region near the
Black Sea, 82

COLLATIA, ancient Sabine city, 1030,
1050

COLOSSUS OF RHODES, 303

CONCINA, NICCOLÒ, Italian
Dominican scholar (1694–1762),
professor of metaphysics at Padua
and Vico's correspondent, 974

CONFUCIUS, Latin name for K'ung
Fu-tse, Chinese sage (551–
479 BC), 50, 427

CONRAD III, Holy Roman Emperor
(1138–52), 972